Contemporary World Fiction

Contemporary World Fiction

A Guide to Literature in Translation

JURIS DILEVKO, KEREN DALI, AND GLENDA GARBUTT

AN IMPRINT OF ABC-CLIO, LLC
Santa Barbara, California • Denver, Colorado • Oxford, England

Library of Congress Cataloging-in-Publication Data

Dilevko, Juris.
Contemporary world fiction : a guide to literature in translation/ Juris Dilevko, Keren Dali, and Glenda Garbutt.
p. cm.
Includes bibliographical references and index.
ISBN 978–1–59158–353–0 (acid-free paper); 978–1–59884–909–7 (ebook)
1. Fiction–20th century–Translations into English–Bibliography. 2. Fiction–21st century–Translations into English–Bibliography. I. Dali, Keren. II. Garbutt, Glenda. III. Title.
Z5917.T7D55 2011
[PN3503]
016.80883′048—dc22 2010052517

ISBN: 978–1–59158–353–0
EISBN: 978–1–59884–909–7

15 14 13 12 11 1 2 3 4 5

This book is also available on the World Wide Web as an eBook.
Visit www.abc-clio.com for details.

Libraries Unlimited
An Imprint of ABC-CLIO, LLC

ABC-CLIO, LLC
130 Cremona Drive, P.O. Box 1911
Santa Barbara, California 93116-1911

This book is printed on acid-free paper ∞

Manufactured in the United States of America

Contents

Preface

According to newspaper reports in late 2008, "Horace Engdahl, the permanent secretary of the Swedish Academy, the organization that awards the Nobel Prize in Literature, gave an interview to the Associated Press" in which he suggested that an author from the United States would not be receiving the award in question in 2008. One of the reasons, he said, was that "[t]he U.S. is too isolated, too insular. They don't translate enough and don't really participate in the big dialogue of literature. That ignorance is restraining" (McGrath, 2008; Rich, 2008). His remarks gave rise to some degree of controversy as well as to reflections about the place of translated fiction in literary life. Regardless of whether Engdahl is correct about the situation in the United States, translated fiction opens diverse avenues to different cultures; to different ways of being, thinking, and feeling; and to different social, historical, and political circumstances.

We hope that this volume provides convenient access to a wealth of fiction translated from numerous world languages into English. Aimed at academic libraries that support world literature classes and collections; Readers' Advisory (RA) librarians in public libraries; and individual readers as they search for new books to read, this guide contains bibliographical essays that contextualize some of the major non-English literary traditions and annotated entries for works of fiction by more than 1,000 authors whose works have been translated into English.

Although this volume now appears as a finished product, a reference tool of this kind is never complete. New titles translated into English from different world languages appear almost every day. Chad W. Post, "the director of Open Letter, a new press based at the University of Rochester that focuses exclusively on books in translation," calculates that 280 fiction titles were translated into English and published in the United States in 2008; 285 titles in 2009; and some 225 titles in 2010 (Post, 2010; Rich, 2008).

In addition, Larry Rohter (2010) reports that, through the aegis of various cultural agencies and private foundations, many nations, frustrated at the non-existent or slow pace that their authors are translated into English, formalized long-term plans with a view to "underwriting the training of translators, encouraging their writers to tour in the United States, submitting to American marketing and promotional techniques they may have previously shunned and exploiting existing niches in the publishing industry." For example, Dalkey Archive Press entered into arrangements with "official groups" and "financing agencies" in Slovenia, Israel, Catalonia, Switzerland, and Mexico to publish a number of book series written by authors from those respective countries and regions. Some contracts call for up to 24 books over six years; some are for fewer titles. As the publisher of Dalkey Archive noted, this recent trend of subsidization is an important one with significant ramifications, because when publishers partner with "consulates, embassies and book institutes of other countries," the net effect is to stimulate "a considerable level of interest and a feeling that something much bigger is going on than 'here is a book by someone I've never heard of before.' "

In the "Introduction" below, we indicate how librarians and library users can keep up with the ever-growing number of translated books.

Although a concerted effort was made to ensure that the information in this volume is accurate, mistakes, omissions, and inaccuracies are inevitable in any project of this scope. Nonetheless, we hope that this volume will help readers gain some sense of the richness of translated fiction.

REFERENCES

McGrath, Charles. (2008, October 5). "Lost in Translation? A Swede's Snub of U.S. Lit." *The New York Times Book Review*. Available at http://www.nytimes.com (accessed October 20, 2008).

Post, Chad W. (2010, January 16). "2008, 2009, and 2010 Translation Database." (Three Percent website). Available at http://www.rochester.edu/College/translation/threepercent/index.php?s=database (accessed December 7, 2010).

Rich, Motoko. (2008, October 19). "Translation is Foreign to U.S. Publishers." *The New York Times Book Review*. Available at http://www.nytimes.com (accessed October 20, 2008).

Rohter, Larry. (2010, December 8). "Translation as Literary Ambassador." Available at http://www.nytimes.com (accessed December 8, 2010).

Introduction

A book such as this is much needed at the beginning of the twenty-first century. The fact that the world is globalizing is a trite concept by now, but it is nonetheless true. Our world is shrinking in every way imaginable. As people travel more; as they increasingly receive their formal education abroad; as they seek and find employment in countries thousands of miles from where they were born; and as they are able to follow events instantaneously in far-flung locales through the power of the Internet and social networking technologies, they necessarily become more interested in and concerned about other cultures and countries. However, what people in North America often hear or read about other cultures and countries is filtered through Western perspectives and sensibilities: the view of the outsider. How do we get beyond the sometimes one-dimensional view of what has often been referred to as the Western gaze? One way is to sample some of the stories of other countries and cultures as told by those individuals who live in those countries or cultures and/or speak the language of those countries or cultures. The aim of this guide is to facilitate such an exploration of other countries and cultures as told through stories written in the original languages of those countries and cultures. Here, readers will find an array of "insider" voices—insiders who have written novels and short stories that provide North American readers with the opportunity to hear from, learn about, and perhaps better understand our globalized world. As Edith Grossman (2010) has eloquently written in *Why Translation Matters*, translation "represents a concrete literary presence with the crucial capacity to ease and make more meaningful our relationships to those with whom we may not have had a connection before," helping readers "to see from a different angle, to attribute new value to what once may have been unfamiliar."

PURPOSE, SCOPE, AND SELECTION CRITERIA

This volume, which focuses on works of fiction translated into English from world languages, is conceived as a tool for academic and public libraries as well as the readers who use those institutions. Its purpose is not to create a comprehensive encyclopedia of major contemporary authors representing world literatures. We do not intend to compete with encyclopedic sources or guides such as the *Columbia Guides to Literature Since 1945* or the Babel Guides series. Instead, the purpose of our volume is to present a large and diverse sampling of contemporary world authors and their books translated into

English from 1980–2010. We certainly do not claim to include every author and every title translated from a non-English language in this period. Readers will understand how impossible that would be.

However, we tried to include as many authors as possible; thus, each author is represented by one main annotation. For those authors who have seen more than one of their works translated into English, we selected what appeared to be the most notable of those works. For example, Per Petterson is represented by his acclaimed *Out Stealing Horses*, although he very well could also have been represented by *To Siberia*. Other titles by the author are generally listed with brief descriptions or comments at the end of the annotation. Ultimately, this is a matter of subjective judgment.

We also tried to include translated authors not covered in mainstream media reviewing sources, although, again, this does not mean that we neglected mainstream reviews. In addition, a strong attempt was made to include authors from as many countries and languages as possible in order to achieve balanced representation, although, again, not all countries are represented for reasons of availability of materials as well as space limitations.

An analysis of "all translated titles reviewed in *Publishers Weekly* during 2004 and 2005" showed that this trade journal reviewed 132 translated titles in 2004 (out of 5,588 total reviews) and 197 translated titles in 2005 (out of 5,521 total reviews) (Maczka & Stock, 2006, p. 50). Of these translated books, the most popular languages were French (81 titles), followed by German (56), Spanish (39), Italian (21), Japanese (19), Dutch (13), Russian (13), Portuguese (10), and Swedish and Hebrew (nine each). In total, books in 34 languages were translated, including Chinese (seven), Polish (four), Arabic (three), and Icelandic (one) (Maczka & Stock, 2006, p. 51). In other words, about 59.9 percent of non-English books translated into English that were reviewed by *Publishers Weekly* from 2004–2005 were originally written in French, German, Spanish, and Italian.

Because of the influence of *Publishers Weekly* and because reviewed books tend to be purchased in greater quantities by libraries than nonreviewed books, the argument could be made that it is very likely that the percentages of nation-specific translated fiction and nonfiction on library shelves—especially public library shelves—broadly mirror the percentages discussed above. Our volume can be used to reinforce or alter those percentages. Certainly, many people will find some of their favorite translated authors and fiction titles missing; others will perhaps scratch their heads in amazement that we overlooked such and such a title. But the books that are included here will allow interested readers and librarians a chance to begin to explore the wide range of translated fiction available in diverse languages.

Some of the genres common in North America, such as romance, horror fiction, or fantasy, are not widely represented in translated literature—although elements of those genres can often be found in translated work (e.g., the magical realism movement resulted in many titles with fantastic elements). Although these genres are noted (check the subject index for the terms *paranormal*, *horror*, and *speculative*), the selection will be limited. On the other hand, detective and mystery stories, thrillers, and suspense fiction are popular worldwide, as are novels with certain themes or story types, such as coming-of-age. However, the bulk of fiction translated into English is comprised of books that may be referred to as mainstream and/or literary fiction.

The Library of Congress Classification (LCC) was used as a basis for finding major languages and literatures of the world. Using the web version of LCC (http://classificationweb.net), we utilized the search function (keyword search) to locate "Individual authors or works" within specific literatures (e.g., "African" or "Russian" or "French"). The keyword search was used as a jumping-off point to the appropriate LCC schedules. Then, we sifted through the respective schedules and related tables, identifying call number ranges for specific languages and time periods in class P for Languages and Literatures. For example, "Swedish literature—Individual authors or works—1961–2000" corresponded to the following call number range: PT9876.1-9876.36; and "Swedish literature—Individual authors or works—2001" corresponded to the following call number range: PT9877.1-9877.36. Using the call number ranges derived from LCC Web, we subsequently ran multiple searches in The Harvard

University Library holdings (Hollis Catalog) to identify specific authors and titles for each language. In most cases, the call number ranges defined through LCC Web ensured that we covered authors whose creative proliferation fell into the time period after 1980.

However, it was impossible to eliminate all older authors through LCC ranges alone; therefore, manual elimination by using Hollis searches was performed. We excluded authors whose works were extensively published and translated before 1980, even if these authors continued to be published and translated after 1980. Again, there are exceptions.

The primary arrangement of this book is by language rather than by country, although the two coincide in some cases. Language ties often better reflect cultural cohesion than national borders or geographies. For example, the primary arrangement is by German literature rather than by literature from Germany. Here, German literature includes secondary division by country: German literature from Austria; German literature from Germany; and German literature from Switzerland. Similarly, the primary arrangement is by Arabic literature and the secondary division is by country: Arabic literature from Iraq; Arabic literature from Egypt; Arabic literature from Yemen; and so on.

No method of arrangement of world literature is without flaws and limitations, and ours is no exception. Organizing by language groups has resulted in some groupings that may not initially resonate with readers. For example, literature of the Caribbean islands can be found in two chapters—that covering Spanish-language translations and that covering French-language translations. And countries, such as Belgium, where French is spoken as well as Dutch, are mentioned in Chapter 8 and in Chapter 9. However, we feel that this arrangement best reflects the commonalities and cohesion of various types of world literature. In addition to the detailed table of contents, indexes and chapter keys are provided to assist readers in navigating the guide, and references in chapter introductions comment on the locations of related groupings.

In all the Hollis searches, which were performed by using the expanded search function, the following limiters were applied: Language: English; Format: Books; and Year Range: 1980–2006. The call number ranges ensured the retrieval of works originally written in specific languages of interest by individual authors writing in these languages; the limiter by Language (English) ensured that only translations or bilingual editions (including the original and the translation) were retrieved. The initial searches were performed between April 2005 and March 2006. A comprehensive list of authors and titles was created. This list was later supplemented by information derived from various sources, including but not limited to the following: the Babel Guides series; the Wilson Authors series (e.g., *World Authors, 1995–2000*); the *Columbia Guides to Literature Since 1945* series; resources incorporated into the *Literature Resource Centre Online* (Thomson-Gale); *Timetables of World Literature* by G. T. Kurian; numerous Internet resources; and more recently translated books from the years 2007, 2008, 2009, and the early part of 2010. For books translated in these more recent years, we included some of the titles that were mentioned by mainstream reviewing sources, such as *The New York Times Book Review* and *The New Yorker*, or featured on the Three Percent website.

From these assembled titles, we chose the books that are included in the following chapters. We focused on novels, although there are also collections of short stories. Children's books are typically absent in this volume.

Some regions, such as India and Africa, produce an immense body of fiction in English. While belonging to the category of world literature, such books are not translated per se. Our assumption is that regardless of the country of origin, literature originally written in English does not encounter the same problems of access and promotion as it makes its way to North America as does translated fiction. It is not English-language books from abroad but rather translated fiction specifically that often remains out of the public eye. In addition, books written in English are generally published with a world audience in mind, whereas those written in a non-English language are likely written for a smaller and more cohesive audience, which means that in some ways, they offer readers a truer representation of their cultures of origin. Therefore, books from such English-speaking countries as

Australia or New Zealand as well as books from India and Africa originally written in English are considered outside the scope of this volume.

The following databases were used to locate popular and literary criticism about the selected titles: ProQuest; Expanded Academic; Factiva; Literature Resource Centre; JSTOR; Literature Online; and Global Books in Print. In addition, print sources and Internet-only sources, such as Amazon.com, were also used. Our annotations are based on these reviews and external sources. Although we read some of the books that appear here, we do not want to mislead readers into thinking that we read every title. We did not. Instead, we relied on numerous external sources (as described in the previous sentences) for a majority of the annotations. Some of the annotations (and discussions of related titles) are short; some are longer (e.g., *The Redbreast* by Jo Nesbø; *Silence of the Grave* by Arnaldur Indriđason; *The Kindly Ones* by Jonathan Littell; *The Terra-Cotta Dog* by Andrea Camilleri; *Out* by Natsuo Kirino; *Snow* by Orhan Pamuk; *Out Stealing Horses* by Per Petterson; and others). Typically, these longer annotations (and discussions of related titles) represent books that were read in their entirety. But we hope that all contain at least one interesting fact that may be of interest to potential readers. Finally, readers will discover that, for some of the annotated titles, there are other (either earlier or later) editions.

ARRANGEMENT OF CHAPTERS AND ENTRIES

Outside of this introduction, the book is divided into nine chapters, which—as stated previously—group titles by language and cultural groups and/or geography. The overall arrangement of chapters is as follows:

- Chapter 1: Africa: African Vernacular, Afrikaans, French, and Portuguese
- Chapter 2: The Arab World: Middle East, Trans-Caucasus, and Western/Central Asia
- Chapter 3: East Asia: China, Japan, and Korea
- Chapter 4: South Asia: India, Pakistan, Bangladesh, Nepal, and Other South Asian Countries
- Chapter 5: The Mediterranean: Greece, Israel, and Italy
- Chapter 6: Russia and Central and Eastern Europe
- Chapter 7: The Iberian Peninsula and Latin America
- Chapter 8: Northern Europe: Low Countries, Scandinavia, and Baltic Countries
- Chapter 9: Western Europe: Austria, Germany, France, Switzerland, French-Speaking Belgium, and French-Speaking Caribbean

The annotated entries within chapters are generally arranged geographically (by country), but in the case of Africa, language group became the primary organizational dictate. With regard to countries or languages within one region, we opted for alphabetical organization. Of course, no geographic arrangement is perfect, and some readers may quibble with our decisions.

A "key" at the beginning of each chapter is intended to inform readers of the original languages covered and help them navigate and locate titles from certain countries—meaning the country of origin for the author (rather than the settings represented in the books).

At the beginning of each chapter, you will also find a brief overview of the contents of the chapter and a quick glance at earlier translated fiction from the region in question. A bibliographic essay follows, discussing reference sources and monographs about some of the world literatures mentioned in that chapter. Each of the described books in these essays was individually examined. These essays are in no way meant to be exhaustive—merely indicative of some items that interested readers may use to learn more about a specific literary tradition and its authors.

The annotated author/title entries in this volume include information about an author's name in direct order; a title; a translator; place of publication and publisher; genre/literary style/story type; an annotation; related title(s) by the same author; one or two subject keywords; original language; and a list of other translated books written by the author. Not every entry includes all this information. Each entry also includes a subheading entitled "Source(s) Consulted for Annotation" where we give credit to any sources used, paraphrased, or quoted to produce the annotation. We cite many reviews from *Publishers Weekly*, *Library Journal*, and *Booklist* under this heading. Of course, these reviews appear in the publications cited, but they also appear on the Amazon website and in the electronic version of Global Books in Print.

Using WorldCat and bibliographic databases named in the methodology section, we verified the accuracy of bibliographic information provided for the cited entries and sources. But various databases have different degrees of completeness and their own unique formats for data representation. The same review from *Publishers Weekly* can be indexed as "anonymous" in Expanded Academic and have a reviewer's name attached to it in ProQuest; the date of publication can be indexed as "Summer" in Expanded Academic and as "1 July" in ProQuest. Because we utilized a variety of databases, we cannot guarantee complete consistency in how certain cited sources are represented throughout the volume. Certain bibliographic details could not be verified; these were omitted.

There are a number of indexes at the end of this guide where readers will be able to find listings of, among other things, authors, titles, and subjects.

FORMS OF AUTHORS' NAMES

The representation of names of authors whose original languages are written in non-Roman alphabets (i.e., Arabic, Greek, Hebrew, Slavic Cyrillic, and the languages of India and South Asia) presented a challenge. For these language groups, many author names are followed by an alternative form provided in parentheses. The basic form of names is derived from WorldCat catalog records for the corresponding title and facilitates the retrieval of authors' works in most North American catalogs. The alternative (in parentheses) form of a name is based on the form of an author's name that can be found on a book cover, in publishers' catalogs, and in acquisitions tools (e.g., Global Books in Print). While WorldCat relies on Library of Congress (LC) authority records and LC-established forms of names, publishers do not necessarily follow LC conventions. We provide alternative forms of names for non-Roman names in order to facilitate the retrieval of authors' works in sources other than library catalogs. We verified alternative forms of names by using the actual items or book covers online. However, when neither items nor covers were accessible, we relied on information contained in the Responsibility field of WorldCat bibliographic records.

Alphabetization of the entries is based on the form of name found in the "Author(s)" field of WorldCat bibliographic records, where the name can be presented in either direct or inverted order, according to the cataloging rules for a specific language.

A FEW WORDS ABOUT TRANSLATED FICTION

When *The New York Times Book Review* published its list of the 10 best fiction and nonfiction books of 2007, it was striking that of the five fiction books on the list, two were translated fiction. Forty percent of what *The New York Times Book Review*—perhaps the most influential and widely read book review journal in the United States—considered to be the best fiction for 2007 was originally published in a non-English language. These two books were *Out Stealing Horses* by Per Petterson, a former librarian and bookseller, and *The Savage Detectives* by Roberto Bolaño (both discussed in this guide). Petterson's work was translated from the Norwegian. Bolaño, a Chilean writer, originally wrote in Spanish. In 2008, Bolaño's *2666* was named one of the five best fiction books of the year by *The New York Times Book Review*, which also included Ma Jian's *Beijing Coma* and Victor Pelevin's *The Sacred Book of the Werewolf* in its list of "100 Notable Books of 2008" (all three are discussed in this guide).

Roberto Bolaño, who died in 2003 and is revered in the Spanish-speaking literary world, is perhaps the most well-known of these acclaimed writers to North American audiences. Writing about *The Savage Detectives*, James Wood (2007) characterized Bolaño as "[t]his wonderfully strange Chilean imaginer" who is "at once a grounded realist and a lyricist of the speculative." Jonathan Lethem (2008), an influential American writer whose most recent novel is *Chronic City*, refers to Bolaño as a "genius" because of his ability to interweave, in *2666*, "a blunt recitation of life's facts—his novels at times evoke biographies, case studies, police or government file—with digressive outbursts of lyricism as piercing as the disjunctions of writers like Denis Johnson, David Goodis or, yes, Philip K. Dick, as well as the filmmaker David Lynch."

Per Petterson, who won the Norwegian Critics Prize for Literature and the 2006 Independent Foreign Fiction Prize, has also received uncommon praise. Thomas McGuane (2007), author of such novels as *Nobody's Angel* and *The Cadence of Grass*, ranks him among the greatest of contemporary writers, specifically referring to *Out Stealing Horses* as "a gripping account of such originality as to expand the reader's own experience of life" that is reminiscent "of the careful and apropos writing of J. M. Coetzee, W. G. Sebald and Uwe Timm" as well as that of Knut Hamsun and Halldór Laxness.

Ma Jian, the Chinese author of such books as *The Noodle Maker* and *Stick Out Your Tongue*, was widely lauded for *Beijing Coma*, which places readers into the mind of Dai Wei, "who has lain in a waking coma, conscious but paralyzed, since he was shot leaving Tiananmen Square" and then takes them on a journey "through his childhood in the Cultural Revolution, his adventures as a lovesick college student and his involvement in the student movement, and then through China's transformative decade, from 1989 to the millennium, as he overhears it from a bed in his aging mother's apartment" (Row, 2008).

And Victor Pelevin—a well-respected Russian writer known for *The Life of Insects* (discussed in this guide), *Buddha's Little Finger*, and *Homo Zapiens*—clearly outdid himself with *The Sacred Book of the Werewolf*, which is narrated "by a shape-shifting nymphet named A Hu-Li, a red-haired Asiatic call girl who is some 2,000 years old but looks 14" (Schillinger, 2008). As this "supernatural creature" and "supervixen" trolls for "investment bankers" at posh hotels, she ponders "the precepts of Confucianism, Buddhism and Sikhism, along with the theories of Wittgenstein, William of Occam, Freud, Foucault and, especially, Berkeley" (Schillinger, 2008).

But neither the five books specifically mentioned here nor any of the others annotated in the following chapters would be accessible to unilingual English-speaking readers were it not for the translator. Thus, the translator takes on a highly significant role, acting as a kind of intermediary between the original text and the translated text. As Suzanne Jill Levine (2009) argues, the translator is, as indicated by the title of her book, a "subversive scribe" who plays a central, not secondary, role in bringing world literature to English-speaking audiences. Moreover, as Anthony Pym (2010) explains in *Exploring Translation Theories*, translators rely on a vast body of theory to situate themselves in relation to their texts.

Thus, it is no surprise that, like writing styles, translating styles vary. A good way to get a sense of this variability is to look at what two of the better known translators of contemporary world fiction have to say about their work. Howard Goldblatt, a prolific translator of such Chinese titles as *Life and Death Are Wearing Me Out* (by Mo Yan) and *The Moon Opera* (by Bi Feiyu), views his primary task as making as much Chinese literature as possible available to English-speaking readers. As he observes, "The satisfaction of knowing I've faithfully served two constituencies keeps me happily turning good, bad, and indifferent Chinese prose into readable, accessible, and—yes—even marketable English books" (Goldblatt, 2002). That does not mean that he does not pay attention to the nuances of Chinese; he most certainly does—and then some. But his overarching aim is accessibility.

A different approach is taken by the equally prolific Margaret Jull Costa, who translates from the Portuguese and Spanish. Noting that she has "an unerring eye for the non-bestseller," she focuses on such writers as Javier Marías, Eça de Queiroz, and José Saramago. She joyously tackles these authors' difficult prose, taking pride "in getting every bit of the sentence to connect syntactically and coherently without losing the rhythm or the reader" and not stopping until "one of those page-long or two-page-long sentences really works in English with no loss of cogency" (qtd. in Doll, 2009). As a result, she often revises her translations "about nine or ten times" simply because she devotes an extraordinary amount of time in trying to burrow into the author's mind for the purpose of "reimagining the text, of allowing the language of the text to become part of my imagination (qtd. in Doll, 2009).

We do not mean to suggest that one of these translators is better than the other; both Goldblatt and Jull Costa are widely and justifiably admired. If readers continue to read international fiction, they will inevitably start to pay attention to the translators of that fiction. They will begin to notice recurring translator names, and they will begin to form their own judgments about translation styles—just as they form their own judgments about the original fiction being translated.

THE RICH HERITAGE OF TRANSLATION

Of course, there has always been a wealth of translation of fiction from non-English languages into English. How do we get a handle on this extensive historical heritage without losing sight of the forest for the trees?

One of the best places to start may be *The Oxford Guide to Literature in English Translation*, edited by Peter France (2000). This 656-page volume not only contains erudite essays on the history and theory of translation but also extensive region-specific essays about translated literatures from, among others, African languages, Celtic languages, Arabic, East Asian languages, Hispanic languages, Indian languages, French, Northern European languages, and West Asian languages. Each major language group is further broken down into subgroups. For example, the section on African languages includes subsections on East African languages; West African languages; languages of South Africa; and Afrikaans. The section on West Asian languages includes subsections on Ancient Mesopotamian literature; classical Persian; Modern Persian; and Turkish. The Arab section discusses translations of the Koran; *The Thousand and One Nights*; and Naguib Mahfouz. Similarly, the section about Hispanic languages includes subsections about medieval Spanish literature; Spanish poetry of the sixteenth and seventeenth centuries; picaresque novels; Latin American fiction in Spanish; Catalan; and Brazilian literature. Each of the essays take a historical approach, painting a nuanced portrait of the evolution of translated works from a specific language group or subgroup from the first extant English translation to the contemporary era. Each subsection in each section is followed by an extensive list of translated works from that language into English, including anthologies, novels, poetry collections, and plays as well as a list of bibliographic sources for further study. An equally extensive index allows the interested reader to easily locate specific translated authors.

For readers more interested in a historical and critical approach to translation, there is absolutely nothing better than *The Oxford History of Literary Translation in English* and the second edition of the *Routledge Encyclopedia of Translation Studies*. Containing essays from dozens of contributors, the five volumes in the *Oxford History of Literary Translation in English* cover the period from the Middle Ages to 2000. Each volume not only explores the role that translations played in "the larger literary culture of the period" under discussion but also looks in detail at specific works and authors that were translated into English during that period. For example, in the third volume of the series (1660–1790), there are overview articles about translation and canon formation; translation and literary innovation; and the publishing and readership of translation. These are followed by articles about translated French literature; Italian literature; Spanish literature; biblical translation and paraphrase; and many other translated literary traditions. In the first volume of the series (to 1550), there are not-to-be-missed articles about such topics as patronage and sponsorship of translation and religious writing and women translators. In volume 4 (1790–1900), indispensable articles include translation, politics, and the law; principles and norms of translation; literatures of the Indian subcontinent; and literatures of Central and Eastern Europe. Each volume concludes with a section containing biographical information about translators working during the relevant timeframe.

The *Routledge Encyclopedia of Translation Studies* will especially be of interest to those people who want to know about various theories of translation as well as the history of translation in non-English speaking countries and regions. It concisely summarizes the different ways of dealing with the many challenges that arise when translating fiction and nonfiction, discussing such topics as adaptation, dialogue interpretation, localization, pseudotranslation, think-aloud protocols, and the unit of translation. It also describes in significant detail the philosophical and ideological issues that translators must consider when deciding which intellectual framework they will use for their translation. Among the many possible approaches to choose from are the interpretive; descriptive vs. committed; functionalist; postcolonial; psycholinguistic and cognitive; and sociological. Finally, it has in-depth essays about the history and tradition of translation in Russia, China, Turkey, Sweden, Iceland, France, Germany, and Hungary—to name only a few.

Once the five-volume *Oxford History of Literary Translation in English*, the one-volume *The Oxford Guide to Literature in English Translation*, and the *Routledge Encyclopedia of Translation Studies* have been thoroughly perused, it may be time to turn to the *Encyclopedia of Literary Translation in English*, a massive two-volume set (containing about 1,700 pages in total) edited by Olive Classe. There are three major types of entries: general and historical surveys of literary translation into English from the major world languages—classical and modern; topics related to the history, theory, and practice of literary translation into English; and writer and work entries, which are "analytical accounts of the treatment in English translation of (a) all the significant translated works by major world authors or (b) single translated works" (Classe, 2000, p. xi). In addition to an alphabetical and chronological list of entries, readers and librarians will be immeasurably helped by a list of writers and works by language. Using this feature, one can easily locate, for example, all the Bengali, Hindi, Modern Greek, Russian, or Japanese writers covered by the encyclopedia. And the sheer number of writers discussed is astounding, including Han Yu (China), Christa Wolf (German), Endre Ade (Hungary), Witold Gombrowicz (Poland), Vasko Popa (Serbo-Croat), Clarice Lispector (Brazil), and Evgenii Zamiatin (Russia). Each author entry contains a biography, a list of that author's translated works into English, and guidance about further readings about the author in question. In addition, one can find survey essays about such relatively obscure topics as Albanian, Catalan, and Finnish literary translations into English. Finally, there is a title index, a translator index, and a general index. As with *The Oxford Guide to Literature in English Translation*, the *Encyclopedia of Literary Translation in English* is the kind of reference source that one could spend years leafing through and even more years reading all the translated works therein contained.

Just as stunning in its breadth and depth is the two-volume *Reference Guide to World Literature* (3rd ed.) published in 2003 by St. James Press and edited by Sara Pendergast and Tom Pendergast. This mammoth reference source, which has over 1,700 pages, is divided into two parts: The first volume provides detailed bio-bibliographic information about world authors (including a list of their translated works), and the second volume contains critical analyses of such classic works of literature as the well-known *Petersburg* by the Russian novelist Andrei Belyi and the less well-known *Snow Country* by the Japanese novelist Kawabata Yasunari. The third edition is particularly to be commended for its emphasis on languages that were less represented in the previous two editions: Arabic, Chinese, and Japanese as well as Thai, Estonian, Dutch, Farsi, Belarusian, Kurdish, Kreol, Persian, and

Ukrainian. Writers come from such countries as Indonesia, Ivory Coast, Mozambique, Syria, Tunisia, Iran, and Morocco. The introduction to the two-volume set also emphasizes that it has expanded its coverage of contemporary women's writers to include such authors as the Nicaraguan poet and novelist Gioconda Belli and the Indian novelist Qurratulain Hyder, who writes in Urdu.

KEEPING CURRENT WITH ELECTRONIC AND PRINT RESOURCES

Notwithstanding the general excellence of the foregoing books—by virtue of their publication dates in the early 2000s—they obviously do not cover post-2000 developments. How, then, can one keep up? We recommend the following electronic sources: the website for *Booktrust*; the website for the *Center for Literary Translation* at Columbia University; the Three Percent website (part of the Open Letter publishing initiative at the University of Rochester); and *Words Without Borders*, subtitled *The Online Magazine for International Literature*. Brief descriptions about what you will find at these websites appear in the paragraphs below, and URLs for them are provided at the end of the chapter. The following print sources are also valuable: *Translation Review*, with its sister publication *Annotated Books Received*; *World Literature Today*; and ongoing series from both Dalkey Archive Press and AmazonCrossing of world literature in translation. Again, brief descriptions of these sources appear below.

Booktrust, a website produced in the United Kingdom, features annotated lists of recommended, forthcoming, and recently published translated novels. There is an extensive review archive of translated fiction as well as overviews of publishers specializing in translated fiction.

The website for the *Center for Literary Translation* at Columbia University is also useful for its list of publishing houses specializing in translations as well as journals and magazines that feature translated authors. Equally noteworthy is its list of translation resources by country. For example, someone interested in contemporary literature from Finland, Germany, or Turkey can be linked to relevant sites, which not only contain general information about developments in that literary tradition but also information about translations into English.

The Three Percent website (so named because "only about 3% of all books published in the United States are works in translation") is a treasure trove of information about recently translated fiction. Overseen by Chad W. Post, the director of Open Letter Press, Three Percent defines itself on its website as "A resource for international literature at the University of Rochester." To say it is a resource is quite an understatement. Not only does the site contain informed news and commentary about the state of translations (e.g., the economics of publishing translations), but it also provides detailed lists of all translated titles published each year in the United States. These lists have invaluable information about the number of fiction and poetry books translated each year into English, but also quantitative information about the languages from which books are translated and the publishers of translated works. By glancing at the list of publishers, readers can get a good sense of the key players in the world of translated fiction and poetry. For example, in 2008, 2009, and 2010, top publishers of translated titles were, among others, Dalkey Archive, New Directions, Vertical, Europa Editions, Open Letter, Archipelago Books, Green Integer, Overlook, White Pine, Toby Press, Ugly Duckling, and American University at Cairo Press. But perhaps the most important feature of the Three Percent website is its review section, which has hundreds of articles about new translated fiction and is constantly expanding.

Words Without Borders is also important. Here, again, there are extensive reviews about recently translated literature into English. One can discover *Missing Soluch* by Mahmoud Dowlatabadi, a novel about rural village life in Iran, translated from the Farsi; *The Model* by Lars Saabye Christensen, a novel about the lengths an artist will go to remain an artist, translated from the Norwegian; *Allah Is Not Obliged* by Ivory Coast author Ahmadou Kourouma, a novel about the tragic fate of child soldiers, translated from the French; and *Paradise Travel* by Jorge Franco, a book about illegal Colombian immigrants in the United States, translated from the Spanish. Likewise, there are special issues about such topics as Francophone Africa; Seoul searching; the groves of Lebanon; the Balkans; checkpoints: literature from Iraq; writing from North Korea; and the Lusophone world. To round out the offerings, there are interviews with international authors as well as lesson plans and study guides about world literatures for educators. *Words Without Borders* also put together an anthology of fiction and non-fiction originally written in Arabic, Persian, Turkish, and Urdu. Entitled *Tablet & Pen: Literary Landscapes from Modern Middle East* and edited by Reza Aslan, it was subsequently published in 2010 by W. W. Norton to resounding acclaim (Rohter, 2010).

Translation Review, which is the official publication of the American Literary Translators Association (ALTA), contains—according to its website—"in-depth interviews with translators; articles that deal with the evaluation of existing translations; profiles on small, commercial, and university publishers of foreign literature in translation; [and] comparative studies of multiple translations into English of the same work." Recent articles have covered such topics as modern Arabic poetry in English translation and on translating *The Prison Diary* of Ho Chi Minh. Perhaps of greater interest to librarians is *Annotated Books Received*, also published by the ALTA. This publication, which is only available online at the ALTA website and appears twice a year, "lists recent books in English translation, with a brief annotation for each book listed." Each of the issues "covers more than 100 book titles, organized by language area, and includes an index of translators and publishers." This is a superb way to find out about recent translations of, for example, the work of Silvia Molina, a Mexican writer, or the Guadeloupean novelist Maryse Condé and to keep abreast of translations from Czech, Icelandic, Tamil, and Italian.

World Literature Today (WLT), formerly called *Books Abroad*, serves much the same purpose as *Translation Review*, but it contains many more articles and book reviews. A typical issue of *WLT*, which is published quarterly, has about 100 pages, with issues of more than 150–200 pages not being uncommon. A random issue from 2003 contains articles discussing the Hungarian writer Imre Kertész; the international children's literature movement; Swedish writer Kerstin Ekman; Maltese playwright Francis Ebejer; Latin American writers in perspective; and new poetry from Chile, Romania, and the United States. Another random issue from 2008 contains essays about politics and contemporary Danish fiction; voices of the feminine in Brazilian literature; and Senegalese novelist Ousmane Sembène, author of *The Black Docker*, among other translated works. In addition, there are special issues that focus on a single writer (such as Colombian author Alvaro Mutis or Nigerian author Chimamanda Ngozi Adichie) or a single theme (such as endangered languages; graphic literature; or inside China). Worth highlighting in this regard is a recent 2010 issue of *WLT*, which is devoted to world science fiction. Perhaps most importantly, there is a book review section that has to be seen to be believed. It contains reviews not only of translated works but also of nontranslated works in their original languages. Here, one can learn about translated work by Japanese novelist Miri Yu concerning the growing problem of teenage violence (*Gold Rush*) and Korean novelist Yi In-hwa, who has written a historical mystery called *Everlasting Empire*.

Moreover, we want to point readers to a new series that promises to provide annual updates about translated European fiction. Dalkey Archive Press, a major publisher of translated literature, has been much praised for *Best European Fiction 2010*, edited by Aleksandar Hemon, a Bosnian American writer well-known for his novel *The Lazarus Project*, and introduced by Zadie Smith, author of *White Teeth*, among others. Containing translated work from authors from such countries as Estonia, Switzerland, Slovenia, Liechtenstein, Macedonia, Latvia, Slovakia, and numerous others, the first installment of this annual anthology is a rich source of information about contemporary writers working in non-English European languages. One can imagine Dalkey Archive—or another publisher—undertaking similar anthologies about East Asian, South American, and Middle Eastern fiction.

As mentioned in the "Preface," Dalkey Archive is also working closely with governmental and non-govermental entities from diverse countries and regions to publish numerous translated series of full-length fiction titles by authors writing in the languages spoken in those countries and regions. For example, Dalkey's Slovenian series includes books such as *Necropolis* by Boris Pahor and *You Do Understand* by Andrej Blatnik (Rohter, 2010).

Finally, we draw readers' attention to the AmazonCrossing imprint of Amazon, established in 2010. Devoted to world literature (both fiction and non-fiction) in translation, AmazonCrossing, according to its website, relies on "customer feedback and other data from Amazon sites to identify exceptional works that deserve a wider, global audience." Its first published title was Tierno Monénembo's historical novel *The King of Kahel* (originally written in French), soon followed by other novels such as Oliver Pötzsch's *The Hangman's Daughter* (a historical thriller originally written in German); Lin Zhe's *Old Town* (a wide-ranging novel of family history originally written in Chinese); Oksana Zabuzko's *Field Work in Ukrainian Sex* (originally written in Ukrainian), widely hailed as a contemporary classic of Ukrainian literature (AmazonCrossing, 2010); and Martin Redrado's *No Reserve: The Limit of Absolute Power* (a non-fiction work originally written in Spanish), a social and economic analysis of contemporary developments in Argentina.

INTERNATIONAL AWARDS

Now that you are fully up-to-date with the new translated fiction titles mentioned in these sources, you may also want to keep an eye on the annual literary awards from such countries as France, Germany, or Spain. The winners of major literary prizes in these countries are often strong candidates for translation into English. For example, the 2006 winner of the Prix Goncourt, France's highest literary honor, was Jonathan Littell's *Les Bienveillantes*; it was translated into English in 2009 as *The Kindly Ones* (discussed in this guide). The 2008 Prix Goncourt winner, *Syngué Sabour* by Atiq Rahimi, an exiled Afghani writer living in France who has previously written books in Dari, was translated into English as *The Patience Stone* (discussed in this guide). His prize-winning novel is "a poetic, and sometimes crude, monologue by a woman sitting with her dying 'war hero' husband" that becomes an eloquent account of "the oppression of women in Afghanistan" (Lichfield, 2008).

The 2007 winner of the Prix Goncourt, *Alabama Song* by Gilles Leroy, is a sensitively wrought and psychologically acute examination of the tumultuous and tragic life of Zelda Sayre Fitzgerald, wife of F. Scott Fitzgerald. It will no doubt eventually be translated into English, since it has already been translated into more than 25 other languages. English translations will also likely be made of the 2009 Goncourt winner, *Trois Femmes Puissantes*, by French-Senegalese author Marie NDiaye, a riveting account of displacement, exile, and suffering; and of the 2010 Goncourt winner, *La Carte et le Territoire* by Michel Houellebecq, an unsettling and astute consideration of the ethics of living and dying (discussed in this guide).

Just as important—if not more—is the annual Nobel Prize for Literature. Announced in the first weeks of October, the Nobel Prize for Literature often goes to authors who write in non-English languages. (A complete list of Nobel Laureates in Literature is listed at the Nobel Prize web address given in the reference list below.) Some of these authors' novels, plays, or poems already exist in English prior to their winning the Nobel Prize, but it is almost always the case that—subsequent to the award—there is a concerted effort to translate or reissue their entire past and future corpus. Recent laureates include the Portuguese author José Saramago (1998); the Turkish writer Orhan Pamuk (2006); the French writer J.-M. G. Le Clézio (2008); Herta Müller, originally from Romania but writing in German (2009); and the Peruvian author Mario Vargas Llosa (2010). Readers who would like to have as much detail as possible about each of the Nobel Prize winners in literature should welcome with open arms four volumes published in 2007 in the Dictionary of Literary Biography series: *Nobel*

Prize Laureates in Literature, Part 1: Agnon–Eucken (Vol. 329); *Nobel Prize Laureates in Literature, Part 2: Faulkner–Kipling* (Vol. 330); *Nobel Prize Laureates in Literature, Part 3: Lagerkvist–Pontoppidian* (Vol. 331); *Nobel Prize Laureates in Literature, Part 4: Quasimodo–Yeats* (Vol. 332). Each of the entries contains a substantial overview and critical analysis of the author in question, a complete list of his or her works, and some combination of official acceptance speeches, banquet speeches, presentation speeches, and autobiographical statements. The entry for Saramago is about 30 pages, while the entry for Frans Eemil Sillanpää, the first Finnish writer to be awarded the Nobel Prize (in 1939), is 10 pages. In fact, the Dictionary of Literary Biography series, which had over 340 volumes by the middle of 2008 and shows no signs of stopping, publishes numerous volumes about world literature. For example, Volume 326 in the series was *Chinese Fiction Writers, 1900–1949* and Volume 346 was *20th-Century Arabic Writers*.

Saramago, of course, is known for such novelistic parables as *Blindness*, *Seeing*, and *The Cave*, which explore the underpinnings of social and political power (all discussed in this guide). In these works, he typically imagines "a fanciful, what if? sort of premise" and then logically wends his way through all its "possible ramifications" to a resolution (Rafferty, 2006). In *The Cave*, Saramago ruminates on the all-pervasive power of a modern-day shopping and entertainment center that not only destroys an artisanal way of life but also presents itself as the one true path toward truth and salvation. In *Blindness*, an inexplicable epidemic of blindness envelopes an entire nation, plunging everyone except one person into a phantasmagoric and violent landscape that calls into question the basis of their humanity. In *Seeing*, no less than 83 percent of the population of a nameless country chooses to leave their ballots blank during an election, giving rise to fears of a mysterious revolution whose target may be the professionalization of government.

Pamuk is well-known for his elegiac accounts of the Turkish experience. Whether his setting is the sophisticated metropolis of Istanbul (the novels *Black Book* and *The Museum of Innocence* as well as the autobiographical *Istanbul: Memories and the City*); the Ottoman empire in the sixteenth century (the novel *My Name Is Red*, discussed in this guide); or a small provincial town in Anatolia cut off from the rest of the world by a seemingly interminable winter storm and driven by tensions between fundamentalist Muslims, Kurds, and secularists (the novel *Snow*, discussed in this guide), his books provide what Margaret Atwood (2004) calls "an in-depth tour of the divided, hopeful, desolate, mystifying Turkish soul," with a view toward "narrating his country into being."

Le Clézio may be the least well-known of recent Nobel laureates. He has lived in such various locations as Mauritius and Nigeria; written "his doctoral thesis for the University of Perpignan on the early history of Mexico"; "taught at colleges in Mexico City, Bangkok, Albuquerque and Boston"; "lived among the Embera Indians in Panama"; and "published translations of Mayan sacred texts" (Lyall, 2008). It is therefore no surprise that his writing is equally wide ranging, encompassing such themes as "exile and self-discovery, . . . cultural dislocation and globalization, . . . [and] the clash between modern civilization and traditional cultures" (Lyall, 2008). His most famous works are *Wandering Star*, a novel which considers the parallels between Jewish and Palestinian refugees; *Onitsha*, partly based on the author's childhood in Nigeria; and *Desert*, a magisterial examination of Saharan nomad culture and French urban life as seen through the eyes of a young woman (all three books are discussed in this guide).

CONCLUSION

Translated fiction encourages a new way of looking at things. If you read one or two of the novels that we annotate in the following pages and if you read about one or two aspects of one or more non-English literary traditions as discussed in the bibliographic essays, this volume will have done its job. Under the spell of some of the authors mentioned in the following chapters, you will have—to paraphrase Atwood—narrated into being for yourself a new country (or countries) and a new culture (or cultures) without leaving your favorite reading chair or nook. You will have a better understanding of the world writ large as you engage with such books as Pamuk's *Snow*; Saramago's *Seeing*; Le Clézio's *Wandering Star*; Petterson's *Out Stealing Horses*; Bolaño's *2666*; Jian's *Beijing Coma*; and Pelevin's *The Sacred Book of the Werewolf*. Just by reading these seven books, you will feel some of the issues of importance in diverse geographic regions of the world. Think how much you will additionally gain by exploring the approximately 1,000 annotated entries that comprise the remainder of this volume.

REFERENCES

"10 Best Books of 2007." (2007, December 9). *The New York Times Book Review*. Available at http://www.nytimes.com (accessed January 4, 2008).

"100 Notable Books of 2008." (2008, December 7). *The New York Times Book Review*. Available at http://www.nytimes.com (accessed December 8, 2008).

AmazonCrossing. (2010). "World Literature in Translation." Available at http://www.amazon.com/gp/feature.html?ie=UTF8&docId=1000507571 (accessed December 9, 2010).

Atwood, Margaret. (2004, August 15). "Headscarves to Die For." Review of *Snow* by Orhan Pamuk (trans. by Maureen Freely). *The New York Times Book Review*. Available at http://www.nytimes.com (accessed September 7, 2006).

Baker, Mona, and Saldanha, Gabriela. (Ed.). (2008). *Routledge Encyclopedia of Translation Studies* (2nd ed.). London: Routledge.

Booktrust Translated Fiction. (2009). Available at http://www.translatedfiction.org.uk/Home (accessed July 21, 2009).

Center for Literary Translation at Columbia University. (2009). Available at http://www.centerforliterarytranslation.org/index.html (accessed July 21, 2009).

Classe, Olive. (Ed.). (2000). *Encyclopedia of Literary Translation into English* (2 vols.). London: Fitzroy Dearborn.

Doll, Megan. (2009, November). "An Interview with Margaret Jull Costa." *Bookslut*. Available at http://www.bookslut.com (accessed December 18, 2009).

France, Peter. (Ed.). (2000). *The Oxford Guide to Literature in English Translation*. Oxford: Oxford University Press.

France, Peter, and Gillespie, Stuart. (Eds.) (2006–2011). *The Oxford History of Literary Translation in English* (5 vols.). New York: Oxford University Press.

Goldblatt, Howard. (2002, April 18). "The Writing Life." *The Washington Post Book World*. Available at http://www.washingtonpost.com (accessed December 18, 2009).

Grossman, Edith. (2010). *Why Translation Matters*. New Haven, CT: Yale University Press. (Quotation taken from promotional material on Yale University Press website).

Lethem, Jonathan. (2008, November 9). "The Departed." Review of *2666* by Roberto Bolaño (trans. by Natasha Wimmer). *The New York Times Book Review*. Available at http://www.nytimes.com (accessed November 10, 2008).

Levine, Suzanne Jill. (2009). *The Subversive Scribe: Translating Latin American Fiction*. Champaign, IL: Dalkey Archive Press.

Lichfield, John. (2008, November 11). "Award: 2008 Prix Goncourt." Available at http://newpagesblog.blogspot.com/2008/11/award-2008-prix-goncourt.html (accessed November 26, 2008).

Lyall, Sarah. (2008, October 10). "French Writer Wins Nobel Prize." *The New York Times*. Available at http://www.nytimes.com (accessed October 14, 2006).

Maczka, Michelle, and Stock, Riky. (2006). "Literary Translation in the United States: An Analysis of Translated Titles Reviewed by *Publishers Weekly*." *Publishing Research Quarterly* 22(2): 49–54.

McGuane, Thomas. (2007, June 24). "In a Lonely Place." Review of *Out Stealing Horses* by Per Petterson (trans. by Anne Born). *The New York Times Book Review*. Available at http://www.nytimes.com (accessed January 4, 2008).

Nobel Prize. (2008). "All Nobel Laureates in Literature." Available at http://nobelprize.org (accessed May 6, 2008).

Pendergast, Sara, and Pendergast, Tom. (Eds.). (2003). *Reference Guide to World Literature* (3rd ed.). (2 vols.). Detroit, MI: St. James Press.

Pym, Anthony. (2010). *Exploring Translation Theories*. New York: Routledge.

Rafferty, Terrence. (2006, April 9). "Every Nonvote Counts." Review of *Seeing* by José Saramago (trans. by Margaret Jull Costa). *The New York Times Book Review*. Available at http://www.nytimes.com (accessed April 10, 2006).

Rich, Motoko. (2008, October 19). "Translation is Foreign to U.S. Publishers." *The New York Times Book Review*. Available at http://www.nytimes.com (accessed October 20, 2008).

Rohter, Larry. (2010, December 8). "Translation as Literary Ambassador." Available at http://www.nytimes.com (accessed December 8, 2010).

Row, Jess. (2008, July 13). "Circling the Square." Review of *Beijing Coma* by Ma Jian. *The New York Times Book Review*. Available at http://www.nytimes.com (accessed November 27, 2008).

Schillinger, Liesl. (2008, September 26). "Demonic Muse." Review of *The Sacred Book of the Werewolf* by Victor Pelevin. Available at http://www.nytimes.com (accessed November 27, 2008).

Three Percent. (2008). A resource for international literature at the University of Rochester. Available at http://www.rochester.edu/College/translation/threepercent (accessed October 12, 2008).

Translation Review. (1978–ongoing). Official Publication of the American Literary Translators Association (ALTA). Published by The University of Texas at Dallas, Richardson, TX. Available at http://www.utdallas.edu/alta/publications/translation-review (accessed May 5, 2008).

Walsh, S. Kirk. (2006, August 17). "Cast Adrift by Grief, Mourning Becomes Arvid." Review of *In the Wake* by Per Petterson (trans. by Anne Born). *The New York Times Book Review*. Available at http://www.nytimes.com (accessed December 16, 2007).

Wood, James. (2007, April 15). "The Visceral Realist." Review of *The Savage Detectives* by Roberto Bolaño (trans. by Natasha Wimmer). *The New York Times Book Review*. Available at http://www.nytimes.com (accessed January 4, 2008).

Words Without Borders: The Online Magazine for International Literature. (2003–ongoing). Available at http://wordswithoutborders.org (accessed May 14, 2008).

World Literature Today. (1927–ongoing). Formerly known as *Books Abroad* until end of 1976. Published at the University of Oklahoma, Norman, OK. Available at http://www.ou.edu/worldlit (accessed May 5, 2008).

CHAPTER 1

Africa: African Vernacular, Afrikaans, French, and Portuguese

Languages groups:	**Countries represented:**	
African Vernacular	Algeria	Mauritius
Kikuyu	Angola	Morocco
Swahili	Cameroon	Mozambique
Yoruba	Cape Verde	Nigeria
Zulu	Congo, Republic of	Rwanda
Afrikaans	(Congo-Brazzaville)	Senegal
French	Cote de Ivoire (Ivory Coast)	South Africa
Portuguese	Djibouti, Republic of	Tanzania
	Egypt	Togo
	Kenya	Tunisia
	Mali	Zaire

INTRODUCTION

This chapter contains annotations of books translated from the languages of Africa. It is subdivided into four parts: translations from African vernacular languages; Afrikaans; French; and Portuguese. Please note that North African countries where Arabic is spoken—such as Egypt, Sudan, and Morocco—are also covered in Chapter 2.

Among the African vernacular-language books mentioned here are Sibusiso Nyembezi's *The Rich Man of Pietermaritzburg* (translated from Zulu) and *Wizard of the Crow* by Ngugi wa Thiong'o (translated from Kikuyu). Readers who wish to gain insight about the contemporary political situation in some African nations may want to begin with these books. The Yoruba classic *The Forest of a Thousand Daemons* by D. O. Fagunwa and translated by the Nobel Prize–winning author Wole Soyinka is indispensable for a sound appreciation of the themes and structures of African literature.

Of the many translated Afrikaans titles, Mark Behr's *The Smell of Apples* and Marlene van Niekerk's *Agaat* are particular standouts. Both paint a vivid picture of the tragic consequences of the apartheid system—both on the personal and broader social levels. Behr translated his own novel, something for which André Philippus Brink was also well-known. Brink—who is perhaps one of the most visible novelists writing in Afrikaans—self-translated *The Ambassador*, among others.

A large number of the translated titles in this chapter were originally written in French, reflecting France's extensive colonial presence in Africa. The aftermath of this difficult historical situation is imaginatively presented in, for example, Ahmadou Kourouma's *Waiting for the Vote of the Wild Animals* and Patrice Nganang's *Dog Days: An Animal Chronicle*. Readers may also enjoy Bernard Binlin Dadié's *An African in Paris*; Ousmane Sembène's *Black Docker*; and Faïza Guène's *Kiffe Kiffe Tomorrow*—all three of which speak to the experiences of Africans from former French colonies who visit or live in France.

Portugal also had African colonies, so some novelists from Angola and Mozambique write in Portuguese. Two of the most notable are Jose Eduardo Agualusa, author of *The Book of Chameleons*, and Mia Couto, whose works include *Sleepwalking Land* and *The Last Flight of the Flamingo*. Readers may find it interesting to look for similarities and differences in the worldviews of African-Portuguese and African-French authors. They may also find it useful to compare some of the translated novels written in French by African authors in the 1950s, such as Camara Laye's *Black Child* and Ferdinand Oyono's *Houseboy*, with more recent titles from the 1990s and early 2000s.

Earlier Translated Literature

Much of the pre-twentieth-century heritage of African literature exists in the form of oral narratives, many of which are available in the Oxford Library of African Literature series. Among the noteworthy titles in this series are *Wisdom from the Nile: A Collection of Folkstories*; *The Zande Trickster*; *Akamba Stories*; *The Heroic Recitations of the Bahima of Ankole*; and *The Xhosa Ntsomi*. Other comparatively well-known narratives are *Sunjata* and *The Ozidi Saga*.

In the early twentieth century, African novels began to appear in vernacular languages. Groundbreaking texts include the translations of Thomas Mofolo's *Chaka: An Historical Romance* and *The Traveller of the East* (both written in Sesotho); T. N. Maumela's *Mafangambiti: The Story of a Bull* (written in Venda); A. C. Jordan's *The Wrath of the Ancestors* (written in Xhosa); and John Dube's *Jeqe the Bodyservant of King Tshaka* (written in Zulu).

SOURCES CONSULTED

France, Peter. (Ed.). (2000). "African Languages." In *The Oxford Guide to Literature in English Translation*, pp. 127–138. Oxford: Oxford University Press.

Klein, Leonard S. (Ed.). (1988). *African Literatures in the 20th Century: A Guide*. Harpenden, Herts, UK: Oldcastle Books.

BIBLIOGRAPHIC ESSAY

African literature cannot merely be reduced to the well-known novels of Nigerian author Chinua Achebe (e.g., *Things Fall Apart* and *Anthills of the Savannah*); the plays, poems, and dramas of the Nigerian Wole Soyinka, winner of the Nobel Prize for Literature in 1986; or the novels of Nuruddin Farah, a Somalian awarded the 1998 Neustadt International Prize for Literature. Nor is it sufficient to equate African literature with the works of such Botswana or South African writers as Bessie Head, Alan Paton, Nadine Gordimer, or J. M. Coetzee (winner of the Nobel Prize for Literature in 2003).

To be sure, these are some of the most well-known African writers, but this may be because they write in English. For readers interested in pursuing the English-language tradition in African writing, much bio-bibliographic information about these and many other authors can be found in the Dictionary of Literary Biography series—three volumes of *Twentieth-Century Caribbean and Black African Writers* (1992, 1993, 1996; vols. 117, 125, 157), all edited by Bernth Lindfors and Reinhard Sander—as well as in *South African Writers*, edited by Paul A. Scanlon (2000; vol. 225). In addition, there are two excellent literary histories in the Longman Literature in English series: *Southern African Literatures* by Michael Chapman, which covers South Africa, Malawi, Namibia, Zambia, and Zimbabwe, and *African Literatures in English: East and West* by Gareth Griffiths, which expertly positions Achebe and other writers from Kenya, Uganda, and nearby countries as "the culmination of a longer and more continuous tradition" where earlier writers "employed forms such as letters, journals, essays, legal prose, histories and ethnographies" (p. 109). These books can be supplemented by *The Columbia Guide to East African Literature in English Since 1945*, edited by Simon Gikandi and Evan Mwangi, which includes bio-bibliographic entries about authors from Ethiopia, Kenya, Somalia, Tanzania, and Uganda as well as thematic entries about topics such as Christian missions, autobiography, and popular literature; and *The Columbia Guide to Central African Literature in English Since 1945*, edited by Adrian A. Roscoe, which includes bio-bibliographic information about authors from Malawi, Zambia, and Zimbabwe as well as a historical overview about British colonialism.

But much of African literature is also written in French and Portuguese, not to mention such indigenous languages as Wolof, Sesotho, Hausa, San, Silozi, Lango, Diola, and Taureg. France was a major colonial power in Africa, especially in North Africa, West Africa, and the Sahel (e.g., Algeria, Morocco, Senegal, Mali, Niger, Burkina Faso, Chad, Mauritania, Ivory Coast, Togo, Benin, Gabon, Central African Republic, Congo-Brazzaville, and Cameroon). Portugal was a colonial power in Angola, Cape Verde, Guinea-Bissau, Mozambique, and São Tomé and Príncipe. Even Spain had colonies: Equatorial Guinea and Spanish Sahara (now referred to as Western Sahara and "claimed" by Morocco). As for indigenous languages, Kenyan writer Ngugi wa Thiong'o strongly believes that a true African literary identity can only be retained by writing in African languages. Obiajunwa Wali, in a 1963 article called "The Dead End of African Literature," concurred: "[U]ntil [African] writers and their Western midwives accept the fact that any true African literature must be written in African languages, they would be merely pursuing a dead end, which can only lead to sterility, uncreativity, and frustration."

To get a good introductory sense of the numerous literary traditions in Africa in non-English languages, we recommend that readers begin with the *Encyclopedia of African Literature*, edited by Simon Gikandi. Indeed, it is from this authoritative reference source that information about Ngugi's views and Wali's quotation (see above) are taken (p. 282). In addition to substantial bio-bibliographic information about such writers as Mongo Beti (born in Cameroon, writing in French); Patrick Chakaipa (born in Zimbabwe, writing in Shona); Mariama Bâ (born in Senegal, writing in French); Daniel Olorunfemi Fagunwa (born in Nigeria, writing in Yoruba); Xuanhenga Xitu (born in Angola, writing in Portuguese); Mia Couto (born in Mozambique, writing in Portuguese); Gakaara wa Wanjau (born in Kenya; writing in Gikuyu); and Camara Laye (born in Guinea, writing in French), readers will find authoritative articles on such topics as Sahelian literatures in African languages; Sahelian literatures in French; Gikuyu literature; South African literature in African languages; Islam in African literature; Swahili literature; Shona and Ndebele literature; West African literatures in French; Yoruba literature; North African literature in Arabic; North African literature in French; Central African literatures in French; realism and magical realism; Portuguese language literature; Afrikaans literature; Ethiopian literature; homosexuality; literature in Hausa; and oral literature and performance.

More detailed information about African authors is available in the two-volume reference work *African Writers*, edited by Brian Cox. Here, readers will find extensive bio-bibliographic and bio-critical articles (with available English-language translations indicated) about writers such as Mohammed Dib (Algeria); Ferdinand Oyono (Cameroon); Okot p'Bitek (Uganda); and Thomas

Mokopu Mofolo (Lesotho). Similar in purpose and broad scope is *Postcolonial African Writers: A Bio-Bibliographical Critical Sourcebook*, edited by Pushpa Naidu Parekh and Siga Fatima Jagne, which has many entries not found in Cox's *African Writers* (e.g., Senegalese writer Aminata Sow Fall; Cameroon writer Calixthe Beyala; and Mozambique writer Ungulani Ba Ka Khosa).

Three other reference books are noteworthy. *African Authors: A Companion to Black African Writing, 1300–1973*, edited by Donald E. Herdeck, has brief biographical entries for hundreds of authors, but its chief value lies in its series of appendices: critical essays about the development of contemporary African literature, black writers and the African revolution, vernacular writing in southern Africa, and key Afro-Caribbean writers; authors categorized by chronological period, genre, country of origin, and European and African language(s) employed; and an analytical table surveying anthologies of African writing according to the number of authors, selections, and total pages. On the other hand, *African Literatures in the 20th Century: A Guide*, edited by Leonard S. Klein, provides overviews of African literature by individual country. Finally, *African Literature and Its Times*, edited by Joyce Moss, gives excellent contextual information about such famous African novels as Mariama Bâ's *So Long a Letter*; Ferdinand Oyono's *Houseboy*; Sembène Ousmane's *God's Bit of Wood*; and Yacine Kateb's *Nedjma*.

After readers have sampled some of the fictional works by some of the authors mentioned here, they will no doubt want much more information about African literature as a whole. For this purpose, the two volumes of *The Cambridge History of African and Caribbean Literature*, edited by F. Abiola Irele and Simon Gikandi, are ideal. Here, readers will be treated to definitive chapters about such topics as Africa and orality; the folktale and its extensions; festivals, ritual, and drama in Africa; African oral epics; African literature in Arabic; the Swahili literary tradition; African-language literatures of southern Africa; the emergence of written Hausa literature; literature in Yoruba; Gikuyu literature; African literature in French; Francophone literatures of the Indian Ocean; African literatures in Spanish; literature in Afrikaans; African literatures in Portuguese; and African literature and postindependence disillusionment. This is a reference work that will be consulted and read decades from now—not only for its extensive bibliographies and judicious analysis but also for the staggering amount of factual information on every page.

We also want to draw attention to histories that are either shorter or more specialized. The first is *A History of Twentieth-Century African Literatures*, edited by Oyekan Owomoyela, which conveniently has separate chapters on French-language fiction, French-language poetry, French-language drama, Portuguese literature, African-language literatures, African women writers, and publishing in Africa. Albert Gérard's *African Language Literatures: An Introduction to the Literary History of Sub-Saharan Africa* is another valuable book, especially because it approaches African literary history from a thematic perspective, viewing it in terms of its Saba inheritance (i.e., its Ethiopian heritage); the legacy of Islam (as seen in the Faluni, Hausa, Wolof, and Swahili traditions); and the impact of the West. A more theoretical perspective on the African literary heritage is adopted by F. Abiola Irele in *The African Imagination: Literature in Africa and the Black Diaspora*, which argues that African literary production—no matter the language it is written in—has at its core the desire to serve nationalist aspirations through the "dominant symbols" of "celebration of community" (p. 74). Irele's brilliant analysis should be read together with *Thresholds of Change in African Literature: The Emergence of a Tradition*, edited by Kenneth W. Harrow, which examines the so-called first-generation novels of témoignage (novels of witness); second-generation novels of revolt; and third-generation novels of postrevolt in order to form a comprehensive model of African literature. And it would be remiss not to mention Odile Cazenave's *Rebellious Women: The New Generation of Female African Novelists*, which has superb discussions about the novels of Calixthe Beyala, Véronique Tadjo, and Angèle Rawiri.

For readers primarily interested in South African literature, we recommend Christopher Heywood's *A History of South African Literature*, which considers the Khoisan, Nguni-Sotho, Anglo-Afrikaner, and Indian oral and literary traditions as well as their "merging through bodily and literary creolisation, from precolonial to present times" (p. vii). Prominently featured are such novelists as Thomas Mofolo and Solomon Tshekisho Plaatje. Also noteworthy is C. N. van der Merwe's *Breaking Barriers: Stereotypes and the Changing of Values in Afrikaans Writing, 1875–1990*, which traces the development and eventual destruction of ethnic, gender, and racial stereotypes in Afrikaans literature. Extensive discussions about numerous aspects of literature from North African and Sahelian literatures are contained in *Camel Tracks: Critical Perspectives on Sahelian Literatures*, edited by Debra Boyd-Buggs and Joyce Hope Scott, which contains chapters on such topics as Sahelian oral literatures, the relationship of literature and politics, and literature by Sahelian women. Ahmed S. Bangura's *Islam and the West African Novel: The Politics of Representation* is the perfect complement to *Camel Tracks* because it focuses "on the imaginative responses to Islam by black African novelists" such as Sembène Ousmane, Aminata Sow Fall, and Ibrahim Tahir (p. 3).

One of the best books on Portuguese-language (Lusophone) literature in Africa is *The Postcolonial Literature of Lusophone Africa*, edited by Patrick Chabal, which not only contains detailed overviews about Portuguese and Creole literatures since 1974–1975 in Mozambique, Angola, Guinea-Bissau, Cape Verde, and São Tomé and Príncipe but also "makes deep forays into the colonial and pre-colonial periods" so as to provide a "cultural and historical context within which this literature developed" (p. 1). Readers will learn about such Angolan writers as Manuel dos Santos Lima and José Eduardo Agualusa as well as Mozambique novelists Luís Bernardo Honwana, Suleiman Cassamo, and Mia Couto, among many others. Another valuable contribution to Lusophone studies is Hilary Owen's *Mother Africa, Father Marx: Women's Writing of Mozambique, 1948–2002*, which analyzes the writings of such Mozambique women writers as Noémia de Sousa, Lina Magaia, Lília Momplé, and Pauline Chiziane.

One of the most accessible and wide-ranging texts dealing with French-language writing in Africa is Patrick Corcoran's *The Cambridge Introduction to Francophone Literature*. In addition to helpful introductory essays about the concept of *Francophonie*, there are overviews of French-language literature from the Maghreb region (Morocco, Algeria, and Tunisia); Sub-Saharan Africa; Oceania; the Middle East; and the Caribbean. But the highlight of this book are the individual essays about such Maghreb novelists as Mohammed Dib, Kateb Yacine, Driss Chraïbi, Albert Memmi, Rachid Boudjedra, Assia Djebar, and Tahar Ben Jelloun; Sub-Saharan novelists Henri Lopes, Ahmadou Kourouma, Sony Labou Tansi, and Ken Bugul; Oceania writers Ananda Devi (Mauritius), Axel Gauvin (La Réunion), and Raharimanana (Madagascar); Middle East novelists Amin Maalouf (Lebanon) and Albert Cossery (Egypt); and Patrick Chamoiseau (Martinique in the Caribbean), whose 1992 novel *Texaco* is considered a classic.

Corcoran's book should be read in conjunction with *Introduction to Francophone African Literature: A Collection of Essays*, edited by Olusola Oke and Sam Ade Ojo, which is particularly valuable for its two chapters about early 1920s Francophone novels by such writers as Bakary Diallo, Ousmane Socé, and Paul Hazoumé. Even more wide-ranging in its historical approach to Francophone African writing is Christopher L. Miller's *Nationalists and Nomads: Essays on Francophone African Literature and Culture*. As its title indicates, *Themes in African Literature in French: A Collection of Essays*, edited by Sam Ade Ojo and Olusola Oke, takes a thematic approach to French-language African literature, focusing on political disillusionment, the growth of sociopolitical consciousness, and antiheroes in the novels of Mongo Beti, Alioum Fantouré, and Yves-Emmanuel Dogbe, among others. Readers should also pay special attention to the CARAF (Caribbean and African Literature Translated from French) series published by the University of Virginia Press. Featuring the emerging voices of Francophone African literature, the series includes such critically acclaimed novels as Patrice Nganang's *Dog Days: An Animal Chronicle* and Ahmadou Kourouma's *Waiting for the Vote of the Wild Animals*.

Absolutely essential for a complete understanding of African literatures is the four-volume series called Women Writing Africa, published by The Feminist Press at the City University of New York and edited by numerous individuals. Each of the four volumes focuses on one African region: volume one covers the African South (i.e., Botswana, Lesotho, Namibia, South Africa, Swaziland, and Zimbabwe); volume two covers the African West and the Sahel (i.e., Benin, Burkina Faso, Ivory Coast, Gambia, Ghana, Guinea-Conakry, Liberia, Mali, Niger, Nigeria, Senegal, and Sierra Leone); volume three covers the African East (i.e., Kenya, Malawi, Tanzania, Uganda, and Zambia); and volume four covers the African North (i.e., Algeria, Egypt, Mauritania, Morocco, and the Sudan). One of the great virtues of this series is that it collects the writings of women in all the languages spoken in their respective regions from the earliest times to the present. For example, *Women Writing Africa: The Eastern Region* has material in 32 languages, including Kiswahili, Gikuyu, and Chimambwe; *Women Writing Africa: West Africa and the Sahel* has material in 20 languages, including Hausa, Wolof, Diola, and Igbo; and *Women Writing Africa: The Southern Region* has material in such indigenous languages as Xhosa, Zulu, and Setswana. Each text is introduced by a brief note, allowing readers to understand the social and cultural context of the anthologized item. Significantly, these four volumes range across many oral and literary forms, such as letters, lamentations, ritual and ceremonial words, lullabies, maiden songs, petitions, work songs, anecdotes, speeches, reminiscences, autobiographies, and folktales. As the editors point out, the series is a groundbreaking work of cultural reclamation—made all the more valuable by the extensive historical overviews at the beginning of each of the volumes.

A similar kind of cultural reclamation is performed by *Oral Epics from Africa: Vibrant Voices from a Vast Continent*, edited by John William Johnson and colleagues, which collects 19 oral epics mainly from West Africa as well as six from Central and North Africa. Another invaluable book is Albert S. Gérard's *Four African Literatures: Xhosa, Sotho, Zulu, Amharic*, which, as its title indicates, provides a much-needed historical consideration of four indigenous literary traditions. Just as crucial is *Literatures in African Languages: Theoretical Issues and Sample Surveys*, edited by B. W. Andrzejewski, which looks extensively at literary traditions in the Fula, Mande, Twi, Hausa, Giiz, Cushitic, Tswana, and San languages.

By now, readers will have realized just how culturally diverse African literature really is. Thus, we would like to conclude by recommending *The Rienner Anthology of African Literature*, edited by Anthonia C. Kalu, which exemplifies this diversity in one volume of about 1,000 pages. It contains poems, songs, and narratives that constitute the oral tradition from North Africa, West Africa, Central Africa, East Africa, and South Africa; autobiographies of the slave trade; extracts from novels and short stories by such English-language writers as Chinua Achebe and Nadine Gordimer; extracts from novels and short stories by such French-language writers as Camara Laye, Mariama Bâ, and Sembène Ousmane; extracts from Thomas Mofolo's novel *Chaka*, written in Sesotho; and poetry from Maria Manuela Margarido, who was born in São Tomé and Príncipe and writes in Portuguese. After perusing Kalu's anthology, readers should be eager to consult one or more of the reference sources or monographs listed here for in-depth information. But for readers who simply cannot wait to discover all the riches of the various African literary traditions, *The Undergraduate's Companion to African Writers and Their Web Sites*, compiled by Miriam E. Conteh-Morgan, may be a useful stopgap measure.

SELECTED REFERENCES

Andrzejewski, B. W., Piłaszewicz, S., and Tyloch, W. (Eds.). (1985). *Literatures in African Languages: Theoretical Issues and Sample Surveys*. New York: Cambridge University Press.

Bangura, Ahmed S. (2000). *Islam and the West African Novel: The Politics of Representation*. Boulder, CO: Lynne Rienner Publishers.

Boyd-Buggs, Debra, and Scott, Joyce Hope. (Eds.). (2003). *Camel Tracks: Critical Perspectives on Sahelian Literatures*. Trenton, NJ: Africa World Press.

Cazenave, Odile. (2000). *Rebellious Women: The New Generation of Female African Novelists*. Boulder, CO: Lynne Rienner Publishers.

Chabal, Patrick. (Ed.). (1996). *The Postcolonial Literature of Lusophone Africa*. Evanston, IL: Northwestern University Press.

Chapman, Michael. (1996). *Southern African Literatures*. Harlow, Essex, UK: Longman.

Conteh-Morgan, Miriam E. (2005). *The Undergraduate's Companion to African Writers and Their Web Sites*. Westport, CT: Libraries Unlimited.

Corcoran, Patrick. (2007). *The Cambridge Introduction to Francophone Literature*. New York: Cambridge University Press.

Cox, C. Brian. (Ed.). (1997). *African Writers*. (2 vols.). New York: Charles Scribner's Sons.

Daymond, M. J.; Driver, Dorothy; Meintjes, Sheila; Molema, Leloba; Musengezi, Chiedza; Orford, Margie; and Rasebotsa, Nobantu. (Eds.). (2003). *Women Writing Africa: The Southern Region*. New York: The Feminist Press at the City University of New York.

Gérard, Albert S. (1981). *African Language Literatures: An Introduction to the Literary History of Sub-Saharan Africa*. Harlow, Essex, UK: Longman.

Gérard, Albert S. (1971). *Four African Literatures: Xhosa, Sotho, Zulu, Amharic*. Berkeley, CA: University of California Press.

Gikandi, Simon. (Ed.). (2003). *Encyclopedia of African Literature*. London: Routledge.

Gikandi, Simon, and Mwangi, Evan. (Eds.). (2007). *The Columbia Guide to East African Literature in English Since 1945*. New York: Columbia University Press.

Griffiths, Gareth. (2000). *African Literatures in English: East and West*. Harlow, Essex, UK: Longman.

Harrow, Kenneth W. (Ed.). (1994). *Thresholds of Change in African Literature: The Emergence of a Tradition*. Portsmouth, NH: Heinemann.

Herdeck, Donald E. (Ed.). (1973). *African Authors: A Companion to Black African Writing, 1300–1973*. Washington, DC: Black Orpheus Press.

Heywood, Christopher. (2004). *A History of South African Literature*. New York: Cambridge University Press.

Irele, F. Abiola. (2001). *The African Imagination: Literature in Africa and the Black Diaspora*. Oxford: Oxford University Press.

Irele, F. Abiola, and Gikandi, Simon. (Eds.). (2004). *The Cambridge History of African and Caribbean Literature*. (2 vols.) New York: Cambridge University Press.

Johnson, John William; Hale, Thomas A.; and Belcher, Stephen. (Eds.). (1997). *Oral Epics from Africa: Vibrant Voices from a Vast Continent*. Bloomington, IN: Indiana University Press.

Kalu, Anthonia C. (Ed.). (2007). *The Rienner Anthology of African Literature*. Boulder, CO: Lynne Rienner Publishers.

Klein, Leonard S. (Ed.). (1988). *African Literatures in the 20th Century: A Guide*. Harpenden, Herts, UK: Oldcastle Books.

Lihamba, Amandina; Moyo, Fulata L.; Mulokozi, M. M.; Shitemi, Naomi L.; and Yahya-Othman, Saïda. (Eds.). (2007). *Women Writing Africa: The Eastern Region*. New York: The Feminist Press at the City University of New York.

Miller, Christopher L. (1998). *Nationalists and Nomads: Essays on Francophone African Literature and Culture*. Chicago: University of Chicago Press.

Moss, Joyce. (Ed.). (2000). *African Literature and Its Times*. Detroit, MI: Thompson Gale.

Ojo, Sam Ade, and Oke, Olusola. (Eds.). (2000). *Themes in African Literature in French: A Collection of Essays*. Ibadan, Nigeria: Spectrum Books.

Oke, Olusola, and Ojo, Sam Ade. (Eds.). (2000). *Introduction to Francophone African Literature: A Collection of Essays*. Ibadan, Nigeria: Spectrum Books.

Owen, Hilary. (2007). *Mother Africa, Father Marx: Women's Writing of Mozambique, 1948–2002*. Lewisburg, PA: Bucknell University Press.

Owomoyela, Oyekan. (Ed.). (1993). *A History of Twentieth-Century African Literatures*. Lincoln, NE: University of Nebraska Press.

Parekh, Pushpa Naidu, and Jagne, Siga Fatima. (Eds.). (1998). *Postcolonial African Writers: A Bio-Bibliographical Critical Sourcebook*. Westport, CT: Greenwood Press.

Roscoe, Adrian A. (Ed.). (2008). *The Columbia Guide to Central African Literature in English Since 1945*. New York: Columbia University Press.

Sutherland-Addy, Esi, and Diaw, Aminata. (Eds.). (2005). *Women Writing Africa: West Africa and the Sahel*. New York: The Feminist Press at the City University of New York.

van der Merwe, C. N. (1994). *Breaking Barriers: Stereotypes and the Changing of Values in Afrikaans Writing, 1875–1990*. Amsterdam, The Netherlands: Rodopi.

ANNOTATIONS FOR TRANSLATED BOOKS FROM AFRICA

African Vernacular Languages

D. O. Fagunwa. ***Forest of a Thousand Daemons: A Hunter's Saga.***
Translated by Wole Soyinka. New York: Random House, 1982. 140 pages.
Genres/literary styles/story types: mainstream fiction; magical realism; quest
A group of hunters go on a quest to find a magical object that will purportedly bring fame and peace to any town that possesses it. But they soon realize that there is no easy answer to their problems. The novel—a landmark in Yoruba fiction—has been compared with *The Odyssey*, early medieval romances, and *Pilgrim's Progress*. An integral part of the book are traditional African songs, proverbs, spells, and imaginary creatures.
Subject keywords: philosophy; social problems
Original language: Yoruba
Source consulted for annotation:
Abe, Ezekiel A. *Journal of Reading* 35 (October 1991): 171.
Another translated book written by D. O. Fagunwa: *Expedition to the Mount of Thought*

Ben R. Mtobwa. ***Dar es Salaam by Night.***
Translated by Felicitas Becker. Nairobi, Kenya: Spear Books, 1999. 177 pages.
Genres/literary styles/story types: crime fiction; urban fiction
This is urban fiction at its grittiest—a no-holds-barred look at the underside of life in Tanzania's largest city. It tells the story of Rukia, a stunning 20-year-old prostitute. Peterson, a wealthy foreigner, has fallen for Rukia, but Rukia's shady childhood friends—Hasara and Hasira—suddenly appear, scheming to kill Peterson for his money. As this tangled tale unfolds, Peterson's long-lost mother Nunu reappears and makes a revelation that has profound implications.
Subject keyword: urban life
Original language: Swahili
Sources consulted for annotation:
Litprom Literature & Translation (http://www.litprom.de).
Mwangi, Evan. *Daily Nation*, 17 October 1999 (http://www.nationaudio.com).

Sibusiso Nyembezi. ***The Rich Man of Pietermaritzburg.***
Translated by Sandile Ngidi. Laverstock, Wiltshire, UK: Aflame Books, 2008. 200 pages.
Genres/literary styles/story types: mainstream fiction; rags to riches
A flimflam man comes to a small rural village with promises of a better, more modern future. He convinces some of the villagers to sell their cattle and thus accumulate capital, but others—especially the educated and women—are not duped by his self-serving and mellifluous words.
Subject keyword: rural life
Original language: Zulu
Source consulted for annotation:
Global Books in Print (online) (reviews from *Booklist* and *School Library Journal*).

Ngugi wa Thiong'o. ***Wizard of the Crow.***
Translated by the author. New York: Pantheon Books, 2006. 768 pages.
Genres/literary styles/story types: mainstream fiction; postcolonial fiction
This satiric novel depicts a country called the Free Republic of Aburiria, which some commentators have seen as a stand-in for Kenya during the era of President Daniel arap Moi. Sycophantic ministers plan on constructing a skyscraper in honor of their nation's leader. Unbelievable chaos ensues as everyone tries to profit from the impending project, which is called "Marching to Heaven."

Businessmen plot to win contracts; the poor jostle for menial jobs. Looming in the distance is an implacable international financial organization that must be assuaged. But its onerous conditions for lending money occasion protests and riots. Against this backdrop, a beggar with an M.B.A. and a radical feminist fall in love. As Jeff Turrentine writes, the author "scrutinize[s] his homeland by borrowing the same postcolonial magnifying glass that writers like Salman Rushdie and Derek Walcott have trained on India and the Caribbean."
Subject keywords: politics; power
Original language: Kikuyu
Source consulted for annotation:
Turrentine, Jeff. *The New York Times Book Review*, 10 September 2006 (online).
Some other translated books written by Ngugi wa Thiong'o: *The River Between*; *Devil on the Cross*; *Matigari*

Afrikaans (South Africa)

Mark Behr. *The Smell of Apples.*
Translated by the author. New York: St. Martin's Press, 1995. 200 pages.
Genres/literary styles/story types: mainstream fiction; coming-of-age
Marnus Erasmus, the novel's narrator, is the 10-year-old son of a general who serves in the South African military and is considered to be a national hero. As Marcus grows up in the Cape Town of the early 1970s, his once-idyllic life slowly unravels as he loses faith in his father and the nation's apartheid policy. When Marnus witnesses his father sexually molesting his best friend, Frikkie, the disintegration of Marnus's illusions is complete. The book, which demonstrates the inseparability of political issues and personal concerns, has been made into a film.
Subject keywords: power; social problems
Original language: Afrikaans
Sources consulted for annotation:
Amazon.com (all editorial reviews).
Berona, David A. *Library Journal* 120 (August 1995): 113.
Luis, Fiona. *Boston Globe*, 26 December 1995, p. 57.
Medalie, David. *Journal of Southern African Studies* 23 (September 1997): 507.
Morphet, Tony. *World Literature Today* 70 (Winter 1996): 226.
Rochman, Hazel. *Booklist* 92 (1 September 1995): 51.
Steinberg, Sybil S. *Publishers Weekly* 242 (17 July 1995): 218.
Some other books written by Mark Behr: *Embrace*; *Kings of the Water*

André Philippus Brink. *The Ambassador.*
Translated by the author. New York: Summit Books, 1986. 288 pages.
Genre/literary style/story type: mainstream fiction
Stephen Keyter, a mid-level employee of the South African embassy in France, thinks he has uncovered an affair between ambassador Paul van Heerden and Nicolette; he writes a denunciatory report regarding the ambassador's activities. Although the ambassador was not having an affair at the time Stephen sent his report, he eventually does so, causing the breakdown of his personal and professional life.
Subject keywords: politics; power
Original language: Afrikaans
Sources consulted for annotation:
Stade, George. *The New York Times*, 29 June 1986, p. A21.
Steinberg, Sybil S. *Publishers Weekly* 229 (21 February 1986): 155.
Sutherland, John. *Los Angeles Times*, 18 May 1986, p. 15.

Some other books written by André Philippus Brink: *A Chain of Voices*; *An Act of Terror*; *Imaginings of Sand*; *The Other Side of Silence*; *Cape of Storms: The First Life of Adamastor*; *The Right of Desire*; *Devil's Valley*; *A Dry White Season*; *The Wall of the Plague*; *Praying Mantis*; *Before I Forget*; *States of Emergency*; *Rumors of Rain*; *An Instant in the Wind*; *Looking on Darkness*

Tom Dreyer. *Equatoria.*
Translated by Michiel Heyns. Laverstock, Wiltshire, UK: Aflame Books, 2008. 160 pages.
Genres/literary styles/story types: adventure; quest
In the first decades of the twentieth century, two American scientists are hired by a Belgian zoo to capture and bring back the fabled okapi, a rarely seen and shy animal that has both zebra- and giraffe-like characteristics and is only found in the isolated forests of the Congo. But their scientific idealism must contend with the tragic realities of colonialism, tribal politics, and the rubber industry.
Subject keywords: colonization and colonialism; power
Original language: Afrikaans
Source consulted for annotation:
Global Books in Print (online) (reviews from *Booklist*, *Library Journal*, and *Publishers Weekly*).
Another translated book written by Tom Dreyer: *Polaroid*

Elsa Joubert. *Poppie* (or *Poppie Nongena*).
Translated by the author. New York: W. W. Norton, 1985. 359 pages.
Genre/literary style/story type: mainstream fiction
Based on a true story, this novel is a searing indictment of South Africa's unyielding pass laws, which caused many people to remain perpetual and poverty-stricken outsiders. Getting a pass meant that one had to have a job, but getting a job meant that one had to have a pass. For those with neither pass nor job, the tragic impossibility of it all was often overwhelming. Thus, Poppie—a recent widow and the protagonist of this book—struggles valiantly to provide for her family, caught in the inexorable crush of apartheid on the margins of Cape Town.
Subject keyword: social problems
Original language: Afrikaans
Sources consulted for annotation:
Amazon.com (all editorial reviews).
Kalem, T. E. *Time* 121 (14 February 1983): 87.
Publishers Weekly 231 (27 February 1987): 160.
Some other books written by Elsa Joubert: *To Die at Sunset*; *The Last Sunday*; *Isobelle's Journey*

Dalene Matthee. *Fiela's Child.*
Translated by the author. New York: Alfred A. Knopf, 1986. 350 pages.
Genre/literary style/story type: mainstream fiction
Fiela Kimoetie loves her family and her way of life in an area of South Africa called the Long Kloof region. One day, she finds a three-year-old white boy on her farm. She and her husband do not know where he has come from, but it does not matter. They name him Benjamin, and he spends the next nine years in the family. When census workers appear, they are startled by what they find. Benjamin is removed from the farm and is claimed by the van Rooyens family, who rename him Lukas.
Related title by the same author:
Readers may also enjoy *The Day the Swallows Spoke*, which focuses on Araminta, a small-town real-estate agent who becomes involved in the shady world of diamond trafficking when she is given six diamonds by a Zimbabwe couple who wishes to emigrate to South Africa.
Subject keyword: family histories

Original language: Afrikaans
Sources consulted for annotation:
Back cover of the book for *The Day the Swallows Spoke.*
Bauermeister, Erica. *500 Great Books by Women* (Amazon.com).
Davis, Isabel. *Newsday*, 18 May 1986, p. 15.
Graeber, Laurel. *The New York Times*, 20 September 1992, p. 52.
Koestler, Frances A. *The Washington Post*, 2 June 1986, p. B9.
Sabor, Peter. *Library Journal* 111 (15 May 1986): 79.
Steinberg, Sybil S. *Publishers Weekly* 229 (28 March 1986): 49.
The Washington Post, 1 June 1986, p. X13.
Some other books written by Dalene Matthee: *Circles in a Forest*; *The Mulberry Forest*; *The Day the Swallows Spoke*; *Dreamforest*; *Driftwood*

Deon Meyer. *Dead Before Dying.*
Translated by Madeleine van Biljon. New York: Little, Brown, 1999. 342 pages.
Genres/literary styles/story types: crime fiction; police detectives
In Cape Town, things are not going well for police captain Mat Joubert. Despondent after the sudden loss of his wife—who was also a police officer—he no longer seems to have a reason to live or work. But he is soon assigned a new case, where he must solve a seemingly random series of murders committed with a firearm from the Boer War era.
Subject keyword: urban life
Original language: Afrikaans
Sources consulted for annotation:
Hoffert, Barbara. *Library Journal* 131 (January 2006): 72.
Hughes, Frank. *The Southland Times*, 21 August 1999, p. 26.
Publishers Weekly 253 (27 March 2006): 55.
Terpening, Ronnie H. *Library Journal* 131 (1 May 2006): 72.
Wilkinson, Joanne. *Booklist* 102 (1 May 2006): 37.
Yager, Susanna. *The Sunday Telegraph*, 18 April 1999, p. 14.
Some other translated books written by Deon Meyer: *Dead at Daybreak*; *Heart of the Hunter*

John Miles. *Deafening Silence: Police Novel.*
Translated by Eithne Doherty. Cape Town, South Africa: Human & Rousseau, 1996. 300 pages.
Genres/literary styles/story types: crime fiction; police detectives
This novel focuses on the experiences of a black policeman, Tumelo John Moleko, who—after being attacked by a white colleague—undertakes a long, painful, and ultimately unsuccessful process to get a semblance of justice. It is based on the true story of Richard Motasi, who died in murky circumstances after his case was taken up by Lawyers for Human Rights.
Subject keywords: power; politics
Original language: Afrikaans
Sources consulted for annotation:
Lord, Gill. *Cape Argus*, 15 September 1997 (from Factiva databases).
de Waal, Shaun. *Electronic Mail & Guardian* (South Africa), 13 October 1997 (applicable URL no longer works).

Karel Schoeman. *Take Leave and Go.*
Translated by the author. North Pomfret, VT: Sinclair-Stevenson/Trafalgar Square, 1993. 279 pages.
Genre/literary style/story type: mainstream fiction

Adriaan, a brooding and melancholy poet who has recently published a new book, yearns for his lover, Stefan, who has moved to Canada. Psychologically adrift in a claustrophobic Cape Town, he watches as numerous other friends and acquaintances make plans to leave an increasingly isolated South Africa. His prospects dim further when the museum at which he works is forced to close. Struggling to see meaning in a nihilistic universe, he visits an older poet, who has totally withdrawn from society. George Packer referred to Karel Schoeman as South Africa's Proust because of the author's sensitive depiction of the "inner lives" of bewildered South Africans who are "painfully estranged from a country they once knew."
Subject keyword: writers
Original language: Afrikaans
Sources consulted for annotation:
Amazon.com (review from *Kirkus Reviews*).
Financial Times, 10 April 1993, p. 18.
Packer, George. *The New York Times Book Review*, 12 September 1993, p. 37.
Publishers Weekly 240 (10 May 1993): 51
Some other books written by Karel Schoeman: *Promised Land*; *Take Leave and Go*; *This Life*

Dan Sleigh. *Islands*.
Translated by André Brink. Orlando, FL: Harcourt, 2002. 758 pages.
Genres/literary styles/story types: historical fiction; literary historical
When the Dutch colonized South Africa in the second half of the seventeenth century, terrible things happened, especially to the native Goringhaicona people. The history of this tragic episode is told through the lives of an aging native leader, his niece, and her daughter. The book calls into question many of the founding myths of South Africa, showing the brutality and arrogance of the Dutch in regard to both indigenous inhabitants and the environment.
Subject keywords: colonization and colonialism; indigenous culture
Original language: Afrikaans
Sources consulted for annotation:
Amazon.com (review from *Publishers Weekly*).
Drabelle, Dennis. *The Washington Post*, 10 April 2005, p. 7.
Rochman, Hazel. *Booklist* 101 (1 January/15 January 2005): 823.
St. John, Edward B. *Library Journal* 130 (January 2005): 100.
Stynen, Ludo. *World Literature Today* 79 (May/August 2005): 83.

Wilma Stockenström. *The Expedition to the Baobab Tree*.
Translated by J. M. Coetzee. London: Faber and Faber, 1983. 111 pages.
Genres/literary styles/story types: mainstream fiction; feminist fiction
A young tribal woman is sold into slavery, her numerous owners treat her as a sexual object, and her existence is marked by a series of pregnancies. Ultimately, she finds herself alone and free under the welcoming arms of a baobab tree, where she contemplates her past and the nature of existence. Renowned South African author André Brink wrote that this novel "is a harrowing exposé of the humiliations inflicted on the female body—and a moving celebration of the indomitable nature of the female mind."
Subject keyword: social problems
Original language: Afrikaans
Sources consulted for annotation:
Book's inside flap.
Hill, Douglas. *The Globe and Mail* (Toronto), 7 April 1984, E19.

Marita Van der Vyver. ***Entertaining Angels.***
Translated by Catherine Knox. New York: Dutton, 1994. 213 pages.
Genre/literary style/story type: mainstream fiction
Griet Swart—who has survived divorce, miscarriage, stillbirth, and separation from her two stepchildren—attempts suicide, but her plan to end her life is thwarted by a dead cockroach that she finds in the oven into which she has stuck her head. Instead of killing herself, she decides to clean the oven and is almost overwhelmed by fumes. Combining humor, fairy tales, and tragic-comedy, the novel explores Griet's complex and never-dull life.
Subject keyword: social problems
Original language: Afrikaans
Sources consulted for annotation:
Burkhardt, Joanna M. *Library Journal* 119 (December 1994): 135.
Carey, Jacqueline. *The New York Times Book Review*, 8 January 1995, p. 77.
Madrigal, Alix. *The San Francisco Chronicle*, 8 January 1995, p. REV4.
Scott, Whitney. *Booklist* 91 (1 January 1995): 802.
Steinberg, Sybil S. *Publishers Weekly* 241 (21 November 1994): 68.
Some other translated books written by Marita Van der Vyver: *Childish Things*; *Breathing Space*; *Travelling Light*; *Short Circuits*

Etienne Van Heerden. ***The Long Silence of Mario Salviati.***
Translated by Catherine Knox. New York: ReganBooks, 2002. 435 pages.
Genres/literary styles/story types: mainstream fiction; magical realism
This novel is set in a fictional town called Yearsonend in the Karoo, which is often referred to as a semidesert region of South Africa. Wrapped in mysteries and enigmas, Yearsonend is not your average run-of-the-mill place. For example, there is the sudden appearance of a mermaid sculpture, which causes no end of complexities. The National Gallery of Cape Town—in the person of art administrator Ingi Friedlander—wants to purchase it from the local artist in whose yard it sits but is rebuffed. Not accustomed to taking no for an answer, Ingi tries to get to the bottom of the town's strangeness, violence, and general antipathy. Eventually, she discovers that stonecutter Mario Salviati is the key to understanding Yearsonend.
Subject keyword: rural life
Original language: Afrikaans
Sources consulted for annotation:
Amazon.com (book description).
Huntley, Kristine. *Booklist* 99 (15 February 2003): 1051.
Montgomery, Isobel, and Williams, Ranti. *The Observer*, 1 March 2003, p. 30.
Rice, Xan. *The Times*, 22 February 2003 (from Factiva databases).
Stuhr, Rebecca. *Library Journal* 128 (January 2003): 160.
Zaleski, Jeff. *Publishers Weekly* 249 (23 December 2002): 45.
Some other translated books written by Etienne Van Heerden: *Ancestral Voices*; *Mad Dog and Other Stories*; *Leap Year*; *Casspirs and Camparis: A Historical Entertainment*; *Kikuyu*

Marlene Van Niekerk. ***Agaat.***
Translated by Michiel Heyns. Portland, OR: Tin House Books, 2010. 581 pages.
Genres/literary styles/story types: mainstream fiction; women's lives
Critics raved about this glorious novel that recounts life on a South African farm in the last half of the twentieth century, as remembered by a 70-year-old woman—Milla de Wet—who in the mid-1990s is suffering from a neurological disease. At death's door, she is cared for by her one constant

companion, who has been with her through thick and thin: Agaat, an indigenous female whom Milla found abandoned as a child. Taking Agaat under her wing, Milla made her at once a domestic helper; governess to her son Jakkie; and sounding board. At death's door, Milla is more than ever dependent on the strength, knowledge, and grace of Agaat, who tends to each of her needs even though Milla has lost all power of speech. Liesl Schillinger observed that a book like *Agaat* is "the reason people read novels, and the reason authors write them."

Related title by the same author:

Readers may also wish to explore *Triomf*, which Rob Nixon called "a riotous portrait of a burned-out family of hillbilly Afrikaners struggling haphazardly to adapt to the new South Africa." The family in question is the incestuous Benades clan, who in the early 1990s live in slum-like squalor trying to eke out a living repairing refrigerators. Their neighborhood was built on top of the razed Sophiatown, a beacon of multicultural tolerance before it fell victim to apartheid politics. Thus, the Benades family—a seething in-bred cauldron of racist and intolerant behavior—is a fitting symbol for the tragedy of South African history. They are also extremely hilarious.

Subject keyword: family histories

Original language: Afrikaans

Sources consulted for annotation:

Nixon, Rob. *The New York Times Book Review*, 1 March 2004 (online).

Rochman, Hazel. *Booklist* 100 (1 December 2003): 648.

Schillinger, Liesl. *The New York Times Book Review*, 23 May 2010 (online).

Steinglass, Matt. *The Washington Post*, 2 May 2004, p. T7.

Toerien, Barend J. *World Literature Today* 69 (Spring 1995): 423.

Another translated book written by Marlene Van Niekerk: *Triomf*

French

Nathacha Appanah. *Blue Bay Palace.*

Translated by Alexandra Stanton. Laverstock, Wiltshire, UK: Aflame Books, 2009. 164 pages.

Genres/literary styles/story types: mainstream fiction; coming-of-age

On the island of Mauritius, Maya is a poor 16-year-old Indian woman. She works as a receptionist at an upscale hotel, catering to every whim and fancy of often boorish Western tourists. She falls in love with Dave, a wealthy Brahmin who works in the hotel's restaurant, and they start a passionate affair. Some three years later, Dave meekly marries a woman chosen by his parents. As Maya comes to grips with the unfairness of the caste system, her love for Dave becomes increasingly obsessive and sexually frenzied: she threatens his wife, sleeps with his gardener, and continues to see Dave. Eventually, she reaches the brink of madness, and it is almost inevitable that murder is the only solution to her dilemma. Some critics have invoked Marguerite Duras to describe the intensity of passion found in this novel.

Subject keyword: social problems

Original language: French

Sources consulted for annotation:

Aflame Books (book description), http://www.aflamebooks.com.

King, Adele. *World Literature Today* (January 2005) (online).

Krygier, Sarah. *School Library Journal* (1 June 2009) (online).

Amadou Hampaté Bâ. *The Fortunes of Wangrin.*

Translated by Aina Pavolini Taylor. Bloomington, IN: Indiana University Press, 1999. 272 pages.

Genre/literary style/story type: mainstream fiction

This novel explores the confrontation between oral and written cultures in the countries of West Africa colonized by the French. Wangrin is an educated and multilingual man determined to

succeed. As he works his way up in the civil service, he hatches a variety of schemes and plots to enrich himself, taking advantage of the muddled, corrupt, and chaotic conditions of colonial rule to exploit the French and his own indigenous people.
Subject keywords: colonization and colonialism; indigenous culture
Original language: French
Sources consulted for annotation:
Adepitan, Titi. *Canadian Literature* 175 (Winter 2002): 147.
Johnston, Bonnie. *Booklist* 96 (1 November 1999): 507.
Steinberg, Sybil S. *Publishers Weekly* 246 (25 October 1999): 51.
Another translated book written by Amadou Hampaté Bâ: *Kaïdara*

Mariama Bâ. *Scarlet Song.*
Translated by Dorothy S. Blair. Harlow, Essex, UK: Longman, 1986. 171 pages.
Genres/literary styles/story types: mainstream fiction; women's lives
This book recounts the doomed love story between Mirelle, a French diplomat's daughter, and Ousmane, a poverty-stricken Senegalese Muslim. They have kept their passion hidden from their respective families, but eventually they decide to marry, naïvely believing that love will sustain them. But ancient codes and patriarchal customs intervene, leaving Mirelle alone and bereft.
Related title by the same author:
Readers may also enjoy *So Long a Letter*, a classic of African fiction. Here, the widowed Ramatoulaye Fall writes a letter to her friend Aissatou about the betrayal she experienced at the hands of her husband, who takes a younger second wife in accordance with polygamous practices.
Subject keyword: social problems
Original language: French
Sources consulted for annotation:
Book's inside flap.
Enotes.com (introduction; themes), http://www.enotes.com/long-letter.
Ochshorn, Kathleen. *St. Petersburg Times*, 30 December 2001, p. 4D.
Another translated book written by Mariama Bâ: *So Long a Letter*

Tahar Ben Jelloun. *Corruption.*
Translated by Carol Volk. New York: New Press, 1995. 136 pages.
Genre/literary style/story type: mainstream fiction
In Casablanca, Mourad is the rare virtuous and upright man, struggling to maintain his professional and personal integrity in a society where bribery is the norm. His wife Hlima continually rages against the state of poverty that she and her children have found themselves in because of her husband's honesty. His colleagues and friends do not understand why he does not better his family's financial position by being part of the web of corruption that surrounds him. Eventually, he succumbs to temptation—his defenses weakened by incessant internal debates about the principles and philosophies of correct action in a degraded world.
Related title by the same author:
For anyone interested in the psychological and philosophical implications of immigration, *Leaving Tangier* and *A Palace in the Old Village* are must-reads. In *Leaving Tangier*, Spain is the promised land for many Moroccans who risk their lives in flimsy and overcrowded boats that often capsize, drowning all those on board. Some of Azel's friends have met this terrifying fate, so Azel's journey to Spain—as the lover of a rich Spaniard—is less fraught with immediate mortal danger. But as he and his lover settle in Barcelona, he quickly discovers that the hardships of immigration are multidimensional. He is no less immune from despair, self-loathing, and alienation than anyone else. In *A Palace in the Old Village*, a Moroccan man on the verge of retirement contemplates the future. He has lived and worked in France

for some 40 years, carefully accumulating a nest egg to see him through his old age. He decides that his best course of action is to return to his native village and build the most sumptuous house possible—a symbol of achievement that will serve as a welcoming beacon to his far-flung family members. The novel describes a clash of generations and values that is as painful as it is timeless.
Subject keyword: social problems
Original language: French
Sources consulted for annotation:
Eder, Richard. *Los Angeles Times*, 19 October 1995, p. 4.
Glaser, Sheila. *The Village Voice*, 7 November 1995, p. SS6.
McCulloch, Alison. *The New York Times Book Review*, 12 April 2009 (online).
Penguin Press website (book description), http://us.penguingroup.com
Seaman, Donna. *Booklist* 92 (15 October 1995): 383.
Steinberg, Sybil S. *Publishers Weekly* 242 (11 September 1995): 75.
Some other translated books written by Tahar Ben Jelloun: *This Blinding Absence of Light*; *The Last Friend*; *The Sacred Night*; *The Sand Child*; *Silent Day in Tangier*; *State of Absence*; *Solitaire*; *Leaving Tangier; A Palace in the Old Village*

Anouar Benmalek. *The Lovers of Algeria.*
Translated by Joanna Kilmartin. Saint Paul, MN: Graywolf Press, 2004. 278 pages.
Genres/literary styles/story types: mainstream fiction; women's lives
Anna, a Swiss circus entertainer, and Nasreddine, an Algerian, fall in love, have twins, and get married. As the two are returning from their civil marriage ceremony in 1955, their bus is stopped, and Nasreddine is arrested by French soldiers who wrongly suspect him of being a member of the Front de Liberation Nationale (FLN). Unable to withstand the pain of torture during interrogation, Nasreddine gives the French the names of possible FLN sympathizers. Released from jail, he returns home to find his twins murdered and his wife gone. In 1997, Anna decides that she must return to Algeria to find the graves of her children and Nasreddine.
Subject keywords: politics; power
Original language: French
Sources consulted for annotation:
Ermelino, Louisa. *Entertainment Weekly* 778 (13 August 2004): 95.
Hopkinson, Amanda. *The Independent*, 19 October 2001, p. 5.
Muldoon, Moira. *Austin American-Statesman*, 22 August 2004, p. K5.
Tangalos, Sofia A. *Library Journal* 129 (August 2004): 63.
White, Emily. *The Washington Post*, 5 September 2004, p. T4.
Zaleski, Jeff. *Publishers Weekly* 251 (5 July 2005): 37.
Another translated book written by Anouar Benmalek: *The Child of an Ancient People*

Mongo Beti (pseudonym for Alexandre Biyidi-Awala). *The Story of the Madman.*
Translated by Elizabeth Darnel. Charlottesville, VA: University of Virginia Press, 2001. 190 pages.
Genre/literary style/story type: mainstream fiction
The tragicomic elements of postcolonial rule are explored in this satiric novel by a Cameroonian writer that is set in the late 1980s in a fictional African country. As governments change at a dizzying pace—as corrupt dictators come and go—a chief and his two sons are caught in the middle. As they struggle to navigate the treacherous shoals of modernity, they must also pay heed to the exigencies of tradition. In the end, what—if any values—will predominate?
Related titles by the same author:
Readers may also enjoy *Lament for an African Pol*, which describes a small-scale rebellion against a chief who enjoys the support of colonial authorities. Also of interest may be *The Poor Christ of*

Bomba, which focuses on the attempts of Father Drumont to bring Christianity to a group of indigenous people. The novel is in the form of a diary kept by Drumont's cook.
Subject keywords: colonization and colonialism; indigenous culture
Original language: French
Sources consulted for annotation:
Amazon.com (book description).
Célérier, Patricia-Pia. Afterword (contained in edition cited above).
Djiffack, Andre. *The International Journal of African Historical Studies* 35 (2002): 229.
Global Books in Print (online) (review from *Choice* for *Lament for an African Pol*).
Jack, Belinda. *Francophone Literatures: An Introductory Survey* (p. 245).
Some other translated books written by Mongo Beti: *The Poor Christ of Bomba*; *Perpetua and the Habit of Unhappiness*; *Lament for an African Pol*; *Remember Ruben*; *King Lazarus*; *Mission to Kala*

Calixthe Beyala. *Your Name Shall Be Tanga.*
Translated by Marjolijn de Jager. Portsmouth, NH: Heinemann, 1996. 137 pages.
Genres/literary styles/story types: mainstream fiction; women's lives
A young woman lies dying in a prison cell in the fictional city of Iningue. She is unable to speak, she seems to have no name, and she exists in age somewhere between childhood and adulthood. She shares her cell with a foreigner named Anna-Claude, who has been labeled insane and has been arrested for participating in protests against the government. Anna-Claude names her cellmate Tanga, and as she persuades Tanga to tell her unbearably horrific story, Anna-Claude metamorphoses into her cellmate, thereby empowering Tanga and revealing an uncommon sense of solidarity.
Subject keywords: identity; social problems
Original language: French
Sources consulted for annotation:
Amazon.com (book description).
Heinemann.com, http://www.heinemann.com/books-multimedia.aspx.
Kalisa, Marie-Chantal. *Humanities and Social Sciences Online* (July 1997), http://www.h-net.org.
Some other translated books written by Calixthe Beyala: *The Sun Hath Looked Upon Me*; *Loukoum: The "Little Prince" of Belleville*

Aziz Chouaki. *The Star of Algiers.*
Translated by Ros Schwartz and Lulu Norman. Saint Paul, MN: Graywolf Press, 2005. 213 pages.
Genre/literary style/story type: mainstream fiction
This is the story of a young man's dream to become a famous musician in 1990s Algeria. Moussa Massy has updated traditional Kabyle music by drawing inspiration from Michael Jackson. Thus, he thinks that his hardscrabble days living in a crowded apartment are finally over. But Islamic fundamentalists are none too pleased with Moussa, who finds himself increasingly isolated. As he sinks ever deeper into an abyss of illicit substances, his quest to leave Algeria for France becomes chimerical and futile.
Subject keyword: power
Original language: French
Sources consulted for annotation:
Olszewski, Lawrence. *Library Journal* 129 (December 2004): 98.
Publishers Weekly 251 (29 November 2004): 23.

Bernard Binlin Dadié. *An African in Paris.*
Translated by Karen C. Hatch. Urbana, IL: University of Illinois Press, 1994. 153 pages.

Genre/literary style/story type: mainstream fiction
This novel turns the tables on Western writers visiting Africa who try to explain Africa and Africans to Western readers. Tanhoé Bertin travels to Paris, where he sets out to find and describe the inhabitants of Paris. At the end of the day, he recognizes the fundamental similarities among all peoples.
Subject keyword: power
Original language: French
Source consulted for annotation:
The translator's introduction to the book.
Some other translated books written by Bernard Binlin Dadié: *Climbié*; *Hands*

Mohammed Dib. ***The Savage Night.***
Translated by C. Dickson. Lincoln, NE: University of Nebraska Press, 2001. 191 pages.
Genres/literary styles/story types: mainstream fiction; short stories
Exploring the tragic circumstances associated with Algerian history, especially the revolt against French colonial rule and its aftermath, the author—who is considered one of the giants of Algerian literature—shrewdly captures the many ironies and horrors of oppression. Some of these 13 stories have been compared with the work of Paul Bowles. Dib's translator writes that he juxtaposes "the gentle, luminous side of humanity and the savage darkness that lurks in all of us."
Subject keyword: social problems
Original language: French
Sources consulted for annotation:
Amazon.com (book description).
The translator's introduction to the book.
Another translated book written by Mohammed Dib: *Who Remembers the Sea*

Fatou Diome. ***The Belly of the Atlantic.***
Translated by Ros Schwartz and Lulu Norman. London: Serpent's Tail, 2006. 256 pages.
Genres/literary styles/story types: mainstream fiction; coming-of-age
On Niodior, a small Senegalese island, Madické dreams of a successful soccer career and wants to emigrate to France. His sister Salie already lives in Paris, so he hopes she will facilitate his plans. But Salie's French reality is a far cry from her brother's vision of an utopian ideal. The book also captures the vibrancy and sadness of Niodior, where political exiles are sent by the Senegalese government.
Subject keywords: social problems; urban life
Original language: French.
Source consulted for annotation:
Serpent's Tail website (book description), http://www.serpentstail.com.

Boubacar Boris Diop. ***Murambi: The Book of Bones.***
Translated by Fiona McLaughlin. Bloomington, IN: Indiana University Press, 2006. 181 pages.
Genres/literary styles/story types: historical fiction; literary historical
Cornelius Uvimana is a history teacher in the Republic of Djibouti during the 1994 genocide in Rwanda. Learning about the death of his family, he returns home, only to discover that his father was a key participant in the atrocities. As Cornelius struggles to write about the genocide, he is confronted with complex questions about his responsibility to the victims and their memory.
Subject keywords: power; politics
Original language: French
Sources consulted for annotation:
Gagiano, Annie. LitNet.com, http://www.litnet.co.za.

Indiana University Press (book review), http://www.iupress.indiana.edu.
Julien, Eileen. Foreword to the book.
McLaughlin, Fiona. Introduction to the book.

Tahar Djaout. *The Watchers.*
Translated by Marjolijn de Jager. St. Paul, MN: Ruminator Books, 2002. 206 pages.
Genre/literary style/story type: mainstream fiction
This novel casts a jaundiced eye on governmental bureaucracy. Hoping to revive an age-old arts-and-craft tradition, Mahfoudh Lemdjad sets his sights on redesigning a loom. He typically works late into the night, which arouses the suspicion of his neighbor, Menouar Ziada, who convinces himself that Mahfoudh is a threat to the government. As the paperwork, bribery, and suspicions pile up and as Mahfoudh is caught in a tangle of often ridiculous misconceptions, the loom becomes an all-too-real symbol of a fraught past.
Related title by the same author:
Readers may also enjoy *The Last Summer of Reason*, in which the bookseller Boualem Yekker must courageously stand his ground against the growing political threat of radical theocracy.
Subject keywords: power; politics
Original language: French
Sources consulted for annotation:
Farley, Amy. *The Village Voice*, 16 October/22 October 2002, p. 56.
Green, John. *Booklist* 99 (15 September 2002): 207.
Publishers Weekly 249 (21 October 2002): 57.
University of Nebraska Press website (book description), http://www.nebraskapress.unl.edu.
Another translated book written by Tahar Djaout: *The Last Summer of Reason*

Assia Djebar. *So Vast the Prison.*
Translated by Betsy Wing. New York: Seven Stories Press, 1999. 363 pages.
Genres/literary styles/story types: mainstream fiction; women's lives
Isma's affair with a student is discovered by her husband Leo, who attacks her with a broken bottle and tries to blind her. After she leaves Leo, she begins to make a film about Berber mountain women. The novel draws important linkages between personal and sociocultural oppression.
Related titles by the same author:
Readers may also enjoy *Children of the New World*, which takes place on a single day in May 1956 in the village of Blida during Algeria's war for independence. After a fragment from a bomb kills an old woman in her home, the villagers realize that their future may not be as bright as they once had hoped. Also of interest may be *Angels of Catastrophe* and *Women of Algiers in Their Apartment*—both of which chronicle the ongoing legacy of oppression and blighted lives in contemporary Algeria.
Subject keyword: social roles
Original language: French
Sources consulted for annotation:
Amazon.com (all editorial reviews).
Burns, Erik. *The New York Times Book Review*, 13 February 2000, p. 21.
Dixler, Elsa. *The New York Times Book Review*, 5 March 2006 (online).
Global Books in Print (online) (jacket description for *Angels of Catastrophe*; reviews from *Choice* and *Publishers Weekly* for *Women of Algiers in Their Apartment*).
Mallory, Heather. *Ms.* (August/September 2001): 82.
Mortimer, Mildred. *World Literature Today* 75 (Summer 2001): 107.
Murphy, Richard. *Review of Contemporary Fiction* 21 (Fall 2001): 202.
Steinberg, Sybil S. *Publishers Weekly* 246 (25 October 1999): 50.

Some other translated books written by Assia Djebar: *Women of Algiers in Their Apartment*; *Children of the New World: A Novel of the Algerian War*; *Fantasia, an Algerian Cavalcade*; *A Sister to Scheherazade*; *The Mischief*; *Far from Medina*; *Nadia*; *The Tongue's Blood Does Not Run Dry*; *Angels of Catastrophe*

Emmanuel Boundzéki Dongala. *Johnny Mad Dog.*
Translated by Maria Louise Ascher. New York: Farrar, Straus and Giroux, 2005. 321 pages.
Genres/literary styles/story types: mainstream fiction; coming-of-age
Set in an African country divided by fierce ethnic rivalries, this book contains almost unbearable scenes of violence and mass murder. Laokolé is a 16-year-old girl who aspires to be an engineer, but she must flee with wounded members of her family when their city is attacked by armed militias. Johnny, also 16, is a member of one such militia—the Death Dealers and the Roaring Tigers—who impose a reign of terror on the city. Luisita Lopez Torregrosa noted that the author, who escaped from Congo-Brazzaville in 1997 and now teaches in the United States, uses a language that is "rude," "raw," and "lyrical," forcing readers to see "the extremes of Africa as he wants us to see them."
Subject keyword: war
Original language: French
Sources consulted for annotation:
Amazon.com (book description).
Green, John. *Booklist* 101 (15 April 2005): 1429.
Publishers Weekly 252 (14 March 2005): 43.
Rungren, Lawrence. *Library Journal* 130 (1 April 2005): 84.
Simon, Denise. *Black Issues Book Review* 7 (May/June 2005): 69.
Torregrosa, Luisita Lopez. *The New York Times Book Review*, 10 July 1005, p. 16.
Valdes, Marcela. *Publishers Weekly* 252 (13 June 2005): 26.
Some other translated books written by Emmanuel Boundzéki Dongala: *Little Boys Come from the Stars*; *The Fire of Origins*

Gaston-Paul Effa. *All That Blue.*
Translated by Anne-Marie Glasheen. London: BlackAmber, 2002. 95 pages.
Genres/literary styles/story types: mainstream fiction; coming-of-age
In French colonial Cameroon, it was customary to give to the local Catholic church a child who would be educated for the priesthood. Thus, at age five, Douo Papus is sacrificed to the nuns by his stoic father and despairing mother. He is not allowed to see his family while growing up; at age 15, he is sent to Paris to begin his life as a monk. As he recalls his youth, Douo attempts to deal with the pain that he has suffered and to understand the man that he has become.
Subject keywords: family histories; religion
Original language: French
Sources consulted for annotation:
Amazon.com (book description).
Back cover of the book.
Evaristo, Bernardine. *Writers Talk Books*, http://www.britishcouncil.org/arts-literature-literature-matters-bevaristo.htm.
Another translated book written by Gaston-Paul Effa: *Ma*

Ali Ghanem. *The Seven-Headed Serpent.*
Translated by Alan Sheridan. San Diego, CA: Harcourt Brace Jovanovich, 1986. 326 pages.
Genres/literary styles/story types: mainstream fiction; coming-of-age

Allawa was born in a village in the Algerian mountains, living in accordance with seemingly timeless traditions. But as the war for Algerian independence became more intense, Allawa and his family move to the city of Constantine, where Allawa falls in love with the cinema and later emigrates to France, finding work as a filmmaker.
Subject keyword: rural life
Original language: French
Source consulted for annotation:
From the flyleaf.
Another translated book written by Ali Ghanem: *A Wife for My Son*

Faïza Guène. *Kiffe Kiffe Tomorrow* (or *Just Like Tomorrow*).
Translated by Sarah Adams. Orlando, FL: Harcourt, 2006. 179 pages.
Genres/literary styles/story types: mainstream fiction; coming-of-age
Doria is a Muslim teenager living in the outskirts of Paris. Her housing project is called Paradise, but life in Paradise is anything but enchanting. Doria's father, an alcoholic, shuttles back and forth between France and Morocco, where he has a second wife with whom he dreams of having a son. While her uneducated mother tries to make a living by taking on low-paid cleaning jobs, Doria is failing at school. Despite their difficulties and an overriding sense of doom, mother and daughter try to remain optimistic as they traverse the strangeness that is their adopted country. Doria's authentic voice drew favorable comparisons with J. D. Salinger's Holden Caufield in *The Catcher in the Rye*.
Subject keywords: culture conflict; social problems
Original language: French
Sources consulted for annotation:
Publishers Weekly 253 (3 April 2006): 35.
Rochman, Hazel. *Booklist* 102 (1 June 2006): 36.
Rosenfeld, Lucinda. *The New York Times Book Review*, 23 July 2006 (online).

Yasmina Khadra (pseudonym of Mohammed Moulessehoul). *The Swallows of Kabul*.
Translated by John Cullen. New York: Nan A. Talese/Doubleday, 2004. 195 pages.
Genre/literary style/story type: mainstream fiction
What is it like to live in an Afghanistan ruled by the Taliban? In his position as a jailer, Atiq Shaukat guards soon-to-be-executed prisoners, but he cannot escape the specter of death even at home, where his wife is terminally ill. Meanwhile, the marriage of Mohsen Ramat and Zunaira comes to a tragic end when Moshen participates in a public stoning—an act that ultimately leads to his wife being accused of murder. When Zunaira becomes a prisoner whom the increasingly despondent Atiq must guard, tragedy is inevitable.
Related titles by the same author:
Readers may also be interested in *The Attack*, in which the wife of an Arab-Israeli surgeon becomes a suicide bomber, and *The Sirens of Baghdad*, which explores the life of a university student in Iraq.
Subject keywords: social problems; religion
Original language: French
Sources consulted for annotation:
Adams, Lorraine. *The New York Times Book Review*, 21 May 2006 (online).
Amazon.com (book description).
Keane, Edward. *Library Journal* 129 (January 2004): 157.
Levy, Michele. *World Literature Today* 79 (January/April 2005): 81.
Maslin, Janet. *The New York Times*, 15 April 2006 (online).
Maslin, Janet. *The New York Times*, 26 April 2007 (online).

Olson, Ray. *Booklist* 100 (1 February 2004): 950.
Todaro, Lenora. *The New York Times Book Review*, 29 February 2004, p. 7.
Walch, Robert. *America* 190 (24 May/31 May 2004): 29.
Zaleski, Jeff. *Publishers Weekly* (1 December 2003): 40.
Some other translated books written by Yasmina Khadra: *Autumn of the Phantoms*; *The Attack*; *Double Blank*; *Wolf Dreams*; *Morituri*; *In the Name of God*; *The Sirens of Baghdad*; *Dead Man's Share*

Out El Kouloub. *Three Tales of Love and Death.*
Translated by Nayra Atiya. Syracuse, NY: Syracuse University Press, 2000. 137 pages.
Genres/literary styles/story types: mainstream fiction; short stories
Each of the three stories in this collection focuses on failed or doomed love. Socioeconomic inequalities, a forced seduction, and a supposed death play large roles in these tales, recounting the tragic lives of individuals living in marginalized social conditions.
Subject keywords: rural life; urban life
Original language: French
Sources consulted for annotation:
Al-Nowaihi, Magda. *The Middle East Journal* 55 (Spring 2001): 339.
Kahf, Mohja. *World Literature Today* 75 (Winter 2001): 192.
Some other translated books written by Out el Kouloub: *Zanouba*; *Ramza*

Ahmadou Kourouma. *Waiting for the Vote of the Wild Animals.*
Translated by Carrol F. Coates. Charlottesville, VA: University of Virginia Press, 2001. 277 pages.
Genre/literary style/story type: mainstream fiction
This novel is a powerful satire about the pompous, arrogant, corrupt, and self-aggrandizing President Koyaga, leader of a fictional African country that is meant to be Togo. Part of the satire and irony comes from the fact that it is told in the form of a traditional praise-song by Bongo, whom Koyaga has appointed to be the chronicler of his achievements.
Related titles by the same author:
Readers may also gravitate toward *Allah Is Not Obliged*, which recounts the life of the barely educated Birahima, who—after his mother dies from cancer—becomes a child soldier in Liberia and Sierra Leone. Also of interest may be *Monnew*, which focuses on a tribal king who does not realize his own complicity in colonial rule.
Subject keywords: politics; power
Original language: French
Sources consulted for annotation:
African Business 287 (May 2003): 64.
Busby, Margaret. *The Independent*, 19 April 2003, p. 32.
Caute, David. *The Spectator* 292 (10 May 2003): 42.
Daoust, Phil. *The Guardian*, 15 March 2003, p. 27.
Global Books in Print (online) (synopsis/book jacket for *Waiting for the Vote of the Wild Animals*; review from *Choice* for *Monnew*; reviews from *Booklist* and *Publishers Weekly* for *Allah Is Not Obliged*).
Some other translated books written by Ahmadou Kourouma: *Monnew*; *The Suns of Independence*; *Allah Is Not Obliged*

Werewere Liking. *The Amputated Memory.*
Translated by Marjolijn de Jager. New York: Feminist Press at the City University of New York, 2007. 446 pages.

Genres/literary styles/story types: mainstream fiction; women's lives

This book focuses on 80-year-old Halla Njoke, who recalls the serpentine path of her life in a country resembling Cameroon. After being raped by her father and bearing his child, she attends a missionary school, learns about the system of French colonialism and its myriad tentacles, and becomes a fervent anticolonial activist and then a writer. Pointing to the fact that the book includes songs, folklore, and much dialogue, critics have noted that *The Amputated Memory* could also be staged as a play. The author's *It Shall Be of Jasper and Coral and Love-Across-a-Hundred-Lives*, which consists of two novels, is a rich evocation of patriarchy through a blend of facts, fiction, and myths.

Subject keywords: politics; power

Original language: French

Source consulted for annotation:

Global Books in Print (online) (reviews from *Booklist*, *Library Journal*, and *Publishers Weekly* for *The Amputated Memory*; review from *Choice* for *It Shall Be of Jasper and Coral*).

Another translated book written by Werewere Liking: *It Shall Be of Jasper and Coral and Love-Across-a-Hundred-Lives: Two Novels*

Henri Lopes. *The Laughing Cry: An African Cock and Bull Story.*

Translated by Gerald Moore. Columbia, LA: Readers International, 1987. 257 pages.

Genre/literary style/story type: mainstream fiction

This satiric novel recounts the life and times of an African dictator and the subsequent impoverishment of the country as a result of his rule. It is told by the man chosen by the president to oversee his palace—a political neophyte who is much more interested in carnal pleasures than the intricacies of power. The author was prime minister of Congo-Brazzaville between 1973 and 1976.

Subject keywords: politics; power

Original language: French

Source consulted for annotation:

Mutter, John. *Publishers Weekly* 231 (27 March 1987): 43.

Another translated book written by Henri Lopes: *Tribaliks: Contemporary Congolese Stories*

Alain Mabanckou. *African Psycho.*

Translated by Christine Schwartz Hartley. London: Serpent's Tail. 2008. 176 pages.

Genre/literary style/story type: mainstream fiction

The reviewer for *Time Out New York* magazine called this novel a "pulp fiction vision of Frantz Fanon's 'wretched of the earth.' " Gregoire Nakobomayo wants to kill his girlfriend Germaine, and he sets out to do so with painstaking detail—even going so far as to engage in telepathic communication with Angoualima, a deceased serial killer. Of course, his carefully prepared plans consistently go awry.

Related title by the same author:

Readers may also enjoy *Broken Glass*. At the behest of the owner, a failed Congolese teacher chronicles the life and times of a down-at-the-heels bar called Credit Gone Away. As the teacher lovingly memorializes the bar's denizens, he plans his own suicide by drowning.

Subject keyword: urban life

Original language: French

Source consulted for annotation:

Serpent's Tail website (book description), http://www.serpentstail.com.

Another translated book written by Alain Mabanckou: *Broken Glass*

Leïla Marouane. *The Abductor.*

Translated by Felicity McNab. London: Quartet Books, 2000. 193 pages.

Genre/literary style/story type: mainstream fiction
Aziz Zeitoun and his wife Nayla have six daughters, who are the narrators of this novel. In a fit of rage, Aziz divorces his wife, although he soon has second thoughts. But according to Islamic law, he can only remarry her if she first remarries another man and then divorces him. Thus, they choose a new husband for Nayla whom they think will play along with the scheme. But their carefully laid plans are derailed when the chosen husband disappears with Nayla.
Subject keyword: family histories
Original language: French
Sources consulted for annotation:
Kempf, Andrea. *Library Journal* 126 (15 November 2001): 128.
Zaleski, Jeff. *Publishers Weekly* 248 (11 June 2001): 59.

Rachid Mimouni. *The Honor of the Tribe.*
Translated by Joachim Neugroschel. New York: HarperCollins, 1992. 173 pages.
Genre/literary style/story type: mainstream fiction
When modernization comes to an Algerian village, tragedy ensues. Proud of his new position as a mid-level administrator, Omar el Mabrouk returns to Zitouna, his native village. He has big plans for Zitouna, which he wants to turn into a notable town, commensurate with his new exalted sense of self.
Subject keywords: family histories; rural life
Original language: French
Sources consulted for annotation:
Amazon.com (review from *Kirkus Reviews*).
Bautz, Mark. *The Washington Times*, 19 July 1992, p. B8.
Partello, Peggy. *Library Journal* 117 (15 June 1992): 102.
Steinberg, Sybil S. *Publishers Weekly* 239 (25 May 1992): 37.
The Virginia Quarterly Review 69 (Winter 1993): 22.
Another translated book written by Rachid Mimouni: *The Ogre's Embrace*

Malika Mokeddem. *Of Dreams and Assassins.*
Translated by K. Melissa Marcus. Charlottesville, VA: University of Virginia Press, 2000. 124 pages.
Genres/literary styles/story types: mainstream fiction; women's lives
Based in part on the author's own life, this novel considers the oppression of women and their lack of rights in postindependence Algeria. Kenza Meslem, the book's heroine, was born in Montpellier, France, which her mother was visiting at the time. When her mother returns home to Algeria, she finds that her husband has remarried. With no rights to the custody of her child, she disappears. But Kenza grows up yearning for her mother, eventually leaving Algeria for Montpellier to search for her.
Related titles by the same author:
Readers may also be interested in *Century of Locusts*, which focuses on Mahmoud's quest for vengeance after his wife was raped and murdered. Also of interest may be *The Forbidden Woman*, which is an autobiographical novel describing the author's rebellion against fundamentalism. It charts her gradual awakening, educational progress, and eventual career as a medical doctor in France.
Subject keyword: social problems
Original language: French
Sources consulted for annotation:
Amazon.com (book description).
Blackburn, Steven. *The Muslim World* 92 (Fall 2002): 492.

Geesey, Patricia. *The International Fiction Review* 30 (2003): 100.
Global Books in Print (online) (reviews from *Booklist* and *Choice* for *Century of Locusts*; review from *Booklist* for *The Forbidden Woman*).
Some other translated books written by Malika Mokeddem: *The Forbidden Woman*; *Century of Locusts*

Tierno Monénembo. *The Oldest Orphan.*
Translated by Monique Fleury Nagem. Lincoln, NE: University of Nebraska Press, 2004. 96 pages.
Genres/literary styles/story types: mainstream fiction; coming-of-age
This novel recounts aspects of the 1994 genocide in Rwanda. The 15-year-old narrator, Faustin, has been sentenced to death and tells his story from a Kigali prison. Witness to unspeakable atrocities, he recounts his horrific past, struggling to make sense of a senseless existence.
Subject keywords: social problems; war
Original language: French
Sources consulted for annotation:
Amazon.com (from the inside flap).
King, Adele. Introduction to the book.
Some other translated books written by Tierno Monénembo: *The Bush Toads; The King of Kahel*

V. Y. Mudimbe. *Before the Birth of the Moon.*
Translated by Marjolijn de Jager. New York: Simon & Schuster, 1989. 203 pages.
Genres/literary styles/story types: mainstream fiction; political thrillers
This novel is a love story with political aspects or a political novel with romantic aspects. Set in 1960s Zaire, a high-ranking government official falls in love with a prostitute. His increasing obsession with her has disturbing implications for his personal and professional life—even threatening the existence of the government.
Subject keyword: politics
Original language: French
Sources consulted for annotation:
Giddings, Paula. *Essence* 19 (January 1989): 30.
Phillips, Julie. *The Seattle Times*, 30 April 1989, p. K7.
Publishers Weekly 238 (6 September 1991): 93.
The Washington Post, 19 February 1989, p. X12.
Some other translated books written by V. Y. Mudimbe: *The Rift*; *Between Tides*

Patrice Nganang. *Dog Days: An Animal Chronicle.*
Translated by Amy Baram Reid. Charlottesville, VA: University of Virginia Press, 2006. 232 pages.
Genres/literary styles/story types: mainstream fiction; urban fiction
Set in the capital city of Yaounde, this novel takes the pulse of Cameroon, as seen through the eyes of a dog who—through detailed and rigorous observations of the quotidian habits and eccentricities of humans—penetrates the mysteries of urban life and offers a riveting account of the sociocultural condition of contemporary Africa.
Subject keywords: politics; urban life
Original language: French
Source consulted for annotation:
Global Books in Print (online) (review from *Library Journal*).

Ousmane Sembène. *Black Docker.*
Translated by Ros Schwartz. London: Heinemann, 1987. 120 pages.

Genre/literary style/story type: mainstream fiction
This novel tells the semiautobiographical story of a dock worker and his ambitions to better his life. Diaw Falla is a much respected member of the immigrant African community in 1950s Marseilles. His work on the docks sustains and finances his dream of becoming a writer. As he pours all his spiritual and emotional energy into his book, he must constantly face the endless trials and vexing tribulations of an immigrant's life, especially racism.
Subject keywords: culture conflict; writers
Original language: French
Source consulted for annotation:
Back cover of the book.
Some other translated books written by Ousmane Sembène: *Xala*; *God's Bits of Wood*; *The Last of the Empire: A Senegalese Novel*; *Niiwam and Taaw*; *Tribal Scars and Other Stories*; *The Money-Order, with White Genesis*

Robert Solé. *The Alexandria Semaphore*.
Translated by John Brownjohn. London: Harvill, 2001. 294 pages.
Genre/literary style/story type: historical fiction
Set in nineteenth-century Egypt, this novel focuses on Maxime Touta, a Syrian Greek Catholic living in Alexandria. Against the backdrop of the building of the Suez Canal, Maxime pursues his twin goals of becoming a journalist and wooing Nada, a refugee. This novel is part of a trilogy that also includes *The Photographer's Wife* and *Birds of Passage*. In *The Photographer's Wife*, after Dora Sawaya marries Milo Touta, a photographer, she becomes immersed in his world, creating new photography techniques that go well beyond the tried and true approaches of her husband.
Subject keywords: politics; social roles
Original language: French
Sources consulted for annotation:
Amazon.com (book description; book inside flap).
Goring, Rosemary. *Sunday Herald*, 24 June 2001, p. 10.
Kempf, Andrea Coron. *Library Journal* 126 (15 November 2001): 98.
Lively, Penelope. *The Spectator*, 14 July 2001, p. 33.
Pollard, Michael. *The Guardian*, 13 March 1999, p. 010.
Steinberg, Sybil S. *Publishers Weekly* 246 (20 September 1999): 71.
Some other translated books written by Robert Solé: *The Photographer's Wife*; *Birds of Passage*

Sony Lab'Ou Tansi (Sony Labou Tansi). *The Seven Solitudes of Lorsa Lopez*.
Translated by Clive Wake. Portsmouth, NH: Heinemann, 1995. 129 pages.
Genre/literary style/story type: mainstream fiction
In this delicious comic novel recounting the endemic corruption of postcolonial Africa, things are not going well in the town of Valancia. Lorsa Lopez thinks that his wife has infected him with lice, so he kills her. But he did not count on the town's outrage. In the best traditions of Aristophanes' *Lysistrata*, Estina Bronzario organizes a sex strike to denounce vestiges of patriarchy, social inequalities, and the general malaise permeating Valancia.
Subject keyword: social problems
Original language: French
Sources consulted for annotation:
Amazon.com (book description).
Baker, Phil, et al. *The Sunday Times*, 14 January 1996 (from Factiva databases).
King, Chris. *The Nation* 262 (25 March 1996): 34.

Simson, Maria. *Publishers Weekly* 242 (30 October 1995): 57.
Another translated book written by Sony Lab'Ou Tansi: *The Antipeople*

Mustapha Tlili. *Lion Mountain.*
Translated by Linda Coverdale. New York: Arcade, 1990. 180 pages.
Genres/literary styles/story types: historical fiction; women's lives
This political novel, which evokes recent Tunisian history, revolves around the struggle of Horia El-Gharib to preserve her people's traditions and customs during the colonial and postcolonial eras. She is dynamic and committed—an implacable foe of modernization and Western values. Critics have pointed to the novel's similarities with Albert Camus's *The Plague* insofar as both are philosophical explorations of alienation.
Subject keywords: colonization and colonialism; rural life
Original language: French
Sources consulted for annotation:
Mihram, Danielle. *Library Journal* 115 (15 May 1990): 98.
Steinberg, Sybil S. *Publishers Weekly* 237 (16 March 1990): 61.

Abdourahman A. Waberi. *In the United States of Africa.*
Translated by David and Nicole Ball. Lincoln, NE: University of Nebraska Press, 2009. 134 pages.
Genre/literary style/story type: mainstream fiction
This novel is a no-holds-barred satire whose central premise is that the promised land is no longer the United States of America but the United States of Africa. Refugees from Western economic and cultural poverty now flock to Africa, where they hope to find redemption and start a more prosperous life. An African physician, working in France to help the residents of that poverty-stricken country, adopts a young girl. Raised in wealthy Africa, she travels back to France to try and discover her heritage.
Related title by the same author:
Readers may also enjoy *The Land Without Shadows*, a collection of 17 short stories that portrays precolonial, colonial, and postcolonial life in Djibouti, shining a light on numerous economic and cultural aspects of this little-known country, especially the poor and marginalized. The book makes extensive use of oral tradition, along with literary references to such classic writers as William Shakespeare and Samuel Beckett.
Subject keywords: politics; power
Original language: French
Sources consulted for annotation:
The Complete Review (book review), http://www.complete-review.com.
Global Books in Print (online) (synopsis/book jacket for *In the United States of Africa*).
University of Virginia Press website (book description), http://www.upress.virginia.edu.
Another translated book written by Abdourahman A. Waberi: *The Land Without Shadows*

Amin Zaoui. *Banquet of Lies.*
Translated by Frank Wynne. London: Marion Boyars, 2008. 240 pages.
Genres/literary styles/story types: mainstream fiction; coming-of-age
Koussaila, an Algerian, is torn between two worlds. He has undergone a rambunctious and torrid sexual education—to say the least—thanks to his aunt, a nun, his grandmother, a teacher's wife, and a Jewish neighbor. Will his future lie with the traditions and mores of Islam or will he adopt the often perfervid and independent ways of the West? Will his touchstone be the Koran or *Madame Bovary*?
Subject keyword: identity
Original language: French

Sources consulted for annotation:
Bendict, Jay. *Vulpes Libri* website (book review), http://vulpeslibris.wordpress.com.
Global Books in Print (online) (synopsis/book jacket).

Norbert Zongo. *The Parachute Drop.*
Translated by Christopher Wise. Trenton, NJ: Africa World Press, 2004. 173 pages.
Genre/literary style/story type: mainstream fiction
As noted by the translator, this book is "one of the few sustained meditations on the psychology of the African dictator." It is based on Burkina Faso's Blaise Compaore. The author, who was publisher and editor of the newspaper *L'Indépendant*, was killed in a car bombing, which was determined to be politically motivated.
Subject keywords: politics; power
Original language: French
Source consulted for annotation:
The translator's preface to the book.

Portuguese

Jose Eduardo Agualusa. *The Book of Chameleons.*
Translated by Daniel Hahn. New York: Simon & Schuster, 2008. 180 pages.
Genres/literary styles/story types: mainstream fiction; magical realism
Have you ever considered what might happen if Jorge Luis Borges were reincarnated as a gecko? Here is your answer. The gecko tells the story of Felix Ventura, who makes a healthy living by creating—out of whole cloth—storied pasts for the nouveau riche of Angola. But this wonderful and remunerative scheme soon begins to unravel when the imaginary past becomes less than imaginary in the present.
Related title by the same author:
Readers may also enjoy *Creole*, which focuses on the adventures of Fradique Mendes, a nobleman who—in the course of his ramblings in Angola and Brazil—falls in love with a former slave.
Subject keywords: politics; power
Original language: Portuguese
Source consulted for annotation:
Global Books in Print (online) (reviews from *Booklist* and *Publishers Weekly* for *The Book of Chameleons*; synopsis/book jacket for *Creole*).
Some other translated books written by Jose Eduardo Agualusa: *Creole*; *My Father's Wives*

Germano Almeida. *The Last Will and Testament of Senhor da Silva Araújo.*
Translated by Sheila Faria Glaser. New York: New Directions, 2004. 152 pages.
Genre/literary style/story type: mainstream fiction
When Señor da Silva dies, his nephew—who had hoped to be his uncle's sole heir—is in for quite a shock. Not only is the will almost 400 pages long, but it reveals a tangled past; among the revelations are sexual escapades and a child born out of wedlock. As the novel unfolds, Señor da Silva's numerous secrets are revealed, creating a rich portrait of a man whose hidden life belied his stiff and staid exterior. The author is from Cape Verde.
Subject keyword: family histories
Original language: Portuguese
Sources consulted for annotation:
Amazon.com (book description).
Publishers Weekly 45 (14 June 2004): 45.

Mia Couto. ***Sleepwalking Land.***
Translated by David Brookshaw. London: Serpent's Tail, 2006. 213 pages.
Genres/literary styles/story types: mainstream fiction; magical realism
When Muidinga and Tuahir stumble upon a corpse-filled bus, they find mysterious notebooks belonging to Kindzu. These are no ordinary notebooks, and as Muidinga and Tuahir read them, the landscape begins to kaleidoscopically swirl, taking on the shifting features of Mozambique's geography. Uzodinma Iweala praised this novel for creating "a dreamscape of uncertainty where characters and readers alike marvel not at the abnormal becoming normal but at the way we come to accept the impossible as reality."
Related titles by the same author:
Readers may also enjoy *The Last Flight of the Flamingo*, which Rob Nixon called a "witty magic realist whodunit" that offers "a sly commentary on the politically surreal." When the body parts of peacekeepers from the United Nations start turning up in the village of Tizangara, Massimo Risi, an Italian, is sent to investigate. Also of interest may be *Under the Frangipani*, in which a dead man haunts the body of a police inspector looking into a murder at a refuge for the aged. Couto is considered by many to be Mozambique's foremost novelist.
Subject keywords: philosophy; war
Original language: Portuguese
Sources consulted for annotation:
Amazon.com (book description).
Drabelle, Dennis. *Chicago Sun-Times*, 2 October 2005, p. 8.
Global Books in Print (online) (review from *Publishers Weekly* for *Under the Frangipani*).
Iweala, Uzodinma. *The New York Times Book Review*, 30 July 2006 (online).
Nixon, Rob. *The New York Times Book Review*, 17 July 2005, p. 25.
Stone, Misha. *Booklist* 101 (1 June/15 June 2005): 1760.
Some other translated books written by Mia Couto: *The Last Flight of the Flamingo*; *Voices Made Night*; *Every Man Is a Race*; *Under the Frangipani*; *A River Called Time*

Lília Momplé. ***Neighbours: The Story of a Murder.***
Translated by Richard Bartlett and Isaura de Oliveira. Oxford: Heinemann, 2001. 134 pages.
Genre/literary style/story type: political thrillers
South Africa's apartheid policy had devastating implications for Mozambique's citizens, as this novel makes clear. In Maputo, South African government agents raid the wrong residence in search of African National Congress (ANC) members, who have found refuge with sympathizers.
Subject keyword: family histories
Original language: Portuguese
Source consulted for annotation:
Gagiano, Annie. LitNet.com, http://www.litnet.co.za.

Ondjaki. ***Good Morning Comrades.***
Translated by Stephen Henighan. Emeryville, ON: Biblioasis, 2008. 120 pages.
Genres/literary styles/story types: mainstream fiction; coming-of-age
This novel focuses on Ndalu, a 12-year-old boy who lives in Angola at a time when Cubans seem to be running the entire country. He is taught by Cubans, and his essay topics have to do with Cuban issues. As a result, he is more than a little perplexed by his family's servant, who believes that Angola was better off under the Portuguese.
Related title by the same author:
Readers may also enjoy *The Whistler*, in which an itinerant moves into a deserted village church. His main claim to fame is whistling, and as he whistles, his songs and melodies invoke the history of the various peoples of the surrounding region.

Subject keywords: politics; power
Original language: Portuguese
Source consulted for annotation:
Global Books in Print (online) (review from *School Library Journal* for *The Whistler*; synopsis/book jacket for *Good Morning Comrades*).
Another translated book written by Ondjaki: *The Whistler*

Pepetela (pen name for Arthur Carlos Mauricio Pesta). *Yaka.*
Translated by Marga Holness. Portsmouth, NH: Heinemann, 1996. 307 pages.
Genres/literary styles/story types: historical fiction; literary historical
Angola's complicated political and social history is explored through the life of Alexandre Semedo, whose father was sent to Angola after committing murder in Portugal. In many respects, Angola was to Portugal what Australia originally was to England: a place to send prisoners. Because of this tortured history, a multitiered social pecking order evolved, further complicating Angolan cultural and economic relations.
Subject keyword: family histories
Original language: Portuguese
Sources consulted for annotation:
Amazon.com (review from *Midwest Book Review*).
Moser, Gerald M. *World Literature Today* 71 (Autumn 1997): 845.
New Internationalist 281 (July 1996): 32.
Simson, Maria. *Publishers Weekly* 243 (6 May 1996): 74.
Some other translated books written by Pepetela: *The Return of the Water Spirit*; *Mayombe*; *Ngunga's Adventures: A Story of Angola*

José Luandino Vieira. *The Loves of João Vêncio.*
Translated by Richard Zenith. San Diego, CA: Harcourt Brace Jovanovich, 1991. 64 pages.
Genre/literary style/story type: mainstream fiction
João Vêncio, a former seminarian turned thief, tenderly recounts three of his love affairs as he awaits sentencing for murder. His story is told against the background of a vibrant Angolan shanty town, providing a good sense of the social and cultural diversity of the country.
Related title by the same author:
Readers may also enjoy *The Real Life of Domingos Xavier*, another short novel which was originally written in 1961 but not published until more than a decade later. It is ostensibly about a tractor driver, Domingos Xavier, who is brought to a police station and tortured to death. As his wife frantically searches for him, the book depicts the harrowing social conditions that inspired the Angolan revolution.
Subject keyword: urban life
Original language: Portuguese
Sources consulted for annotation:
Shreve, Jack. *Library Journal* 116 (January 1991): 157.
Young, Glynn. *St. Louis Post-Dispatch*, 12 May 1991, p. 5C.
Some other translated books written by José Luandino Vieira: *Luuanda*; *The Real Life of Domingos Xavier*

CHAPTER 2

The Arab World: Middle East, Trans-Caucasus, and Western/Central Asia

Language groups:	Countries represented:	
Arabic	Algeria	Lebanon
Persian	Armenia	Libya
Trans-Caucasus and Central Asian languages	Azerbaijan	Morocco
Armenian	Egypt	Palestine
Azerbaijani (Azeri)	Georgia	Saudi Arabia
Georgian	Iran (Persia)	Sudan
Kyrgyz	Iraq	Syria
Turkish	Jordan	Turkey
	Kyrgyzstan	United Arab Emirates
		Yemen

INTRODUCTION

This chapter contains annotations of books from the countries of the Arab world (e.g., Algeria, Egypt, Iraq, Jordan, Lebanon, Morocco, Saudi Arabia, Sudan, Syria, and Yemen) and Western and Central Asia (e.g., Turkey, Iran, Armenia, and Georgia). The predominant languages represented in this chapter are Arabic, Turkish, and Persian, with a handful of titles in Armenian and Georgian.

Many readers are familiar with the novels of the Egyptian Nobel Prize laureate Naguib Mahfouz, especially his *Cairo Trilogy* (*Palace Walk*, *Palace of Desire*, and *Sugar Street*), but there are numerous other Egyptian writers worth exploring, such as Ibrahim Aslan (*Nile Sparrows*); Alla Al Aswany (*The Yacoubian Building* and *Chicago*); Yusuf Idris (*City of Love and Ashes*); and Latifa al-Zayyat (*The Open Door*).

And just as Egyptian writing should not be reduced to Mahfouz alone, so should Arabic writing not be seen wholly in terms of Egyptian authors. Readers may find much to ponder in such Iraqi writers as Fadhil al-Azzawi (*The Last of the Angels*), Betool Khedairi (*A Sky So Close*), and Iqbal al-Qazwini

(*Zubaida's Window*); such Lebanese writers as Hassan Daoud (*The House of Mathilde*) and Elias Khoury (*Gate of the Sun* and *Yalo*); the Jordanian author Abdelrahman Munif, who chronicles the social, cultural, and political transformation of a Persian Gulf country after the discovery of oil, in three magnificent volumes (*Cities of Salt*, *The Trench*, and *Variations on Night and Day*); Saudi Arabian writer Ibrahim Nasrallah (*Prairies of Fever*); Sudanese author Tayeb Salih, whose *Season of Migration to the North* has inspired countless other novelists; and Syrian writer Halim Barakat (*The Crane*).

There are also numerous writers from Iran. Some translated late twentieth- and early twenty-first-century Persian novels mentioned in this chapter include Mahmoud Dowlatabadi's *Missing Soluch*; Shahriar Mandanipour's *Censoring an Iranian Love Story*; Naveed Noori's *Dakhmeh*; Shahrnush Parsipur's *Women Without Men*; and Iraj Pezeshkzad's *My Uncle Napoleon*.

With regard to contemporary translated Turkish novels, many people recognize the name of Nobel Prize winner Orhan Pamuk, known for such novels as *Snow*, *My Name is Red*, and *The Museum of Innocence*. But there are many other translated Turkish writers who deserve a wide audience, including Adalet Agaoglu (*Curfew*); Elif Shafak (*The Flea Palace*); and Mehmet Murat Somer (*The Prophet Murders*).

Earlier Translated Literature

The Arabic nonscriptural prose tradition can be traced back to two key works: the ever-popular *Thousand and One Nights* and the lesser-known *Muqaddimah*, a philosophical analysis of world history by Ibn Khaldun (1332–1406). Some readers may find that these classic translated texts are excellent complements to the contemporary novels mentioned previously, but they should also not forget that the Arabic fictional tradition includes important novels written before the 1980s: such pre–World War II titles as Taha Husayn's *An Egyptian Childhood* and Tawfiq al-Hakim's *Return of the Spirit* as well as such post–World War II translated titles as Abdelrahman al-Sharqawi's *Egyptian Earth*; Gamal al-Ghitani's *The Zafarani Files*; and Idwar al-Kharrat's *City of Saffron* and *Girls of Alexandria*.

Likewise, there is a strong Persian novelistic tradition. Some notable early twentieth-century novels are Sadiq Hidayat's *The Blind Owl*; Jalal Al-e Ahmad's *Lost in the Crowd*; Ghulam Husayn Sa'idi's *Fear and Trembling*; and Simin Daneshvar's *A Persian Requiem*. And contemporary Turkish literature owes a singular debt to Yashar Kemal, who—by virtue of such works as *Salman the Solitary*; *Memed, My Hawk*; and *They Burn the Thistles*—is to the modern Turkish novel what Naguib Mahfouz is to the modern Egyptian novel.

SOURCES CONSULTED

France, Peter. (Ed.). (2000). "Arabic" and "West Asian Languages." In *The Oxford Guide to Literature in English Translation*, pp. 138–158, 610–624. Oxford: Oxford University Press.

Jayyusi, Salma Khadra. (Ed.). (2005). *Modern Arabic Fiction: An Anthology*. New York: Columbia University Press.

BIBLIOGRAPHIC ESSAY

The Arab World

One of the best places to start learning about the riches of the Arabic literary tradition is with Sama Khadra Jayyusi's *Modern Arabic Fiction: An Anthology*. This 1,056-page book not only contains English translations of a large number of Arab fiction writers (almost all from the twentieth century), but it also has an elegant and erudite introductory essay of more than 60 pages that discusses the social and cultural context of Arab fiction. Here, readers will find coverage of such topics as Arabic fictional genres in classical times; the rise of the novel in Arabic; and Egypt's literary centrality. Major authors about whom valuable background information is provided are: Jurji Zaydan; Muhammad Husain Haykal; Naguib Mahfouz; Ibrahim Nasrallah; Edward al-Kharrat; Yusuf Idris; Zakaria Tamir; Gamal al-Ghitani; and 'Abd al-Rahman Munif, author of the widely hailed *Cities of Salt*. There are short stories from more than 100 writers, including Faruq Wadi and Hussa Yusuf. There are also extracts from the novels of more than 25 writers, such as Hanna Mina, Radwa Ashour, Emile Habiby, and Ghada Samman. Other readers will find *The Anchor Book of Modern Arabic Fiction*, edited by Denys Johnson-Davies, to be more manageable. At slightly less than 500 pages, it nevertheless contains short stories and novel extracts of almost 80 writers from 14 countries, including Edwar al-Kharrat, Sonallah Ibrahim, Haggag Hassan Oddoul, Ghassan Kanafani, and Tayeb Salih.

After getting a taste of the diversity of Arab fiction from these two anthologies, readers may wish to learn more about the Arab literary tradition as a whole. For this purpose, we recommend *The Arabic Literary Heritage: The Development of Its Genres and Criticism* by Roger Allen. Readers will be presented with a majestic overview of the physical, historical, and intellectual context of Arab literature, with chapters devoted to sacred texts, poetry, prose, and drama. This is a must-have book. For those interested in a substantially more in-depth treatment of the various historical periods in Arab literature, Cambridge University Press has published a six-volume series entitled The Cambridge History of Arabic Literature. Two of the more interesting volumes in this series are *Arabic Literature in the Post-Classical Period*, edited by Roger Allen and D. S. Richards (2006), and *Modern Arabic Literature*, edited by M. M. Badawi (1992). Also noteworthy is the two-volume *Encyclopedia of Arabic Literature*, edited by Julie Scott Meisami and Paul Starkey, which contains more than 800 pages of material on numerous authors (including some North African writers writing mainly in French), literary movements, and literary subjects, with each entry containing a list of further readings. An accessible way to find out more about early Arab writers is *Arabic Literary Culture, 500–925*, edited by Michael Cooperson and Shawkat M. Toorawa. It is part of the Dictionary of Literary Biography series (published by Gale), which also contains a volume entitled *Twentieth-Century Arabic Writers* (2008; vol. 346).

Another essential book is Roger Allen's *The Arabic Novel: An Historical and Critical Introduction* (2nd ed.). In about 260 pages, he provides an in-depth look at the principal themes in the modern Arabic novel, touching on the impact of oil; the relationship of country and city; family roles and the status of women; and the individual and freedom. Allen then critically analyzes 12 representative novels, including the works of Halim Barakat and Ghassan Kanafani. If this book is unavailable, readers will want to explore Matti Moosa's *The Origins of Modern Arabic Fiction* (2nd ed.). In 13 chapters, Moosa traces the historical antecedents and milestones of Arab fiction, ranging from the work of Salim al-Bustani to Numan Abduh al-Qasatili to such Egyptian modernists as Naguib Mahfouz, winner of the Nobel Prize for Literature in 1988. Moosa's book can be productively supplemented by Sabry Hafez's *The Genesis of Arabic Narrative Discourse: A Study in the Sociology of Modern Arabic Literature*.

Egyptian writers play a prominent part in any discussion of Arab fiction, so we recommend two books that focus specifically on Egyptian novels. The first is *The Modern Egyptian Novel: A Study in Social Criticism* by Hilary Kilpatrick. Here, we are introduced to such lesser-known novelists as Taha Husain, Adil Kamal, and Abd al-Hakim Qasim as well as the more well-known Mahfouz. Samah Selim's *The Novel and the Rural Imaginary in Egypt, 1880–1985* will appeal to those who wish to view Egyptian novels through the prism of contemporary critical literary theory. Of especial importance in Selim's book are chapters about the so-called village novel and the landmark novel by 'Abd al-Rahman al-Sharqawi entitled *The Land*, translated in English as *Egyptian Earth*. Equally compelling is *Arab Culture and the Novel: Genre, Identity, and Agency in Egyptian Fiction* by Muhammad Siddiq, an examination of the tension between individualism and normative traditionalism in Arab novels.

Of course, Egypt is by no means the only Arab country that produces fiction. For an excellent overview of other novelists, we invite readers to consult *Contemporary Arab Fiction: Innovation from Rama to Yalu* by Fabio Caiani, which contains insightful discussions of the Iraqi novelist Fu'ad al-Takarli; the Lebanese author Ilias Khouri; and the Morrocan novelist Muhammad Barrada, among others. Another valuable book is Ibrahim Taha's *The Palestinian Novel*. So too is Debbie Cox's *Politics, Language, and Gender in the Algerian Arabic Novel* as well as *Opening the Gates: A Century of Arab Feminist Writing*, edited by Margot Badran and Miriam Cooke. For readers interested in postmodern approaches to Arab fiction, we can think of no better title than *The Experimental Arabic Novel: Postcolonial Literary Modernism in the Levant* by Stefan G. Meyer. Chapters and sections deal with such topics as existentialism and the fragmentation of narrative voice; magical realism: Salim Barakat; cultural and historical counternarrative: Abdelrahman Munif; fragmented reportage: Ghada Samman; the dynamics of war and sexuality; and the limits of masculine perspective. For a feminist perspective on the writers of Algeria, Morocco, and Tunisia, Suzanne Gauch's *Liberating Shahrazad: Feminism, Postcolonialism, and Islam* is a bracing look at the intersection of Arab literature (and filmmaking) and the media-saturated and globalized world. For the most up-to-date information about many of these writers, some readers may find that *The Undergraduate's Companion to Arab Writers and Their Web Sites*, compiled by Dona S. Straley, suits their needs.

While the books mentioned here deal primarily with the novel, the short story also has an important place in the Arab literary tradition. Two titles that extensively discuss this topic are *The Quest for Identities: The Development of the Modern Arabic Short Story* by Sabry Hafez and *The Modern Arabic Story: Shahrazad Returns* (2nd ed.) by Mohammad Shaheen. Hafez's treatment of the subject is thematic. He surveys realistic, romantic, and experimental writers, highlighting the work of Mahmud Taymur, Yahya Haqqi, Mahmud Kamil, Bishr Faris, and Ibrahim Aslan, among others. In contrast, Shaheen's book is a unique amalgam of critical essays and short story translations, where writers such as Michael 'Aflaq, Najib Surur, and Akram Haniyyah are featured.

Turkey

Many people do not know anything about Turkish literature beyond the fact that Orhan Pamuk won the Nobel Prize for Literature in 2006. We therefore suggest that readers begin with three anthologies: *An Anthology of Turkish Literature*, edited by Kemal Silay; *An Anthology of Short Stories*, introduced by Ali Alparslan; and *Twenty Stories by Turkish Women Writers*, translated by Nilufer Mizanoglu Reddy. Having discovered that Turkey has a substantial literary tradition, readers can now turn to the three-volume *Encyclopedia of Turkish Authors: People of Literature, Culture and Science* by Ihsan Isik to find out more about some of the authors whose work they read about in the anthologies. As they flip through the pages of the encyclopedia, they will certainly run across additional author names that will intrigue them. As Isik remarks in the introduction, the encyclopedia contains 2,023 writers, carefully selected as being of interest to the Western world from a larger 10-volume encyclopedia published for the Turkish market.

We also recommend three critical studies about Turkish fiction. The first is *Rapture and Revolution: Essays on Turkish Literature* by Talat S. Halman. This book is a series of essays by one of the foremost authorities on Turkish literature. If a reader has time for only one critical overview and assessment of Turkish literature, this is it. Subjects covered include Islamic themes in Turkish poetry; the death and rebirth of myths in Near Eastern literatures; Turkish literature in the 1960s; the evolution of Turkish drama; big town blues: peasants "abroad" in Turkish literature; and Yunus Emre's Humanism. Our second suggestion is Kenan Cayir's *Islamic Literature in Contemporary Turkey: From Epic to Novel*, which examines the rise of literary fiction associated with post-1980s Islamist movement. Third, we recommend *Autobiographical Themes in Turkish Literature: Theoretical and Comparative Perspectives*, an edited collection of essays about the place of autobiography in the writings of such authors as Pamuk, Mahmud Darwish, Latife Tekin, and Ahmet Midhat.

Armenia

When considering Armenian literature, there is absolutely no better place to start than *A Reference Guide to Modern Armenian Literature, 1500–1920*, compiled by Kevork B. Bardakjian. This 714-page volume contains an overview about the history of Armenian literature from 1500 to 1990; alphabetized bio-bibliographic entries for hundreds of authors born between 1500 and 1920; and extensive bibliographies of Armenian literature and critical studies. Each of the six introductory chapters—devoted to the sixteenth, seventeenth, eighteenth, nineteenth, early twentieth, and late twentieth centuries—begins with a section entitled "Overview of the Armenian Realities of the Age," thus focusing attention on the interconnections between history, political, social, and cultural life. Also noteworthy is that each of the bio-bibliographic entries contains a list of that author's works that have been translated—whether into English, French, Spanish, or other languages—as well as an extensive list of criticism pertaining to that author. Bardakjian's comprehensive text will be a landmark for years to come.

Still, there will be some who want additional details. For these individuals, we suggest three books. The first is Srbouhi Hairapetian's *A History of Armenian Literature: From Ancient Times to the Nineteenth Century*. As its title indicates, this book focuses on areas and time periods not covered by Bardakjian. Thus, we have chapters on Armenian folk literature; the creation of the Armenian alphabet; religious literature; Armenian historiography from the fifth to the eighth century; sacred music; the Armenian folk epic; medieval Armenian prose, lamentations, and verse; and bardic lyricism. Some of the authors covered are Pavstos Buzand, Davit Anhagt, Sahak Partev, and Tovman Artzruni. The second book is Victoria Rowe's *A History of Armenian Women's Writing: 1880–1922*, which is another significant addition to our understanding of Armenian culture. Rowe performs invaluable work in discussing the social and cultural conditions for the rise of Armenian women's writing in the late nineteenth century and early twentieth century, critically analyzing the writings of Srpuhi Dussap, Sibyl and Mariam Khatisian, Marie Beylerian, Shushanik Kurghinian, and Zabel Yesayian. The third book is Marc Nichanian's *Writers of Disaster: Armenian Literature in the Twentieth Century*. In this first volume of a projected four-volume set, Nichanian writes about the historical novels of Yeghishé Charents, Gurgen Mahari, Zabel Esayan, and Vahan Totovents.

We have saved the best for last: a three-volume anthology called *The Heritage of Armenian Literature*, edited by Agop J. Hacikyan, Gabriel Basmajian, Edward S. Franchuk, and Nourhan Ouzounian. Each of the volumes not only has substantial translated extracts from the key works of the included authors but also extensive overviews about the authors, genres, and historical periods under discussion. The first volume is called *From the Oral Tradition to the Golden Age*; the second is called *From the Sixth to the Eighteenth Century*; and the final volume bears the name *From the Eighteenth Century to Modern Times*. In total, there are more than 2,500 pages of text. It is the kind of monumental and definitive scholarly accomplishment that deserves the widest possible audience.

Iran (Persia)

If we had to choose only one book to read about Iranian (Persian) literature, it would undoubtedly be Jan Rypka's *History of Iranian Literature*, written with numerous collaborators. There are extensive chapters on Ancient Eastern Iranian culture; the culture of the ancient Medes and Persians; the history of Persian literature up to the beginning of the twentieth century (with sections, for example, about the tolerance of Persian poetry, eros and its expression, the form of the epic and didactic poem, and quatrain poets); Persian literature of the twentieth century; Tajik literature from the sixteen century to the present; Iranian folk literature; and Persian literature in India. There is coverage of the Arsacids; the Samanid Period; the Ghaznavid Period; the Seljuq Period; and the Mongols, the Timurids, and the Safavids. There is also ample discussion of fables, shadow plays, humor, and riddles. It is a wide-ranging and deeply learned book that represents the very best of dedicated and meticulous scholarship. Equally fascinating and sweeping in its scope is Edward G. Browne's four-volume *A Literary History of Persia*, which starts with the discovery of inscriptions and documents of Ancient Persia in the Achæmenian Period and goes up to 1924. For those individuals only interested in Persian literature from the beginning of the ninth century up to the end of the fifteenth century, A. J. Arberry's *Classical Persian Literature* cannot be overlooked. And for those intrigued by the way in which an Indian scholar deals with the topic, it is imperative to read Nabi Hadi's *History of Indo-Persian Literature*, which can be productively supplemented by his *Dictionary of Indo-Persian Literature*.

But valuable as these books are, they pale in comparison to the monumental 18-volume *A History of Persian Literature*, published by I. B. Tauris and under the general editorship of Ehsan Yarshater. Two volumes of this series had appeared by 2009: *General Introduction to Persian Literature*, edited by J. T. P. de Bruijn, and *The Literature of Pre-Islamic Iran*, edited by Ronald E. Emmerick and Maria Macuch. The first-mentioned volume—conceived as a broad introductory overview to the subject—contains essays dealing with topics such as: pre-Islamic Iranian and Indian influences on Persian literature; Hellenistic influences in classical Persian literature; Arabic influences on Persian literature; and Persian literature and the arts of the book. Each of the subsequent volumes will discuss in more detail the cultural background, literary movements, and major authors of a given chronological period.

Central Asia and Georgia

It is difficult to find English-language sources about the literatures of the countries of Central Asia: Kazakhstan; Kyrgyzstan; Uzbekistan; Tajikistan; and Turkmenistan. But readers will be rewarded if they look at some of the following books: *The Oral Art and Literature of the Kazakhs of Russian Central Asia* by Thomas G. Winner; *The Voice of the Steppe: Modern Kazakh Short Stories*, translated into English from Russian; *Patron, Party, Patrimony: Notes on the Cultural History of the Kirghiz Epic Tradition* by Daniel Prior; *Manas: The Kyrgyz Heroic Epos in Four Parts*, translated by Walter May; *Essays on Uzbek History, Culture, and Language*, edited by Bakhtiyar A. Nazarov and Denis Sinor; *The Modern Uzbeks: From the Fourteenth Century to the Present: A Cultural History* by Edward Allworth; *Tradition and Society in Turkmenistan: Gender, Oral Culture and Song* by Carole Blackwell; and *At the Foot of the Blue Mountains: Stories by Tajik Authors*. An excellent source about Georgian literature is the revised edition of Donald Rayfield's *The Literature of Georgia: A History*.

SELECTED REFERENCES

Allen, Roger. (1998). *The Arabic Literary Heritage: The Development of Its Genres and Criticism*. Cambridge, UK: Cambridge University Press.

Allworth, Edward. (1990). *The Modern Uzbeks: From the Fourteenth Century to the Present: A Cultural History*. Stanford, CA: Hoover Institution Press.

Allworth, Edward. (1995). *The Arabic Literary Heritage: The Development of Its Genres and Criticism* (2nd ed.). Syracuse, NY: Syracuse University Press.

Arberry, A. J. (1958/1994). *Classical Persian Literature*. Richmond, Surrey, UK: Curzon Press.

Badran, Margot, and Cooke, Miriam. (Eds.). (1990). *Opening the Gates: A Century of Arab Feminist Writing*. Bloomington, IN: Indiana University Press.

Bardakjian, Kevork B. (2000). *A Reference Guide to Modern Armenian Literature, 1500–1920*. Detroit, MI: Wayne State University Press.

Blackwell, Carole. (2001). *Tradition and Society in Turkmenistan: Gender, Oral Culture and Song*. Richmond, Surrey, UK: Curzon Press.

Browne, Edward G. (1902/1964). *A Literary History of Persia* (4 vols.). Cambridge, UK: Cambridge University Press.

Caiani, Fabio. (2007). *Contemporary Arab Fiction: Innovation from Rama to Yalu*. London: Routledge.

Cayir, Kenan. (2007). *Islamic Literature in Contemporary Turkey: From Epic to Novel*. New York: Palgrave Macmillan.

Cooperson, Michael, and Toorawa, Shawkat M. (Eds.). (2005). *Arabic Literary Culture, 500–925* (Volume 311 of the *Dictionary of Literary Biography*). Detroit, MI: Gale.

Cox, Debbie. (2002). *Politics, Language, and Gender in the Algerian Arabic Novel*. Lewiston, NY: Edwin Mellen Press.

de Bruijn, J. T. P. (Ed.). (2009). *General Introduction to Persian Literature*. London: I. B. Tauris.

Emmerick, Ronald E., and Macuch, Maria. (Eds.). (2009). *The Literature of Pre-Islamic Iran*. London: I. B. Tauris.

Gauch, Suzanne. (2007). *Liberating Shahrazad: Feminism, Postcolonialism, and Islam*. Minneapolis, MN: University of Minnesota Press.

Hacikyan, Agop J.; Basmajian, Gabriel; Franchuk, Edward S.; and Ouzounian, Nourhan. (Eds.). (2000–2005). *The Heritage of Armenian Literature* (3 vols.). Detroit, MI: Wayne State University Press.

Hadi, Nabi. (1995). *Dictionary of Indo-Persian Literature*. New Delhi: Abhinav Publications.

Hadi, Nabi. (2001). *History of Indo-Persian Literature*. New Delhi: Iran Culture House.

Hafez, Sabry. (1993). *The Genesis of Arabic Narrative Discourse: A Study in the Sociology of Modern Arabic Literature*. London: Saqi.

Hafez, Sabry. (2007). *The Quest for Identities: The Development of the Modern Arabic Short Story*. London: Saqi.

Hairapetian, Srbouhi. (1995). *A History of Armenian Literature: From Ancient Times to the Nineteenth Century*. Delmar, NY: Caravan Books.

Halman, Talat S. (2007). *Rapture and Revolution: Essays on Turkish Literature*. Syracuse, NY: Syracuse University Press and Crescent Hill Publications.

Isik, Ihsan. (2005). *Encyclopedia of Turkish Authors: People of Literature, Culture and Science*. Ankara, Turkey: Elvan Publishing.

Jayyusi, Salma Khadra. (Ed.). (2005). *Modern Arabic Fiction: An Anthology*. New York: Columbia University Press.

Denys Johnson-Davies, Denys. (Ed.). (2006). *The Anchor Book of Modern Arabic Fiction*. New York: Anchor Books.

Kilpatrick, Hilary. (1974). *The Modern Egyptian Novel: A Study in Social Criticism*. London: Ithaca Press.

Meisami, Julie Scott, and Starkey, Paul. (2005). *Encyclopedia of Arabic Literature* (2 vols.). London: Routledge.

Meyer, Stefan G. (2001). *The Experimental Arabic Novel: Postcolonial Literary Modernism in the Levant*. Albany, NY: State University of New York Press.

Moosa, Matti. (1997). *The Arabic Literary Heritage: The Development of Its Genres and Criticism*. Boulder, CO: Lynne Rienner Publishers.

Nichanian, Marc. (2002). *Writers of Disaster: Armenian Literature in the Twentieth Century (Volume One: The National Revolution)*. Princeton, NJ: Taderon Press for the Gomidas Institute.

Prior, Daniel. (2000). *Patron, Party, Patrimony: Notes on the Cultural History of the Kirghiz Epic Tradition*. Bloomington, IN: Indiana University Research Institute for Inner Asian Studies.

Rayfield, Donald. (1999). *The Literature of Georgia: A History* (rvd. ed.). Oxford: Oxford University Press.

Reddy, Nilufer Mizanoglu. (1988). *Twenty Stories by Turkish Women Writers*. Bloomington, IN: Indiana University Turkish Studies.

Rowe, Victoria. (2003). *A History of Armenian Women's Writing: 1880–1922*. London: Cambridge Scholars Press.

Rypka, Jan. (1968). *History of Iranian Literature*. Dordrecht, The Netherlands: D. Reidel Publishing Company.

Shaheen, Mohammad. (2002). *The Modern Arabic Story: Shahrazad Returns* (2nd ed.). New York: Palgrave Macmillan.

Siddiq, Muhammad. (2007). *Arab Culture and the Novel: Genre, Identity, and Agency in Egyptian Fiction*. London: Routledge.

Silay, Kemal. (Ed.). (1996). *An Anthology of Turkish Literature*. Bloomington, IN: Indiana University Turkish Studies and Turkish Ministry of Culture Joint Series.

Straley, Dona S. (2004). *The Undergraduate's Companion to Arab Writers and Their Web Sites*. Westport, CT: Libraries Unlimited.

Taha, Ibrahim. (2002). *The Palestinian Novel: A Communication Study*. London: Routledge.

Talattof, Kamran. (2000). *The Politics of Writing in Iran: A History of Modern Persian Literature*. Syracuse, NY: Syracuse University Press.

Winner, Thomas. (1958). *The Oral Art and Literature of the Kazakhs of Russian Central Asia*. Durham, NC: Duke University Press.

ANNOTATIONS FOR BOOKS TRANSLATED FROM ARABIC

Algeria

al-Tahir Wattar (Tahir Wattar). *The Earthquake*.
Translated by William Granara. London: Saqi, 2000. 179 pages.
Genre/literary style/story type: mainstream fiction
In postindependence Algeria, Shaykh Abdelmajid Boularwah is none too pleased with the general direction of the new government. He fears the erosion of traditional social values, so he journeys to Constantine, his place of birth, hoping to stem the tide of modernity and atheism that he sees slowly permeating the Algerian soul and landscape. His attempts prove unsuccessful, and his despair ultimately leads him to suicide. Some critics have said that this novel reminds them of James Joyce's *Ulysses*.
Subject keywords: family histories; social problems
Original language: Arabic
Sources consulted for annotation:
Amazon.com (book description).
Bland, Sally. *Middle East News Online*, 26 March 2001 (from Factiva databases).
Boullata, Issa J. *World Literature Today* 74 (Autumn 2000): 904.

Egypt

Ibrahim Abd al-Majid (Ibrahim Abdel Meguid). *The Other Place*.
Translated by Farouk Abdel Wahab. Cairo, Egypt: American University in Cairo Press, 1997. 299 pages.
Genre/literary style/story type: mainstream fiction
In the Gulf states, there is easy money to be made. Thus, professionals and manual laborers flock there, little knowing what really awaits them: an outlandishly corrupt culture floating on a sea of petrodollars, where local elites and representatives of Western oil companies think only about how to further enrich themselves. This novel, which focuses on an Egyptian from Alexandria, critiques the effects of consumerism and invasive capitalist values on indigenous culture, the environment, and human emotions.
Subject keyword: modernization
Original language: Arabic
Source consulted for annotation:
Book front flap.
Some other translated books written by Ibrahim Abd al-Majid: *Birds of Amber*; *No One Sleeps in Alexandria*

Ibrahim Aslan. *Nile Sparrows*.
Translated by Mona El-Ghobashy. Cairo, Egypt: American University in Cairo Press, 2004. 112 pages.

Genre/literary style/story type: mainstream fiction
This novel majestically portrays the everyday life of Egyptians as it traces a grandson's search for his missing grandmother. Hanem, the 100-year-old family matriarch, has vanished from her village in the area of Warraq. As Mr. Abdalla, her grandson, sets off to find her, he also embarks on a journey through his family's past—a journey that forces him to come to terms with his own fast-eroding life.
Related title by the same author:
Readers may also enjoy *The Heron*, a lyrical meditation on the pervasiveness of corruption. In the tense atmosphere of the day just before the so-called bread riots that nearly capsized the government of Anwar Sadat in 1977, residents of one impoverished neighborhood watch and wait, taking note of how the newly rich go about their business, trying their own hand at money-making schemes, and speculating about whether things will ever really change.
Subject keywords: family histories; rural life
Original language: Arabic
Source consulted for annotation:
Amazon.com (book descriptions for both books; all editorial reviews).
Some other translated books written by Ibrahim Aslan: *The Heron*; *Evening Lake and Other Stories*

Ala Aswani (Alaa Al Aswany). *The Yacoubian Building*.
Translated by Humphrey Davies. Cairo, Egypt: American University in Cairo Press, 2004. 253 pages.
Genre/literary style/story type: mainstream fiction
This novel, which focuses on the residents of the titular apartment building, is invariably compared to Naguib Mahfouz's *The Cairo Trilogy* and *Miramar*. But as Pankaj Mishra writes, it is much more blunt in its assessment of "the physical and moral rot of contemporary Egypt." Unsparing in its denunciation of the corruption and hypocrisy of contemporary Egypt, the novel holds up a mirror to the multidimensional inequities of a class-based society; the oppression of women; the rise of radical Islam; and wide-ranging business and government corruption.
Related title by the same author:
Readers may also wish to explore *Chicago*, which, as Amy Virshup observes, interweaves "the stories of a half-dozen Egyptians living in Chicago and connected to the histology department at the University of Illinois Medical Center." The result is a tragic-comic world full of bewildered and tormented characters: the devoutly religious mix with aficionados of pornography, who in turn mix with political radicals working for regime change.
Subject keywords: social problems; urban life
Original language: Arabic
Sources consulted for annotation:
Global Books in Print (online) (reviews from *Booklist*, *Library Journal*, and *Publishers Weekly* for *Chicago*).
Mishra, Pankaj. *The New York Times Magazine*, 27 April 2008 (online).
Virshup, Amy. *The New York Times Book Review*, 15 October, 2008 (online).
Some other translated books written by Ala Aswani: *Chicago*; *Friendly Fire: Ten Tales of Today's Cairo*

Salwá Bakr. *The Golden Chariot*.
Translated by Dinah Manisty. Reading, UK: Garnet, 1995. 195 pages.
Genres/literary styles/story types: mainstream fiction; women's lives
This novel focuses on Aziza, who is imprisoned for the murder of her abusive stepfather. As she becomes acquainted with the other women in her prison ward, she reveals the treachery, perfidy,

and crimes of her former friends, whose lives she unsparingly dissects. Critics have invoked *The Arabian Nights* when discussing *The Golden Chariot*, which they see as interrogating the very premises of conventional wisdom about madness and criminal behavior in a patriarchal and socio-economically oppressive society.
Subject keywords: power; social problems
Original language: Arabic.
Sources consulted for annotation:
Arab.net. Egypt. Salwa Bakr (applicable URL no longer works).
Booth, Marilyn. *British Journal of Middle Eastern Studies* 23 (November 1996): 232.
EurospanBookstore.com (book review), http://www.eurospanbookstore.com.
Some other translated books written by Salwá Bakr: *The Wiles of Men and Other Stories*; *Such a Beautiful Voice*

Muhammad Bisati (Mohamed el-Bisatie). *A Last Glass of Tea and Other Stories*.
Translated by Denys Johnson-Davies. Boulder, CO: Lynne Rienner Publishers, 1998. 139 pages.
Genres/literary styles/story types: mainstream fiction; short stories
Set in the Nile Delta, these 24 short stories examine crucial social issues, including generational conflict, polygamy, sexual abuse, and the tyranny of ancient customs.
Related titles by the same author:
Readers may also enjoy *Over the Bridge*, in which a government official develops a lucrative scheme to make money by first creating a bogus police department for an imaginary city and then pocketing the nonexistent department's payroll. Also of interest may be *Clamor of the Lake*, which explores the lives of a husband and wife whose dreary and desolate lives are made bearable by the objects they find on the beach.
Subject keywords: family histories; rural life
Original language: Arabic
Sources consulted for annotation:
American University in Cairo Press (book descriptions), http://www.aucpress.com.
Dawood, Ibrahim. *World Literature Today* 73 (Spring 1999): 383.
Some other translated books written by Muhammad Bisati: *Houses Behind the Trees*; *Clamor of the Lake*; *Over the Bridge*; *Hunger*

Saad Elkhadem. *One Night in Cairo: An Egyptian Micronovel with Footnotes*.
Toronto, ON: York Press, 2001. 41 pages. [bilingual edition: Arabic & English].
Genres/literary styles/story types: mainstream fiction; experimental fiction
This book focuses on the alienation and isolation experienced by someone who, after living abroad, returns to Egypt. The author's most famous work is the *Trilogy of the Flying Egyptian*, which explore the emotional and psychological states of an Egyptian living in the West.
Subject keyword: social problems
Original language: Arabic
Sources consulted for annotation:
Cassis, A. F. *International Fiction Review* 29 (January 2002): 97.
Dahab, F. Elizabeth. *Canadian Ethnic Studies Journal* 38 (Summer 2006): 72.
Haywood, John A. *World Literature Today* 69 (Autumn 1995): 860.
Kadhim, Hussein. *World Literature Today* 71 (Summer 1997): 646.
Peters, Issa. *World Literature Today* 68 (Autumn 1994): 873.
Some other books in English written by Saad Elkhadem: *Trilogy of the Flying Egyptian* (*Canadian Adventures of the Flying Egyptian*; *Chronicle of the Flying Egyptian in Canada*; *Crash Landing of the Flying Egyptian*); *Wings of Lead*; *The Plague*; *The Blessed Movement*

Sulayman Fayyad (Soleiman Fayyad). ***Voices.***
Translated by Hosam Aboul-Ela. London: Marion Boyars, 1993. 112 pages.
Genres/literary styles/story types: mainstream fiction; women's lives
This novel, which is set in the rural Egyptian village of Darawish, revolves around Hamid al-Bahairi, who has made his fortune in Paris as an upscale hotelier and shopowner. Married to Simone, a sophisticated Frenchwoman, and the father of two children, he becomes homesick and returns to his native village. But his homecoming is poisoned by the jealousy of family members and marred by cultural and religious conflicts, which eventually turn fatal when a crime is committed against Simone by the village women with the full support of their husbands and village elders.
Subject keywords: culture conflict; rural life
Original language: Arabic
Sources consulted for annotation:
Haywood, John. *World Literature Today* 68 (Summer 1994): 627.
Steinberg, Sybil S. *Publishers Weekly* 239 (12 October 1992): 65.

Gamal al-Ghitani. ***The Zafarani Files.***
Translated by Farouk Abdel Wahab. Cairo, Egypt: American University of Cairo Press, 2009. 335 pages.
Genre/literary style/story type: mainstream fiction
Strange things are going on in Zafarani alley. Every resident male, except one, is impotent; every resident female, except one, who has sex with any other man will render that man impotent. It is all part of a diabolical plan woven by a deranged sheikh, who institutes a series of rules and regulations first about personal conduct and then slowly expands his edicts to encompass the political world.
Related title by the same author:
Readers may also be interested in *Zayni Barakat*, which tells the story of Egypt's Mamluk dynasty but also draws parallels to Egypt under Nasser. Not only is corruption all-pervasive in both eras but so is a psychologically debilitating climate of fear.
Subject keywords: power; urban life.
Original language: Arabic.
Sources consulted for annotation:
Amazon.com (book description).
Head, Gretchen. *Daily Star*, 24 July 2004 (from Factiva databases).
Kakutani, Michiko. *The New York Times*, 22 February 1991, p. 26.
MacFarquhar, Neil. *The New York Times*, 12 September 2004, p. 28.
Post, Chad W. Three Percent website (book review), http://www.rochester.edu/College/translation/threepercent.
Some other translated books written by Gamal al-Ghitani: *Zayni Barakat*; *A Distress Call*

Yahyá Haqqi (Yahya Hakki). ***The Lamp of Umm Hashim and Other Stories.***
Translated by Denys Johnson-Davies. Cairo, Egypt: American University in Cairo Press, 2004. 88 pages.
Genres/literary styles/story types: mainstream fiction; short stories
The author is credited with being one of the giants of Egyptian literature. According to the American Univeristy in Cairo Press website, he was among the first "to practice genres of creative writing that were new to the traditions of classical Arabic." He is widely known for the title story of this collection, which recounts the tale of a foreign-educated Egyptian doctor who returns home and "tries to come to terms with two divergent cultures."
Subject keyword: culture conflict

Original language: Arabic
Sources consulted for annotation:
Amazon.com (book description).
American University in Cairo Press website (book description), http://www.aucpress.com.
Some other translated books written by Yahyá Haqqi: *Good Morning! and Other Stories*; *Blood and Mud: Three Novelettes*

Sun Allah Ibrahim (Sun'allah Ibrahim). ***The Committee.***
Translated by Mary St. Germain and Charlene Constable. Syracuse, NY: Syracuse University Press, 2001. 166 pages.
Genres/literary styles/story types: thriller; political thriller
Set in the Egypt of Anwar Sadat, this novel conjures up the ghosts of George Orwell, Franz Kafka, and Albert Camus. An unnamed narrator faces undefined accusations before a shadowy committee. His punishment is to choose a leading Arab and then write an essay about that leading figure. Not content with assigning the essay, the committee also appoints one of its members to keep a close watch on the narrator. Inevitably, the narrator murders his tormentor.
Related title by the same author:
Readers may also be interested in *Zaat*, which explores the eponymous heroine's life in Egypt starting in the 1950s under Nasser. She works in a newspaper's Department of News Monitoring and Assessment, so the novel—in a collage style reminiscent of John Dos Passos' *USA* trilogy—incorporates headlines, news articles, obituaries, and other ephemera to present a multidimensional view of social and cultural life in Cairo.
Subject keywords: power; politics
Original language: Arabic
Sources consulted for annotation:
Boullata, Issa J. *World Literature Today* 76 (Spring 2002): 243.
Caso, Frank. *Booklist* 98 (15 November 2001): 547.
Global Books in Print (online) (synopsis/book jacket).
Salih, Sabah A. *The Middle East Journal* 56 (Summer 2002): 512.
Zaleski, Jeff. *Publishers Weekly* 248 (29 October 2001): 34.
Some other translated books written by Sun Allah Ibrahim: *The Smell of It & Other Stories*; *Zaat*

Yusuf Idris. ***City of Love and Ashes.***
Translated by R. Neil Hewison. Cairo, Egypt: American University in Cairo Press, 1999. 166 pages.
Genres/literary styles/story types: mainstream fiction; literary historical
In 1952 Cairo, as Egypt yearns for national independence, Hamza and Fawziya—fervent radicals and revolutionaries—must find their way through a tumultuous political landscape and a minefield of personal emotions.
Related title by the same author:
Readers may also be interested in *The Sinners*, where the discovery of the corpse of a baby causes mass indignation. In a quest to find the guilty party, villagers take it upon themselves to snoop into the lives of others.
Subject keyword: politics
Original language: Arabic
Sources consulted for annotation:
Amazon.com (all editorial reviews).
American University in Cairo Press (book review), http://www.aucpress.com.
Global Books in Print (online) (book jacket for *The Sinners*).

Some other translated books written by Yusuf Idris: *The Sinners*; *The Piper Dies and Other Stories*; *A Leader of Men*; *The Language of Pain and Other Stories*; *Rings of Burnished Brass*; *The Cheapest Nights and Other Stories*

Idwar Kharrat (Edwar al-Kharrat). *Rama and the Dragon*.
Translated by Ferial Ghazoul and John Verlenden. Cairo, Egypt: American University in Cairo Press, 2002. 327 pages.
Genre/literary style/story type: mainstream fiction
Mikhail is madly in love with the sensual and exotic Rama. They are in every way opposites. Not only are they from different parts of Egypt, but they also adhere to different religions: Copt and Muslim. Thus, the novel becomes as much a philosophical excursion into differences and similarities as a stark rendering of passion.
Subject keyword: religion
Original language: Arabic
Sources consulted for annotation:
Amazon.com (book description).
Fayed, Shaimaa & Marei, Jehan. *Egypt Today*, 1 February 2003 (from Factiva databases).
Some other translated books written by Idwar Kharrat: *City of Saffron*; *Girls of Alexandria*; *Stones of Bobello*

Ibrahim Kuni (Ibrahim al-Koni). *Anubis: A Desert Novel*.
Translated by William M. Hutchins. Cairo, Egypt: American University in Cairo Press, 2005. 184 pages.
Genres/literary styles/story types: adventure; quest
This novel invokes Anubis, the ancient Egyptian god of the dead, to tell the story of a young man who seeks his long-lost father in the harsh and unyielding desert. He must combat not only physical harships but also spiritual ones. The author is of Tuareg descent.
Related title by the same author:
Readers may also enjoy *The Bleeding of the Stone*, which was characterized by *Kirkus Reviews* as an "ecological fable, political statement, and lyrical lament for the past." A Bedouin goatherder must deal with tourists who shatter the peace of his solitary life in their quest to view ancient cave paintings and get a glimpse of the rare mouflon.
Subject keyword: identity
Original language: Arabic
Sources consulted for annotation:
Amazon.com (book description).
Global Books in Print (online) (reviews from *Booklist*, *Choice*, and *Kirkus Reviews* for *The Bleeding of the Stone*).
Some other translated books written by Ibrahim Kuni: *The Bleeding of the Stone*; *Seven Veils of Seth*; *Gold Dust*

Najib Mahfuz (Naguib Mahfouz). *The Cairo Trilogy* (*Palace Walk*; *Palace of Desire*; *Sugar Street*).
Translated by William Maynard Hutchins. New York: Alfred A. Knopf, 2001. 1,313 pages.
Genres/literary styles/story type: mainstream fiction; literary historical
Taken together, the three parts of this trilogy recount the life of three generations of an Egyptian family during the period 1900–1950. This is a sweeping narrative of domestic drama, infighting, and social and cultural hypocrisy. Characters variously deal with such issues as oppression, sexual awakening, and political revolution, among many other topics. The author has been compared with

Balzac, Dickens, and Tolstoy for the all-encompassing verve, bluntness, and compassion with which he portrays Egyptian society.
Subject keywords: family histories; politics
Original language: Arabic
Sources consulted for annotation:
Dyer, Richard. *Boston Globe*, 28 January 1992, p. 27.
Holroyd, Michael. *New Statesman* 17 (16 August 2004): 39.
Johnson, Stanley. *The Oregonian*, 12 March 1995, p. E5.
Kempf, Andrea. *Library Journal* 126 (15 November 2001): 128.
McCormick, Marion. *The Gazette*, 13 January 1990, p. K10.
"Naguib Mahfouz." *Contemporary Authors Online*. Thomson Gale, 2006.
Upchurch, Michael. *Knight Ridder Tribune News Service*, 1 June 2005, p. 1.
Wald-Hopkins, Christine. *Arizona Daily Star*, 11 August 1991, p. 10E.
World Literature Today 79 (May/August 2005): 45.
Zafris, Jim. *The Plain Dealer*, 2 March 1997, p. 10E.
Some other translated books written by Najib Mahfuz: *Arabian Nights and Days*; *Children of the Alley*; *The Harafish*; *Adrift on the Nile*; *The Journey of Ibn Fattouma*; *The Beginning and the End*; *The Time and the Place and Other Stories*; *Wedding Song*; *Midaq Alley*; *The Thief and the Dogs*; *Akhenaten, Dweller in Truth*; *The Beggar*; *Autumn Quail*; *Respected Sir*

Abd al-Hakim Qasim (Abdel-Hakim Kassem). *The Seven Days of Man*.
Translated by Joseph Norment Bell. Evanston, IL: Hydra Books/Northwestern University Press, 1996. 218 pages.
Genres/literary styles/story types: adventure; quest
This book recounts the evolution from traditionalism to modernity of a Nile Delta village as well as the seven-stage pilgrimage of the narrator Abdel-Aziz to the shrine of a Sufi saint. Some critics praised the novel for its lyrical writing and philosophical reflections about the spiritual history of mankind.
Subject keywords: modernization; rural life
Original language: Arabic
Sources consulted for annotation:
Amazon.com (review from *Kirkus Reviews*).
Boullata, Issa J. *World Literature Today* 71 (Winter 1997): 215.
Another translated book written by Abd al-Hakim Qasim: *Rites of Assent: Two Novellas*

Muhammad Yusuf Quayd (Yusuf al-Qa'id). *War in the Land of Egypt*.
Translated by Olive and Lorne Kenny and Christopher Tingley. Brooklyn, NY: Interlink Books, 1998. 192 pages.
Genre/literary style/story type: mainstream fiction
A village leader does not want his son to go to war, so he turns to the services of a middleman to find a substitute who can take the place of his son in the army. Masri, who never speaks in the novel, is the unfortunate person selected. The story is told from the viewpoint of Masri's father, the leader of the village; the middleman; the village watchman; an officer in the army; and, finally, an investigator. Critics have invoked Franz Kafka to describe the sense of tragic absurdity permeating this book.
Subject keywords: rural life; social roles
Original language: Arabic
Sources consulted for annotation:
Amazon.com (all editorial reviews).

Cline, David. *Booklist* 94 (1 April 1998): 1302.
New Internationalist 386 (January/February 2006): 31.
Rejwan, Nissim. *Jerusalem Post*, 27 October 1989, p. 17.
Whittaker, Peter. *New Internationalist* 378 (May 2005): 30.
Some other translated books written by Muhammad Yusuf Quayd: *The Days of Drought*; *News from the Meneisi Farm*

Miral Tahawi (Miral al-Tahawy). ***Blue Aubergine.***
Translated by Anthony Calderbank. Cairo, Egypt: American University in Cairo Press, 2002. 125 pages.
Genres/literary styles/story types: mainstream fiction; women's lives
Set in the 1980s and 1990s, this novel follows the life of Nada, a young Bedouin woman whose troubled childhood has left her with few social skills. Her search to find meaning in life first leads to Islamic traditionalism, then to a semblance of Western emancipation. As she tries to assert her independence, her quest for affection and understanding remains elusive.
Subject keyword: social roles
Original language: Arabic
Sources consulted for annotation:
Amazon.com (book description).
The Washington Post, 17 June 2002, p. C4.
Another translated book written by Miral Tahawi: *The Tent*

Baha Tahir (Bahaa' Taher). ***Aunt Safiyya and the Monastery.***
Translated by Barbara Romaine. Berkeley, CA: University of California Press, 1996. 124 pages.
Genre/literary style/story type: mainstream fiction
This book is set in a small Egyptian village in 1967, the year of the Arab-Israeli war. It explores such themes as the condition of women and the tradition of blood fueds as well as relations between Muslims and Christian Copts. It seems foreordained that Safiyya, a young orphan girl, will marry Harbi, but instead, she is forced to wed the elderly and wealthy local chieftain. Eventually, she bears a son. But her husband—convinced that his child will be kidnapped by a vengeful Harbi—imprisons and tortures him. Harbi escapes, kills Safiyya's husband, and, years later—recognizing that Safiyyah's son is compelled to avenge his father's murder—takes refuge with local Coptic monks, who play a prominent part in attempting to reconcile the fueding factions.
Subject keywords: religion; rural life
Original language: Arabic
Sources consulted for annotation:
Lively, Penelope. *The New York Times Book Review*, 30 June 1996 (online).
Peters, Issa. *World Literature Today* 71 (Winter 1997): 216.
Simson, Maria. *Publishers Weekly* 243 (8 April 1996): 63.
Some other translated books written by Baha Tahir: *Love in Exile*; *Sunset Oasis*

Latifah Zayyat (Latifa al-Zayyat). ***The Open Door.***
Translated by Marilyn Booth. Cairo, Egypt: American University in Cairo Press, 2000. 364 pages.
Genres/literary styles/story types: mainstream fiction; coming-of-age
When Egyptian society as a whole undergoes a political and nationalistic awakening in the 1950s, Layla also becomes more politically and sexually aware. As Layla—along with a diverse group of friends—struggles to assimilate the profound social and cultural transformations all around her, she must also pay attention to her middle-class upbringing, which calls for an ever-upward trajectory through a successful marriage.

Subject keywords: power; social roles
Original language: Arabic
Sources consulted for annotation:
Amazon.com (book description).
Kahf, Mohja. *World Literature Today* 76 (Winter 2002): 227.
Another translated book written by Latifah Zayyat: *The Owner of the House*

Iraq

Dayzi Amir (Daisy al-Amir). ***The Waiting List: An Iraqi Woman's Tales of Alienation.***
Translated by Barbara Parmenter. Austin, TX: Center for Middle Eastern Studies, University of Texas at Austin, 1994. 79 pages.
Genres/literary styles/story types: mainstream fiction; women's lives
These short stories, which are set in Iraq, Cyprus, and Lebanon, focus on the psychological and intellectual difficulties that women experience in times of conflict, war, and exile.
Subject keyword: social problems
Original language: Arabic
Sources consulted for annotation:
Amazon.com (all editorial reviews).
Ms. (January 1995): 68.

Sinan Antun (Sinan Antoon). ***I'jaam.***
Translated by Rebecca C. Johnson and the author. San Francisco, CA: City Lights, 2007. 97 pages.
Genre/literary style/story type: mainstream fiction
This is a highly imaginative work that is built around the ways that words change meaning once diacritical marks are added in Arabic. A mysterious manuscript without these marks is discovered at Iraqi's Interior Ministry. When it is decoded and transcribed, it turns out to be the biographical legacy of an imprisoned activist who expressed his ongoing political opposition through the series of word games that constitute the essence of the manuscript.
Subject keywords: politics; power
Original language: Arabic.
Source consulted for annotation:
Pierpont, Claudia Roth. "Found in Translation." *The New Yorker* (18 January 2010) (online).

Fadil Azzawi (Fadhil al-Azzawi). ***The Last of the Angels.***
Translated by William M. Hutchins. Cairo, Egypt: American University in Cairo Press, 2007. 304 pages.
Genres/literary styles/story types: mainstream fiction; magical realism
Strange and wonderful things happen in Kirkuk (Iraq) just before the overthrow of the monarchy. This novel focuses on Hameed Nylon, a former chauffeur who lost his oil-industry job after being the subject of unfounded sexual rumors and who subsequently becomes a radical activist. According to the publisher's website, other memorable characters in this "satiric, picaresque, and apocalyptic" novel include a sheep butcher who "travels to the Soviet Union to find his long-lost brothers, and returns home to great acclaim (and personal fortune) in an airship" and Burhan Abdullah, a young boy who "discovers an old chest in the attic of his family's house that lets him talk to angels."
Related title by the same author:
Readers may also be interested in the autobiographical *Cell Block Five*, which focuses on Aziz, who becomes a prisoner without any charges being filed against him. As he awaits his fate in the

company of political prisoners, he is offered various pieces of advice about how to survive and bring about his release.
Subject keywords: politics; power
Original language: Arabic
Source consulted for annotation:
American University in Cairo Press (book descriptions), http://www.aucpress.com.
Another translated book written by Fadil Azzawi: *Cell Block Five*

Batul Khudayri (Betool Khedairi). ***A Sky So Close.***
Translated by Muhayman Jamil. New York: Pantheon Books, 2001. 241 pages.
Genres/literary styles/story types: mainstream fiction; coming-of-age
This novel centers on a young Iraqi girl born to an English mother and an Iraqi father. After her father suffers a heart attack, the family moves from a small village to Baghdad just as the Iraq-Iran war begins. While the war rages, the narrator becomes obsessed with ballet. After her father dies, she falls in love with a Christian Iraqi solider, whom she eventually leaves to take care of her dying mother who wishes to return home to England.
Subject keywords: culture conflict; family histories
Original language: Arabic
Sources consulted for annotation:
Karkabi, Barbara. *Houston Chronicle*, 1 May 2003, p. 01.
Maiello, Michael. *The New York Times Book Review*, 12 August 2001, p. 22.
Schurer, Norbert. *Winston-Salem Journal*, 24 March 2002, p. 20.
Van Til, Cheryl. *Library Journal* 126 (1 June 2001): 216.
Zaleski, Jeff. *Publishers Weekly* 248 (2 July 2001): 53.
Zeilstra, Linda. *Booklist* 97 (15 May 2001): 1732.
Another translated book written by Batul Khudayri: *Absent*

Aliyah Mamduh (Alia Mamdouh). ***Naphtalene: A Novel of Baghdad.***
Translated by Peter Theroux. New York: The Feminist Press at the City University of New York, 2005. 214 pages.
Genres/literary styles/story types: mainstream fiction; coming-of-age
This novel tells the story of Huda, a nine-year-old girl growing up in Baghdad in the 1940s. Life is not easy in a household with a brutal father and an ill mother; things only get worse when her father replaces her mother with a second wife. But there are epheremal joys and poignant moments to be discovered in the surrounding neighborhood, and Huda finds constant solace in the comforting words and presence of her grandmother.
Related title by the same author:
Readers may also enjoy *The Loved Ones*, which focuses on Suhaila, who is visited by innumerable friends when she is hospitalized in Paris. The visitors provide a multidimensional picture of Suhaila's tortured and tangled exile's life—its many lows as well as its few compensations.
Subject keyword: urban life
Original language: Arabic
Sources consulted for annotation:
American University in Cairo Press (book description), http://www.aucpress.com.
Boullata, Issa. J. *World Literature Today* 80 (March/April 2006): 54.
Dixler, Elsa. *The New York Times Book Review*, 4 September 2005, p. 16.
Engberg, Gillian. *Booklist* 101 (15 May 2005): 1637.
Mamdouh, Alia. *Orlando Sentinel*, 17 July 2005.
Publishers Weekly 252 (23 May 2005): 57.

Straight, Susan. *Ms.* 15 (Summer 2005): 89.
Some other translated books written by Aliyah Mamduh: *Mothballs*; *The Loved Ones*

Salim Matar (Selim Matar). *The Woman of the Flask.*
Translated by Peter Clark. Cairo, Egypt: American University in Cairo Press, 2005. 152 pages.
Genres/literary styles/story types: mainstream fiction; magical realism
Adam is an Iraqi who flees to Switzerland during Saddam's tyrannical régime. One of the few possessions he carries with him is a flask that belonged to his deceased father. Upon opening it, he discovers a ravishing and enchanting woman. The novel blends the stories of Adam's ancestors as told by the woman in the flask, with accounts of his current life as a computer programmer in Switzerland.
Subject keyword: family histories
Original language: Arabic
Sources consulted for annotation:
Amazon.com (book description).
Sarhan, Hada. *Middle East News Online*, 26 February 2001 (from Factiva databases).

Buthaynah Nasiri (Buthaina Al Nasiri). *Final Night.*
Translated by Denys Johnson-Davies. Cairo, Egypt: American University in Cairo Press, 2008. 136 pages.
Genres/literary styles/story types: mainstream fiction; short stories
According to the publisher's website, this collection of short stories reflects the author's "deeply felt nostalgia for Iraq." She is "less interested in the position of women in society than in that of people in general and the sufferings they experience between birth and the end of life." Now living in Cairo, the author also publishes books by other Iraqi writers.
Subject keyword: identity
Original language: Arabic
Source consulted for annotation:
American University in Cairo Press (book description), http://www.aucpress.com.

Iqbal Qazwini (Iqbal al-Qazwini). *Zubaida's Window: A Novel of Iraqi Exile.*
Translated by Amira Nowaira. New York: Feminist Press at The City University of New York, 2008. 137 pages.
Genres/literary styles/story types: mainstream fiction; women's lives
As Zubaida drinks tea and watches the United States invasion of Iraq on television from her Berlin apartment in 2003, she remembers the Baghdad that she once knew with a mix of nostalgia and horror. She lost her younger brother to the Iraq-Iran War, and she is at risk of losing her own soul in a strange land that is isolated and alienated from all that she holds dear.
Subject keywords: social problems; war
Original language: Arabic
Sources consulted for annotation:
Feminist Press at The City University of New York (book description), http://www.feministpress.org.
Global Books in Print (online) (reviews from *Booklist* and *Publishers Weekly*).

Sumayyah Ramadan (Somaya Ramadan). *Leaves of Narcissus.*
Translated by Marilyn Booth. Cairo, Egypt: American University in Cairo Press, 2002. 111 pages.
Genres/literary styles/story types: mainstream fiction; women's lives

This novel traces the psychological breakdown of Kimi, an Egyptian who has left her upper-class family to study literature at Dublin's Trinity College. Here, she discovers such writers as James Joyce, Oscar Wilde, and Samuel Beckett. She spirals downward into a depression and debilitating mental anguish and is eventually hospitalized.
Subject keyword: identity
Original language: Arabic
Sources consulted for annotation:
Amazon.com (book description).
Fayed, Shaimaa. *Egypt Today*, 1 March 2003 (from Factiva database).

Nawal Sadawi (Nawal El Saadawi). *Innocence of the Devil.*
Translated by Sherif Hetata. Berkeley, CA: University of California Press, 1994. 233 pages.
Genres/literary styles/story types: mainstream fiction; women's lives
Ganat, who is a patient in a mental hospital, and Narguiss, who is the head nurse of the hospital, were once very close. Narguiss has been sentenced to a life in exile because she was found to no longer be a virgin, and Ganat's release from the hospital depends on her ability to relinquish her past relationship with Narguiss. The author, whose work has been compared with Salman Rushdie's *Satanic Verses*, uses elements of magical realism to produce a densely philosophical consideration of patriarchy and social conventions.
Subject keywords: identity; social roles
Original language: Arabic
Sources consulted for annotation:
Allen, M. D. *World Literature Today* 69 (Summer 1995): 637.
Ms. 5 (January 1995): 68.
Steinberg, Sybil S. *Publishers Weekly* 241 (24 October 1994): 54.
Some other translated books written by Nawal Sadawi: *God Dies by the Nile*; *The Circling Song*; *Two Women in One*; *Searching*; *Memoirs of a Woman Doctor*; *The Fall of the Imam*; *Death of an Ex-Minister*; *Love in the Kingdom of Oil*; *She Has No Place in Paradise*; *The Well of Life*; *and, The Thread: Two Short Novels*

Mahmud Said (Mahmoud Saeed). *Saddam City.*
Translated by Ahmad Sadri. London: Saqi, 2004. 130 pages.
Genre/literary style/story type: mainstream fiction
This novel is a thundering denunciation of Saddam Hussein's ruthless regime. Mustafa Ali Noman is a teacher working in Baghdad who is arrested one morning as he arrives at school. Refused all contact with his family, he eventually understands that no one really cares whether he is guilty or innocent. As his psycholoigical torment grows, the prison of his mind becomes almost as terrifying as his physical circumstances. Critics have seen echoes of the works of Franz Kafka, Aleksandr Solzhenitsyn, and Elie Wiesel in this book.
Subject keywords: power; social problems
Original language: Arabic
Source consulted for annotation:
Amazon.com (book description).
Another translated book written by Mahmud Said: *Two Lost Souls*

Samuel Shimon. *An Iraqi in Paris: An Autobiographical Novel*.
Translated by Samira Kawar. London: Banipal Books, 2005. 249 pages.
Genre/literary style/story type: mainstream fiction

Born in an Iraqi village, the author of this autobiographical novel eventually finds himself living a poverty-stricken and quasi-bohemian existence in 1980s France, surviving by his wits and the occasional helping hand from friends and chance acquainatances. Critics have compared the book to Henry Miller's *Tropic of Cancer.*
Subject keywords: social problems; urban life
Original language: Arabic
Sources consulted for annotation:
Tonkin, Boyd. *The Independent*, 25 March 2005, p. 27.
Wilson-Goldie, Kaelen. *Daily Star*, 30 December 2005 (from Factiva databases).

Fuad Takarli (Fuad al-Takarli). ***The Long Way Back.***
Translated by Catherine Cobham. Cairo, Egypt: American University in Cairo Press, 2001. 379 pages.
Genre/literary style/story type: mainstream fiction
Set in the Iraq of the 1960s, this novel chronicles four generations of a single family as well as the wider political events of the period. Among the central characters in the book are three brothers: the alcoholic and alienated Hussayn, the suicidal Mihdat, and the psychologically scarred 'Abd al-Karim.
Subject keywords: family histories; social problems
Original language: Arabic
Sources consulted for annotation:
Amazon.com (book description).
Whittaker, Peter. *New Internationalist* 352 (December 2002): 31.

Jordan

Abd al-Rahman Munif (Abdelrahman Munif). ***Variations on Night and Day.***
Translated by Peter Theroux. New York: Pantheon Books, 1993. 333 pages.
Genres/literary styles/story types: mainstream fiction; literary historical
This is the third novel in a five-part epic set in the fictional country of Mooran, which is a stand-in for Saudi Arabia. The epic as a whole describes the rise of petrodollar culture in a heretofore deeply traditional and religious society, focusing on the profound social and cultural transformations that modernity brought to a people steeped in the ways of the desert. In its historical sweep it has often been compared with William Faulkner's novels set in Yoknapatawpha County, such as *The Sound and The Fury*, *The Hamlet*, *The Town*, and *The Mansion*. The first novel in Munif's series, *Cities of Salt*, is a multidimensional portrait of the arrival of Western oil companies in Mooran and ends with the death of Mooran's founder, Sultan Khureybil. The second novel in the series, *The Trench*, chronicles the ascent of Khureybil's oldest son Khazael to power and his overthrow by Fanar, his younger brother. In *Variations on Night and Day*, Munif explores Fanar's life as a child and teenager, portraying his father's corrupt relationship with British colonialists. The last two novels of the series have yet to be translated into English.
Subject keywords: colonization and colonialism; politics
Original language: Arabic
Sources consulted for annotation:
Ajami, Fouad. *The New York Times*, 5 September 1993, p. A6.
Amazon.com (review from *Kirkus Reviews*).
Kirsch, Jonathan. *Los Angeles Times*, 18 August 1993, p. 3.
Peters, Issa. *World Literature Today* 68 (Spring 1994): 418.
Steinberg, Sybil S. *Publishers Weekly* 240 (5 July 1993): 62.
Upchurch, Michael. *Seattle Times*, 31 October 1993, p. F2.

Some other translated books written by Abd al-Rahman Munif: *Cities of Salt*; *The Trench*; *Endings*; *Variations on Night and Day*

Lebanon

Hudá Barakat (Hoda Barakat). *Disciples of Passion.*
Translated by Marilyn Booth. Syracuse, NY: Syracuse University Press, 2005. 136 pages.
Genre/literary style/story type: mainstream fiction
According to the publisher's website, this book "chronicles the civil war in Lebanon through the troubled and sometimes quasi-hallucinatory mind of a [Christian] young man who has experienced kidnapping, hostage exchange, and hospital internment." As he ekes out his days in an asylum, he recalls his love for a Muslim woman—an idyllic impossibility that seems as remote as the prospect of peace in a devastated land.
Related title by the same author:
Readers may also enjoy *The Tiller of Waters*, which focuses on a family of Lebanese textile merchants, especially Mitri and the Kurdish maid with whom he is in love. According to the pubisher's website, the novel includes "scientific discourse about herbal plants and textile crafts, customs and manners of Arabs, Armenians, and Kurds, mythological figures from ancient Greece, Mesopotamia, Phoenicia, and Arabia, the theosophy of the African Dogons and the medieval Byzantines, and historical accounts of the Crusades in the Holy Land and the silk route to China."
Subject keywords: religion; social problems
Original language: Arabic
Sources consulted for annotation:
Amazon.com (book description; review from *Publishers Weekly*).
American University in Cairo Press (book description), http://www.aucpress.com.
Some other translated books written by Hudá Barakat: *The Stone of Laughter*; *The Tiller of Waters*

Abbas Baydun (Abbas Beydoun). *Blood Test.*
Translated by Max Weiss. Syracuse, NY: Syracuse University Press, 2008. 136 pages.
Genre/literary style/story type: mainstream fiction
After the deaths of his father, brother, and uncle, a young man is thrust into a family leadership role. He soon falls in love with a married woman, but her former relationship with his uncle poses a major stumbling block to his hopes. As he tries to get a better sense of his dead relatives' lives, he discovers that the past, no matter how opaque, will always have significant ramifications.
Subject keyword: family histories
Original language: Arabic
Sources consulted for annotation:
Global Books in Print (online) (review from *Publishers Weekly*).
Syracuse University Press (book description), http://www.syracuseuniversitypress.syr.edu.

Rashid Daif (Rashi al-Daif). *Dear Mr. Kawabata.*
Translated by Paul Starkey. London: Quartet Books, 1999. 166 pages.
Genre/literary style/story type: mainstream fiction
Wounded during the Lebanese Civil War, the dying and unnamed narrator addresses a series of letters to the dead novelist Yasunari Kawabata, who committed suicide in 1972. In these imaginary letters, the protagonist examines his life and Lebanon's history, touching upon such topics as childhood, family, religion, suicide, war, and the nature of death.
Subject keyword: family histories

Original language: Arabic
Sources consulted for annotation:
Adams, Noah. *All Things Considered*, 14 March 2000, p. 1
Amazon.com (book description; review from *Kirkus Reviews*).
Johnston, Bonnie. *Booklist* 96 (15 May 2000): 1727.
Kempf, Andrea. *Library Journal* 126 (15 November 2001): 128.
Rohrbaugh, Lisa. *Library Journal* 125 (1 June 2000): 192.
Waters, Colin. *Sunday Herald*, 15 August 1999, p. 8.
Some other translated books written by Rashid Daif: *Passage to Dusk*; *This Side of Innocence*; *Learning English*

Hassan Daoud. *The House of Mathilde*.
Translated by Peter Theroux. London: Granta Books, 1999. 181 pages.
Genre/literary style/story type: mainstream fiction
Set in a Beirut apartment building in 1983 during the Lebanese war, this novel revolves around the daily lives of the building's assorted residents. Events are narrated from the perspective of a young boy who is wise beyond his years. The collective portrait of the apartment building is a homage to the perseverance and resiliency of average people trying to make the best of a bad situation.
Related title by the same author:
Readers may also enjoy *The Year of the Revolutionary New Bread-Making Machine*, which is set in 1960s Beirut and focuses on a family bakery run by Muhammad's father and uncle. But modernity rears its ugly head in the form of an ingenious bread-making machine. Life will never be the same again for the bakery's employees, whose dreams will inevitably be crushed by the march of progress.
Subject keywords: family histories; urban life
Original language: Arabic
Sources consulted for annotation:
Amazon.com (book description).
Global Books in Print (online) (synopsis/book jacket).
The Herald, 15 May 1999 (from Factiva databases).
Shepherd Smith, Isobel. *The Times*, 1 May 1999 (from Factiva databases).
Another translated book written by Hassan Daoud: *The Year of the Revolutionary New Bread-Making Machine*

Ilyas Khuri (Elias Khoury). *Gate of the Sun*.
Translated by Humphrey Davies. Brooklyn, NY: Archipelago Books, 2005. 539 pages.
Genres/literary styles/story types: mainstream fiction; literary historical
In an attempt to resurrect Yunes, a Palestinian fighter, from a coma as he lies in a field hospital, Khalil, a doctor, tells him a series of stories about the tragic fate of Palestinians. *Gate of the Sun*—which has been compared to *The Book of One Thousand and One Nights* because of its spellbinding interweaving of personal, social, and political history—thus limns the tragedy and intermittent joys experienced by Palestinians since 1948. Critics were unanimous in calling this book a modern classic.
Related title by the same author:
Readers may also be interested in *Yalo*, where the eponymous protagonist—a Lebanese calligrapher who has fallen on hard times in Paris—is convinced to return to Lebanon as an all-purpose bodyguard of an arms dealer. But his life becomes even more chaotic and confused than before. Not only does Yalo and the wife of his employer quickly become lovers, but he also robs and attacks the strangers that he sees having sex at a secret hideaway in a nearby forest. The novel raises thorny questions about the nature of violence, passion, war, and human motivations.

Subject keywords: politics; power
Original language: Arabic
Sources consulted for annotation:
Adams, Lorraine. *The New York Times Book Review*, 15 January 2006 (online).
Driscoll, Brendan. *Booklist* 102 (1 February 2006): 29.
El-Youssel, Samir. *Orlando Sentinel*, 12 March 2006, p. F4.
Freeman, John. *Times Union*, 19 March 2006, p. J4.
LeBor, Adam. *The New York Times Book Review*, 2 March 2008 (online).
Publishers Weekly 252 (21 November 2005): 27.
Rhodes, Fred. *Middle East* 365 (March 2006): 64.
Some other translated books written by Ilyas Khuri: *Little Mountain*; *The Journey of Little Gandhi*; *Gates of the City*; *Yalo*

Amin Maalouf. *The Gardens of Light.*
Translated by Dorothy S. Blair. Brooklyn, NY: Interlink Books, 1999. 242 pages.
Genre/literary style/story type: historical fiction
This novel describes the life of Mani, the founder of Manicheaism, often described as a Gnostic religion. Mani, who originally lived in Babylon under the Persian empire in the third century, enjoyed success in India before returning home, where the Persian king, Shapur I, allowed the new religion to flourish. Maalouf's book is a multihued and richly textured account of sociocultural ferment and turbulenece.
Subject keyword: religion
Original language: Arabic
Sources consulted for annotation:
Back cover of the book.
Steinberg, Sybil S. *Publishers Weekly* 245 (7 December 1998): 51.
Some other translated books written by Amin Maalouf: *Balthasar's Odyssey*; *Leo Africanus*; *The Rock of Tanios*; *The First Century After Beatrice*; *Samarkand*; *Ports of Call*

Imili Nasr Allah (Emily Nasrallah). *Flight Against Time.*
Translated by Issa J. Boullata. Austin, TX: Center for Middle Eastern Studies, University of Texas at Austin, 1997. 186 pages.
Genre/literary style/story type: mainstream fiction
When Radwan Abu Yusef and his wife Raya decide to flee the Lebanese civil war, they visit family and friends who have long since left for Prince Edward Island (Canada) and New York. While the eldery couple are in North America, the war worsens. What will they lose or gain by returning? By staying? As they confront these existential questions, the memory of their native village becomes a touchstone and psychological refuge.
Subject keywords: aging; identity
Original language: Arabic
Sources consulted for annotation:
Amazon.com (book description).
Kirchhoff, H. J. *The Globe and Mail* (Toronto), 26 January 1998, p. C7.
Some other translated books written by Imili Nasr Allah: *A House Not Her Own*; *The Fantastic Strokes of Imagination*

Ghadah Samman (Ghada Samman). *The Square Moon: Supernatural Tales.*
Translated by Issa J. Boullata. Fayetteville, AR: University of Arkansas Press, 1998. 203 pages.
Genres/literary styles/story types: mainstream fiction; women's lives

Using elements of the fantastic, these short stories explore the inner lives and frustrations of women in a patriarchal culture. Who can say that madness really is madness? Who can say with certainty what perversion really is? As these women walk the tightrope of psychological and emotional well-being, they provide insight into crucial questions of normalcy, convention, and expectations.
Subject keyword: identity
Original language: Arabic
Sources consulted for annotation:
Accad, Evelyne. *World Literature Today* 73 (Autumn 1999): 811.
Boullata, Issa. *Booklist* 95 (15 December 1998): 727.
Some other translated books written by Ghadah Samman: *Beirut, '75*; *The Night of the First Billion*; *Beirut Nightmares*

Hanan Shaykh (Hanan al-Shaykh). *Beirut Blues.*
Translated by Catherine Cobham. New York: Anchor Books, 1995. 371 pages.
Genre/literary style/story type: mainstream fiction
Told through a series of unsent letters written by Asmahan, a young woman, this novel is an elegy for a once-vibrant and now-dying Beirut. As Asmahan struggles to decide whether to emigrate, her letters become increasingly fevered and impassioned—filled with both love and hate for the city that is an indelible part of her soul.
Related title by the same author:
Readers may also enjoy *The Locust and The Bird*, which recounts the tortured family history of Kamila, a young woman of 14 who is forced to marry an older man. Years later, Kamila leaves her family behind and begins a new life with Muhammad, her first love.
Subject keyword: social problems
Original language: Arabic
Sources consulted for annotation:
Allen, M. D. *World Literature Today* 70 (Spring 1996): 465.
Harris, Michael. *Los Angeles Times*, 24 September 1995, p. 6.
Ingraham, Janet. *Library Journal* 120 (1 September 1995): 205.
Needham, George. *Booklist* 91 (1 June 1995): 1724.
Powell, Rosalind. *The Observer*, 12 May 1996, p. 16.
Saliba, Therese. *Ms.* (May 1995): 76.
Steinberg, Sybil S. *Publishers Weekly* 242 (10 April 1995): 52.
World Literature Today 80 (March/April 2006): 41.
Some other translated books written by Hanan Shaykh: *Women of Sand and Myrrh*; *The Story of Zahra*; *Only in London*; *I Sweep the Sun Off Rooftops*; *The Locust and the Bird*

Iman Humaydan Yunus (Iman Humaydan Younes). *B as in Beirut.*
Translated by Max Weiss. Northampton, MA: Interlink Books, 2007. 229 pages.
Genres/literary styles/story types: mainstream fiction; women's lives
This novel focuses on the psychological consequences of the Lebanese war on four women living in a Beirut apartment building. Emotionally traumatized by the random destruction and brutality of the fighting, one of the women never goes anywhere without her suitcases. Forced to accommodate themselves to the omnipresent violence, none of the women lead a normal life.
Related title by the same author:
Readers may also enjoy *Wild Mulberries*, which focuses on a young woman growing up in a mountain village in an area famous for the cultivation of silk worms.
Subject keywords: social problems; war
Original language: Arabic

Source consulted for annotation:
Global Books in Print (online) (review from *Publishers Weekly* for *B as in Beirut*; synopsis/book jacket for *Wild Mulberries*).
Another translated book written by Iman Humaydan Yunus: *Wild Mulberries*

Libya

Ahmad Ibrahim Faqih (Ahmed Fagih). ***Valley of Ashes.***
London: Kegan Paul International, 2000. 141 pages.
Genres/literary styles/story types: mainstream fiction; women's lives
Jamila, who lives in a small desert village, wishes to become a teacher—a choice for which she is mercilessly pilloried and mocked. Her quest to expand her intellectual and emotional horizons is met with hostility at every turn. How far will her perseverance take her, and what will be the ultimate cost of her yearning for independence? Many critics consider Faqih to be in the front rank of Libyan authors.
Subject keywords: culture conflict; rural life
Original language: Arabic
Sources consulted for annotation:
Amazon.com (book description).
The Guardian, 19 August 2000, p. 11.
Some other translated books written by Ahmad Ibrahim Faqih: *Libyan Stories: Twelve Short Stories from Libya*; *Charles, Diana, and Me, and Other Stories*; *Who's Afraid of Agatha Christie? and Other Stories*; *Gardens of the Night: A Trilogy*

Morocco

Laylá Abu Zayd (Leila Abouzeid). ***The Last Chapter.***
Translated by Leila Abouzeid and John Liechety. Cairo, Egypt: American University in Cairo Press, 2000. 163 pages.
Genres/literary styles/story types: mainstream fiction; women's lives
This book explores the multiple dilemmas experienced by a young Moroccan woman who strives to assert her independence in the late twentieth centruy. She chooses to be single; she chooses to have gainful employment outside the home; and she valiantly works toward realizing her ideals of a just and compassionate world.
Subject keywords: identity; social roles
Original language: Arabic
Sources consulted for annotation:
Amazon.com (book description).
Barber, Peggy. *Booklist* 97 (15 March 2001): 1353.
Some other translated books written by Laylá Abu Zayd: *Year of the Elephant: A Moroccan Woman's Journey Toward Independence*; *The Director and Other Stories from Morocco*

Muhammad Baradah (Mohamed Berrada). ***Fugitive Light.***
Translated by Issa J. Boullata. Syracuse, NY: Syracuse University Press, 2002. 171 pages.
Genre/literary style/story type: mainstream fiction
This book recounts the loves and losses of the now aged artist Al Ayshuni. While working in Tangiers, he fell in love with Ghaylana, who disappeared from his life when her family arranged her marriage to another man. Al Ayshuni's memories of these past events are awakened by a visit from Ghaylana's daughter, Fatima.
Subject keyword: aging

Original language: Arabic
Source consulted for annotation:
Barber, Peggy. *Booklist* 99 (1 October 2002): 300.
Another translated book written by Muhammad Baradah: *The Game of Forgetting*

Mohammed Mrabet. *Marriage with Papers.*
Translated by Paul Bowles. Bolinas, CA: Tombouctou Books, 1986. 79 pages.
Genre/literary style/story type: mainstream fiction
This autobiographical novel recounts the protagonist's relationship with his wife Zohra, who is portrayed as being obsessed with material possessions. The husband suspects that his wife is trying to poison him, so the couple begins to live apart without divorcing. Mrabet's 10 fiction books, which explore the dissonance between modernity and tradition, have been translated by Paul Bowles from Moghrebi (Moroccan Arabic). Fascinated with Mrabet's genius for storytelling, Bowles—who lived in Morocco for more than 50 years and was a prolific author perhaps most well-known for the novel *The Sheltering Sky*—encouraged Mrabet to tape his stories and then translated them.
Subject keyword: family histories
Original language: Arabic
Sources consulted for annotation:
Dawood, Ibrahim. *World Literature Today* 64 (Spring 1990): 264.
"Mohammed ben Chaib el Hajjam." *Contemporary Authors Online*, Gale, 2002.
Some other translated books written by Mohammed Mrabet: *The Boy Who Set the Fire & Other Stories*; *Love with a Few Hairs*; *The Lemon*; *Harmless Poisons, Blameless Sins*; *The Beach Café & The Voice*; *The Big Mirror*; *Three Tales*

Muhammad Shukri (Mohamed Choukri). *Streetwise.*
Translated by Ed Emery. London: Saqi, 1996. 164 pages.
Genres/literary styles/story types: mainstream fiction; coming-of-age
This semiautobiographical novel recounts the author's poverty-stricken existence in Tangiers. There is little reason for him to remain at home, where his father exerts a violent reign. Thus, he takes to the streets, becoming part of an underworld where sex and drugs are freely available. But eventually, he resolves to turn his life around, enrolling in an elementary school to learn how to read and write.
Subject keywords: social problems
Original language: Arabic
Sources consulted for annotation:
Simson, Maria. *Publishers Weekly* 243 (3 June 1996): 78.
Whittaker, Peter. *New Internationalist* 403 (August 2007): 31.

Palestine (Palestinian Autonomous Areas)

Laylá Atrash (Leila al-Atrash). *A Woman of Five Seasons.*
Translated by Nura Nuwayhid Halwani and Christopher Tingley. Brooklyn, NY: Interlink Books, 2002. 170 pages.
Genres/literary styles/story types: mainstream fiction; women's lives
In the fictional Arab country of Barqais, Nadia al-Faqih marries Ihsan Natour but yearns for his brother, Jalal, a political activist. As her husband's wealth and prestige in the oil world grows, Nadia becomes increasingly disillusioned with his lack of scruples, retreating into a world filled with books and her idealized love for Jalal.
Subject keyword: family histories

Original language: Arabic
Sources consulted for annotation:
Amazon.com (book description).
Johnston, Bonnie. *Booklist* 98 (15 April 2002): 1379.
Simawe, Saadi A. *World Literature Today* 77 (April/June 2003): 158.

Imil Habibi (Emile Habiby). ***The Secret Life of Saeed: The Pessoptimist.***
Translated by Salma Khadra Jayyusi and Trevor LeGassick. Brooklyn, NY: Interlink Books, 2002. 169 pages.
Genre/literary style/story type: mainstream fiction
A devastating satire that has been compared to the works of Voltaire and Jonathan Swift, this novel revolves around Saeed, a Palestinian, who decides to stay in Israel after its creation. His family has a long history of pusillanimous behavior, so it is entirely natural that Saeed becomes an informer and collaborator. But nothing every goes right for him; when he flies a flag of surrender in 1967 to demonstrate his loyalty, the gesture is interpreted as a provocation and he is jailed. Eventually, he escapes, ending up in outer space.
Subject keywords: politics; social problems
Original language: Arabic
Sources consulted for annotation:
Amazon.com (book description).
Pierpont, Claudia Roth. "Found in Translation." *The New Yorker* (18 January 2010) (online).
Rhodes, Fred. *Middle East* 338 (October 2003): 65.
Warrell, Beth. *Booklist* 98 (1 January/15 January 2002): 806.
Another translated book written by Imil Habibi: *Saraya, the Ogre's Daughter: A Palestinian Fairy Tale*

Jabra Ibrahim Jabra. ***In Search of Walid Masoud.***
Translated by Roger Allen and Adnan Haydar. Syracuse, NY: Syracuse University Press, 2000. 289 pages.
Genre/literary style/story type: mainstream fiction
This novel focuses on the disappearance of Walid Masoud, whose car is found in the desert on Iraq's border with Syria. Walid's friends and lovers slowly reconstruct his life, portraying a dymamic journalist whose life intersected with important political events and developments.
Subject keyword: writers
Original language: Arabic
Sources consulted for annotation:
Nettles, Maya. *Library Journal* 125 (15 October 2000): 102.
Peters, Issa. *World Literature Today* 75 (Spring 2001): 404.
Quinn, Mary Ellen. *Booklist* 96 (August 2000): 2112.
Steinberg, Sybil S. *Publishers Weekly* 247 (28 August 2000): 56.
Some other translated books written by Jabra Ibrahim Jabra: *Hunters in a Narrow Street*; *The Ship*

Ghassan Kanafani. ***Men in the Sun and Other Palestinian Stories.***
Translated by Hilary Kilpatrick. Boulder, CO: Lynne Rienner Publishers, 1998. 117 pages.
Genres/literary styles/story types: mainstream fiction; short stories
Critics have praised the conciseness and grittiness of this collection's prose, evoking comparisons with Ernest Hemingway. The title story, which takes place some 10 years after the defining events of 1948 in which Palestinians were exiled from their lands, was the basis of the film *The Deceived.*

Deemed a classic of Palestinian literature, it recounts the traumatic smuggler-aided journey of three Palestinians across desert expanses to Kuwait, a country which holds out the promise of work and the chance to regain dignity. Kanafani continues his focus on the fate of Palestinian refugees in *Palestine's Children*, which contains the story "Returning to Haifa," described by Claudia Roth Pierpont as perhaps the first example of a positive portrayal of Israeli settlers in Arab literature.
Subject keywords: social problems; war
Original language: Arabic
Sources consulted for annotation:
Global Books in Print (online) (author information; synopsis/book jacket).
Pierpont, Claudia Roth. "Found in Translation." *The New Yorker* (18 January 2010) (online).
Another translated book written by Ghassan Kanafani: *Palestine's Children*

Sahar Khalifah (Sahar Khalifeh). *Wild Thorns.*
Translated by Trevor LeGassick and Elizabeth Fernea. Brooklyn, NY: Interlink Books, 2000. 207 pages.
Genre/literary style/story type: mainstream fiction
This novel chronicles the intertwined lives of the cousins Usama and Adil. Usama, who espouses idealistic views and is a fervent nationalist, returns to the West Bank and Gaza Strip after being fired from his job in the Arab Gulf states. Adil is more of a realist, committed to supporting his family by any means at his disposal—even working in Israel. Tragedy ensues when Usama attacks a bus convoy carrying Palestinian workers into Israel.
Subject keyword: politics
Original language: Arabic
Sources consulted for annotation:
Amazon.com (reviews from *Kirkus Reviews* and *Midwest Book Review*).
"Sahar Khalifa." Answers.com, http://www.answers.com.
"Wild Thorns: Living Between the Impossible and the Absurd," http://myownlittleworld.com/miscellaneous/writings/wild-thorns.html.
Some other translated books written by Sahar Khalifah: *The Inheritance*; *The Image, the Icon, and the Covenant*

Yahyá Yakhlif. *A Lake Beyond the Wind.*
Translated by May Jayyusi and Christopher Tingley. Brooklyn, NY: Interlink Books, 1999. 215 pages.
Genre/literary style/story type: historical fiction
This novel focuses on the dramatic events of the 1948 conflict between Arabs and Jews in Palestine. Set in Samakh, a village on Lake Tiberias, the book describes the rhythms of daily life that are forever lost once war breaks out. As violence drives out traditions, the inhabitants are dispersed, suffering both physical and emotional exile.
Subject keyword: rural life
Original language: Arabic
Sources consulted for annotation:
Dawood, Ibrahim. *World Literature Today* 74 (Summer 2000): 682.
Steinberg, Sybil S. *Publishers Weekly* 246 (24 May 1999): 68.

Nazik Saba Yarid (Nazik Saba Yared). *Improvisations on a Missing String.*
Translated by Stuart A. Hancox. Fayetteville, AR: University of Arkansas Press, 1997. 133 pages.
Genres/literary styles/story types: mainstream fiction; women's lives
Saada Rayyis, a Christian Arab, is in a hospital recovering from a mastectomy. As she muses upon a past in which she has suffered more than her fair share of prejudice, her emotionally charged family

and personal relationships come to the forefront, allowing her to see the contingenices and ironies of life from a new perspective.
Subject keyword: family histories
Original language: Arabic
Sources consulted for annotation:
Olson, Yvette Weller. *Library Journal* 122 (15 November 1997): 78.
Peters, Issa. *World Literature Today* 72 (Summer 1998): 679.
Robbins, Eric. *Booklist* 94 (15 December 1997): 685.

Saudi Arabia

Hamza Bogary. *The Sheltered Quarter: A Tale of a Boyhood in Mecca.*
Translated by Olive Kenny and Jeremy Reed. Austin, TX: Center for Middle Eastern Studies, University of Texas at Austin, 1991. 119 pages.
Genres/literary styles/story types: mainstream fiction; coming-of-age
According to the publisher's website, this autobiographical novel is funny, sensitive, and compassionate. Narrated by the rougish Muhaisin, the book reflects on life in Mecca before oil was discovered. An elegy of sorts to disappeared traditions, the book nevertheless touches on many thorny social and cultural issues, including the role of women, capital punishment, and the effects of westernization.
Subject keyword: culture conflict
Original language: Arabic
Source consulted for annotation:
The University of Texas Press (book review), http://www.utexas.edu/utpress.

Turki Hamad (Turki al-Hamad). *Adama.*
Translated by Robin Bray. Saint Paul, MN: Ruminator Books, 2003. 292 pages.
Genres/literary styles/story types: mainstream fiction; coming-of-age
Hisham lives in Adama but is not from Adama. He rejects its quiescence and its fierce middle-class aspirations. Thus, he reads voluminously and begins to shape a political philosophy of his own. Fervently idealistic, he becomes involved with the Baathists, a Marxist-oriented group plotting the downfall of the Saudi Arabian governing elite. As his involvement grows, so does his disillusionment. Caught in a no-man's-land of social upheaval, Hisham must assert his independence and core values.
Subject keywords: politics; power
Original language: Arabic
Sources consulted for annotation:
Amazon.com (book description).
Cheuse, Alan. *All Things Considered*, 23 December 2003, p. 1.
Hirsch, Deborah. *Madison Capital Times*, 2 January 2004, p. 9A.
Tonkin, Boyd. *The Independent*, 17 May 2003, p. 25.
Another translated book written by Turki Hamad: *Shumaisi*

Ibrahim Nasr Allah (Ibrahim Nasrallah). *Prairies of Fever.*
Translated by May Jayyusi and Jeremy Reed. Brooklyn, NY: Interlink Books, 1993. 155 pages.
Genre/literary style/story type: mainstream fiction
In an isolated Saudi Arabian village, five strangers barge into Muhammad Hammad's house in the middle of the night, claiming that he is dead and demanding that he pay his own funeral expenses. Of course, he is frightened, disturbed, and uncertain of his own existence—all the more so because

his uncannily identical roommate has vanished. For Muhammad, a visiting teacher in the village, the search for his colleague turns into a search for self-identity and a way to break away from the claustrophobia of village life.
Subject keywords: identity; rural life
Original language: Arabic
Sources consulted for annotation:
Amazon.com (review from *Kirkus Reviews*).
Amireh, Amal. *World Literature Today* 68 (Spring 1994): 419.

Ghazi Abd al-Rahman Qusaybi (Ghazi A. Algosaibi). ***An Apartment Called Freedom.***
Translated by Leslie McLoughlin. London: Kegan Paul International, 1996. 241 pages.
Genres/literary styles/story types: mainstream fiction; coming-of-age
Five young men share an apartment in 1950s Cairo. Imbued with the revolutionary fervor and ardent idealism of nascent Egyptian nationalism, they draft a multiclause constitution designed to ensure that the mini-state of their apartment adheres to firm democratic principles. As Egypt strives to assert its independence and establish a modern identity, so do the five young men. But perils are everywhere, especially in the form of changing sexual mores.
Subject keywords: identity; politics
Original language: Arabic
Sources consulted for annotation:
Amazon.com (book description).
Stothard, Peter. *The Times*, 18 July 1996, p. 1.
Some other translated books written by Ghazi Abd al-Rahman Qusaybi: *A Love Story*; *Seven*

Raja Abd Allah Sani (Rajaa Alsanea). ***Girls of Riyadh.***
Translated by Rajaa Alsanea and Marilyn Booth. New York: Penguin, 2007. 286 pages.
Genres/literary styles/story types: mainstream fiction; women's lives
Focusing on the lives of five wealthy young women, this novel caused outrage in Saudi Arabia. Mary-Lou Zeitoun characterized it as "[o]ne part *Sex and the City*, three parts soap opera with a pinch of Jane Austen." She referred to the protagonists as "Saudi Barbies" who "like to shop, especially in London and Paris"; who routinely use technologies such as instant messaging and online chat rooms; and who pursue graduate degrees abroad. But their freedom and independence end when they return to Riyadh and their families, where they must adhere to rigid patriarchal rules and customs.
Subject keywords: identity; social roles
Original language: Arabic
Sources consulted for annotation:
Rochman, Hazel. *Booklist* 103 (1 June/15 June 2007): 36.
Zeitoun, Mary-Lou. *The Globe and Mail* (Toronto), 21 July 2007, p. D5.

Sudan

Tayeb Salih. ***Season of Migration to the North.***
Translated by Denys Johnson-Davies. New York: New York Review of Books, 2009. 184 pages.
Genre/literary style/story type: mainstream fiction
Originally published in 1966, this novel has been uniformly praised as one of the most influential books ever to appear in Africa. Two of the central themes, developed with abiding grace, are the legacy of colonialism on postcolonial independence as well as the impact of Western modernity and sociocultural practices on a traditional land. Recently returned to Sudan after receiving an

education in England, the narrator must cope with the aftermath of the disappearance and likely death of Mustafa, a Sudanese man of a previous generation also educated in England. As he assumes the care of Mustafa's wife and children, he discovers Mustafa's startling history and is forced to confront the paradoxes and ironies underlying political and moral rhetoric.
Subject keywords: colonization and colonialism; family histories
Original language: Arabic
Sources consulted for annotation:
Global Books in Print (online) (reviews from *Choice* and *Publishers Weekly*).
The New York Review of Books website (book description), http://www.nybooks.com.

Syria

Halim Barakat. *The Crane.*
Translated by Bassam Frangieh and Roger Allen. Cairo, Egypt: American University in Cairo Press, 2008. 168 pages.
Genres/literary styles/story types: mainstream fiction; coming-of-age
It is a long way from a small Syrian village to the campus of an American university in the 1960s, political protests, and a life in Washington, D.C. As the author nostalgically recounts his poignant childhood and adolescence in Syria—emblematically represented by a wounded crane—he also develops inner strength that allows him to forge ahead.
Subject keywords: rural life; urban life
Original language: Arabic
Source consulted for annotation:
American University in Cairo Press (book description), http://www.aucpress.com.

Ulfat Idlibi. *Sabriya: Damascus Bitter Sweet.*
Translated by Peter Clark. Brooklyn, NY: Interlink Books, 1997. 186 pages.
Genres/literary styles/story types: mainstream fiction; women's lives
This novel begins with the lavish funeral of Sabriya's father and Sabriya's suicide the next day. It then continues as a diary, recounting the various large and small ways that women experience oppression in the Arab world. Unable to marry the man she loves, Sabriya mourns the death of one brother in the 1920s and struggles with the patriarchal edicts of another brother. She gives up her aspirations to be a teacher and fills her despair-ridden days caring for her aging parents.
Subject keywords: family histories; social roles
Original language: Arabic
Sources consulted for annotation:
Amazon.com (review from *Kirkus Reviews*).
Financial Times, 4 November 1995, p. 14.
McPhee, Jenny. *The New York Times*, 7 September 1997, p. 25.
Peters, Issa. *World Literature Today* 72 (Winter 1998): 198.
Another translated book written by Ulfat Idlibi: *Grandfather's Tale*

Muhammad Kamil Khatib (Muhammad Kamil al-Khatib). *Just Like a River.*
Translated by Maher Barakat and Michelle Hartman. Brooklyn, NY: Interlink Books, 2003. 120 pages.
Genres/literary styles/story types: mainstream fiction; women's lives
This is a polyphonic novel that gives insight into 1980s Syria. When the daughter of a middle-class family falls in love with a radical university professor, tradition and modernity inevitably collide.
Subject keywords: identity; social roles

Original language: Arabic
Sources consulted for annotation:
Middle East 334 (May 2003): 65.
Olson, Ray. *Booklist* 99 (1 March 2003): 1145.

Hanna Minah (Hanna Mina). ***Fragments of Memory: A Story of a Syrian Family.***
Translated by Olive Kenny and Lorne Kenny. Austin, TX: Center for Middle Eastern Studies, University of Texas at Austin, 1993. 180 pages.
Genres/literary styles/story types: mainstream fiction; coming-of-age
Told through the eyes of a small boy, this autobiographical novel follows the plight of a poor family that tries to eke out a meager existence in a small Syrian village under the impress of feudalism in the 1920s and 1930s. The father is a chronic alcoholic and hapless Don Juan whose moneymaking plans are doomed to failure: a smuggling scheme is thwarted; a harvest is destroyed by locusts; the family loses its home and must live outdoors; and the children become beggars.
Subject keywords: family histories; rural life
Original language: Arabic
Sources consulted for annotation:
Amazon.com (all editorial reviews).
Maier, John. *International Journal of Middle East Studies* 27 (November 1995): 533–536.
Another translated book written by Hanna Minah: *Sun on a Cloudy Day*

United Arab Emirates

Muhammad Murr (Muhammad al Murr). ***Dubai Tales.***
Translated by Peter Clark. London: Forest Books, 1991. 154 pages.
Genre/literary style/story type: mainstream fiction
When consumerism comes to the United Arab Emirates, it does so with a vengeance, wreaking havoc among and between families and spouses, upsetting long-cherished notions about honor and traditional values, and providing endless fodder to explore the contradictions, paradoxes, and hypocrisy of a society all too willing to embrace Western lifestyles.
Subject keyword: modernization
Original language: Arabic
Sources consulted for annotation:
Kaganoff, Penny. *Publishers Weekly* 238 (31 May 1991): 67.
Solomon, Charles. *Los Angeles Times*, 7 July 1991, p. BR10.
Another translated book written by Muhammad Murr: *The Wink of the Mona Lisa, and Other Stories from the Gulf*

Yemen

Muhammad Abd al-Wali (Mohammad Abdul-Wali). ***They Die Strangers.***
Translated by Abubaker Bagader and Deborah Akers. Austin, TX: Center for Middle Eastern Studies, University of Texas at Austin, 2001. 138 pages.
Genres/literary styles/story types: mainstream fiction; short stories
This collection contains 13 short stories and the title novella. All explore the experiences of poverty-stricken Yemenis who seek a better life elsewhere in the 1950s and 1960s. In the novella, a Yemeni man has been a shopkeeper in Ethopia for some 10 years, financially supporting his family back home and hoping to someday return in triumph. But his real life is closely tied to Ethopia, where he has earned a reputation as a philanderer and roué—a testimony to the bittersweet alientation and rootlessness of exile.

Subject keyword: social problems
Original language: Arabic
Sources consulted for annotation:
Amazon.com (book description).
The Complete Review (book review), http://www.complete-review.com.
Saad al-Jumli, Mohammed and Rollins, Barton J. *World Literature Today* 71 (1 January 1997): 39.
Saldana, Stephanie. *The Daily Star*, 9 January 2002 (from Factiva databases).

Zayd Muti Dammaj (Zayd Mutee Dammaj). *The Hostage.*
Translated by May Jayyusi and Christopher Tingley. Brooklyn, NY: Interlink Books, 1994. 151 pages.
Genres/literary styles/story types: mainstream fiction; coming-of-age
In 1948, Yemen is caught up in the throes of an unsuccessful coup. As the governor tries to ensure his political survival, strategic machinations are the order of the day. A teenage boy is kidnapped and taken to the palace to convince the clan of which he is a member to remain loyal to the governor. In his new role as a palace servant, he meets Sharifa Hafsa, the beguiling and steely sister of the governor. Sharifa's power and fragility exert a magnetic attraction on the boy, and he not only experiences a sexual awakening but also an initiation into a pervasive culture of corruption.
Subject keywords: politics; power
Original language: Arabic
Sources consulted for annotation:
Carapico, Sheila. *The Middle East Journal* 49 (Spring 1995): 347.
Hutchison, Paul E. *Library Journal* 119 (August 1994): 126.

ANNOTATIONS FOR BOOKS TRANSLATED FROM PERSIAN (IRAN)

Jalal Al Ahmad (Jalal al-e Ahmad). *By the Pen.*
Translated by M. R. Ghanoonparvar. Austin, TX: Center for Middle Eastern Studies, University of Texas at Austin, 1988. 126 pages.
Genre/literary style/story type: historical fiction
In sixteenth-century Isfahan, the scribes Asadollah and Abdozzaki are swept up in a series of raucous social and political events. According to Michael Hillmann, while the central story line concerns "a specific period in the reign of Safavid Shah 'Abbas the Great (ruled 1587–1629)," there is a historic parallel to "the rise and fall of Mohammad Mosaddeq (1882–1967)."
Subject keywords: politics; religion
Original language: Persian
Sources consulted for annotation:
Beard, Michael. *The Middle East Journal* 44 (Summer 1990): 524.
The Complete Review (book review), http://www.complete-review.com.
Hillmann, Michael Craig. Introduction to the book.
Another translated book written by Jalal Al Ahmad: *The School Principal*

Mahshid Amirshahi. *Suri & Co.: Tales of a Persian Teenager.*
Translated by Jutta E. Knörzer. Austin, TX: Center for Middle Eastern Studies, University of Texas at Austin, 1995. 87 pages.
Genres/literary styles/story types: mainstream fiction; coming-of-age
As the title indicates, Suri, a teenage girl, is the focal point of this collection of eight short stories, which take place in the late 1960s and early 1970s prior to the 1979 Iranian Revolution. Suri enjoys all the privileges of an upper-class existence, and she also has all the characteristics and personality flaws associated with that type of life. As she holds ever tighter to her material and decadent world,

its superficiality becomes ever more apparent, and it is almost inevitable that the Western values personified by Suri will be overthrown by a sociocultural movement that sees itself as an agent of purification and virtue.
Subject keywords: identity; social roles
Original language: Persian
Sources consulted for annotation:
Amazon.com (all editorial reviews).
Rahimieh, Nasrin. *World Literature Today* 70 (Winter 1996): 234.

Simin Danishvar (Simin Daneshvar). *Savushun: A Novel About Modern Iran* (or ***A Persian Requiem*).**
Translated by M. R. Ghanoonparvar. Washington, DC: Mage Publishers, 1990. 387 pages.
Genres/literary styles/story types: historical fiction; women's lives
When Allied forces occupy Iran during World War II, political and cultural differences come starkly to the forefront. Some Iranians want to help the British army by selling its soldiers grain and other foodstuffs; others are adamantly and idealistically opposed to any aid whatsoever. Zari, her husband Yusef, and Yusef's brother are on opposite sides of this issue; indeed, it is a rift that is replicated in hundreds of other villages and among thousands of other Iranians, cutting to the core of Iran's social and historical identity. Critics have observed that this novel is indispensable for a thorough understanding of contemporary Iran.
Subject keywords: family histories; politics
Original language: Persian
Sources consulted for annotation:
Amazon.com (all editorial reviews).
Karimi-Hakkak, Ahmad. *The Middle East Journal* 45 (Autumn 1991): 699.
Kempf, Andrea. *Library Journal* 126 (15 November 2001): 128.
Modarressi, Taghi. *The Washington Post*, 18 November 1990, p. X7.
Some other translated books written by Simin Danishvar: *Daneshvar's Playhouse: A Collection of Stories*; *Sutra & Other Stories*

Mahmud Dawlat'abadi (Mahmoud Dowlatabadi). *Missing Soluch*.
Translated by Kamran Rastegar. Brooklyn, NY: Melville House, 2007. 375 pages.
Genres/literary styles/story types: mainstream fiction; women's lives
Unremittingly bleak and tragic, this novel is an unsparing indictment of life in an Iranian village in the late twentieth century. One critic compared it to John Steinbeck's *East of Eden*. Mergan's husband Soluch disappears, leaving her to fend for herself with her two sons and daughter. Merely surviving is difficult enough for Mergan's impoverished family, but village politics complicate matters even more. Wealthy residents want to lay claim to a piece of land that has always been allotted to the poor. Abbas and Abrau, Mergan's two sons, succumb to the lure of quick riches, selling off their shares. But Mergan refuses to sell. As she and her 12-year-old daughter Hajer sink even further into poverty, Mergan is forced to marry Hajer to an older man. Both Mergan and Hajer are raped, and Hajer is locked up by her new husband at home. For both women, life is nothing but a vast prison with little—if any—hope.
Subject keyword: family histories
Original language: Persian
Sources consulted for annotation:
Global Books in Print (online) (review from *Publishers Weekly*).
Melville House website, http://www.mhpbooks.com.

Ismail Fasih (Esmail Fassih). *Sorraya in a Coma.*
Translated by the author. London: Zed Books, 1985. 287 pages.
Genre/literary style/story type: mainstream fiction
This book explores the isolating effect of the Iranian revolution on Iranian exiles living in Paris. Many of them have been educated in the West and thus feel comfortable with its liberal ideals, but they also have a deep affinity for their heritage and traditions. Thus, they are caught on the horns of a dilemma, perplexed at the religious direction of the revolution that many of them once embraced as a necessary rejection of consumerist and modern values.
Subject keyword: modernization
Original language: Persian
Source consulted for annotation:
Preface to the book.

Davud Ghaffarzadegan. *Fortune Told in Blood.*
Translated by M. R. Ghanoonparvar. Austin, TX: University of Texas Press, 2008. 71 pages.
Genre/literary style/story type: mainstream fiction
During the bloody Iran-Iraq war of the 1980s, two Iraqi soldiers from different socioeconomic backgrounds witness mayhem and destruction from their observation post high up on a mountain. They would much rather be elsewhere: the former law student dreams of his soon-to-be wife; the struggling landlowner ponders his failed literary studies. But here they are in the mountains, and their desolation, revulsion, and isolation are only exacerbated by a military inspection conducted by a member of the Republican Guard, who accuses them of being cowards—of failing to fire on the enemy below. Inevitably, a violent confrontation ensues—one that pits the principles of humanity against what is presented as the call of duty.
Subject keywords: politics; power
Original language: Arabic
Sources consulted for annotation:
The Complete Review (book review), http://www.complete-review.com.
Univeristy of Texas Press website, http://www.utexas.edu/utpress.

Hushang Gulshiri (Hushang Golshiri). *The Prince.*
Translated by James Buchan. London: Harvill Secker, 2005. 152 pages.
Genre/literary style/story type: historical fiction
Prince Ehtejab, the last of a long line of autocratic and despotic Qajar princes of Persia, is dying. But he has not been able to match his predecessors for cruelty and corruption. As he nears death, the numerous palace portraits of his extended family come to life in a seemingly endless phantasmagoria, upbraiding the prince for his cowardice and many other weaknesses.
Subject keyword: power
Original language: Persian
Sources consulted for annotation:
Amazon.com (all editorial reviews).
Asfour, Lana. *New Statesman* 19 (9 January 2006): 41.
Church, Michael. *The Independent*, 29 December 2005, p. 42.
Davis, Dick. *The Guardian*, 1 April 2006, p. 17.
Another translated book written by Hushang Gulshiri: *Black Parrot, Green Crow*

Shahriyar Mandani'pur (Shahriar Mandanipour). *Censoring an Iranian Love Story.*
Translated by Sara Khalili. New York: Alfred A. Knopf, 2009. 295 pages.

Genre/literary style/story type: mainstream fiction

This novel is both a romance and a postmodern commentary about writing a love story that would meet the approval of Iranian censors. The book's two protagonists are Sara and Dara, who are forced into all kinds of furtive maneouvers to avoid societal disapproval of their budding passion. Dara, who has been incarcerated because he sells and watches videos of Western movies, may not be the most suitable match for Sara, who must choose between him and Sinbad, a successful businessman. Michiko Kakutani summarizes the book as "a darkly comic view of the Kafkaesque absurdities" of life in contemporary Iran.

Subject keywords: politics; power

Original language: Persian

Sources consulted for annotation:

Global Books in Print (online) (reviews from *Booklist*, *Library Journal*, and *Publishers Weekly*).

Kakutani, Michiko. *The New York Times*, 30 June 2009 (online).

Shukuh Mirzadahgi (Shokooh Mirzadegi). ***That Stranger within Me: A Foreign Woman Caught in the Iranian Revolution.***

Translated by Esmail Nooriala. Bethesda, MD: Ibex, 2002. 191 pages.

Genres/literary styles/story types: mainstream fiction; women's lives

In an Iran convulsed by revolutionary fervor, a Czech archaeologist must come to terms with the death of her husband. Against the dreary backdrop of Tehran's central morgue, she is forced to confront her past, hoping against hope for a redemptive epiphany.

Subject keyword: family histories

Original language: Persian

Sources consulted for annotation:

Balgamwalla, Sabrina. *The Middle East Journal* 57 (Autumn 2003): 703.

Mirzadegi, Shokook. Back cover of book.

Naveed Noori. ***Dakhmeh.***

New Milford, CN: Toby Press, 2003. 189 pages.

Genre/literary style/story type: mainstream fiction

Upon the death of his mother and against the wishes of his family, Arash decides to return to Iran from the United States to live out the remainder of his life. But he struggles to find his place in a country that he no longer recognizes. Adrift and alienated, he seeks refuge in his memories and the workings of his mind, but he cannot find peace. His quixotic aspirations to transform Iranian society along Western lines are doomed to failure, and he is imprisoned and tortured for writing derisive comments about Iranian political leaders on banknotes.

Subject keywords: politics; social problems

Original language: Persian

Sources consulted for annotation:

Publishers Weekly 250 (21 July 2003): 176.

Rosdahl, Lyle D. *Library Journal* 128 (15 September 2003): 93.

Shahrnush Parsipur. ***Women Without Men.***

Translated by Kamran Talattof and Jocelyn Sharlet. Syracuse, NY: Syracuse University Press, 1998. 131 pages.

Genres/literary styles/story types: mainstream fiction; women's lives

This novel, which contains elements of magical realism and Persian myths, follows the serpentine paths of five women who want to reject men and marriage. To do so, they establish a refuge in a walled garden in Karaj, a river town near Tehran.

Related title by the same author:
Readers may also enjoy *Touba and the Meaning of Night*, which traces the history of twentieth-century Iran through the eyes of Touba, a resilient woman who, after two failed marriages, earns money as a carpet maker and finds solace in Sufism.
Subject keyword: social roles
Original language: Persian
Sources consulted for annotation:
Chadwell, Faye A. *Library Journal* 124 (January 1999): 156.
Global Books in Print (online) (reviews from *Booklist*, *Library Journal*, and *Publishers Weekly*).
Hanaway, William L. *World Literature Today* 73 (Summer 1999): 587.
Johnston, Bonnie. *Booklist* 95 (15 December 1998): 727.
Kirchner, Bharti. *Seattle Times*, 3 July 2005, p. J5.
Steinberg, Sybil S. *Publishers Weekly* 245 (26 October 1998): 44.
Another translated book written by Shahrnush Parsipur: *Touba and the Meaning of Night*

Iraj Pizishkzad (Iraj Pezeshkzad). *My Uncle Napoleon*.
Translated by Dick Davis. Washington, DC: Mage Publishers, 1996. 507 pages.
Genre/literary style/story type: mainstream fiction
This deliciously comedic and poignant novel focuses on an eccentric snob with an invented heroic past who worships Napoleon and Hitler and hates the English. It is narrated by his 13-year-old nephew, who is in love with his cousin Layli, who just happens to be the daughter of none other than the absurdly megalomaniac Uncle Napoleon. Critics have invoked the names of P. G. Wodehouse and Anita Loo to describe the humor of this book.
Subject keyword: family histories
Original language: Persian
Sources consulted for annotation:
Adams, Phoebe-Lou. *The Atlantic Monthly* 278 (August 1996): 93.
Hanaway, William L. *World Literature Today* 71 (Winter 1997): 217.
Javadi, Hasan. *The Middle East Journal* 51 (Autumn 1997): 618.
Kempf, Andrea. *Library Journal* 126 (15 November 2001): 128.
Rogers, Michael. *Library Journal* 131 (1 April 2006): 133.
Rubin, Merle. *The Christian Science Monitor*, 12 Feb 1997, p. 12.
Steinberg, Sybil S. *Publishers Weekly* 243 (3 June 1996): 64.

Muniru Ravanipur (Moniru Ravanipur). *Satan's Stones*.
Translated by M. R. Ghanoonparvar. Austin, TX: University of Texas Press, 1996. 77 pages.
Genres/literary styles/story types: mainstream fiction; short stories
Iran is not just synonymous with Tehran, and the stories in this collection provide a glimpse of life in less populated areas, especially desert regions—where existence is unremittingly austere and harsh, where the burden of survival often falls on women, and where the bonds of humanity fray easily.
Subject keywords: power; rural life
Original language: Persian
Sources consulted for annotation:
Ghanoonparvar, M. R. Introduction to the book.
Publishers Weekly 243 (26 August 1996): 91.
Another translated book written by Muniru Ravanipur: *Kanizu*

Ghulam Husayn Saidi (Gholam-Hossein Saedi). *Fear and Trembling*.
Translated by Minoo Southgate. Washington, DC: Three Continents Press, 1984. 121 pages.

Genres/literary styles/story types: mainstream fiction; short stories
This book is set in Iran's remote gulf coast region, where the cultures of Somalia and Zanzibar have had a strong influence on the traditions of small local villages. In six stories, the author explores the collective psyche of a people living in a harsh environment, where heat, famine, disease, and perpetual water shortages foster a litany of physical and psychological ailments.
Subject keywords: rural life; social problems
Original language: Persian
Source consulted for annotation:
Southgate, Minoo. Introduction to the book.
Another translated book written by Ghulam Husayn Saidi: *Dandil: Stories from Iranian Life*

Guli Taraqqi (Goli Taraghi). ***A Mansion in the Sky and Other Short Stories.***
Translated by Faridoun Farrokh. Austin, TX: University of Texas Press, 2003. 154 pages.
Genres/literary styles/story types: mainstream fiction; short stories
This collection of stories describes the author's childhood in Tehran before the Iranian Revolution as well as his family's exile. Emotional and psychological scars abound as they leave behind a familiar culture, plunging into an angst-ridden unknown.
Subject keywords: culture conflict; family histories
Original language: Persian
Source consulted for annotation:
Amazon.com (all editorial reviews).
Another translated book written by Guli Taraqqi: *Winter Sleep*

ANNOTATIONS FOR BOOKS TRANSLATED FROM LANGUAGES OF THE TRANS-CAUCASUS AND CENTRAL ASIA

Armenia

Andranik Andreasean (Antranig Antreassian). ***Death and Resurrection: A Novel of the Armenian Massacres.***
Translated by Jack Antreassian. New York: Ashod Press, 1988. 313 pages.
Genre/literary style/story type: historical fiction
This novel recapitulates the numerous horrors of the Armenian genocide in the late 1910s and early 1920s. Characterized by deporatations, forced labor, and untold massacres of innocent civilians, the genocide cut a devastating swath of destruction through the Armenian people. The book also recounts episodes of sporadic resistance, where scattered guerilla groups fought essentially futile battles against the Ottoman Empire, and concludes with Armenia becoming part of the Soviet Union. The frightful legacy of the genocide—a term whose very use is contested—still roils contemporary social and political relationships between Turkey and Armenia.
Subject keyword: war
Original language: Armenian
Sources consulted for annotation:
Avakian, Arra S. *World Literature Today* 63 (Spring 1989): 359.
Back cover of the book.
Another translated book written by Andranik Andreasean: *The Cup of Bitterness*

Azerbaijan

Mir Jalal. ***Dried-Up in Meetings & Other Short Stories.***
Translated by Hasan Javadi. Sherman Oaks, CA: Azerbaijan International, 1998. 91 pages.

Genres/literary styles/story types: mainstream fiction; short stories
According to the translator, Jalal's scathing fiction reveals the insularity of government officials as they live their lives in a world governed solely by bureaucratic rules and administrative niceties. The stories in this collection touch on such themes as corruption; the psychology of bullying; the idolatry of the West; Azerbaijan's Islamic heritage; and tradition-bound views of women.
Subject keywords: power; social roles
Original language: Azerbaijani
Source consulted for annotation:
The translator's introduction.

Georgia

Grigol Abasize (Grigol Abashidze). *Lasharela: A Georgian Chronicle of the 13th Century.*
Translated by Sergei Sosinski. Moscow: Progress Publishers, 1981. 405 pages.
Genre/literary style/story type: historical fiction
This novel chronicles Georgian history of the thirteenth century under the reign of Lasha. Readers get glimpses of feudal life, the role of clergy, and ongoing conflicts with Turkey, Persia, and the Mongols during what historians refer to as Georgia's golden age. Lasha was much loved by his people, but then he broke the code of honor by stealing the wife of a military officer who had saved his life. According to Viktor Shklovskii, *Lasharela* is "a prologue to the long night of Genghis Khan's invasion," which is described in the author's subsequent book, fittingly entitled *A Long Night*.
Subject keyword: power
Original language: Georgian/Russian
Source consulted for annotation:
Introduction to the book.

Kyrgyzstan

Chingiz Aitmatov. *The Place of the Skull.*
Translated by Natasha Ward. New York: Grove Press, 1989. 310 pages.
Genre/literary style/story type: mainstream fiction
This novel, which evokes Bulgakov's *The Master and Margarita* and Dostoyevsky's *The Brothers Karamazov*, was almost univerisally acclaimed. Seemingly disparate plot lines, characters, and events are linked by a group of steppe wolves, who have been displaced and cornered by mercenary antelope hunters and drug traffickers. The first part of the book centers on a fervently idealistic deacon's son, Avdiy Kallistratov, who travels to Kazakhstan on an ultimately doomed quest to morally reform a group of drug smugglers through unorthodox Christian beliefs. In the second part, which takes place in the mountains of Kyrgyzstan, a hardworking and upright citizen encounters a she-wolf that irreversibly damages his life. Despite numerous references to Christianity, there is little possibility of redemption and reconciliation in this bleak book, where evil always enjoys the upper hand.
Related titles by the same author:
Readers may also enjoy *Jamilia*, which is a heartbreaking love story about Jamilia's hopeless love for Daniyar during World War II in a small village in the Caucasus. Jamilia's husband is at the front, and the little news she gets from him is in the form of perfunctory and soulless letters. Thus, she passes her time helping Daniyar, a returned and wounded solidier, with often backbreaking labor, dreaming of the elusive and illusory possibilities of a future whose premises are more than nebulous. Critical praise also greeted *The Day Lasts More Than a Hundred Years*, a plaintive and melancholic account—with a vast historical sweep—of the unyielding starkness of life in remote Kazakhstan as refracted through the events surrounding the death, funeral procession, and attempted burial of a villager.

Subject keyword: religion
Original language: Russian
Sources consulted for annotation:
Clark, Tom. *Los Angeles Times*, 18 June 1989, p. 4.
Global Books in Print (online) (synopsis/book jacket).
Zirin, Mary F. *The Library Journal* 114 (15 February 1989): 175.
Some other translated books written by Chingiz Aitmatov: *The Day Lasts More Than a Hundred Years*; *Tales of the Mountains and Steppes*; *The White Ship*; *Mother Earth and Other Stories*; *Farewell Gul'sary!*; *Piebald Dog Running Along the Shore and Other Stories*; *The Cranes Fly Early*; *Jamilia*

ANNOTATIONS FOR BOOKS TRANSLATED FROM TURKISH

Adalet Agaoglu. *Curfew.*
Translated by John Goulden. Austin, TX: Center for Middle Eastern Studies, University of Texas at Austin, 1997. 250 pages.
Genre/literary style/story type: mainstream fiction
In 1980, political tensions are running high in Turkey: the imposition of martial law and curfews quickly follows a military coup. As the Turkish government tries to maintain its grip on power, seven people cope as best they can with the changed social circumstances that military rule brings. Their hopes and dreams, their tangled personal relationships, and their indomitable human spirit are all revealed in the wee hours of one morning before the new curfew takes effect.
Subject keywords: politics; power
Original language: Turkish
Sources consulted for annotation:
Global Books in Print (online) (review from *Choice*).
Teymour, Ali D. *The Middle East Journal* 52 (Spring 1998): 308.
Another translated book written by Adalet Agaoglu: *Summer's End*

Erendiz Atasü. *The Other Side of the Mountain.*
Translated by Erendiz Atasü and Elizabeth Maslen. London: Milet Publishing, 2000. 283 pages.
Genres/literary styles/story types: mainstream fiction; women's lives
Only after her mother's death does a daughter learn about her previous life. In the early 1900s, her mother was an idealistic student in Cambridge, determined to bring the fruits of Western education to a modernizing Turkey under the leadership of Ataturk. But the resolve and fervency of Turkey's secularization process eventually disippated, and as the daughter—who is also the narrator of this novel—considers her own generation, she finds that the visionary outlook of yesteryear has been replaced by the pedestrian concerns associated with warfare, survival, and internal strife.
Subject keywords: culture conflict; family histories
Original language: Turkish
Sources consulted for annotation:
Amazon.com (about the author; book description).
Nelson, Elizabeth. "Turkish Author Erendiz Atasu," http://www.suite101.com/european-literature.

Ilyas Halil. *Unregulated Chicken Butts and Other Stories.*
Translated by Joseph S. Jacobson. Salt Lake City, UT: University of Utah Press, 2002. 181 pages.
Genres/literary styles/story types: mainstream fiction; short stories
In 35 short stories, the author—who emigrated to Montréal in 1964—writes with enthusiasm and verve about the plight of exiled Turks. Boundlessly optimistic, restless, and energetic, they spend their days concocting get-rich schemes and shaking their heads at the absurdities of Western life.

Subject keyword: culture conflict
Original language: Turkish
Source consulted for annotation:
Shelnutt, Eve. *Web: The Contemporary West* 8 (Spring 1991).
Some other translated books written by Ilyas Halil: *Wanted: Infidel Employees*; *Shoeshine Ramadan and Other Stories*; *Temple for Rent*; *The Drunken Grass and Other Stories*; *Dog Hunt*; *White Coffee Shop Journal and Other Stories*; *Dissatisfied*; *Naked Yula*

Bilge Karasu. *Death in Troy.*
Translated by Aron Aji. San Francisco, CA: City Lights Books, 2002. 165 pages.
Genres/literary styles/story types: mainstream fiction; coming-of-age
Structured as a series of 13 interconnected stories, this book portrays various aspects of the coming-of-age of Mushfik Hanim. As he tries to find his way in a male-dominated world where desires and passions are sublimated and repressed, Mushfik must deal with his overbearing father, his overprotective mother, and his yearning for another boy.
Subject keywords: identity; social roles
Original language: Turkish
Sources consulted for annotation:
Amazon.com (book description; *Publishers Weekly*).
Çaliskan, Sveda. *World Literature Today* 77 (October/December 2003): 155.
Spinella, Michael. *Booklist* 98 (August 2002): 1921.
Some other translated books written by Bilge Karasu: *Night*; *The Garden of Departed Cats*

Yasar Kemal (Yashar Kemal). *Salman the Solitary.*
Translated by Thilda Kemal. London: Harvill, 1998. 310 pages.
Genre/literary style/story type: mainstream fiction
Set against the backdrop of World War I and the Armenian genocide in Turkey, the novel focuses on Ismail Agha, a Kurdish man. As Ismail and the female members of his family flee their homeland, they come across a dying boy, Salman, whom they rescue. He becomes part of the family as they start their lives anew in a distant village. Salman grows to worship Ismail, who in turn reveres him as his only son until Zero, Ismail's wife, gives birth to Mustafa. Tension, jealously, and rivalry mark the relationships between the boys—an ongoing conflict that brings difficult familial and historical questions to the forefront. Kemal is often referred to as Turkey's most illustrious writer. Two of his most famous books (*Memed, My Hawk* and *They Burn the Thistles*) are published in the New York Review of Books (NYRB) Classics series.
Subject keywords: family histories; rural life
Original language: Turkish
Sources consulted for annotation:
Amazon.com (book description).
Johnston, Bonnie. *Booklist* 94 (1 March 1998): 1092.
Sage, Lorna. *The Observer*, 14 December 1997, p. 17.
Sutherland, John. *Sunday Times*, 14 December 1997, p. B8.
Some other translated books written by Yasar Kemal: *Memed, My Hawk*; *The Sea-Crossed Fisherman*; *They Burn the Thistles*; *The Undying Grass*; *Iron Earth, Copper Sky*; *Anatolian Tales*; *Murder in the Ironsmiths Market*; *The Wind from the Plain*; *To Crush the Serpent*; *The Legend of the Thousand Bulls*; *The Saga of a Seagull*; *The Birds Have Also Gone*; *The Legend of Ararat*; *Tanhai*

Perihan Magden. *Two Girls.*
Translated by Brenda Freely. London: Serpent's Tail, 2005. 249 pages.

Genre/literary style/story type: mainstream fiction

It is the summer before Behiye begins her studies at Bosphorus University in Istanbul, and she is not happy with her life. Concerned about her weight, perpetually angry, and eager to flee her stultifying and abusive family, she dreams of a more perfect and despair-free world. Her hopes seem to be on the verge of becoming reality when she falls in love with a young woman, Handan. Eventually, they make plans to join Handan's father in Australia. But Behiye is once again left on the outside looking in when Handan discovers that she is attracted to men. What, then, is one to think when a series of young men are killed? Who is ultimately to blame?

Subject keywords: identity; social roles

Original language: Turkish

Sources consulted for annotation:

Amazon.com (book description).

Erasing Clouds Book Reviews, http://www.erasingclouds.com.

News from Nowhere: Liverpool's Radical & Community Bookshop, http://www.newsfromnowhere .org.uk.

Another translated book written by Perihan Magden: *The Messenger Boy Murders*

Aras Ören. *Please, No Police.*

Translated by Teoman Sipahigil. Austin, TX: Center for Middle Eastern Studies, University of Texas at Austin, 1992. 136 pages.

Genre/literary style/story type: mainstream fiction

Originally published in 1980, this novel is an example of the genre known in Germany as "the literature of guest workers." For the past five decades, the phenomenon of the guest worker has played a vital role in the economies of both developed and developing countries in Europe. Millions of Turks immigrated to Germany in search of work and a better life. *Please, No Police* chronicles the lives of Turkish men and women who struggle to survive in a country that is more than ambivalent about their presence and contribution.

Subject keyword: social problems

Original language: Turkish

Source consulted for annotation:

Phillips, Alice H. G. *Current History* 92 (January 1993): 43.

Orhan Pamuk. *Snow.*

Translated by Maureen Freely. New York: Alfred A. Knopf, 2004. 425 pages.

Genre/literary style/story type: mainstream fiction

Critics have observed that a quiet grace and abiding respect for all characters permate this elegant book. Ka, an exiled poet who lives in Germany, returns to Istanbul for his mother's funeral and then travels to the rural town of Kars, where numerous young women have committed suicide because they adamantly persisted in publicly wearing head scarves. But Kars is also the town where Ipek, Ka's childhood sweetheart, lives. She is now divorced from her husband and runs a hotel. Ka is thrust into the middle of a smoldering political situation in Kars, which is exacerbated by an endless snowstorm that cuts the town off from the rest of the country. The fear of Islamic fundamentalism leads to a short-lived military coup. While Ka tries to situate himself within the abstruse cross-currents of the town's festering drama, he also courts Ipek, convinced that only Ipek's love will save him from a dreary existence back in Germany. Ultimately, his naïveté results in tragedy for all concerned. When the snow finally stops and he leaves Kars by himself, he can only sob as he looks out the window of his train. Touching on thorny social and cultural issues, Pamuk weaves a deep and enthralling narrative.

Related titles by the same author:
Readers may also want to explore the author's nonfiction memoir, *Istanbul: Memories and the City*, an elegiac yet ultimately clear-eyed account of the physical, emotional, and psychological geography of Istanbul. Also of interest may be *My Name Is Red*, in which the author contemplates the divided Turkish soul through an exploration of the effects of the introduction of Italian Renaissance painting into the upper reaches of late sixteenth-century Ottoman aristocracy, marked by its devotion to more traditional Islamic art forms. In polyphonic chapters where the voices of classically trained miniaturists explain through myths and legends the positives and negatives associated with Western approaches to style, perspective, chiaroscuro, individuality, and originality, a stunning picture of a lost world emerges. It is a world characterized both by exalted notions of divinity and bitter artistic rivalries that sometimes lead to murder. Finally, *The Museum of Innocence* traces, in 83 chapters, the obsessive passion of Kemal for Fusun, a shopgirl, through objects that are associated with Fusun. In 2010, Pamuk opened a museum in Istanbul with 83 displays of everyday objects—a real-life analogue and visual talisman of the book.
Subject keywords: politics; social problems
Original language: Turkish
Sources consulted for annotation:
Azimi, Negar. *The New York Times Magazine*, 1 November 2009 (online).
De Bellaigue, Christopher. *The New York Times Book Review*, 12 June 2005.
Eder, Richard. *The New York Times*, 10 August 2004 (online).
Howard, Maureen. *The New York Times*, 1 November 2009 (online).
Kloszewski, Marc. *Library Journal* 129 (July 2004): 73.
Schmidt, Heidi Jon. *People Weekly* 62 (13 September 2004): 55.
Wyatt, Neal. *Library Journal* 132 (1 February 2007): 108.
Some other translated books written by Orhan Pamuk: *My Name Is Red*; *The White Castle*; *The New Life*; *The Black Book*; *The Museum of Innocence*

Elif Shafak. *The Flea Palace*.
Translated by Müge Göçek. London: Marion Boyars, 2004. 444 pages.
Genre/literary style/story type: mainstream fiction
Every apartment building has its own history, and the Bonbon Palace is no exception. It was built on top of a cemetery and houses a motley assortment of residents—all caught in the malignant grip of an ever-growing heap of garbage in the courtyard. The novel follows the faltering lives of the residents as they try to stave off physical, emotional, financial, and psychological decline.
Related title by the same author:
Shafak has also written novels in English, including *The Saint of Incipient Insanities*, which focuses on three male graduate students (a Turk from Istanbul; a Moroccan; and a Spaniard) in Massachusetts and their attempts to navigate American culture and deal with the women in their lives.
Subject keywords: social problems; urban life
Original language: Turkish
Sources consulted for annotation:
Adams, Lorraine. *The New York Times Book Review*, 21 January 2007 (online).
Adil, Alev. *The Independent*, 25 June 2004, p. 23.
Global Books in Print (synopsis; reviews from *Booklist*, *Library Journal*, and *Publishers Weekly*).
Some other translated books written by Elif Shafak: *The Saint of Incipient Insanities*; *The Gaze*

Mehmet Murat Somer. *The Prophet Murders*.
Translated by Kenneth Dakan. London: Serpent's Tail, 2008. 224 pages.
Genres/literary styles/story types: crime fiction; amateur detectives

When a series of seemingly accidental deaths rock an Istanbul nightclub frequented by transvestites, the owner of the club is more than a little suspicious, but the police are of little use. Thus, the dynamic owner embarks on her own investigation, discovering the religious underpinnings of the mysterious deaths of the women who worked for her.
Subject keyword: urban life
Original language: Turkish
Source consulted for annotation:
Global Books in Print (online) (reviews from *Booklist* and *Publishers Weekly*).

Latife Tekin. *Berji Kristin: Tales from the Garbage Hills.*
Translated by Ruth Christie and Saliha Paker. London: Marion Boyars, 1993. 160 pages.
Genre/literary style/story type: mainstream fiction
This novel recounts the lives of poverty-stricken squatters who built the ironically named community of Flower Hill on top of a dump on the outskirts of Istanbul in the 1960s. It portrays their daily struggles for dignity and self-respect as well as the harsh conditions of their meager lives.
Subject keywords: power; urban life
Original language: Turkish
Sources consulted for annotation:
Amazon.com (*500 Great Books by Women*; book description; review from *Kirkus Reviews*).
Publishers Weekly 239 (17 August 1992): 490.
Another translated book written by Latife Tekin: *Dear Shameless Death*

CHAPTER 3

East Asia: China, Japan, and Korea

Language groups:	Korean	Japan
Chinese (Mandarin)	**Countries represented:**	Korea (North and South)
Japanese	China	Taiwan

INTRODUCTION

This chapter contains annotations of books translated from the primary languages of three East Asian countries: China, Japan, and Korea.

The translated Chinese books mentioned here are by contemporary authors who have received a relatively large amount of media attention as well as by those who have not. In the former category are Nobel Prize winner Gao Xingjian (*One Man's Bible* and *Soul Mountain*); Yu Hua (*Brothers*); Ma Jian (*The Noodle Maker* and *Beijing Coma*); and Mo Yan (*The Republic of Wine* and *Life and Death Are Wearing Me Out*). In the latter category are Wang Anyi (*The Song of Everlasting Sorrow*); Ran Chen (*A Private Life*); Yan Lianke (*Serve the People!*); and Wang Shuo (*Please Don't Call Me Human*).

Among the contemporary Japanese novelists mentioned in this chapter are the ever-popular Haruki Murakami, internationally known for such titles as *Kafka on the Shore*; Kobo Abe (*The Woman in the Dunes*; *The Ark Sakura*; and *Kangaroo Notebook*); and Nobel Prize winner Kenzaburo Oe (*Somersault*). But these three authors are only the tip of the iceberg. Names that may soon become as equally familiar as Murakami, Abe, and Oe are Natsuo Kirino, whose psychological thrillers *Out* and *Grotesque* have attracted much recent attention; Miyuki Miyabe, whose books *All She Was Worth* and *Crossfire* are often discussed in the same breath as Kirino's works; Yoshihiro Tatsumi, whose superb *A Drifting Life* is considered to be a classic of the manga form; and Yasutaka Tsutsui, whose *Salmonella Men on Planet Porno and Other Stories* has drawn rave reviews.

This chapter concludes with Korean fiction writers. Some contemporary novelists to keep in mind are Hahn Moo-Sook (*And So Flows History*); Lee Seung-U (*The Reverse Side of Life*); Yi Munyol

(*Our Twisted Hero*); and Park Kyong-ni (*The Curse of Kim's Daughters*); and Kim Young-Ha (*I Have The Right to Destroy Myself*).

Earlier Translated Literature

The Chinese fictional tradition builds on a tremendously rich heritage, especially the so-called Six Classical Novels. Originally published in a period that spans the early sixteenth century to the late eighteenth century, these panoramic and often multivolume works bring together elements of adventure, history, philosophy, romance, satire, and allegory. Collectively, they can be said to depict the political, social, religious, and cultural evolution of China up to 1800. Translated numerous times throughout the twentieth century, recent English-language versions of these novels are entitled *Three Kingdoms*; *Outlaws of the Marsh*; *The Journey to the West*; *The Plum in the Golden Vase*; *The Scholars*; and *The Story of the Stone*. Many critics observe that of these six novels, the two most appreciated are *The Journey to the West* (translated in four volumes by Anthony Yu) and *The Story of the Stone* (translated in five volumes by David Hawkes and John Minford). Other famous Chinese novels include Yu Li's *The Carnal Prayer Mat* and E Liu's *The Travels of Lao Ts'an*. In the middle decades of the twentieth century, some of the most renowned Chinese authors are She Lao (*Rickshaw*; *Ma and Son*; and *Cat Country*); Eileen Chang (*The Rice-Sprout Song* and *Naked Earth*); and Jin Ba (*Family* and *Cold Nights*).

Just as contemporary Chinese novels draw strength from a diverse past, so do Japanese novels. Readers who gravitate to Murakami and Kirino may therefore want to experience such Japanese translated classics as *The Tale of Genji*, an eleventh-century masterpiece by Shikibu Murasaki, and the late seventeenth-century short story collection *Five Women Who Loved Love* by Saikaku Ihara. Important twentieth-century writing has been produced by such renowned novelists as 1968 Nobel Prize winner Yasunari Kawabata (*Sound of the Mountain* and *The Izu Dancer and Other Stories*); Yukio Mishima (*Spring Snow*; *Runaway Horses*; and *The Decay of the Angel*); Jun'ichiro Tanizaki (*The Makioka Sisters*); and Soseki Natsume (*Kokoro*).

For readers interested in classic Korean novels in English translation, a good place to begin are the short stories and novels of Hwang Sun-Won, author of such titles as *The Descendants of Cain* and *Trees on a Slope*—both of which poignantly describe the wrenching transformations in Korean society after World War II and during the Korean War. Also significant is the short story collection *The Wings* by Yi Sang, who died in 1937.

SOURCES CONSULTED

France, Peter. (Ed.). (2000). "East Asian Languages." In *The Oxford Guide to Literature in English Translation*, pp. 222–250. Oxford: Oxford University Press.

Mostow, Joshua. (Ed.). (2003). *The Columbia Companion to Modern East Asian Literature*. New York: Columbia University Press.

BIBLIOGRAPHIC ESSAY

For all intents and purposes, readers and librarians would be very well-versed about the literatures of China, Japan, and Korea if they only consulted one book: *The Columbia Companion to Modern East Asian Literature*, edited by Joshua Mostow. We do not exaggerate one iota when we say that this book is really that good and complete. Following a general introduction, there are three substantial sections on each of the three literatures in question. Each of the sections has either four or five thematic essays that cover various aspects of literary history, followed by lengthy and authoritative entries about individual authors, works, and literary movements. There are about 50 entries for Japanese literature; about 40 for Chinese literature; and about 30 for Korean literature. In the Japan section, the thematic essays cover such topics as: the problem of the modern subject; nation and nationalism; gender, family, and sexualities in modern literature; and the social organization of modern Japanese literature. In the thematic essays in the China and Korea sections, the same breadth of coverage is evident, with in-depth articles about literary communities and the production of literature (China); modern Chinese literature as an institution; and the literature of territorial division (Korea). In reality, the entries—which include information about available translations—are detailed mini-essays. For Japan, some of the subjects covered are: Meiji women writers; the debate over pure literature; Miyamoto Yuriko and socialist writers; wartime fiction; occupation-period fiction; Kobo Abe; the 1960s and 1970s boom in women's writing; Haruki Murakami; and modern Okinawan literature. For China, entries range across such topics as the debate on revolutionary literature; same-sex love in recent Chinese literature; martial arts fiction and Jin Yong; Mo Yan and *Red Sorghum*; the Taiwan nativists; scar literature and the memory of trauma; avant-garde fiction in China; post-Mao urban fiction; and the return to recluse literature, as represented by the works of Gao Xingjian, the Nobel Prize winner for Literature in 2000. Korean entries introduce such authors as Yi Kwangsu, Kim Tongni, and Yang Kwija. After browsing in *The Columbia Companion to Modern East Asian Literature*, readers will certainly want to rush out and read three or four of the novels mentioned therein.

China

Of course, one book is never enough on a subject that is truly of interest. Readers for whom Chinese literature is a passion will be ecstatic to discover *A History of Contemporary Chinese Literature* by Hong Zicheng. Written by an eminent Chinese scholar; reprinted numerous times in China; and finally translated into English, the book provides a history of Chinese poetry, prose, and drama in the period between 1949 and 1999, vibrantly contextualizing and explaining the various literary environments of these five decades. Important chapters and subsections about Chinese fiction include: the literary thought of Mao Zedong; the state of typology in fiction; contemporary forms of rural fiction; urban fiction and fiction of industrial themes; beyond the mainstream; the thought liberation tide; educated youth fiction in the reconsideration of history; root-seeking and the artistic forms of fiction; writers of New Realism in fiction; the fiction of woman writers; and the overall situation of literature in the 1990s. Readers will be pleased to discover such 1980–1990s writers as Chi Li, Liu Heng, Ah Cheng, Dai Houying, Zhang Chengzhi, Han Shaogong, Zhang Wei, Wang Anyi, Shen Rong, and Zhang Min. Many of these writers "ponder the massive influence of material existence on the life of the individual" who struggles to find a place for spiritual and philosophical concerns in the midst of what often appears as unceasing commercialization (p. 448).

Equally valuable is the second edition of C. T. Hsia's *A History of Modern Chinese Fiction*, which has the virtue of beginning its coverage in the 1910s with Lu Xun, who is described as "[t]he earliest practitioner of Western-style fiction" and is "generally regarded as the greatest modern Chinese writer" (p. 28). Three important post-Xun realist fiction writers are intelligently analyzed in *Fictional Realism in Twentieth-Century China: Mao Dun, Lao She, Shen Congwen* by David Der-wei Wang. Mao Dun is presented as someone who shows "how realism is conditioned by political and historical factors, and how the claim to reflect always contains the hidden mandate to conceal and exclude, thereby pointing to power struggles in the text as well as in reality" (p. 23). On the other hand, Lao She "depicts the real by subverting its closure with melodramatic tears and hysterical laughter," while Shen Congwen's seemingly conservative fiction masks a longing for utopia (p. 23).

Another superb way to deepen one's understanding about Chinese literature is through anthologies. The standard work of this kind remains *The Columbia Anthology of Traditional Chinese Literature*, edited by Victor H. Mair. It contains examples of divinations; inscriptions; philosophical and religious writings; classic verse; lyrics and aria; elegies and rhapsodies; folk songs and ballads; parables and allegories; anecdotal fiction; so-called tales of the strange; short stories; and extracts from early and sometimes anonymous novels. It proves beyond a shadow of a doubt that Chinese literature "is not a seamless, monotonous fabric"; in the process, it criticizes literary historians "who emphasize only standard genres and elite writers" and thereby "perpetuat[e] a false image of what Chinese literature might be for our own age" (p. xxiii). Mair's anthology of the vast range of traditional Chinese literature should be read in conjunction with *The Columbia Anthology of Modern Chinese Literature*, edited by Joseph S. M. Lau and Howard Goldblatt. More than half the book is devoted to fiction from three time periods: 1918–1949, 1949–1976, and post-1976. In addition to classic modern fiction from Lu Xun, Mao Dun, Lao She, and Shen Congwen, there is work from Ba Jin, Ding Ling, Hua Tong, Liu Yichang, Wang Meng, Xi Xi, Gao Xingjian, Mo Yan, Wang Anyi, and Yu Hua.

Readers specifically interested in Chinese women writers will no doubt be pleased to learn about *Writing Women in Modern China: An Anthology of Women's Literature from the Early Twentieth Century*, edited by Amy D. Dooling and Kristina M. Torgeson, and *Writing Women in Modern China: The Revolutionary Years, 1936–1976*, edited by Amy D. Dooling. Both these volumes deserve high praise for including detailed biographical information about the anthologized authors as well as substantial critical introductions analyzing the role and importance of women writers in Chinese cultural life. Readers thus gain a good understanding about the historical circumstances in which such authors as Yang Gang, Yang Jiang, Bai Wei, Zong Pu, Lu Yin, and Ding Ling wrote. Also of importance is *A Place of One's Own: Stories of Self in China, Taiwan, Hong Kong, and Singapore*, edited by Kwok-Kan Tam and colleagues. As the title indicates, the notion of Chinese literature is expanded to include Taiwan, Hong Kong, and Singapore. After perusing these anthologies, readers may be ready for *Modern Chinese Women Writers: Critical Appraisals*, edited by Michael S. Duke, which is an invaluable critical assessment of writers such as Chen Ruoxi, Li Ang, Zhang Kangkang, Zhu Lin, and Shen Rong.

One way for readers and librarians to tap into the most up-to-date developments in Chinese fiction might be to keep an eye on books published by Cambria Press (New York). We say this based on the two following titles: *Feminism and Global Chineseness: The Cultural Production of Controversial Women Authors* by Aijun Zhu and *The Jin Yong Phenomenon: Chinese Martial Arts Fiction and Modern Chinese Literary History*, edited by Ann Huss and Jianmei Liu. The first book analyzes such wildly successful and controversial contemporary writers as Wei Hui, Li Ang, and Li Bihua. Published in late 1999, Wei Hui's novel *Shanghai Baby* became a much-talked-about Chinese bestseller in 2000 with its "bold and sensational presentation of female sexuality" (p. 113). It was interpreted as "a response to cultural conflicts in contemporary China between the status of male-centered literary tradition, the shaky position of feminism, and the rising power of popular culture" (pp. 112–113). Much the same could be said of the effect of Li Ang and Li Bihua on cultural life in Taiwan and Hong Kong, respectively. But another popular phenomenon in China is the martial arts novel, as represented by the work of Jin Yong. Jin Yong's translated novels have gained wide popularity, especially in the wake of Ang Lee's film *Crouching Tiger, Hidden Dragon*. Fans of martial arts fiction will therefore want to read every page of *The Jin Yong Phenomenon: Chinese Martial Arts Fiction and Modern Chinese Literary History* in order to better situate him within the Chinese literary canon.

Japan

Japanese literature is every bit as rich as Chinese literature. To fully appreciate its historical roots, it is imperative that readers first consult *The Princeton Companion to Classical Japanese Literature* by Earl Miner, Hiroko Odagiri, and Robert E. Morrell. In addition to a literary history that spans the time period 645 to 1868; chronologies (i.e., periods; regnal and era names; annals of works and events); biographical information about major authors and works; and an overview of literary genres (e.g., waka, sutras), there are sections explaining time and annual celebrations; ranks and offices; and architecture, clothing, armor, and arms. In other words, *The Princeton Companion* provides the kind of practical information necessary for an informed reading of classical Japanese literature. After thoroughly familiarizing themselves with this work, readers can then more fully appreciate the vast learning that is on display on every page of the three volumes of Jin'ichi Konishi's *A History of Japanese Literature*. Filled with fascinating details about Japanese literature in the archaic and ancient ages, the early middle ages, and the high middle ages, it is the product of a lifetime of meticulous scholarship and an extraordinary breadth of sustained study. For a comprehensive one-volume literary history, we suggest Shuichi Kato's *A History of Japanese Literature: From the Man'yoshú to Modern Times*.

Exemplary discussions of individual Japanese novelists are contained in Donald Keene's *Five Modern Japanese Novelists*. Here, readers will get valuable contextual and critical insight about Jun'ichiro Tanizaki, Yasunari Kawabata, Yukio Mishima, Kobo Abe, and Ryotaro Shiba. This book should be supplemented with two volumes in the Dictionary of Literary Biography series: *Japanese Fiction Writers, 1868–1945*, edited by Van C. Gessel (1997; vol. 180), and *Japanese Fiction Writers Since World War II*, also edited by Van C. Gessel (1997; vol. 182). There is detailed bio-bibliographic information about such well-known writers such as Kenzaburo Oe (winner of the Nobel Prize for Literature in 1994) and Haruki Murakami but also about such relatively little-known authors as Kita Morio, Shiina Rinzo, Uno Chiyo, and Noma Hiroshi. *Japanese Fiction Writers Since World War II* also features overviews (reprinted from *Japanese Literature Today*) about developments in Japanese literature in each of the years between 1987 and 1995. *Modern Japanese Writers*, edited by Jay Rubin, is also noteworthy, especially for its lengthy articles about the so-called atomic bomb writers and the controversial novelist and short story writer Osamu Dazai, who is often compared to Ernest Hemingway. John Lewell's *Modern Japanese Novelists: A Biographical Dictionary* can also be a valuable source of information for lesser-known novelists. Also, readers will be fascinated by *Japanese Women Writers: A Bio-Critical Sourcebook*, edited by Chieko I. Mulhern, and *Japanese Women Fiction Writers: Their Culture and Society, 1890s to 1990s: English Language Sources*, compiled by Carol Fairbanks. In fact, these last two reference texts should be used together. Mulhern's text has bio-bibliographic information about 58 female writers from the ninth century to about 1990. Fairbanks's text begins with the statement that there are "[o]ver three hundred works of fiction by ninety-seven Japanese women writers from the 1890s to the 1990s . . . available in English: 64 novels, 217 short stories and novellas, and 24 excerpts from novels" (p. ix). Her book aims to provide information about all these authors and their translated works. Arranged in alphabetical order by author, each entry contains the titles (and summaries) of translated works as well as a list of "secondary sources covering a wide range of subjects, including critical commentary, theoretical approaches, comparisons with other authors (Japanese and Western), literary movements, social and political issues; gender roles, or historical contexts" (p. x).

Two unique anthologies should also be consulted. The first is *Modanizumu: Modernist Fiction from Japan, 1913–1938*, edited by William J. Tyler, which not only contains substantial extracts from often overlooked writers such as Inagaki Taruho, Abe Tomoji, and Kajii Motojiro but also detailed introductions about various aspects of the literary modernist period in Japanese literature. The second is *Partings at Dawn: An Anthology of Japanese Gay Literature*, edited by Stephen D. Miller, which highlights "numerous literary works dating from the classical court culture of the Heian Period (794–1185) up to modern times that will be of interest to anyone concerned with understanding the various meanings ascribed to sexual and emotional relations between members of the same sex in Japan" (p. 11). As the back cover of the book indicates, "The renowned 17th century writer Ihara Saikaku is well represented with his stories of samurai and their boyloves." Among other authors included are Hiruma Hisao and Yukio Mishima.

Finally, no discussion of Japanese culture and literature can overlook manga. To get some sense of the manga phenomena and the way that it has permeated all aspects of Japanese culture, we recommend *Adult Manga: Culture and Power in Contemporary Japanese Society* by Sharon Kinsella and *Japanese Visual Culture: Explorations in the World of Manga and Anime*, edited by Mark W. MacWilliams. This last book is particularly salient, with wide-ranging and informative essays about such topics as manga in

Japanese history; characters, themes, and narrative patterns in the manga of Osamu Tezuka; teenage girls, romance comics, and contemporary Japanese culture; narratives of the Second World War in Japanese manga, 1957–1977; and medieval genealogies of manga and anime horror.

Korea

The best way to grasp the complexities and sophistication of Korean literature is through *A History of Korean Literature*, edited by Peter H. Lee, and *Understanding Korean Literature* by Kim Hunggyu. We recommend that readers start with Hunggyu's book, which explains the relationship among oral, classical Chinese, and vernacular Korean literatures; the history of the Korean language and its various literary styles; the genres of Korean literature, including the classic novel, new novel, and modern novel; and the various phases of Korean literature. Readers can then immerse themselves in Lee's volume, which contains elegant and definitive essays about the Korean language; major literary forms, prosody, and themes in Korean poetry; the shift from oral to written literature; literary genres and works in Chinese and the vernacular from the beginning of the C.E. era to the end of the nineteenth century; detailed overviews about fiction and poetry written by men and women in various periods of the twentieth century; and a concluding chapter about the literature of North Korea. Whenever people talk about Korean culture and literature, Lee's book will always be mentioned as a landmark.

For a landmark of a different kind, the next place to turn is Ann Sung-Hi Lee's book *Yi Kwang-Su and Modern Korean Literature*, which not only contains a translation of Kwang-su's *The Heartless* (thought by many scholars to be one of the most important Korean novels of the twentieth century) but also a detailed consideration of the historical and cultural forces and issues that laid the groundwork for the development of Korean fiction in the late nineteenth and early twentieth centuries. There is a wealth of information about other Korean novelists, poets, and playwrights in *Who's Who in Korean Literature*, compiled by the Korean Culture and Arts Foundation. Here, readers will discover novelists such as Soo-Kil Ahn, Sun-Won Hwang, and In-Hoon Choi.

Finally, we wish to draw attention to the tremendously diverse array of fiction contained in the following anthologies: *Modern Korean Literature: An Anthology, 1908–1965*, edited by Chung Chong-Wha; *Unspoken Voices: Selected Short Stories by Korean Women Writers*, edited by Jin-Young. Choi; *A Ready-Made Life: Early Masters of Modern Korean Fiction*, edited by Kim Chong-un and Bruce Fulton; *Modern Korean Fiction: An Anthology*, edited by Bruce Fulton and Youngmin Kwon; and the expanded edition of *Land of Exile: Contemporary Korean Fiction*, edited by Marshall R. Pihl, Bruce Fulton, and Ju-Chan Fulton.

SELECTED REFERENCES

Choi, Jin-Young. (Ed.). (2002). *Unspoken Voices: Selected Short Stories by Korean Women Writers*. Dumont, NJ: Homa & Sekey Books.

Chong-un, Kim, and Fulton, Bruce. (Eds.). (1998). *A Ready-Made Life: Early Masters of Modern Korean Fiction*. Honolulu, HI: University of Hawai'i Press.

Chong-Wha, Chung. (Ed.). (1995). *Modern Korean Literature: An Anthology, 1908–1965*. London: Kegan Paul.

Dooling, Amy D. (Ed.). (2005). *Writing Women in Modern China: The Revolutionary Years, 1936–1976*. New York: Columbia University Press.

Dooling, Amy D., and Torgeson, Kristina M. (Eds.). (1998). *Writing Women in Modern China: An Anthology of Women's Literature from the Early Twentieth Century*. New York: Columbia University Press.

Duke, Michael S. (Ed.). (1989). *Modern Chinese Women Writers: Critical Appraisals*. Armonk, NY: M. E. Sharpe.

Fairbanks, Carol. (Ed.). (2002). *Japanese Women Fiction Writers: Their Culture and Society, 1890s to 1990s: English Language Sources*. Lanham, MD: Scarecrow Press.

Fulton, Bruce, and Kwon Youngmin. (Eds.). (2005). *Modern Korean Fiction: An Anthology*. New York: Columbia Press.

Hsia, C. T. (1971). *A History of Modern Chinese Fiction*. (2nd ed.). New Haven, CT: Yale University Press.

Hunggyu, Kim. (1997). *Understanding Korean Literature*. (Trans. by Robert J. Fouser). Armonk, NY: M. E. Sharpe.

Huss, Ann, and Liu, Jianmei. (Eds.). (2007). *The Jin Yong Phenomenon: Chinese Martial Arts Fiction and Modern Chinese Literary History*. Youngstown, NY: Cambria Press.

Kato, Shuichi. (1997). *A History of Japanese Literature: From the Man'yoshú to Modern Times*. (New abridged ed.). Richmond, Surrey, UK: Japan Library.

Keene, Donald. (2003). *Five Modern Japanese Novelists*. New York: Columbia University Press.

Kinsella, Sharon. (2000). *Adult Manga: Culture and Power in Contemporary Japanese Society*. Richmond, Surrey, UK: Curzon Press.

Konishi, Jin'ichi. (1984–1991) *A History of Japanese Literature*. (3 vols.). New Haven, CT: Yale University Press.

Korean Culture and Arts Foundation. (1996). *Who's Who in Korean Literature*. Elizabeth, NJ: Hollym.

Lau, Joseph S. M., and Goldblatt, Howard. (Eds.). (2007). *The Columbia Anthology of Modern Chinese Literature*. (2nd ed.). New York: Columbia University Press.

Lee, Ann Sung-Hi. (2005). *Yi Kwang-Su and Modern Korean Literature*. Ithaca, NY: East Asia Program Cornell University.

Lee, Peter H. (Ed.). (2003). *A History of Korean Literature*. New York: Cambridge University Press.

Lewell, John. (1993). *Modern Japanese Novelists: A Biographical Dictionary*. New York: Kodansha International.

MacWilliams, Mark W. (Ed.). (2008). *Japanese Visual Culture: Explorations in the World of Manga and Anime*. Armonk, NY: M. E. Sharpe.

Mair, Victor H. (Ed.). (1994). *The Columbia Anthology of Traditional Chinese Literature*. New York: Columbia University Press.

Miller, Stephen D. (Ed.). (1996). *Partings at Dawn: An Anthology of Japanese Gay Literature*. San Francisco, CA: Gay Sunshine Press.

Miner, Earl; Odagiri, Hiroko; and Morrell Robert E. (1985). *The Princeton Companion to Classical Japanese Literature*. Princeton, NJ: Princeton University Press.

Mostow, Joshua. (Ed.). (2003). *The Columbia Companion to Modern East Asian Literature*. New York: Columbia University Press.

Mulhern, Chieko I. (Ed.). (1994). *Japanese Women Writers: A Bio-Critical Sourcebook*. Westport, CT: Greenwood Press.

Pihl, Marshall R.; Fulton, Bruce; and Fulton, Ju-Chan. (Eds.). (2007). *Land of Exile: Contemporary Korean Fiction*. (expanded ed.). Armonk, NY: M. E. Sharpe.

Rubin, Jay. (Ed.). (2001). *Modern Japanese Writers*. New York: Charles Scribner's Sons.

Tam, Kwok-Kan; Yip, Terry Siu-Han; and Dissanayake, Wimal. (Eds.). (1999). *A Place of One's Own: Stories of Self in China, Taiwan, Hong Kong, and Singapore*. Oxford: Oxford University Press.

Tyler, William J. (Ed.). (2008). *Modanizumu: Modernist Fiction from Japan, 1913–1938*. Honolulu, HI: University of Hawai'i Press.

Wang, David Der-wei. (1992). *Fictional Realism in Twentieth-Century China: Mao Dun, Lao She, Shen Congwen*. New York: Columbia University Press.

Zhu, Aijun. (2007). *Feminism and Global Chineseness: The Cultural Production of Controversial Women Authors*. Youngstown, NY: Cambria Press.

Zicheng, Hong. (2007). *A History of Contemporary Chinese Literature*. (Trans. by Michael M. Day). Leiden, The Netherlands: Brill.

ANNOTATIONS FOR TRANSLATED BOOKS FROM CHINA

Acheng (Ah Cheng). *Three Kings: Three Stories from Today's China*.
Translated by Bonnie McDougall. London: Collins-Harvill, 1990. 223 pages.
Genres/literary styles/story types: mainstream fiction; short stories
These stories transpose and rework motifs and images from folktales and legends into contemporary settings. A chess prodigy loses a game to an older man. A forester—whose soul and spirit reside in

an enchanted tree—is compelled by governmental authorities to destroy the tree; he perishes along with it. A newly appointed teacher in a rural area loses his job after trying to teach his students to think independently.
Subject keyword: social problems
Original language: Chinese
Sources consulted for annotation:
Choice 31 (April 1994): 1249.
Cohn, Don. *Far Eastern Economic Review* 150 (8 November 1990): 40.
Another translated book written by Acheng: *Unfilled Graves*

Bei Ai (Ai Bei). ***Red Ivy, Green Earth Mother.***
Translated by Howard Goldblatt. Salt Lake City, UT: Peregrine Smith Books, 1990. 146 pages.
Genres/literary styles/story types: mainstream fiction; women's lives
The three short stories and novella that constitute this book take place after the Chinese Cultural Revolution of the late 1960s and early 1970s, when free economic zones and nascent democratic principles were introduced in China. Bei's middle-class heroines live in a fast-changing but still male-dominated society clouded by political uncertainty, cultural confusion, and hypocrisy. In the novella "Red Ivy," Ji Li—a mayor's daughter who is the niece of a high-ranking party member—works in a women's correctional facility. Her view is that while life in prison is harsh, it is in many ways preferable to a life of so-called freedom that is free in name only. The three short stories take place in domestic settings, where women live in deep unhappiness and often in a suicidal fever brought on by marital infidelities, abusive husbands, and smothering despotic parents—all exacerbated by political corruption.
Subject keywords: politics; power
Original language: Chinese
Sources consulted for annotation:
Amazon.com (book description).
Dean, Kitty Chen. *Library Journal.* 115 (August 1990): 136.
Kaganoff, Penny. *Publishers Weekly* 237 (24 August 1990): 58.
Mullen, Bill. *Chicago Tribune*, 9 September 1990, p. 7.
Solomon, Charles. *Los Angeles Times*, 30 September 1990, p. 14.

Alai. ***Red Poppies.***
Translated by Howard Goldblatt and Sylvia Li-chun Lin. Boston: Houghton Mifflin, 2002. 433 pages.
Genre/literary style/story type: historical fiction
The days of feudal Tibet are passing; soon, the Chinese will invade Tibet and bring poppy seeds—both a source of prosperity and a scourge for the native population. The narrator of the novel is an adolescent Young Master, the second son of a Tibetan ruler. He is notorious for his eccentric behavior, mood swings, and strange antics, but he turns out to be a prophet who has a deep understanding of the fragility of human existence. This book, which has been compared to the works of Gabriel García Márquez and Salman Rushdie, can be understood as an elegy for a vanishing way of life.
Subject keywords: politics; power
Original language: Chinese
Sources consulted for annotation:
Crossette, Barbara. *The New York Times Book Review*, 12 May 2002, p. 18.
Hilton, Isabel. *Los Angeles Times*, 8 December 2002, p. R3.
Shoup, Sheila. *School Library Journal* 48 (May 2002): 179.
Wu, Fatima. *World Literature Today* 77 (April/June 2003): 92.

Feiyu Bi (Bi Feiyu). ***The Moon Opera.***
Translated by Howard Goldblatt and Sylvia Li-chun Lin. Boston: Houghton Mifflin Harcourt, 2007. 128 pages.
Genre/literary style/story type: mainstream fiction
Politics, jealousy, intrigue, and oppression are present in every sphere of life; the opera is no different. This novel recounts the tangled and tragic tale of an opera singer who scalds her understudy with boiling water. After earning her living as a teacher for some two decades, she returns to the stage at the behest of a factory-owner millionaire.
Related title by the same author:
Readers may also enjoy *Three Sisters*, which examines the quest for power and influence through the lives of Yumi, Yuxiu, and Yuyang—each of whom employs a different character trait to achieve fame and popularity.
Subject keyword: identity
Original language: Chinese
Sources consulted for annotation:
Amazon. com (product description).
Fantastic Fiction website (book description), http://www.fantasticfiction.co.uk.
Another translated book written by Feiyu Bi: *Three Sisters*

Naiqian Cao (Cao Naiqian). ***There's Nothing I Can Do When I Think of You Late at Night.***
Translated by John Balcom. New York: Columbia University Press, 2009. 232 pages.
Genres/literary styles/story types: mainstream fiction; short stories
There is isolated—and then there is isolated. This collection of interlinked stories describes a location that most definitely falls into the second category and is based on an actual village to which the author was exiled during the Cultural Revolution. In Wen Clan Caves, life is rudimentary and abysmally harsh. Despair permeates every aspect of life, as do sordid passions that explode into violence. The stark, bleak lives of the villagers have an uncompromising and raw realism that makes them tragic figures from another age. This book, which the translator referred to as an example of "austere lyricism" in his introduction, has been compared to such classic works as *Go Down, Moses* by William Faulkner; *Winesburg, Ohio* by Sherwood Anderson; and Erskine Caldwell's fiction.
Subject keyword: rural life
Original language: Chinese
Sources consulted for annotation:
Columbia University Press website (book description), http://cup.columbia.edu.
The Complete Review (book review), http://www.complete-review.com.
Hardenberg, Wendy. Three Percent website, http://www.rochester.edu/College/translation/threepercent.

Hsien-liang Chang (Zhang Xianliang). ***Getting Used to Dying.***
Translated by Martha Avery. New York: HarperCollins, 1991. 291 pages.
Genre/literary style/story type: mainstream fiction
Blending the real and the hallucinatory fantastic, this book is set against the background of political events in communist China from the 1950s to the 1980s and a visit to the United States. During the Chinese Cultural Revolution, people were jailed for being educated, literate, and having had property-owning relatives or parents, among other things. Partly autobiographical, this novel is a grim journey into the psyche of a nameless protagonist who has been imprisoned for 22 years.
Subject keywords: politics; power
Original language: Chinese

Sources consulted for annotation:
Dean, Kitty Chen. *Library Journal* 115 (December 1990): 167.
Dirlam, Sharon. *Los Angeles Times*, 3 February 1991, p. 6.
Price, Ruth. *Chicago Tribune*, 3 February 1991, p. 6.
Steinberg, Sybil S. *Publishers Weekly* 237 (16 November 1990): 43.
Some other translated books written by Hsien-liang Chang: *Mimosa and Other Stories*; *Half of Man Is Woman*

S. K. Chang (Chang Hsi-kuo). *The City Trilogy: Five Jade Disks, Defenders of the Dragon City, Tale of a Feather.*
Translated by John Balcom. New York: Columbia University Press, 2003. 407 pages.
Genre/literary style/story type: speculative fiction
This science-fiction trilogy by a Taiwanese writer is situated in imaginary Sunlon City, which is a world unto itself with distinctive traditions, regulations, and cultural practices. In *Five Jade Disks*, the Huhui people defend Sunlon from a clan of Shan warriors; in *Defenders of the Dragon City*, the Shan make a second attempt to defeat Sunlon. Tyrannical Mayor Ma ascends to power in *Tale of a Feather*, and the city—torn by political rivalry and intrigue—ends up in ruins. The book is recommended for fans of Tolkien.
Subject keywords: politics; power
Original language: Chinese
Sources consulted for annotation:
Cannon, Peter. *Publishers Weekly* 250 (10 March 2003): 57.
Cassada, Jackie. *Library Journal* 128 (15 April 2003): 129.
Schroeder, Regina. *Booklist* 99 (1 May 2003): 1586.
Another translated book written by S. K. Chang: *Chess King*

Jo-hsi Ch'en (Ruoxi Chen). *The Execution of Mayor Yin, and Other Stories From the Great Proletarian Cultural Revolution.*
Translated by Nancy Ing and Howard Goldblatt. Bloomington, IN: Indiana University Press, 2004. 202 pages.
Genres/literary styles/story types: mainstream fiction; short stories
The author is a Taiwanese-born writer who returned to China to participate in the Maoist reforms of the 1960s after receiving her graduate degree in the United States—only to leave for Hong Kong and then Canada a few years later. This collection of stories deals with daily life in China during the Cultural Revolution. As the raging paranoia engendered by the revolution reaches its crest, a woman spies on her neighbor to prove her marital infidelity and ensure that she receives a just punishment. In another story, parents agonize over their four-year-old son's fate after he utters a silly sentence about Mao while playing.
Subject keywords: politics; power
Original language: Chinese
Sources consulted for annotation:
Douglas, Carol Anne. *Off Our Backs* 9 (30 September 1979): 3.
Kinkley, J. C. *Choice* 42 (March 2005): 1225.
Some other translated books written by Jo-hsi Ch'en: *The Short Stories of Chen Ruoxi, Translated from the Original Chinese: A Writer at the Crossroad*; *The Old Man and Other Stories*

Ran Chen. *A Private Life.*
Translated by John Howard-Gibbon. New York: Columbia University Press, 2004. 214 pages.
Genres/literary styles/story types: mainstream fiction; women's lives

This novel traces the sexual awakening and maturation of Niuniu, who first falls in love with a male school teacher; then has a lesbian experience with an older neighbor, the widow Ho; and finally finds true love in college with Yin Nan. Disowned by her father, she becomes an outcast, finding strength and refuge in her mother and lovers. But after her mother and the widow Ho die and after Yin Nan disappears during the mayhem of the Tiananmen Square massacre, Niuniu withdraws to the hallucinatory world of her dreams, visions, and memories. The novel provides an in-depth analysis of the mindset and psyche of a woman fleeing from a hostile environment to the soothing solitariness of an internal world.
Subject keyword: family histories
Original language: Chinese
Sources consulted for annotation:
Tangalos, Sofia A. *Library Journal* 129 (August 2004): 64.
Williams, P. F. *Choice* 42 (February 2005): 1019.
Zaleski, Jeff. *Publishers Weekly* 251 (31 May 2004): 50.

Yuanbin Chen (Chen Yuanbin). *The Story of Qiuju*.
Translated by Anna Walling. Beijing: Chinese Literature Press, 1995. 206 pages.
Genres/literary styles/story types: mainstream fiction; short stories
One of the four stories in this collection is about a pregnant and uneducated peasant woman who displays astounding fortitude when she defends her husband in front of a scornful village ruler, thus ensuring justice for her family. A movie based on this story was awarded the Golden Rooster, China's highest cinematic award, as well as the Golden Lion Prize at the Venice International Film Festival.
Subject keywords: family histories; rural life
Original language: Chinese
Sources consulted for annotation:
Amazon.com (book description).
Oon, Clarissa. *Straits Times*, 15 January 2003 (from Factiva databases).
Yuen, Lowell. *Straits Times*, 29 November 1992 (from Factiva databases).

Naishan Cheng (Cheng Naishan). *The Banker.*
Translated by Britten Dean. San Francisco, CA: China Books & Periodicals, 1992. 459 pages.
Genre/literary style/story type: historical fiction
This is the first novel in a trilogy that chronicles three generations of a well-to-do Chinese family in Shanghai. Set against the backdrop of what is referred to as the Second Sino-Japanese War, which roughly coincided with World War II, it focuses on Zhu Jingchen's ascension from modest beginnings to bank president. But his savvy financial leadership is no match for the multifaceted political situation that China finds itself in, and he is eventually arrested for his political views.
Subject keywords: family histories; war
Original language: Chinese
Sources consulted for annotation:
Mintz, Kenneth. *Library Journal* 118 (1 March 1993): 106.
Publishers Weekly 240 (8 February 1993): 80.
Some other translated books written by Naishan Cheng: *The Blue House*; *The Piano Tuner*

Zijian Chi (Chi Zijian). *Figments of the Supernatural.*
Translated by Simon Patton. Sydney, Australia: James Joyce Press, 2004. 206 pages.
Genres/literary styles/story types: mainstream fiction; women's lives
Told from a feminist perspective, the stories in this collection describe life and culture in northern China. A representative story is "Fine Rain at Dusk on Grieg's Sea," which alternates between

Norway, the homeland of composer Edvard Grieg, and Mona, a tiny town in China's countryside. While in Norway, the narrator hears Grieg's music mixed with the sound of rain, and she realizes that she has heard this same enchanting melody in her hometown in China.
Subject keywords: identity; social roles
Original language: Chinese
Sources consulted for annotation:
Boland, Rosita. *Irish Times*, 10 June 2004, p. 16.
Ping, Wang. MCLC Resource Center (book review), http://mclc.osu.edu.
Another translated book written by Zijian Chi: *A Flock in the Wilderness*

Jicai Feng (Feng Jicai). *The Three-Inch Golden Lotus*.
Translated by David Wakefield. Honolulu, HI: University of Hawai'i Press, 1994. 239 pages.
Genres/literary styles/story types: historical fiction; literary historical
A family's history is told through a social and historical exploration of the ancient custom of foot-binding. The head of the Tong family is an antiques dealer who yearns for perfection. When Tong sees the feet of Fragrant Lotus, he knows that he has glimpsed heaven, so he insists on marrying her to one of his sons. Fragrant Lotus assumes a prominent place within the Tong family until the practice of foot-binding is abolished and bound feet are considered repulsive.
Subject keywords: family histories; social roles
Original language: Chinese
Sources consulted for annotation:
Amazon.com (review from *Kirkus Reviews*).
Chen, Jianguo. *World Literature Today* 69 (Summer 1995): 643.
Dean, Kitty Chen. *Library Journal* 119 (15 March 1994): 100.
Publishers Weekly 241 (31 January 1994): 81.
Sullivan, Mary Ellen. *Booklist* 90 (15 March 1994): 1326.
Some other translated books written by Jicai Feng: *Chrysanthemums and Other Stories*; *The Miraculous Pigtail*

Xingjian Gao (Gao Xingjian). *One Man's Bible*.
Translated by Mabel Lee. New York: HarperCollins, 2002. 450 pages.
Genre/literary style/story type: mainstream fiction
The events of this semiautobiographical novel begin in 1996–1997 in Hong Kong when the narrator has a torrid four-day-long affair with a woman who forces him to confront his past. Told in flashbacks and using stream of consciousness, the book is a harrowing account of the Chinese Cultural Revolution in the 1960s and 1970s and the narrator's participation in the psychological cruelties that were an everyday part of that era. In a perfervid atmosphere governed by fear and paranoia, the very idea of humanity changed profoundly. Critics have compared Gao to such writers as Anchee Min, Ha Jin, and Milan Kundera.
Related title by the same author:
Readers should also experience *Soul Mountain*, which is a semiautobiographical novel about a journey through a mountainous region of China that Gao undertook in the early 1980s after he had been misdiagnosed with lung cancer and was the subject of rumors that he was about to be imprisoned.
Subject keywords: philosophy; politics
Original language: Chinese
Sources consulted for annotation:
Bates, Milton J. *World Literature Today* 78 (January/April 2004): 76.
Bernstein, Richard. *The New York Times*, 18 October 2002 (online).

Kristof, Nicholas D. *The New York Times Book Review*, 24 December 2000 (online).
Quanm Shirley N. *Library Journal* 127 (August 2002): 142.
Zaleski, Jeff. *Publishers Weekly* 249 (5 August 2002): 51.
Some other translated books written by Xingjian Gao: *Soul Mountain*; *Buying a Fishing Rod for My Grandfather; One Man's Bible; Return to Painting; The Case for Literature*

Hua Gu (Gu Hua). *Virgin Widows.*
Translated by Howard Goldblatt. Honolulu, HI: University of Hawai'i Press, 1996. 165 pages.
Genres/literary styles/story types: mainstream fiction; women's lives
Through parallel stories of two women living 100 years apart, the author explores the question of widowhood and remarriage. When the aging and violent husband of Guihua Yao dies, she wishes to marry one of her husband's employees, but her choice encounters broad community opposition. Qingyu Yang—whose youthful marriage to the son of aristocrats rescued her from a life of poverty—chooses to remain chaste after her husband's death, thus honoring his memory and ensuring her continued economic survival.
Subject keywords: identity; social roles
Original language: Chinese
Source consulted for annotation:
Sorenson, Simon. *World Literature Today* 72 (Winter 1998): 203.
Some other translated books written by Hua Gu: *Pagoda Ridge and Other Stories*; *Small Town Called Hibiscus*

Xiaolu Guo. *Village of Stone.*
Translated by Cindy Carter. London: Chatto & Windus, 2004. 183 pages.
Genre/literary style/story type: mainstream fiction
When a package of dried eel arrives for Coral from her native village, this mysterious gift unleashes a stream of unhappy memories. Coral has made a new life for herself in Beijing in the company of her boyfriend, Red, but she is instantly whisked back to her lonely and tragic existence as an orphan raised by grandparents who did not talk to one another.
Subject keywords: rural life; urban life
Original language: Chinese
Sources consulted for annotation:
Amazon.com (book description).
Danny Yee's Book Reviews (book review), http://dannyreviews.com.
Morgan, Vivienne. *Birmingham Post*, 24 April 2004, p. 53.

Shaogong Han (Han Shaogong). *A Dictionary of Maqiao.*
Translated by Julia Lovell. New York: Columbia University Press, 2003. 322 pages.
Genre/literary style/story type: mainstream fiction
Based on the author's experiences working in rural China during the Cultural Revolution, this tragicomic novel is set in the imaginary village of Maqiao. Written in the form of a dictionary with 111 entries, it explores the many absurd decisions taken by China's leadership during this period of violent political upheaval, including Mao's plan to standardize the Chinese language. Critics have compared the author to François Rabelais.
Subject keywords: power; rural life
Original language: Chinese
Sources consulted for annotation:
Ehrenreich, Ben. *The Village Voice*, 17 September/23 September 2003, p. 96.
Quan, Shirley N. *Library Journal* 128 (15 June 2003): 101.

Wolff, Katherine. *The New York Times Book Review*, 13 August 2003, p. 17.
Wu, Fatima. *World Literature Today* 78 (September/December 2004): 85.
Zaleski, Jeff. *Publishers Weekly* 250 (16 June 2003): 49.
Another translated book written by Shaogong Han: *Homecoming? and Other Stories*

Ying Hong (Hong Ying). *Peacock Cries at the Three Gorges.*
Translated by Mark Smith and Henry Zhao. London: Marion Boyars, 2004. 334 pages.
Genre/literary style/story type: mainstream fiction
This is the story of reincarnated lovers set against the construction of the Three Gorges Dam project on the Yangtze River. Dr. Liu, a research geneticist, is married to the director of this mammoth and environmentally controversial project. Unexpectedly discovering that her husband is being unfaithful to her, she leaves both her job and marriage. When she visits her aunt, Liu becomes acquainted with her aunt's son, Yueming, who is an artist and fervently against Three Gorges. As their relationship deepens, so does Liu's understanding about the stakes involved in the dam project.
Subject keywords: family histories; politics
Original language: Chinese
Sources consulted for annotation:
Amazon.com (book description).
Tangalos, Sofia A. *Library Journal* 129 (December 2004): 100.
Some other translated books written by Ying Hong: *Daughter of the River*; *K: The Art of Love*; *Summer of Betrayal*; *A Lipstick Called Red Pepper: Fiction About Gay & Lesbian Love in China*

Chunming Huang (Huang Chun-ming). *The Taste of Apples: Taiwanese Stories* (or ***The Drowning of an Old Cat and Other Stories***).
Translated by Howard Goldblatt. New York: Columbia University Press, 2001. 251 pages.
Genres/literary styles/story types: mainstream fiction; short stories
Written in the style of Anton Chekhov, the nine stories in this collection describe life in rural Taiwan, focusing on the poor, the marginalized, and the eccentric. The author's cast of characters struggle to eke out an existence at the crossroads of modernity and tradition, caught in a no-man's-land of psychological desolation and bleakness.
Subject keywords: rural life; culture conflict
Original language: Chinese.
Sources consulted for annotation:
Amazon.com (book description).
Kinkley, Jeffrey C. *World Literature Today* 75 (Summer 2001): 142.
Rubin, Merle. *Los Angeles Times*, 2 July 2001, p. E3.

Pingwa Jia (Jia Pingwa). *Turbulence.*
Translated by Howard Goldblatt. Baton Rouge, LA: Louisiana State University Press, 1991. 507 pages.
Genre/literary style/story type: mainstream fiction
As the Chinese economy went into capitalist overdrive in the 1980s, it seems everyone wanted to try their hand at entrepreneurship. Rural villages were no exception. And it is in these rural villages that the effects of capitalist mayhem can best be seen, as age-old traditions are left behind. As some individuals sell their souls for success and profit, they struggle to retain some semblance of humanity. As others battle the corruption of entrenched interests and try to find their own place in the sun, they too must calculate just exactly what they lose and what they gain by adherence to contemporary mores and less-than-ethical practices. This epic novel has received almost unanimous critical acclaim for its portrayal of a village on the cusp of irreversible change.

Subject keywords: rural life; modernization
Original language: Chinese
Sources consulted for annotation:
Amazon.com (book description; review from *Kirkus Reviews*).
Duckworth, Michael. *Asian Wall Street Journal*, 18 October 1991, p. 13.
Library Journal 116 (August 1991): 145.
Publishers Weekly 238 (30 August 1991): 66.
Some other translated books written by Pingwa Jia: *The Heavenly Hound*; *Heavenly Rain*

Rong Jiang (Jiang Rong; pseudonym for Lu Jiamin). *Wolf Totem.*
Translated by Howard Goldblatt. New York: Penguin, 2008. 527 pages.
Genre/literary style/story type: mainstream fiction
This novel was described by Adrienne Clarkson, a former governor general of Canada, as "a passionate argument about the complex interrelationship between nomads and settlers, animals and human beings, nature and culture." As noted by Pankaj Mishra, it focuses on "the education of an intellectual from China's majority Han community living with nomadic herders in the grasslands of Inner Mongolia." Chen Zhen is the intellectual in question, and as he learns more about his environment, the book becomes not only "an indictment of Han imperialism" but also "a guide to the troubled self-images of [the Chinese people] as they stumble, grappling with some inconvenient truths of their own, into modernity."
Subject keyword: rural life
Original language: Chinese
Sources consulted for annotation:
BeijingReview.com.cn (Q&A with Authors), http://www.bjreview.com.cn/books/node_10094.htm.
Mishra, Pankaj. *The New York Times Book Review*, 4 May 2008 (online).

Yong Jin (Louis Cha). *The Deer and the Cauldron: A Martial Arts Novel.*
Translated by John Minford and Rachel May. New York: Oxford University Press, 1997–2002. 3 vols.
Genres/literary styles/story types: historical fiction; epics
As the reviewer on the website YellowBridge observes, Jin Yong is "the unrivaled giant of the modern martial arts (wuxia) genre." First serialized in a Hong Kong newspaper, his 14 novels now appear in this three-volume book, which focuses on the ribald adventures of Trinket during the mid-eighteenth century under the Qing dynasty. The Qing were originally Manchus, a Tartar people, so cabals formed against them, including the Red Flower Society. According to the YellowBridge reviewer, "the book is very much like a typical Hong Kong movie where the movie director has never bothered to decide whether the movie is a comedy or drama, a kung fu spectacular or a tender love story, an uplifting message-filled narrative or horror movie. It is simply all of that and it switches between them at great speed."
Subject keyword: power
Original language: Chinese
Sources consulted for annotation:
Amazon.com (book description).
The Economist 359 (14 April 2001): 80.
YellowBridge.com (book review), http://www.yellowbridge.com.
Some other translated books written by Yong Jin: *The Book and the Sword: A Martial Arts Fox Volant of the Snowy Mountain*; *Heaven Sword & Dragon Sabre*; *The Legendary Couple*

Ang Li (Li Ang). *The Butcher's Wife.*
Translated by Howard Goldblatt and Ellen Yeung. London: Peter Owen, 2003. 142 pages.

Genre/literary style/story type: mainstream fiction; women's lives
Using Taiwan as her setting, the author fictionalizes a murder that occurred in 1930s Shanghai. When her father dies, Lin Shi is forced for economic reasons to marry a brutal pig butcher who delights in the screams of the pigs that he kills as well as those of his wife, whom he viciously rapes on a regular basis. Lin Shi is thus compelled to choose between starving on the streets and putting up with her horrific plight, which becomes even more horrific when her cries of agony during forced sex are interpreted as expressions of selfish sexual pleasure that disturb the community. When she hears this accusation, she pledges total silence, which only serves to increase the wrath of her husband even further. The conclusion is as inevitable as it is gruesome.
Subject keywords: rural life; power
Original language: Chinese
Sources consulted for annotation:
Rogers, Michael. *Library Journal* 128 (15 February 2003): 174.
See, Carolyn. *Los Angeles Times*, 17 November 1986, p. 6.
Solomon, Charles. *Los Angeles Times*, 2 September 1990, p. 14.

Pi-hua Li (Lillian Lee). *Farewell My Concubine* (*Farewell to My Concubine*).
Translated by Andrea Lingenfelter. London: Penguin, 1993. 255 pages.
Genre/literary style/story type: mainstream fiction
Set against the turbulent and violent history of modern China, this novel recounts the relationship of two men—Xiaolou Duan and Dieyi Cheng—who have been trained from childhood to be Peking Opera performers. Xiaolou's physical stature and power destine him for male roles, while Dieyi's talents are more suited for female roles. As the world of opera consumes their lives, Dieyi becomes enamored with Xiaolou. But his feelings are unrequited when Xiaolou falls in love with a prostitute.
Subject keywords: identity; social roles
Original language: Chinese
Sources consulted for annotation:
Li, Cherry W. *Library Journal* 118 (15 October 1993): 89.
Liu, Timothy. *Lambda Book Report* 4 (November 1993): 33.
Steinberg, Sybil S. *Publishers Weekly* 240 (16 August 1993): 88.
Another translated book written by Pi-hua Li: *The Last Princess of Manchuria*

Qiao Li (Li Qiao). *Wintry Night.*
Translated by Taotao Liu and John Balcom. New York: Columbia University Press, 2001. 291 pages.
Genre/literary style/story type: mainstream fiction
This novel, which takes place between 1890 and 1945, chronicles the austere lives of a Chinese family who establishes the village of Fanzai Wood in a mountainous area of Taiwan. As farmers, they must contend with poverty and soul-destroying storms. Later, they must also deal with the complexities of the Japanese occupation, especially when two of the grandchildren of the original settlers are forced to join the Japanese army and sent to the Philippines, where they witness untold horrors.
Subject keyword: family histories
Original language: Chinese
Sources consulted for annotation:
Amazon.com (book description).
Kaske, Michelle. *Booklist* 97 (1 March 2001): 1227.
Kinkley, Jeffrey C. *World Literature Today* 75 (Summer 2001): 130.
Quan, Shirley N. *Library Journal* 126 (15 April 2001): 132.
Steinberg, Sybil S. *Publishers Weekly* 248 (5 February 2001): 66.

Rui Li (Li Rui). ***Silver City.***
Translated by Howard Goldblatt. New York: Metropolitan Books, 1997. 276 pages.
Genre/literary style/story type: mainstream fiction
For over a century, the Li and Bai families have struggled for supremacy in Silver City and control of its salt mines. This book explores every aspect of the prolonged conflict between the two clans. To say the least, it is a seething and violent animosity based on traditional blood and honor codes that reaches a brutal nadir when a majority of the male members of the Li family are executed by a communist firing squad in 1951.
Subject keywords: family histories; politics
Original language: Chinese
Sources consulted for annotation:
Amazon.com (review from *Kirkus Reviews*).
Caso, Frank. *Booklist* 94 (1 November 1997): 455.
Duke, Michael S. *World Literature Today* 73 (Winter 1999): 209.
Steinberg, Sybil S. *Publishers Weekly* 244 (27 October 1997): 54.
Williams, Janis. *Library Journal* 122 (15 October 1997): 92.

Yongping Li (Li Yung-p'ing). ***Retribution: The Jiling Chronicles.***
Translated by Howard Goldblatt and Sylvia Li-chun Lin. New York: Columbia University Press, 2003. 246 pages.
Genres/literary styles/story types: mainstream fiction; women's lives
During an annual festival in the imaginary town of Jiling, Changseng is raped while she is making an offering to a Buddhist deity. Distraught, she commits suicide. Her husband, the local coffin maker, unleashes a thunderclap of furious violence against the loved ones of the rapist. The book is told from multiple perspectives, with each of the townspeople contributing their memories and insights about the tragic events.
Subject keyword: social problems
Original language: Chinese
Sources consulted for annotation:
Amazon.com (book description).
Quan, Shirley N. *Library Journal* 128 (1 November 2003): 124.
Wong, Timothy C. *World Literature Today* 78 (September/December 2004): 85.

Xiaosheng Liang (Liang Xiaosheng). ***Panic and Deaf: Two Modern Satires.***
Translated by Hanming Chen. Honolulu, HI: University of Hawai'i Press, 2001. 157 pages.
Genre/literary style/story type: mainstream fiction
In the first novella, Yao Chungang, whom some critics describe as a Chinese everyman along the lines of Arthur Miller's Willy Loman, cannot cope anymore with the mind-boggling changes of 1990s China—gradually becoming both literally and figuratively impotent. The second novella, which for some critics has evoked Franz Kafka's *The Metamorphosis*, takes place on the day that the protagonist is to be promoted at work. But he wakes up to the baffling reality that he can no longer hear. Undaunted by this bizarre turn of events, he assumes his new position, implementing ridiculous policies whose only purpose is to mask his new disability.
Subject keywords: identity; social roles
Original language: Chinese
Sources consulted for annotation:
Amazon.com (book description).
Berry, Michael. *Persimmon: Asian Literature, Arts, and Culture* (Winter 2002) (applicable URL no longer works).

Wong, Timothy C. *World Literature Today* 75 (Summer 2001): 130.
Another translated book written by Xiaosheng Liang: *The Black Button*

Lianke Yan (Yan Lianke). *Serve the People!*
Translated by Julia Lovell. New York: Black Cat/Grove/Atlantic, 2008. 217 pages.
Genre/literary style/story type: mainstream fiction
This novel is a combination of erotic and satiric fiction. Wu Dawang has memorized all of Mao's writings, and he is also an excellent cook. What additional qualities does a soldier need to get promoted? As Wu begins his new job as the right-hand man of a military commander, he becomes the object of lust of the commander's wife. Blindly obedient, he fulfills all her needs and fantasies, serving the people as best he is able until the unexpected happens. As Liesl Schillinger writes, their "dalliance sometimes reminds the reader (a bit) of Emma Bovary and Rodolphe, playacting at obsession until their game, by accident, turns serious."
Subject keywords: politics; power
Original language: Chinese
Sources consulted for annotation:
Global Books in Print (online) (reviews from *Booklist*, *Library Journal*, and *Publishers Weekly*).
Schillinger, Liesl. *The New York Times Book Review*, 4 May 2008 (online).

Heng Liu (Liu Heng). *Green River Daydreams*.
Translated by Howard Goldblatt. New York: Grove Press, 2001. 332 pages.
Genre/literary style/story type: mainstream fiction
Guanghan Cao, a scion of a wealthy family, returns home after having attended university in France. He brings a French engineer (nicknamed Big Road) with him in order to help him build and operate a match factory. But Guanghan's parents and brother have other plans for him, including marriage to Yunan. Of course, he rebels against traditional strictures and expectations, experiments with explosives, and joins a political rebellion. Tragedy looms when Yunan and Big Road fall in love.
Subject keywords: family histories; politics
Original language: Chinese
Sources consulted for annotation:
Amazon.com (book description).
Cooper, Tom. *Library Journal* 126 (15 June 2001): 104.
Johnston, Bonnie. *Booklist* 97 (1 June/15 June 2001): 1842.
Zaleski, Jeff. *Publishers Weekly* 248 (11 June 2001): 55.
Some other translated books written by Heng Liu: *Black Snow: A Novel of the Beijing Demimonde*; *The Obsessed*

Suola Liu (Liu Sola). *Chaos and All That*.
Translated by Richard King. Honolulu, HI: University of Hawai'i Press, 1994. 134 pages.
Genres/literary styles/story types: mainstream fiction; women's lives
Haha Huang is currently a student in London. In order not to forget her past, she begins a novel recounting her life during the Cultural Revolution, especially its more absurd moments. As a child, she remembers learning how to curse in a specific way so as to gain entry into the Red Guards; the ignominy of communal outhouses; and abstruse ideological debates surrounding the issue of house pets.
Subject keyword: rural life
Original language: Chinese
Sources consulted for annotation:
Bogenschutz, Debbie. *Library Journal* 119 (1 November 1994): 110.

Hassan, Ihab. *World Literature Today* 69 (Spring 1995): 432.
Simson, Maria. *Publishers Weekly* 241 (19 September 1994): 64.
Sullivan, Mary Ellen. *Booklist* 91 (1 November 1994): 477.
Another translated book written by Suola Liu: *Blue Sky Green Sea and Other Stories*

Jian Ma (Ma Jian). *The Noodle Maker.*
Translated by Flora Drew. New York: Farrar, Straus and Giroux, 2005. 181 pages.
Genre/literary style/story type: mainstream fiction
In a dystopian world where the government keeps close tabs on citizens' private lives in a bid to control both their deeds and thoughts, absurdity reigns: an entrepreneur opens an illegal crematorium; an actress performs a suicidal act onstage; and a painter loses his creativity through a dog's incantation. These bizarre episodes are recounted by Sheng to his friend Vlazerim, who makes money from selling his blood, over dinner and drinks in a claustrophobic Beijing apartment. The novel is a biting satire that calls to mind the work of Gao Xingjian, Nikolai Gogol, Pedro Juan Gutiérrez, and Italo Calvino.
Related title by the same author:
Readers may also wish to explore *Beijing Coma*, which focuses on Dai Wei, who lies in a coma in his mother's apartment after being injured during the Tiananmen Square revolutionary incident. He recalls the serpentine path of his life, which has run alongside many important historical events in the latter half of the twentieth century.
Subject keywords: politics; power
Original language: Chinese
Sources consulted for annotation:
Publishers Weekly. 251 (22 November 2004): 37.
Row, Jess. *The New York Times Book Review*, 13 July 2008 (online).
Seaman, Donna. *Booklist* 101 (1 January/15 January): 819.
Tepper, Anderson. *The New York Times Book Review*, 27 March 2005, p. 23.
Welin, Joel. *Sarasota Herald Tribune*, 3 April 2005, p. E4.
Some other translated books written by Jian Ma: *Beijing Coma*; *Stick Out Your Tongue*

Mian Mian. *Candy.*
Translated by Andrea Lingenfelter. Boston: Little, Brown, 2003. 279 pages.
Genres/literary styles/story types: mainstream fiction; coming-of-age
Sex, alcoholism, drugs, prostitution, dysfunctional relationships, and AIDS are key elements of this book. Hong, a 19-year-old high school dropout, flees Shanghai and makes her way to a free economic zone in pursuit of her dream of becoming a writer. But things do not work out as planned. Compelled to work as a prostitute, she begins a dissolute life and starts a hopeless relationship with Saining, a guitarist. Hong is a poster child of the generation that came of age in the late 1980s and early 1990s: lost, confused, and yearning for human kindness, freedom, and truth. This novel was banned by the Chinese government.
Subject keyword: social problems
Original language: Chinese
Sources consulted for annotation:
Areddy, Jim. *Far Eastern Economic Review* 167 (5 February 2004): 48.
Peiffer, Prudence. *Library Journal* 128 (15 May 2003): 126.
Zaleski, Jeff. *Publishers Weekly* 250 (26 May 2003): 46.

Yan Mo (Mo Yan). *The Republic of Wine.*
Translated by Howard Goldblatt. New York: Arcade, 2000. 355 pages.

Genres/literary styles/story types: mainstream fiction; magical realism

In this highly inventive phantasmagoria, a fictitious Chinese province called Liquorland is plagued by promiscuity, drunkenness, and cannibalism. Violence and debauchery assume such outrageous proportions that a special investigator, Ding Gou'er, is sent from Beijing to investigate. But Ding is dragged into the very depths of alcoholism, depravity, and depraved sex that he is supposed to examine. Part of the novel is presented as correspondence between an esteemed writer, Mo Yan, and a graduate student delving into the gritty details of cannibalism. As the plot unfolds, the real and the imaginary increasingly blur.

Related title by the same author:

Readers may also enjoy *Life and Death Are Wearing Me Out*, in which the five narrators are animal reincarnations of Ximen Nao, a young landowner murdered by an enraged zealot during the first stages of the communist revolution. As Jonathan Spence points out, the book is "a kind of documentary" that begins at the end of the Chinese Civil War, sweeps through the dislocations of the Cultural Revolution, and concludes with the triumph of capitalist principles.

Subject keywords: politics; urban life

Original language: Chinese

Sources consulted for annotation:

The Economist 359 (14 April 2001): 80.

Spence, Jonathan. *The New York Times Book Review*, 4 May 2008 (online).

Steinberg, Sybil S. *Publishers Weekly* 247 (27 March 2000): 53.

Some other translated books written by Yan Mo: *Red Sorghum: A Novel of China*; *Big Breasts and Wide Hips*; *Shifu, You'll Do Anything for a Laugh*; *Life and Death Are Wearing Me Out*; *Explosions and Other Stories*; *The Garlic Ballads*

Hualing Nie (Hualing Nieh). *Mulberry and Peach: Two Women of China.*

Translated by Jane Parish Yang with Linda Lappin. New York: Feminist Press at the City University of New York, 1998. 231 pages.

Genres/literary styles/story types: mainstream fiction; women's lives

After experiencing numerous political and social upheavals in the China in the period from 1940–1970, Helen Mulberry Sang flees to the United States. But life is strange and alienating in her new country, so she develops a persona, called Peach, to help her cope. While Peach does everything to integrate into the American mainstream, Mulberry resists. The book alternates between Peach's thoughts—contained in a letter to an immigration officer whom she is trying to outwit—and diary entries made by Mulberry.

Subject keywords: culture conflict; social problems

Original language: Chinese

Sources consulted for annotation:

Amazon.com (book description).

Kaganoff, Penny. *Publishers Weekly* 234 (28 October 1988): 72.

Ofstedal, Julie. *Review-Fiction*, http://voices.cla.umn.edu.

Some other translated books written by Hualing Nie: *Eight Stories by Chinese Women*; *The Purse, and Three Other Stories of Chinese Life*

Anyi Wang (Wang Anyi). *The Song of Everlasting Sorrow: A Novel of Shanghai.*

Translated by Michael Berry and Susan Chan Egan. New York: Columbia University Press, 2008. 440 pages.

Genre/literary style/story type: mainstream fiction

This novel follows the life of Wang Qiyao, a young woman whose photo appeared on a magazine cover and who was subsequently one of the runner-ups in a beauty contest. Her social ascent

continues as the mistress of a wealthy man, but after he dies, she experiences a rude fall, drifting anonymously through the few remaining tumbledown and labyrinthine old neighborhoods of Shanghai. As the city gradually takes on a modern and futuristic architectural garb and as it razes the chaotic longtang and replaces them with gleaming towers, the novel thoughtfully considers—in the words of Francine Prose—"the question of what endures and what remains the same," being "particularly illuminating and incisive on the subject of female friendship, on what draws girls and women together and then drives them apart."
Subject keywords: modernization; urban life
Original language: Chinese
Sources consulted for annotation:
Global Books in Print (online) (review from *Publishers Weekly*).
Prose, Francine. *The New York Times Book Review*, 4 May 2008 (online).

Shuo Wang (Wang Shuo). *Please Don't Call Me Human.*
Translated by Howard Goldblatt. New York: Hyperion, 2000. 289 pages.
Genre/literary style/story type: mainstream fiction
Faced with dispiriting losses during a recent Olympics, China is determined to find a new hero to restore its sports glory. Thus, a National Mobilization Committee is formed to identify the next big thing. The hero-to-be is someone named Tang Yuanbao, a pedi-cab driver descended from a former boxing legend, who is still alive at the venerable age of 111. Under the watchful eye of the Committee, Tang is completely transformed, readied, and packaged for his expected date with fame and glory. Will he become the long-sought-after champion and, if so, at what cost? The author has been compared with Jack Kerouac and William Burroughs, among others. This novel was banned in China.
Subject keywords: politics; power
Original language: Chinese
Sources consulted for annotation:
The Economist 359 (14 April 2001): 80.
Steinberg, Sybil S. *Publishers Weekly* 247 (19 June 2000): 60.
Some other translated books written by Shuo Wang: *Playing for Thrills*; *The Troubleshooters*

Xi Xi. *Marvels of a Floating City and Other Stories.*
Translated by Eva Hung, John and Esther Dent-Young. Hong Kong: Research Centre for Translation, Chinese University of Hong Kong, 1997. 106 pages.
Genres/literary styles/story types: mainstream fiction; short stories
Each of the three stories in this collection limns the 1997 political transition in Hong Kong from British to Chinese rule. The first story is about the paintings of René Magritte and their connection to Hong Kong. The second story is a surrealist tale of a town that almost overnight becomes a mighty pillar of economic growth. The final story is a modern version of the ancient Chinese play *Circle of Chalk*, where two women go to court to determine which of them is the mother of a child.
Subject keyword: modernization
Original language: Chinese
Sources consulted for annotation:
Amazon.com (book description).
Kinkley, Jeffrey C. *World Literature Today* 72 (Spring 1998): 455.
Some other translated books written by Xi Xi: *A Girl Like Me, and Other Stories*; *Flying Carpet: A Tale of Fertillia*

Lihong Xiao (Hsiao Li-Hung). *A Thousand Moons on a Thousand Rivers.*
Translated by Michelle Wu. New York: Columbia University Press, 2000. 304 pages.

Genre/literary style/story type: mainstream fiction
In 1970s Taiwan, the winds of change are almost gale-force. As agriculture gives way to industrialization and as traditional Buddhist values and ethics fight to retain a place in a materialistic onslaught, Zhenguan and Daxin, childhood sweethearts, struggle with their feelings, become disillusioned, and affirm their enduring love.
Subject keyword: modernization
Original language: Chinese
Sources consulted for annotation:
Donald, Colin. *The Herald*, 4 April 2000, p. 18.
Williams, Philip F. C. *World Literature Today* 74 (Summer 2000): 580.

Xinran. *Sky Burial: An Epic Love Story of Tibet*.
Translated by Julia Lovell and Esther Tyldesley. New York: Nan A. Talese/Doubleday, 2005. 206 pages.
Genres/literary styles/story types: historical fiction; literary historical
In 1958, a few weeks after their wedding, Shu Wen's husband Kejun joins the People's Liberation Army and departs for Tibet on a unification mission. Soon afterward, he is reported killed in unknown circumstances, and Shu Wen makes a pilgrimage to Tibet, determined to uncover the truth. She spends three decades there, unearthing unsettling facts about her husband and how he fell victim to a clash of cultures. Shu Wen returns to China in the 1990s but finds it alien, distant, and drenched in political and social chaos. Her journey has brought her neither peace nor closure.
Subject keywords: culture conflict; social problems
Original language: Chinese
Sources consulted for annotation:
Amazon.com (book description).
Calhoun, Ada. *The New York Times Book Review*, 14 August 2005, p. 14.
Publishers Weekly 252 (16 May 2005): 34.
Seaman, Donna. *Booklist* 101 (July 2005): 1903.

Geling Yan. *The Lost Daughter of Happiness*.
Translated by Cathy Silber. New York: Hyperion East, 2001. 288 pages.
Genres/literary styles/story types: historical fiction; literary historical
Based on a true story, this novel tells about how Fusang is kidnapped and made to work as a prostitute in San Francisco's Gold Rush Era. She is extremely popular—eventually attracting the attention of the gangster Ah Ding, who steals her away. As they try to outrun their tangled pasts, they must steer a course through the treacherous currents of a Chinatown that is a cauldron of animosity and violence.
Related title by the same author:
Readers may also be interested in *The Uninvited*, which takes place in the turbocharged world of Chinese economic expansion. Dan manages to keep body and soul together by gate-crashing government banquets for the free food available there. But his placid life is overturned when he inadvertently stumbles upon political corruption.
Subject keyword: social problems
Original language: Chinese
Sources consulted for annotation:
Gambone, Philip. *The New York Times Book Review*, 13 May 2001 (online).
Global Books in Print (online) (reviews from *Library Journal* and *Publishers Weekly* for *The Lost Daughter of Happiness*; synopsis/book jacket for *The Uninvited*).
Another translated book written by Geling Yan: *The Uninvited*

Hua Yu (Yu Hua). *Brothers*.
Translated by Eileen Chow and Carlos Rojas. New York: Pantheon, 2009. 656 pages.
Genre/literary style/story type: mainstream fiction
This sprawling novel is nothing less than a social and cultural history of contemporary China from the 1960s to the first decade of the twentieth century. It encompasses such key events as Mao Zedong's Cultural Revolution, which began in 1966, as well as the years of gung ho and ultimately savage entrepreneurship when China opened itself up to Western-style capitalism. The two emblematic figures of the book are Li Guangtou and his half-brother Song Gang, whose fates wildly diverge as the social and economic underpinnings of China shift. Where Li Guangtou is a risk-taking, gregarious, and boastful rebel, Song Gang is a humble, taciturn, and law-abiding citizen who is content with very little. The opening pages of the novel reveal Li Guangtou's character: In a rudimentary and communal latrine where only a thin partition separates the women's section from the men's, he is caught trying to sneak a peek at the nether regions of women by extending his body as far down into the nausea-inducing pit as possible. He claims to have gotten a good glimpse of Lin Hong, who is reputed to be the town's most beautiful young woman. But when Li Guangtou sets out to try and conquer her heart, she flatly rejects him, choosing instead to marry Song Gang because of his steadiness and loyalty. Lin Hong's rejection of Li Guangtou is one of the factors that inspires him to become a successful businessman with far-flung interests. His fortune and influence grows —a mirror image of the rollicking excesses and economic power that characterized China in the late 1990s and early 2000s. Meanwhile, Song Gang and Lin Hong stagnate—the former losing his job and his health; the latter stuck in an old-fashioned factory whose director makes lecherous advances. Their loving and idyllic life, symbolized by the once-prestigious gleaming bicycle on which Song Gang took Lin Hong to work each day, is now a mere nothing in comparison with the westernized lifestyles of their affluent neighbors, with their designer clothes and technological marvels. Li Guangtou's riches keep multiplying, reaching unprecedented heights when he decides to organize a beauty contest for virgins. As the town becomes the center of international attention, it is invaded not only by thousands of women claiming to be virgins but also by a series of charlatans who offer artificial hymens. Easy money is made by one and all—except an increasingly frustrated and pensive Song Gang, who realizes that Lin Hong deserves better. Thus, in an attempt to make money for Lin Hong, he sets out on a cross-country odyssey, trying to sell penis- and breast-enhancing creams. With Song Gang gone, his wife finally succumbs to the advances of Li Guangtou, laying the groundwork for a tragic denouement when Song Gang returns.
Related titles by the same author:
Readers may also enjoy *To Live!*, which focuses on Fugui, a carefree young husband and father with a penchant for other women. But Fugui's insouciant life quickly turns tragic as almost everyone in his immediate and extended family dies. Also noteworthy may be *Cries in the Drizzle*, which takes up many of the same themes as *Brothers*, focusing on provincial life in 1970s China.
Subject keywords: family histories; politics
Original language: Chinese
Sources consulted for annotation:
Global Books in Print (online) (reviews for all novels except *Brothers* from *Booklist*, *Library Journal*, and *Publishers Weekly*).
Mishra, Pankaj. *The New York Times Magazine*, 25 January 2009 (online).
Some other translated books written by Hua Yu: *Cries in the Drizzle*; *Chronicle of a Blood Merchant*; *To Live!*

Ailing Zhang (Eileen Chang). *Lust, Caution: The Story*.
Translated by Julia Lovell. New York: Anchor Books, 2007. 68 pages.
Genres/literary styles/story types: thrillers; political thrillers

Set in World War II Shanghai during its occupation by the Japanese, this noir novel features Jiazhi, a student activist, whose undercover job it is to bring about the death of Mr. Yi, a prominent member of the occupational government. Will her feelings for Yi prevent her from achieving her task?
Subject keywords: social problems; urban life
Original language: Chinese
Sources consulted for annotation:
Amazon.com (book description).
Dupuy, Claire. *Birmingham Post*, 5 January 2008, p. 18.
Some other translated books written by Ailing Zhang: *Traces of Love and Other Stories*; *The Rice-Sprout Song*; *Naked Earth: A Novel About China*; *Love in a Fallen City*; *The Rouge of the North*

Dachun Zhang (Chang Ta-Chun). ***Wild Kids: Two Novels About Growing Up.***
Translated by Michael Berry. New York: Columbia University Press, 2000. 255 pages.
Genres/literary styles/story types: mainstream fiction; coming-of-age
This collection of stories focuses on streetwise and consumerist Taiwanese adolescents whose disdain for family and teachers is viscerally palpable. The first story describes the friendship between a brother and sister as they plot and scheme to make their way through a shape-shifting urban landscape. In the second story, 14-year-old Hou Shichun, a school dropout, runs away from home—only to find himself involved in the chaotic life of a Taipei gang. Critics have found echoes of J. D. Salinger and Grace Paley in these stories.
Subject keyword: urban life
Original language: Chinese
Sources consulted for annotation:
The Economist 359 (14 April 2001): 80.
Gordon, Emily. *Newsday*, 17 September 2000, p. B14.
McLane, Maureen. *The New York Times Book Review*, 17 September 2000, p. 25.
Steinberg, Sybil S. *Publishers Weekly* 247 (31 July 2000): 66.

Jie Zhang (Zhang Jie). ***As Long as Nothing Happens, Nothing Will.***
Translated by Gladys Yang, Deborah J. Leonard, and Zhang Andong. New York: Grove Weidenfeld, 1991. 196 pages.
Genres/literary styles/story types: mainstream fiction; short stories
The absurdities of the bureaucratic mindset are deliciously exposed in this collection of stories. In a dysfunctional hospital, patients waiting for life-saving surgery die because elevators are out of order; nurses suffer from anemia; and doctors have enuresis. In another story, a tour leader and a professor have stark differences of opinion about the priority that should be given to an individual's need to use the bathroom. In a third story, culture elites exploit a naïve rural artist.
Subject keyword: social problems
Original language: Chinese
Sources consulted for annotation:
Amazon.com (review from *Kirkus Reviews*).
Campbell, Don G. *Los Angeles Times*, 4 August 1991, p. 6.
Cudar, David. W. *St. Petersburg Times*, 28 July 1991, p. 7D.
Steinberg, Sybil S. *Publishers Weekly* 238 (31 May 1991): 58.
Some other translated books written by Jie Zhang: *Heavy Wings*; *Love Must Not Be Forgotten*

Wei Zhang (Zhang Wei). ***The Ancient Ship.***
Translated by Howard Goldblatt. New York: HarperCollins, 2008. 451 pages.
Genre/literary style/story type: historical fiction

This novel focuses on three families in the town of Wali, chronicling their intertwined and tragic stories and thus recounting the multifaceted sweep of Chinese history after 1949. As reform, counterreform, and modernization movements transform daily life for everyone in Wali, the undercurrents and underside of the town are revealed.
Subject keywords: family histories; rural life
Original language: Chinese
Source consulted for annotation:
Global Books in Print (online) (product description; review from *Booklist*).

Qingwen Zheng (Cheng Ch'ing-wen). *Three-Legged Horse.*
Translated Carlos G. Tee and others. New York: Columbia University Press, 1999. 225 pages.
Genres/literary styles/story types: mainstream fiction; short stories
Set in Taiwan during the twentieth century, these stories deal with universal human suffering and affliction: alienation, lack of self-confidence, threatening authority, unhappy love, separation, and selfishness. In one story, a young female university lecturer with a malformed hand draws strength and comfort from coconut palms. In another story, a despotic matriarch who lost her husband at age 38 orders her daughters-in-law not to sleep with their husbands until they reach the same age. In a third story, a former Japanese collaborator comes to terms with his past by carving three-legged horses as he awaits death.
Subject keyword: social roles
Original language: Chinese
Sources consulted for annotation:
Cao, Guanlong. *The New York Times Book Review*, 7 March 1999, p. 15.
Chen Dean, Kitty. *Library Journal* 124 (January 1999): 161.
Columbia University Press (book review), http://cup.columbia.edu.
Spinella, Michael. *Booklist* 95 (15 December 1998): 724.
Steinberg, Sybil S. *Publishers Weekly* 245 (9 November 1998): 57.

Tianwen Zhu (Chu T'ien Wen). *Notes of a Desolate Man.*
Translated by Howard Goldblatt and Sylvia Li-chun Lin. New York: Columbia University Press, 1999. 169 pages.
Genre/literary style/story type: mainstream fiction
Shao is a 40-year-old Taiwanese gay man whose friend Ah Yao recently died of AIDS in Tokyo. Together with his lover Yongjie, he copes as best he can with the omnipresent specter of death, trying to conjure away pain, bleakness, and desolation by the act of writing.
Subject keywords: identity; social roles
Original language: Chinese
Sources consulted for annotation:
Kinkleym Jeffrey C. *World Literature Today* 74 (Winter 2000): 234.
Olson, Ray. *Booklist* 95 (1 June/15 June 1999): 1785.
Steinberg, Sybil S. *Publishers Weekly* 246 (24 May 1999): 66.

ANNOTATIONS FOR TRANSLATED BOOKS FROM JAPAN

Kobo Abe. *Kangaroo Notebook.*
Translated by Maryellen Toman Mori. New York: Alfred A. Knopf, 1996. 183 pages.
Genre/literary style/story type: speculative fiction
The author is well-known for his surreal and nihilistic perspectives on Japanese society. His work has been compared with that of the filmmaker David Lynch. In this novel, radishes begin to sprout

from a man's legs, and things only get worse when he goes to the hospital to solve this perplexing dilemma. His hospital bed, which has a mind of its own, takes him on a trip to what appears to be hell, where he meets a motley assortment of depraved individuals.

Related titles by the same author:

Readers may also enjoy *The Ark Sakura*, which focuses on an outcast who constructs what he perceives to be an impregnable fortress in an abandoned quarry. He is a survivalist, and like all survivalists, he is convinced that the apocalypse is coming. Thus, his next task is to select the handful of individuals who will ride out the coming storm in his shelter. Also of interest may be *The Woman in the Dunes*, where a man is tricked into living and working with a woman who lives at the bottom of an escape-proof sandpit. Endlessly shoveling sand, he eventually reconciles himself to his fate. *The Woman in The Dunes* may profitably be read in conjunction with Paul Auster's *The Music of Chance*, where two gamblers who have lost a debt to a pair of eccentric millionaires agree to build a totally useless wall out of a seemingly never-ending heap of gargantuan stones. Eventually, they begin to consider themselves as indentured servants.

Subject keywords: identity; social roles

Original language: Japanese

Sources consulted for annotation:

Amazon.com (book description; review from *Kirkus Reviews*).

Dean, Kitty Chen. *Library Journal* 121 (1 April 1996): 114.

Graeber, Laurel. *The New York Times Book Review*, 24 August 1997, p. 24.

Iwamoto, Yoskio. *World Literature Today* 71 (Winter 1997): 228.

Pearl, Nancy. *Booklist* 92 (15 April 1996): 1419.

Steinberg, Sybil S. *Publishers Weekly* 243 (11 March 11 1996): 44.

White, Edmund. *The New York Times Book Review*, 10 April 1988 (online).

Some other translated books written by Kobo Abe: *The Box Man*; *Inter Ice Age 4*; *Beyond the Curve*; *The Ruined Map*; *The Woman in the Dunes*; *The Ark Sakura*; *The Face of Another*; *Secret Rendezvous*

Hiroyuki Agawa. *The Citadel in Spring: A Novel of Youth Spent at War.*

Translated by Lawrence Rogers. Tokyo: Kodansha International, 1990. 254 pages.

Genres/literary styles/story types: mainstream fiction; coming-of-age

Koji Obata works as a cryptographer for the Japanese navy. While stationed in China, he reads in a newspaper that Hiroshima has been destroyed. When he returns, almost all his family is dead, and he enters a nightmarish landscape where bleakness and violence are the normal state of affairs.

Subject keyword: war

Original language: Japanese

Sources consulted for annotation:

Samuel, Yoshiko Yokochi. *The Journal of Asian Studies* 50 (November 1990): 949.

Steinberg, Sybil S. *Publishers Weekly* 237 (30 November 1990): 56.

Some other translated books written by Hiroyuki Agawa: *Devil's Heritage*; *Burial in the Clouds*

Shinya Arai (Arai Shinya). *Shoshaman: A Tale of Corporate Japan.*

Translated by Chieko Mulhern. Berkeley, CA: University of California Press, 1991. 224 pages.

Genre/literary style/story type: mainstream fiction

This is an example of what the Japanese call a "business novel." Michio Nakasato has worked his way up the corporate ladder, but at what cost? He meets a former lover who has become successful as a self-employed businesswoman—all the while raising a child whom he discovers is his own. Thus, the inevitable soul-searching crisis occurs. Has Michio wasted his life? Is he an unimaginative

and robotic drone? Has Japanese society made him the man he is, and can he do anything about it now?
Subject keywords: identity; social problems
Original language: Japanese
Sources consulted for annotation:
Amazon.com (book description).
Goff, Janet. *Japan Quarterly* 39 (April 1992): 272.
Kaganoff, Penny. *Publishers Weekly* 238 (10 May 1991): 276.

Sawako Ariyoshi. *Kabuki Dancer.*
Translated by James R. Brandon. Tokyo: Kodansha International, 2001. 348 pages.
Genres/literary styles/story types: historical fiction; literary historical
This novel explores the history of Kabuki theater through the personal story of Okuri, her family, dance troupe, and lovers. The history of the late sixteenth and early seventeenth century—with its violence, political machinations, and social upheaval—is a vivid presence in this book.
Subject keyword: social problems
Original language: Japanese
Sources consulted for annotation:
Amazon.com (book description; reviews from *Kirkus Reviews* and *Publishers Weekly*).
Parker, Patricia L. *World Literature Today* 69 (Spring 1995): 437.
Woodhouse, Mark. *Library Journal* 119 (1 May 1994): 135.
Some other translated books written by Sawako Ariyoshi: *The Twilight Years*; *The Doctor's Wife*; *The River Ki*

Shunshin Chin (Chin Shunshin). *The Taiping Rebellion.*
Translated by Joshua A. Fogel. Armonk, NY: M. E. Sharpe, 2001. 713 pages.
Genre/literary style/story type: historical fiction
Set in nineteenth-century China, this novel focuses on the Qing dynasty and the rebellion against it by the Society of God Worshippers. Lian Weicai, a powerful Chinese merchant, encourages his son to join the uprising. The book is rich in cultural, social, and political detail about the period in question.
Subject keywords: politics; power
Original language: Japanese
Sources consulted for annotation:
Cooper, Tom. *Library Journal* 125 (1 September 2000): 248.
Reference and Research Book News 16 (May 2001) (from Proquest databases).
Another translated book written by Shunshin Chin: *Murder in a Peking Studio*

Shusaku Endo. *Deep River.*
Translated by Van C. Gessel. New York: New Directions, 1994. 216 pages.
Genre/literary style/story type: mainstream fiction
A group of Japanese tourists—each in their own way wounded spiritually or psychologically—travels to India. Kiguchi, plagued by nightmarish memories of his participation in the failed Japanese invasion of a remote part of eastern India in 1944 during World War II, wishes to pay homage to his fallen comrades. Isobe, who failed to love his wife while she was alive, seeks her reincarnation in the hope of making amends. Numada, a tuberculosis survivor, explores the spiritual succor that his relationship with animals has given him. Mitsuko, who failed to seduce a young priest while in college, searches for him among the poor and dying in Varanasi.

Subject keywords: culture conflict; religion
Original language: Japanese
Sources consulted for annotation:
Harris, Michael. *Los Angeles Times*, 22 May 1995, p. 4.
Hutchison, Paul E. *Library Journal* 120 (15 February 1995): 180.
Schenk, Leslie. *World Literature Today* 70 (Winter 1996): 240.
Seaman, Donna. *Booklist* 91 (15 March 1995): 1307.
Some other translated books written by Shusaku Endo: *The Samurai*; *Wonderful Fool*; *Scandal*; *Volcano*; *Foreign Studies*; *The Final Martyrs*; *The Girl I Left Behind*; *Silence*; *When I Whistle*; *Song of Sadness*; *The Golden Country*

Meisei Goto. *Shot by Both Sides.*
Translated by Tom Gill. Oxford: Counterpoint Press, 2008. 224 pages.
Genre/literary style/story type: mainstream fiction
This novel focuses on middle-aged Akaki, an exile from North Korea now living near Soka, Japan. But the past is all-powerful, and Akaki undertakes a journey back to North Korea, recalling the seminal events that compelled his family to flee, visiting friends and neighbors, in the process always keeping an eye out for the talismanic coat that was a constant companion of his youth.
Subject keyword: family histories
Original language: Japanese
Source consulted for annotation:
Global Books in Print (online) (review from *Publishers Weekly*).

Natsuki Ikezawa. *A Burden of Flowers.*
Translated by Alfred Birnbaum. Tokyo: Kodansha International, 2001. 280 pages.
Genres/literary styles/story types: crime fiction; suspense
Two siblings leave Japan and their less-than-fulfilling home life to carve out futures for themselves elsewhere. Tetsuro Nishijima, a heroin addict struggling to stay sober, is framed by police in Bali, Indonesia, and arrested on a serious drug charge. Fearing execution, he struggles to retain his sanity as Kaoru, his sister, who has taken up residence in Paris, rushes to help her brother.
Subject keyword: family histories
Original language: Japanese
Sources consulted for annotation:
Amazon.com (book description).
Wilkinson, Joanne. *Booklist* 98 (15 December 2001): 704.
Woods, Paula L. *Los Angeles Times*, 28 February 2002, p. E3.
Zaleski, Jeff. *Publishers Weekly* 249 (14 January 2002): 40.
Another translated book written by Natsuki Ikezawa: *Still Lives*

Otohiko Kaga. *Riding the East Wind.*
Translated by Ian Hideo Levy. Tokyo: Kodansha International, 1999. 454 pages.
Genre/literary style/story type: historical fiction
This novel focuses on the failed diplomacy leading up to Japan's attack on Pearl Harbor. Ken Kurushima's parents are Alice, an American, and Saburo Kurushima, a Japanese diplomat who is patterned after Saburo Kurusu, a U.S. envoy who unwittingly became part of a ploy by the Japanese government to hide its plan of attack. Thus, Ken—who is now a Japanese fighter pilot—has to face painful choices in every aspect of his life as a soldier and man.
Subject keyword: family histories
Original language: Japanese

Sources consulted for annotation:
Amazon.com (book description; review from *Kirkus Reviews*).
Cooper, Tom. *Library Journal* 124 (December 1999): 187.
Highbridge, Dianne. *The New York Times Book Review*, 5 December 1999, p. 45.
Hoover, Danise. *Booklist* 96 (15 October. 1999): 420.
Japan Quarterly 47 (January/March 2000): 107.
Samuel, Yoshiko Yokochi. *World Literature Today* 74 (Spring 2000): 358.
Steinberg, Sybil S. *Publishers Weekly* 246 (27 September 1999): 69.

Takeshi Kaiko. *Five Thousand Runaways*.
Translated by Cecilia Segawa Seigle. New York: Dodd, Mead & Co., 1987. 191 pages.
Genre/literary style/story type: mainstream fiction
In the title story, a run-of-the-mill middle-aged businessman from Tokyo who has never done anything unpredictable or outlandish in his life suddenly disappears. In another story, an AWOL Vietnamese soldier chooses complete social isolation instead of subservience to a degrading and alienating conformity. Turning their backs on rigid social straitjackets, the author's protagonists are committed to individuality and freedom.
Subject keywords: identity; social roles
Original language: Japanese
Sources consulted for annotation:
Meras, Phyllis. *Providence Journal*, 27 September 1987, p. I7.
Steinberg, Sybil S. *Publishers Weekly* 232 (28 August 1987): 66.
Some other translated books written by Takeshi Kaiko: *Into a Black Sun*; *Darkness in Summer*; *Panic and the Runaway: Two Stories*

Hitomi Kanehara. *Snakes and Earrings*.
Translated by David James Karashima. New York: Dutton, 2005. 120 pages.
Genres/literary styles/story types: mainstream fiction; coming-of-age
This novel has been compared with *Less Than Zero* by Bret Easton Ellis and *Trainspotting* by Irvine Welsh. It depicts the violence and haunting bleakness at the core of Japan's youth culture through the story of 19-year-old Lui and her lover, Ama, as they face starvation, sexual exploitation, and desolation among the squalid circumstances of big-city life.
Subject keywords: social problems; urban life
Original language: Japanese
Sources:
Amazon.com (*Audiofile*; book description).
Karbo, Karen. *Entertainment Weekly*, 27 May 2005, p. 146.
Olson, Ray. *Booklist* 101 (15 April 2005): 1432.
Peiffer, Prudence. *Library Journal* 130 (15 March 2005): 72.

Natsuo Kirino. *Out*.
Translated by Stephen Snyder. New York: Random House, 2005. 416 pages.
Genres/literary styles/story types: crime fiction; urban fiction
Yayoi works the night shift at a factory that makes box lunches. After strangling Kenji—her abusive husband who has squandered much of their money gambling and philandering at Tokyo nightclubs—she turns to three of her female factory colleagues for help—Masako, Kuniko, and Yoshie—all of whom are caught in tenuous personal circumstances of their own. With Masako taking the lead, the three women dismember and dispose of Kenji's body, but after the body parts are unexpectedly discovered, the police arrest Satake, the yakuza-connected owner of the clubs Kenji had been frequenting.

Satake is none too pleased because his arrest ruins his businesses. Once released, he embarks on a doomed yet frightful course of spiraling revenge, killing Kuniko and engaging in a terrifying psychological duel with Masako, who in the meantime has decided to go into the business of dismembering other dead corpses that members of the Japanese underworld wish to dispose of. *Out* has been compared with the works of Edgar Allan Poe, Nikolai Gogol, and Fyodor Dostoyevsky, especially *Crime and Punishment*. Adjectives such as stark, macabre, bleak, gruesome, grisly, and disturbing are commonly used to describe this book. Some critics mention that Kirino's moral vision is steeped in such writers as Jean-Paul Sartre and Simone de Beauvoir. Despite its persistently dark overtones, graphic violence, and sado-masochistic elements, *Out* is almost unanimously referred to as a noir masterpiece—for its inventive plot, psychological insights, and withering look at corrosive political and economic institutions.

Related titles by the same author:

The author's 2008 novel *Real World* continues the noir tradition: The protagonist kills for philosophical reasons. When Worm, a high school student, murders his mother, he becomes a hero in a Japan obsessed by success and consumer goods. As Kathryn Harrison notes, Kirino's favorite American author is Flannery O'Connor, and she thus provides readers with "a tour through the grotesque and the extreme"—in the process, outdoing Dostoyevsky in the creation of an austere moral universe. Also of interest may be *Grotesque*, which centers on the murder of two aging prostitutes in Tokyo and recounts their inexorable decline from their youthful hopes and dreams. Readers who appreciate Kirino's vision may also wish to explore the works of Miyuki Miyabe.

Subject keywords: social problems; urban life

Original language: Japanese

Sources consulted for annotation:

Bissy, Carrie. *Booklist* 99 (July 2003): 1870.

Cannon, Peter. *Publishers Weekly* 250 (26 May 2003): 52.

Harrison, Kathryn. *The New York Times Book Review*, 20 July 2008, pp. 1, 10.

Harrison, Sophie. *The New York Times Book Review*, 15 April 2007 (online).

Samul, Ron. *Library Journal* 128 (15 June 2003): 101.

Tate, Greg. *The Village Voice*, 17 September/23 September 2003, p. 97.

Wolff, Katherine. *The New York Times Book Review*, 17 August 2003, p. 16.

Some other translated books written by Natsuo Kirino: *Grotesque*; *Soft Cheeks*; *Real World*

Morio Kita (pseudonym). *Ghosts*.

Translated by Dennis Keene. Tokyo: Kodansha International, 1991. 193 pages.

Genres/literary styles/story types: mainstream fiction; coming-of-age

This is the story of an anonymous protagonist who embarks on a search for all that he has lost. His father and sister have died; his mother leaves him in the care of relatives; he has few possessions. Thus, he finds grace and inner peace by collecting insects and climbing mountains. This essentially plotless book has been compared to the work of Marcel Proust in the way that random moments and everyday events trigger larger epiphanies.

Subject keyword: family histories

Original language: Japanese

Sources consulted for annotation:

Amazon.com (book description; review from *Kirkus Reviews*).

Keane, Kevin. *Japan Quarterly* 39 (April 1992): 259.

Perushek, D. E. *Library Journal* 117 (1 March 1992): 117.

Schoenberger, Karl. *Los Angeles Times*, 22 March 1992, p. BR2.

Steinberg, Sybil S. *Publishers Weekly* 238 (13 December 1991): 46.

Some other translated books written by Morio Kita: *The House of Nire*; *The Adventures of Kupukupu the Sailor*

Kenzo Kitakata. ***Ashes.***
Translated by Emi Shimokawa. New York: Vertical, 2003. 224 pages.
Genres/literary styles/story types: crime fiction; urban fiction
This book is in the tradition of Japanese gangster novels. The yakuza Tanaka is beset on all sides. One of the main leaders of the criminal syndicate is dying, so Tanaka must take proactive measures to strengthen his place in the underworld, lest he be swept away by the violent convulsions that are sure to shake the foundations of his criminal milieu.
Related titles by the same author:
Readers may also enjoy *The City of Refuge*, which centers on Koji, whose love for a woman leads him to series of murders and even to kidnapping. Also of interest may be *The Cage*, in which Takino—a former yakuza now managing a supermarket—is convinced to help others escape the mob's influence. Noteworthy too is *Winter Sleep*, in which a former prison inmate turned painter attempts to teach an escaped prisoner the beauties of art.
Subject keyword: urban life
Original language: Japanese
Sources consulted for annotation:
Global Books in Print (online) (reviews from *Library Journal* for *Ashes*; synopsis/book jackets).
Vertical Press (book descriptions for *Ashes*, *The Cage*, and *Winter Sleep*), http://www.vertical-inc .com.
Some other translated books written by Kenzo Kitakata: *The City of Refuge*; *Winter Sleep*; *The Cage*; *When Time Attains Thee*

Satoko Kizaki. ***The Sunken Temple.***
Translated by Carol A. Flath. Tokyo: Kodansha International, 1993. 203 pages.
Genres/literary styles/story types: speculative fiction; fantasy
Set in the imaginary village of Hie on the northern coast of Japan's largest island, Honshu, this brooding story about parallel worlds is inspired by two Japanese legends. In the first legend, Taro Urashima is a guest in the underwater kingdom of a beautiful sea princess. When he decides to return home, he discovers that all the members of his family have perished. The second legend is about a princess who leaves her ocean home to marry a man on land. When she becomes pregnant, she asks her husband to promise to let her give birth in secrecy. But he does not keep his promise and thus sees her in her true form, which causes her to abandon him and returns to the sea.
Subject keyword: identity
Original language: Japanese
Sources consulted for annotation:
Amazon.com (review from *Kirkus Reviews*).
Copeland, Rebecca L. *Japan Quarterly* 41 (April 1994): 223.
Ryan, Marleigh Grayer. *World Literature Today* 68 (Autumn 1994): 888.
Steinberg, Sybil S. *Publishers Weekly* 241 (24 January 1994): 42.
Another translated book written by Satoko Kizaki: *The Phoenix Tree and Other Stories*

Yumiko Kurahashi. ***The Woman with the Flying Head and Other Stories.***
Translated by Atsuko Sakaki. Armonk, NY: M. E. Sharpe, 1998. 157 pages.
Genres/literary styles/story types: speculative fiction; paranormal
The author has been compared to Edgar Allan Poe and E. T. A Hoffman. These dark and phantasmagoric tales—partly inspired by Noh theater, mythology, and biographical elements—explore

aspects of the erotic and the absurd. In one story, a man places a horrific witch's mask on his fiancée's face, only to see her slowly die.
Subject keyword: identity
Original language: Japanese
Sources consulted for annotation:
Lofgren, Erik R. *World Literature Today* 72 (Summer 1998): 689.
Steinberg, Sybil S. *Publishers Weekly* 244 (20 October 1997): 54.
Williams, Janis. *Library Journal* 122 (December 1997): 158.
Another translated book written by Yumiko Kurahashi: *The Adventures of Sumiyakist Q*

Kaoru Kurimoto. *The Guin Saga* (vol. 1: *The Leopard Mask*; vol. 2: *Warrior in the Wilderness*; vol. 3: *The Battle of Nospherus*; vol. 4: *Prisoner of the Lagon*).
Translated by Alexander O. Smith with Elye J. Alexander (vols. 1–3); Alexander O. Smith (vol. 4). New York: Vertical, 2003–2004.
Genres/literary styles/story types: speculative fiction; fantasy
Part fantasy, part thriller, this set of action-adventure books focuses on Remus and Rinda, royal twins who escape from Palos, which has been invaded by the Mongaul. In the Forest of Rood, they are rescued by Guin, a memory-less warrior who wears a leopard mask. The trio prepares to mount resistance against the Mongaul, but fate has other plans for them.
Subject keyword: power
Original language: Japanese
Sources consulted for annotation:
Cannon, Peter. *Publishers Weekly* 250 (14 April 2003): 53.
Cassada, Jackie. *Library Journal* 128 (15 April 2003): 129.

Senji Kuroi. *Life in the Cul-De-Sac*.
Translated by Philip Gabriel. Berkeley, CA: Stone Bridge Press, 2001. 231 pages.
Genres/literary styles/story types: mainstream fiction; short stories
This book of interlinked stories depicts the lives of four families—all of whom reside on the same street in a Tokyo suburb. Here, they struggle with alienation, futility, and a general sense of gnawing anxiety as they go about their humdrum lives characterized by burdensome marriages, thankless eldercare, and decaying authority structures.
Subject keywords: family histories; urban life
Original language: Japanese
Sources consulted for annotation:
Amazon.com (book description).
Barta-Moran, Ellie. *Booklist* 97 (15 April 2001): 1535.
Cooper, Tom. *Library Journal* 126 (July 2001): 124.
Iwamoto, Yoshio. *World Literature Today* 75 (Summer 2001): 137.
Japan Quarterly 48 (July/September 2001): 108.

Saiichi Maruya. *Grass for My Pillow*.
Translated by Dennis Keene. New York: Columbia University Press, 2002. 345 pages.
Genre/literary style/story type: mainstream fiction
In 1940, Shokichi Hamada does not believe in the ideals animating Japanese society and thus refuses to be drafted to fight in World War II. Instead, he simply adopts a new identity, becoming a vagabond peddler and salesman, going from village to village in rural Japan. Twenty years later, Shokichi is married and has seemingly found a sinecure as a clerk in a university, but his past catches up to him, and he experiences firsthand the costs of personal integrity.

Subject keywords: identity; war
Original language: Japanese
Sources consulted for annotation:
Amazon.com (book description).
The New Yorker 78 (11 November 2002): 189.
Some other translated books written by Saiichi Maruya: *Rain in the Wind: Four Stories*; *Singular Rebellion*; *A Mature Woman*

Seicho Matsumoto. *Inspector Imanishi Investigates*.
Translated by Beth Cary. New York: Soho Press, 1989. 313 pages.
Genres/literary styles/story types: crime fiction; police detectives
Seicho Matsumoto is one of Japan's most popular mystery writers; his novels have been compared to those of Georges Simenon and P. D. James. Eitaro Imanishi—a Tokyo homicide inspector who writes haiku, does not swear, and is the epitome of politeness—must resolve the case of a man found beaten and crushed in a railroad stockyard.
Subject keyword: urban life
Original language: Japanese
Sources consulted for annotation:
Goff, Janet. *Japan Quarterly* 38 (January 1991): 110.
Johnson, George. *The New York Times*, 30 September 1990: A46.
Mitgang, Herbert. *The New York Times*, 2 September 1989: A15.
Some other translated books written by Seicho Matsumoto: *Points and Lines*; *The Voice and Other Stories*

Miyuki Miyabe. *All She Was Worth*.
Translated by Alfred Birnbaum. Tokyo: Kodansha International, 1996. 296 pages.
Genres/literary styles/story types: crime fiction; police detectives
This novel is described on the back cover as "a journey through the dark side of Japan's consumer-crazed society." And indeed it is. A Tokyo police offer named Shunsuke Honma investigates the disappearance of Shoko Sekine, who is really not Shoko Sekine at all but someone who has murdered Sekine and then assumed her identity. The mystery revolves around the astronomical amounts of debt that Japanese men and women are willing to accumulate in order to have access to luxuries. The novel also gives insight into the intricacies of Japan's system of residential and work-related registration—a system that makes it difficult to escape from one's past.
Related title by the same author:
Readers may also be interested in *Crossfire*, in which Junko Aoki, a beautiful young woman wants to use her pyrokinetic abilities as a kind of a last-ditch justice system to punish the guilty and the depraved. Thus, she inevitably meets Sergeant Chikako Ishizu, a Tokyo police officer specializing in arson.
Subject keyword: urban life
Original language: Japanese
Sources consulted for annotation:
Amazon.com (book description).
Back cover of the book.
Jefferson, Margo. *The New York Times*, 4 February 2005, p. C1.
Publishers Weekly 252 (28 November 2005): 26.
Samul, Ron. *Library Journal* 130 (December 2005): 107.
Sennett, Frank. *Booklist* 102 (1 January/15 January): 68.
Some other translated books written by Miyuki Miyabe: *Brave Story*; *Crossfire; Shadow Family; The Devil's Whisper; The Book of Heroes; The Sleeping Dragon*

Teru Miyamoto. ***Kinshu: Autumn Brocade.***
Translated by Roger K. Thomas. New York: New Directions, 2005. 196 pages.
Genre/literary style/story type: mainstream fiction
Aki and Yasuaki are divorced, but they meet again by chance at a resort in the mountains. Aki divorced Yasuaki at the behest of her father when Yasuaki had an affair with a bar hostess, who afterward committed suicide. Aki married again, but her new husband, a professor, was also unfaithful. Her only solace is her relationship with her son, who is both mentally and physically disabled. Because neither Aki nor Yasuaki have found peace in their lives, they write a series of letters to each other, allowing them to come to terms with the past.
Subject keywords: identity; social roles
Original language: Japanese
Sources consulted for annotation:
Amazon.com (book description).
Publishers Weekly 252 (29 August 2005): 34.
Quan, Shirley N. *Library Journal* 130 (1 October 2005): 68.
Stirling, Claire. *Calgary Herald*, 4 February 2006, p. F4.
Another translated book written by Teru Miyamoto: *River of Fireflies*
Tsutomu Mizukami. ***The Temple of the Wild Geese and Bamboo Dolls of Echizen: Two Novellas.***
Translated by Dennis Washburn. Champaign, IL: Dalkey Archive Press, 2008. 208 pages.
Genre/literary style/story type: mainstream fiction
To characterize these razor-sharp and mysteriously elegant tales, the *Booklist* reviewer asks readers to "[i]magine a Dostoyevsky novel boiled down to pulp-thriller dimensions with no loss but, rather, a distillation of literary merit." In the first novella, a Buddhist priest and his mistress experience both joys and agonies in an isolated temple in northern Japan. Inevitably, the situation becomes unsustainable and leads to murder. In the second novella, a bamboo carver and a prostitute whom his father used to visit begin a life together in a mountain hamlet.
Subject keywords: rural life; social roles
Original language: Japanese
Source consulted for annotation:
Global Books in Print (online) (reviews from *Booklist* and *Publishers Weekly*).

Haruki Murakami. ***Kafka on the Shore.***
Translated by Philip Gabriel. New York: Alfred A. Knopf, 2005. 436 pages.
Genres/literary styles/story types: mainstream fiction; coming-of-age
Surreal and philosophical are just some of the many adjectives applied to this novel about two vastly different individuals on a quest to understand themselves better. As they wend their way through a dreamlike yet ultimately real Japan, they yearn to find a fleeting serenity that is only granted to a lucky few. On the one hand, there is 15-year-old Kafka Tamura, who runs away from home to avoid a disturbing prophecy from coming true and eventually meets an enigmatic librarian and her no-less-enigmatic clerk—both of whom help him grapple with and stumble toward adulthood. On the other hand, there is the elderly Satoru Nakata, who has lost a large portion of his cognitive functions as a result of a mysterious event during World War II and who has recently committed a murder but can converse with cats and affect the weather.
Related title by the same author:
Readers may also enjoy *After Dark*, which takes place during a single night in Tokyo and features two diametrically opposed sisters: one sleeps all the time; the other disdains anything to do with sleep.
Subject keywords: aging; war

Original language: Japanese
Sources consulted for annotation:
Amazon.com (book description; *Bookmarks Magazine*; all editorial reviews).
Cheuse, Alan. *World Literature Today* 80 (January/February 2006): 27.
Global Books in Print (online) (review from *Booklist* for *After Dark*).
Maslin, Janet. *The New York Times*, 31 January 2005 (online).
Miller, Laura. *The New York Times Book Review*, 6 February 2005 (online).
Publishers Weekly 251 (December 2004): 42.
Seymenliyska, Elena. *The Guardian*, 8 October 2005, p. 19.
Some other translated books written by Haruki Murakami: *A Wild Sheep Chase*; *The Wind-Up Bird Chronicle*; *Norwegian Wood*; *Hard-Boiled Wonderland and the End of the World*; *After the Quake*; *The Sputnik Sweetheart*; *South of the Border, West of the Sun*; *Dance Dance Dance*; *The Elephant Vanishes*; *Blind Willow, Sleeping Woman*; *After Dark*

Ryu Murakami. *In the Miso Soup*.
Translated by Ralph McCarthy. Tokyo: Kodansha International, 2003. 180 pages.
Genres/literary styles/story types: crime fiction; suspense
Kenji is a self-employed tour guide in Shinjuku, a Tokyo area well-known as the epicenter of the sex trade. Just before New Year's Eve, he encounters a psychopathic American client named Frank, who is possibly the world's strongest man, not to mention a cold-blooded murderer who counts a schoolgirl and a homeless man among his recent victims. As Kenji guides Frank through Shinjuku, who will get the better of whom?
Related title by the same author:
Readers may also enjoy *Coin Locker Babies*, which focuses on two infant boys who are abandoned by their mothers in the coin lockers of a train station. Their fates later in life are as bleak as their beginnings. One becomes a pole vaulter whose hobbies include strange drugs and even stranger murders; the other works as a prostitute in a chemically poisoned area outside of Tokyo until one of his customers discovers his musical talents, setting him on the road to an ephemeral celebrity.
Subject keywords: social problems; urban life
Original language: Japanese
Sources consulted for annotation:
Amazon.com (book description; from the inside flap).
Global Books in Print (online) (reviews from *Library Journal* and *Publishers Weekly* for *Coin Locker Babies*).
Samuel, Yoshiko Yokochi. *World Literature Today* 78 (September/December 2004): 88.
Sennett, Frank. *Booklist* 100 (1 December 2003): 647.
Sittenfeld, Curtis. *The New York Times Book Review*, 11 January 2004, p. 20.
Some other translated books written by Ryu Murakami: *Sixty-Nine*; *Coin Locker Babies*; *Almost Transparent Blue*; *Piercing*; *Popular Hits of the Showa Era*

Kenji Nakagami. *The Cape and Other Stories from the Japanese Ghetto*.
Translated by Eve Zimmerman. Berkeley, CA: Stone Bridge Press, 1999. 191 pages.
Genres/literary styles/story types: mainstream fiction; short stories
The author belongs to the burakumin caste, members of which were historically treated as outcasts; they continue to be socially and economically disadvantaged in modern Japan. The title novella focuses on Akiyuki, whose fate is sealed from the moment of his birth. His vagabond and poverty-stricken father has other children, and it is almost inevitable that Akiyuki commits incest

with one of his half-sisters, who is working as a prostitute. Critics have said that Nakagami's fiction contains echoes of Émile Zola and Frank Norris.
Subject keywords: family histories; urban life
Original language: Japanese
Sources consulted for annotation:
Klise, James. *Booklist* 95 (1 May 1999): 1577.
Morris, Mark. *The New York Times Book Review*, 24 October 1999, p. 23.
Samuel, Yoshiko Yokochi. *World Literature Today* 73 (Autumn 1999): 824.
Steinberg, Sybil S. *Publishers Weekly* 246 (12 April 1999): 55.
Another translated book written by Kenji Nakagami: *Snakelust*

Asa Nonami. *The Hunter.*
Translated by Juliet Winters Carpenter. New York: Kodansha America, 2007. 269 pages.
Genres/literary styles/story types: crime fiction; police detectives
Takako Otomichi is a female police detective whose colleagues are not accustomed to women in their tightly knit brotherhood. Thus, her task is made all the more difficult when she investigates the murder of a businessman who has met a fiery death. Of course, it is no ordinary death, and, of course, it is no ordinary suspect when suspicion falls on a ferocious dog-wolf who has been trained to viciously attack its victims.
Related title by the same author:
Readers may also enjoy *Now You're One of Us*, which explores the life of Noriko, a new bride who is uncertain of her place in her husband's family, especially when she learns that her in-laws were complicit in the murder of at least one other family.
Subject keyword: urban life
Original language: Japanese
Source consulted for annotation:
Global Books in Print (online) (reviews from *Booklist*, *Library Journal*, and *Publishers Weekly*).
Some other translated books written by Asa Nonami: *Now You're One of Us*; *Body*

Kenzaburo Oe. *Somersault.*
Translated by Philip Gabriel. New York: Grove Press, 2003. 570 pages.
Genres/literary styles/story types: thrillers; political thrillers
This book was inspired by the 1995 sarin gas attack (by the religious cult Aum Shinrikyo) in Tokyo that killed 12 people and injured hundreds more. In this novel, a cult led by Patron and Guide is riven by factionalism—so much so that when its radical wing makes plans to take over a nuclear plant, the leaders renounce their beliefs. But 10 years later, when the radical wing murders Guide, Patron resurrects what is left of the cult and makes deadly plans to announce its rebirth. In the best traditions of Fyodor Dostoyevsky, the novel deals with thorny questions about faith, duplicity, and the power of charismatic individuals.
Related title by the same author:
Readers may also enjoy *The Changeling*, a novel which is partly based on Oe's psychological and emotional relationship with his brother-in-law, Goro, before and after he committed suicide. As he listens to the recordings that Goro made, Oe's own life becomes tantalizingly real.
Subject keywords: religion; social problems
Original language: Japanese
Sources consulted for annotation:
Amazon.com (book description; all editorial reviews).
Cameron, Lindsley. *The New Yorker* 72 (14 October 1996): 44.
"Oe Kenzaburo." *Contemporary Authors Online*. Gale databases, 2006.

Olson, Ray. *Booklist* 99 (1 December 2002): 629.
Quan, Shirley N. *Library Journal* 127 (December 2003): 180.
Zaleski, Jeff. *Publishers Weekly* 250 (6 January 2003): 36.
Some other translated books written by Kenzaburo Oe: *Nip the Buds, Shoot the Kids*; *An Echo of Heaven*; *Rouse Up O Young Men of the New Age!*; *Teach Us To Outgrow Our Madness: Four Short Novels*; *A Quiet Life*; *The Crazy Iris and Other Stories of the Atomic Aftermath*; *The Pinch Runner Memorandum*; *A Healing Family*; *A Personal Matter*; *The Silent Cry*; *The Catch and Other War Stories*; *The Changeling*

Yoko Ogawa. *The Housekeeper and the Professor.*
Translated by Stephen Snyder. New York: Picador, 2009. 192 pages.
Genre/literary style/story type: mainstream fiction
Seemingly every critic alive has raved about this book, which has been variously described as charming, radiant, elegant, gorgeous, poignant, and touching. The plot concerns a mathematics teacher whose cognitive functions are severely impaired after a car accident in 1975. Although he can remember theorems that he developed 30 years ago, his short-term memory does not extend past 80 minutes. He lives in a cottage located on the property of his elderly sister-in-law, who despairs of finding someone to take care of him. Indeed, nine housekeepers from the Akebono Housekeeping Agency have already quit, overwhelmed by the arduousness and strangeness of the task. But then, in 1992, along comes the 10th housekeeper, a single mother with a 10-year-old son whom the professor takes to calling Root. As the housekeeper prepares his meals and cleans the cottage, a compelling and profound relationship develops among these three individuals. As they introduce themselves and reintroduce themselves again after each block of 80 minutes; as Root begins to spend more time with the professor; as the professor attempts to remember things by pinning notes to his suit; and as the professor eloquently holds forth on the meaning of random numbers (e.g., the housekeeper's birthday, the uniform number of his favorite baseball player), a mysterious and interconnected universe slowly unfolds.
Related title by the same author:
Readers may also enjoy *Hotel Iris*. Mari, a 17-year-old girl, works at her mother's small, dilapidated hotel. She falls in love with a poverty-stricken and widowed translator whom they have had to expel from the hotel for dissolute behavior and with whom she begins a torrid, violent, and dangerous affair.
Subject keywords: aging; identity
Original language: Japanese
Sources consulted for annotation:
Overbye, Dennis. *The New York Times Book Review*, 1 March 2009 (online).
Picador Macmillan website, http://us.macmillan.com/Picador.aspx.
Some other translated books written by Yoko Ogawa: *The Diving Pool*; *Hotel Iris*

Hikaru Okuizumi. *The Stones Cry Out.*
Translated by James Westerhoven. New York: Harcourt Brace, 1998. 138 pages.
Genre/literary style/story type: mainstream fiction
Tsuyoshi Manase has horrific memories of a tragic event that occurred on the Philippine island of Leyte at the end of World War II: Sick and dying Japanese soldiers were executed in a cave. A bookseller by trade, he devotes his spare time to geology, neglects his family, and is generally miserable. But Manase is brutally dragged back to reality when one of his sons is killed in a cave. As the past presses in on the present, questions begin to be raised about Manase's complicity in his son's murder.
Subject keywords: family histories; war

Original language: Japanese
Sources consulted for annotation:
Amazon.com (book description; review from *Kirkus Reviews*).
Ferguson, William. *The New York Times Book Review*, 4 July 1999, p. 15.
Johnston, Bonnie. *Booklist* 95 (15 November 1998): 568.
Parker, Patricia. *World Literature Today* 73 (Autumn 1999): 825.
Quan, Shirley N. *Library Journal* 123 (15 October 1998): 100.
Steinberg, Sybil S. *Publishers Weekly* 245 (7 December 1998): 50.

Arimasa Osawa. *Shinjuku Shark.*
Translated by Andrew Clare. New York: Vertical, 2008. 288 pages.
Genres/literary styles/story types: crime fiction; police detectives
Samejima is an aloof and ostracized Tokyo police detective whose overly persistent pursuit of yakuza corruption relegates him to patrol duty. With no partner and no career-advancement prospects, his only satisfaction comes from his zealously compulsive approach to hunting criminals as well as the fact that he has inside information that would damage the credibility of the police force. When police officers start being killed in pairs, only Samejima's relentless efforts can save the day. Also of interest may be *The Poison Ape*, in which Samejima finds himself thrust into the middle of the Taiwanese underworld.
Subject keyword: urban life
Original language: Japanese
Source consulted for annotation:
Global Books in Print (online) (reviews from *Booklist*, *Library Journal*, and *Publishers Weekly* for *Shinjuku Shark*; synopsis/book jacket for *The Poison Ape*).
Another translated book written by Arimasa Osawa: *The Poison Ape*

Kappa Senoo (Kappa Senoh). *A Boy Called H: A Childhood in Wartime Japan.*
Translated by John Bester. Tokyo: Kodansha International, 1999. 528 pages.
Genres/literary styles/story types: mainstream fiction; coming-of-age
The title of this novel gives a good summary of its contents but not its enduring power. What was it like for H to live in Kobe both before and during the war? What changed? How does a child and young adolescent understand and cope with those changes? What happened to his friends and family as a result of the war? What social habits and mores were irretrievably lost? What was the psychological and emotional impact of strictly enforced wartime regulations? The novel presents answers to these questions from a child's perspective, making them all the more powerful and stark.
Subject keywords: family histories; war
Original language: Japanese
Sources consulted for annotation:
Levine, Steven I. *Library Journal* 125 (1 April 2000): 113.
Noguchi, Mary Goebel. *Japan Quarterly* 47 (April/June 2000): 98.
Rochman, Hazel. *Booklist* 96 (15 February 2000): 1084.
Zaleski, Jeff et al. *Publishers Weekly* 247 (14 February 2000): 182.

Harumi Setouchi. *The End of Summer.*
Translated by Janine Beichman in collaboration with Alan Brender. Tokyo: Kodansha International, 1989. 151 pages.
Genres/literary styles/story types: mainstream fiction; short stories
This collection of four stories examines various aspects of a strange love triangle. Tomoko is an interior designer who is having an affair with Shingo, a married man whose wife interacts with

him only on such rare occasions as holidays and family gatherings. But then Tomoko restarts a liaison with Ryota, a man with whom she had a relationship in the past that broke up her marriage. When she subsequently runs into Shingo with his wife, the tangle and tension of her romantic life intensifies.
Subject keywords: identity; social roles
Original language: Japanese
Sources consulted for annotation:
Brettschneider, Cathie. *Belles Lettres* 5 (Summer 1990): 20.
Solomon, Charles. *Los Angeles Times*, 9 May 1993, p. 13.
Another translated book written by Harumi Setouchi: *Beauty in Disarray*

Ryotaro Shiba. ***The Last Shogun: The Life of Tokugawa Yoshinobu.***
Translated by Juliet Winters Carpenter. Tokyo: Kodansha International, 1998. 255 pages.
Genre/literary style/story type: historical fiction
The title of this book says it all, and critics have said that this detailed and wide-ranging historical novel brings to mind the works of James Michener. It follows Yoshinobu's early education at the hands of his father; his eventual ascent to power in 1867; his accomplishments as Shogun, including his establishment of international ties during a period of Japanese isolationism and his westernization of the government.
Subject keywords: politics; power
Original language: Japanese
Sources consulted for annotation:
Amazon.com (all editorial reviews).
Goff, Janet. *Japan Quarterly* 46 (January 1999): 105.
Stuttaford, Genevieve, et al. *Publishers Weekly* 245 (20 April 1998): 53.
Tanabe, Kunio Francis. *The Washington Post*, 19 July 1998, p. X9.
Some other translated books written by Ryotaro Shiba: *Kukai the Universal: Scenes from His Life*; *Drunk as a Lord: Samurai Stories*

Soji Shimada. ***The Tokyo Zodiac Murders.***
Translated by Ross and Shika MacKenzie. Tokyo: IBC Publishing, 2004. 251 pages.
Genres/literary styles/story types: crime fiction; private investigators
Kiyoshi Mitarai is not only a private detective but also an astrologer. These dual skills come in handy when he attempts to solve a series of bizarre murders apparently committed by the artist Heikichi Umezawa some 40 years ago. Umezawa was obsessed with discovering the essence of beauty, so he killed many of his female relatives to create a woman (Azoth) who would be the embodiment of perfection. Aided by a series of maps and other clues scattered throughout the book, readers are encouraged to solve the so-called Zodiac Murders alongside Mitarai.
Subject keyword: identity
Original language: Japanese
Sources consulted for annotation:
Amazon.com (book description).
Samul, Ron. *Library Journal* 130 (August 2005): 60.

Ikko Shimizu. ***The Dark Side of Japanese Business: Three Industry Novels.***
Translated by Tamae K. Prindle. Armonk, NY: M. E. Sharpe, 1995. 277 pages.
Genre/literary style/story type: mainstream fiction
Industry or business novels are a well-known genre in Japan. The drama of internal corporate struggles and financial machinations; the fight to retain a vestige of independence in the face of

takeovers, corruption, and brutal battles over market share; and the personal cost of devoting one's life to the never-satisfied maw of ambition and profitability—these are the elements that make the genre a compelling force in Japan. In North America, a comparable genre is the corporate (or business) thriller. Thus, readers who liked Joseph Finder's *Paranoia* and *Company Man* may be open to Shimizu's works.
Subject keyword: power
Original language: Japanese
Sources consulted for annotation:
Sawhill, Ray. *The New York Times Book Review*, 13 October 1993, p. 35.
Sender, Henry. *Far Eastern Economic Review*, 18 April 1996, p. 69.

Junzo Shono. *Evening Clouds.*
Translated by Wayne P. Lammers. Berkeley, CA: Stone Bridge Press, 2000. 222 pages.
Genre/literary style/story type: mainstream fiction
If you are tired of action novels or hip treatises about bleak urban landscapes, you will love this novel. It depicts domestic moments in the life of the Oura family on the outskirts of Tokyo. There is almost no drama—just a series of moments that capture the grace of a quiet existence, when one has found inner peace and when one lives in harmony with the environment. No pleasure is too simple or too prosaic; everything becomes endowed with an abiding elegance and perfection, including eating, cooking, gardening, and watching the ever-changing sky with its scudding clouds.
Subject keywords: family histories; urban life
Original language: Japanese
Sources consulted for annotation:
Amazon.com (book description).
Johnston, Bonnie. *Booklist* 96 (15 May 2000): 1731.
Publishers Weekly 247 (15 May 2000): 88.
Ryan, Marleigh Grayer. *World Literature Today* 75 (January 2001): 108.
Another translated book written by Junzo Shono: *Still Life and Other Stories*

Ayako Sono. *No Reason for Murder.*
Translated by Edward Putzar. New York: ICG Muse, 2003. 422 pages.
Genres/literary styles/story types: crime fiction; suspense
Fujio Uno is everyone's worst nightmare: an alienated misfit who is a gruesome serial killer. Yukiko Hata is probably the only woman whom he has been unable to seduce, and it is for this reason that he sees her as a beacon of hope in his wretched life. But her principles and morality lead to her downfall.
Subject keyword: urban life
Original language: Japanese
Sources consulted for annotation:
Amazon.com (book description).
Mansfield, Stephen. *The Japan Times*, 21 March 2004 (from Factiva databases).
Stone Bridge Press. Heian Books (book description), http://www.stonebridge.com.
Another translated book written by Ayako Sono: *Watcher from the Shore*

Koji Suzuki. *Dark Water.*
Translated by Glynne Walley. New York: Vertical, 2004. 279 pages.
Genres/literary styles/story types: speculative fiction; horror
As Jeff Zaleski writes, Suzuki is sometimes referred to as a Japanese Stephen King for his tales of "quiet psychological terror" that explore "the darkness within the human psyche." They are filled

with an "understated dread" and "a sort of creepy normality" because he infuses "everyday settings" with "horrific supernatural events." In this collection, all the stories center around water: drips, leaks, islands, underwater caves. Because the most normal of settings give rise to the strangest events, there is an eerie sense of foreboding and fear on almost every page.
Subject keyword: identity
Original language: Japanese
Sources consulted for annotation:
The Complete Review (book review), http://www.complete-review.com/reviews/japannew/suzukik3.htm.
Zaleski, Jeff. *Publishers Weekly* 251 (11 October 2004): 58.
Some other translated books written by Koji Suzuki: *Ring*; *Spiral*; *Loop*

Randy Taguchi. *Outlet.*
Translated by Glynne Walley. New York: Vertical, 2003. 269 pages.
Genres/literary styles/story types: crime fiction; amateur detectives
Yuki Asakura's brother Taka is dead—the apparent victim of starvation. Determined to find out the true circumstances surrounding his death, Yuki makes strange discoveries about herself: She can smell death on others, and she can also heal through sex.
Subject keyword: identity
Original language: Japanese
Sources consulted for annotation:
Amazon.com (all editorial reviews).
Publishers Weekly 250 (29 September 2003): 43.
Woodhead, Cameron. *The AGEReview*, 26 June 2004, p. 5.

Akimitsu Takagi. *Honeymoon to Nowhere.*
Translated by Sadako Mizuguchi. New York: Soho Press, 1995. 277 pages.
Genres/literary styles/story types: crime fiction; private investigators
Etsuko Ogata does not want to enter into an arranged marriage with Tetsuya Higuchi, a lawyer selected by her father. Instead, she becomes the fiancée of the university teacher Yoshihiro Tsukamoto. Her father is not pleased, and he employs the services of a private investigator to discover her fiancée's family history. And what a history it is: links to a war criminal and arson. This disturbing information does not dissuade Etsuko from marrying Yoshihiro, but on the first night of their honeymoon, a mysterious phone call draws him from her side and out into the night. Yoshihiro is later found strangled to death, and Saburo Kirishima, a long-ago flame of Etsuko, must solve the crime. The author is consistently said to be among the front rank of Japan's crime writers.
Subject keyword: family histories
Original language: Japanese
Sources consulted for annotation:
Amazon.com (book description; all editorial reviews).
Herbert, Rosemary. *Boston Herald*, 18 July 1999, p. 78.
Munger, Katy. *The Washington Post*, 25 July 1999, p. X8.
Williams, Janis. *Library Journal* 124 (August 1999): 147.
Zaleski, Jeff. *Publishers Weekly* 246 (31 May 1999): 71.
Some other translated books written by Akimitsu Takagi: *The Tattoo Murder Case*; *No Patent on Murder*; *The Informer*

Genichiro Takahashi. *Sayonara, Gangsters.*
Translated by Michael Emmerich. New York: Vertical, 2004. 311 pages.

Genres/literary styles/story types: mainstream fiction; postmodernism

Somewhere in the future, names have disappeared. People just do not have them anymore. Thus, to avoid confusion, people begin naming themselves and each other according to meaningful things in their lives. One woman calls herself "Nakajima Miyuki Song Book" and a poetry teacher christens himself "Sayonara, Gangsters." After an opening section dealing with the death of the daughter of "Sayonara, Gangsters" from a previous marriage, the novel focuses on life at the poetry school, where famous Latin poets have become household appliances and where gangsters yearning to write poetry are killed by squads of police.

Subject keyword: identity

Original language: Japanese

Sources consulted for annotation:

Amazon.com (book description).

The Japan Times, 18 July 2004 (from Factiva databases).

Keeley, Brian. *Far Eastern Economic Review*, 4 November 2004, p. 63.

Sugiyama, Chiyono. *The Daily Yomiuri*, 27 June 2004, p. 20.

Zaleski, Jeff. *Publishers Weekly* 251 (29 March 2004): 3.

Takako Takahashi. *Lonely Woman.*

Translated by Maryellen Toman Mori. New York: Columbia University Press, 2004. 155 pages.

Genres/literary styles/story types: mainstream fiction; feminist fiction

Each of the five stories in this collection limns the desolation experienced by young, single Japanese women. On the borderline of madness and struggling to find meaning in a nihilistic universe, they often confront nightmarish situations with bone-chilling and terror-inducing solutions.

Subject keyword: identity

Original language: Japanese

Sources consulted for annotation:

Amazon.com (book description).

Beichman, Janine. *The Washington Times*, 30 May 2004, p. B8.

Leber, Michele. *Booklist* 100 (1 March 2004): 1135.

Richie, Donald. *The Japan Times*, 18 January 2004 (from Factiva databases).

Yoshihiro Tatsumi. *A Drifting Life.*

Translated by Taro Nettleton. Montréal, PQ: Drawn & Quarterly Publications, 2009. 855 pages.

Genres/literary styles/story types: graphic novels; coming-of-age

Critics generally agree that Tatsumi is one of the masters of manga. He tells poignant stories about life in Japan after World War II. Not only does he write sensitively about the psychological and emotional repercussions of Hiroshima, but he also focuses in short story collections—such as *Abandon the Old in Tokyo*—on those sad and lonely individuals who were not part of Japan's economic ascendancy in the 1970s. His masterpiece is the autobiographical *A Drifting Life*, which in addition to being a social and cultural history of the tragedies and absurdities of Japanese life is also a worthy descendant of James Joyce's *A Portrait of the Artist as a Young Man*. Readers may wish to compare Tatsumi's work with one of the relatively little-known pioneers of American graphic novels, Lynd Ward, whose six woodcut novels—all produced in the late 1920s and 1930s—are *Gods' Man*, *Madman's Drum*, *Wild Pilgrimage*, *Prelude to a Million Years*, *Song Without Words*, and *Vertigo*. Lynd's novels are now available in two volumes in the Library of America series.

Subject keywords: politics; urban life

Original language: Japanese

Sources consulted for annotation:

Garner, Dwight. *The New York Times*, 15 April 2009 (online).

Global Books in Print (online) (reviews for all books from *Booklist*, *Library Journal*, and *Publishers Weekly*).
Some other translated books written by Yoshihiro Tatsumi: *Good-Bye*; *Abandon the Old in Tokyo*; *Infierno*; *The Push Man and Other Stories*

Yuko Tsushima. *Woman Running in the Mountains.*
Translated by Geraldine Harcourt. New York: Pantheon, 1991. 275 pages.
Genres/literary styles/story types: mainstream fiction; coming-of-age
Takiko is unmarried and pregnant, but she is determined to keep her baby despite the fierce resistance of her unsupportive and often violent family. Set in a cut-throat consumerist society that disapproves of moral lapses, Takiko experiences a kind of inner freedom at the same time that she becomes a social outcast. When she meets a man with a Down syndrome child, she may have finally found a true emotional home.
Subject keywords: family histories; social problems
Original language: Japanese
Sources consulted for annotation:
Mitgang, Herbert. *The New York Times*, 23 March 1991, p. 15.
Rubin, Merle. *The Christian Science Monitor*, 14 May 1991, p. 13.
Some other translated books written by Yuko Tsushima: *The Shooting Gallery & Other Stories*; *Child of Fortune*

Yasutaka Tsutsui. *Salmonella Men on Planet Porno and Other Stories.*
Translated by Andrew Driver. New York: Pantheon Books, 2008. 272 pages.
Genres/literary styles/story types: speculative fiction; postmodernism
The reviewer in *Library Journal* called this metafictional collection "a cross between the music group the B-52s, Thomas Pynchon's *V.*, Ryu Murakami's *Coin Locker Babies*, and James Turner's graphic novel *Nil: A Land Beyond Belief*." One eccentric story follows another: Scientists discover a planet where literally everything is about sex; a tree determines dreams; everyone stops smoking; the media become obsessed with the trivial life of a dull man; and an efficiency consultant destroys the last vestiges of happiness. Strange as it may seem, Tsutsui's work has some affinities with that of José Saramago; they both ask the question "What would happen if . . . ?"
Related titles by the same author:
Readers may also enjoy *What the Maid Saw: Eight Psychic Tales*, which focuses on Nanase, an 18-year-old maid who is telepathic but is doomed to live among the petty cares, cavils, and concerns of her employers. In one scene, she saves herself from rape by bouncing a would-be rapist's evil thoughts back at him and subsequently driving him to madness. Also of interest may be *Hell*, in which the author envisions hell as an emotionless place where the mere act of thinking of someone conjures up that person.
Subject keyword: social roles
Original language: Japanese
Sources consulted for annotation:
Bohoslawec, Piero. *The Financial Times*, 13 October 2007 (online).
Global Books in Print (online) (reviews from *Library Journal* and *Publishers Weekly*).
Lezard, Nicholas. *The Guardian*, 11 October 2008 (online).
McCaffery, Larry, and Gregory, Sinda. *Review of Contemporary Fiction* 22 (1 July 2002): 202.
Regier, Kerry. *The Vancouver Sun*, 20 October 1990, p. D19.
Some other translated books written by Yasutaka Tsutsui: *What the Maid Saw: Eight Psychic Tales*; *The African Bomb and Other Stories*; *Portraits of Eight Families*; *Hell*; *A Girl Who Runs Through Time*

Eimi Yamada (Amy Yamada). *Trash*.
Translated by Sonya Johnson. Tokyo: Kodansha International, 1994. 372 pages.
Genres/literary styles/story types: mainstream fiction; women's lives
Koko, a Japanese woman, lies handcuffed in bed, contemplating her life—which revolves around an African-American lover and his teenage son. The bustle and excitement of New York have not given her what she wants—only a vague sense of doom and addiction.
Subject keywords: culture conflict; social roles
Original language: Japanese
Sources consulted for annotation:
Bumiller, Elisabeth. *The Washington Post*, 1 June 1991, p. D1.
Steinberg, Sybil S. *Publishers Weekly* 241 (7 November 1994): 64.
Vicarel, Jo Ann. *Library Journal* 119 (December 1994): 136.
Vivinetto, Gina. *St. Petersburg Times*, 30 April 1995, p. 6D.
Some other translated books written by Eimi Yamada: *Bedtime Eyes*; *After School Keynotes*

Taichi Yamada. *Strangers*.
Translated by Wayne P. Lammers. New York: Vertical, 2003. 203 pages.
Genres/literary styles/story types: speculative fiction; horror/paranormal
Hideo Harada is a scriptwriter, middle-aged, divorced, and estranged from his 19-year-old son; he eats and sleeps in his office. Orphaned at age 12, Hideo returns one day to Asakusa, his childhood neighborhood, where he meets his dead father, who takes Hideo home with him to see his mother. Hideo returns again and again to spend time with his deceased family. Only when Kei, his girlfriend, comments that he has become much more pale of late does Hideo realize that there is something wrong with his life.
Subject keywords: family histories; urban life
Original language: Japanese
Sources consulted for annotation:
Poole, Steven. *The Guardian*, 5 March 2005, p. 27.
Riordan, Kate. *Time Out*, 13 January 2005, p. 65.
Thwaite, Anthony. *The Sunday Telegraph*, 13 February 2005, p. 16.
Another translated book written by Taichi Yamada: *In Search of a Distant Voice*

Seishi Yokomizo. *The Inugami Clan*.
Translated by Yumiko Yamazaki. Berkeley, CA: Stone Bridge Press, 2007. 309 pages.
Genres/literary styles/story types: crime fiction; police detectives
The author is one of Japan's most popular crime writers. This novel features Detective Kindaichi and takes place in the 1940s against a background of gangland murders and revenge killings.
Subject keyword: urban life
Original language: Japanese
Source consulted for annotation:
Global Books in Print (online) (synopsis).

Banana Yoshimoto. *Goodbye, Tsugumi*.
Translated by Michael Emmerich. New York: Grove Press, 2002. 186 pages.
Genres/literary styles/story types: mainstream fiction; coming-of-age
While waiting for Maria's father to divorce his wife, Maria and her unmarried mother are living and working in a seaside inn operated by Maria's aunt and uncle. The story focuses on the developing relationship between Maria and Tsugumi, her sickly and spoiled cousin.
Subject keyword: family histories
Original language: Japanese

Sources consulted for annotation:
Amazon.com (book description).
Freeman, John. *St. Petersburg Times*, 4 August 2002, p. 4D.
Reale, Michelle. *Library Journal* 127 (15 June 2002): 98.
Spurling, John. *The Sunday Times*, 18 August 2002 (from Factiva databases).
Wynn, Judith *Boston Herald*, 15 September 2002, p. 038.
Zaleski, Jeff. *Publishers Weekly* 249 (8 July 2002): 29.
Some other translated books written by Banana Yoshimoto: *Kitchen*; *Asleep*; *NP*; *Lizard*; *Hard-boiled & Hard Luck*; *Amrita*

Akira Yoshimura. *Storm Rider.*
Translated by Philip Gabriel. New York: Harcourt, 2004. 367 pages.
Genres/literary styles/story types: adventure; quest
When Hikotaro, a 13-year-old orphan, is pulled from a raging sea by American sailors, he is taken to San Francisco. Rechristened Hikozo, he yearns for his homeland. But he is unable to return because of a law forbidding Japanese who have lived abroad to re-enter Japan. A rich American adopts Hikozo, giving him the privileges and power he never dreamed of. The U.S. Civil War, the Taiping Rebellion, and the Meiji Restoration figure prominently as background material.
Subject keyword: family histories
Original language: Japanese
Sources consulted for annotation:
Amazon.com (book description).
Green, Roland. *Booklist* 100 (1 May 2004): 1548.
Keeley, Brian. *Far Eastern Economic Review*, 9 September 2004, p. 55.
Zaleski, Jeff. *Publishers Weekly* 251 (22 March 2004): 59.
Some other translated books written by Akira Yoshimura: *On Parole*; *Shipwrecks*; *One Man's Justice*

Miri Yu. *Gold Rush.*
Translated by Stephen Snyder. New York: Welcome Rain, 2002. 286 pages.
Genres/literary styles/story types: crime fiction; suspense
The corruption, hypocrisy, and desolation of contemporary Japanese society are stunningly laid bare in this intensely violent novel that has evoked comparisons with Dostoyevsky's *Crime and Punishment*. Fourteen-year-old Kazuki Yuminaga murders his abusive father in order to take over his gambling empire. But things are not that simple: He must contend with his father's girlfriend and opposition from company executives.
Subject keyword: urban life
Original language: Japanese
Sources consulted for annotation:
Amazon.com (book description).
Olson, Ray. *Booklist* 98 (1 May 2002): 1485.
Quan, Shirley N. *Library Journal* 127 (1 May 2002): 136.
Zaleski, Jeff. *Publishers Weekly* 249 (25 March 2002): 38.

ANNOTATIONS FOR TRANSLATED BOOKS FROM KOREA

Chong-nae Cho (Cho Chong-Rae). *Playing with Fire.*
Translated by Chun Kyung-Ja. Ithaca, NY: East Asia Program, Cornell University, 1997. 188 pages.
Genre/literary style/story type: mainstream fiction

Hwang is a happily married father and businessman. At the end of a seemingly ordinary work day, he receives a telephone call from a man who knows his dark and secret past as Bae Jamsu. Hwang is the name he gave himself after the end of the war to hide not only his communist past but also his part in the death of 39 members of a rival family. But the son of one of the murdered members of this family has tracked Bae Jamsu down and begins to exact revenge.
Subject keyword: war
Original language: Korean
Sources consulted for annotation:
Amazon.com (book description).
Crown, Bonnie R. *World Literature Today* 72 (Winter 1998): 212.
Another translated book written by Chong-nae Cho: *The Land of the Banished*

Son-jak Cho (Cho Sun Jak). *The Preview and Other Stories.*
Translated by Kim Chan Young and David R. Carter. Fremont, CA: Asian Humanities Press, 2003. 243 pages.
Genres/literary styles/story types: mainstream fiction; short stories
The ostensibly successful economic development of South Korea in the postwar era conceals a harsh reality: endemic poverty, moral corruption, and the failure to see beyond the comforting rhetoric of achievement and glory that laid the groundwork for the often gaudy excesses of a consumption-obsessed society. These stories capture that multidimensional hypocrisy, focusing on marginalized individuals and social misfits.
Subject keyword: social problems
Original language: Korean
Source consulted for annotation:
Amazon.com (book description).

Mu-suk Han (Hahn Moo-Sook). *And So Flows History.*
Translated by Young-Key Kim-Renaud. Honolulu, HI: University of Hawai'i Press, 2005. 282 pages.
Genre/literary style/story type: historical fiction
The Cho family was once a mighty clan, but when the family patriarch rapes a young slave, its downfall begins. Focusing on three generations of the Chos, the book paints a vivid portrait of Korean history, including the Donghak Peasant Revolution in 1894 and the 35-year-long Japanese occupation of Korea in the first part of the twentieth century. Important questions such as nationalism and the nature of class struggle are invoked, as are the effects of westernization, especially missionary work.
Subject keyword: family histories
Original language: Korean
Sources consulted for annotation:
Amazon.com (about the author; book description).
Back cover of the book.
Carolan, T. *Choice* 43 (February 2006): 1011.
Some other translated books written by Mu-suk Han: *Encounter: A Novel of Nineteenth-Century Korea*; *The Hermitage of Flowing Water and Nine Others*; *In the Depths*

Sung-won Han (Han Sung-won). *Father and Son.*
Translated by Yu Young-nan and Julie Pickering. Dumont, NJ: Homa & Sekey Books, 2002. 285 pages.
Genre/literary style/story type: mainstream fiction

This book examines the social, historical, intellectual, and emotional legacy left by parents to their children in an age of rapid industrialization. The poet and publisher Chu-ch'ôl despairs about his rebellious and disrespectful son Yun-gil. When Chu-ch'ôl and his wife attend the funeral of Chu-ch'ôl's brother, both are anxious not only because Yun-gil is being sought by government authorities but also because Chu-ch'ôl's cousin Chu-ôn, a government agent, will be at the funeral. How could father and son have become such strangers?
Subject keywords: family histories; social problems
Original language: Korean
Sources consulted for annotation:
Amazon.com (book description).
Young-nan, Yu. The translators' note to the book.

Sog-yong Hwang (Hwang Sok-yong). *The Guest.*
Translated by Kyung-Ja Chun and Maya West. New York: Seven Stories Press, 2005. 237 pages.
Genre/literary style/story type: mainstream fiction
After the Korean War, two brothers immigrate to the United States. But they cannot so easily leave their memories behind. Horrific violence is a constant presence in their lives. When one of the brothers dies, the other returns to Korea—only to discover that his dead brother was involved in the bloodshed.
Related title by the same author:
In *The Old Garden*, a political prisoner is released after 18 years in captivity. Obviously, nothing is as he remembers it, so he becomes a wandering lost soul among the catacombs of modernity, hoping to discover the wellsprings of his youthful passion for rebellion.
Subject keyword: war
Original language: Korean
Sources consulted for annotation:
Donovan, Deborah. *Booklist* 102 (15 October 2005): 30.
Global Books in Print (online) (synopsis/book jacket).
Publishers Weekly 252 (29 August 2005): 31.
Ramzy, Austin. *Time International* 167 (9 January 2006): 47.
Some other translated books written by Sog-yong Hwang: *The Shadow of Arms*; *The Old Garden*

Sok-kyong Kang (Kang Sok-Kyong). *The Valley Nearby.*
Translated by Choi Kyong-do. Portsmouth, NH: Heinemann, 1997. 317 pages.
Genres/literary styles/story types: mainstream fiction; women's lives
This novel traces the passionate and persistent attempts of a rural woman to balance traditions and her yearning for freedom; her resistance to the socially expected role of an obedient housewife; and her hope for a better future for her daughter. As noted by Bonnie R. Crown, the book is especially valuable "for its descriptions and discussions of Korean esthetics, the making of pottery, folk art, nature and the environment, food, Buddhism, and other aspects of Korean culture."
Subject keywords: family histories; social roles
Original language: Korean
Sources consulted for annotation:
Amazon.com (book description).
Crown, Bonnie R. *World Literature Today* 72 (Summer 1998): 694.

Chu-yong Kim (Kim Joo-young). *The Sound of Thunder.*
Translated by Chun Kyung-Ja. Seoul, Korea: Si-sa-yong-o-sa, 1990. 326 pages.

Genres/literary styles/story types: mainstream fiction; women's lives
This novel chronicles the desperately bleak and ravaged life of a young widow caught in the maelstrom of the Korean war. She has experienced every indignity imaginable, and now—in the aftermath of the war—she must cope with emotional, psychological, and physical trauma that is seemingly never-ending. As she struggles to find a place to call home, her memories of loss becoming overwhelming.
Subject keyword: war
Original language: Korean
Source consulted for annotation:
Kyung-ja, Chun. Preface to the book.

Won-il Kim (Kim Wŏn-il). *Evening Glow.*
Translated by Agnita M. Tennant. Fremont, CA: Asian Humanities Press, 2003. 261 pages.
Genre/literary style/story type: mainstream fiction
Kapsu, now a resident of Seoul, was born in a small Korean town that was seized by communists in 1948. During the invasion, Kapsu's father fervently embraced the utopian ideals of the conquerors, perceiving them as liberators and joining in the euphoric violence of the time. Some 30 years after these events, Kapsu returns to revisit his childhood home and try to make peace with a past characterized by violence and anguish.
Subject keyword: social problems
Original language: Korean
Sources consulted for annotation:
Amazon.com (book description).
Back cover of the book.
Another translated book written by Won-il Kim: *The Wind and the River*

Jo Kyung-Ran (Kyung-Ran Jo). *Tongue.*
Translated by Chi-Young Kim. New York: Bloomsbury, 2009. 224 pages.
Genre/literary style/story type: mainstream fiction; women's lives
Jeong Ji-won, a renowned chef and founder of a cooking school, must start anew when her longtime lover leaves her for one of her students. Thus, she goes back to first principles, rediscovering the pleasures of Italian cooking and the resiliency of her soul.
Subject keyword: identity
Original language: Korean
Source consulted for annotation:
McCulloch, Alison. *The New York Times Book Review*, 6 August 2009 (online).

Kyong-ni Pak (Park Kyong-ni). *The Curse of Kim's Daughters.*
Translated by Choonwon Kang et al. Paramus, NJ: Homa & Sekey Books, 2004. 299 pages.
Genres/literary styles/story types: historical fiction; literary historical
Songsu Kim is orphaned when his mother commits suicide and his father abandons him. Taken in by Pongjay, his uncle, he marries Punshi, the woman whom his uncle has chosen for him. For a time, things go well: He inherits a pharmacy and becomes an investor in a fishing fleet. But Songsu and Punshi's first child, a son, dies, and the lives of their five daughters are cursed by accusations of infanticide, madness, and domestic tragedy. This book is set against the background of important historical events in pre-1950s Korea.
Subject keyword: family histories
Original language: Korean

Sources consulted for annotation:
Amazon.com (book description).
Back cover of the book.
Scott, Whitney. *Booklist* 100 (July 2004): 1819.
Another translated book written by Kyong-ni Pak: *Land*

Wan-so Pak (Pak Wanso). *My Very Last Possession and Other Stories.*
Translated by Kyung-Ja Chun. Armonk, NY: M. E. Sharpe, 1999. 220 pages.
Genres/literary styles/story types: mainstream fiction; short stories
According to Janice P. Nimura, each of the stories in this collection "offer glimpses of a society at once anchored in and imprisoned by strict Confucian mores and buffeted by war, political unrest and massive emigration." What does hypocrisy feel like? What would real healing involve? What does it mean to be kind? The author has built a solid reputation as an eloquent and insightful analyst of the hopes and excesses of postwar modernization in South Korea.
Subject keyword: modernization
Original language: Korean
Sources consulted for annotation:
Haboush, JaHyun Kim. *The Journal of Asian Studies* 59 (November 2000): 1055.
Knowlton, Edgar C. *World Literature Today* 74 (Winter 2000): 244.
Nimura, Janice P. *The New York Times Book Review*, 10 October 1999, p. 23.
Steinberg, Sybil S. *Publishers Weekly* 246 (21 June 1999): 56.
Some other translated books written by Wan-so Pak: *A Sketch of the Fading Sun*; *The Naked Tree*; *Three Days in That Autumn*

Cho Se-hui (Se-hui Cho). *The Dwarf.*
Translated by Bruce and Ju-chan Fulton. Honolulu, HI: University of Hawai'i Press, 2006. 224 pages.
Genres/literary styles/story types: mainstream fiction; short stories
A bestseller in Korea, this collection of 12 interlinked stories centers on the difficult circumstances in which a poverty-stricken family find themselves during the so-called Korean industrial boom of the 1970s. The author delivers an eloquent portrait of hubris and economic struggle where the rich get richer and the poor get poorer. Writing in *Words Without Borders*, Hayun Jung called *The Dwarf* "an imaginative cross between stark socio-political fiction and magical realism, used to deeply moving effect."
Subject keywords: power; urban life
Original language: Korean
Source consulted for annotation:
University of Hawai'i Press website (book description), http://www.uhpress.hawaii.edu.

Chang-sun Son (Jang-Soon Sohn). *A Floating City on the Water.*
Translated by Jin-Young Choi. Paramus, NJ: Homa & Sekey Books, 2005. 178 pages.
Genre/literary style/story type: mainstream fiction
The partition of Korea affected families in numerous tragic ways. While in Paris, Sujin—who was born in South Korea—falls in love with a young man who turns out to be her brother, born earlier in North Korea. On finding out their true identities, they part ways: Hansuk remains in France while Sujin—who, unbeknownst to Hansuk, is pregnant—returns to South Korea, where she bears Hyung-woo. Twenty years later, son and father meet.
Subject keyword: family histories
Original language: Korean
Source consulted for annotation:
Amazon.com (book description).

Kwi-ja Yang (Yang Gui-ja). *Contradictions.*
Translated by Stephen Epstein and Kim Mi-Young. Ithaca, NY: East Asia Program, Cornell University, 2005. 172 pages.
Genres/literary styles/story types: mainstream fiction; women's lives
Struggling to capture the essence of happiness, Jin-jin An must decide between two men who profess to love her but who could not be more different. At the same time, she must somehow manage relationships with her less-than-pleasant mother; her brother, who thinks of himself as a gangster in training; and her father, who, when he is not drinking, is slipping into madness.
Subject keyword: family histories
Original language: Korean
Sources consulted for annotation:
Amazon.com (book description).
Saran, Mishi. *Far Eastern Economic Review* 168 (December 2005): 72.
Some other translated books written by Kwi-ja Yang: *A Distant and Beautiful Place*; *Strength from Sorrow*

Chung Yeun-hee. *One Human Family and Other Stories.*
Translated by Hyun-jae Yee Sallee. Buffalo, NY: White Pine Press, 2008. 191 pages.
Genres/literary styles/story types: mainstream fiction; short stories
This collection of four stories and a novella explores the continuing legacy of the Korean War. Animosities still linger, as evidenced by a group of senior citizens at a nursing home who suspect that a new arrival collaborated with the enemy. In another story, a child mistakes discarded condoms for balloons—an error that creates new wounds and opens up old ones.
Subject keywords: politics; war
Original language: Korean
Sources consulted for annotation:
Global Books in Print (online) (synopsis/book jacket).
White Pine Press (book description), http://www.whitepine.org.

Cho'ng-jun Yi (Yi Ch'ŏng-jun). *The Prophet and Other Stories.*
Translated by Julie Pickering. Ithaca, NY: East Asia Program, Cornell University, 1999. 189 pages.
Genres/literary styles/story types: mainstream fiction; short stories
This collection of five stories—all of which deal with the various ways that ordinary individuals survive during times of political and cultural crises—grows out of the traumatic history of modern Korea: occupation by a foreign power; the Korean War and subsequent partition; dictatorship under the military; rapid modernization and the concomitant erosion of a panoply of traditional practices; and the painful transition to an accelerated capitalist economy that brings in its wake an ever-increasing emphasis on materialism.
Subject keyword: social problems
Original language: Korean
Sources consulted for annotation:
Back cover of the book.
Crown, Bonnie R. *World Literature Today* 74 (Winter 2000): 244.
Some other translated books written by Chong-jun Yi: *Your Paradise*; *The Wounded*

Ho-ch'ol Yi (Lee Ho-Chul). *Panmunjom and Other Stories.*
Translated by Theodore H. Hughes; with two stories translated by Bruce and Ju-Chan Fulton. Norwalk, CT: EastBridge, 2005. 219 pages.
Genres/literary styles/story types: mainstream fiction; short stories

According to the publisher's website, the author is considered to be "one of South Korea's most prominent contemporary writers." The book is written in "an astonishing variety of literary styles" so as to offer an audience multiple perspectives from which to view "the devastating impact authoritarian rule, draconian anticommunism, and . . . national division have had on the everyday lives of Koreans" over the last 50 years. Yi was himself imprisoned for his outspoken support of human rights in the 1970s and 1980s.
Subject keywords: politics; power
Original language: Korean
Sources consulted for annotation:
Amazon.com (book description).
Hughes, Theodore. Introduction to the book.
Another translated book written by Ho-chol Yi: *Southerners, Northerners*

In-hwa Yi (Yi In-hwa). *Everlasting Empire.*
Translated by Yu Young-nan. White Plains, NY: EastBridge, 2002. 264 pages.
Genres/literary styles/story types: crime fiction; historical mysteries
This book, which has elements of historical fiction and mystery, has been compared to the work of Umberto Eco. An ancient manuscript is found, but there is some dispute about its authenticity, especially since it purports to give insight into the political machinations, philosophies, and cultural context of Korean life in the late eighteenth and early nineteenth centuries.
Subject keywords: philosophy; power
Original language: Korean
Sources consulted for annotation:
Amazon.com (book description).
Back cover of the book.
Knowlton, Edgar C. *World Literature Today* 77 (April/June 2003): 99.

Mun-yol Yi (Yi Munyol). *Our Twisted Hero.*
Translated by Kevin O'Rourke. New York: Hyperion East, 2001. 122 pages.
Genre/literary style/story type: mainstream fiction
Inspired by events in Kwangju in 1980 when South Korean soldiers killed numerous democracy advocates, this intensely psychological novel focuses on two boys in a small rural school. Twelve-year-old Han Pyongt'ae is starting the fifth grade. Ceaselessly bullied by another student, he succumbs to his fate, passively biding his time until a new teacher arrives. An allegory about two opposing political systems, the book has drawn comparisons with William Golding's *Lord of the Flies*.
Subject keywords: politics; power
Original language: Korean
Sources consulted for annotation:
Crown, Bonnie R. *World Literature Today* 76 (Winter 2002): 138.
Leber, Michele. *Booklist* 97 (1 January/15 January 2001): 920.
Obejas, Achy. *The Village Voice* 46 (10 July 2001): 71.
Quan, Shirley N. *Library Journal* 126 (January 2001): 158.
Steinberg, Sybil S. *Publishers Weekly* 247 (11 December 2000): 64.
Some other translated books written by Mun-yol Yi: *Hail to the Emperor!*; *The Poet*; *An Appointment with My Brother*

Sung-u Yi (Lee Seung-U). *The Reverse Side of Life.*
Translated by Yoo-Jung Kong. London: Peter Owen, 2006. 208 pages.

Genres/literary styles/story types: mainstream fiction; postmodernism
The life of a famous fictional South Korean writer, Bugil Bak, comes under scrutiny when a journalist is asked to write about him. In many ways, Bak resembles Lee Seung-U, so part of the fun involves the author attempting to sort through Bak's life, especially his early years, which were marked by the disappearance of his mother and father as well as his relationship with religion. Critics raved about the author's elegant and inventive metafictional sleights of hand.
Subject keyword: writers
Original language: Korean
Sources consulted for annotation:
Back cover of the book.
The Complete Review (book review), http://www.complete-review.com.
Peter Owen Publishers (book description), http://www.peterowen.com.
Another translated book written by Sung-u Yi: *The Prviate Life of Plants*

Tong-ha Yi (Dong-ha Lee). ***Toy City.***
Translated by Chi-Young Kim. St. Paul, MN: Koryo Press, 2007. 214 pages.
Genre/literary style/story type: mainstream fiction
This novel is the melancholic coming-of-age story of an adolescent boy in the aftermath of the Korean War. When circumstances force him to become the economic mainstay of his family, he grudgingly accepts his role and soon discovers that the only person he can count on is himself. As he encounters painful moment after painful moment, he nevertheless finds solace in the simple pleasures of childhood.
Subject keyword: rural life
Original language: Korean
Source consulted for annotation:
Koryo Press website (book description), http://www.koryopress.com.
Another translated book written by Tong-ha Yi: *Shrapnel and Other Stories*

Kim Yong-Ha (Young-ha Kim). ***I Have The Right to Destroy Myself.***
Translated by Chi-Young Kim. Orlando, FL: Harcourt, 2007. 119 pages.
Genres/literary styles/story types: crime fiction; suspense
In 1990s Korea, an unnamed narrator who is obsessed with the painting *The Death of Marat* engages in an odd profession: helping others commit suicide. Se-Yeon sleeps with two brothers, disappears, metamorphoses into various other women, and finally resurfaces as a client of the narrator. Critics have invoked Stephen Crane's novels *Maggie: A Girl of the Streets* and *George's Mother* as points of comparison to this novel.
Subject keyword: urban life
Original language: Korean
Source consulted for annotation:
Global Books in Print (online) (reviews from *Booklist* and *Publishers Weekly*).

CHAPTER 4

South Asia: India, Pakistan, Bangladesh, Nepal, and Other South Asian Countries

Language groups:		**Countries represented:**
Assamese	Nepali	Bangladesh
Bengali	Oriya (Uriya)	Burma
Burmese	Punjabi	India
Gujarati	Rajasthani	Indonesia
Hindi/Hindustani	Sinhalese	Laos
Indonesian	Tamil	Malaysia
Kannada	Telugu	Nepal
Lao	Thai/Siamese	Pakistan
Malaysian	Urdu	Sri Lanka
Marathi	Vietnamese	Thailand
		Vietnam

INTRODUCTION

This chapter contains annotations of books translated from languages that are spoken in India, Pakistan, and Bangladesh, including Assamese, Bengali, Gujarti, Hindi/Hindustani, Marathi, Oriya, Punjabi, Rasjasthani, Telugu, and Urdu. Also discussed are translations from Burmese, Indonesian, Lao, Malaysian, Nepali, Sinhalese, Tamil, Thai/Siamese, and Vietnamese.

Taken as a group, the authors and novels mentioned in this chapter are little known to English-speaking audiences. Still, a few may elicit recognition. For example, there is Taslima Nasrin, a Bengali author whose novel *Shame* caused much consternation; Manoj Das, who writes both in Oriya and English; Qurratulain Hyder, an Urdu writer whose novel *River of Fire* has received international acclaim, earning comparisons with the work of Gabriel García Márquez; Mahasweta Devi, whose *Imaginary Maps: Three*

Stories was translated in 1995 by Gayatri Chakravarty Spivak, a widely respected Indian postcolonial literary critic; Pramoedya Ananta Toer, an Indonesian author renowned for his four-volume *Buru Quartet*; and Tran Vu, a Vietnamese author who has received media attention in *The New York Times Book Review* and *Atlantic Monthly* for his short story collection *The Dragon Hunt*.

Earlier Translated Literature

For readers who wish to explore further in the literature of the Indian languages, an indispensable starting point is a popular translated text originally written in Sanskrit: *The Bhagavad Gita*, readily available as a Penguin paperback or in the Oxford World's Classics series. Many people know that Bengali author Rabindranath Tagore won the Nobel Prize in 1913; indeed, his self-translation of *Gitanjali* is widely known and read. But there are other less famous translated Indian texts that are noteworthy. These include Bankim Chandra Chatterjee's *The Poison Tree* from the nineteenth century and Bibhutibhushan Bandhopadhyay's *Pather Panchali: Song of the Road* (the basis of a 1955 film) from the twentieth century.

SOURCES CONSULTED

France, Peter. (Ed.). (2000). "Indian Languages." In *The Oxford Guide to Literature in English Translation*, pp. 447–466. Oxford: Oxford University Press.

BIBLIOGRAPHIC ESSAY

Typically, when readers think of Indian and South Asian literature, they associate it with such writers as Anita Desai, Bharati Mukherjee, Vikram Seth, Amitav Ghosh, Jhumpa Lahiri, Arundhati Roy, Monica Ali, and Salman Rushdie, who write in English. To be sure, these are significant writers—about whom more bio-bibliographic information can be found in such sources as the volume in the Dictionary of Literary Biography series entitled *South Asian Writers in English*, edited by Fakrul Alum (2006; vol. 323); *South Asian Literature in English: An Encyclopedia*, edited by Jaina C. Sanga; and *South Asian Literature in English: An A-to-Z Guide*, also edited by Jaina C. Sanga. But it would be a huge mistake to think that English-language literature from India and other countries of South Asia completely defines or captures the complexity of this area. All public and academic libraries—no matter their size—should therefore make every effort to acquire all 14 volumes that comprise the Global Encyclopaedic Literature Series published in New Delhi, India, by Global Vision Publishing House. These 14 volumes are divided into five sets: *Encyclopaedic Dictionary of Punjabi Literature* (2 vols.); *Encyclopaedic Dictionary of Pâli Literature* (2 vols.); *Encyclopaedic Dictionary of Sanskrit Literature* (5 vols.); *Encyclopaedic Dictionary of Asian Novels and Novelists* (3 vols.); and *Encyclopaedic Dictionary of Urdu Literature* (2 vols.). Each of the volumes in each of the five sets provides invaluable insight into the various literatures written in non-English languages from this region.

The ideal way to appreciate the vast and intricate mosaic of vernacular languages present in the region is to first look at the three-volume *Encyclopaedic Dictionary of Asian Novels and Novelists*, which provides convenient bio-bibliographic information about 222 Asian novels, 289 novelists, and 37 prominent Asian languages, including Assamese, Bengali, Burmese, Dogri, Gujarati, Hindi, Kashmiri, Kazakh, Malaysian, Sindhi, Tajik, Tamil, Thai, and Vietnamese, not to mention Indonesian, Chinese, and Turkish. Turn next to the two-volume *Encyclopaedic Dictionary of Urdu Literature* or the two-volume *Encyclopaedic Dictionary of Punjabi Literature*, which have detailed bio-bibliographic entries about authors, works, literary movements, and genres in Urdu and Punjabi literature, respectively. If the foregoing volumes are principally concerned with authors and works from the nineteenth and twentieth centuries, then the two-volume *Encyclopaedic Dictionary of Pâli Literature*, which contains more than 600 entries, and the five-volume *Encyclopaedic Dictionary of Sanskrit*

Literature, which marshals information about some 1,150 authors and 1,100 significant literary works, will introduce readers to literary traditions with roots extending as far back as 2000 B.C.E.

India and Pakistan

Among its many other virtues, Nalini Natarajan's *Handbook of Twentieth-Century Literatures of India* is published in the United States and thus may be more easily accessible than the reference texts mentioned. If libraries can only afford one book on non-English Indian literature, this is the wise choice. It contains articles about twentieth-century Assamese, Bengali, Gujarati, Hindi, Kannada, Malayalam, Marathi, Panjabi, Tamil, Telugu, Urdu, and Marathi literatures, indicating where authors from these traditions have been translated into English. For those interested in a historical overview of Indian literature ranging back to the Indian epic, classical drama, and lyric poetry, a compact and highly readable work is *The Literatures of India: An Introduction* by Edward C. Dimock Jr. and colleagues. In 17 chapters and more than 1,000 pages, *Literary Cultures in History: Reconstructions from South Asia*, edited by Sheldon Pollock, provides eloquent testimony about the way in which the past and present intersect in various South Asian literatures. Chapter titles include: Three Moments in the Genealogy of Tamil Literary Culture; Critical Tensions in the History of Kannada Literary Culture; Multiple Literary Cultures in Telugu; The Literary Culture of Premodern Kerala; The Two Histories of Literary Culture in Bengal; Work and Persons in Sinhala Literary Culture; and A Long History of Urdu Literary Culture. Also of interest might be *Indian Fiction in English Translation*, edited by Shubha Tiwari, which includes critical appraisals of the works of such authors as Qurratulain Hyder, Intizar Husain, Pratibha Ray, and Manoj Das.

Some readers will not be satisfied with chapter-length treatments of some of these literatures, no matter how expertly written. For these individuals, additional historical detail about the Urdu literary tradition can be gained from Muhammad Sadiq's *A History of Urdu Literature*; Ali Jawad Zaidi's *A History of Urdu Literature*; and M. S. Jain's *Muslim Ethos as Reflected in Urdu Literatures*. On the other hand, those interested in Punjabi literature will invariably gravitate to Sant Singh Sekhon's two-volume *A History of Panjabi Literature* or his one-volume *A History of Punjabi Literature*, co-authored with Kartar Singh Duggal.

Once readers become well-acquainted with some of the key figures and movements in South Asian literature, they will be happy to learn of the existence of anthologies. Perhaps the most wide-ranging and useful anthology is the three-volume *Modern Indian Literature: An Anthology*, edited by K. M. George. The first volume not only contains detailed historical introductions and critical analyses of 22 literary traditions (ranging from Bengali to Dogri to Kashmiri to Konkani to Manipuri to Nepali to Oriya to Rajasthani to Sanskrit) but also examples of English-language translations from these traditions. The second and third volumes feature fiction and plays, respectively, and again the editor has taken care to include translations from all 22 literatures. Equally noteworthy are the two volumes of *The Oxford India Anthology of Modern Urdu Literature*, edited by Mehr Afshan Farooqi. The first volume concentrates on poetry and prose miscellany, while the second volume contains short stories and novel extracts from such authors as Balwant Singh, Ghulam Abbas, Hajira Masroor, Khalida Husain, Qurratulain Hyder, Khadija Mastoor, and Shamsur Rahman Faruqi. A more compact anthology, which mainly includes translated literature from Benagli, Hindi, and Urdu, is *The Picador Book of Modern Indian Literature*, edited by Amit Chaudhuri. Another valuable compilation is *Hidden in the Lute: An Anthology of Two Centuries of Urdu Literature*, selected and translated by Ralph Russell. Readers specifically interested in women's writing will be drawn toward the two-volume *Women Writing in India: 600 B.C. to the Present*, edited by Susie Tharu and K. Lalitha, as well as *So That You Can Know Me: An Anthology of Pakistani Women Writers*, edited by Yasmin Hameed and Asif Aslam Farrukhi.

Thailand, Malaysia, Indonesia, and Vietnam

A marvelous anthropologically based introduction to Thai literature is Herbert P. Phillips's *Modern Thai Literature: With an Ethnographic Interpretation*. Phillips not only provides necessary contextual background to understand the community of contemporary Thai writers but also includes representative translated samples of their writings arranged according to such themes as religion, family, fun, and the search for respectability; the internationalization of Thailand and the development ethos; the deterioration of Thai life; the politicization of experience; and the search for the good life. With regard to the literature of Malaysia, no better book could be hoped for than Vladimir Braginsky's *The Heritage of Traditional Malay Literature: A Historical Survey of Genres, Writings, and Literary Views*, which traces the "ideological evolution" of Malay literature through three stages from the seventh to the nineteenth century: "the adoption of Buddhism and Hinduism and their syncretization, the Malayization of Indianized culture, [and] the initial Islamization during which the external adoption of the new religion played a dominant role, and its subsequent deepening" (p. 34). An excellent understanding of the Indonesian literary tradition can be gained through A. Teeuw's two-volume *Modern Indonesian Literature*. The first volume covers the period from about 1920 to 1965; the second volume spans 1965 to 1978. For the most up-to-date information about Indonesia, we are extremely lucky to have Stefan Danerek's *Tjerita and Novel: Literary Discourse in Post New Order Indonesia*, which focuses on Indonesian authors of the 1990s and early 2000s, introducing writers such as Taufik I. Jamil, Oka Rusmini, Ayu Utami, Eka Kurniawan, Abidah El Khalieqy, Anggie Widowati, and Nova Riyanti Yusuf.

As with all the literatures considered in this chapter, Vietnamese literature has a multifaceted lineage. Thus, it is particularly gratifying to be able to recommend Maurice M. Durand and Nguyen Tran Huan's *An Introduction to Vietnamese Literature*. There is an excellent overview of the historical and social situation in Vietnam, which was "a province of China from the second century B.C.E. to the tenth century C.E., under Chinese suzerainty from then until the end of the nineteenth century, and under French rule from then until 1954, when the communist régime took over in North Vietnam" (p. 1). Chinese influences are thus pervasive in Vietnamese culture, and the book adroitly examines the development of indigenous Vietnamese literature between the sixteenth and nineteenth centuries. The book concludes with a critical analysis of such major twentieth-century Vietnamese novelists as Nhat Linh and Khai Hung.

SELECTED REFERENCES

Bhattacharya, J. N., and Sarkar, Nilanjana. (Eds.). (2004). *Encyclopaedic Dictionary of Sanskrit Literature*. (5 vols.). New Delhi, India: Global Vision Publishing House.

Braginsky, Vladimir. (2004). *The Heritage of Traditional Malay Literature: A Historical Survey of Genres, Writings, and Literary Views*. Singapore: Institute of Southeast Asian Studies.

Chaudhuri, Amit. (Ed.). (2001). *The Picador Book of Modern Indian Literature*. London: Picador.

Danerek, Stefan. (2006). *Tjerita and Novel: Literary Discourse in Post New Order Indonesia*. Lund, Sweden: Centre for Languages and Literatures, Lund University.

Dimock Jr., Edward C.; Gerow, Edwin; Naim, C. M.; Ramanujan, A. K.; Roadarmel, Gordon; and van Buitenen, J. A. B. (1974). *The Literatures of India: An Introduction*. Chicago: University of Chicago Press.

Durand, Maurice M., and Huan, Nguyen Tran. (1985). *An Introduction to Vietnamese Literature*. (Trans. by D. M. Hawke). New York: Columbia University Press.

Farooqi, Mehr Afshan. (2008). *The Oxford India Anthology of Modern Urdu Literature* (2 vols.). Oxford: Oxford University Press.

George, K. M. (Ed.). (1992–1994). *Modern Indian Literature: An Anthology*. (3 vols.). New Delhi, India: Sahitya Akademi.

Hameed, Yasmin, and Farrukhi, Asif Aslam. (Eds.). (1997). *So That You Can Know Me: An Anthology of Pakistani Women Writers*. Reading, Berkshire, UK: Garnet.

Jain, M. S. (2000). *Muslim Ethos as Reflected in Urdu Literatures*. Jaipur, India: Rawat Publications.

Malhotra, R. P. (Ed.). (2005). *Encyclopaedic Dictionary of Asian Novels and Novelists*. (3 vols.). New Delhi, India: Global Vision Publishing House.

Malhotra, R. P., and Arora, Kuldeep. (Eds.). (2003). *Encyclopaedic Dictionary of Punjabi Literature*. (2 vols.). New Delhi, India: Global Vision Publishing House.

Natarajan, Nalini. (Ed.). (1996). *Handbook of Twentieth-Century Literatures of India*. Westport, CT: Greenwood Press.

Phillips, Herbert P. (1987). *Modern Thai Literature: With an Ethnographic Interpretation*. Honolulu, HI: University of Hawai'i Press.

Pollock, Sheldon. (Ed.). (2003). *Literary Cultures in History: Reconstructions from South Asia*. Berkeley, CA: University of California Press.

Russell, Ralph. (Ed.). (1995). *Hidden in the Lute: An Anthology of Two Centuries of Urdu Literature*. Manchester, UK: Carcanet.

Sadiq, Muhammad. (1964). *A History of Urdu Literature*. London: Oxford University Press.

Samiuddin, Abida. (Ed.). (2007). *Encyclopaedic Dictionary of Urdu Literature*. (2 vols.). New Delhi, India: Global Vision Publishing House.

Sanga, Jaina C. (Ed.). (2004). *South Asian Literature in English: An Encyclopedia*. Westport, CT: Greenwood Press.

Sanga, Jaina C. (Ed.). (2003). *South Asian Literature in English: An A-to-Z Guide*. Westport, CT: Greenwood Press.

Sekhon, Sant Singh. (1993). *A History of Panjabi Literature*. (2 vols.). Patiala, India: Punjabi University Press.

Sekhon, Sant Singh, and Duggal, Kartar Singh. (1992). *A History of Punjabi Literature*. New Delhi, India: Sahitya Akademi.

Singh, N. K., and Baruah, B. (Eds.). (2003). *Encyclopaedic Dictionary of Pâli Literature*. (2 vols.). New Delhi, India: Global Vision Publishing House.

Teeuw, A. (1967–1979). *Modern Indonesian Literature*. (2 vols.). The Hague, Netherlands: Martinus Nijhoff.

Tharu, Susie, and Lalitha, K. (Eds.). (1993). *Women Writing in India: 600 B.C. to the Present*. (2 vols.). New York: The Feminist Press at the City University of New York.

Tiwari, Shubha. (Ed.). (2005). *Indian Fiction in English Translation*. New Delhi, India: Atlantic Publishers & Distributors.

Zaidi, Ali Jawad. (1993). *A History of Urdu Literature*. New Delhi, India: Sahitya Akademi.

ANNOTATIONS FOR BOOKS TRANSLATED FROM LANGUAGES OF INDIA, PAKISTAN, AND BANGLADESH

Assamese

Homena Baragohañi (Homen Borgohain). *Pita Putra*.
Translated by Ranjita Biswas. New Delhi, India: National Book Trust, 1999. 203 pages.
Genre/literary style/story type: mainstream fiction
This novel portrays the shift of generations in the remote village of Mohghuli during India's troubled road to independence. Written with an undercurrent of poignant lyricism, it tells the story of three sons rebelling against their father, Sivanath, who clings to traditional ways, yearning for an idealized past that did not and does not exist. As Sivanath becomes increasingly isolated in his conjured-up world whose values even he does not fully support, his three sons become what Ananda Bormudoi calls "a dramatic projection" of his "divided self." The book is structured so events are often told by multiple narrators—a technique that allows readers to see the hypocrisy permeating rural life in Assam.
Subject keywords: family histories; rural life
Original language: Assamese

Sources consulted for annotation:
Bormudoi, Ananda. Introduction to the book.
The Hindu (19 November 2000) (from Factiva databases).
Some other translated books written by Homena Baragohañi: *The Field of Gold and Tears*; *The Sunset*

Mamani Rayachama Goswami (Mamoni Raisom Goswami, Indira Goswami). *The Moth-Eaten Howdah of the Tusker* (or ***The Worm-Eaten Howdah of a Tusker***).
Translated by the author. New Delhi, India: Rupa, 2004. 362 pages.
Genres/literary styles/story types: mainstream fiction; women's lives
Set in a Hindu Vaishnavite monastery (sattra) ruled by an abbot according to traditional religious customs, this novel depicts the fate of Giribala, the daughter of the abbot and a teenaged widow whose spirit is crushed by patriarchal worldviews. After her husband dies, Giribala is compelled to return to the sattra, where she is locked up. Her brother Indranath, the future abbot, is depicted as a benevolent humanist eager to overturn religious orthodoxies; he tries to help Giribala by asking her to assist a European scholar who has come to the sattra to study ancient manuscripts. But after she and the scholar are found together unchaperoned and although nothing sexual has transpired, Giribala must undergo a harsh penance and ultimately commits suicide. Indranath eventually realizes that the feudal economic order underpinning religious-based conservatism was responsible for his sister's death and must therefore be overthrown if progress is to occur. When landless peasants rebel against the established order, Indranath commits suicide, riding into their midst in a semi-catonic state that symbolically atones for his sister's death and becomes a harbinger of change. Considered an Assamese classic, the book is steeped in what the authors of *Indira Goswami & Her Fictional World* label a "somber, penumbral and horrid atmosphere."
Subject keywords: rural life; social roles
Original language: Assamese
Source consulted for annotation:
Essays by Hiren Gohain, Bhishma Sahni, and Gobinda Prassad Sarma in *Indira Goswami & Her Fictional World: The Search for the Sea* (New Delhi, India: B. R. Publishing, 2002).
Some other translated books written by Mamani Rayachama Goswami: *The Shadow of Kamakhya*; *A Saga of South Kamrup*; *Shadow of Dark God*; *The Sin*; *Pages Stained with Blood*

Silabhadra (Sheelabhadra, pseudonym of R. M. Dutta Choudhury). *Agomoni Ferry Crossing.*
Translated by Nagen Dutta. New Delhi, India: B. R. Publishing, 2000. 96 pages.
Genre/literary style/story type: mainstream fiction
A man has a dream about his long-ago life as a road contractor on the lonely national highway that connects Assam with the rest of India. He sets up his base of operations at Agomoni Ferry Crossing, which—as Nagen Dutta writes in the introduction to this novel—became "a whole new world," where "[e]verything earthly, including love, greed, fear, violence and vanity" mark the fabric of everyday life. In 25 short chapters, the author describes a variegated cast of characters working on the highway as well as their interactions among themselves and with nearby residents. Exposed to the full range of human peccadilloes, misery, and joys during his time as a contractor, the author gains a better sense of his own place in the world and about the pervasive power of serendipity that ensured that he would become a road contractor. If his father's bicycle had not broken down outside the home of an engineer in 1913; if the engineer had not offered him a pump to fix the bicycle; and if the engineer had not convinced the father to open a brick field, the author would not have become a road contractor whose experiences in rural Assam allowed him to possess uncommon insight into the human condition.
Subject keyword: modernization

Original language: Assamese
Source consulted for annotation:
Dutta, Nagen. Preface to the book.
Another translated book written by Silabhadra: *Behag: A Collection of Stories*

Bengali

Anita Agnihotri. *Those Who Had Known Love.*
Translated by Rani Ray. New Delhi, India: Srishti Publishers, 2000. 204 pages.
Genres/literary styles/story types: mainstream fiction; women's lives
This is a melodic, lyrical, and philosophical reflection on love, politics, and the realities of Indian life. Rukmini grows up in Calcutta, where—amid an atmosphere of political ferment—she falls in love with her childhood friend Phalgun. It is an idyllic love and courtship, where classical music and the poetry of Rabindranath Tagore figure prominently. But as Rukimini becomes increasingly devoted to her career and travels across India, she comes face-to-face with implacable and almost insurmountable social difficulties.
Subject keyword: social problems
Original language: Bengali
Sources consulted for annotation:
Agnihotri, Anita. Author's Preface in the book.
Indiaclub.com (book description), http://www.indiaclub.com.
Another translated book written by Anita Agnihotri: *Forest Interludes: A Collection of Journals and Fiction*

Bani Basu. *The Enemy Within.*
Translated by Jayanti Datta. New Delhi, India: Orient Longman, 2002. 170 pages.
Genre/literary style/story type: mainstream fiction
According to Jayanti Datta, this novel chronicles the "haunting futility" of the Naxalite Movement, which "left an indelible imprint on the Bengali psyche." The Marxist-oriented Naxalites led a short-lived peasant uprising in the late 1960s and early 1970s centered around land reform.
Subject keyword: social problems
Original language: Bengali
Source consulted for annotation:
Datta, Jayanti. Translator's note to the book.
Another translated book written by Bani Basu: *The Birth of the Maitreya*

Sucitra Bhattacarya (Suchitra Bhattacharya). *Dahan: The Burning.*
Translated by Mahua Mitra. New Delhi, India: Srishti Publishers, 2001. 265 pages.
Genres/literary styles/story types: mainstream fiction; women's lives
Romita, a young married woman, is attacked by four men in front of many witnesses, but only one person comes to her rescue. The incident makes Romita re-examine her relationship with her husband, and it also serves as a springboard for an analysis about the place of women in a patriarchal society with clearly demarcated boundaries and regulations that dare not be questioned.
Subject keywords: social problems; social roles
Original language: Bengali
Source consulted for annotation:
Indiaclub.com (about the author; book description), http://www.indiaclub.com.
Some other translated books written by Sucitra Bhattacarya: *Autumn Bird*; *Falling Apart*; *I Am Madhabi*

Mahasweta Devi. ***Imaginary Maps.***
Translated by Gayatri Chakravarty Spivak. New York: Routledge, 1995. 248 pages.
Genres/literary styles/story types: mainstream fiction; short stories
This collection of three stories centers on the wretched social and cultural conditions in which tribal people in India live. It focuses on the destruction of their habitats, the plight of women, and the tenuousness of their poverty-stricken existence in the face of urbanization and globalization.
Subject keyword: rural life
Original language: Bengali
Source consulted for annotation:
Global Books in Print (online) (review from *Library Journal*).

Sunil Gangopadhyaya (Sunil Gangopadhyay). ***First Light.***
Translated by Aruna Chakravarti. New York: Penguin Books, 2001. 753 pages.
Genre/literary style/story type: historical fiction
This novel is a historical epic of India in the late nineteenth and early twentieth centuries, when a series of historical, political, and social events fundamentally altered the Indian landscape. At the center of the book is Rabindranath Tagore, who achieved international literary fame. According to Aruna Chakravarti, the book's title refers to "Rabindranath's creative inspiration," which is presented as "a powerful symbol of awakening" and "the first stirrings of resentment against foreign rule and the growth of a nationalist consciousness."
Subject keywords: politics; power
Original language: Bengali
Source consulted for annotation:
Chakravarti, Aruna. Introduction to the book.
Some other translated books written by Sunil Gangopadhyaya: *Arjun*; *Those Days*; *Fear and Other Stories*; *East-West*; *The Youth*; *Heaven's Gates*; *Ranu o Bhanu: The Poet and His Muse*; *The Lovers and Other Stories*

Begum Jahan Ara. ***A Fragment of a Journey.***
Translated by Bela Dutt Gupta. Dhaka, Bangladesh: Taran Publishers, 1992. 152 pages.
Genre/literary style/story type: historical fiction
This novel is a firsthand account of the harrowing events surrounding the Bangladeshi Liberation War of 1971—a conflict between West Pakistan (now Pakistan) and East Pakistan that resulted in East Pakistan's independence as the new nation of Bangladesh. Caught in the raging turmoil, Monira narrates her family's struggle to survive and their desperate attempt to escape the horrors of the war. In the face of shocking brutality, Monira nevertheless displays a profound humanity and compassion for the poverty-stricken individuals she meets during her pell-mell flight.
Subject keywords: family histories; war
Original language: Bengali
Sources consulted for annotation:
Back cover of the book.
Gupta, Bela Dutt. Foreword to the book.

Shirshendu Mukhopadhyay. ***Woodworm.***
Translated by Shampa Banerjee. Madras, India: Macmillan India, 1996. 106 pages.
Genre/literary style/story type: mainstream fiction
According to Nabaneet Dev Sen, this novel portrays "a modern Indian man's abstract philosophical crisis" as he searches for "his true identity, beyond the biological, social, geographical and temporal definitions." By dint of persistent efforts, Shyam Chakrabarty has reached a middle-level managerial

position in Calcutta. But when his superior refers to him as a bastard, Shyam's world slowly begins to disintegrate. He resigns his position, alienates his friends, becomes obsessed with an unattainable female secretary, and develops an all-consuming hatred for the deafening noise of motorcycles—so much so that he uses a mirror to blind a motorcyclist, causing his death. As Shyam takes stock of his actions and their implications, he becomes a tragic figure, wandering the streets—a broken and hollow man seeking psychological and physical death.
Subject keywords: social roles; urban life
Original language: Bengali
Sources consulted for annotation:
Dev Sen, Nabaneeta. Introduction to the book.
Lago, Mary. *World Literature Today* 71 (Spring 1977): 457.
Some other translated books written by Sirshendu Mukhopadhyay: *Canker*; *Waiting for Rain*; *Tomorrow I Promise*; *Relationships: Short Stories*

Tasalima Nasarina (Taslima Nasrin). *Shame.*
Translated by Kankabati Datta. Amherst, NY: Prometheus Books, 1997. 302 pages.
Genre/literary style/story type: mainstream fiction
Politics pervades every aspect of this novel, which provides a scathing picture of social oppression and religious fervor. A member of the Bengali Muslim community, Nasrin describes the campaign of persistent violence conducted against Bangladeshi Hindus by Bangladeshi Muslims in the wake of the destruction of a medieval mosque in Ayodhya in 1992. The story focuses on Maya, a young Hindu woman who is kidnapped, and her brother Suranjan. Bangladeshi religious leaders issued a fatwa against the author.
Subject keywords: politics; social problems
Original language: Bengali
Sources consulted for annotation:
Dhar, Sujoy. *Global Information Network*, 29 November 2003, p. 1.
Edmonton Journal, 28 August 2002, p. C4.
Ingraham, Janet. *Library Journal* 122 (1 November 1997): 117.
Steinberg, Sybil S. *Publishers Weekly* 244 (29 September 1997): 68.
Some other translated books written by Tasalima Nasarina: *Shodh: Getting Even*; *Selected Columns*; *Homecoming*

Rajlukshmee Debee. *The Touch-Me-Not Girl.*
Translated by the author. Mumbai, India: Disha Books, 1997. 170 pages.
Genres/literary styles/story types: mainstream fiction; coming-of-age
This book recounts the childhood and adolescence of Lajklata, as viewed by her girlfriend Gitika. What do such concepts as friendship, love, wealth, and idealism mean in a time of sociopolitical crisis?
Subject keywords: politics; social problems
Original language: Bengali
Sources consulted for annotation:
Back cover of the book.
Indiaclub.com (book description), http://www.indiaclub.com.

Mainula Ahasana Sabera (Moinul Ahsan Saber). *The Human Hole.*
Translated by Suresh Ranjan Basak. Dhaka, Bangladesh: Bangla Academy, 2001. 109 pages.
Genre/literary style/story type: mainstream fiction

According to the preface and introduction of this book, its central theme is "the essential loss of man's simplicity and genuine passion," which can only be rediscovered in the authentic surroundings of nature. Each of the linked novellas features a man and a woman who move from civilization into a natural setting, where they experience prelapsarian innocence. They are able to emerge—if only temporarily—from the roles that society has imposed upon them, reveling in the immediacy of life and emotion.
Subject keyword: philosophy
Original language: Bengali
Sources consulted for annotation:
Basak, Suresh Ranjan. Translator's introduction to the book.
Rashid, M. Harunur. Preface to the book.

Gujarati

Dhruva Bhatta (Dhruv Bhatt). *Oceanside Blues.*
Translated by Vinod Meghani. New Delhi, India: Sahitya Akademi, 2001. 188 pages.
Genre/literary style/story type: mainstream fiction
A young engineer is tasked with surveying the semi-isolated Saurashtra region of Gujarat state. As he goes about his job in this area that abuts the Arabian Sea, he contemplates what will be lost and what will be gained when the forces of science and modernization—driven by an insatiable thirst for profit—invade outlying parts of India. The novel contains descriptions of some of the traditions, folklore, and legends of Saurashtra.
Subject keyword: social problems
Original language: Gujarati
Sources consulted for annotation:
Back cover of the book.
Bhatt, Druv. Author's foreword to the book.
Indiaclub.com (book description), http://www.indiaclub.com.

Harindra Dave. *Henceforth.*
Translated by Bharati Dave. Madras, India: Macmillan India, 1996. 86 pages.
Genre/literary style/story type: mainstream fiction
In an effort to escape his hectic urban life, the novel's protagonist retreats to Urad, a small seaside village, where he spends time thinking about his relationship with Manjari. The sea becomes a powerful character in this book—its immensity and grandeur a calming antidote to the hurly-burly of the chaotic city. As he begins to experience the peace and serenity of his new surroundings, the value and virtues of rural life assume a profound significance.
Subject keyword: rural life
Original language: Gujarati
Source consulted for annotation:
Bharati, Dharmveer. Introduction to the book.
Another translated book written by Harindra Dave: *Where Are You, My Madhav?*

Yôsepha Mekavana (Joseph Macwan). *The Stepchild.*
Translated by Rita Kothari. New Delhi, India: Oxford University Press, 2004. 240 pages.
Genre/literary style/story type: mainstream fiction
The Dalits—untouchables in the Indian caste system—face mind-boggling oppression and discrimination. This novel focuses on the lives of four marginalized members of that community. Two couples struggle to eke out a living; have numerous conflicts with landowners and members of the other castes; and are inevitably caught up in social and political turbulence.

Subject keyword: social problems
Original language: Gujarati
Sources consulted for annotation:
Back cover of the book.
Introduction to the book.

Pannalal Nanalal Patel (Pannalal Patel). ***Endurance, a Droll Saga.***
Translated by V. Y. Kantak. New Delhi, India: Sahitya Akademi, 1995. 428 pages.
Genres/literary styles/story types: mainstream fiction; coming-of-age
During a famine in Gujarat at the beginning of the twentieth century, Raju oversees the education and development of Kalu, who is transformed—as the translator of the book comments—from a "puny, sentimentalism-prone, schoolboyish young man" into a mature and socially aware adult.
Subject keyword: social problems
Original language: Gujarati
Source consulted for annotation:
Kantak, V. Y. Translator's note to the book.

Hindi/Hindustani

Mannu Bhandari. ***The Great Feast.***
Translated by Richard Alan Williams. New Delhi, India: Radha Krishna, 1981. 146 pages.
Genre/literary style/story type: mainstream fiction
This novel chronicles the events surrounding the death of Bisesar, who is in every respect an anonymous young man. But because the death, which could either be a suicide or a murder, occurs just before an election, it is ruthlessly exploited by almost everyone. Politicians on both sides, police, and the hovering media all want to turn this tragic event to their advantage.
Subject keyword: politics
Original language: Hindi/Hindustani
Sources consulted for annotation:
Amazon.com (book description).
Bhattacharjee, Biprodas. *The Statesman*, 8 April 2003, p. 1.
Some other translated books written by Mannu Bhandari: *Bunty*; *The Dusk of Life & Other Stories*

Kamleshwar. ***Partitions.***
Translated by Ameena Kazi Ansari. New York: Penguin Books, 2006. 367 pages.
Genre/literary style/story type: historical fiction
This novel, which focuses on the 1947 Partition of India, has been described on the Indiaclub website as a "boldly provocative saga . . . that relentlessly probes our underlying assumptions of history and truth, religion and nationalism." It features an unnamed judge who must determine the degree of complicity of such well-known tyrants as Adolf Hitler and Saddam Hussein as well as other lesser-known figures, such as Hernando Cortez and Lord Mountbatten, for the murders that they caused and the countries that they ravaged.
Subject keywords: politics; power
Original language: Hindi/Hindustani
Source consulted for annotation:
Indiaclub.com (book description), http://www.indiaclub.com.
Some other translated books written by Kamleshwar: *Summer Days: A Collection of Short Stories*; *The Defamed Alley*; *The Street With Fifty-Seven Lanes*

Bhisham Sahni. *Tamas*.
Translated by the author. New Delhi, India: Penguin Books, 2001. 352 pages.
Genre/literary style/story type: historical fiction
Based on real events, the novel recounts the story of the trusting and naïve Nashu. He is tricked by a manipulative Muslim politician to slaughter a pig. But when the dead animal turns up on the front steps of the mosque the next morning, the outrage of Muslims is boundless. A full-scale slaughter breaks out in the small town of Tamas, with Hindus, Sikhs, and Muslims indulging in wanton violence that foreshadows the large-scale bloodshed and chaos that will result from the 1947 Partition of India.
Subject keywords: rural life; social problems
Original language: Hindi/Hindustani
Sources consulted for annotation:
Indiaclub.com (book description), http://www.indiaclub.com.
Introduction to the book.
Some other translated books written by Bhisham Sahni: *The Boss Came to Dinner and Other Stories*; *The Mansion*; *Basanti*

Vinod Kumar Sukla (Vinod Kumar Shukla). *The Servant's Shirt*.
Translated by Satti Khanna. New Delhi, India: Penguin Books, 1999. 249 pages.
Genre/literary style/story type: mainstream fiction
A withering exploration of servitude and resistance, this novel focuses on Santu and Sampat, who are just beginning their married life in a small town in the central Indian state of Madhya Pradesh in the 1960s. Santu, a low-level clerk for the tax department, must contend with arcane regulations and stultifying bureaucracy. On the domestic front, Sampat deals with a leaking roof and the landlord's wife.
Subject keywords: family histories; rural life
Original language: Hindi/Hindustani
Sources consulted for annotation:
Indiaclub.com (book description), http://www.indiaclub.com.
Introduction to the book.

Krishna Baldev Vaid. *The Diary of a Maidservant*.
Translated by Sagaree Sengupta. New York: Oxford University Press, 2008. 264 pages.
Genres/literary styles/story types: mainstream fiction; women's lives
As the title of this novel indicates, Shanti is a young woman working as a maidservant. To pass the time and stimulate her mind, she begins to keep a diary. Here, she not only recounts the daily difficulties and struggles that she must contend with while doing her job but also her innermost thoughts, dreams, and aspirations. In so doing, she develops unique insight into her social and cultural milieu.
Subject keyword: family histories
Original language: Hindi
Source consulted for annotation:
Global Books in Print (online) (synopsis/book jacket).
Some other translated books written by Krishna Baldev Vaid: *Steps in the Darkness*; *The Broken Mirror*

Omprakash Valmiki. *Joothan: An Untouchable's Life*.
Translated by Arun Prabha Mukherjee. New York: Columbia University Press, 2003. 208 pages.
Genre/literary style/story type: realism

This book is not fiction; rather, it is the author's autobiography of the life of what are referred to in Indian society as "untouchables"—members of low castes. From a legal standpoint, the caste system was done away with in 1949, but the type of social and cultural stratification that marginalizes Dalits is still an ongoing problem. *Joothan* explores the abject and degrading reality of Dalit life in the 1950 as well as the gradual political awakening of Dalits through the work of the politician B. R. Ambedkar. This book is included here because there are very few accounts of Dalit life by a Dalit.
Subject keyword: social problems
Original language: Hindi
Source consulted for annotation:
Columbia University website (book description), http://cup.columbia.edu.

Nirmal Verma. *The Last Wilderness.*
Translated by Pratik Kanjilal. New Delhi, India: Indigo Publishing, 2002. 293 pages.
Genre/literary style/story type: mainstream fiction
This novel is a philosophical meditation about what remains to be done when the end of life is near. What is one's obligation and duty before one leaves this world? Set in a small town in the Himalayas, the book examines the lives of—in the words of Indiaclub.com—"[a]n ageing [sic] civil servant who lives only in memory, a German woman once taken for a spy, a doctor who visits patients on horseback and a philosopher who has taken to growing apples."
Subject keywords: aging; rural life
Original language: Hindi/Hindustani
Source consulted for annotation:
Indiaclub.com (book description), http://www.indiaclub.com.
Some other translated books written by Nirmal Verma: *Maya Darpan and Other Stories*; *The Crows of Deliverance*; *Indian Errant: Selected Stories of Nirmal Verma*

Kannada

U. R. Anantha Murthy. *Bharathipura.*
Translated by P. Sreenivasa Rao. Madras, India: Macmillian India, 1996. 222 pages.
Genre/literary style/story type: mainstream fiction
Jagannatha is a rich landholding atheist who has experienced the bracing effects of modernity and progress while visiting England. When he returns to his small village in southern India, he tries to implement Western-style social and cultural reforms, focusing on making life better for the most poverty-stricken of his fellow citizens. But his efforts are marred by the persistence of caste hierarchies.
Subject keyword: rural life
Original language: Kannada
Source consulted for annotation:
Rao, Susheela N. *World Literature Today* 71 (Spring 1997): 457–458.
Another translated book written by U. R. Anantha Murthy: *Samskara*

Marathi

Jayavant Dvarkanath Dalvi (Jayawant Dalvi). *Leaves of Life.*
Translated by P. A. Lad. Mumbai, India: Disha Books, 1998. 196 pages.
Genre/literary style/story type: mainstream fiction
According to Susheela N. Rao, this is "an autobiographical memoir" that examines "the disintegration and disappearance of a whole indigenous way of life under the impact of an alien culture in the name of progress." An unnamed narrator returns to his native village—only to find that it is no longer the idyllic place that he remembers.

Subject keywords: culture conflict; rural life
Original language: Marathi
Source consulted for annotation:
Rao, Susheela N. *World Literature Today* 74 (Winter 2000): 239.
Another translated book written by Jayavant Dvarkanath Dalvi: *Chakra*

Kiran Nagarkar. *Seven Sixes Are Forty-Three.*
Translated by Shubha Slee. Portsmouth, NH: Heinemann, 1995. 177 pages.
Genres/literary styles/story types: mainstream fiction; coming-of-age
Kushank Purandare is a struggling writer waiting for the world to recognize him, getting by with the help of his friends and acquaintances. As he waits, he recalls his childhood and adolescence, invoking such themes as hopelessness, suffering, and alienation. Critics have commented on the striking presence of sexual themes and language—elements which reshaped Marathi literature. The author writes in both Marathi and English.
Subject keyword: social problems
Original language: Marathi
Sources consulted for annotation:
Sharma, Kalpana. *The Hindu*, 5 March 2006, p. 1.
Rao, Susheela N. *World Literature Today* 70 (Summer 1996): 767.
Sarang, V. *World Literature Today* 56 (Winter 1982): 187.
Some other translated books written by Kiran Nagarkar: *Ravan & Eddie*; *Cuckold*; *God's Little Soldier*

Oriya (Uriya)

Manoj Das. *Chasing the Rainbow: Growing Up in an Indian Village.*
Translated by the author. New Delhi, India: Oxford University Press, 2004. 160 pages.
Genres/literary styles/story types: mainstream fiction; coming-of-age
These short stories take place in a number of Indian villages and towns where the author lived between ages four and 14: Sankhari; Gunupur, Jamalpur; Jaleswarpur; and Mirgoda. As with many of the author's stories, two themes predominate: rural Indian village life before the advent of modernity and the effect of change on ordinary villagers. As the author himself states, he wishes to depict rural India before the emergence of "a class of professional power-seekers eager to measure and artificially readjust the values and institutions governing village life on the Procrustean bed of the ideologies which in reality were nothing better than their personal interests." The stories nostalgically describe a world where children were raised communally. The author, who writes both in English and Oriya, is very much concerned with preserving traditional culture and mores.
Subject keywords: rural life; social problems
Original language: Oriya/Uriya
Sources consulted for annotation:
"A Note from the Publisher" in *The Dusky Horizon and Other Stories.*
Author's preface to *Chasing the Rainbow.*
Some other translated books written by Manoj Das: *The Dusky Horizon*; *Farewell to a Ghost*; *The Vengeance and Other Stories*; *Cyclones*; *The Miracle and Other Stories*; *Bulldozers and Fables and Fantasies for Adults*; *The Crocodiles Lady*; *A Tiger at Twilight*; *A Song for Sunday and Other Stories*; *The Lady Who Died One and a Half Times and Other Fantasies*; *Mystery of the Missing Cap and Other Stories*

Gopinath Mohanty. *The Survivor.*
Translated by Bikram K. Das. Madras, India: Macmillan India, 1995. 223 pages.

Genre/literary style/story type: mainstream fiction
Recently wedded, Balidatta and Sarojini are young and on the cusp of great personal transformations. He is an ambitious and determined clerk who slowly but surely climbs the corporate ladder, ending up at the very pinnacle of his company. Sarojoni undertakes a similar climb, conquering her lack of education and illiteracy to become the head of a woman's association and the badminton partner of an influential man who later dies and who may be the father of the child that she later bears. Has the struggle for power and success all been worth it?
Subject keywords: family histories; power
Original language: Oriya/Uriya
Sources consulted for annotation:
Mohanty, Niranjan. *World Literature Today* 71 (Summer 1997): 650.
Mohapatra, Sitakanth. Introduction to the book.
Some other translated books written by Gopinath Mohanty: *Paraja*; *The Ancestor*; *High Tide, Ebb Tide*; *The Bed of Arrows and Other Stories*; *Ants and Other Stories*

Chandra Sekhar Rath (Chandrasekhar Rath). *Astride the Wheel.*
Translated by Jatindra Kumar Nayak. New Delhi, India: Oxford University Press, 2003. 179 pages.
Genre/literary style/story type: mainstream fiction
According to the Indiaclub website, this novel explores the life of Sanatan Dase, "a fifty-year-old servitor of the Lakshminarayan temple" who must regularly deal with "his wife's continuous complaints, the petty social insults . . . and the endless shortages in his life." But then he "leaves behind the claustrophobic brahmin settlement, its caste hierarchies, trivial preoccupations and repetitive rituals to travel with Sanatan Dase to Dakhineswar, Varanasi, Vrindavan, and finally to Puri." His pilgrimage "coincides with a journey into an inner world of profound mystical experience."
Subject keyword: religion
Original language: Oriya/Uriya
Sources consulted for annotation:
Indiaclub.com (about the author; book description), http://www.indiaclub.com.
Mohanty, Prafulla Kumar. Introduction to the book.
Another translated book written by Chandra Sekhar Rath: *Chandrasekhar Rath*

Punjabi

Amrita Pritam. *Blank Sheets.*
Translated by Krishna Gorowara. New Delhi, India: B. R. Publishing, 1984. 92 pages.
Genres/literary styles/story types: mainstream fiction; coming-of-age
Pankaj, who has just celebrated his 24th birthday, suddenly discovers that his mother was not married when she gave birth to him. He grew up knowing nothing of his father and now begins to question everything that he thought he knew about his mother. As he struggles to deal with his illegitimacy, he is often overwhelmed by his emotions.
Subject keyword: family histories
Original language: Punjabi
Source consulted for annotation:
Gorowara, Krishna. (1992). Introduction to the book.
Some other translated books written by Amrita Pritam: *A Line in Water*; *49 Days*; *Doctor Dev.*; *That Man*; *Two Faces of Eve.*; *The Haunted House and the Thirteenth Sun*; *Death of a City*; *Shadows of Words*; *A Statement of Agony*; *The Rising Sun*; *Flirting with Youth*; *Village No. 36*

Gurdial Singh. *Night of the Half Moon.*
Translated by Pushpinder Syal and Rana Nayar. Madras, India: Macmillan India, 1996. 151 pages.
Genre/literary style/story type: mainstream fiction
Moddan Singh returns to his small village in the Malva region of the Punjab after having served a long prison sentence for murder. During his incarceration, he nostalgically dreamt of home, but on his return, he finds that his perceptions of his friends and family have indelibly been altered by his confinement. He struggles with his good friend Ruldu; his new wife Dani; and his mother Bebe.
Subject keywords: family histories; rural life
Original language: Punjabi
Sources consulted for annotation:
Hashmi, Alamgir. *World Literature Today* 71 (Spring 1997): 460.
Maini, Darshan Singh. (1996). Introduction to the book.
Some other translated books written by Gurdial Singh: *The Last Flicker*; *Parsa*; *The Survivors*

Fakhr Zaman (Fakhar Zaman). *The Prisoner.*
Translated by Khalid Hasan. London: Peter Owen, 1996. 118 pages.
Genre/literary style/story type: mainstream fiction
In July 1977, the Pakistani government of Prime Minister Zulfikar Ali Bhutto was overthrown by General Mohammad Zia ul-Haq in a military coup. This novel recounts the author's imprisonment as a supporter of Bhutto through the story of Z, a journalist, who is falsely accused of murder and is awaiting execution by hanging.
Subject keyword: politics
Original language: Punjabi
Sources consulted for annotation:
Amazon.com (review from *Kirkus Reviews*).
Rahman, Tariq. *World Literature Today* 71 (Autumn 1997): 874.
Steinberg, Sybil S. *Publishers Weekly* 243 (30 September 1996): 62.
Some other translated books written by Fakhr Zaman: *The Lost Seven and Dead Man's Tale*; *The Lowborn*; *The Outcast (The Alien)*

Rajasthani

Vijayadanna Detha (Vijaydan Detha). *The Dilemma and Other Stories.*
Translated by Ruth Vanita. New Delhi, India: Manushi Prakashan, 1997. 169 pages.
Genres/literary styles/story types: mainstream fiction; women's lives
This is a collection of stories and tales that examine the power dynamics in relationships between women and men. In one story, Beeja—a girl who was raised as a boy by a father who wanted a son—marries Teeja. Their wedding night reveals the truth, but they nevertheless choose to live together. When they are driven from their village, a supernatural entity offers to change Beeja into a man so she and Teeja may share a life of traditional domestic bliss. But things do not work out as planned, and the relationship can only be saved when Beeja is changed back into a woman.
Subject keywords: power; rural life
Original language: Rajasthani
Sources consulted for annotation:
Amazon.com (book description).
Roy, Nilanjana S. *Business Standard*, 29 January 1998, p. 7.
Shaw, Marion. *Journal of Gender Studies* 9 (November 2000): 360.

Telugu

Balivada Kantarava (Balivada Kantha Rao). ***The Secret of Contentment and Other Telugu Short Stories.***

Translated by Sujata Patnaik. New Delhi, India: Sterling Paperbacks, 2002. 166 pages.

Genres/literary styles/story types: mainstream fiction; short stories

According to the book's foreword, this is a collection of 18 short stories by an author renowned for his "genuine humanism" and ability to give "startling insights into the oddities of human nature." Recognized as "landmarks in the tradition of the Indian short story," they accurately describe the social realities of Indian life.

Subject keyword: social problems

Original language: Telugu

Sources consulted for annotation:

Indiaclub.com (about the author; book description), http://www.indiaclub.com.

Sivaramkrishna, M. Foreword to the book.

Urdu

Ghulam Abbas. ***Hotel Moenjodaro & Other Stories.***

Translated by Khalid Hasan. New Delhi, India: Penguin Books, 1996. 242 pages.

Genres/literary styles/story types: mainstream fiction; short stories

According to Khlaid Hassan, this book is "one of the most disturbing allegories of our time." After Captain Adam Kahn, a Pakistani astronaut, lands on the moon, national celebrations break out, especially at the Hotel Moenjodaro, where international jetsetters have gathered. But in a rural village, the local mullah informs his congregation that science is an affront to the mysteries of religion. Violence and unrest sweep the country as religious leaders inveigh against all aspects of modernity. Eventually, the government is overthrown, but the various religious factions are beset by internal conflicts. Nevertheless, a harsh new regime that denounces westernization assumes control of every aspect of social and cultural life, imposing dress codes, forbidding the use of English, closing universities, instituting religious education, putting severe restrictions on the appearance and activities of women, forcing men to be bearded, and banning pictures. But when the new regime tries to rewrite the history of Islam, civil war ensues, quickly followed by a foreign invasion.

Subject keywords: modernization; social problems

Original language: Urdu

Sources consulted for annotation:

Hasan, Khalid. (1996). Introduction to the book.

Hasan, Khalid. *Friday Times*, 1 November 2002, http://www.sasnet.lu.se/ghulamabbas.html.

Another translated book written by Ghulam Abbas: *The Women's Quarter and Other Stories from Pakistan*

Abdussamad (Abdus Samad). ***A Strip of Land Two Yards Long.***

Translated by Jai Ratan. New Delhi, India: Sahitya Akademi, 1997. 239 pages.

Genre/literary style/story type: mainstream fiction

This novel focuses on the tragic effects of the Partition of India on a family in Bihar. Caught up in the general violence and the struggle to migrate to a safe place, family members become stateless, destitute, emotionally scarred, and profoundly alienated from each other and their heritage.

Subject keyword: family histories

Original language: Urdu

Source consulted for annotation:
Indiaclub.com (book description), http://www.indiaclub.com.
Another translated book written by Abdussamad: *Dawn of Dreams*

Altaf Fatimah (Altaf Fatima). *The One Who Did Not Ask.*
Translated by Rukhsana Ahmad. Portsmouth, NH: Heinemann, 1993. 334 pages.
Genres/literary styles/story types: mainstream fiction; women's lives
Set against the backdrop of the Partition of India, this novel is the coming-of-age story of Gaythi Ara Jahangir, the daughter of an upper-class Muslim family. According to Fawzia Afzal-Khan, she is "a spirited, independent-thinking feminist" whose "egalitarian idealism" and "stubborn strength" animate her struggles against "the conventional pieties of her mother and older sister's world." But her idealism is eventually shattered by social pressures.
Subject keyword: social roles
Original language: Urdu
Source consulted for annotation:
Afzal-Khan, Fawzia. *World Literature Today* 69 (Winter 1995): 224.

Asad Muhammad Khan. *The Harvest of Anger and Other Stories.*
Translated by Aquila Ismail. Karachi, Pakistan: Oxford University Press, 2002. 184 pages.
Genres/literary styles/story types: mainstream fiction; short stories
This collection of 12 stories examines such themes as death, Sufism, and memory. Critics have invoked *A Thousand and One Nights* to characterize the author's approach to storytelling.
Subject keyword: social problems
Original language: Urdu
Sources consulted for annotation:
Amazon.com (all editorial reviews).
Qader, Nasrin. *The Journal of Asian Studies* 62 (August 2003): 986.

Ismat Cughtai (Ismat Chughtai). *The Crooked Line.*
Translated by Tahira Naqvi. Portsmouth, NH: Heinemann, 1995. 335 pages.
Genres/literary styles/story types: mainstream fiction; women's lives
In this partly autobiographic novel, Shamman, the heroine, struggles to find a way through the political and religious complexities of Indian life. According to Alamgir Hashmi, the author traces her "inner development and social existence in exuberant detail, from childhood to middle age and maturity."
Subject keyword: social problems
Original language: Urdu
Sources consulted for annotation:
Amazon.com (all editorial reviews).
Hashmi, Alamgir. *World Literature Today* 70 (Spring 1996): 471–472.
Some other translated books written by Ismat Cughtai: *The Quilt & Other Stories*; *The Heart Breaks Free & The Wild One*; *Lifting the Veil: Selected Writings of Ismat Chughtai*

Abdullah Hussein (Abdullah Husain). *The Weary Generations.*
Translated by the author. London: Peter Owen, 1999. 334 pages.
Genres/literary styles/story types: historical fiction; literary historical
This novel chronicles the love story of Naim Ahmad Khan and Azra against the backdrop of the British Raj. Naim joins the British Army and fights in World War I in an effort to restore honor to his father, who has been falsely accused of treason. After losing an arm in the war, Naim, now a

decorated hero, returns home to his village of Roshan Pur. He marries Azra, a rich man's daughter who reluctantly leaves her parents' home in Delhi to take her place by her husband's side. But they drift apart as Naim becomes involved in Muslim political movements and is eventually jailed.
Subject keywords: politics; power
Original language: Urdu
Sources consulted for annotation:
Amazon.com (review from *Kirkus Reviews*).
Jaggi, Maya. *The Guardian*, 1 July 2000, p. 11.
Noor, Ronny. *World Literature Today* 74 (Winter 2000): 246.
Spurling, John. *Sunday Times*, 18 March 1999, p. 3.
Some other translated books written by Abdullah Hussein: *Émigré Journeys*; *Stories of Exile and Alienation*; *Downfall by Degrees and Other Stories*

Qurratulain Haidar (Qurratulain Hyder). *River of Fire*.
Transcreated by the author. New York: New Directions, 1999. 428 pages.
Genres/literary styles/story types: historical fiction; postcolonial fiction
Aamer Hussein, writing in *The Times Literary Supplement* (London), has said that this book "is to Urdu fiction what *A Hundred Years of Solitude* is to Hispanic literature" and that the author "has a place alongside her exact contemporaries, Milan Kundera and Gabriel García Márquez, as one of the world's major living writers." According to the book's jacket description, the novel describes "the fates of four recurring characters over two and a half millennia: Gautam, Champa, Kamal, and Cyril—Buddhist, Hindu, Muslim, and Christian." Touching upon many important aspects of Indian history and Hindi culture, it details the chicanery of colonial machinations that resulted in the Partition of India and deals compassionately with the effect of the Partition on Muslims.
Subject keywords: philosophy; power
Original language: Urdu
Sources consulted for annotation:
Amazon.com (book description; all editorial reviews).
Rao, Susheela N. *World Literature Today* 73 (Summer 1999): 597.
Zaleski, Jeff. *Publishers Weekly* 243 (23 September 1996): 74.
Some other translated books written by Qurratulain Haidar: *Fireflies in the Mist*; *A Season of Betrayals: A Short Story and Two Novellas*; *The Street Singers of Lucknow and Other Stories*; *A Woman's Life*; *My Temples, Too*; *The Exiles*

Intizar Husain. *The Seventh Door and Other Stories*.
Translated and edited by Muhammad Umar Memon and others. Boulder, CO: Lynne Rienner Publishers, 1998. 235 pages.
Genres/literary styles/story types: mainstream fiction; short stories
The partition of India and the subsequent founding of Pakistan have given rise to a rich literature. This collection is particularly to be recommended for its stylistic elegance, which Amardeep Singh describes as running the gamut from "the stark fatalism of Kafka" to "an almost Beckettian sense of futility and circularity." As a result, the author's "engagement with the epistemological problem represented by Pakistan in the immediate post-Partition era is far more interesting than Salman Rushdie's renderings in *Midnight's Children* and *Shame*."
Subject keyword: social problems
Original language: Urdu
Sources consulted for annotation:
Bose, Tirthankar. *Pacific Affairs* 72 (Winter 1999/2000): 605.
Singh, Amardeep. *Contemporary South Asia* 8 (July 1999): 240.

Some other translated books written by Intizar Husain: *Chronicle of the Peacocks: Stories of Partition, Exile and Lost Memories*; *Basti*; *Leaves and Other Stories*; *Circle and Other Stories*; *An Unwritten Epic and Other Stories*

Khadijah Mastur. *Cool, Sweet Water.*
Translated by Tahira Naqvi. Oxford: Oxford University Press, 1999. 187 pages.
Genres/literary styles/story types: mainstream fiction; short stories
This is a collection of 15 short stories and excerpts from two of the author's novels. According to the book's back cover, Mastur voices her "deep concern for the lives of ordinary people, especially women left behind in their society's scramble for modernization" in a style that could be described as "scathing, uncompromising realism."
Subject keyword: social problems
Original language: Urdu
Sources consulted for annotation:
Amazon.com (all editorial reviews and synopsis).
Indiaclub.com (book description), http://www.indiaclub.com.
Another translated book written by Khadijah Mastur: *Inner Courtyard (Aangan)*

Naiyer Masud. *Essence of Camphor.*
Translated by Muhammad Umar Memon and others. New York: New Press, 1999. 187 pages.
Genre/literary style/story type: mainstream fiction
The author, who has translated Franz Kafka into Urdu, has written a collection that many critics have described as being Kafkian in nature, with touches of magical realism. The protagonists are lonely and alienated—anomalous outcasts in a bleak world. In one story, a stuttering boy is sent away to live with a clown because his father has remarried and does not wish that his new wife should have to deal with him.
Subject keywords: identity; social roles
Original language: Urdu
Sources consulted for annotation:
Chadwell, Faye A. *Library Journal* 125 (15 February 2000): 201
Coppola, Carlo. *World Literature Today* 74 (Winter 2000): 240.
Harris, Michael. *Los Angeles Times*, 22 August 2000, p. 3.
Igloria, Luisa. *Virginian-Pilot*, 11 June 2000, p. E4.
Quinn, Mary Ellen. *Booklist* 96 (1 March 2000): 1195.
Steinberg, Sybil S. *Publishers Weekly* 247 (27 March 2000): 54.
Some other translated books written by Naiyer Masud: *Snake Catcher*; *The Myna from Peacock Garden*

Shaukat Siddiqi. *God's Own Land: A Novel of Pakistan.*
Translated by David J. Matthews. Sandgate, UK: Paul Norbury/UNESCO, 1991. 245 pages.
Genre/literary style/story type: mainstream fiction
As with Qurratulain Hyder's *River of Fire*, this novel is considered by many critics to be an Urdu classic. Against the background of poverty-stricken neighborhoods in Karachi and Lahore, it features a sister and brother who try to deal with tragic events that rip their family apart, including the murder of their mother by their stepfather.
Subject keyword: family histories
Original language: Urdu
Source consulted for annotation:
Indiaclub.com (book description), http://www.indiaclub.com.

ANNOTATIONS FOR TRANSLATED BOOKS FROM OTHER SOUTH ASIAN COUNTRIES

Burma

P. Nop (Nai Yen Ni). ***Tangay, the Setting Sun of Ramanya.***
Translated by Eveline Willi. Bangkok, Thailand: Song Sayam, 1997. 142 pages.
Genre/literary style/story type: mainstream fiction
This novel, which is based on true events as recounted by refugees and aid workers, is about the little-known Mon people, who have long struggled for freedom and independence from Burma (Myanmar).
Subject keyword: culture conflict
Original language: Mon
Sources consulted for annotation:
Amazon.com (book description).
Kaowao Newsgroup. Literature, Culture and Ethnic Identity. *Interview: An Evening with Nai Yen Ni*, http://www.kaowao.org/interview-6.php.
Preface to the book.

Thein Pe Myint. ***Sweet and Sour: Burmese Short Stories.***
Translated by Usha Narayanan. New Delhi, India: Sterling Publishers, 1999. 173 pages.
Genres/literary styles/story types: mainstream fiction; short stories
Accoridng to Paul Sharrad, these works of short fiction—which are set just before and after the transition to Burmese independence from colonial rule—"range from comic love matches through satires of the rich and powerful to sympathetic portraits of poor but honest workers wrestling with temptation."
Subject keyword: power
Original language: Burmese
Sources consulted for annotation:
Amazon.com (book description).
Sharrad, Paul. *World Literature Today* 73 (Autumn 1999): 814.

Nu Nu Yi. ***Smile as They Bow.***
Translated by Alfred Birnbaum and Nu Nu Yi. New York: Hyperion, 2008. 160 pages.
Genre/literary style/story type: mainstream fiction
This novel recalls Ben Jonson's famous early seventeenth century play *Bartholomew Fair*, which was centered around a raucous summer fair in London that attracted a motley array of participants and gawkers. In Jonson's play, chicanery, dubious amusements, and love triangles make for an uproarious spectacle. In *Smile As They Bow*, the setting is an annual festival and fair in a small Burmese village. Here also there is a welter of complications and riotous entertainment, with Daisy Bond, a transvestite, in the middle of things. Plying his trade as a spiritual medium, he falls in love with his assistant, who in turn is attracted to a beautiful and poverty-stricken beggar.
Subject keyword: social roles
Original language: Burmese
Sources consulted for annotation:
Global Books in Print (online) (reviews from *Booklist* and *Publishers Weekly*).
Saunders, Kate. *The Times*, 17 October 2008 (online).

Indonesia

Mochtar Lubis. ***Tiger!***
Translated by Florence Lamoureux. Singapore: Select Books, 1991. 128 pages.

Genre/literary style/story type: mainstream fiction

When a group of villagers embarks on a search for damar—a particularly valuable resin that is an important component of such items as batik and incense—they are literally and figuratively stalked by their sins, which assume the form of a tiger. Thus, their journey turns into a nightmarish trek through a landscape of recrimination and betrayal, where each man must face up to the mistakes of his past. Accoring to Koh Buck Song, this book is a "political allegory" and an "uncompromising attack on hypocrisy and inequities." The author was imprisoned for his political views.

Subject keywords: politics; power

Original language: Indonesian

Source consulted for annotation:

Song, Koh Buck. *Strait Times*, 2 February 1991; 28 December 1991 (from Factiva databases).

Some other translated books written by Mochtar Lubis: *Twilight in Djakarta*; *A Road with No End*; *The Outlaw and Other Stories*

Y. B. Mangunwijaya. *Durga/Umayi.*

Translated by Ward Keeler. Seattle, WA: University of Washington Press, 2004. 212 pages.

Genres/literary styles/story types: historical fiction; literary historical

This book recounts Indonesian history from a satiric, ironic, and allegorical perspective. A village woman becomes one of President Sukarno's servants in the preindependence 1930s, where one of her tasks is to clean bathrooms. After serving for a brief time as a cook during the revolutionary era, she is raped by Dutch soldiers and then undergoes two plastic surgeries. She turns into what Jennifer Lindsay calls "a morally-challenged 'career woman' wheeling and dealing in arms and drugs and living a life of totally absurd opulence."

Subject keywords: politics; social problems

Original language: Indonesian

Sources consulted for annotation:

Amazon.com (book description).

Lindsay, Jennifer. *The Jakarta Post*, 1 August 2004, p. 6.

Another translated book written by Y. B. Mangunwijaya: *The Weaverbirds*

Ismail Marahimin. *And the War Is Over.*

Translated by John H. McGlynn. Baton Rouge, LA: Louisiana State University Press, 1986. 173 pages.

Genre/literary style/story type: historical fiction

This book is an in-depth exploration of how colonialism affected Indonesia. The Japanese invasion of Indonesia during World War II marked the end of Dutch colonialism. A turbulent period ensued, with Indonesia declaring independence in 1949. But the maelstrom of events in the period 1945–1949 had profound consequences, as the Japanese set up prison camps for the Dutch and embarked on conscription campaigns. On the island of Sumatra, in the small village of Teratakbuluh, Indonesians are caught between two colonial orders, trying as best they can to survive, watching as traditional practices erode, and struggling to adapt to life-altering changes.

Subject keywords: colonization and colonialism; rural life

Original language: Indonesian

Sources consulted for annotation:

Amazon.com (book description).

Lewis, L. M. *Library Journal* 112 (1 April 1987): 164.

Mukherjee, Bharati. *The Washington Post*, 21 June 1987, p. X10.

A. A. Pandji Tisna (Anak Agung Pandji Tisna). *The Rape of Sukreni.*

Translated by George Quinn. Jakarta, Indonesia: Lontar Foundation, 1998. 124 pages.

Genre/literary style/story type: mainstream fiction

Using plot elements and language influenced by traditional Balinese theater, the author explores the negative consequences of commercialism and consumerism on Balinese customs and traditions. Bali is often imagined as an idyllic island oasis, but this book portrays its inhabitants as subservient to a capitalist ethos that demands that they turn their backs on a set of traditional values and mores that have served them well for centuries. Thus, having sold their souls, they think it is almost inevitable that retribution will swoop down upon them, laying bare their compromises and shallowness.

Subject keyword: modernization

Original language: Indonesian

Sources consulted for annotation:

Back cover of the book.

Quinn, George. Introduction to the book.

Pramoedya Ananta Toer. *This Earth of Mankind.*

Translated by Max Lane. New York: William Morrow, 1991. 367 pages.

Genre/literary style/story type: historical fiction

The author, a longtime political prisoner, is best known for his *Buru Quartet*, of which *This Earth of Mankind* is the first volume. Subsequent volumes are *Child of All Nations*; *Footsteps*; and *House of Glass*. The quartet chronicles the effects of Dutch colonialism on Indonesia from the late nineteenth century to the end of World War I. In *This Earth of Mankind*, Minke is a Javanese writer who has been educated in Europe. His marriage to Annelies, who is of mixed racial heritage, causes much consternation. As the young couple struggle with various types of social and legal threats, their lives and any chance for happiness are utterly destroyed. In *Child of All Nations*, Minke tries to recover from the murder of his wife, but his attempts to expose the perfidy of the Dutch colonial regime are stonewalled. In *Footsteps*, Minke becomes radicalized—first as a journalist and then as the publisher of Indonesia's first indigenous newspaper. In *House of Glass*, the narrator is Police Commissioner Tuan Pangemanann, who becomes Minke's implacable enemy, persecuting by any means possible the nascent revolutionary movement that Minke symbolizes.

Subject keywords: politics; power

Original language: Indonesian

Sources consulted for annotation:

Amazon.com (book descriptions and editorial reviews for all novels in the *Buru Tetralogy*).

Chadwell, Faye. A. *Library Journal* 129 (1 March 2004): 110.

Jaggi, Maya. *The Guardian*, 18 December 2004, p. 27.

Olson, Ray. *Booklist* 100 (1 February 2004): 952.

Zaleski, Jeff. *Publishers Weekly* 251 (26 January 2004): 231.

Some other translated books written by Pramoedya Ananta Toer: *The Girl from the Coast*; *This Earth of Mankind*; *The Fugitive*; *House of Glass*; *Footsteps*; *Child of All Nations*; *A Heap of Ashes*; *It's Not an All Night Fair*; *All That Is Gone*

Ahmad Tohari. *The Dancer: A Trilogy of Novels.*

Translated by René T. A. Lysloff. Jakarta, Indonesia: Lontar Foundation, 2003. 469 pages.

Genre/literary style/story type: historical fiction

According to Nancy I. Cooper, this trilogy is noteworthy not only for its "intriguing characters and labyrinthine plots" but also for its ability to provide "deeper explorations of Javanese cultural dynamics, particularly gender identity, and their relationship to political developments." The central conflict is between "local indigenous" values and traditions, as represented by "a sexually charged dancing girl," and "national . . . ideals of modernization and religious reform," as embodied in the main male character.

Subject keywords: politics; power
Original language: Indonesian
Source consulted for annotation:
Cooper, Nancy I. *Journal of Southeast Asian Studies* 35 (1 October 2004): 531.

Laos

Uthin Bunnyavong (Outhine Bounyavong). *Mother's Beloved: Stories from Laos.*
Translated and edited by Bounheng Inversin and Daniel Duffy. Seattle: University of Washington Press, 1999. 163 pages.
Genres/literary styles/story types: mainstream fiction; short stories
These 14 short stories give a good sense of life in Laos before and after the 1975 communist revolution, which overthrew the constitutional monarchy that had been established in 1954 after a long period of French colonial rule. As W. Fry states, they focus on such topics as "women's basketball, traditional Lao lamvong dancing, hunting, bird watching, tree cultivation, urban development, giving rides to strangers, unexploded ordnance in the Plain of Jars, bribery, personal honesty, dogs, valor in combat and the threat of environmental degradation." Two of the more powerful stories concern the destruction of trees and the killing of birds. One critic evoked Ernest Hemingway to describe the author's stylistic approach.
Subject keyword: rural life
Original language: Lao
Sources consulted for annotation:
Fry, W. *Pacific Affairs* 74 (Spring 2001): 132.
Noor, Ronny. *World Literature Today* 74 (Autumn 2000): 810–811.

Malaysia

Abdul Samad Said. *Salina.*
Translated by Harry Aveling. Kuala Lumpur, Malaysia: Dewan Bahasa dan Pustaka, Ministry of Education Malaysia, 1991. 531 pages.
Genre/literary style/story type: mainstream fiction
Set in Kampung Kambing, a Singapore slum, during World War II, this book chronicles the lives of the prostitute Salina as well as other poverty-stricken individuals as they attempt to survive World War II and its aftermath. As the reviewer in *The (New) Strait Times* wrote, the author uses "brief dialogue, flashbacks, sequential episodes, and interior monologues" to create a "meticulous study of individuals and their common social context."
Subject keyword: social problems
Original language: Malaysian
Sources consulted for annotation:
The New Straits Times, 11 March 1998, p. 6 (from Factiva databases).
The Strait Times, 7 October 1993 (from Factiva databases).
Some other translated books written by Abdul Samad Said: *The Morning Post*; *Lazy River*

Ishak Haji Muhammad. *The Son of Mad Mat Lela.*
Translated by Harry Aveling. Singapore: Federal Publications, 1983. 106 pages.
Genres/literary styles/story types: mainstream fiction; coming-of-age
Bulat is an infant who was deserted by his birth parents. Adopted by Mat Lela, a man considered insane by his neighbors, he is soon kidnapped by Johari and Permai. When their marriage fails, Bulat must find refuge with his stepfather. But when the stepfather remarries, he is cast out of his home by his new stepmother and begins to travel around the Malayan Peninsula.

Subject keyword: culture conflict
Original language: Malaysian
Sources consulted for annotation:
Aveling, Harry. *Journal of the South Pacific Association for Commonwealth Literature and Language Studies* 36 (1993), http://wwwmcc.murdoch.edu.au/ReadingRoom/litserv/SPAN/36/Aveling.html.
Back cover of the book.
Thomas, Phillip L. Foreword to the book.
Another translated book written by Ishak Haji Muhammad: *The Prince of Mount Tahan*

Keris Mas. *Jungle of Hope.*
Translated by Adibah Amin. Kuala Lumpur, Malaysia: Dewan Kahasa dan Pustaka, Ministry of Education, 1990. 269 pages.
Genre/literary style/story type: mainstream fiction
Pak Kia and Zaidi are two brothers who embody two very different approaches to modernity. While Pak Kia resists change and supports traditional ways, Zaidi embraces progress and urbanization. Pak Kia and a handful of others flee into the jungle to escape what they consider to be a degrading and soul-destroying contemporary world.
Subject keywords: culture conflict; social problems
Original language: Malaysian
Source consulted for annotation:
Tan, Sunny. *New Straits Times*, 27 February 2001, p. 06.
Another translated book written by Keris Mas: *Blood and Tears*

Nepal

Shankar Koirala. *Khairini Ghat: Return to a Nepali Village.*
Translated by Larry Hartsell. Kathmandu: Pilgrims Book House, 1996. 101 pages.
Genre/literary style/story type: mainstream fiction
Against the background of modernization and technological change in rural areas, this book recounts the story of Bhaktabire, the illiterate eldest son of a village elder in a small Nepali village. After spending 10 years in Calcutta (India), he returns home—only to find that his father has remarried in the hopes of having another son as heir. As Bhaktabire struggles to fit back into village life, he must also win over the affections of his father.
Subject keywords: family histories; rural life
Original language: Nepali
Source consulted for annotation:
Back cover of the book.

Vijaya Malla. *Kumari Shobha.*
Translated by Philip H. Pierce. Kathmandu: Royal Nepal Academy, 2001. 158 pages.
Genre/literary style/story type: mainstream fiction
Enthroned and revered as Nepal's Living Goddess, Kumari, the novel's heroine, accepts the traditional belief that the man she takes as her husband will die an unnatural death. But Upendra is unconcerned about such superstitions, soliciting her hand and staunchly believing that they will have a long and happy life together. Exploring an important part of Nepal's cultural and religious heritage, the book offers unique insight into the country's intriguing social and psychological dynamics.
Subject keyword: religion

Original language: Nepali
Sources consulted for annotation:
"From the Publisher" in the book.
Karmacharya, Madhav Lal. Foreword to the book.
Pierce, Philip H. Forward by the translator (in the book).

Manuja Babu Misra (Manuj Babu Mishra). *The Dream Assembly: A Transcendental March Towards Reality.*
Translated by Mohan Mishra. Kathmandu: Bagar Foundation Nepal, 2001. 148 pages.
Genre/literary style/story type: mainstream fiction
In the Katmandu neighborhood of Bauddha stands what is referred to as The Memorial Building. According to the introductory material in this novel, it is here that the "spiritual souls" of "immortal beings who have gone far beyond the disciplinary boundary of time and death" meet to "hold talks and discussions for the well-being and prosperity of mankind." These souls are collectively given the name of the "dream assembly." Socrates, Buddha, Confucius, Bacon, Plato, Vincent Van Gogh, Dante, Christ, and William Shakespeare—to name only a few—converse about such topics as "art, music, literature, culture, tradition, civilization, philosophy, science, and politics."
Subject keyword: philosophy
Original language: Nepali
Sources consulted for annotation:
Back cover of the book.
Mishra, Manuj Babu. "A Few Words about My Book" in the book.
Sharma, Tara Nath. "Brief Statement" in the book.
Silwal, Nakul. "Publisher's Note" in the book.

Sri Lanka

Rupa Amarasekara (Rupa Amarasekera). *Revolt of an Era.*
Translated by the author. Colombo, Sri Lanka: S. Godage and Bros, 1993. 128 pages.
Genre/literary style/story type: mainstream fiction
According to the preface and cover description, this novel explores the lives "of a widowed young mother and her seven children" who struggle to survive in the modern world. The main focus is on "the eternal struggle of women, young and old, against the turmoils they face to keep the home fires burning" and "to preserve family ties."
Subject keyword: family histories
Original language: Sinhalese
Sources consulted for annotation:
Amarasekara, Rupa. Preface to the book.
Back cover of the book.

Ranjit Dharmakirti. *Robert Knox.*
Translated by E. M. G. Edirisinghe. Colombo, Sri Lanka: Vijitha Yapa Book Shop, 1999. 200 pages.
Genres/literary styles/story types: adventure; survival and disaster stories
This novel reimagines the historical episode of the capture of 19 British sailors in 1659 on Ceylon by Rajasinghe II, the King of Kandy. Among the captives were Captain Robert Knox and his son. The father succumbed to malaria, but the son eventually escaped. He would go on to write *An Historical Relations of the Island of Ceylon*, the inspiration for Daniel Defoe's *Robinson Crusoe*. In his novel *Robert Knox*, Dharmakirti returns to Knox's autobiography, supplementing it with tales and legends from oral traditions.

Subject keyword: culture conflict
Original language: Sinhalese
Sources consulted for annotation:
Back cover of the book.
Dharmakirti, Ranjit. Foreword to the book.
Edirisinghe, E. M. G. Translator's note in the book.

Dambane Gunavardhana (Dambane Gunawardhana). *Hunting Grounds.*
Translated by Kusum Disanayaka. Atlanta, GA: Dayawansa Jayakody International, 1997. 127 pages.
Genre/literary style/story type: historical fiction
The first group of people known to have inhabited Sri Lanka was the Vaedda people. The author, a member of the Vaedda community, recounts a tragic story of dispossession: Vaedda hunters between 1910 and 1950 were forced off their traditional hunting grounds. The novel sees contemporary society as a new type of hunting ground—a vicious and violent world characterized by fierce competitive pressures.
Subject keyword: modernization
Original language: Sinhalese
Sources consulted for annotation:
Back cover of the book.
Disanayaka, Kusum. Translator's note to the book.
Gunawardhana, Dambane. "A Note from the Author" in the book.
Kahandagamage, Piyasena. Preface to the book.

Charu Nivedita. *Zero Degree.*
Translated by Pritham Chakravarthy and Rakesh Khanna. Chennai, India: Blaft Publications, 2008. 248 pages.
Genres/literary styles/story types: mainstream fiction; postmodernism
According to the publisher's website, this novel is a work of "transgressive fiction that unflinchingly probes the deepest psychic wounds of humanity." It features a "mad patchwork of phone sex conversations, nightmarish torture scenes, tender love poems, numerology, mythology, and compulsive name-dropping of Latin American intellectuals." Readers may also be interested in *The Blaft Anthology of Tamil Pulp Fiction*, which includes 17 stories by bestselling Tamil writers of genre fiction.
Subject keywords: identity; social roles
Original language: Tamil
Source consulted for annotation:
Blaft Publications (book descriptions for both mentioned items), http://www.blaft.com.

Ediriweera R. Sarachchandra (Ediriwira Sarachchandra). *Curfew and a Full Moon.*
Freely rendered into English by the author. Singapore: Heinemann Asia, 1987. 223 pages.
Genre/literary style/story type: historical fiction
According to the cover, this book examines an early 1970s student rebellion from the perspective of both faculty and students at the University of Ceylon. As the author explores the way in which students moved away from intellectual pursuits toward political radicalization, he evokes "the atmosphere of subversion, jungle insurgency, and ruthless repression" that characterized the period.
Subject keywords: politics; power
Original language: Sinhalese
Source consulted for annotation:
Back cover of the book.

Some other translated books written by Ediriweera R. Sarachchandra: *With the Begging Bowl*; *Foam Upon the Stream: A Japanese Elegy*

Thailand

Botan (pseudonym for Supa Sirising). ***Letters from Thailand.***
Translated by Susan F. Kepner. Chiang Mai, Thailand: Silkworm Books, 2002. 410 pages.
Genre/literary style/story type: mainstream fiction
This novel focuses on a man who desperately clings to his ethnic identity to avoid cultural assimilation. Suang U has immigrated to Thailand, and he recounts his new life through letters that he writes to his mother back home in China. After only one year, he has achieved success: He has married his boss's daughter; he is placed in charge of the expanding business; and he has a son whom he adores. But because he does not wish to lose his Chinese heritage, he slowly begins to see only the negative aspects of the Thai people. Likewise, his marriage turns into a disappointment when his wife bears him three daughters but no more sons.
Subject keywords: culture conflict; family histories
Original language: Thai/Siamese
Sources consulted for annotation:
Amazon.com (book description).
Baker, Chris. *Bangkok Post*, 29 June 2002, p. 3.

Chat Kopchitti (Chart Korpjitti). ***The Judgment.***
Translated by Phongdeit Jiangphatthana-Kit and Marcel Barang. Pak Chong, Nakhon Rachasima, Thailand: Howling Books, 2003. 318 pages.
Genre/literary style/story type: mainstream fiction
According to Marcel Barang, this book is "a powerful social satire, which uses all the shades of irony . . . to plead the cause of an innocent victim and denounce the corrupted values of an insensitive and cruel society." The novel chronicles the fall of Fak, who "embodies the basic values of Thai Buddhist culture," from honored monk to "garrulous drunkard" to his death.
Subject keyword: social problems
Original language: Thai/Siamese
Source consulted for annotation:
Barang, Marcel. Foreword to the book.
Some other translated books written by Chat Kopchitti: *Mad Dogs & Co.*; *No Way Out*; *Time*

K. (Kanha) Surangkhanang. ***The Prostitute.***
Translated by David Smyth. Kuala Lumpur, Malaysia: Oxford University Press, 1994. 229 pages.
Genres/literary styles/story types: mainstream fiction; women's lives
Reun, a simple country girl, is seduced by a young man from Bangkok and forced into prostitution. Working in a sordid brothel, she falls in love with a man who promises to marry her and thus save her from future degradation. But he abandons her before the marriage can occur, and Reun is left alone and pregnant. Eventually, she and a fellow prostitute run away, rent a house, and try to raise Reun's child in impoverished circumstances. After Samorn falls sick and dies, Reun returns to prostitution as a means to care for her daughter.
Subject keyword: social problems
Original language: Thai/Siamese
Sources consulted for annotation:
Back cover of the book.
Smyth, David. Introduction to the book.

Khamman Khonkhai (Khammaan Khonkhai). *The Teachers of Mad Dog Swamp.*
Translated by Gehan Wijeyewardene. St. Lucia, Australia: University of Queensland Press, 1982. 263 pages.
Genre/literary style/story type: mainstream fiction
Teachers have come to a small village in Ubon Province in the Isan region of northeast Thailand. They are initially met with distrust by the villagers, but bonds of mutual respect slowly develop between the two groups. The novel also focuses on the tensions that arise because of the destruction of the surrounding forests by rapacious profiteers who have political backing. On the one hand, the teachers acquiesce to the construction of a new school using the controversial lumber. On the other hand, a teacher's attempt to provide documentation about the logging leads to a tragic end when his friendship with a local girl is used as an excuse to kill him.
Subject keywords: politics; rural life
Original language: Thai/Siamese
Sources consulted for annotation:
Lefferts Jr., Leedom H. *The Journal of Asian Studies* 44 (February 1985): 468.
Wijeyewardene, Gehan. Translator's introduction to the book.
Another translated book written by Khamman Khonkhai: *Teacher Marisa*

Khamphun Bunthawi (Kampoon Boontawee). *A Child of the Northeast.*
Translated by Susan Fulop Kepner. Bangkok, Thailand: Editions Duangkamol, 1994. 483 pages.
Genre/literary style/story type: mainstream fiction
This autobiographical novel chronicles the hardships of 1930s village life among the Isan people, who live in Northeast Thailand along the Laotian border. The story's protagonist is an eight-year-old boy named Koon. According to the translator, the book presents "an altruistic view of life," where "virtue is synonymous with honesty, kindness, hospitality, cheerfulness, industry, generosity, and courage."
Subject keywords: family histories; rural life
Original language: Thai/Siamese
Source consulted for annotation:
Kepner, Susan Fulop. Translator's introduction to the book.

M. R. Kukrit Pramoj (Kukrit Pramoj). *Four Reigns.*
Translated by Tulachandra. Chang Mai, Thailand: Silkworm Books, 2000. 663 pages.
Genre/literary style/story type: historical fiction
This novel, which has drawn comparisons with Tolstoy's *War and Peace*, explores the lives of minor court figures from the end of King Chulalongkorn's reign in the late nineteenth century through the reign of King Ananda Mahidol in 1946. Two of the central characters are Ploi and her mother. When they move to the royal palace, Ploi receives an extensive social and cultural education at the hands of the many court women and other wives of the king. Eventually, she falls in love with the brother of one of her best friends, and her mothers dies in the throes of childbirth. Some of the issues covered are feudalism, polygamy, and arranged marriages.
Subject keyword: social problems
Original language: Thai/Siamese
Sources consulted for annotation:
Back cover of the book.
Pramoj, Kukrit. Preface to the book.
ThingsAsian.com. (book review), http://www.thingsasian.com.
Some other translated books written by Kukrit Pramoj: *Many Lives*; *Red Bamboo*

Nikhom Raiyawa (Nikom Rayawa). ***High Banks, Heavy Logs.***
Translated by Richard C. Lair. Ringwood, Australia: Penguin Books, 1991. 160 pages.
Genre/literary style/story type: mainstream fiction
This novel is a philosophical meditation on human worth and the purpose of life. A wood-carver ponders life as he watches logging operations on the Yom River. As the forces of modernization and presumed progress come to this isolated area in the form of the forestry industry, he observes the disintegration of his community and its traditions.
Subject keywords: modernization; rural life
Original language: Thai/Siamese
Sources consulted for annotation:
The Straits Times, 8 June 1991 (from Factiva databases).
Sun Herald, 12 May 1991, p. 108 (from Factiva databases).

Praphatson Sewikun (Praphatsorn Seiwikun). ***Time in a Bottle.***
Translated by Phongdeit Jiangphatthanarkit and Marcel Barang. Bangkok, Thailand: Thai Modern Classics, Chaiyong Limthongkun Foundation of Sonthi Limthongkun, 1996. 251 pages.
Genres/literary styles/story types: mainstream fiction; coming-of-age
Generation gaps exist in every society and in every era, and 1960s-1970s Thailand is no exception. Nat, now an adult, recalls his troubled childhood and adolescence growing up in a middle-class household. The focus is on his high school and early university years, which coincided with Thailand's democracy movement.
Subject keywords: social problems; urban life
Original language: Thai/Siamese
Sources consulted for annotation:
Barang, Marcel. Postscript to the book.
Seiwikun, Praphatson. Foreword to the book.

Wimon Sainimnuan. ***Snakes.***
Translated by Phongdeit Jiangphatthanarkit. Bangkok, Thailand: TMC, 1996. 220 pages.
Genre/literary style/story type: mainstream fiction
Inspired by John Steinbeck's *The Grapes of Wrath*, this novel is a denunciation of corrupt Buddhist monks against the backdrop of political venality and unbridled consumerism. Abbot Nian is not only a beheader of sacred statues but also a seducer and murderer who will stop at nothing to increase the supposed prestige of his temple.
Subject keywords: politics; power
Original language: Thai/Siamese
Sources consulted for annotation:
Barang, Marcel. "Postscript" to the book.
Thaifiction.com. (book review), http://www.thaifiction.com.

Win Lieowarin (Win Lyovarin). ***Democracy, Shaken & Stirred.***
Translated by Prisna Boonsinsukh. Bangkok, Thailand: 113 Company, 2003. 319 pages.
Genres/literary styles/story types: historical fiction; literary historical
Two old men on opposing sides in Thai political struggles recall bygone events of the past 60 years as they sit in a park in 1992. Long ago, one of them was a rebellious activist; the other, a policeman. But now their worldviews coincide more than they differ. What brought them together? How did their philosophies evolve?
Subject keywords: politics; power
Original language: Thai/Siamese

Sources consulted for annotation:
Back cover of the book.
Morris, Ron. 2bangkok.com (book review), http://www.2bangkok.com.

Vietnam

Bao Ninh. *The Sorrow of War: A Novel of North Vietnam.*
Translated by Phan Thanh Hao. New York: Pantheon Books, 1995. 233 pages.
Genre/literary style/story type: mainstream fiction
At the end of the Vietnam War, Kien is part of a group of individuals who recover the corpses of soldiers. It is the kind of work that is psychologically diffcult because it brings up suppressed memories and activates a range of emotions, causing frustration, pain, and anger. For a very different look at the question of the recovery of the corpses of soldiers, readers may be interested in Lee Child's *Tripwire*, which goes into grisly detail about many aspects of this process.
Subject keyword: war
Original language: Vietnamese
Sources consulted for annotation:
Glick, Ira D. *The American Journal of Psychiatry* 157 (December 2000): 2070.
Shaw, Michael T. *Marine Corps Gazette* 79 (April 1995): 92.
Steinberg, Sybil S. *Publishers Weekly* 241 (19 December 1994): 45.
Taylor, Gilbert. *Booklist* 91 (1 February 1995): 990.

Lê Đoàn (Doan Le). *The Cemetery of Chua Village and Other Stories.*
Translated by Rosemary Nguyen, with additional translations by Duong Tuong and Wayne Karlin. Willimantic, CT: Curbstone Press, 2005. 189 pages.
Genres/literary styles/story types: mainstream fiction; short stories
These 10 stories are about life in modern-day Vietnam. In his introduction to the volume, Wayne Karlin writes that they are at once allegories and "gently complex satire[s]" where "a frustrated petitioner, unable to obtain housing can change not only into a fly, but into a gay fly (or a fly pretending to be gay); the dead can mirror the snobberies and passions of the living; [and] a man can try to reason out the complexities of his relationship with his father's clone."
Subject keyword: social problems
Original language: Vietnamese
Sources consulted for annotation:
Amazon.com (book description).
Upchurch, Michael. *Chicago Tribune*, 20 February 2005, p. 3.

Thu Huong Duong (Duong Thu Huong). *Beyond Illusions.*
Translated by Nina McPherson and Phan Huy Duong. New York: Hyperion East, 2002. 247 pages.
Genre/literary style/story type: mainstream fiction
Linh is married to Nguyen, a journalist who used to be a professor. Together with their daughter, they have a seemingly happy and prosperous life. But Linh discovers that her husband has made a number of compromises to advance his career and his socioeconomic status. As a result, she begins an affair with an older man, a composer, whom she believes has retained his ideals. Her disillusionment knows no bounds when she learns that he too has made accommodations with existing power structures and authorties.
Subject keywords: politics; power
Original language: Vietnamese

Sources consulted for annotation:
Amazon.com (book description).
Bose, Sudip. *The New York Times Book Review*, 17 March 2002, p. 25.
Johnston, Bonnie. *Booklist* 98 (1 January/15 January): 808.
Quan, Shirley N. *Library Journal* 127 (January 2002): 150.
Zaleski, Jeff. *Publishers Weekly* 248 (17 December 2001): 65.
Some other translated books written by Thu Huong Duong: *Novel Without a Name*; *Paradise of the Blind*; *Memories of a Pure Spring*; *No Man's Land*

Anh Thái Ho (Ho Anh Thai). *The Women on the Island.*
Translated by Phan Thanh Hao, Celeste Bacchi, and Wayne Karlin. Seattle, WA: University of Washington Press, 2000. 155 pages.
Genres/literary styles/story types: mainstream fiction; women's lives
In the 1980s, a group of women are working in a foresty operation on Cat Bac Island. During the Vietnam War, they played an integral part in keeping the Ho Chi Minh Trail open and functioning, enduring all kinds of hardship. But as the capitalist model takes root in Vietnam, they feel themselves increasingly marginalized and useless. Desperate and lonely, they are easy prey for charlatans and swindlers. As Michael Harris writes, this is a novel about "the reemergence of individual desires in a people who for decades had subordinated everything to the collective struggle." Critics have invoked Aleksandr Solzhenitsyn's *Cancer Ward* to describe the novel's atmosphere.
Subject keyword: social problems
Original language: Vietnamese
Sources consulted for annotation:
Harris, Michael. *Los Angeles Times*, 18 September 2001, p. E3.
Pearl, Nancy. *Booklist* 97 (1 May 2001): 1669.
Some other translated books written by Anh Thai Ho: *Behind the Red Mist*; *Legend of the Phoenix and Other Stories from Vietnam*

Luu Lê (Le Luu). *A Time Far Past.*
Translated by Ngo Vinh Hai. Amherst, MA: University of Massachusetts Press, 1997. 272 pages.
Genre/literary style/story type: mainstream fiction
This book recounts the saga of Giang Minh Sai from the 1960s to the 1980s, a tumultuous period in Vietnamese history. He is married at age 10 to a girl named Tuyet in a small rural village. The unhappy child-husband finds solace in his studies, growing up to be a political activist. But when he falls in love with Huong, the village is scandalized, and he enlists in the army, becoming a hero for shooting down a helicopter and gaining information from the pilot. With the war is over, Sai ends his marriage to Tuyet. He moves to Hanoi, where he embarks on another unsuccessful marriage, and then returns home to his village—only to drown himself in his work.
Subject keyword: family histories
Original language: Vietnamese
Sources consulted for annotation:
Banerian, James. *World Literature Today* 71 (Autumn 1997): 877.
Dean, Kitty Chen. *Library Journal* 122 (15 March 1997): 90.
Duffy, Dan. *The Nation* 265 (7 July 1997): 31.
Steinberg, Sybil S. *Publishers Weekly* 244 (28 April 1997): 49.

Minh Khuê Lê (Le Minh Khue). *The Stars, the Earth, the River.*
Translated by Bac Hoai Tran and Dana Sach. Willimantic, CT: Curbstone Press, 1997. 231 pages.
Genres/literary styles/story types: mainstream fiction; short stories

Told from the perpective of young women, this collection of short stories debunks many of the stereotypes associated with Vietnam. In fact, it is much like every other place in the world, home to major and minor hypocricies, selfishness, narcissistic behavior, cheating, lying, and self-serving ambition. The author participated as a young woman in the North Vietnamese war effort and also worked as journalist.
Subject keywords: identity; social roles
Original language: Vietnamese
Sources consulted for annotation:
Amazon.com (all editorial reviews).
Banerian, James. *World Literature Today* 72 (Winter 1998): 214.
Gerstler, Amy. *The Village Voice* 42 (8 April 1997): 49.
Steinberg, Sybil S. *Publishers Weekly* 244 (24 March 1997): 61.

Van Kháng Ma (Ma Van Khang). *Against the Flood.*
Translated by Phan Thanh Hao and Wayne Karlin. Willimantic, CT: Curbstone Press, 2000. 309 pages.
Genre/literary style/story type: mainstream fiction
In contemporary Hanoi, Khiem is a book editor who aspires to literary greatness; his wife has had numerous affairs. Hoan, a proofreader, has long admired Khiem for his moral and ethical rectitude. Soon, they begin an affair. It is an auspicious time in their lives, especially since Khiem has just published what he considers to be his best work: a novel called *The Haven*. But the book attracts much ideological criticism—so much so that the book is banned and Khiem loses his job. Hoan is also disgraced, and she is forced to survive by selling opium.
Subject keywords: politics; writers
Original language: Vietnamese
Sources consulted for annotation:
Banerian, James. *World Literature Today* 75 (Spring 2001): 327.
Bromberg, Judith. *National Catholic Reporter* 37 (6 April 2001): 10.
Steinberg, Sybil S. *Publishers Weekly* 247 (18 September 2000): 89.

Huy Thiep Nguyen (Nguyen Huy Thiep). *The General Retires and Other Stories.*
Translated by Greg Lockhart. Singapore: Oxford University Press, 1992. 192 pages.
Genres/literary styles/story types: mainstream fiction; short stories
These eight stories present a stark portrait of the corrosive realities of contemporary Vietnam. Like Balzac, the author is merciless in his examination of personal and social foibles. His characters are often violent and evil, indulging in every type of imaginable vice. The title story portrays a man who has given his entire life to a political cause—only to find himself completely disillusioned and sickened by the immorality surrounding him.
Subject keyword: social problems
Original language: Vietnamese
Sources consulted for annotation:
Duiker, William J. *Pacific Affairs* 67 (Fall 1994): 467.
Nguyen, Dinh-Hoa. *World Literature Today* 68 (Winter 1994): 224.
Tran, Qui-Phiet. *Studies in Short Fiction* 32 (Winter 1995): 108.
Another translated book written by Huy Thiep Nguyen: *Crossing the River*

Khai Nguyen (Nguyen Khai). *Past Continuous.*
Translated by Phan Thanh Hao and Wayne Karlin. Willimantic, CT: Curbstone Press, 2001. 159 pages.

Genres/literary styles/story types: mainstream fiction; short stories
The narrator tells the stories of three people who played significant roles on behalf of the North Vietnamese during the Vietnam War. Taken together, the experiences of an undercover operative, a female army leader, and a Catholic priest provide rich insight into the psychology and emotions animating the protracted struggle against the United States and South Vietnam.
Subject keyword: war
Original language: Vietnamese
Sources consulted for annotation:
Amazon.com (book description).
Banerian, James. *World Literature Today* 76 (Spring 2002): 146.
Quan, Shirley N. *Library Journal* 126 (December 2001): 174.

Thich Nhat Hanh. *The Moon Bamboo.*
Translated by Vo-Dinh Mai and Mobi Ho. Berkeley, CA: Parallax Press, 1989. 179 pages.
Genres/literary styles/story types: mainstream fiction; short stories
Always hovering in the background of this collection of four stories is the Vietnam War, but the focus is on the saving grace of children. A blind girl is rescued by a mysterious boy; another girl metamorphoses into a fish to save family and friends. The author is a renowned Buddhist teacher who was nominated for the Nobel Peace Prize in 1967. He has also written many books in English, including *Living Buddah, Living Christ*.
Subject keyword: philosophy
Original language: Vietnamese
Sources consulted for annotation:
Bagby, Jeanne S. *Library Journal* 114 (July 1989): 110.
"Thich Nhat Hanh." *Contemporary Authors Online*. Gale databases, 2002.
Some other translated books written by Thich Nhat Hanh: *Hermitage Among the Clouds*; *The Stone Boy and Other Stories*; *The Hermit and the Well*; *The Pine Gate*

Vu Tran (Tran Vu). *The Dragon Hunt: Five Stories.*
Translated by Nina McPherson and Phan Huy Duong. New York: Hyperion, 1999. 146 pages.
Genres/literary styles/story types: mainstream fiction; short stories
Many critics lauded this collection for its frankness and sense of drama, calling it some of the best literary work to be produced in Vietnam. Francine Prose noted echoes of Ernest Hemingway and Marguerite Duras in some of the stories, particularly praising "The Coral Reef" for its vividness and verisimilitude. Here, the author adroitly recounts the terror and panic of hundreds of boat people clinging to overcrowded vessels; with neither food nor water, tragedy looms during every stage of the voyage. Other stories recount the effects of deep emotional and psychological scars. In "Gunboat on the Yangtze," a blind cello player and his sister turn to incest and rape, while in "The Back Streets of Hoi An," a woman's lover can only talk about genocide during intimate moments.
Subject keyword: war
Original language: Vietnamese
Sources consulted for annotation:
Adams, Phoebe-Lou. *The Atlantic Monthly* 283 (April 1999): 114.
Amazon.com (review from *Kirkus Reviews*).
Prose, Francine. *The New York Times Book Review*, 20 June 1999, p. 19.
Spinella, Michael. *Booklist* 95 (15 February 1999): 1043.
Steinberg, Sybil S. *Publishers Weekly* 246 (11 January 1999): 53.
Williams, Janice. *Library Journal* 124 (1 March 1999): 112.

CHAPTER 5

The Mediterranean: Greece, Israel, and Italy

Language groups:	Italian	Israel
Greek	**Countries represented:**	Italy
Hebrew	Greece	

INTRODUCTION

This chapter contains annotations of books from countries in the Mediterranean region: Greece, Israel, and Italy. The languages covered are Modern Greek, Hebrew, and Italian.

Of the three translated fiction traditions discussed in this chapter, Modern Greek is perhaps the least known. Among the noteworthy authors that deserve wider recognition are Apostolos Doxiadis (*Uncle Petros and Goldbach's Conjecture*); Rhea Galanki (*I Shall Sign as Loui*); Amanda Michalopoulou (*I'd Like*); Alexis Stamatis (*The Seventh Elephant* and *American Fugue*); and Vassilis Vassilikos (*The Few Things I Know About Glafkos Thrassakis*).

On the other hand, the names of many of the Israeli authors writing in Hebrew mentioned in this chapter may be familiar to at least some readers: Aharon Appelfeld (*The Conversion*); David Grossman (*To the End of the Land* and *See Under: Love*); Etgar Keret (*The Bus Driver Who Wanted to Be God and Other Stories*); Amos Oz (*The Same Sea*); Anton Shammas (*Arabesques*); and A. B. Yehoshua (*The Liberated Bride* and *A Woman in Jerusalem*). That is not to say that there are no unknown or little known translated authors of Hebrew fiction—for example, Gail Hareven (*The Confessions of Noa Weber*); Savyon Liebrecht (*A Man and a Woman and a Man*); and Ronit Matalon (*Bliss*).

Knowledge of translated Italian fiction lies somewhere in the middle between these two poles. On the one hand, almost everyone recognizes such important figures as Umberto Eco, author of *The Name of the Rose*, and Andrea Camilleri, author of the Inspector Montalbano series of mysteries. They are as famous as Grossman and Oz—if not more so. But writers such as Niccolò Ammaniti (*I'm Not Scared*); Antonia Arslan (*Skylark Farm*); Alessandro Boffa (*You're an Animal, Viskovitz!*); Aldo Busi (*The Standard Life of a Temporary Pantyhose Salesman*); Andrea Canobbio (*The Natural Disorder of Things*); Gianrico Carofiglio (*Reasonable Doubts*); and Amara Lakhous (*Clash of Civilizations Over an Elevator in Piazza Vittorio*) are likely as unknown in the English-speaking world as the Greek writers Michalopoulou and Stamatis.

Earlier Translated Literature

For readers interested in delving into the historical traditions of the literatures included in this chapter, there is a wealth of material, especially translations from Ancient Greek. There are the epic poems *The Iliad* and *The Odyssey*, attributed to Homer; the plays of Aeschylus, Sophocles, Euripides, and Aristophanes; the philosophical texts of Plato and Aristotle; the histories of Herodotus, Thucydides, and Xenophon; the biographies of Plutarch; the romances of Heliodorus and Longus; and the fables of Aesop. Three significant mid- and late twentieth-century translated novels from Modern Greek are Kostas Tachtsis's *The Third Wedding*; Stratis Tsirkas's three-volume *Drifting Cities*; and Nikos Kazantzakis's *The Last Temptation*.

Before and during the British Mandate (1920–1948; i.e., before the birth of Israel), Hebrew literature flourished in Palestine. Three important translated novelists from this period are Josef Hayyim Brenner (*Breakdown and Bereavement* and *Out of the Depths*); S. Y. Agnon, a Nobel Prize laureate in the mid-1960s (*A Simple Story* and *A Book That Was Lost and Other Stories*); and Moshe Shamir (*King of Flesh and Blood* and *My Life with Ishmael*).

Any discussion of translated Italian literature must include Dante Alighieri's epic *The Divine Comedy* (consisting of the *Inferno*, *Purgatorio*, and *Paradiso*) and Giovanni's Boccaccio's novel-cycle *The Decameron*—both of which are readily available in Penguin and Oxford World's Classics paperback versions. Dante's work has been translated both as poetry and prose and has attracted such famous translators as Dorothy L. Sayers and Robert Pinsky. *The Decameron* also has provided hours of reading enjoyment to all lovers of good books. Noteworthy too are nineteenth-century Italian authors, such as Giovanni Verga, whose fame may be partly traced to the fact that three of his novels were translated by D. H. Lawrence (*Master Don Gesualdo*; *Little Novels of Sicily*; and *Cavalleria Rusticana*).

With regard to early twentieth-century Italian fiction, readers may want to discover the novels of Grazia Deledda—arguably one of the most forgotten of Nobel Prize laureates (in 1926). Among her translated titles are *After the Divorce*; *Cosima*; and *The Woman and the Priest*. Mid-twentieth-century fiction is dominated by such authors as Alberto Moravia (*The Time of Indifference*) and Cesare Pavese (*The Moon and the Bonfire*). Perhaps the two most recognized translated Italian novels of the late 1950s and early 1960s are Giuseppe Tomasi di Lampedusa's *The Leopard*, an account of Garibaldi's Italian unification movement as experienced by a Sicilian aristocratic family, and Giorgio Bassani's *The Garden of the Finzi-Continis*, which chronicles Jewish life during the reign of Mussolini. Other renowned modern Italian writers are Italo Calvino (*The Baron in the Trees*; *Invisible Cites*; and *If on a Winter's Night a Traveller*); Primo Levi (*The Periodic Table*); and Elsa Morante (*History: A Novel*).

SOURCES CONSULTED

France, Peter. (Ed.). (2000). "Greek," "Hebrew and Yiddish," and "Italian." In *The Oxford Guide to Literature in English Translation*, pp. 348–394, 395–404, 467–502. Oxford: Oxford University Press.

Hainsworth, Peter, and Robey, David. (Eds.). (2002). *The Oxford Companion to Italian Literature*. Oxford: Oxford University Press.

BIBLIOGRAPHIC ESSAY

Greece

There is little doubt that the most comprehensive overview of Modern Greek literature is contained in the second edition of *An Introduction to Modern Greek Literature* by Roderick Beaton. Unstintingly praised by critics for its thorough analysis of major writers and for its extensive bibliography that identifies English-language translations, Beaton's book covers the period between 1821 ("the conventional date of the Greek revolt against the ruling Ottoman empire" [p. 25]) and 1998. Modern Greek literature is of course best known for such poets as C. P. Cavafy; Odysseus Elytis (winner of the Nobel Prize for Literature in 1979); George Seferis (winner of the Nobel Prize for Literature in 1963); and Yannis Ritsos, but Beaton's book gives equal time to fiction writers—resurrecting long-forgotten novels, such as *Leander* by Panayotis Soutsos, but appropriately focusing on the works of such comparatively better-known writers as Grigorios Xenopoulos, Ioannis Kondylakis, Kosmas Politis, Margarita Lymberaki, Stratis Tsirkas, Dido Sotiriou, and Nikos Kazantzakis, who is universally recognized for his *Zorba the Greek* (or *The Life and Times of Alexis Zorbas*). The perfect counterpart to Beaton's book is *The Other Self: Selfhood and Society in Modern Greek Fiction* by Dimitris Tziovas, which astutely contextualizes and analyzes such significant modern Greek novels as *The Murderess* by Alexandros Papadiamantis; *Condemned* by Konstantinos Theotokis; *Vasilis Arvanitis* by Stratis Myrivilis; *The Third Wedding* by Kostas Tachtsis; *Fool's Gold* by Maro Douka; and *Achilles' Fiancée* by Alki Zei.

Of course, older literary histories are also valuable, and this is certainly the case with *A History of Modern Greek Literature* by Linos Politis and *A History of Modern Greek Literature* by C. Th. Dimaras. These two books are very different in scope from Beaton's effort because both Politis and Dimara extend the history of Modern Greek literature back to the eleventh century—bringing to light Greek folksongs; Byzantine romances; epics such as *Digenìs Akritas*; the pastoral poetry of the Cretan period (1570–1669); and the Modern Greek enlightenment of the eighteenth century. Many of the writers referred to by Beaton, Tziovas, Politis, and Dimaras are anthologized in *Modern Greek Writing: An Anthology in English Translation*, edited by David Ricks. As Ricks writes in the preface, the purpose of the volume is "to whet the reader's appetite for more" so that "struck by a particular selection, the interested reader will go on to track down the volumes of poetry, the short stories and the novels from which the present selection comes and thus enlarge his or her sense of what modern Greece has contributed to the republic of letters" (p. 15).

Israel

Perhaps the ideal way to gain an introduction to Hebrew literature—and to differentiate it from American Jewish literature, British Jewish literature, and Yiddish literature—is to read the overview articles about these topics that are contained in *Jewish Writers of the Twentieth Century*, edited by Sorrel Kerbel. In the essay about Hebrew literature, readers will discover such late nineteenth-century novelists as Mendele Moykher Sforim, Y. H. Brenner, and U. N. Gnessin as well as such twentieth-century voices as Amos Oz, A. B. Yehoshua, David Grossman, Orly Castel-Bloom, Yehudit Katzir, Savyon Liebrecht, and Shmuel Yosef Agnon, who won the Nobel Prize for Literature in 1966. If readers wish to have extensive bio-bibliographic information about these and other writers, they can then turn to the individual author entries that constitute the bulk of Kerbel's rewarding reference book.

Another excellent entry point into some of the classics of Hebrew writing is *Middle Eastern Literatures and Their Times*, edited by Joyce Moss. Such important Hebrew novels as S. Y. Agnon's *Only Yesterday*; David Grossman's *See Under: Love*; A. B. Yehoshua's *Mr. Mani*; and Aharon Appelfield's *Badenheim 1939* are not only critically analyzed but historically and socially contextualized. As its title indicates, this volume also includes detailed articles about novels written in Arabic (e.g., *Cities of Salt* by Abd-al-Rahman Munif); Persian (e.g., *Once Upon a Time* by Muhammad Ali Jamalzadah); and Turkish (e.g., *Memed, My Hawk* by Yasar Kemal).

For a more detailed approach to the vast sweep of Hebrew literature, we recommend two books by Eisig Silberschlag: *From Renaissance to Renaissance: Hebrew Literature from 1492–1970* and *From Renaissance to Renaissance: Hebrew Literature in the Land of Israel 1870–1970*. Readers will quickly discover that an important event in Hebrew literature was "the exile from Spain" in 1492, which provided "the root of a mystical and—subsequently—rationalist revolution in Hebrew literature"; which "color[ed] the first blush of dawn in the cultural regeneration of Jewry in Turkey and in Palestine, in Italy and in Holland—in the countries which absorbed the influx of Jewish refugees from the Iberian peninsula"; and which "reached its full fruition" in Italy and Germany in the eighteenth century, in Eastern Europe in the nineteenth century, and in Israel and the United States in the twentieth century (p. ix). Some of the writers discussed in these histories are given more detailed consideration in Todd Hasak-Lowy's *Here and Now: History, Nationalism, and Realism in Modern Hebrew Fiction*, which insightfully analyzes the novels of S. Y. Abramovitz, S. Y. Agnon, and S. Yizhar. Equally worthwhile is *Reading Hebrew Literature: Critical Discussions of Six Modern Texts*, edited by Alan Mintz, which considers canonical prose and poetry by M. J. Berdyczewski, Saul Tchernichowsky, U. Z. Greenberg, S. Y. Agnon, Amalia Kahana-Carmon, and Dahlia Ravikovitch.

Published in the mid-1970s, Silberschlag's two literary histories obviously do not touch on developments in Hebrew literature in the late 1970s and beyond. To get a good sense of the vibrant and dynamic nature of contemporary Hebrew literature, we suggest *The Boom in Contemporary Israeli Fiction*, edited by Alan Mintz, which contains essays about magic realism in the Israeli novel; the politics of gender in contemporary Israeli fiction; and Israel's fantastic fiction of the Holocaust. Mintz's *Translating Israel: Contemporary Hebrew Literature and Its Reception in America* is also a fascinating book, with stellar overviews of Israeli literature in the period between 1970 and 1995 as well as sensitive readings of such novelists as David Grossman and A. B. Yehoshua. Readers should not overlook Risa Domb's *Identity and Modern Israeli Literature*, which discusses such fiction writers as Yoram Kaniuk, Nathan Shaham, and Gabriela Avigur-Rotem. Nor should they neglect Gershon Shaked's *Modern Hebrew Fiction*, which thoughtfully and elegantly discusses Hebrew prose fiction from 1880 to the 1990s and focuses on such topics as Hebrew social realism; romanticism and westernization; local color fiction; and the transformation of literary realism and the struggle for a national narrative in the post-1940 era.

The topic of Hebrew women writers is majestically addressed by Wendy I. Zierler's *And Rachel Stole the Idols: The Emergence of Modern Hebrew Women's Writing*. This is literary history at its best, resurrecting such neglected novelists as Sarah Feige Meinkin Foner, Hava Shapiro, and Devorah Baron, described as "the first major woman writer of Hebrew prose fiction" (p. 171). Readers will also want to explore *No Room of Their Own: Gender and Nation in Israeli Women's Fiction* by Yael S. Feldman as well as the anthology entitled *Contemporary Israeli Women's Writing*, edited by Risa Domb, which contains samples of the prose of such comparatively lesser-known authors as Maya Bejerano, Ruth Almog, Leah Aini, Dorit Peleg, Orna Coussin, Michal Govrin, and Chana Bat Shahar. Of course, there are anthologies that provide a broader range of Hebrew authors of both sexes; one such text is *The Oxford Book of Hebrew Short Stories*, edited by Glenda Abramson.

Of extraordinary importance is the two-volume *Holocaust Literature: An Encyclopedia of Writers and Their Work*, which contains in-depth bio-bibliographic and bio-critical information about approximately 300 writers who have dealt with one or more aspects of the Holocaust in their books. One of its many significant features is a series of appendices that categorize writers by their language of composition (e.g., Hebrew, Yiddish, English, German); the genre in which they wrote (e.g., diary, fiction, nonfiction prose); and the themes present in their works (e.g., bystanders; guilt; religious and secular healing; indifference to saving Jews; Nazi camp universe; survivor psychology; moral imperative to remember; and universalizing the Holocaust). Among the many Hebrew-language authors included are Jenny Aloni, David Grossman, Haim Gouri, Tanya Hadar, Amos Oz, and Elie Wiesel, who also writes in Yiddish.

Wiesel's use of both Hebrew and Yiddish (and also of French) leads to the vexed question of the relationship between Hebrew and Yiddish. Before the Haskalah (Jewish Enlightenment), the two languages enjoyed a "mutually productive interaction." But in the wake of the teachings of German Jewish philosopher Moses Mendelssohn (1729–1786), who argued that "if Jews were ever to achieve civil emancipation in the countries in which they lived, they would have to embrace the values of the

European enlightenment, which valued reason and science over faith and superstition and demanded moderate secularization together with European education," Yiddish was rejected as "a corrupt . . . jargon spoken only by illiterates and criminals" (Sherman, *Writers In Yiddish*, p. xv). But Yiddish persisted; world-renowned authors, such as Isaac Bashevis Singer, as well as such lesser-known figures as Sholem Asch and Rachel Korn wrote in that language. Extensive bio-bibliographic information about these and many other Yiddish writers is available in the *Dictionary of Literary Biography* volume entitled *Writers in Yiddish*, edited by Joseph Sherman (2007; vol. 333).

We want to conclude this section by emphasizing the immense value of Rachel Feldhay Brenner's *Inextricably Bonded: Israeli Arab and Jewish Writers Re-Visioning Culture*. Undertaking a "juxtaposition of Israeli Jewish and Israeli Arab texts" that she hopes will "illuminate aspects of meaning obfuscated" by a more typical "conformist, programmatic interpretive reading," Brenner argues that "in contrast to the dominant ideology of separation," the stories and novels of Israeli Jewish and Israeli Arab writers "reveal an inextricable bonding between Israeli Jews and Israeli Arabs." As she compares the fiction of such Israeli Jewish authors as S. Yizhar; A. B. Yehoshua; Amos Oz; and David Grossman with the fiction of Attalah Mansour (e.g., *In a New Light*); Emile Habiby (e.g., *The Pessoptimist*); and Anton Shammas (e.g., *Arabesques*)—who together "practically constitute[] the corpus of Israeli Arab literature in Hebrew"—she notes that "these literatures of dissent suggest a concept of identity grounded in the acknowledgement of an ineluctable and irreversible interpenetration of the Jewish and Arab selves at profound psychological and ethical levels" (pp. 13–14).

Italy

One of the most accessible and informative ways to be introduced to Italian literary culture is through *Modern Italian Literature* by Ann Hallamore Caesar and Michael Caesar. This book begins with the late seventeenth century, examines literary production in various Italian city-states, moves to the literature of Italian unification during the nineteenth century, and concludes with a detailed consideration of the effects of modernism, fascism, minimalist postmodernism, and the ideology of the marketplace on late twentieth-century writing. Specific topics examined include: journalism, theater and the book trade in Venice; war, technology, and the arts; narratives of selfhood; the social condition of the intellectuals; and testing the limits of the novel. Equally informative and accessible is *The Cambridge Companion to the Italian Novel*, edited by Peter Bondanella and Andrea Ciccarelli. Here, readers will not only gain insight into such famous twentieth-century Italian novelists as Luigi Pirandello, Primo Levi, Umberto Eco, and Italo Calvino, but they will also learn about the contexts and frameworks out of which and in which these writers wrote. For example, there are essays about the forms of long prose fiction in late medieval and early modern Italian literature; popular fiction between Italian unification and World War I; feminist writing in the twentieth century; the Italian novel and the cinema; and frontier, exile, and migration in the contemporary Italian novel. The book concludes with an engaging look at Italian mystery writing, as represented by Leonardo Sciascia, Enrico Brizzi, Andrea Camilleri, and Carlo Lucarelli.

Of course, no one can hope to fully appreciate classic or contemporary Italian novels without understanding Italy. For this purpose, there is *The Cambridge Companion to Modern Italian Culture*, edited by Zygmunt G. Baránski and Rebecca J. West, where readers will find authoritative historical and critical essays about the role of Catholicism, socialism, communism, language, drama, design, art, fashion, music, and film in the development of Italian culture over the past 150 years. Aware of all this background, readers can now confidently turn to the some of the numerous translated Italian novels annotated in *The Babel Guide to Italian Fiction in English Translation* by Ray Kennoy and Fiorenza Conte.

After sampling some Italian fiction listed in Kennoy and Conte's book—perhaps Alberto Moravia's *The Conformist* or Roberto Calasso's *The Marriage of Cadmus and Harmony*—there is a strong possibility that readers will wish to explore further in the realm of Italian literature, especially its origins in the twelfth and thirteenth centuries. *The Cambridge History of Italian Literature*, edited by Peter Brand and Lino Pertile, is a gold mine for this purpose. There are lucid and entertaining analyses of such canonical authors as Dante, Boccaccio, and Petrarch—not to mention detailed bibliographies and substantial historical overviews of developments in poetry, prose, and drama in each century up to the 1990s. For yet more insight about issues in early Italian literature, Teodolinda Barolini's *Dante and the Origins of Italian Literary Culture* is the perfect complement to Brand and Pertile's book.

Just as one could not go wrong in consulting any of the aforementioned books, the following reference sources are models of their kind. By far the most exhaustive of them is the two-volume *Encyclopedia of Italian Literary Studies*, edited by Gaetana Marrone, with contributions from 221 international scholars and critics. Its approximately 2,000 pages contain vivid and meticulous entries on hundreds of authors, broad literary subjects, and significant works. Some of the topics covered include: detective fiction; lesbian and gay writing; migration literature; printing and publishing; Russian influences; utopian literature; popular culture and literature; oral literature; and book culture. Each entry assesses critically the topic or person in question, presenting a list of an author's selected works and/or further readings.

For smaller libraries that may not be able to afford the *Encyclopedia of Italian Literary Studies*, we recommend a combination of *Italian Literature and Its Times*, edited by Joyce Moss, and *The Oxford Companion to Italian Literature*, edited by Peter Hainsworth and David Robey. *Italian Literature and Its Times* concentrates on about 50 important literary works, explaining them in terms of their historical, social, political, psychological, economic, and cultural contexts (p. vii). Thus, the entry about Andrea Camilleri's detective novel *Excursion to Tindari* features sections on the Sicilian Mafia, criminal prosecution of the Mafia, and the Sicilian dialect; the entry about Umberto Eco's *The Name of the Rose* contains sections about the rise of monasteries and the Franciscans; and the entry on Luigi Pirandello's *Six Characters in Search of an Author* situates it within the framework of the rise of fascism. With nearly 2,400 entries, *The Oxford Companion to Italian Literature* is a substantial and captivating mini-encyclopedia that—along with biographical and critical entries on hundreds of authors—succinctly elucidates literary genres and types (e.g., science fiction, colonial literature, bestiaries); literary movements, themes, and issues (e.g., Arthurian literature, the Baroque, semiotics); cultural contexts and institutions (e.g., existentialism, feminism, chivalry, nuns); language (e.g., slang, dialect); social and political context (e.g., feudalism, communes, Jesuits); non-Italian writing and influences (e.g., Italian writers in Switzerland, Latin influences); and the relationship of literature with other arts (e.g., opera, comics, cookery books).

We also wish to draw attention to three volumes in the Dictionary of Literary Biography series: *Italian Novelists Since World War II, 1945–1965*, edited by Augustus Pallotta (1997; vol. 177); *Italian Novelists Since World War II, 1965–1995*, edited by Augustus Pallotta (1999; vol. 196); and *Italian Prose Writers, 1900–1945*, edited by Luca Somigli and Rocco Capozzi (2002; vol. 264). These volumes should be supplemented by *The Feminist Encyclopedia of Italian Literature* and *Italian Women Writers: A Bio-Bibliographical Sourcebook*, both edited by Rinaldina Russell and both of which contain thorough biographical information and critical analyses about such authors as Anna Banti, Laura Cereta, St. Catherine of Siena, Moderata Fonte, Natalia Ginzburg, Gina Lagorio, Dacia Maraini, Maria Messina, Elsa Morante, Ada Negri, Antonia Pulci, and Annie Vivanti. Struck by the large number of pre-1900 (and pre-1700) women writers in Italy contained in these two reference books, many readers will no doubt want to turn to Virginia Cox's *Women's Writing in Italy, 1400–1650* for additional background and context.

SELECTED REFERENCES

Abramson, Glenda. (Ed.). (1996). *The Oxford Book of Hebrew Short Stories*. Oxford: Oxford University Press.

Baránski, Zygmunt G., and West, Rebecca J. (Eds.). (2001). *The Cambridge Companion to Modern Italian Culture*. New York: Cambridge University Press.

Barolini, Teodolinda. (2006). *Dante and the Origins of Italian Literary Culture*. New York: Fordham University Press.

Beaton, Roderick. (1999). *An Introduction to Modern Greek Literature*. (2nd ed.). Oxford: Clarendon Press.

Bondanella, Peter, and Ciccarelli, Andrea. (Eds.). (2003). *The Cambridge Companion to the Italian Novel*. New York: Cambridge University Press.

Brand, Peter, and Pertile, Lino. (Eds.). (1999). *The Cambridge History of Italian Literature*. (rev. ed.). New York: Cambridge University Press.

Brenner, Rachel Feldhay. (2003). *Inextricably Bonded: Israeli Arab and Jewish Writers Re-Visioning Culture*. Madison, WI: University of Wisconsin Press.

Caesar, Ann Hallamore, and Caesar, Michael. (2007). *Modern Italian Literature*. Malden, MA: Polity.

Cox, Virginia. (2008). *Women's Writing in Italy*. Baltimore, MD: Johns Hopkins University Press.

Dimaras, C. Th. (1972). *A History of Modern Greek Literature*. (Trans. by Mary P. Gianos). Albany, NY: State University of New York Press.

Domb, Risa. (Ed.). (2008). *Contemporary Israeli Women's Writing*. London: Vallentine Mitchell.

Domb, Risa. (2006). *Identity and Modern Israeli Literature*. London: Vallentine Mitchell.

Feldman, Yael S. (1999). *No Room of Their Own: Gender and Nation in Israeli Women's Fiction*. New York: Columbia University Press.

Hainsworth, Peter, and Robey, David. (Eds.). (2002). *The Oxford Companion to Italian Literature*. Oxford: Oxford University Press.

Hasak-Lowy, Todd. (2008). *Here and Now: History, Nationalism, and Realism in Modern Hebrew Fiction*. Syracuse, NY: Syracuse University Press.

Kennoy, Ray, and Conte, Fiorenza. (1995). *The Babel Guide to Italian Fiction in English Translation*. London: Boulevard.

Kerbel, Sorrel. (Ed.). (2003). *Jewish Writers of the Twentieth Century*. New York: Fitzroy Dearborn.

Kremer, S. Lillian. (Ed.). (2003). *Holocaust Literature: An Encyclopedia of Writers and Their Work*. (2 vols.). New York: Routledge.

Marrone, Gaetana. (Ed.). (2007). *Encyclopedia of Italian Literary Studies*. (2 vols.). New York: Routledge.

Mintz, Alan. (Ed.). (1997). *The Boom in Contemporary Israeli Fiction*. Hanover, NH: Brandeis University Press and University Press of New England.

Mintz, Alan. (Ed.). (2003). *Reading Hebrew Literature: Critical Discussions of Six Modern Texts*. Hanover, NH: Brandeis University Press and University Press of New England.

Mintz, Alan. (Ed.). (2001). *Translating Israel: Contemporary Hebrew Literature and Its Reception in America*. Syracuse, NY: Syracuse University Press.

Moss, Joyce. (Ed.). (2005). *Italian Literature and Its Times*. Detroit, MI: Thompson Gale.

Mintz, Alan. (Ed.). (2004). *Middle Eastern Literatures and Their Times*. Detroit, MI: Thompson Gale.

Politis, Linos. (1973). *A History of Modern Greek Literature*. Oxford: Clarendon Press.

Ramras-Rauch, Gila, and Michman-Melkman, Joseph. (Eds.). (1985). *Facing the Holocaust: Selected Israeli Fiction*. Philadelphia, PA: The Jewish Publication Society.

Ricks, David. (Ed.). (2003). *Modern Greek Writing: An Anthology in English Translation*. London: Peter Owen Publishers.

Russell, Rinaldina. (Ed.). (1997). *The Feminist Encyclopedia of Italian Literature*. Westport, CT: Greenwood Press.

Russell, Rinaldina. (Ed.). (1994). *Italian Women Writers: A Bio-Bibliographical Sourcebook*. Westport, CT: Greenwood Press.

Shaked, Gershon. (2000). *Modern Hebrew Fiction*. (Trans. by Yael Lotan). Bloomington, IN: Indiana University Press.

Silberschlag, Eisig. (1973). *From Renaissance to Renaissance: Hebrew Literature from 1492–1970*. New York: Ktav Publishing.

Silberschlag, Eisig. (1977). *From Renaissance to Renaissance: Hebrew Literature in the Land of Israel 1870–1970*. New York: Ktav Publishing.

Tziovas, Dimitris. (2003). *The Other Self: Selfhood and Society in Modern Greek Fiction*. Lanham, MD: Lexington Books.

Zierler, Wendy I. (2004). *And Rachel Stole the Idols: The Emergence of Modern Hebrew Women's Writing*. Detroit, MI: Wayne State University Press.

ANNOTATIONS FOR TRANSLATED BOOKS FROM GREECE

Petros Ampatzoglou (Petros Abatzoglou). ***What Does Mrs. Freeman Want?***
Translated by Kay Cicellis. Normal, IL: Dalkey Archive Press, 2005. 111 pages.
Genre/literary style/story type: mainstream fiction
The unnamed Greek narrator of this novel is a typical man—self-obsessed and patriarchal to the core. Of course, he has an image of what the ideal woman should be like, but Mrs. Freeman, a married English woman, in no way resembles this ideal. The narrator is nevertheless fascinated by her independent spirit and sparkling verve. The book dissects cultural incompatibilities and divergent worldviews as they play out in a domestic milieu.
Subject keywords: culture conflict; social roles
Original language: Greek
Sources consulted for annotation:
Dalkey Archive Press (book description), http://www.dalkeyarchive.com
Kedros Publishers series of Greek novels in English translation. "Other Books in This Series" review.

Lili Bita. ***The Scorpion and Other Stories.***
Translated by Robert Zaller in collaboration with the author. New York: Pella Publishing, 1998. 208 pages.
Genres/literary styles/story types: mainstream fiction; women's lives
The setting of this novel is the 1940s, the most turbulent period of modern Greek history. After being occupied by Italy and Germany during World War II, Greece underwent a prolonged civil war between communists and royalists. The author examines the way in which these tumultuous events were reflected in domestic life, spotlighting the trials and tribulations of growing up female in a patriarchal culture. Women are invariably destroyed by the very people expected to love and protect them, although revenge, redemption, and liberation are occasionally possible. In one story, Antonia is ruthlessly beaten by her father after she is suspected of being inhabited by the devil. In another story, Stasa's mother mutilates her with scissors after she discovers her daughter's affection for an enemy soldier.
Subject keywords: power; social roles
Original language: Greek
Sources consulted for annotation:
Spencer, Sharon. *World Literature Today* 73 (Summer 1999): 569.
Zaller, Robert. Translator's introduction to the book.

Soteres Ph. Demetriou (Sotiris Dimitriou). ***May Your Name Be Blessed.***
Translated by Leo Marshall. Birmingham, UK: Centre for Byzantine, Ottoman & Modern Greek Studies, University of Birmingham, 2000. 84 pages.
Genre/literary style/story type: mainstream fiction; women's lives
The events in this novel, which spans about 50 years from 1944 to 1993, are presented through the eyes of three related narrators: Alexo, a 15-year-old girl, who travels in the company of other women from the Greek village of Povla to Albania to exchange goods for food; Sophia, Alexo's sister, left to recuperate in the home of her Albanian relatives and unable to return home due to a border closure; and Sophia's grandson, who finally realizes his dream of repatriating to Greece—only to find himself treated as an illegal immigrant. As the cover and introduction of this book make clear, this is a multifaceted narrative about the differences between urban and rural life as well as the effects of "constant movement and displacement" and the destruction of personal relationships "by political adversity and social prejudice."

Subject keywords: family histories; social problems
Original language: Greek
Sources consulted for annotation:
Back cover of the book.
Tziovas, Dimitris. Introduction to the book.
Another translated book written by Soteres Ph. Demetriou: *Woof, Woof, Dear Lord and Other Stories*

Maro Douka. *Fool's Gold.*
Translated by Roderick Beaton. Athens, Greece: Kedros, 1991. 325 pages.
Genres/literary styles/story types: mainstream fiction; coming-of-age
According to the publisher, this novel is about "an impressionable girl's unflinching search for a true identity, both for herself and for her country." Myrsini Panayoutou is the daughter of an affluent Athenian family. Her university years coincided with the dictatorship that followed the coup of April 1967. Idealistic and rebellious, Myrsini becomes involved with the underground resistance movement and engaged to a political prisoner.
Subject keywords: identity; politics
Original language: Greek
Source consulted for annotation:
Kedros Publishers series of Greek novels in English translation. "Other Books in This Series" review.
Another translated book written by Maro Douka: *Come Forth, King*

Apostolos K. Doxiades (Apostolos Doxiadis). *Uncle Petros and Goldbach's Conjecture.*
Translated by the author. New York: Bloomsbury, 2000. 209 pages.
Genre/literary style/story type: mainstream fiction
This novel takes as its starting point a 250-year-old mathematical conjecture proposed by Christian Goldbach. It has remained unresolved since the eighteenth century, evading the greatest scientific minds. One such mind is this novel's Uncle Petros, a mathematical genius whose life was blighted by his unsuccessful attempts to solve the conjecture. As a result, he tries to dissuade his nephew from becoming a mathematician, explaining to him how an intellectual challenge can became a morbid fixation and how all-consuming scientific endeavor can turn into self-destructive folly.
Subject keyword: identity
Original language: Greek
Sources consulted for annotation:
The Australian, 10 May 2000 (from Factiva databases).
Gilpin, Sam. *The Sunday Times*, 1 July 2001 (from Factiva databases).
Savvas, Minas. *World Literature Today* 74 (1 July 2000): 684.

Rea Galanake (Rhea Galanaki). *I Shall Sign as Loui.*
Translated by Helen Dendrinou Kolias. Evanston, IL: Northwestern University Press, 2000. 201 pages.
Genre/literary style/story type: historical fiction
This book resurrects the life of Andreas Rigopoulos (1821–1889), who was a staunch fighter for Greek independence and democratic governance. Born in Patras, Rigopolous went to Italy to study, becoming a supporter of Garibaldi and reading widely in such authors as Karl Marx and Victor Hugo. Combining fact and fiction, the novel consists of letters written during the last week of his life to the fictional Louisa, a sophisticated and cultured married woman with whom he once was in love. The letters contain his reflections on his travels to Europe and America as well as his thoughts about the historical struggle of the Greeks for liberation from the Turks.

Related title by the same author:
Readers may also gravitate toward *The Life of Ismail Ferik Pasha*, which recounts the history of Crete in the nineteeth century. When Crete revolts against the Ottoman empire, a Cretan boy is kidnapped and taken to Egypt; in captivity, he is forced to adopt Islam and undergoes military training. Later, he is sent back to Crete to help subdue another revolt. Haunted by his past, he attempts to find his brother and come to terms with his divided soul.
Subject keywords: politics; power
Original language: Greek
Sources consulted for annotation:
Beyerle, Shaazka. *Europe*, 1 March 2001, p. 47.
Dendrinou Kolias, Helen. Translator's Preface to the book.
Global Books in Print (reviews from *Kirkus Reviews* and *Publishers Weekly*).
Savvas, Minas. *World Literature Today* 75 (1 April 2001): 409.
Some other translated books written by Rea Galanake: *Eleni or Nobody*; *The Life of Ismail Ferik Pasha*

Giorges Giatromanolakes (Yoryis Yatromanolakis). *The Spiritual Meadow.*
Translated by Mary Argyraki. Sawtry, Cambs, UK: Dedalus, 2000. 182 pages.
Genres/literary styles/story types: mainstream fiction; magical realism
This novel is a satire about the so-called Regime of the Colonels (1967–1974) and its devastating impact on the human psyche. It tells the story of Theodore P., a humanities teacher sent to work on the fictitious island of Porphyri. As Theodore describes his anguish when faced with the stifling and dictatorial atmosphere of his new school, he also recalls his past life and tries to imagine the future. Undertaking a voyage through the pages of ancient and modern Greek history, he describes his involvement in crucial military campaigns; how he survived a disastrous flood; his encounters with famous politicians and poets; and how he was swallowed and set free by a whale.
Subject keywords: identity; politics
Original language: Greek
Sources consulted for annotation:
Amazon.com (review from *Kirkus Reviews*).
Argyraki, Mary. Translator's introduction to the book.
Back cover of the book.
Bien, Peter. *World Literature Today* 74 (Autumn 2000): 906.
Some other translated books written by Giorges Giatromanolakes: *History of a Vendetta*; *Eroticon*; *A Report of a Murder*

Ioanna Karystiani. *Swell.*
Translated by Konstantine Matsoukas. New York: Europa Editions, 2010. 272 pages.
Genres/literary styles/story types: adventure; survival and disaster stories
Captain Mitsos Avgustìs has spent some 12 years at sea without seeing his family and loved ones. Like the sea-wandering Ulysses after the Trojan War, Avgustis on his return to land must come to terms with the life he left behind—in all its glory and in all its abjectness.
Subject keyword: identity
Original language: Greek
Source consulted for annotation:
Europa Editions (book description), http://www.europaeditions.com.
Another translated book written by Ioanna Karystiani: *The Jasmine Isle*

Alexandros Kotzias. *The Jaguar.*
Translated by H. E. Criton. Athens, Greece: Kedros, 1991. 143 pages.

Genre/literary style/story type: mainstream fiction
Despite its social and historical underpinnings, this novel is a satire of hypocrisy and self-righteousness. In the first part of the book, Dimitra recounts her activities as a member of the resistance during World War II. She was also subjected to persecution as a communist during the Greek Civil War of the 1940s. In the second part, her sister-in-law Philio arrives from America to claim an inheritance, triggering the question of who has been more true to lofty social and political ideals.
Subject keywords: politics; social roles
Original language: Greek
Source consulted for annotation:
Back cover of the book.

Menes Koumantareas (Menis Koumandareas). *Their Smell Makes Me Want To Cry.*
Translated by Patricia Felisa Barbeito and Vangelis Calotychos. Birmingham, UK: Centre for Byzantine, Ottoman & Modern Greek Studies, University of Birmingham, 2004. 252 pages.
Genre/literary style/story type: mainstream fiction
Euripedes works in a barbershop that is a community gathering spot. Here, all and sundry come to tell their stories: a political activist, a gigolo, blue-collar workers, and professionals. As they ponder the vicissitudes of life, they are more than aware of the funeral home next door.
Subject keyword: aging
Original language: Greek
Sources consulted for annotation:
Back cover of the book.
Barbeito, Patricia Felisa, and Calotychos, Vangelis. Foreword to the book.
Another translated book written by Menes Koumantareas: *Koula*

Petros Markaris. *Deadline in Athens: An Inspector Costas Haritos Mystery* (or *The Late-Night News*).
Translated by David Connolly. New York: Grove Press, 2004. 295 pages.
Genres/literary styles/story types: crime fiction; police detectives
Costas Haritos, a former prison guard under a less-than-savory political regime, is now a successful police inspector. But he has a hard time coping with workplace politics and being diplomatic with superiors; nothing much pleases him about the state of the contemporary world. When Janna Karayoryi, a famous television journalist, is murdered just before she was to report a scoop, Haritos must orient himself within the prevailing cynicism of the media world—rife with its own kind of back-biting, vicious competition, and corrupt politics. When Janna's successor is also murdered, Haritos knows that the corruption involves the highest levels of Greek society.
Subject keyword: urban life
Original language: Greek
Sources consulted for annotation:
Amazon.com (book description).
Klett, Rex E. *Library Journal* 129 (1 September 2004): 121.
"Petros Markaris." *Contemporary Authors Online*. Thomson Gale, 2006.
Sennett, Frank. *Booklist* 100 (August 2004): 1906.
Another translated book written by Petros Markaris: *Zone Defence*

Tefcros Michaelides. *Pythagorean Crimes.*
Translated by Lena Cavanagh. Las Vegas, NV: Parmenides Publishing, 2008. 300 pages.
Genres/literary styles/story types: crime fiction; historical mysteries

This mystery revolves around the murder of mathematician Stefanos Kantartzis in 1929. Michael Igerinos, his friend and also a mathematician, is the prime suspect because the murdered man had had relationships with Igerinos's former wife and mistress. As the novel progresses, early twentieth-century Greek history assumes an increasingly important role, as does mathematical history, especially an international congress of mathematicians held in Paris in 1900.
Subject keywords: politics; social roles
Original language: Greek
Sources consulted for annotation:
The Complete Review (book review), http://www.complete-review.com.
Global Books in Print (online) (review from *Publishers Weekly*).

Amanda Michalopoulou. *I'd Like.*
Translated by Karen Emmerich. Champaign, IL: Dalkey Archive Press, 2008. 142 pages.
Genres/literary styles/story types: mainstream fiction; postmodernism
As Monica Carter observes, the interlinked stories in this collection feature "hypnotic repetition of objects, characters, places and phrases" whose meaning is often hidden and multidimensional. Everyday events become endowed with a poetic luminescence. Nothing is ever as we imagined it. A widow's decision to live with her sister turns out to be a bad idea; a much-admired and elderly writer turns out not to be exactly as one of his fans envisioned him. The author has been compared with Marguerite Duras.
Subject keyword: identity
Original language: Greek
Sources consulted for annotation:
Carter, Monica. Three Percent website (book review), http://www.rochester.edu/College/translation/threepercent.
Dalkey Archive Press (book description), http://www.dalkeyarchive.com.
Global Books in Print (online) (review from *Publishers Weekly*).

Eugenia Phakinou (Eugenia Fakinou). *Astradeni.*
Translated by H. E. Criton. Athens, Greece: Kedros, 1991. 239 pages.
Genres/literary styles/story types: mainstream fiction; coming-of-age
Eleven-year-old Astradeni lives on the island of Symi (in the Aegean Sea close to Rhodes), where community life is guided by tradition and infused with folk magic and religious beliefs. When financial hardships prompt her family to move to Athens, she undergoes an emotional and psychological transformation. No longer able to derive strength and inspiration from contact with nature, she must acclimatize herself to the alienating environment of the city, with its frenzied pursuit of a consumerist lifestyle.
Subject keywords: rural life; urban life
Original language: Greek
Source consulted for annotation:
Kedros Publishers series of Greek novels in English translation. "Other Books in This Series" review.
Another translated book written by Eugenia Phakinou: *The Seventh Garment*

Spyros Plaskovites (Spyros Plaskovitis). *The Façade Lady of Corfu.*
Translated by Amy Mims. Athens, Greece: Kedros, 1995. 320 pages.
Genre/literary style/story type: mainstream fiction
Middle-aged Anghelina Dassiou, a salesperson in a Corfu hotel, longs for the lost beauty of Corfu before it was turned into a major tourist attraction by foreign investors and local millionaires. Dinos

Hairetis, who was born on Corfu but moved away, is a guest at the hotel. Disaffected, drifting, and disillusioned, he is torn between past and present and between the global economy and the preservation of the cultural heritage of the Greek islands. When he falls in love with Anghelina, he begins to make changes in his life.
Subject keyword: modernization
Original language: Greek
Source consulted for annotation:
Back cover of the book.

Dido Soteriou (Dido Sotiriou). *Farewell Anatolia.*
Translated by Fred A. Reed. Athens, Greece: Kedros, 1991. 310 pages.
Genre/literary style/story type: historical fiction
According to the publisher, this novel focuses on "the death or expulsion of two million Greeks from Turkey by Kemal Attaturk's revolutionary forces in the late summer of 1922." The theme of "paradise lost and of shattered innocence" predominates, especially in the story of Manolis, a Christian, who mourns his childhood friend, a Muslim shepherd boy. The book has been compared with *Birds Without Wings* by Louis de Bernières.
Subject keyword: war
Original language: Greek
Source consulted for annotation:
Kedros Publishers series of Greek novels in English translation. "Other Books in This Series" review.

Ersi Sotiropoulos. *Landscape with Dog.*
Translated by Karen Emmerich. Northampton, MA: Clockroot Books, 2009. 166 pages.
Genres/literary styles/story types: mainstream fiction; short stories
Critics have raved about this collection of short stories: Seventeen minimalist gems about the inability of couples, partners, and loved ones to understand each other and to know what the other is thinking. Emotionally resonant and written with shattering honesty, each of the stories captures the painful gulf that separates our conceptions of ourselves from how others see us.
Related title by the same author:
Also worthwhile may be *Zigzag Through the Bitter Orange Trees*, which has been praised as a graceful and lyrical tapestry that has affinities with William Faulkner, Marguerite Duras, and Federico Fellini. Here, four lonely people are caught in an intricate web of compassion, anger, angst, and self-deception as they struggle to come to terms with a debilitating disease affecting Lia. Lia's brother, her nurse, and a 12-year-old girl give voice to their individual aspirations, providing insight into the contemporary Greek psyche.
Subject keyword: identity
Original language: Greek
Sources consulted for annotation:
Clockroot Books website (book description), http://www.clockrootbooks.com.
The Complete Review (book review), http://www.complete-review.com.
Another translated book written by Ersi Sotiropoulos: *Zigzag Through the Bitter Orange Trees*

Alexes Stamates (Alexis Stamatis). *The Seventh Elephant.*
Translated by David Connolly. London: Arcadia, 2000. 199 pages.
Genre/literary style/story type: mainstream fiction
This novel focuses on a young, hip, rich, and sexy alcoholic. Trying to flee a chain of botched love affairs, he wanders from Athens to London to Munich, where he meets a woman that will change

the entire course of his life. On Holy Saturday, he takes a symbolic and redemptive swim, marking the beginning of a new way of looking at just about everything.

Related title by the same author:

Readers may also be interested in *American Fugue*, which also examines the theme of redemption and self-knowledge. A writer in the depths of despair takes a job at an American university but quickly becomes dissatisfied with life in the college town and flees westward. When his car breaks down in Arizona, Marcelo Diaz, who is on way to Hannibal, Missouri—Mark Twain's birthplace—gives him a ride in his black Mustang. But Diaz dies suddenly, so the writer assumes his identity, continuing Diaz's journey and his rendezvous with Laura, whom he has never met in person.

Subject keyword: identity

Original language: Greek

Sources consulted for annotation:

Amazon.com (book description).

Amazon.co.uk (United Kingdom) (customer reviews for *American Fugue*).

Martin, Alex. *Scotland on Sunday*, 17 December 2000, p. 11.

Some other translated books written by Alexes Stamates: *Bar Flaubert*; *American Fugue*

Thanases Valtinos (Thanassis Valtinos). *Data from the Decade of the Sixties.*

Translated by Jane Assimakopoulos and Stavros Deligiorgis. Evanston, IL: Northwestern University Press, 2000. 307 pages.

Genre/literary style/story type: historical fiction

This novel recreates the tumultuous period of the 1960s in Greece by focusing on the lives of ordinary Greeks. There is no plot and no clearly defined characters. Instead, there is a collage of newspaper clippings; advertisements; archival documents; announcements; obituaries; and personal letters through which readers learn about the private loves, tragedies, and dilemmas of individuals struggling to survive.

Subject keyword: social problems

Original language: Greek

Sources consulted for annotation:

Assimakopoulos, Jane, and Deligiorgis, Stavros. Translators' introduction to the book.

Bien, Peter. *World Literature Today* 75 (Winter 2001): 188.

Another translated book written by Thanases Valtinos: *Deep Blue Almost Black*

Vasiles Vasilikos (Vassilis Vassilikos). *The Few Things I Know About Glafkos Thrassakis.*

Translated by Karen Emmerich. New York: Seven Stories Press, 2002. 356 pages.

Genres/literary styles/story types: mainstream fiction; postmodernism

As Mary Park notes, this novel is a literary hybrid called "autonovegraphy" or "novistory"—a kind of "fictionalized autobiography." It focuses on the life and death of Glafkos Thrassakis, the pen name of Lazarus Lazaridis, a nineteenth-century Greek writer, who is a stand-in for Vassilis Vassilikos. The book recounts episodes in Greek history: occupation during World War II, military dictatorship, and the influence of American foreign policy. It also explores the author's childhood during World War II, the development of his leftist views, and his life as a political exile. But there are also a series of extraordinary elements that provide a touch of the thriller: cannibals, spies, secret clubs, plots to overthrow the government of Montenegro, and insane countesses. The book has been compared to the best writings of Milan Kundera.

Subject keywords: politics; power

Original language: Greek

Sources consulted for annotation:

Hibbard, Allen. *Review of Contemporary Fiction* 23 (1 July 2003): 136.

Montgomery, Isobel. *The Guardian*, 14 May 2005 (from Factiva databases).
Park, Mary. *The New York Times Book Review*, 30 March 2003, p. 14.
Power, Chris. *The Times*, 21 May 2005, p. 11.
Some other translated books written by Vasiles Vasilikos: *Z*; *. . . And Dreams Are Dreams*; *The Coroner's Assistant: A Fictional Documentary*; *The Harpoon Gun*; *The Plant. The Well. The Angel: A Trilogy*; *The Monarch*; *The Photographs*

ANNOTATIONS FOR TRANSLATED BOOKS FROM ISRAEL (HEBREW)

Suzane Adam. *Laundry.*
Translated by Becka Mara McKay. Iowa City, IA: Autumn Hill Books, 2008. 250 pages.
Genre/literary style/story type: mainstream fiction
Ildiko is only five years old, but her life has already become unbearable. She idolizes the older Yutzi, but Yutzi takes advantage of her, reviling and abusing her. Even when Ildiko's family emigrates to Israel from Transylvania (Romania), she continues to be indelibly marked by the events of her childhood, which she eventually recounts to her husband. The legacy of the Holocaust looms large.
Subject keyword: family histories
Original language: Hebrew
Sources consulted for annotation:
Autumn Hill Books (book description), http://www.autumnhillbooks.org.
Global Books in Print (online) (synopsis/book jacket).

Aron Appelfeld (Aharon Appelfeld). *The Conversion.*
Translated by Jeffrey M. Green. New York: Schocken Books, 1998. 228 pages.
Genre/literary style/story type: mainstream fiction
In a small Austrian town in the dying days of the Hapsburg Empire, Karl Hüber renounces his Jewish faith in order to ensure professional and social success. He converts to Christianity and his job with the town council seems safe. But when the town embarks on a plan to raze Jewish stores, he must re-examine his decision. In an attempt to reconcile himself to his faith and his family's traditions, Karl and the woman he loves, Gloria, return to a small village in the Carpathian mountains, but even here, they cannot escape virulent anti-Semitism. As Larry Wolff obersves, this book—in which the Hapsburg Empire "takes on some of the semimythological resonance of the embattled empire in J. M. Coetzee's *Waiting for the Barbarians*"—can be read as "a historical novel about the Austrian past and [as] an allegorical analysis of the significance of religious identity."
Related title by the same author:
Readers may also be interested in *Blooms of Darkness*, in which a mother smuggles her 11-year-old son Hugo out of a Jewish ghetto in an Ukrainian city and leaves him with her friend Mariana, who is a prostitute selling her favors to the German forces. Thus, Hugo spends his time in Mariana's bedroom closet, privy to all her secrets and protected by her connections and the cross he now wears. It is a whole new world for him: a luxuriant debauchery the very opposite of the ordered rationality in which he was raised. Inevitably, he succumbs to the charms of his new surroundings, and she introduces him to sex. But when the Nazis flee and the Soviets gain the upper hand, Hugo ends up protecting Mariana.
Subject keywords: anti-Semitism; family histories
Original language: Hebrew
Sources consulted for annotation:
Amazon.com (all editorial reviews).
Leavitt, David. *The New York Times Book Review*, 21 March 2010 (online).
Steinberg, Sybil S. *Publishers Weekly* 245 (7 September 1998): 81.

Sterling, Eric. *World Literature Today* 73 (Spring 1999): 385.
Wolff, Larry. *The New York Times Book Review*, 24 January 1999, p. 20.
Some other translated books written by Aron Appelfeld: *Badenheim 1939*; *The Age of Wonders*; *The Iron Tracks*; *To the Land of the Cattails (To the Land of the Reeds)*; *Katerina*; *The Immortal Bartfuss*; *Tzili, the Story of a Life*; *For Every Sin*; *The Healer*; *The Retreat*; *Unto the Soul*; *In the Wilderness*; *All Whom I Have Loved*; *Laish*; *Blooms of Darkness*

Haim Beer (Haim Be'er). *The Pure Element of Time.*
Translated by Barbara Harshav. Hanover, NH: University Press of New England, 2003. 282 pages.
Genre/literary style/story type: mainstream fiction
This novel recounts the story of the author's life and development as a writer. First, there was his religious grandmother, who told him wonderful tales about his family's ancestors. Then, there were his mismatached parents—the mother dynamic and educated; the father a mere shell of a man, haunted by the memory of the pogroms and resigned to the overwhelming perfidy of the world.
Subject keyword: family histories
Original language: Hebrew
Sources consulted for annotation:
Beck, Atara. *Canadian Jewish News* 33 (1 May 2003): 39.
Zaleski, Jeff. *Publishers Weekly* 249 (2 December 2002): 35.
Another translated book written by Haim Beer: *Feathers*

Orly Castel-Bloom. *Human Parts.*
Translated by Dalya Bilu. Boston: David R. Godine, 2003. 249 pages.
Genre/literary style/story type: mainstream fiction
The perfect storm of catastrophic events has hit Israel. Not only must the nation deal with what seems to be a daily round of terrorist attacks, but now it must also cope with a massive flu epidemic and unbelievably cold weather. Thus, of course, everyone is anxious and stressed, seeking a way to remain sane in chaotic times and to find a psychological and emotional equilibrium that will allow them to persevere yet again. Referring to this novel as either a dystopia, an allegory, or both, critics have seen parallels with H. G. Wells's *War of the Worlds* or John Wyndham's *The Day of the Triffids*.
Subject keywords: politics; social problems
Original language: Hebrew
Sources consulted for annotation:
Abramowitz, Molly. *Library Journal* 128 (December 2003): 164.
Gladstone, Bill. *Books in Canada* 33 (March 2004): 14.
Mesher, D. *Judaism* 53 (Summer 2004): 310.
Publishers Weekly 252 (11 April 2005): 35.
Zaleski, Jeff. *Publishers Weekly* 250 (22 December 2003): 39.
Another translated book written by Orly Castel-Bloom: *Dolly City*

Chaim Eliav (sometimes rendered as Hayim Eliav). *The Mission.*
Translated by Miriam Zakon. Brooklyn, NY: Shaar Press, 2000. 458 pages.
Genres/literary styles/story types: thrillers; political thrillers
Jeff Handler finds himself in Soviet-era Moscow for professional and personal reasons. His company is in the diamond-buying business, but his grandfather wants him to find religious memorabilia that were abandoned by the family in Moscow a half-century ago. As Handler goes about his business and personal affairs, he arouses the suspicions of the KGB.
Subject keyword: family histories
Original language: Hebrew

Source consulted for annotation:
Book description by http://www.discountseforim.com.
Some other translated books written by Chaim Eliav: *The Runaway: A Frightening Disappearance, a Cult, and a Desperate Search*; *The Envelope*; *In the Spider's Web: Decades After the War a Jew Is Enmeshed in International Nazi Intrigue*; *The Persecution: Intrigue and Suspense and a City Entangled in Danger*

Assaf Gavron. *Almost Dead.*
Translated by James Lever with the author. New York: HarperCollins, 2010. 336 pages.
Genre/literary style/story type: mainstream fiction
Critics have been unanimous in referring to this book as a satire to end all satires. In an Israel wracked by tumult, torment, and violence, Eitan Einoch, a businessman, has the uncanny knack of surviving bombing attempts. He emerges safe from separate attacks on a minibus and a café and is unharmed when a hitchhiker he has picked up is shot. His seeming good fortune attracts media attention, and he quickly becomes a celebrity and symbol of resilience. But not everyone is pleased with Einoch's luck: Fahmi Sabih, a suicide bomber, and his brother are committed Palestinian revolutionaries and are more than a little perplexed at Einoch's charmed life. Inevitably, there will be one more attack on Einoch.
Related title by the same author:
Readers may also want to look forward to the English-language publication of Gavron's *Hydromania*, which is set some 60 years in the future when three companies control the worldwide supply of fresh water and rain. The world has been turned topsy-turvy: China, Japan, and Hungary are key powers, the United States is in decline, and Israel's territory has shrunk considerably. Everyone and everything is experiencing a severe dearth of water—a situation that may be alleviated by an invention that allows the collection and purification of rainwater. But, as always, politics are a complicating factor.
Subject keywords: politics; power
Original language: Hebrew
Sources consulted for annotation:
Assafgavron.com (author's website), http://assafgavron.com.
HarperCollins website (book description), http://harpercollins.com.
Luchterhand (publisher's website), http://www.randomhouse.de.
Waxman, Jeff. Three Percent website (book review), http://www.rochester.edu/College/translation/threepercent.

David Grossman. *To the End of the Land.*
Translated by Jessica Cohen. New York: Alfred A. Knopf, 2010. 576 pages.
Genre/literary style/story type: mainstream fiction
Critics have labeled this book a majestic achievement, all the more so given its personal resonance for the author, whose son was killed during the 2006 Lebanon war. In the novel, Ora fears that Ofer, her son, an enlistee in the Israeli army, will be killed in combat. But she has a plan. She will simply go hiking for a month in the Galilee region, and because she will be incommunicado while she is away, military authorities will not be able to reach her with news of her son's possible death. As a result, her son will live. She goes with Avram, Ofer's father, though not her husband. As Ora and Avram physically make their way through a starkly luminous countryside, they also traverse a psychological and emotional maelstrom, recalling significant personal and historical events that have made them who they are and have affected Israel's definition and image of itself. Colm Toibin marveled at the elegance and power of Grossman's "antiwar" masterpiece, observing that, admidst the novel's tragic sweep, "it is filled with original and unexpected detail about domestic life, about

the shapes and shadows that surround love and memory, and about the sharp and desperate edges of loss and fear."

Related title by the same author:

Readers may also enjoy *See Under: Love*. Here, Momik is a young boy who has been kept in the dark about the death camps. Thus, he creates his own story about those horrific events, pieced together from randomly gleaned information. Eventually, Momik becomes a writer, with plans to create an encyclopedia of the Holocaust for children. However, he gives up on this idea and instead creates a story that draws inspiriation from the fact that his great-uncle, Anshell Wasserman, was a famous children's author who was imprisoned in one of the camps. Momik's novel describes how when a German officer discovered who one of his prisoners was, he forced Wasserman to recount a new episode of one of his serial adventure stories each night.

Subject keywords: family histories; war

Original language: Hebrew

Sources consulted for annotation:

Finucan, Stephen. *The Toronto Star*, 20 November 2010 (online).

Toibin, Colm. *The New York Times Book Review*, 26 September 2010 (online).

White, Edmund. *The New York Times Book Review*, 16 April 1989 (online).

Some other translated books written by David Grossman: *Her Body Knows*; *The Book of Intimate Grammar*; *Be My Knife*; *The Zigzag Kid*; *Duel*; *Someone to Run With*; *The Smile of the Lamb; See Under: Love*

Batya Gur. *Bethlehem Road Murder: A Michael Ohayon Mystery.*

Translated by Vivian Eden. New York: HarperCollins, 2004. 356 pages.

Genres/literary styles/story types: crime fiction; police detectives

Chief Superintendent Michael Ohayon must discover who killed a Yemenite woman in the Jerusalem neighborhood of Baka, an area known for its diverse immigrant population and often violent confrontations. Things get even more perplexing when Ohayon links the woman's death to the kidnapping of babies in the 1950s. The author of the Ohayon mysteries has been compared with Agatha Christie. Some other books in the series are *Murder Duet*; *Literary Murder*; *The Saturday Morning Murder*; *Murder on a Kibbutz*; and *Murder in Jerusalem*.

Subject keyword: social problems

Original language: Hebrew

Sources consulted for annotation:

Amazon.com (book description).

Halkin, Talya. *Jerusalem Post*, 22 May 2005, p. 8.

Ott, Bill. *Booklist* 101 (1 January/15 January 2005): 827.

Pearl, Nancy. *Library Journal* 129 (1 November 2004): 62.

Publishers Weekly 251 (8 November 2004): 39.

Stasio, Marilyn. *The New York Times Book Review*, 12 December 2004, p. 26.

Gail Hareven. *The Confessions of Noa Weber.*

Translated by Dalya Bilu. Brooklyn, NY: Melville House, 2009. 330 p.

Genre/literary style/story type: mainstream fiction

Noa Weber is a successful Israeli feminist author of thrillers who finds it difficult to understand what can only be described as her all-encompassing and obsessive love for Alek, a Russian émigré some years older than her whom she met in 1972. She marries him, partly to escape her military obligations, and remains transfixed with him despite the fact that he is untrue to her and returns to Russia. Thus, Noa writes to Hagar, her 29-year-old daughter, hoping to solve for herself the mystery of her unshakeable attachment to Alek.

Subject keywords: identity; power
Original language: Hebrew
Sources consulted for annotation:
Global Books in Print (online) (reviews from *Library Journal* and *Publishers Weekly*).
Melville House website, http://www.mhpbooks.com.

Shulamith Hareven. ***Thirst: The Desert Trilogy (The Miracle Hater; Prophet; After Childhood).***
Translated by Hillel Halkin with the author. San Francisco, CA: Mercury House, 1996. 185 pages.
Genres/literary styles/story types: historical fiction; literary historical
Set in biblical times—after the Hebrew exodus and during the years of wandering in the desert—these three novellas focus on the ordinary individuals who partook in those seminal events. For one reason or another, they quickly lose their religious belief as well as their awe of Moses and other leaders. They are skeptics—alienated outsiders on a historically charged landscape whose very presence calls into question traditional accounts. There is Eshkhar, who as a boy is treated cavalierly by Joshua and who becomes an embittered man disdainful of God and the whole idea of miracles. There is Hivai and also Salu—both of whom are cast out from a community of faith.
Subject keyword: religion
Original language: Hebrew
Source consulted for annotation:
Dickstein, Lore. *The New York Times Book Review*, 15 December 1996 (online).
Some other translated books written by Shulamith Hareven: *City of Many Days*; *Twilight and Other Stories*

Yael Hedaya. ***Accidents.***
Translated by Jessica Cohen. New York: Metropolitan Books/Henry Holt, 2005. 453 pages.
Genre/literary style/story type: mainstream fiction
Yonaton Luria is a widower in his 50s who can no longer write. Still grieving his wife's death, he finds it increasingly difficult to take care of his 10-year-old daughter. Shira Klein is a writer in her 30s who not only has trouble dealing with her success but also with the death of her father. As these two emotionally and psychologically wounded individuals move toward each other, they must overcome their fears about love.
Subject keywords: social roles; writers
Original language: Hebrew
Sources consulted for annotation:
Abramowitz, Molly. *Library Journal* 130 (1 September 2005): 131.
Bibel, Barbara. *Booklist* 101 (August 2005): 1992.
O'Neill, Joseph. *The Atlantic Monthly* 296 (December 2005): 133.
Publishers Weekly 252 (11 July 2005): 57.
Another translated book written by Yael Hedaya: *Housebroken: Three Novellas*

Yoel Hoffmann. ***The Shunra and the Schmetterling.***
Translated by Peter Cole. New York: New Directions, 2004. 128 pages.
Genres/literary styles/story types: mainstream fiction; coming-of-age
Written with the grace and elegance of haiku, this novel is a paean to childhood. It is a quasi-memoir that recounts a boy's experiences in an Israeli village, the lives of his neighbors, his hopes and dreams, and his recognition about the inevitable passing of time.
Subject keyword: rural life
Original language: Hebrew

Sources consulted for annotation:
Amazon.com (book description).
Cohen, Leslie. *World Literature Today* 79 (May/August 2005): 109.
Mostly Fiction Book Reviews, http://www.mostlyfiction.com.
Proctor, Minna. *Artforum* 11 (Summer 2004): 4.
Some other translated books written by Yoel Hoffmann: *The Heart Is Katmandu*; *Bernhard*; *The Christ of Fish*; *Katschen & the Book of Joseph*

Shifra Horn. *The Fairest Among Women.*
Translated by Hebrew H. Sacks. New York: St. Martin's Press, 2001. 293 pages.
Genres/literary styles/story types: mainstream fiction; magical realism
Rosa, whose life spanned the period from about 1940 to the mid-1990s, had three husbands, eight children, and numerous grandchildren. Thus, her family history is rich in unexpected and extraordinary events—where facts meld with fiction and where exaggerations and absurdities often metamorphose into folktales and legends that assume mythic form.
Subject keyword: family histories
Original language: Hebrew
Sources consulted for annotation:
Amazon.com (book description).
Cohen, Ellen R. *Library Journal* 126 (1 April 2001): 132.
Pearl, Nancy. *Booklist* 97 (1 May 2001): 1665.
Zaleski, Jeff. *Publishers Weekly* 248 (25 June 2001): 48.
Some other translated books written by Shifra Horn: *Four Mothers*; *Tamara Walks on Water*; *Ode to Joy*

Yoram Kaniuk. *The Last Jew: Being the Tale of a Teacher Henkin and the Vulture, the Chronicles of the Last Jew, the Awful Tale of Joseph and His Offspring, the Story of Secret Charity, the Annals of the Moshava, All Those Wars, and the End of the Annals of the Jews.*
Translated by Barbara Harshav. New York: Grove Press, 2006. 522 pages.
Genre/literary style/story type: mainstream fiction
In the aftermath of World War II and the Holocaust, Ebenezer Schneerson discovers that he can no longer remember anything about his personal life, but he can remember simply everything about the long sweep of Jewish history and culture. As he travels through Europe and Israel, everyone wants to exploit him for his all-encompassing memory.
Subject keywords: anti-Semitism; family histories
Original language: Hebrew
Sources consulted for annotation:
Abramowitz, Molly. *Library Journal* 130 (December 2005): 113.
Amazon.com (book description; review from *Publishers Weekly*).
Christensen, Bryce. *Booklist* 102 (15 December 2005): 23.
Mitgang, Herbert. *The New York Times*, 19 May 1982, p. C21.
Some other translated books written by Yoram Kaniuk: *The Story of Aunt Shlomzion the Great*; *Confessions of a Good Arab*; *His Daughter*; *Rockinghorse*; *Adam Resurrected*; *Himmo, King of Jerusalem*; *The Acrophile*

Etgar Keret. *The Bus Driver Who Wanted To Be God and Other Stories.*
Translated by Dalya Bilu and Miriam Schlesinger. New York: Thomas Dunne Books, 2001. 182 pages.
Genres/literary styles/story types: mainstream fiction; short stories

The author is considered to be one of the trendsetters in contemporoary Israeli fiction. The 22 stories in this collection are characterized by inventive language, off-kilter approaches to everyday events, wickedly astute satire, and delicious irony. Two of the more keenly observed stories are about a bus driver who is meticulously precise about his schedule and a convenience store that is located at the entrance to hell.

Related title by the same author:

Readers may also enjoy *The Nimrod Flipout*, which contains 30 stories that have been characterized by Emily Gitter as being "what Rod Serling might have sounded like had he decided to make *The Twilight Zone* a comedy set in Israel, with each episode lasting just a few minutes." In one story, a man's girlfriends always break up with him as if on cue when they hear something on the radio; in another story, a woman turns into a hirsute soccer-loving man.

Subject keyword: urban life

Original language: Hebrew

Sources consulted for annotation:

Amazon.com (book description; all editorial reviews).

Anastas, Benjamin. *The New York Times Book Review*, 28 October 2001, p. 33.

Beller, Thomas. *The New York Times Book Review*, 7 May 2006 (online).

Cohen, Leslie. *World Literature Today* 76 (Spring 2002): 245.

Gitter, Emily. *The New Standard*, 5 April 2008 (reprinted from *Forward*).

Global Books in Print (online) (review from *Publishers Weekly* for *The Nimrod Flipout*)

Green, John. *Booklist* 98 (15 October 2001): 382.

Zaleski, Jeff. *Publishers Weekly* 248 (17 September 2001): 53.

Some other translated books written by Etgar Keret: *The Nimrod Flipout*; *Jetlag: Five Graphic Novellas*; *Gaza Blues: Different Stories*; *How To Make a Good Script Great*; *Kneller's Happy Campers*; *Missing Kissinger*; *The Girl on the Fridge*

Alona Kimchi. *Lunar Eclipse*.

Translated by Yael Lotan. London: Toby Press, 2000. 276 pages.

Genres/literary styles/story types: mainstream fiction; short stories

The protagonists of these five stories are needy, deluded, disturbed, and often quite simply mad. Sometimes, they hate themselves; sometimes, they hate others. All are in pain and all engage in various forms of self-destruction: infecting each other with AIDS; trying to keep boredom at bay through dangerous activities; juggling a career with bouts of bulimia. Critics have been virtually unanimous in prasing the work of this author.

Subject keywords: identity; social roles

Original language: Hebrew

Sources consulted for annotation:

Margolis, David. *The Jerusalem Report*, 25 March 2002, p. 39.

The Toby Press (book description), http://www.tobypress.com.

Another translated book written by Alona Kimchi: *Weeping Susannah*

Haim Lapid. *Breznitz*.

Translated by Yael Lotan. London: Toby Press, 2000. 232 pages.

Genres/literary styles/story types: crime fiction; police detectives

Dan Breznitz, whose personal life is coming apart at the seams, works in Tel Aviv as a homicide detective. When an Arab schoolteacher is found to be in possession of an ear that came from a badly decomposed body, it seems to be an open-and-shut case. But Breznitz dismisses the suspect's confession and embarks on a serpentine quest to uncover the victim's identity and killer. Critics have said that the author's work provides insightful analysis about the relationship between Israeli police and Arabs.

Subject keywords: social problems; urban life
Original language: Hebrew
Sources consulted for annotation:
Amazon.com (book description).
Margolis, David. *The Jerusalem Report*, 11 February 2002, p. 48.
Raphael, Lev. *Knight Ridder Tribune News Service*, 15 May 2002, p. 1.
Another translated book written by Haim Lapid: *The Crime of Writing*

Savyon Liebrecht. *A Man and a Woman and a Man.*
Translated by Marsha Pomerantz. New York: Persea Books, 2001. 249 pages.
Genre/literary style/story type: mainstream fiction
While visiting their dying parents at a Tel Aviv nursing home, two individuals meet in the parking lot and begin an 18-day relationship. Hamutal, whose mother has Alzheimer's disease, has been sent by an orderly to tell Saul that his father's stock of diapers is running out. As both of them struggle with the meaning of death and memory, they also begin to explore the fragility of love.
Subject keyword: aging; family histories
Original language: Hebrew
Sources consulted for annotation:
Amazon.com (book description).
Kalb, Deborah. *The Washington Post*, 19 August 2001, T8.
Rochman, Hazel. *Booklist* 97 (July 2001): 1981.
Rohrbaugh, Lisa. *Library Journal* 126 (August 2001): 162.
Zaleski, Jeff. *Publishers Weekly* 248 (30 July 2001): 62.
Some other translated books written by Savyon Liebrecht: *Apples from the Desert*; *A Good Place for the Night*

Ronit Matalon. *Bliss.*
Translated by Jessica Cohen. New York: Metropolitan Books, 2003. 262 pages.
Genre/literary style/story type: mainstream fiction
This novel focuses on the lives of two very different women who have been friends since childhood. Ofra has lived most of her life vicariously through her politically active counterpart, Sarah, who is outraged at the Israeli treatment of Arabs. While Ofra babysits, Sarah photographs the miseries of life in Gaza, takes up the cause of a murdered child, and has an affair with an Arab man. Soon, Ofra despairs of her friend's single-mindedess; she has her own painful world to grapple with in the form of relatives in France who have lost one of their sons to AIDS.
Subject keywords: family histories; politics
Original language: Hebrew
Sources consulted for annotation:
Abramowitz, Molly. *Library Journal* 128 (August 2003): 133.
Amazon.com (book description).
Eder, Richard. *The New York Times Book Review*, 10 August 2003, p. 5.
Linfield, Susie. *Los Angeles Times*, 10 August 2003, R12.
Publishers Weekly 250 (11 August 2003): 258.
Seaman, Donna. *Booklist* 99 (August 2003): 1956.
Another translated book written by Ronit Matalon: *The One Facing Us*

Aharon Megged. *Foiglman.*
Translated by Marganit Weinberger-Rotman. New Milford, CT: Toby Press, 2003. 277 pages.
Genre/literary style/story type: mainstream fiction

Zvi Arbel is an Israeli historian who has just published a book about the mid-seventeenth-century Khmelnytsky Uprising in what is modern-day Ukraine. As Ukrainians struggled to free themselves from Polish rule, many thousands of Jews were killed. Zvi receives a book of poetry, published in Yiddish by a Polish Holocaust survivor named Shmuel Foiglman, as a memento of thanks for his historical efforts. Shmuel soon appears at Zvi's home and Zvi works diligently to find an Israeli publisher for Shmuel's poetry. He also begins to realize that Shmuel is an authentic representation of the history that he has studied all his life.
Subject keywords: anti-Semitism; writers
Original language: Hebrew
Sources consulted for annotation:
Amazon.com (book description).
Ben-Dat, Mordechai. *Canadian Jewish News* 35 (26 May 2005): 4.
Cohen, George. *Booklist* 100 (1 December 2003): 647.
Goldman, Morris. *Jerusalem Post*, 2 January 2004, p. 04.
Wilson, Frank. *Knight Ridder Tribune News Service*, 31 December 2003, p. 1.
Some other translated books written by Aharon Megged: *Asahel*; *Living on the Dead*; *Mandrakes from the Holy Land*; *The Short Life*; *Fortunes of a Fool*

Sami Michael. ***A Trumpet in the Wadi.***
Translated by Yael Lotan. New York: Simon & Schuster, 2003. 244 pages.
Genres/literary styles/story types: mainstream fiction; coming-of-age
In the Arab quarter of Haifa in 1982, two Christian Arab sisters—Mary and Huda—live with their mother and grandfather, who is from Egypt. Huda falls in love with Alex, an immigrant of Russian Jewish descent, who is an accomplished trumpet player living in their apartment building. Mary must contend with the advances of their landlord's son, eventually settling for marriage with her Muslim cousin.
Subject keywords: identity; social roles
Original language: Hebrew
Sources consulted for annotation:
Abramowitz, Molly. *Library Journal* 128 (July 2003): 124.
Amazon.com (book description).
DeCandido, GraceAnne A. *Booklist* 99 (July 2003): 1866.
Mort, Jo-Ann. *Chicago Tribune*, 8 August 2003, p. 1.
Publishers Weekly 250 (28 July 2003): 78.
See, Carolyn. *The Washington Post*, 22 August 2003, p. C7.
Some other translated books written by Sami Michael: *Refuge*; *Victoria*

Amos Oz. ***The Same Sea.***
Translated by Nicholas de Lange in collaboration with the author. New York: Harcourt, 2001. 201 pages.
Genre/literary style/story type: mainstream fiction
When Nadia Danon, wife of Albert and mother to Rico, succumbs to ovarian cancer, the people she leaves behind struggle to make sense of their own lives. Rico travels to Tibet and Bangladesh, searching to understand the meaning of alientation, loneliness, memory, and death. Meanwhile, Albert lusts for Dita, Rico's girlfriend, who has little choice but to move into Albert's home when she loses all her money to a swindling film producer.
Related title by the same author:
Readers may also be interested in *Fima*, which focuses on Efraim Nisan (Fima), a man in his 50s who lives a squalid existence in a dingy apartment in Jerusalem. As he tries to cope with everyday

minutiae and as he argues with the radio and constantly pores over his newspapers, his thoughts nevertheless soar toward the higher planes of philosophy and ethics. Many critics have seen him as a symbolic Israeli everyman caught in the throes of an untenable situation—waiting to live, waiting to act, waiting to show himself to be fully human when tragic events strike.
Subject keywords: family histories; identity
Original language: Hebrew
Sources consulted for annotation:
Amazon.com (book description; *The New Yorker*).
Dickstein, Morris. *The Nation* 274 (21 January 2002): 27.
Hoffman, William M. *The New York Times Book Review*, 28 October 2001, p. 12.
Pearl, Nancy. *Library Journal* 127(15 November 2002): 128.
Prose, Francine. *The New York Times Book Review*, 24 October 1993 (online).
Santo, Philip. *Library Journal* 128 (August 2001): 164.
Seaman, Donna. *Booklist* 99 (15 October 2001): 383.
Sterling, Eric. *World Literature Today* 75 (Summer 2001): 110.
Zaleski, Jeff. *Publishers Weekly* 248 (3 September 2001): 54.
Some other translated books written by Amos Oz: *To Know a Woman*; *A Perfect Peace*; *Fima*; *Black Box*; *Don't Call It Night*; *The Hill of Evil Counsel*; *Elsewhere, Perhaps*; *Where the Jackals Howl and Other Stories*; *Until Daybreak: Stories from the Kibbutz*; *Unto Death*; *My Michael*; *Touch the Water, Touch the Wind*; *Panther in the Basement*; *Rhyming Life and Death*; *The Amos Oz Reader*

Sayed Qashu (Sayed Kashua). *Dancing Arabs*.
Translated by Miriam Schlesinger. New York: Grove Press, 2004. 227 pages.
Genres/literary styles/story types: mainstream fiction; coming-of-age
Growing up in the Arab-Israeli village of Tira, the novel's Palestinian protagonist is a young man adrift, spending his time daydreaming about renowned accomplishments. Because his grandfather fought against Israeli independence in 1948 and his father detonated a bomb in a cafeteria, it makes sense that his family hopes that he too will become a national hero, especially when he is offered a scholarship to a prestigious Jewish school. But they are shocked to discover that his greatest yearning is to become Jewish.
Subject keywords: family histories; identity
Original language: Hebrew
Sources consulted for annotation:
Amazon.com (book description).
Driscoll, Brendan. *Booklist* 100 (15 March 2004): 1265.
Shihade, Magid. *Arab Studies Quarterly* 27 (Winter 2005): 89.
Stuhr, Rebecca. *Library Journal* 129 (15 May 2004): 114.
Wilson, Charles. *The New York Times Book Review*, 16 May 2004, p. 28.
Zaleski, Jeff. *Publishers Weekly* 251 (3 May 2004): 171.
Another translated book written by Sayed Qashu: *Let It Be Morning*

Dorit Rabinyan. *Strand of a Thousand Pearls*.
Translated by Yael Lotan. New York: Random House, 2001. 264 pages.
Genre/literary style/story type: mainstream fiction
This novel describes the tangled lives of a Persian family in Israel. After Solly Azizyan and Iran marry, they have four daughters—all of whom present unique challenges. Lizzie masturbates in public; Sofia marries a businessman who deals in tear gas; Matti is psychotic, constantly yearning for her stillborn twin; and Marcelle marries the love of her life—only to reject him on the day after the wedding. Some critics have seen parallels with Jeffrey Eugenides's *The Virgin Suicides*.

Subject keyword: family histories
Original language: Hebrew
Sources consulted for annotation:
Amazon.com (book description).
Da Costa, Erica. *Los Angeles Times*, 23 June 2002, p. R12.
Knapp, Kem. *St. Louis Post-Dispatch*, 14 July 2002, p. F10.
Olson, Yvette W. *Library Journal* 127 (1 April 2002): 142.
See, Carolyn, *The Washington Post*, 5 July 2002, p. C4.
Zaleski, Jeff. *Publishers Weekly* 249 (18 March 2002): 72.
Some other translated books written by Dorit Rabinyan: *Persian Brides*; *Our Weddings*

Haim Sabato. *Adjusting Sights*.
Translated by Hillel Halkin. New Milford, CT: Toby Press, 2006. 154 pages.
Genre/literary style/story type: historical fiction
Two young Jewish men go off to fight in the Arab-Israeli war of 1973, but only Haim returns. Religion provides him with a way to cope with his pain, but he nevertheless wonders what happened to his friend Dov. Sabato continues his semiautobiographical approach in *From the Four Winds*, which focuses on immigrant camps in 1950s Israel, and in *Aleppo Tales*, which consists of three stories about the little-known Jewish community in Syria.
Subject keywords: social problems; war
Original language: Hebrew
Source consulted for annotation:
Toby Press website (book description), http://www.tobypress.com.
Some other translated books written by Haim Sabato: *Aleppo Tales*; *The Dawning of the Day*; *From the Four Winds*

Nathan Shaham. *The Rosendorf Quartet*.
Translated by Dalya Bilu. New York: Grove Weidenfeld, 1987. 357 pages.
Genre/literary style/story type: mainstream fiction
The period between 1936 and 1939 was a tense time in Palestine: strikes, violent uprisings, tax revolts—all to protest against Jewish immigration. Against this background, a string quartet of Jewish refugees makes its way across the countryside—a harbinger of a new cultural flowering that is not met with open arms by all. The first four chapters are told from the perspectives of each of the musicians, while the fifth chapter takes the form of a journal kept by a friend. Some critics have compared this work to William Faulkner's *The Sound and the Fury*.
Subject keywords: culture conflict; social problems
Original language: Hebrew
Sources consulted for annotation:
Amazon.com (reviews from *Kirkus Reviews* and *Publishers Weekly*).
Kosman, Joshua. *San Francisco Chronicle*, 5 July 1992, p. REV-9.
Pearl, Nancy. *Library Journal* 127 (15 November 2002): 128.
Reel, James. *The Arizona Daily Star*, 22 December 1991, p. 12.D.
Some other translated books written by Nathan Shaham: *Bone to the Bone*; *The Other Side of the Wall*

David Shahar. *Summer in the Street of the Prophets* and *A Voyage to Ur of the Chaldees* (*Palace of the Shattered Vessels, Volumes 1 and 2*).
Translated by Dalya Bilu. New York: Weidenfeld & Nicolson, 1988. 434 pages.
Genres/literary styles/story types: historical fiction; literary historical

These two books recount the daily trials and tribulations of a neighborhood in Jerusalem during the British Mandate in the 1920s and 1930s. Although focusing on Gabriel Jonathan Luria, who is descended from the sixteenth-century Jewish mystic Isaac Luria, the novels offer a rich portrait of all who make the neighborhood their home, emphasizing their hopes, dreams, and painful losses. The book has been compared to Marcel Proust's *Remembrance of Things Past.*
Subject keyword: urban life
Original language: Hebrew
Sources consulted for annotation:
Green, Jeff. *Jerusalem Post*, 11 July 1996 (from Proquest databases).
Kaplan, Johanna. *The New York Times*, 21 May 1989, p. A27.
Link, Baruch. *Los Angeles Times*, 1 January 1989, B8.
Some other translated books written by David Shahar: *News from Jerusalem*; *His Majesty's Agent*

Meir Shalev. *The Loves of Judith.*
Translated by Barbara Harshav. Hopewell, NJ: Ecco Press, 1999. 315 pages.
Genres/literary styles/story types: mainstream fiction; magical realism
Zayde recounts the story of his mother, Judith, and the three men who claim to be his father during four lavish meals over a period of 30 years. All three of the men (Moshe, Jacob, and Globerman) met Judith when she accepted employment in the widower Moshe's home after being abandoned by her husband. Critics have raved about the beautiful and bittersweet depictions of love in this book.
Subject keyword: family histories
Original language: Hebrew
Sources consulted for annotation:
Amazon.com (book description; review from *Kirkus Reviews*).
DeCandido, GraceAnne A. *Booklist* 95 (15 February 1999): 1042.
Mort, Jo-Ann. *Los Angeles Times*, 25 May 1999, p. 1.
Rohrbaugh, Lida. *Library Journal* 124 (15 February 1999): 186.
Steinberg, Sybil S. *Publishers Weekly* 246 (25 January 1999): 70.
Some other translated books written by Meir Shalev: *Esau*; *Blue Mountain*; *My Father Always Embarrasses Me*; *Four Meals*

Tseruyah Shalev (Zeruya Shalev). *Husband and Wife.*
Translated by Dalya Bilu. New York: Grove Press, 2001. 311 pages.
Genre/literary style/story type: mainstream fiction
Some marriages are serene refuges from the malignant chaos of the external world. Other marriages embody that malignant chaos. Udi and Na'ama have known each other forever; they married young and are now both on the cusp of forty. Udi works as an outdoor adventure guide; his wife is a social worker. Their relationship is disintegrating, and their preadolescent daughter Noga is caught in the middle. But when Udi suddlenly loses the ability to move his legs and is subsequently diagnosed with conversion disorder (where physical symptoms are due to psychological stress), the rotten core of a carefully constructed life is exposed.
Subject keywords: family histories; identity
Original language: Hebrew
Sources consulted for annotation:
Amazon.com (book description).
Nesbitt, Robin. *Library Journal* 127 (15 May 2002): 128.
Verdone, Jules. *Boston Globe*, 21 August 2002, p. D2.
Zaleski, Jeff. *Publishers Weekly* 249 (17 June 2002): 38.
Another translated book written by Tseruyah Shalev: *Love Life*

Anton Shammas. *Arabesques.*
Translated by Vivian Eden. New York: Harper & Row, 1988. 263 pages.
Genres/literary styles/story types: mainstream fiction; coming-of-age
Unanimous critical acclaim greeted this work of autobiographical fiction that alternates between the narrator's memories of his extended family's pre- and post-1948 life in the small village of Fassuta in Galilee and his own experiences in and reminisces of Israel; the occupied territories; Paris; and, finally, Iowa City, where he attends the University of Iowa's writing program. Despite the hardship, treachery, pain, and violence that permeates Fassuta, it is also a place of wonder for a small boy—full of magical and mysterious occurrences whose repercussions and lessons resonate throughout the decades. In Iowa, the narrator recalls his love of Willa Cather, especially the opening passages of her novel *My Antonia*, situating his quest for unraveling the tangled skeins of the past within a universal framework. The author, who is an Arab Christian, writes in Hebrew and is an Israeli citizen.
Subject keywords: family histories; writers
Original language: Hebrew
Source consulted for annotation:
Gass, William H. *The New York Times Book Review*, 17 April 1988, p. 1.

Benjamin Tammuz. *Minotaur.*
Translated by Kim Parfitt and Mildred Budhy. New York: New American Library, 1981. 210 pages.
Genre/literary style/story type: mainstream fiction
A middle-aged Israeli spy spots a beautiful English girl on a bus. He tracks her down, and they begin an all-consuming seven-year correspondence in which he never reveals his true identity. In the manner of William Faulkner's *The Sound and the Fury* and Lawrence Durrell's *The Alexandria Quartet*, the novel's main events are examined from multiple shifting perspectives.
Subject keywords: identity; power
Original language: Hebrew
Sources consulted for annotation:
Amazon.com (book description).
Publishers Weekly 252 (12 September 2005): 42.
Quammen, David. *The New York Times*, 9 August 1981, p. A12.
Rogers, Michael. *Library Journal* 130 (1 November 2005): 128.
Scheindlin, Dahlia. *Jerusalem Post*, 12 December 1997, p. 03.
Some other translated books written by Benjamin Tammuz: *Requiem for Naaman*; *Castle in Spain*; *Orchard*; *A Rare Cure*; *Meetings with the Angel: Seven Stories from Israel*

A. B. Yehoshua. *The Liberated Bride.*
Translated by Hillel Halkin. Orlando, FL: Harcourt, 2003. 568 pages.
Genre/literary style/story type: mainstream fiction
Yochanan Rivlin is an esteemed professor, and his wife, Hagit, is an equally esteemed judge. He fidgets and fusses; she hides her fragility behind a steel-trap mind. As they travel to an Israeli Arab village to attend the wedding of one of Rivlin's Palestinian students, he becomes obsessed with discovering why his son's marriage has ended, making a complete pest and bother of himself and antagonizing his wife. Part comedy and part tragedy, the novel examines the small daily successes and failures of ordinary people caught in an untenable political situation.
Related titles by the same author:
Readers may also enjoy *A Woman in Jerusalem*, which takes as its starting point the death of Yulia Ragayev, a 48-year-old non-Jewish immigrant to Israel who, as Claire Messud writes, is killed "in a suicide bombing, with no identification on her person other than a pay stub from the bakery where

she worked." When the bakery owner delegates his human resources manager to investigate, the manager becomes caught up in a quixotic quest to valorize Yulia's life. Also of interest may be *Friendly Fire: A Duet*. Yimri has moved to Africa in an attempt to forge a complete new life for himself, but when he finds out that his soldier son has died in the Israeli-occupied West Bank, the past catches up to him, and he is forced to confront thorny political issues.
Subject keywords: politics; social roles
Original language: Hebrew
Sources consulted for annotation:
Amazon.com (book description; review from *The New Yorker*).
Bronner, Ethan. *The New York Times Book Review*, 16 November 2008 (online).
Brown, Robert E. *Library Journal* 128 (1 November 2003): 127.
Eder, Richard. *The New York Times Book Review*, 1 February 2004, p. 9.
Kamenetz, Anya. *The Village Voice*, 12 November/18 November 2003, p. C81.
Messud, Claire. *The New York Times Book Review*, 13 August 2006 (online).
Publishers Weekly 250 (15 September 2003): 40.
Some other translated books written by A. B. Yehoshua: *Five Seasons*; *Mr. Mani*; *A Late Divorce*; *The Lover*; *A Journey to the End of the Millennium*; *Open Heart*; *Three Days and a Child*; *A Woman in Jerusalem*; *Early in the Summer of 1970*; *The Continuing Silence of a Poet*; *Friendly Fire: A Duet*

ANNOTATIONS FOR TRANSLATED BOOKS FROM ITALY

Carmine Abate. *Between Two Seas*.
Translated by Antony Shugaar. New York: Europa Editions, 2008. 209 pages.
Genre/literary style/story type: mainstream fiction
Giorgio Bellusci wants to restore the grandeur of his family's once-famous but now dilapidated inn, which once counted Alexandre Dumas among its visitors. But numerous problems stand in his way. When gangsters try to extort protection money from him, he murders one of them. And when he is released from prison after serving time for his crime, his troubles only multiply. With the inn nearly reconstructed, he must fend off the avenging gangsters who now want to destroy the inn.
Subject keywords: family histories; rural life
Original language: Italian
Source consulted for annotation:
Global Books in Print (online) (review from *Publishers Weekly*).

Simonetta Agnello Hornby. *The Almond Picker*.
Translated by Alastair McEwen. New York: Farrar, Straus and Giroux, 2005. 315 pages.
Genre/literary style/story type: mainstream fiction
This novel focuses on the aftermath of the death of Mennulara, a lifelong domestic for an important family, in the Sicilian town of Roccacolomba in 1963. But she was no ordinary servant. Through unrelenting work and native intelligence, she single-handedly ensured the financial solvency of the Alfallipe household. But her last will and testament was—to say the least—a bit strange, so it is little wonder that the three Alfallipe children wish to contest it. On the other hand, the local Mafia chieftain wants the will executed exactly as Mennulara wanted it. Critics have observed that this novel resembles the family sagas of Isabel Allende and Laura Esquivel, with additional echoes of *One Hundred Years of Solitude* and *The Godfather*.
Subject keyword: family histories
Original language: Italian

Sources consulted for annotation:
De Candido, Grace Anne A. *Booklist* 101 (1 January 2005): 819.
Global Books in Print (online) (synopsis/book jacket).
Kirkus Reviews 73 (1 January 2005): 10.
Publishers Weekly 252 (21 February 2005): 158.
Restaino, Leann. *Library Journal* 130 (1 January 2005): 97.

Niccolò Ammaniti. *I'm Not Scared.*
Translated by Jonathan Hunt. Edinburgh, UK: Canongate, 2003. 200 pages.
Genres/literary styles/story types: mainstream fiction; coming-of-age
Nine-year-old Michele Amitrano lives with his family in the isolated village of Acqua Traverse. In the nearby fields, he and his friends stumble upon a pit where another small boy lies chained and barely alive. Eventually, Michele discovers that the adults of the village have kidnapped the boy, hoping to win a large ransom from his presumably rich parents. As Michele tries to make sense of the tangle of secrets permeating the village, he finds solace in the Bible and comics about the American West.
Related titles by the same author:
Readers may also enjoy *I'll Steal You Away*, in which 12-year-old Pietro Moroni dreams of escaping his isolated village of Ischiano Scalo. But because he is the lone failing student at his school, his chances of flight are minimal. Graziano Biglia, a drug-addicted sex god, yearns to reform and plans to open a store in Pietro's village. *As God Commands* offers yet another take on the desperation and angst of rural life in Italy, when the bank robbery plans of three men living on the margins of society lead to a horrific outcome.
Subject keywords: rural life; social problems
Original language: Italian
Sources consulted for annotation:
Books Briefly Noted. *The New Yorker* (4 January 2010) (online).
Bray, Christopher. *The New York Times Book Review*, 10 September 2006 (online).
Kirkus Reviews 70 (15 December 2002): 1783.
Publishers Weekly 249 (23 December 2002): 44.
Venuti, Lawrence. *The New York Times Book Review*, 16 February 2003, p. 14.
Some other translated books written by Niccolò Ammaniti: *I'll Steal You Away*; *As God Commands*

Antonia Arslan. *Skylark Farm.*
Translated by Geoffrey Brock. New York: Alfred A. Knopf, 2007. 275 pages.
Genre/literary style/story type: historical fiction
This is a compelling account of the 1915 Armenian genocide—a word whose use is entirely appropriate to some but equally inappropriate to others. Yerwant is a Venetian physician with Armenian roots. His family, including Sempad, his pharmacist brother, live peacefully on a farm in Turkey. Unprepared for the unspeakable violence to come, the family is rounded up, the men are killed, and the women begin a death march to Syria. Only a few survive, eventually reaching Yerwant in Italy.
Subject keywords: power; war
Original language: Italian
Sources consulted for annotation:
De Bellaigue, Christopher. *The New York Times Book Review*, 4 February 2007 (online).
Global Books in Print (online) (reviews from *Booklist* and *Publishers Weekly*).

Alessandro Baricco. *Ocean Sea.*

Translated by Alastair McEwen. New York: Alfred A. Knopf, 1999. 241 pages.

Genres/literary styles/story types: mainstream fiction; postmodernism

A motley group of individuals meet at the isolated Almayer Inn, located near the sea. Among the guests are Professor Bartleboom, whose life work is an encyclopedia of limits; Ann Deveria, who is trying to forget her lover; Plasson, a painter who wants to capture the sea in a painting; Elisewin, a fragile girl not made for this world; a priest who is uncannily blunt; and a mysterious sailor. As these characters struggle for redemption and as they try to find what they have been unable to find elsewhere, readers are exposed to a series of numinous tales that are as elusive and multidimesional as life itself.

Related titles by the same author:

Also of interest may be *Silk*, in which a silkworm trader makes a pilgrimage to Japan in the nineteenth century. Equally worthwhile may be *City*, which features Gould, a teenage genius, and Shatzy Shell, a verbose telephone pollster whose idea of a 30-second phone call extends to 30 minutes. When she phones Gould, it is almost inevitable that she is fired after a conversation for the ages.

Subject keyword: identity

Original language: Italian

Sources consulted for annotation:

"Alessandro Baricco." *Contemporary Authors Online*, Thomson Gale, 2006.

Crane, Rufus S. *World Literature Today* 73 (Summer 1999): 508.

Eder, Richard. *The New York Times Book Review*, 28 July 2002 (online).

Global Books in Print (online) (review from *Kirkus Reviews*).

Leiding, Reba. *Library Journal* 124 (1 January 1999): 146.

McPhee, Jenny. *The New York Times Book Review*, 21 March 1999 (online).

Pearl, Nancy. *Booklist* 95 (1 February 1999): 960.

Steinberg, Sybil S. *Publishers Weekly* 246 (4 January 1999): 74.

Some other translated books written by Alessandro Baricco: *Silk*; *Without Blood*; *City*; *An Iliad*; *Lands of Glass*

Stefano Benni. *Timeskipper.*

Translated by Antony Shugaar. New York: Europa Editions, 2008. 272 pages.

Genres/literary styles/story types: mainstream fiction; coming-of-age

On his way to school, a young boy meets a mysterious and umkempt vagabond who endows him with the gift of seeing with great acuity into the future while still experiencing the ordinary grace of present life. Critics have referred to Benni's books as Italian versions of magical realism.

Subject keyword: identity

Original language: Italian

Source consulted for annotation:

Europa Editions (book description), http://www.europaeditions.com.

Another translated book written by Stefano Benni: *Margherita Dolce Vita*

Romano Bilenchi. *The Chill.*

Translated by Anne Goldstein. New York: Europa Editions, 2009. 120 pages.

Genres/literary styles/story types: mainstream fiction; coming-of-age

This is a sublime and masterful novel of adolescence and the discovery of sexuality in a small village in Tuscany, where the petty nature of humanity almost crushes the 16-year-old narrator.

Subject keyword: rural life

Original language: Italian

Sources consulted for annotation:
Books Briefly Noted. *The New Yorker* (November 23, 2009) (online).
Europa Editions (book description), http://www.europaeditions.com.

Luther Blissett (pseudonym). ***Q.***
Translated by Shaun Whiteside. Orlando, FL: Harcourt, 2003. 750 pages.
Genres/literary styles/story types: thrillers; religious thrillers
In the sixteenth-century at the beginning of the Reformation, religious politics was played at the very highest levels with sophistication and panache. This novel features heretics, papal spies, Anabaptists, all manner of deceit and perfidy, and boundless intrigue. It will be enjoyed by fans of Umberto Eco's *The Name of the Rose*. Readers are urged to explore the phenomenon of the Luther Blissett Project, a sociocultural movement dedicated to political activism.
Subject keywords: politics; power
Original language: Italian
Sources consulted for annotation:
Amazon.com (book description; back cover of the book).
Christensen, Bryce. *Booklist* 100 (1 February 2004): 932.
Global Books in Print (online) (review from *Library Journal*).
Zaleski, Jeff. *Publishers Weekly* 251 (2 February 2004): 56.
Another translated book written by Luther Blissett: *54* (as Wu Ming)
Alessandro Boffa. ***You're an Animal, Viskovitz!***
Translated by John Casey, with Maria Santminiatelli. New York: Alfred A. Knopf, 2002. 176 pages.
Genre/literary style/story type: mainstream fiction
As per the title of this deliciously hilarious allegory, Viskovitz is indeed an animal. In fact, he is twenty of them, including a dung bettle, a dormouse, and a scorpion. He is reincarnated over and over again, and on each occasion, he pines for the beautiful Ljuba, who constantly outwits him. Critics have detected echoes of Ovid's *Metamorphoses*, Franz Kafka, and Viktor Pelevin in Boffa's work.
Subject keyword: identity
Original language: Italian
Sources consulted for annotation:
Global Books in Print (online) (review from *Booklist*).
Malin, Irving. *Review of Contemporary Fiction* 22 (Fall 2002): 160.
Williams, Mary Elizabeth. *The New York Times Book Review*, 24 November 2002, p. 32.
Zaleski, Jeff. *Publishers Weekly* 249 (29 April 2002): 44.

Giuseppe Bonaviri. ***Dolcissimo.***
Translated by Umberto Mariani. New York: Italica Press, 1990. 146 pages.
Genres/literary styles/story types: mainstream fiction; magical realism
The residents of the village of Zebulonia, in Sicily, have all disappeared, and Ariet, a physician and former resident, is sent to investigate. Together with Mario Sinus, an ethnologist, they probe the village's distant past, examining its legends, deities, and rituals. As they meet former inhabitants and as they get a sense of the tragedy that befell Zebulonia, they discover the ecological roots of the disaster and a possible path to redemption. Some critics have invoked the work of Gabriel García Márquez in describing this novel.
Subject keyword: social problems
Original language: Italian
Sources consulted for annotation:
Amazon.com (book description; back cover of the book).

Italica Press on the Web (book description), http://www.italicapress.com.
Kaganoff, Penny. *Publishers Weekly* 237 (31 August 1990): 60.
Some other translated books written by Giuseppe Bonaviri: *Nights on the Heights*; *Saracen Tales*

Stefano Bortolussi. *Head Above Water.*
Translated by Anne Milano Appel. San Francisco, CA: City Lights Books, 2003. 184 pages.
Genres/literary styles/story types: mainstream fiction; postmodernism
Cardo Mariano is about to become a father. But when Sol, his partner, finds about his affair with another woman, she returns home to Norway, leaving Cardo alone to ponder his inability to make commitments. As he relives his childhood and adolescence—indelibly marked by feelings of guilt about the drowning of his brother—he sends e-mails to Sol and begins to write a novel about Italian radical politics in the 1960s and 1970s. Soon, he discovers what happened to his own disappeared father, and he eventually returns to Sol, who is the only constant in his troubled life.
Subject keywords: family histories; identity
Original language: Italian
Sources consulted for annotation:
Amazon.com (book description).
Kirkus Reviews 71 (15 September 2003): 1139.
Michael Spinella. *Booklist* 100 (1 November 2003): 478.

Mario Brelich. *The Holy Embrace.*
Translated by John Shepley. Marlboro, VT: Marlboro Press, 1994. 229 pages.
Genre/literary style/story type: historical fiction
This novel is a retelling of the story of Abraham and Sarah, whose marriage is presented as a wretched one because of Sarah's frigidity and narcissism. But when God makes Sarah young and beautiful again, Abraham succumbs to his preordained fate. Readers may also be interested in *Navigator of the Flood*, which retells the story of Noah.
Subject keyword: social roles
Original language: Italian
Sources consulted for annotation:
Amazon.com (review from *Kirkus Reviews*).
Guardiani, Francesco. *Review of Contemporary Fiction* 15 (Spring 1995): 169.
Smothers, Bonnie. *Booklist* 91 (15 November 1994): 577.
Steinberg, Sybil S. *Publishers Weekly* 241 (10 October 1994): 63.
Some other translated books written by Mario Brelich: *Navigator of the Flood*; *The Work of Betrayal*

Gesualdo Bufalino. *Tommaso and the Blind Photographer.*
Translated by Patrick Creagh. London: Harvill Press, 2000. 183 pages.
Genre/literary style/story type: mainstream fiction
Tommaso, a janitor, attempts to unravel the mysteries behind the death of his blind photographer friend Tir, who has taken a series of pictures of famous and influential Italians partaking in a frenzied drug-induced orgy. But it is not easy because Tommaso is also responsible for ensuring the smooth functioning of a meeting of tenants in his building.
Related title by the same author:
Readers may also enjoy *The Plague-Sower*, a novel that hauntingly retells the narrator's two-year stay in a sanitorium in Palermo, where he was treated for tuberculosis.
Subject keywords: power; social roles
Original language: Italian

Sources consulted for annotation:
The Complete Review (book review), http://www.complete-review.com/reviews/italia/bufalg1.htm.
"Gesualdo Bufalino." *Dictionary of Literary Biography Online*. Thomson Gale databases.
Global Books in Print (online) (review from *Choice* for *The Plague-Sower* and review from *Kirkus Reviews* and jacket description for *Tommaso and the Blind Photographer*).
Kaganoff, Penny. *Publishers Weekly* 234 (26 August 1988): 79.
Some other translated books written by Gesualdo Bufalino: *Lies of the Night*; *The Plague-Sorrower*; *Blind Argus, or The Fables of the Memory*; *The Keeper of Ruins and Other Inventions*

Aldo Busi. *The Standard Life of a Temporary Pantyhose Salesman.*
Translated by Raymond Rosenthal. New York: Farrar, Straus and Giroux, 1988. 430 pages.
Genre/literary style/story type: mainstream fiction
Angelo Basarovi, a gay university student of a certain age, goes to work for Celestino Lometto, an unkempt and ethically challenged lout who owns a panty hose factory. As the pair travel across Europe and as Celestino's fortune grows, Angelo assumes the role of a moral compass, especially when Celestino orders him to dispose of the Down syndrome child that his wife has just given birth to. As Angelo—a man who has traditionally been considered an outcast—struggles to save the life of another outcast, he discovers hidden powers and emotions. Some critics have detected echoes of Don Quixote and Sancho Panza in the adventures of Angelo and Celestino.
Related title by the same author:
Readers may also enjoy *Seminar on Youth*. All that Barbaro, a male prostitute, wants to do is sleep, but he finds himself penniless in late 1960s Paris.
Subject keywords: identity; social roles
Original language: Italian
Sources consulted for annotation:
"Aldo Busi." *Contemporary Authors Online*, Gale, 2003.
Cancogni, Annapola. *The New York Times Book Review*, 13 August 1989 (online).
Global Books in Print (online) (reviews from *Booklist*, *Choice*, and *Publishers Weekly*).
Mullenneaux, Lisa. *Library Journal* 113 (1 October 1988): 100.
Some other translated books written by Aldo Busi: *Seminar on Youth*; *Sodomies in Eleven Point*; *Uses and Abuses*

Roberto Calasso. *The Marriage of Cadmus and Harmony.*
Translated by Tim Parks. New York: Alfred A. Knopf, 1993. 403 pages.
Genres/literary styles/story types: historical fiction; literary historical
As the reviewers for *Library Journal* and *Kirkus Reviews* observed, this novel is "[a] reconsideration and recombination of Greek mythology" that "takes apart the old myths to discover the birth of history and modern thinking amid timeless patterns of behavior." As the author "moves effortlessly between the legends and the poets and writers—like Homer, Ovid, and Sophocles—who gave their own spin to the old stories," readers are drawn into an ancient world that, paradoxically, seems very contemporary.
Related titles by the same author:
Also of interest may be *The Ruin of Kasch*, which, as Sunil Khilnani writes, is an exploration of the intricacies of French history in the period 1780–1830 through "a rich texture of stories, meditations, aphorisms and quotations that paint the metamorphosis of the ancient and classical worlds into the modern." Equally worthwhile may be *Ka*, which, again according to Khilnani, is based "on a wealth of Western Indological scholarship" and "navigates the narrative ocean of the Brahmanas, the Upanishads, the Mahabharata and the Puranas, as well as stories of the Buddha."
Subject keyword: philosophy

Original language: Italian
Sources consulted for annotation:
Global Books in Print (online) (review from *Kirkus Reviews*).
Khilnani, Sunil. *The New York Times Book Review*, 23 October 1994 (online).
Khilnani, Sunil. *The New York Times Book Review*, 8 November 1998 (online).
Lefkowitz, Mary. *The New York Times Book Review*, 14 March 1993.
Opello, Olivia. *Library Journal* 118 (1 February 1993): 110.
Steinberg, Sybil S. *Publishers Weekly* 240 (15 February 1993): 217.
Some other translated books written by Roberto Calasso: *The Ruin of Kasch*; *Ka*

Andrea Camilleri. *The Terra-Cotta Dog.*
Translated by Stephen Sartarelli. New York: Penguin, 2003. 331 pages.
Genres/literary styles/story types: crime fiction; police detectives
This series follows the adventures of Inspector Salvo Montalbano, a detective whose jurisdiction covers the Sicilian towns of Vigàta and Montelusa. He is brutally forthright, witty, sardonic, cynical, cranky, and profane—never missing a chance to make a caustic or ribald observation about the chaos and contradictions of Italian politics, his incompetent or obsequious colleagues, and the often futile attempts by various police agencies to put an end to activities associated with the Mafia. He pleads with his administrative superiors not to promote him; reads Spanish literature and adores William Faulkner's *Pylon*; and goes for long swims at sea during particularly stressful moments. He stutters at press conferences, much preferring to talk to the assembled reporters about good food rather than criminal investigations. He has the utmost scorn for the bombast of television newscasters and the mindless glitz of the media in general. Montalbano deals with a motley array of individuals on a daily basis, and they are just as blunt, colorful, and unapologetic of their idiosyncrasies as the inspector himself. Hardly anyone uses euphemisms or meaningless circumlocutions, perhaps yet another reason that Camilleri's novels have gained popularity in a North America, where the theoretical existence of free speech is frequently superseded by the pusillanimous reality of politically correct rectitude and careerism. *The Terra-Cotta Dog* features a high-ranking gangster who makes elaborate arrangements for his own arrest; a hidden cave in the Sicilian countryside stocked with all manner of weaponry and ammunitions, not to mention the bodies of two people killed more than 50 years ago and elaborately arranged in a funerary tableau; and a gun-packing, defrocked priest who lives without electricity but who teaches Montalbano about the nuances of semiotics and Umberto Eco.
Related titles by the same author:
In *The Snack Thief*, the inspector comes face-to-face with the complexities of immigration when an abandoned child begins stealing lunchboxes; his relationship with his longtime girlfriend Livia also comes to the forefront. In *Rounding the Mark*, immigration is again front and center as Montalbano's world-weariness and disillusion reach an apex: his favorite restaurant closes; he is scandalized by the political considerations that interfere with and determine police priorities, especially in the wake of the violent suppression of G8 demonstrators in Genoa; and he bumps up against a dead body during one of his cherished swims.
Subject keywords: politics; power
Original language: Italian
Sources Consulted in Annotation:
Bailey, Paul. *The Guardian*, 14 October 2006, p. 21.
Clements, Toby. *The Daily Telegraph* (London), 3 February 2007, p. 32.
Lipez, Richard. *The Washington Post Book World*, 20 August 2006, p. T13.
Thomas, Mark. *Canberra Times* (Australia), 7 January 2007, p. A8.

Wilson, Laura. *The Guardian*, 14 July, 2007, p. 17.
Some other translated books written by Andrea Camilleri: *The Shape of Water*; *The Snack Thief*; *Excursion to Tindari*; *The Scent of the Night*; *Voice of the Violin*; *Rounding the Mark*; *The Patience of the Spider*; *The Paper Moon*; *August Heat*; *The Wings of the Sphinx*; *The Track of Sand*

Ferdinando Camon. *The Sickness Called Man.*
Translated by John Shepley. Marlboro, VT: Marlboro Press, 1992. 177 pages.
Genre/literary style/story type: mainstream fiction
The narrator of this novel suffers from strange ailments; he visits one therapist after another in search of a cure or at least some greater understanding about his state of health. But it is the numerous styles of psychoanalytic therapy and the various therapists themselves that are the focal point of this book—all with their quirks and idiosyncracies and their own agendas. They are fair game for a delicious satire about futility, randomness, and alientation in an Italy that has lost its faith in Catholicism and the political process.
Subject keywords: identity; social problems
Original language: Italian
Sources consulted for annotation:
Camon, Ferdinando. Author's website: http://www.ferdinandocamon.it.
Global Books in Print (online) (review from *Library Journal*).
Northwestern University Press (book description), http://nupress.northwestern.edu.
Steinberg, Sybil S. *Publishers Weekly* 240 (15 February 1993): 217.
Some other translated books written by Ferdinando Camon: *The Fifth Estate*; *Life Everlasting*; *Memorial*; *The Story of Sirio: A Parable*

Andrea Canobbio. *The Natural Disorder of Things.*
Translated by Abigail Asher. New York: Farrar, Straus and Giroux, 2006. 206 pages.
Genres/literary styles/story types: crime fiction; suspense
Claudio Fratta is a landscape architect specializing in gardens and finding himself in difficult situations. His brother has recently died, and he cannot stop obsessing about how his father was driven to bankruptcy by loan sharks. To top off his list of troubles, he has just seen a murder in the parking lot of a supermarket, and he has had to drive another witness of the same murder to the hospital. But his life may be taking a turn for the better when he is hired to design a garden for Elisabetta Renal and her wheelchair-bound husband. Then again, maybe not. As Claudio struggles to find answers to the mysteries that haunt him, he and Elisabetta, who is mysteriously linked to the aforementioned murder, become lovers.
Subject keyword: urban life
Original language: Italian
Sources consulted for annotation:
Global Books in Print (online) (reviews from *Booklist*, *Library Journal*, and *Publishers Weekly*).
Vida, Vendela. *The New York Times Book Review*, 10 September 2006 (online).

Ottavio Cappellani. *Sicilian Tragedee.*
Translated by Frederika Randall. New York: Farrar, Straus and Giroux, 2008. 340 pages.
Genre/literary style/story type: mainstream fiction
Tino Cagnotto likes to think of himself as a progressive and hip theater director. After falling in love with Bobo, a clerk, he is inspired to stage a radical version of Romeo and Juliet. But, of course, nothing ever goes as planned; there are complications galore, and the book evolves into a satiric look at contemporary Sicilian society, politics, and various cultural milieus.

Related title by the same author:
Readers may also enjoy *Who is Lou Sciortino?*, a humorous book whose subtitle "A Novel About Murder, the Movies, and Mafia Family Values" is a good indication of its contents. Don Lou is a big-time New York mobster who facilitates his grandson's entry into the movie industry. But Don Lou's motives are not entirely pure; he is more interested in money laundering than films.
Subject keywords: identity; social roles
Original language: Italian
Sources consulted for annotation:
Global Books in Print (online) (reviews from *Booklist*, *Library Journal*, and *Publishers Weekly* for both novels).
Leavitt, David. *The New York Times Book Review*, 19 October 2008 (online).
Turrentine, Jeff. *The New York Times Book Review*, 5 August 2007 (online).
Another translated book written by Ottavio Cappellani: *Who is Lou Sciortino?*

Paola Capriolo. *The Woman Watching*.
Translated by Liz Heron. London: Serpent's Tail, 1998. 214 pages.
Genre/literary style/story type: mainstream fiction
Vulpius, a famous actor, is cast in the role of Don Juan's valet. As he performs night after night, he becomes aware that one of the audience members is only watching him at every performance. Of course, all this attention goes to his head. He and his role become one; he literally thinks of nothing else but the adoring gaze of his mysterious admirer; and he withdraws from every aspect of his life except his onstage persona. There are elements of the gothic in this modern-day version of the Narcissus story, and some critics have said that the novel is reminiscent of works by Thomas Mann and Franz Kafka.
Related title by the same author:
Readers may also enjoy *Floria Tosca*, which is set during the Napoleonic wars. Mario Cavaradossi, a liberal painter, is imprisoned and executed for his political beliefs, which causes the singer Floria Tosca to commit suicide.
Subject keywords: identity; social roles
Original language: Italian
Sources consulted for annotation:
Cokal, Susann. *Review of Contemporary Fiction* 18 (Fall 1998): 255.
Global Books in Print (online) (review from *Kirkus Reviews*).
Hainsworth, Peter. *The New York Times Book Review*, 20 December 1998, p. 6.
Steinberg, Sybil S. *Publishers Weekly* 145 (24 August 1998): 47.
Venuti, Lawrence. *The New York Times Book Review*, 24 August 1997 (online).
Some other translated books written by Paola Capriolo: *Floria Tosca*; *A Man of Character*; *The Dual Realm*; *The Helmsman*

Massimo Carlotto. *The Fugitive*.
Translated by Antony Shugaar. New York: Europa Editions, 2008. 162 pages.
Genres/literary styles/story types: crime fiction; suspense
This is an autobiographical novel describing the six-year-long odyssey of the author as a fugitive from Italian justice. Accused of murder, he sought refuge in France and Mexico, where he donned imaginative disguises, integrated himself into various underground communities, and constantly lived on the alert to avoid capture.
Related titles by the same author:
Aware of the background described above, readers may now be interested in turning to some of Carlotto's less autobiographical novels. One of these is *Death's Dark Abyss*, which centers on Silvano Contin, a wine salesman whose family is kidnapped by bank robbers. Also of interest

may be *The Goodbye Kiss*, in which a former terrorist is prepared to do anything and everything in order to return to Italy. Finally, there is a series of books featuring Alligator, a private detective. In *The Master of Knots*, Alligator is thrust into the murky world of the Italian sex trade when a prominent sex worker specializing in S&M is kidnapped.

Subject keywords: identity; social problems

Original language: Italian

Sources consulted for annotation:

Amazon.com (book description; all editorial reviews).

Gerritsen, Tess. *Irish Independent*, 8 January 2005 (from Factiva databases).

Global Books in Print (online) (reviews from *Booklist*, *Library Journal*, and *Publishers Weekly* for all books).

Lewin, Matthew. *The Guardian*, 29 January 2005, p. 29.

McGirr, Michael. *The Sydney Morning Herald*, 9 April 2005, p. 26.

Some other translated books written by Massimo Carlotto: *The Goodbye Kiss*; *Death's Dark Abyss*; *The Colombian Mule*; *Poisonville*

Gianrico Carofiglio. *Reasonable Doubts*.

Translated by Howard Curtis. London: Bitter Lemon Press, 2007. 249 pages.

Genres/literary styles/story types: crime fiction; police detectives

This book, one of a series, features Guido Guerrieri, an Italian defense attorney who is going through a midlife crisis. Against all apparent logic, he elects to defend a former Fascist gang member, Fabio Rayban, who once attacked him. Convicted of drug smuggling, Rayban wants Guerrieri to appeal his sentence. Rayban has a beautiful Japanese wife, Natsu Kawabata, and Guerrieri quickly falls for her, which makes his position as legal counsel all the more tenuous. The Guerrieri series of legal thrillers will appeal to fans of John Grisham and Michael Connelly's *The Lincoln Lawyer*.

Subject keywords: power; social problems

Original language: Italian

Source consulted for annotation:

Global Books in Print (online) (reviews from *Booklist*, *Library Journal*, and *Publishers Weekly*).

Some other translated books written by Gianrico Carofiglio: *The Past Is a Foreign Country*; *Involuntary Witness*; *A Walk in the Dark*

Gianni Celati. *Appearances*.

Translated by Stuart Hood. London: Serpent's Tail, 1991. 126 pages.

Genres/literary styles/story types: mainstream fiction; short stories

Nothing is ever as it appears to be, and the consequences of our actions are always unpredictable. When a man withdraws into himself and stops speaking, he suddenly discovers that he is a magnet for strangers who want to tell him their darkest secrets and aspirations. And when a young bookseller takes pride in being well-read, he is told that such erudition will only scare away potential customers. Critics have called the author a worthy successor to Italo Calvino.

Related title by the same author:

Readers may also enjoy *Voices from the Plains*, which contains 30 stories about unique individuals who have a slightly skewed relationship to the world. In one story, a scholar begins to rewrite all the endings of the numerous novels in his collection because he cannot bear tragic denouements.

Subject keywords: identity; philosophy

Original language: Italian

Sources consulted for annotation:

Global Books in Print (online) (reviews from *Choice* and *Publishers Weekly* for *Voices from the Plains*).

Publishers Weekly 239 (17 August 1992): 493.
Another translated book written by Gianni Celati: *Voices from the Plains*

Andrea De Carlo. *Yucatán.*
Translated by William Weaver. San Diego, CA: Harcourt Brace Jovanovich, 1990. 213 pages.
Genre/literary style/story type: mainstream fiction
A Yugoslavian film director and his entourage set out on an adventure-filled journey to the Yucatan to gather material for their next movie. They are particularly interested in a mysterious underground legend named Camado, who is an expert on drugs, including peyote, and occult practices. But Camado is hard to track down, leading the film director on a merry chase through a ravaged, bleak, and ultimately revealing landscape.
Subject keyword: identity
Original language: Italian
Sources consulted for annotation:
Global Books in Print (online) (synopsis/book jacket).
Rubin, Merle. *The Christian Science Monitor*, 1 June 1990, p. 9.
Steinberg, Sybil S. *Publishers Weekly* 237 (12 January 1990): 47.
Some other translated books written by Andrea De Carlo: *The Cream Train*; *Wind Shift*; *Sea of Truth*

Erri De Luca. *Sea of Memory.*
Translated by Beth Archer Brombert. Hopewell, NJ: Ecco Press, 1999. 118 pages.
Genres/literary styles/story types: mainstream fiction; coming-of-age
In the 1950s, while on summer vacation, a 16-year-old boy from Naples helps his fisherman uncle, who fought in World War II and who now lives on an island near the resort destination of Capri. As they ply the coastal waters baiting hooks and hauling nets, something lies hidden just behind the idyllic scrim of adolescence and the frolicking German tourists: the memory of the war and Italy's unacknowledged complicity in Nazi atrocities. Eventually, the teenaged boy is introduced to Caia, who is a Jewish refugee from Romania whose family was destroyed by the Holocaust. His love for her deepens, especially when Caia becomes unconsolable after hearing tourists singing German military anthems, and he understands that his fate is bound up with understanding Italy's nebulous wartime past.
Subject keywords: anti-Semitism; war
Original language: Italian
Sources consulted for annotation:
Amazon.com (book description; review from *Kirkus Reviews*).
Ferriss, Lucy. *The New York Times Book Review*, 29 August 1999 (online).
Maceri, Domenico. *World Literature Today* 74 (Spring 2000): 429.
Rohrbaugh, Lisa. *Library Journal* 124 (July 1999): 130.
Steinberg, Sybil S. *Publishers Weekly* 246 (5 July 1999): 59.
Some other translated books written by Erri De Luca: *God's Mountain*; *Three Horses*

Luca Di Fulvio. *The Mannequin Man.*
Translated by Patrick McKeown. London: Bitter Lemon Press, 2007. 369 pages.
Genres/literary styles/story types: crime fiction; police detectives
This novel features chief inspector Giacomo Amaldi, who works in a city very much like Genoa. During a month-long garbage strike that turns the city into a fetid swamp, he must deal with a deranged serial killer who is murdering women, taking various body parts, and making a mannequin out of them.
Subject keyword: urban life
Original language: Italian

Source consulted for annotation:
Global Books in Print (online) (reviews from *Booklist*, *Library Journal*, and *Publishers Weekly*).

Francesca Duranti. *The House on Moon Lake.*
Translated by Stephen Sartarelli. New York: Random House, 1986. 181 pages.
Genres/literary styles/story types: mainstream fiction; postmodernism
Belying his aristocratic background, Fabrizio Garrone is a struggling translator who has just finished translating the little-known novel *The House on Moon Lake* by Fritz Oberhofer. His publisher, thinking perhaps to stimulate demand for all things Oberhofer, asks Fabrizio to write Oberhofer's biography. But he quickly finds himself short of material, especially for the last three years of his subject's life; as a result, he begins to invent people and events in Oberhofer's life. Thus, the entirely fictive Maria Lettner, Oberhofer's mistress, is born. But when the biographer—now somewhat chastened by his hoax and wanting to set the record straight—receives a phone call from someone claiming to be Lettner's granddaughter, who calmly informs him that she has a hoard of correspondence between Oberhofer and her grandmother, he knows that something is frightfully amiss.
Subject keywords: identity; writers
Original language: Italian
Sources consulted for annotation:
Harris, Bertha. *The New York Times Book Review*, 24 February 1991 (online).
Ponce, Pedro. *Review of Contemporary Fiction* 21 (Fall 2001): 216.
Shelley Cox. *Library Journal* 111 (1 Oct 1986): 108.
Spinella, Michael. *Booklist* 97 (1 November 2000): 519.
Steinberg, Sybil S. *Publishers Weekly* 230 (1 August 1986): 67.
Some other translated books written by Francesca Duranti: *Happy Ending*; *Personal Effects*; *Left-Handed Dreams*

Umberto Eco. *The Mysterious Flame of Queen Loana.*
Translated by Geoffrey Brock. Orlando, FL: Harcourt, 2005. 469 pages.
Genre/literary style/story type: mainstream fiction
Giambattista Bodoni is a 59-year-old antiquarian book seller and stroke victim who cannot remember anything except for what he has read. He can recite long stretches of philosophical and literary works, but cannot remember the first thing about his family and friends. Thus, his wife suggests that he return to his boyhood home in the hopes that familiar surroundings will stimulate his memory. Here, he discovers the accumulated treasures of his adolescence—books, journals, comics, music, love letters, diaries, school assignments—and he begins to forge a sense of who he was—and is.
Subject keywords: aging; identity
Original language: Italian
Sources consulted for annotation:
Amazon.com (book description).
Cronin, Justin. *The Washington Post*, 17 July 2005, p. F8.
Global Books in Print (online) (reviews from *Library Journal* and *Publishers Weekly*).
Hooper, Brad. *Booklist* 101 (1 March 2005): 1102.
Mallon, Thomas. *The New York Times Book Review*, 12 June 2005 (online).
Some other translated books written by Umberto Eco: *The Island of the Day Before*; *The Name of the Rose*; *Baudolino*; *Foucault's Pendulum*; *The Three Astronauts*; *The Bomb and the General*

Oriana Fallaci. *Inshallah.*
Translated by James Marcus and Oriana Fallaci. New York: Nan A. Talese/Doubleday, 1992. 599 pages.

Genre/literary style/story type: mainstream fiction

The setting of this novel is Beirut, Lebanon, in the aftermath of the October 1983 suicide bombings at American and French military installations. The book, which describes the multifaceted political and social history of Beirut, focuses on the soldiers of the Italian peacekeeping force in the ensuing winter months as they wait for what they believe to be an inevitable third attack. As the level of foreboding increases, as the situation grows more opaque and confused by the hour, the only constant is a snarling and growling nihilism.

Subject keyword: war

Original language: Italian

Sources consulted for annotation:

Dickey, Christopher. *Los Angeles Times*, 10 January 1993, p. 1.

Global Books in Print (online) (reviews from *Booklist* and *Kirkus Reviews*).

Keneally, Thomas. *The New York Times*, 27 December 1992, p. A8.

Steinberg, Sybil S. *Publishers Weekly* 239 (5 October 1992): 54.

Some other translated books written by Oriana Fallaci: *A Man*; *Penelope at War*; *Letter to a Child Never Born*

Elena Ferrante (pseudonym). *Troubling Love.*

Translated by Ann Goldstein. New York: Europa Editions, 2006. 139 pages.

Genres/literary styles/story types: mainstream fiction; women's lives

This novel focuses on Delia, a 45-year-old woman whose mother, Amalia, has drowned—her body naked except for an expensive piece of lingerie. Something does not quite ring true about this scenario, so Delia returns to Naples to delve into the mystery of the paradoxical Amalia, a comely woman who hid her beauty lest she awaken the violently unpredicatbale jealously of her husband.

Related titles by the same author:

Readers may also enjoy *The Days of Abandonment*, which traces the life of Olga after her husband, Mario, leaves his family for the teenaged Carla. Also of interest may be *The Lost Daughter*, in which a middle-aged academic has decidedly mixed amd ultimately frightening feelings about motherhood.

Subject keywords: identity; social roles

Original language: Italian

Source consulted for annotation:

Global Books in Print (online) (reviews from *Booklist*, *Library Journal*, and *Publishers Weekly* for all novels).

Some other translated books written by Elena Ferrante: *The Days of Abandonment*; *The Lost Daughter*

Linda Ferri. *Cecilia.*

Translated by Ann Goldstein. New York: Europa Editions, 2010. 288 pages.

Genres/literary styles/story types: literary historical; women's lives

This novel imaginatively retells the story of Cecilia, an early martyr of the Christian church in the late second century who is referred to as the patron saint of musicians. During the reign of Marcus Aurelius in Imperial Rome, Cecilia is born into a wealthy family. Her father is a prefect; her mother is a worshipper of Isis. Cecilia converts to Christianity and marries Valerian, an aristocrat, but the couple grows apart as Valerian refuses to share his wife's beliefs. The novel is particularly good at investigating the emotional and psychological motivations of Cecilia and her parents.

Related title by the same author:

Readers may also enjoy *Enchantments*, a lyrical coming-of-age novel that follows a young Italian girl—who lives in Paris after World War II—to the cusp of adulthood. In many ways, it can be seen as a secular version of *Cecilia* but without the certainty of faith.

Subject keyword: religion
Original language: Italian
Source consulted for annotation:
Merrihew, Kirstin. *MostlyFiction Book Reviews*, http://bookreview.mostlyfiction.com.
Another translated book written by Linda Ferri: *Enchantments*

Paolo Giordano. *The Solitude of Prime Numbers.*
Translated by Shaun Whiteside. New York: Viking, 2010. 271 pages.
Genre/literary style/story type: mainstream fiction
Probably one of the most eloquently moving books you will ever read, alongside Marianne Wiggins's *Evidence of Things Unseen* (2003). Like Wiggins's novel, Giordano's book is to be treasured, read slowly, and then reread slower still. It is ultimately a love story, complicated by uncommon tragedies. While trying to please her father, Alice Della Rocca has a terrible ski accident that permanently reduces her mobility; she is merely a shell of what she once was. Then there is Mattia, who is so embarrassed by his mentally disabled sister that he abandons her in a park; she disappears, and he never forgives himself. He is a suicide waiting to happen. When these two damaged, scarred, and frightened people meet as adolescents, they cling to each other as if there were no tomorrow. And as other people enter their lives, Mattia and Alice find reasons to reject them, preferring the haunting solitude of their pain to the evanescent joys of normality. As Richard Eder observed, the author "transfigures what ostensibly is a story of injury and defeat" into an aching triumph through the "piercing subtlety" of his writing.
Subject keyword: family histories
Original language: Italian
Sources consulted for annotation:
Eder, Richard. *The New York Times*, 13 March 2010 (online).
Schillinger, Liesl. *The New York Times Book Review*, 11 April 2010 (online).

Amara Lakhous. *Clash of Civilizations Over an Elevator in Piazza Vittorio.*
Translated by Ann Goldstein. New York: Europa Editions, 2008. 144 pages.
Genre/literary style/story type: mainstream fiction
When a man is found dead in the dingy elevator of an apartment building in Rome that is home to a wide variety of immigrants, everyone has an opinion about the crime and everyone has a personal story to tell. As the voice of an Iranian chef mingles with that of a shopkeeper from Bangladesh and as a curmudgeonly professor inveighs against the changes brought about by modern life, readers will no doubt agree with the reviewer for *The New Yorker*, who remarked that the book's "real subject is the heave and crush of modern, polyglot Rome."
Subject keywords: identity; urban life
Original language: Italian
Sources consulted for annotation:
Books Briefly Noted. *The New Yorker* (December 8, 2008) (online).
Global Books in Print (online) (reviews from *Booklist* and *Publishers Weekly*).

Rosetta Loy. *The Water Door.*
Translated by Gregory Conti. New York: Other Press, 2006. 109 pages.
Genres/literary styles/story types: mainstream fiction; coming-of-age
It is difficult for any child to see beyond his or her own threshold to the broader social and historical trends swirling about in the external world. It is doubly difficult when you are the cosseted child of wealthy parents trying to live in Rome during the years of World War II as if very little of importance was going on. But soon, one of the child's playmates disappears; it just happens that the

playmate was Jewish. And then the family's governess leaves; the governess just happened to be German.

Related title by the same author:

Readers may also enjoy *Hot Chocolate at Hanselmann's*, which focuses on Arturo as he tries to survive during the war years in France and then Switzerland. Half-Jewish, he must constantly adopt to an ever-worsening situation and find solace where he can.

Subject keywords: anti-Semitism; urban life

Original language: Italian

Sources consulted for annotation:

Amazon.com (book description; review from *Kirkus Reviews*).

Global Books in Print (online) (review from *Library Journal* for *Hot Chocolate at Hanselmann's*).

Some other translated books written by Rosetta Loy: *Hot Chocolate at Hanselmann's*; *The Dust Roads of Monferrato*

Carlo Lucarelli. *Via Delle Oche*.

Translated by Michael Reynolds. New York: Europa Editions, 2008. 160 pages.

Genres/literary styles/story types: crime fiction; police detectives

Set in 1948, this is the third and final installment of the so-called De Luca Trilogy, which also consists of *The Damned Season* and *Carte Blanche*. Commissario De Luca, who had formerly been a member of Mussolini's secret police force, leads a tangled life in postwar Italy. Can he keep his past a secret? Can he keep his head above water in treacherous political waters to forge a respectable career? As he investigates a death at a Bologna brothel that his colleagues want to classify as a suicide but that he considers a murder, he discovers scandal after scandal at the top echelons of Italian society.

Subject keywords: politics; urban life

Original language: Italian

Source consulted for annotation:

Global Books in Print (online) (reviews for all books from *Booklist*, *Library Journal*, and *Publishers Weekly*).

Some other translated books written by Carlo Lucarelli: *Carte Blanche*; *The Damned Season*; *Day After Day*; *Almost Blue*

Claudio Magris. *A Different Sea*.

Translated by M. S. Spurr. London: Harvill, 1993. 104 pages.

Genre/literary style/story type: mainstream fiction

This novel centers on Enrico Mreule, who is fed up with the hypocrisy and pretentiouness of modern life. In 1909, he leaves his home in the Austrian Empire and travels to Patagonia to become a gaucho. Here, he spends 13 mostly solitary years reading philosophy, tending sheep, and trying to discover the meaning of life. Ultimately dissatisfied by his quest for authenticity, he returns home and becomes a teacher, but his new role does nothing to reconcile him to others.

Related title by the same author:

Readers may also be interested in *Danube*, in which the author traces the history and idiosyncrasies of this significant European river through a series of what Eugen Weber labels as "abstractions, fables, apercus, excursions, quotations, notes and dissertations, snippets and cameos."

Subject keywords: philosophy; rural life

Original language: Italian

Sources consulted for annotation:

Eder, Richard. *Los Angeles Times*, 9 February 1995, p. 10.

Global Books in Print (online) (review from *Kirkus Reviews*).

St. John, Janet. *Booklist* 91 (15 February 1995): 1060.

Steinberg, Sybil S. *Publishers Weekly* 242 (2 January 1995): 60.
Weber, Eugen. *The New York Times Book Review*, 1 October 1989 (online).
Some other translated books written by Claudio Magris: *Inferences from a Sabre*; *Danube*

Valerio Manfredi. *The Talisman of Troy.*
Translated by Christine Feddersen-Manfredi. London: Macmillan, 2004. 275 pages.
Genre/literary style/story type: historical fiction
The ancient world lives on in this historical novel based on Homer's *The Iliad* and *The Odyssey.* Combining history, traditional myths and legends, and vibrant storytelling, the author weaves a spellbinding tale about the real origins of the Trojan War.
Subject keyword: power
Original language: Italian
Sources consulted for annotation:
Amazon.com (book description).
Trink, Bernard. *The Bangkok Post*, 21 January 2005, p. 1.
Wood, Michael. *Coventry Evening Telegraph*, 8 May 2004, p. 25.
Some other translated books written by Valerio Manfredi: *Spartan*; *The Last Legion*; *Trilogy About Alexander the Great: Alexander: Child of a Dream, Alexander: Sands of Ammon, Alexander. Ends of the Earth*; *Tyrant*; *Empire of Dragons*; *The Tower of Solitude*; *Heroes*

Giorgio Manganelli. *Centuria: One Hundred Ouroboric Novels.*
Translated by Henry Martin. Kingston, NY: McPherson, 2005. 213 pages.
Genres/literary styles/story types: mainstream fiction; short stories
What can one say about this extraordinary book that contains 100 very short tales about the widest assortment of characters possible, each captured in the midst of a particularly important event? Critics have referred to the book as maze-like, allusive, absurd, endlessly refractive, and ultimately existential. It all begins to make sense (or does it?) when one knows that an Ouroboros is an ancient mythical, philosophical, and religious symbol for eternity, cyclicity, and self-sufficient unity.
Subject keyword: philosophy
Original language: Italian
Sources consulted for annotation:
Amazon.com (book description; review from *Times Literary Supplement*).
Feeney, Tim. *Review of Contemporary Fiction* 25 (Fall 2005): 138.
Goldsmith, Francisca. *Library Journal* 130 (1 February 2005): 73.
Pekar, Harvey. *Artforum* 12 (June–September 2005): 53.
Another translated book written by Giorgio Manganelli: *All the Errors*

Dacia Maraini. *The Silent Duchess.*
Translated by Dick Kitto and Elspeth Spottiswood. New York: Feminist Press at The City University of New York, 1998. 261 pages.
Genres/literary styles/story types: mainstream fiction; women's lives
Thirteen-year-old Marianna Ucria, deaf and mute, has no choice but to marry her aging uncle. After 27 years of married life and five children, her husband dies, finally allowing her to come into her own as a woman and astute businesswoman.
Related title by the same author:
Readers may also enjoy *Bagheria*, where the author recounts her childhood in a small town near Palermo, Sicily. As she remembers important people and events, she also describes the influence of organized crime on Sicilian culture, society, and values.
Subject keyword: family histories

Original language: Italian
Sources consulted for annotation:
Flanagan, Margaret. *Booklist* 95 (15 November 1998): 567.
Global Books in Print (online) (synopsis/book jacket).
Harrison, Kathryn. *The New York Times Book Review*, 13 December 1998 (online).
Marcus, James. *The New York Times Book Review*, 9 April 1995 (online).
Rohbaugh, Lisa. *Library Journal* 123 (15 September 1998): 113.
Steinberg, Sybil S. *Publishers Weekly* 245 (5 October 1998): 81.
Some other translated books written by Dacia Maraini: *Darkness*; *Woman at War*; *Voices*; *Letters to Marina*; *My Husband*; *Isolina*; *The Violin*; *Memoirs of a Female Thief*; *The Holiday*; *Bagheria*; *The Train*

Paolo Maurensig. *The Lüneburg Variation.*
Translated by Jon Rothschild. New York: Farrar, Straus and Giroux, 1997. 139 pages.
Genres/literary styles/story types: thrillers; political thrillers
Dieter Frisch, a former Nazi but now a respectable businessman in Vienna, is found dead in the center of an elaborate topiary maze, which is in the form of a chessboard. Is it suicide or is it murder? Chess, of course, is the key to Frisch's death. Frisch played against Tabori, a supremely talented opponent before World War II. When Tabori was imprisoned in a concentration camp of which Frisch was the commandant, Frisch forced him to play matches for grisly stakes. This book has invoked comparisons with the work of Paul Auster, Ruth Rendell, and William Styron.
Subject keywords: anti-Semitism; war
Original language: Italian
Sources consulted for annotation:
Bernstein, Richard. *The New York Times*, 17 December 1997, p. E12.
Global Books in Print (online) (reviews from *Booklist*, *Kirkus Reviews*, and *Publishers Weekly*).
Smith, Margaret A. *Library Journal* 122 (August 1997): 133.
Another translated book written by Paolo Maurensig: *Canone Inverso*

Marta Morazzoni. *The Invention of Truth.*
Translated by M. J. Fitzgerald. New York: Alfred A. Knopf, 1993. 99 pages.
Genres/literary styles/story types: historical fiction; literary historical
This novel juxtaposes two very different people—both of whom will leave an indelible mark on cultural history. In 1879, the famed English writer John Ruskin visited the cathedral at Amiens. Awestruck by the majestic sacredness of the cathedral, he ponders timeless questions dealing with truth and beauty. Anne Elisabeth, a seamstress from Amiens who is working on the Bayeux Tapestry, contemplates how to endow it with as much verisimilitude as possible.
Related title by the same author:
Readers may also enjoy *The Alphonse Courrier Affair*, an evocative tale of adultery and rivalry set in a rural village in France in the early years of the twentieth century.
Subject keyword: social roles
Original language: Italian
Source consulted for annotation:
Global Books in Print (online) (reviews from *Booklist*, *Kirkus Reviews*, and *Publishers Weekly* for both books).
Some other translated books written by Marta Morazzoni: *Girl in a Turban*; *The Alphonse Courrier Affair*; *His Mother's House*

Anna Maria Ortese. *The Iguana.*
Translated by Henry Martin. Kingston, NY: McPherson, 1987. 198 pages.

Genres/literary styles/story types: mainstream fiction; magical realism
His mother wants more real estate; his publisher friend wants publishable manuscripts. Thus, a Milan aristocrat, Count Aleardo di Grees, begins a strange and startling voyage to satisfy both. Eventually, he comes across the strangest of islands, inhabited by three brothers and their iguana servant, Estrellita, who has the characteristics of a young girl. Harshly treated by the brothers and forced to live in the most abysmal of conditions, Estrellita becomes an object of fascination and love for the Count, who schemes to release her from her bondage. Critics have referred to the book as a satire and a fable that has much in common with William Shakespeare's *Tempest* and Franz Kafka's *Metamorphosis*.
Related title by the same author:
Readers may also enjoy *A Music Behind the Wall*, a two-volume collection of stories whose common thread is that life would be totally unbearable were it not for dreams, illusions, and fantasies.
Subject keywords: identity; social roles
Original language: Italian
Sources consulted for annotation:
Fuchs, Marcia G. *Library Journal* 112 (1 October 1987): 109.
Global Books in Print (online) (reviews from *Choice* and *Publishers Weekly* for both books).
McNamara, Katherine. *Los Angeles Times*, 25 August 1996, p. 7.
Steinberg, Sybil S. *Publishers Weekly* 232 (11 September 1987): 79.
Venuti, Lawrence. *The New York Times Book Review*, 22 November 1987 (online).
Some other translated books written by Anna Maria Ortese: *The Lament of the Linnet*; *A Music Behind the Wall*

Melissa P. *100 Strokes of the Brush Before Bed* (or ***One Hundred Strokes of the Brush Before Bed*).**
Translated by Lawrence Venuti. New York: Black Cat, 2004. 167 pages.
Genres/literary styles/story types: mainstream fiction; coming-of-age
The least that one can say about this novel is that it caused a ruckus and sensation when first published. Written when the author was 16, it is a fictionalized autobiography of a teenage girl from Sicily who cannot get enough sex. Thus, she indulges in everything—absolutely everything. Nothing is left to the imagination, and no form of sex is left out. At the same time, she feels some degree of shame and guilt for her carnal transgressions, imposing upon herself a nightly penance of 100 brushstrokes of her hair. For readers interested in the relationship between sex and guilt from a different perspective, Catherine Millet's *The Sexual Life of Catherine M.* may be a good choice. The author, an influential presence in the Parisian art world, not only recounts her predilection for orgies but also examines the psychological and emotional reasons for that predilection.
Related title by the same author:
Readers may also wish to explore *The Scent of Your Breath*. Here, the author—who has now chosen to identify herself as Melissa Panarello—focuses her story on how jealously mars a love affair.
Subject keyword: identity
Original language: Italian
Sources consulted for annotation:
Global Books in Print (online) (reviews from *Booklist* and *Publishers Weekly* for *The Sexual Life of Catherine M.*).
Kirkus Reviews 72 (1 August 2004): 709.
Kolhatkar, Sheelah. *The New York Times Book Review*, 13 August 2006 (online).
Raben, Dale. *Library Journal* 129 (August 2004): 69.
Smith, Kyle. *People Weekly* 62 (1 November 2004): 49.

Todaro, Lenora. *The New York Times Book Review*, 7 November 2004 (online).
Zaleski, Jeff. *Publishers Weekly* 251 (20 September 2004): 45.
Another translated book written by Melissa P.: *The Scent of Your Breath*

Roberto Pazzi. *Conclave.*
Translated by Oonagh Stransky. South Royalton, VT: Steerforth Press, 2003. 231 pages.
Genre/literary style/story type: mainstream fiction
The Pope has just died, and the politicking is fierce among the cardinals gathered at the Varican to elect a new pontiff. But after four months of interminable discussions and of the kind of power struggles that would make Machiavelli blush, they cannot reach a decision. They want to leave their enforced sequestration, but there is no escape, especially given a massive infestation of rats. The author has been compared with Italo Calvino for his absurdist perspective on life.
Subject keywords: politics; religion
Original language: Italian
Sources consulted for annotation:
Crane, Rufus S. *World Literature Today* 76 (Winter 2002): 202.
Global Books in Print (online) (synopsis/book jacket).
Parry, Sally E. *Review of Contemporary Fiction* 23 (Fall 2003): 140.
Zaleski, Jeff. *Publishers Weekly* 250 (12 May 2003): 45.
Some other translated books written by Roberto Pazzi: *Searching for the Emperor*; *The Princess and the Dragon*; *Adrift in Time*

Romana Petri. *The Flying Island.*
Translated by Sharon Wood. New Milford, CT: Toby Press, 2002. 106 pages.
Genre/literary style/story type: mainstream fiction
On the isolated island of Pico in the Azores, a female Italian tourist discovers the harsh changes that modernity has brought to a traditional lifestyle imbued with magic and supernatural elements. As she becomes more and more acquainted with the locals who never left, she rues the influx of returning workers who bring with them the value system of consumerist America.
Subject keyword: modernization
Original language: Italian
Sources consulted for annotation:
Geracimos, Ann. *The Washington Times*, 19 January 2003, p. B6.
Global Books in Print (online) (synopsis/book jacket; review from *Kirkus Reviews*).
Library Journal 128 (July 2003): 46.
Some other translated books written by Romana Petri: *An Umbrian War*; *Other People's Fathers*

Giuseppe Pontiggia. *Born Twice.*
Translated by Oonagh Stransky. New York: Alfred A. Knopf, 2002. 191 pages.
Genre/literary style/story type: mainstream fiction
Professor Frigerio has a 30-year-old son born with a severe neurological disorder that has gravely affected his cognitive and intellectual development. Life has been one challenge after another—for both father and son. As Frigerio looks back to his interactions and struggles with often insensitive and uncomprehending administrators and authority figures, he relives the agony, anger, and ambivalence that marked his journey to come to terms with his son's condition. The book has evoked comparisons with *Rouse Up O Young Men of the New Age* by Kenzaburo Oe.
Related title by the same author:

Readers may also be interested in *The Invisible Player*, where a linguistics professor tries to track down the author of an anonymous personal attack on his scholarly work—only to discover a hall of mirrors in which language can be manipulated in a multitude of ways for the basest of purposes.
Subject keyword: family histories
Original language: Italian
Sources consulted for annotation:
Baumel, Judith. *The New York Times Book Review*, 26 February 1989 (online).
Global Books in Print (online) (reviews from *Kirkus Reviews*).
Seaman, Donna. *Booklist* 99 (15 October 2002): 388.
Venuti, Lawrence. *The New York Times Book Review*, 13 October 2002, p. 25.
Zaleski, Jeff. *Publishers Weekly* 249 (30 September 2002): 48.
Some other translated books written by Giuseppe Pontiggia: *The Invisible Player*; *The Big Night*

Giorgio Pressburger. *Teeth and Spies*.
Translated by Shaun Whiteside. London: Granta Books, 1999. 260 pages.
Genres/literary styles/story types: mainstream fiction; postmodernism
This novel is a biography of SG, an Italian of Jewish extraction, as told through his 32 teeth, with each tooth representing a key event in his life. Taken together, the 32 chapters sketch a tangled, tragic, and often humorous history of Eastern Europe.
Related title by the same author:
Readers may also enjoy *The Law of White Spaces*, which is a collection of five stories, each of which features a physician who gradually becomes mad because of his inability to explain a mystery tied to a patient's condition.
Subject keyword: identity
Original language: Italian
Sources consulted for annotation:
Crane, Rufus. *World Literature Today* 73 (Autumn, 1999): 716.
Global Books in Print (online) (synopsis/book jacket for *Teeth and Spies*; review from *Library Journal* for *The Law of White Spaces*).
Montgomery, Isobel. *The Guardian*, 12 August 2000, p. 11.
Some other translated books written by Giorgio Pressburger: *Homage to the Eighth District: Tales from Budapest*; *The Law of White Spaces*; *Snow and Guilt*; *The Green Elephant*

Gianni Riotta. *Prince of the Clouds*.
Translated by Stephen Sartarelli. New York: Farrar, Straus and Giroux, 2000. 287 pages.
Genre/literary style/story type: mainstream fiction
Carlo Terzo studies military strategy without ever having experienced actual combat. Shy and politically naïve, he is packed off to Sicily after World War II. Away from the hustle and bustle of Rome, he plans to write a manual for strategic living and care for his dying wife. But when he meets two young Siciliams imbued with political and social idealism, he finds himself leading a battle between the peasantry and local landowners.
Related title by the same author:
Readers may also enjoy *The Lights of Alborada*, where an Italian prisoner in Texas after World War II has 40 days to stop the wedding of the woman he loves to one of their former teachers.
Subject keyword: power
Original language: Italian
Sources consulted for annotation:
Crane, Rufus S. *World Literature Today* 75 (Winter 2001): 160.

Global Books in Print (online) (synopsis/book jacket for *The Lights of Alborada*).
Pye, Michael. *The New York Times Book Review*, 21 May 2000, p. 21.
Steinberg, Sybil S. *Publishers Weekly* 247 (1 May 2000) 50.
Another translated book written by Gianni Riotta: *The Lights of Alborada*

Leonardo Sciascia. *Equal Danger.*
Translated by Adrienne Foulke. New York: New York Review Books, 2003. 119 pages.
Genres/literary styles/story types: crime fiction; police detectives
According to Sergio Perosa, Sciascia writes "a particular kind of detective fiction where no culprit is ever found and apprehended, where no light can ever be shed, and where intrigues and corruption pervade and envelop society." A perfect example of this is *Equal Danger*, where Inspector Rogas investigates the deaths of two judges and a district attorney, but when he begins to make progress, he is transferred. Also of interest may be *The Day of the Owl* and *Sicilian Uncles*, which focus on the daily activities of organized-crime leaders. The author has also written such true-crime books as *1912 + 1* and *The Moro Affair and the Mystery of Majorana*.
Subject keywords: politics; social problems
Original language: Italian
Sources consulted for annotation:
Farrell, Joe. *The Guardian*, 19 August 2000, p. 9.
Ferrucci, Franco. *The New York Times Book Review*, 24 November 1985 (online).
Global Books in Print (online) (synopses for *Equal Danger* and *The Day of the Owl*).
Grunwald, Eric. *Boston Globe*, 8 August 2004, p. D9.
MacDougall, Carl. *The Herald*, 4 August 2001, p. 12.
Perosa, Sergio. *The New York Times Book Review*, 24 August 1986 (online).
Some other translated books written by Leonardo Sciascia: *Sicilian Uncles*; *Open Doors and Three Novellas*; *The Wine-Dark Sea*; *The Council of Egypt*; *1912 + 1*; *The Moro Affair and the Mystery of Majorana*; *To Each His Own*; *Death of an Inquisitor & Other Stories*; *The Knight and Death & Other Stories*; *The Day of the Owl*

Antonio Tabucchi. *The Missing Head of Damasceno Monteiro.*
Translated by J. C. Patrick. New York: New Directions, 2005. 192 pages.
Genres/literary styles/story types: crime fiction; amateur detectives
A young Portuguese reporter and budding literary scholar is sent by his editor to make sense of the discovery of a headless body near an ecampment of the Roma(ni) people (often, though wrongly, referred to as Gypsies) in Oporto. Here, he meets a diverse array of characters, including a radical lawyer, a prostitute, and a hotel owner—all of whom help him investigate the mistreatment of this oppressed community and to peel back the many layers of police corruption that surround the case.
Related title by the same author:
Readers may also enjoy *Pereira Declares: A Testimony*, which is set in Portugal in the late 1930s. The cultural editor of a Lisbon newspaper is a timid, fearful man, refusing to publish any article that has the least connection to political questions. Instead, he fills his allotted space with literary works that he himself has translated. But his plan backfires when a translation of a story by Balzac is perceived to be offensive to Germans.
Subject keywords: politics; power
Original language: Italian
Sources consulted for annotation:
Global Books in Print (online) (reviews from *Kirkus Reviews* and *Publishers Weekly* for both novels).

Hove, Thomas. *Review of Contemporary Fiction* 20 (Fall 2000): 138.
O'Connell, Alex. *The Times*, 4 May 2000 (from Factiva databases).
Pye, Michael. *The New York Times Book Review*, 20 February 2000, p. 17.
Venuti, Lawrence. *The New York Times Book Review*, 21 July 1996 (online).
Some other translated books written by Antonio Tabucchi: *Letter from Casablanca*; *Indian Nocturne*; *The Edge of the Horizon*; *Little Misunderstandings of No Importance*; *It's Getting Later All the Time: A Novel in the Form of Letters*; *Vanishing Point*; *Pereira Declares: A Testimony*

Susanna Tamaro. *Answer Me.*
Translated by John Cullen. New York: Nan A. Talese/Doubleday, 2001. 215 pages.
Genres/literary styles/story types: mainstream fiction; short stories
These are riveting stories of social isolation and psychological abandonment. In one story, Rosa, a 19-year-old orphan, is an alcoholic struggling to accept that her mother was a prostitute. In another story, a middle-aged woman is secretly relieved that her abusive husband has died.
Related titles by the same author:
Readers may also be interested in *Listen to My Voice*, in which Marta embarks on a journey to discover her long-lost father after finding an old photograph of him. Readers may also enjoy *Anima Mundi*, which focuses on Walter, who yearns to be a writer in Rome but quickly finds out that the literary life is often degrading and vicious.
Subject keyword: family histories
Original language: Italian
Sources consulted for annotation:
Autumn Hill Books (book description), http://www.autumnhillbooks.org.
De Zelar-Tiedman, Christine. *Library Journal* 127 (1 April 2002): 144.
Global Books in Print (online) (review from *Kirkus Reviews* for *Answer Me*; synopsis for *Listen to My Voice*).
Haggas, Carol. *Booklist* 98 (1 March 2002): 1094.
King, Martha. *World Literature Today* 76 (Spring 2002): 218.
Zaleski, Jeff. *Publishers Weekly* 249 (4 February 2002): 50.
Some other translated books written by Susanna Tamaro: *Follow Your Heart*; *Listen to My Voice*; *Anima Mundi*

Simona Vinci. *What We Don't Know About Children* (or *A Game We Play*).
Translated by Minna Proctor. New York: Alfred A. Knopf, 2000. 155 pages.
Genres/literary styles/story types: mainstream fiction; coming-of-age
In a small nondescript town in a nondescript apartment, two teenage boys and three younger girls pass the time exploring their sexuality. Soon, the boys discover pornography magazines, and the seemingly innocent erotic games of the five friends take on a decidedly sinister and violent edge. The book, which some critics have said is more frightening than *Lord of the Flies* because of its pedestrian setting, has also been compared with *The Lover* by Marguerite Duras and *Story of the Eye* by Georges Bataille.
Subject keyword: social problems
Original language: Italian
Sources consulted for annotation:
Amazon.com (book description).
Bernstein, Richard. *The New York Times*, 4 July 2000 (online).
Rozzo, Mark. *Los Angeles Times*, 4 June 2000, p. 10.
Steinberg, Sybil S. *Publishers Weekly* 247 (8 May 2000): 207.
Another translated book written by Simona Vinci: *In Every Sense Like Love*

Sebastiano Vassalli. *The Chimera.*
Translated by Patrick Creagh. New York: Scribner, 1995. 313 pages.
Genres/literary styles/story types: mainstream fiction; women's lives
During the Counter-Reformation in Italy in the early seventeenth century, an orphan girl is burned at the stake in the small village of Zardino. Adopted by a childless couple, the beautiful Antonia soon becomes the cynosure of the village—lusted after by the men and despised by the other women. When she takes a lover, she is accused of being a witch and comes to the attention of religious authorities.
Subject keywords: religion; rural life
Original language: Italian
Sources consulted for annotation:
Berne, Suzanne. *The New York Times Book Review*, 1 October 1995 (online).
Global Books in Print (online) (review from *Kirkus Reviews*).
Lamb, Richard. *The Washington Times*, 24 September 1995, p. B6.
Larson, Dianna. *Booklist* 91 (July 1995): 1862.
Steinberg, Sybil S. *Publishers Weekly* 242 (29 May 1995): 67.
Another translated book written by Sebastiano Vassalli: *The Swan*

Mariolina Venezia. *Been Here a Thousand Years.*
Translated by Marina Harss. New York: Farrar, Straus and Giroux, 2009. 272 pages.
Genre/literary style/story type: mainstream fiction
This novel, which begins in 1861, focuses on the small Italian town of Grottele, recounting the intricate and idiosyncratic lives of the offspring of the six daughters and one son that sprang from the union of Grottele's biggest landowner and Concetta, his mistress. As Carolyn See observes, the book is a loving account of Italian history "through several generations of bumptious peasants who change, over the decades, from somnolent, archetypal figures at one with their livestock and landscape to self-conscious, contemporary human beings ridden with knowledge and anxiety."
Subject keyword: family histories
Original language: Italian
Sources consulted for annotation:
McCulloch, Alison. *The New York Times Book Review*, 6 August 2009 (online).
See, Carolyn. *The Washington Post Book World*, 10 July 2009 (online).

Sandro Veronesi. *The Force of the Past.*
Translated by Alastair McEwen. New York: Ecco Press, 2003. 230 pages.
Genres/literary styles/story types: thrillers; spy thrillers
Gianni Orzean writes children's books, so he is not really ready to be told by an anonymous cabbie that his father was a KGB spy. Gianni had always believed his father to be an army officer—a somewhat typical Italian who supported the Fascist government. As Gianni struggles to uncover the truth, he realizes how little everyone knows about everyone else.
Subject keyword: family histories
Original language: Italian
Sources consulted for annotation:
Cocozza, Paula. *The Independent*, 26 August 2003, p. 15.
Spinella, Michael. *Booklist* 99 (15 February 2003): 1051.
Sullivan, Patrick. *Library Journal* 128 (1 February 2003): 119.
Zaleski, Jeff *Publishers Weekly* 250 (17 March 2003): 53.

Paolo Volponi. *Last Act in Urbino.*
Translated by Peter N. Pedroni. New York: Italica Press, 1995. 302 pages.

Genre/literary style/story type: mainstream fiction
As President Bill Clinton discovered, combining politics and sex is invariably problematic. Giocondini, a chauffeur for the arrogant Count Oddo Oddi-Semproni, and Professor Gaspare Subissoni, an anarchist who has seen better days, have plans for the political independence of Urbino. But when Dirce, a maid whom the count encountered at a brothel and brought back to his palatial home to be his bride, runs away and ends up with Subissoni, the political turns personal.
Subject keywords: politics; power
Original language: Italian
Sources consulted for annotation:
Amazon.com (book description).
Paolucci, A. *Choice* 33 (September 1995): 127.
Simson, Maria. *Publishers Weekly* 242 (20 February 1995): 201.
Some other translated books written by Paolo Volponi: *The Worldwide Machine*; *The Memorandum*; *My Troubles Began*

Wu Ming (pseudonym). ***54.***
Translated by Shaun Whiteside. Orlando, FL: Harcourt, 2005. 549 pages.
Genres/literary styles/story types: thrillers; spy thrillers
To say that this novel is a thriller is an understatement. Set during the Cold War, it features the most unorthdox of characters, including Cary Grant and Lucky Luciano. Politics, history, satire, and pure fun blend to make this book an intellectual feast worthy to be compared with Don DeLillo's *Underworld.* It was written by five writers of the Bologna-based literary foundation Wu Ming, which means "no name" in Mandarin; four of these writers previously wrote *Q* under the pseudonym of Luther Blissett.
Subject keyword: politics
Original language: Italian
Sources consulted for annotation:
Amazon.com (about the author).
Isaacson, Davic. *The Independent on Sunday*, 10 July 2005, p. 26.
Kirkus Reviews 74 (15 May 2006): 494.
Publishers Weekly 253 (6 February 2006): 40.
Sennett, Frank. *Booklist* 102 (1 May 2006): 36.
Another translated book written by Wu Ming: *Q* (as Luther Blissett)

CHAPTER 6

Russia and Central and Eastern Europe

Language groups:

- Albanian
- Belarussian
- Bulgarian
- Croatian
- Czech
- Hungarian
- Macedonian
- Polish
- Romanian
- Russian
- Serbian
- Slovak
- Slovenian
- Ukrainian

Countries represented:

- Albania
- Belarus
- Bosnia and Herzegovina
- Bulgaria
- Croatia
- Czech Republic
- Hungary
- Macedonia
- Montenegro
- Poland
- Romania
- Russia
- Serbia
- Slovakia
- Slovenia
- Ukraine

INTRODUCTION

This chapter contains annotations of books translated from the languages spoken in Russia and Central and Eastern Europe. Some of the languages represented are Albanian, Belarusian, Bulgarian, Croatian, Czech, Hungarian, Macedonian, Polish, Romanian, Russian, Serbian, Slovak, Slovenian, and Ukrainian.

Translated Albanian authors include Ismail Kadaré, who is invariably seen as a future Nobel Prize laureate (*Spring Flowers, Spring Frost* and *The General of the Dead Army*), and Fatos Kongoli (*The Loser*). From Bulgaria, there are such authors as Victor Paskov (*A Ballad for Georg Henig*) and Angel Wagenstein (*Isaac's Torah*); from Croatia, Zoran Feric (*The Death of the Little Match Girl*), Vedrana Rudan (*Night*), and Dubravka Ugrešić (*The Museum of Unconditional Surrender*); and from Serbia, Milorad Pavić (*Last Love in Constantinople: A Tarot Novel for Divination*), Aleksandar Tišma (*The Book of Blam*), and Zoran Zivković (*The Fourth Circle*).

Among the translated Czech authors are such well-known figures as Milan Kundera (*Ignorance* and *Slowness*) and Josef Skvorecký (*The Bride of Texas*) but also such relatively unknown authors as Emil Hakl (*Of Kids and Parents*); Pavel Kohout (*I Am Snowing: The Confessions of a Woman of Prague*);

and Jáchym Topol (*City, Sister, Silver*). Among the translated Hungarian authors are György Dragoman (*The White King*); Péter Esterházy (*Celestial Harmonies*); Imre Kertész (*Liquidation*); and Péter Nádas, whose novel *A Book of Memories* the American critic Susan Sontag raved about.

Some readers may be familiar with at least one translated Polish novelist: the science-fiction master Stanisław Lem, author of such notable titles as *Memoirs Found in a Bathtub* and *Peace on Earth*. But there are numerous other Polish authors to explore, such as Marek Bienczyk (*Tworki*); Ida Fink (*The Journey*); Pawel Huelle (*Who Was David Weiser?*); Jerzy Pilch (*His Current Woman*); and Andrzej Zaniewski (*The Rat*).

When it comes to contemporary translated Russian novels, there is an overabundance of riches. Mystery lovers may be acquainted with Boris Akunin's detective series featuring Erast Fandorin (e.g., *Murder on the Leviathan*). Anatoli Rybakov gained fame with his *The Arbat Trilogy*, a historical epic about life under Stalin during the era of the Soviet Union, and Victor Pelevin attracted much media attention with novels depicting postcommunist Russian life (e.g., *The Life of Insects*; *Homo Zapiens*; and *The Sacred Book of the Werewolf*). But again, there are noteworthy writers beyond this popular handful: Yury Dombrovsky (*The Faculty of Useless Knowledge*); Victor Erofeyev (*Russian Beauty* and *Life with an Idiot*); Andrey Kurkov (*Death and the Penguin*); Sergei Lukyanenko (*The Nightwatch*); Sasha Sokolov (*Astrophobia*); Vladimir Sorokin (*Ice*); Tatyana Tolstaya (*The Slynx*); and Vladimir Voinovich (*Monumental Propaganda*).

Earlier Translated Literature

For readers interested in discovering a small part of the heritage of Central/Eastern European literature, there is the Czech author Jarolsav Hašek (*The Good Soldier Švejk*) and Bohumil Hrabal (*The Little Town Where Time Stood Still* and *I Served the King of England*); the Hungarian writer György Konrád (*The Case Worker* and *The Loser*); the Polish novelist Witold Gombrowicz (*Ferdydurke*); and the Serbian 1961 Nobel Prize laureate Ivo Andrić (*The Bridge Over the Drina*).

The Russian fiction heritage is vast beyond belief. Many critics suggest that an important early landmark is Aleksandr Pushkin's *Eugene Onegin*, often described as a novel-in-verse. Of this text's many translations, one of the most famous is by Vladimir Nabokov. With regard to nineteenth-century novelists, there are giants such as Fyodor Dostoyevsky (*Crime and Punishment*; *The Brothers Karamazov*; and *The Idiot*); Nikolai Gogol (*Dead Souls*); Ivan Goncharov (*Oblomov*); Lev Tolstoy (*War and Peace* and *Anna Karenina*); and Ivan Turgenev (*Fathers and Sons*), who was a particular favorite of Henry James. There is also Mikhail Lermontov, whose novel *A Hero of Our Time* was also translated by Vladimir Nabokov. With regard to the early and mid-twentieth century, some commentators suggest that the two most important Russian novelists were Andrei Bely (*Petersburg*) and Mikhail Bulgakov (*The Master and Margarita*); others would also add Boris Pasternak (*Doctor Zhivago*); Mikhail Sholokhov (*And Quiet Flows the Don*); Aleksandr Solzhenitsyn (*The First Circle*); and Andrey Platonov (*The Foundation Pit*) to this list.

SOURCES CONSULTED

France, Peter. (Ed.). (2000). "Russia" and "Central and East European Languages." In *The Oxford Guide to Literature in English Translation*, pp. 190–221, 582–609. Oxford: Oxford University Press.

Segel, Harold B. (2003). *The Columbia Guide to the Literatures of Eastern Europe Since 1945*. New York: Columbia University Press.

BIBLIOGRAPHIC ESSAY

Central and Eastern Europe

Probably the best place to begin to delve into Central and Eastern European literature is *The Columbia Guide to the Literatures of Eastern Europe Since 1945* by Harold B. Segel. It lives up to its billing as an indispensable guide to the literatures of the region, thoroughly covering authors from Albania (and Kosovo); Bosnia; Bulgaria; Croatia; the Czech Republic; Slovakia; the German Democratic Republic (East Germany); Hungary; Macedonia; Poland; Romania; Serbia (and Montenegro); and Slovenia. There is a substantial 34-page historical and cultural introduction that provides necessary context for fully appreciating the fiction from the countries in this area. Then, there are alphabetically arranged author biographies that critically analyze each writer's major works; at the end of each biography, there is a list of translated works if applicable. An alphabetical author index subdivided by country makes it easy to locate writers from a particular nation. For example, readers can learn about Albanian writer Ismail Kadaré; Czech author Ivan Klíma; Slovak writer Milan Ferko; Slovenian novelist Andrej Blatnik; Romanian poet and novelist Ana Blandiana; Hungarian novelist and short story writer Magda Szabó; and nearly 700 others. A useful bibliography subdivided by country concludes the book. Readers and librarians will be wearing out the pages of this volume for decades to come.

Additional information about authors from many of these countries can be found in three separate volumes of the *Dictionary of Literary Biography*, all edited by Steven Serafin and all with the title *Twentieth-Century Eastern European Writers* (1999, 2000, 2001; vols. 215, 220, 232). In addition to writers from the Czech Republic, Poland, Hungary, and Romania, Serafin's volumes also discuss a large number of authors from Estonia, Latvia, and Lithuania. Also in the Dictionary of Literary Biography series are *South Slavic Writers Before World War II* (1995; vol. 147) and *South Slavic Writers Since World War II* (1997; vol. 181)—both of which are edited by Vasa D. Mihailovich. A recognized expert about South Slavic culture, Mihailovich should also be lauded for producing the monumental *A Comprehensive Bibliography of Yugoslav Literature in English, 1592–1980*, first published in 1984 and with supplements appearing in 1988 and 1992.

Yet more information about these various national literatures can be gleaned from Robert Elsie's two-volume *History of Albanian Literature* (1995); Charles A. Moser's *A History of Bulgarian Literature, 865–1944* (1972); George J. Kovtun's *Czech and Slovak Literature in English* (1988); Josef Nesvadba's *The Lost Face: Best Science Fiction from Czechoslovakia* (1971); Thomas C. Fox's *Border Crossings: An Introduction to East German Prose* (1993); Albert Tezla's edited volume *Ocean at the Window: Hungarian Prose and Poetry Since 1945* (1980); Czeslaw Milosz's *The History of Polish Literature* (2nd ed.) (1983); Sorin Pârvu's *The Romanian Novel* (1992); and Andrew Zawacki's edited volume *Afterwards: Slovenian Writing, 1945–1999* (2000). Cross-cultural perspectives are also important, so it is a pleasure to recommend *A History of Central European Women's Writing*, edited by Celia Hawkesworth. As the title suggests, it contains essays about women writers in various time periods in Hungary, Poland, Croatia, the Czech Republic, Slovakia, and Slovenia, thus enabling comparisons on a region-wide basis.

Russia and Ukraine

While there are numerous histories of Russian literature, the ideal place to start just might be *The Cambridge History of Russian Literature*, edited by Charles A. Moser. Each of the 11 chapters (each of which is about 50 pages long) is by a recognized specialist in the field. The chapters present a wealth of details about such topics as the literature of Old Russia, 988–1730, and the transition to the modern age: sentimentalism and preromanticism, 1790–1820. In addition, the realist, modernist, and socialist realist schools are thoroughly examined against a wide-ranging social and historical background. The same breadth of coverage is evident in *A History of Russian Literature* by Victor Terras, who is particularly thorough when writing about Russian folklore, Old Russian literature from the eleventh to the sixteenth centuries, Byzantine heritage, and the beginnings of Russian prose fiction, folk poetry, and drama in the seventeenth century. Of course, he also discusses at length the philosophical ideas and aesthetics theories informing the literatures of the romantic, realist, and Soviet periods.

Another amazing book is *The Cambridge Introduction to Russian Literature* by Caryl Emerson. If someone is looking for a relatively short, lively, and engaging panorama of the diversity of Russian literature, this title cannot be beat. It succinctly discusses literary heroes and archetypes; traditional narratives, such as the lives of saints and folk epics; neoclassical comedy; the novels of the nineteenth-century romantic era, as represented by Gogol and Pushkin; the realistic novels of Dostoyevsky and Tolstoy; the plays of Chekhov; symbolist and modernist novels; socialist realist novels of the Stalin years; and literature of the post-1956 period, including the detective novels of Boris Akunin.

Having explored these books, readers' appetites may be whetted for additional information. For these individuals, there is the *Reference Guide to Russian Literature*, edited by Neil Cornwell and Nicole Christian. Almost 1,000 pages, this volume contains introductory essays about such topics as postrevolutionary Russian theater; experiment and emigration: Russian literature, 1917–1953; and thaws, freezes, and wakes: Russian literature, 1953–1991. But the real value of this reference source lies in its bio-bibliographic entries on 273 writers and 293 literary works. Equally comprehensive is the *Dictionary of Russian Women Writers*, edited by Marina Ledkovsky and two colleagues, which contains an overview essay about the role of women in Russian literature in the period from 1760–1922. Through detailed and meticulous bio-bibliographic entries, the book discusses 448 women writers who "with a few exceptions, have been forgotten, undervalued, or misread" (p. xxiii). There are also a number of volumes about various periods in Russian literature in the Dictionary of Literary Biography series, published by Gale. We mention the following six titles: *Russian Literature in the Age of Realism*, edited by Alyssa Dinega Gillespie (2003; vol. 277); *Russian Novelists in the Age of Tolstoy and Dostoevsky*, edited by Alexander J. Ogden and Judith E. Kalb (2001; vol. 238); *Twentieth-Century Russian Émigré Writers*, edited by Maria Rubins (2005; vol. 317); *Russian Writers Since 1980*, edited by Marina Balina and Marc Lipovetsky (2004; vol. 285); *Russian Prose Writers Between the World Wars*, edited by Christine Rydel (2003; vol. 272); and *Russian Prose Writers After World War II*, edited by Christine Rydel (2005; vol. 302). Each of these volumes contains substantial biographical information about relevant authors as well as detailed lists of their works, including those that have been translated into English.

For those specifically interested in the classics of Russian literature, no better one-volume survey can be had than *The Cambridge Companion to the Classic Russian Novel*, edited by Malcolm V. Jones and Robin Feuer Miller. There has always been great interest in reading the works of Pushkin, Gogol, Goncharov, Gorky, Dostoyevsky, Tolstoy, Turgenev, Bulgakov, Nabokov, Pasternak, Solzhenitsyn, and Iskander. If these famous names are relatively familiar to you (and even if they are not), you will want to pay close attention to the articles in this book. In addition to concentrating on individual authors, the book also takes a thematic approach, with chapters about the depiction of the city and countryside in classic Russian novels as well as the role of satire, religion, psychology, politics, and philosophy. There are also chapters on novelistic technique, gender, and theory (including the work of Mikhail Bakhtin) as well as carefully selected lists of further readings and a useful chronology of major literary developments.

In the last two decades of the existence of the Soviet Union and during the first two decades of the re-establishment of Russia (Russian Federation), Russian literature underwent a mini-renaissance—at least in the eyes of Western readers. Comprehensive overviews of Soviet literature in the 1970s and 1980s are provided by N. N. Shneidman in *Soviet Literature in the 1970s: Artistic Diversity and Ideological Conformity* and *Soviet Literature in the 1980s: Decade of Transition*. He continues his chronological story in *Russian Literature 1988–1994: The End of an Era*, which not only discusses the effect of glasnost and perestroika on literary endeavors but also focuses on such relatively little known writers as Vladimir Makanin, Andrei Bitov, Vladimir Krupin, Sergei Kaledin, Marina Palei, Aleksandr Kabakov, Viktor Pelevin, Evgenii Popov, Vladimir Sorokin, Valentin Rasputin, Nina Sadur, and Tatyana Tolstaya.

Just by this selected list, one can see that there has been a veritable explosion of Russian fiction—an explosion that continues to this day. Many of the most recent developments on the Russian literary scene are captured in Shneidman's *Russian Literature 1995–2002: On the Threshold of the New Millennium*. Here, Shneidman describes the vibrancy of Russian literary life in eight chapters: The Seniors' Prose; The Mature Generation; The New Writers of the Perestroika Era; Women Writers; The Writers of the Conservative "Patriotic" Camp; The Mystery Novel Writers; and The New Names of 1995–2002. Readers are introduced to such writers as Mikhail Butov, Irina Polianskaia, Nadezhda Khovshchinskaia, Liudmilla Petrushevskaia, Anastasya Verbitskaya, Aleksandra Marinina, Boris Akunin, Polina Dashkova, Oleg Pavlov, Anton Utkin, and Iurii Buida. Especially valuable features of all four of Shneidman's books are the extensive lists of recent Russian fiction translated into English and suggestions for background reading. Two other books about the same time period that are well worth consulting are Robert Porter's *Russia's Alternative Prose* (which has substantial chapters about Eduard Limonov, Viktor Erofeev, and Valeria Narbikova) and M. N. Lipovetsky's *Russian Postmodernist Fiction: Dialogue with Chaos*, which discusses such authors as Sasha Sokolov and Vasily Aksyonov. Lipovetsky's book also contains an appendix that lists all discussed writers, along with succinct biographical information.

Clearly, readers will have understood by the foregoing that much is happening in the world of Russian literature and culture, especially in the last 20 or 30 years. How to put it all in context? To orient oneself within this multifaceted and sophisticated world, we suggest three general works: *The Cambridge Companion to Modern Russian Culture*, edited by Nicholas Rzhevsky; *Consuming Russia: Popular Culture, Sex, and Society Since Gorbachev*, edited by Adele Barker; and *Soviet Popular Culture* by Richard Stites. Rzhevsky's book is especially to be recommended because it includes articles about developments in Russian art, music, theater, and film as well as about the influence of orthodox religion and the rise of popular-culture manifestations.

Another way to approach contemporary Russian culture is through the framework of commercialization and the rapid rise of an entertainment ethos. In the field of literature, these tendencies are explained in such books as *Reading for Entertainment in Contemporary Russia*, edited by Stephen Lovell and Birgit Menzel, and *Russian Pulp: The "Detektiv" and the Russian Way of Crime* by Anthony Olcott. Focusing on the ways that writing, reading, and selling literature has changed in Russia from 1986–2004, Lovell and Menzel's book presents valuable chapters on such various Russian versions of genre fiction as the action thriller, science fiction and fantasy, romance, and historical fiction. Explaining the ongoing popularity of the Russian *detektiv* genre, Olcott situates this genre against a cultural, psychological, and historical context. Russian *detektivs*, he argues, are not to be confused with the Western genres of murder mysteries or detective stories; rather, they should be understood as "a social morality play, the various plots of which all reinforce the notion that society is simultaneously strong—stronger than any individual desire or intention—and yet at the same time very weak, for it can be harmed by the actions of even one of its members" (p. 46). Individuals who have read one or more of the general histories of Russian literature recommended in the previous paragraphs will recognize this as an ongoing theme of Russian fiction.

Last but not least, we cannot forget Ukraine. By far the best overall coverage is provided by *A History of Ukrainian Literature (From the 11th Century to the End of the 19th Century)* by Dmytro Cyzevs'kyj. This book is a model of comprehensiveness, containing chapters about the prehistoric period; the period of the so-called monumental style; the period of the ornamental style; literary baroque; the literature of the national revival; and Ukrainian sentimentalism, romanticism, and realism. As one finishes this more than 600-page book, the overall sense is that Ukrainian literature harbors untold riches. For information about contemporary Ukrainian writers, it is good to discover that Oksana Piaseckyj has produced a reference source entitled *Bibliography of Ukrainian Literature in English and French: Translations and Critical Works, 1950–1986* and that Ed Hogan, along with various colleagues, has produced an anthology of 1980s and 1990s poetry and prose entitled *From Three Worlds: New Ukrainian Writing*.

SELECTED REFERENCES

Barker, Adele. (Ed.). (1999). *Consuming Russia: Popular Culture, Sex, and Society Since Gorbachev*. Durham, NC: Duke University Press.

Cornwell, Neil, and Christian, Nicole. (Eds.). (1998). *Reference Guide to Russian Literature*. London: Fitzroy Dearborn.

Cyzevs'kyj, Dmytro. (1975). *A History of Ukrainian Literature (From the 11th Century to the End of the 19th Century)*. Littleton, CO: Ukrainian Academic Press.

Czerwinski, E. J. (Ed.). (1994). *Dictionary of Polish Literature*. Westport, CT: Greenwood Press.

Emerson, Caryl. (2008). *The Cambridge Introduction to Russian Literature*. New York: Cambridge University Press.

Hawkesworth, Celia. (Ed.). (2001). *A History of Central European Women's Writing*. London: Palgrave.

Hogan, Ed, et al. (Eds.). (1996). *From Three Worlds: New Ukrainian Writing*. Boston: Zephyr Press.

Jones, Malcolm V., and Miller, Robin Feuer. (Eds.). (1998). *The Cambridge Companion to the Classic Russian Novel*. New York: Cambridge University Press.

Ledkovsky, Marina; Rosenthal, Charlotte; and Zirin Mary. (Eds.). (1994). *Dictionary of Russian Women Writers*. Westport, CT: Greenwood Press.

Lipovetsky, M. N. (1999). *Russian Postmodernist Fiction: Dialogue with Chaos*. Armonk, NY: M. E. Sharpe.

Lovell, Stephen, and Menzel, Birgit. (Eds.). (2005). *Reading for Entertainment in Contemporary Russia: Post-Soviet Popular Literature in Historical Perspective*. Munich: Verlag Otto Sagner.

Moser, Charles A. (Ed.). (1992). *The Cambridge History of Russian Literature* (rev. ed.). New York: Cambridge University Press.

Olcott, Anthony. (2001). *Russian Pulp: The "Detektiv" and the Russian Way of Crime*. Lanham, MD: Rowman & Littlefield.

Piaseckyj, Oksana. (1986). *Bibliography of Ukrainian Literature in English and French: Translations and Critical Works, 1950–1986*. Ottawa, ON: University of Ottawa Press.

Porter, Robert. (1994). *Russia's Alternative Prose*. Providence, RI: Berg.

Rzhevsky, Nicholas. (Ed.) (1998). *The Cambridge Companion to Modern Russian Culture*. New York: Cambridge University Press.

Segel, Harold B. (2003). *The Columbia Guide to the Literatures of Eastern Europe Since 1945*. New York: Columbia University Press.

Shneidman, N. N. (1995). *Russian Literature 1988–1994: The End of an Era*. Toronto, ON: University of Toronto Press.

Shneidman, N. N. (2004). *Russian Literature 1995–2002: On the Threshold of the New Millennium*. Toronto, ON: University of Toronto Press.

Shneidman, N. N. (1979). *Soviet Literature in the 1970s: Artistic Diversity and Ideological Conformity*. Toronto, ON: University of Toronto Press.

Shneidman, N. N. (1989). *Soviet Literature in the 1980s: Decade of Transition*. Toronto, ON: University of Toronto Press.

Stites, Richard. (1992). *Soviet Popular Culture*. Cambridge, UK: Cambridge University Press.

Terras, Victor. (1991). *A History of Russian Literature*. New Haven, CT: Yale University Press.

Tezla, Albert. (1970). *Hungarian Authors: A Bibliographical Handbook*. Cambridge, MA: The Belknap Press of Harvard University Press.

ANNOTATIONS FOR TRANSLATED BOOKS FROM CENTRAL AND EASTERN EUROPE

Albania

Ismail Kadaré. ***Spring Flowers, Spring Frost.***
Translated by Jusuf Vrioni (Albanian to French) and David Bellos (French to English). New York: Arcade, 2002. 182 pages.
Genre/literary style/story type: mainstream fiction
Mark Gurabardhi is a painter in Albania after the fall of the communist regime of Enver Hoxha. But life is not getting better; there is only the vaguest semblance of democracy and numerous problems, including taxes, crime, and the reappearance of the time-honored practice of blood debt. In short,

violence and madness reign everywhere. Mark's personal life is also unraveling: His boss is murdered, and his girlfriend disappears along with another friend. And what is one to make of the persistent rumors of files used for blackmail and the marriage of a woman and a snake?
Related titles by the same author:
Readers may also want to explore *The General of the Dead Army*, a searing portrayal of the hubristic aftermath of Italy's invasion of Albania during World War II. An Italian general is dispatched to recover the bodies of Italian soldiers 20 years after the fact. As he and his entourage comb the backroads of Albania in search of buried corpses, he blithely ignores the warnings of a priest that he is infringing on many sociocultural taboos. When the general attends a local wedding feast, he finally realizes that he understands very little—if anything—about the people and country that he has been crisscrossing. Also of interest may be *The Palace of Dreams*, a trenchant allegory set in the Ottoman Empire; the ruler has instituted a system whereby underlings keep a close tab on what people are dreaming and provide him with reports about the most dangerous of those dreams.
Subject keywords: politics; social problems
Original language: Albanian
Sources consulted for annotation:
Adams, Lorraine. *The New York Times Book Review*, 13 November 2005 (online).
Amazon.com (review from *Library Journal*).
Eder, Richard. *The New York Times*, 7 July 2002 (online).
Eder, Richard. *The New York Times*, 26 November 2005 (online).
Eder, Richard. *The New York Times*, 1 October 2008, p. E7.
McAlpin, Matthew L. *Review of Contemporary Fiction* 23 (Spring 2003): 156.
Zaleski, Jeff. *Publishers Weekly* 249 (27 May 2002): 36.
Some other translated books written by Ismail Kadaré: *The Three-Arched Bridge*; *The Pyramid*; *Elegy for Kosovo*; *The File on H.*; *The Concert*; *The Palace of Dreams*; *Chronicle in Stone*; *Doruntine*; *Broken April*; *The Successor*; *The Wedding; The Accident*

Fatos Kongoli. *The Loser.*
Translated by Robert Elsie and Janice Mathie-Heck. Bridgend, UK: Seren Books, 2008. 220 pages.
Genre/literary style/story type: mainstream fiction
Thesar Lumi is an impoverished young man who could have left Albania for Italy but instead finds himself in the bleakest of situations. When he attends university in Tirana, the capital of Albania, he befriends Ladi, the son of a politically prominent family. Things briefly look up, but then Lumi makes the mistake of having an affair with Sonia, a cousin of Ladi. His fate is now sealed, and he must work in a cement factory and exist, as E. J. Van Lanen observes, "in a world where people have little to do but fight over the detritus of their ruined lives."
Subject keyword: power
Original language: Albanian
Sources consulted for annotation:
Global Books in Print (online) (synopsis/book jacket).
Van Lanen, E. J. Three Percent website (book review), http://www.rochester.edu/College/translation/threepercent.

Belarus

Ales' Adamovich. *Khatyn. The Punitive Squads: The Joy of the Knife or The Hyperboreans and How They Live.*
Translated by Glenys Kozlov, Frances Longman, and Sharon McKee. Moscow: Progress Publishers, 1988. 478 pages.

Genres/literary styles/story types: mainstream fiction; coming-of-age
Flera, a former partisan, reminisces about World War II and Nazi atrocities in Belarus. As a young man, he dug up a revolver belonging to a dead soldier in a pile of barbed wire and ran away from home to join local guerrillas fighting the Germans. The novel, which was made into the film *Come and See*, traces Flera's brutal coming-of-age amid the horrors of war.
Subject keyword: war
Original language: Belarusian

Vasil' Bykau (Vasil Bykov). *Sign of Misfortune* (or ***Portent of Disaster*).**
Translated by Alan Myers. New York: Allerton Press, 1990. 240 pages.
Genre/literary style/story type: mainstream fiction
Stepanida and Petroc are two elderly peasants living in rural Belarus. Along with the rest of the country, they endured the harsh conditions associated with the collectivization movement of the 1930s. During World War II, they must deal with the Nazi occupation and local collaborationists. Despite their overwhelmingly hopeless life, they withstand humiliation after humiliation with abiding resiliency, courage, and grace.
Subject keywords: rural life; war
Original language: Belarusian
Sources consulted for annotation:
Steinberg, Sybil S. *Publishers Weekly* 237 (23 February 1990): 204.
Sweedler, Ulla. *Library Journal* 115 (1 March 1990): 113.
Some other translated books written by Vasil' Bykau: *Pack of Wolves*; *The Ordeal*; *His Battalion*; *and, Live until Dawn*; *Alpine Balla*

Bosnia and Herzegovina

Muharem Bazdulj. *The Second Book*.
Translated by Oleg Andric. Evanston, IL: Northwestern University Press, 2005. 142 pages.
Genres/literary styles/story types: historical fiction; short stories
These short stories provide glimpses into the hearts and minds of some of the world's most important literary and historical figures: the near-insane Nietzsche, wrestling with philosophical questions while coping with the irascible minutiae of life; Egyptian Pharaoh Amenhotep IV's quest for divine revelation; and the sibling rivalry of William and Henry James.
Subject keyword: philosophy
Original language: Bosnian
Sources consulted for annotation:
Amazon.com (book description).
Mihailovich, Vasa D. *World Literature Today* 73 (Winter 1999): 170.

Vuk Drašković. *Knife*.
Translated by Milo Yelesiyevich. New York: Serbian Classics Press, 2000. 413 pages.
Genre/literary style/story type: mainstream fiction
Alija Osmanovic believes that Serbs were responsible for killing his Bosnian Muslim family during World War II. Upon reaching adulthood, he vows vengeance. But when he discovers that he was born a Serb and that the people who raised him were responsible for his family's death, he has a major crisis. Alija's story parallels that of Milan Vilenjak, whose family was murdered by Atif Tanovic. Milan's pursuit of Atif leads him to discover that killers can experience remorse and that a man who committed heinous acts at a certain point in his life is no longer that same man decades later.
Subject keywords: politics; power

Original language: Serbian
Sources consulted for annotation:
Amazon.com (book description; review from *Kirkus Reviews*).
Levy, Michele F. *World Literature Today* 74 (Autumn 2000): 887.

Miljenko Jergović. *Sarajevo Marlboro.*
Translated by Stela Tomasevic. New York: Archipelago Books, 2004. 195 pages.
Genres/literary styles/story types: mainstream fiction; short stories
Life was almost unbearable in Sarajevo during the Yugoslav war in the early 1990s. These 29 stories provide a stark assessment of how the average citizen coped—or tried to cope—with such seemingly mundane yet important events as shortages of water and food, and how the act of reading was both a psychological and emotional lifeline.
Subject keywords: social problems; war
Original language: Bosnian
Sources consulted for annotation:
Hunt, Laird. *Review of Contemporary Fiction* 24 (Summer 2004): 138.
Roncevic, Mirela. *Library Journal* 129 (January 2004): 161.
Vidan, Aida. *World Literature Today* 75 (Winter 2001): 170.

Meša Selimović. *The Fortress.*
Translated by E. D. Goy and Jasna Levinger. Evanston, IL: Northwestern University Press, 1999. 406 pages.
Genres/literary styles/story types: historical fiction; literary historical
Ahmet Shabo returns to Sarajevo after the seventeenth-century Battle of Chocim against the Ottoman Empire. But the town and his family have been brought to their knees by a plague. Ahmet finds it difficult to fit in. He loses his job when he insults a powerful person, and one of his fellow soldiers is imprisoned for daring to speak his mind. As Ahmet works to free his friend, he begins to understand the problems and paradoxes of the ethnic-based warrior culture in which he has been raised.
Subject keywords: politics; power
Original language: Serbo-Croatian
Sources consulted for annotation:
Amazon.com (review from *Kirkus Reviews*).
Levy, Michele. *World Literature Today* 74 (Spring 2000): 437.
Pinker, Michael. *Review of Contemporary Fiction* 20 (Summer 2000): 177.
Steinberg, Sybil S. *Publishers Weekly* 246 (16 August 1999): 61.
Some other translated books written by Meša Selimović: *Death and the Dervish*; *The Island*

Sasa Stanisic. *How The Soldier Repairs the Gramophone.*
Translated by Anthea Bell. New York: Grove/Atlantic, 2008. 304 pages.
Genres/literary styles/story types: mainstream fiction; coming-of-age
Aleksandar Krsmanovic and his family now live in Germany, having fled the violence besetting Bosnia-Herzegovina. As he tries to come to terms with his new life, Aleksandar recalls his past, adhering to the lessons of his dead grandfather who told him to rely on his imagination in times of distress. Thus, he constructs his very own personal world—an imaginary refuge that follows its own rules and has its own timeframes.
Subject keywords: family histories; identity
Original language: German
Source consulted for annotation:
Global Books in Print (online) (reviews from *Library Journal* and *Publishers Weekly*).

Nenad Veličković. *Lodgers*.
Translated by Celia Hawkesworth. Evanston, IL: Northwestern University Press, 2005. 193 pages.
Genres/literary styles/story types: mainstream fiction; coming-of-age
In the war-torn Sarajevo of the early 1990s, Maja—a teenager whose family has found shelter in the city museum after their building was demolished—describes how her Muslim father, a dedicated museum curator, struggles to save as many treasures as he can and keep them out of the hands of thieves who want to sell them for food and other daily necessities.
Subject keyword: social problems
Original language: Yugoslavian (as per cover)
Sources consulted for annotation:
Debeljak, Aleš. *World Literature Today* 80 (July/August 2006): 72.
Northwestern University Press (book description), http://www.nupress.northwestern.edu.
Pinker, Michael. *Review of Contemporary Fiction* 26 (Spring 2006): 148.

Bulgaria

Georgi Gospodinov. *Natural Novel*.
Translated by Zornitsa Hristova. Normal, IL: Dalkey Archive Press, 2005. 136 pages.
Genres/literary styles/story types: mainstream fiction; experimental fiction
When the wife of Georgi Gospodinov becomes pregnant and it is clear that Georgi is not the father, the only answer is divorce. But plot summary barely touches on the inventiveness of this book, which is a scrapbook-style mélange containing what amounts to rough sketches, half-baked ideas, and drafts for a novel. The author's purpose is to examine the very act of writing: how does one reconcile spontaneity and the desire to produce a work of lasting value?
Subject keywords: philosophy; writers
Original language: Bulgarian
Sources consulted for annotation:
Amazon.com (review from *Publishers Weekly*).
The New Yorker 81 (14 March 2005): 134.
Reynolds, Susan Salter. *Los Angeles Times*, 20 February 2005, p. R11.
Tepper, Anderson. *The New York Times Book Review*, 5 June 2005, p. 28.
Wright, Heather. *Library Journal* 130 (1 February 2005): 68.

Viktor Paskov (Victor Paskov). *A Ballad for Georg Henig*.
Translated by Robert Sturm. London: Peter Owen, 1990. 132 pages.
Genre/literary style/story type: mainstream fiction
In Sofia, Bulgaria, in the 1950s, most everyone lives in straightened circumstances. When the parents of a small boy want a violin made for their son, they naturally turn to a former musician and famous violin maker, George Henig. A few years later, Victor's mother yearns to have a sideboard in their apartment. When Victor's father visits Henig in the hopes of using his workshop for the sideboard project, he finds him on the verge of death, unable to afford to buy food. This is a haunting tale of solitude and the slow evisceration of beauty and culture under totalitarianism.
Subject keywords: identity; social problems
Original language: Bulgarian
Sources consulted for annotation:
Moser, C. A. *Choice* 28 (April 1991): 1317.
Steinberg, Sybil S. *Publishers Weekly* 238 (19 April 1991): 55.

Angel Wagenstein. *Isaac's Torah.*
Translated by Elizabeth Frank and Deliana Simeonova. New York: Handsel Books, 2008. 320 pages.
Genre/literary style/story type: mainstream fiction
As indicated on the cover page, this novel follows Isaac Jacob Blumenfeld as he lives through world wars and concentration camps—an odyssey that takes him to five countries. But despite his tragic experiences, his tale is permeated with irony, humor, and cheery anecdotes. Some critics have marveled that the book, which could easily have turned into a melancholic dirge about loss, is instead a vibrant affirmation of the resiliency and power of Jewish life.
Subject keywords: anti-Semitism; war
Original language: Bulgarian
Source consulted for annotation:
Witte, Phillip. Three Percent website (book review), http://www.rochester.edu/College/translation/threepercent.

Croatia

Slavenka Drakulić. *S.: A Novel About the Balkans.*
Translated by Marko Ivić. New York: Viking, 1999. 201 pages.
Genre/literary style/story type: mainstream fiction
Based on survivor interviews, this is a gut-wreching novel that describes how Serbian soldiers systematically raped captured Muslim and Croatian women during the Balkan wars in the late twentieth century. Critics have compared this book to Primo Levi's *Survival in Auschwitz.*
Subject keyword: war
Original language: originally published in German; then Croatian; translated from Serbo-Croatian
Sources consulted for annotation:
Cooper, Rand Richards. *The New York Times Book Review,* 2 April 2000, p. 15.
Johnston, Bonnie. *Booklist* 96 (1 January/15 January 2000): 876.
Library Journal 126 (January 2001): 53.
Pearl, Nancy. *Library Journal* 128 (1 March 2003): 144.
Roncevic, Mirela. *Library Journal* 124 (December 1999): 184.
Steinberg, Sybil S. *Publishers Weekly* 246 (29 November 1999): 53.
Some other translated books written by Slavenka Drakulić: *Marble Skin*; *Holograms of Fear*; *The Taste of a Man*; *As If I Am Not There*

Zoran Feric. *The Death of the Little Match Girl.*
Translated by Tomislav Kuzmanovic. Iowa City, IA: Autumn Hill Books, 2008. 196 pages.
Genres/literary styles/story types: crime fiction; suspense
In 1992, on the small Adriatic island of Rab, a Romanian transvestite prostitute is murdered. Thus, the seemingly idyllic, magical, and placid life of Rab, a part of Croatia, is shattered forever, as secret after secret is revealed. Mysterious events abound, including exorcisms and an outbreak of leukemia. Romanian undercover agents hover, and there is more than a whiff of political scandal and gothic debauchery.
Subject keyword: family histories
Original language: Croatian
Source consulted for annotation:
Autumn Hill Books (book description), http://www.autumnhillbooks.org.

Slobodan Novak. *Gold, Frankincense, and Myrrh.*
Translated by Celia Hawkesworth. Iowa City, IA: Autumn Hill Books, 2008. 271 pages.

Genre/literary style/story type: mainstream fiction
An exasperating 100-year-old woman awaits death on the island of Rab. Her property has been expropriated, and there is nothing much for her to do. As she lies on her bed—ill, slovenly, and perpetually complaining—a man keeps watch over her, recalling the history of the island and its people, tracing connections between families and events and between sorrows and joys. Critics have compared this novel to works by Anton Chekhov and Samuel Beckett.
Subject keyword: family histories
Original language: Croatian
Sources consulted for annotation:
Autumn Hill Books (book description), http://www.autumnhillbooks.org.
Global Books in Print (online) (review from *Publishers Weekly*).

Vedrana Rudan. ***Night.***
Translated by Celia Hawkesworth. Normal, IL: Dalkey Archive Press, 2004. 211 pages.
Genres/literary styles/story types: mainstream fiction; feminist fiction
To put it mildly, Tonka Babic is a blunt and often rude contrarian—a feminist who hates feminism. As she watches television one evening, she rants and raves against just about everything, including Western-style consumerism, the institution of marriage, and pusillanimous journalists.
Subject keyword: social problems
Original language: Croatian
Sources consulted for annotation:
Driscoll, Brendan. *Booklist* 101 (1 December 2004): 637.
Lacey, Josh. *The Guardian*, 11 December 2004, p. 226.
Roncevic, Mirela. *Library Journal* 129 (December 2004): 102.

Antun Šoljan. ***A Brief Excursion and Other Stories.***
Translated by Ellen Elias-Bursac. Evanston, IL: Northwestern University Press, 1999. 252 pages.
Genres/literary styles/story types: mainstream fiction; short stories
This book is composed of a novel and six short stories. In the novel, legendary fifteenth-century Istrian frescoes take center stage, becoming the object of covetousness by just about everyone connected with the field of archaelogy and art history. According to the publisher's website, the characters in the short stories "are stirred to action by a chimera of longing only to find, at the end of their efforts, the stark landscape of self-knowledge and loss."
Subject keyword: rural life
Original language: Croatian
Sources consulted for annotation:
Northwestern University Press (book description), http://nupress.northwestern.edu.
Powell's Books (book review), http://www.powells.com.
Some other translated books written by Antun Šoljan: *Luka*; *The Other People on the Moon*

Igor Štiks. ***A Castle in Romagna.***
Translated by Tomislav Kuzmanovic. Iowa City, IA: Autumn Hill Books, 2006. 103 pages.
Genre/literary style/story type: historical fiction
The more things change, the more they stay the same. In 1992, a young Bosnian tours an Italian Renaissance castle, where the guide, a fellow refugee, draws parallels between his fraught love affair in the 1940s with the daughter of a Yugoslav police officer and that of a Rennaissance poet who fell in love with his host's wife.
Subject keyword: identity
Original language: Croatian

Sources consulted for annotation:
Autumn Hill Books (book description), http://www.autumnhillbooks.com.
Global Books in Print (online) (synopsis/book jacket).

Dubravka Ugrešić. *The Museum of Unconditional Surrender.*
Translated by Celia Hawkesworth. New York: New Directions, 1999. 238 pages.
Genres/literary styles/story types: mainstream fiction; experimental fiction
Critics could not say enough good things about this fragmentary and elusive novel about the experience of exile. Because every aspect of the immigrant's or refugee's former life is torn brusquely apart, it is entirely appropriate that this book is a sort of collage of disparate memories, styles, and forms without apparent rhyme nor reason. And just as the traumatized immigrant or refugee painstakingly and slowly builds a new and meaningful life from the resources at hand in a new country of residence, so do the random assortment of facts and descriptions in this book gradually begin to assume a coherent and unified shape: an eloquent disquisition about loss and gain, youth and aging, sorrow and beauty.
Related title by the same author:
Readers may also enjoy *The Ministry of Pain*, in which a group of Croats, Serbs, and Bosnians living in Amsterdam undertakes a game of what can only be described as Yugo-Nostalgia at the behest of a language and literature teacher. Although intended as a therapeutic device, the game has unanticipated consequences.
Subject keywords: family histories; identity
Original language: Croatian
Sources consulted for annotation:
Agovino, Michael J. *The New York Times Book Review*, 14 May 2006 (online).
Amazon.com (book description).
Global Books in Print (online) (reviews from *Booklist* and *Publishers Weekly* for *The Ministry of Pain*; review from *Library Journal* for *Nobody's Home*).
Malin, Irving. *Review of Contemporary Fiction* 20 (Spring 2000): 187.
Zaleski, Jeff. *Publishers Weekly* 249 (14 January 2002): 39.
Some other translated books written by Dubravka Ugrešić: *The Ministry of Pain*; *In the Jaws of Life*; *Fording the Stream Of Consciousness*; *Lend Me Your Character*; *Nobody's Home*; *Baba Yaga Laid an Egg*

Czech Republic

Michal Ajvaz. *The Golden Age.*
Translated by Andrew Oakland. Champaign, IL: Dalkey Archive Press, 2010. 329 pages.
Genres/literary styles/story types: speculative fiction; postmodernism
In the tradition of Jonathan Swift's *Gulliver's Travels*, this book is the story of a modern traveler who writes about the world he found on a small Atlantic island. It was a strange world, to be sure, consisting of people who were content to placidly watch events unfold around them, not differentiating between what actually was or is and what only appears to be. Even stranger still, their central activity is the development and creation of something called the Book, where everyone can write what he or she pleases, correcting others, making references to this or that, footnoting, and linking. This same concern for the fantastic is evident in Ajvaz's *The Other City*, an extraordinary journey through a mysterious Prague that lies just below the surface of the real one.
Subject keywords: philosophy
Original language: Czech

Source consulted for annotation:
Dalkey Archive Press website (book descriptions), http://www.dalkeyarchive.com.
Another translated book written by Michal Ajvaz: *The Other City*

Emil Hakl. ***Of Kids and Parents.***
Translated by Marek Tomin. Prague, Czech Republic: Twisted Spoon Press, 2008. 154 pages.
Genre/literary style/story type: mainstream fiction
When an eldery man, a former scientist, takes a meandering walk with his middle-aged son, a writer, through Prague streets, they talk about everything and nothing: urban legends; World War II; the Prague Spring of 1968; the Croatian Ustasi; transience and the inevitability of change and death. When father and son part company, it may be for the last time; their quiet and melancholy ramble may have been the last act in a turbulent historical drama. Ray Olson in *Booklist* called this novel "a small, *Waiting for Godot*-ish gem."
Subject keyword: family histories
Original language: Czech
Sources consulted for annotation:
Global Books in Print (online) (review from *Booklist*).
Tonkin, Boyd. *The Independent*, 27 June 2008 (online).

Bohumil Hrabal. ***Too Loud a Solitude.***
Translated by Michael Henry Heim. San Diego, CA: Harcourt Brace Jovanovich, 1990. 98 pages.
Genre/literary style/story type: mainstream fiction
Hanta has been a paper compactor for 35 long years. In a dank and depressing Prague basement, his job consists of destroying books considered subversive by the communist regime. Hanta tries to save as many books as he can by taking them home, where they become his sole source of joy and companionship. But he soon discovers that his job is threatened: A new compacting machine is about to be introduced. Critics have invoked T. S. Eliot's J. Alfred Prufrock and James Thurber's Walter Mitty when discussing this novel.
Related titles by the same author:
Readers may also enjoy *Dancing Lessons for the Advanced in Age*, in which an eldery man, a shoemaker by trade, launches into a prolonged excursus—one long sentence—about history, ethics, and culture. Also of interest may be *I Served the King of England*, a political satire about the successes and failures of a Czech waiter; it was made into a much-loved film.
Subject keywords: identity; social problems
Original language: Czech
Sources consulted for annotation:
Amazon.com (book description).
Bednar, Marie. *Library Journal* 115 (15 September 1990): 100.
Berens, Emily. *The Spectator* 266 (6 April 1991): 34.
Global Books in Print (online) (review from *Booklist* for *Dancing Lessons*; review from *Publishers Weekly* for *I Served the King of England*).
Nathanson, Donald L. *The American Journal of Psychiatry* 153 (December 1996): 1640.
Rogers, Michael. *Library Journal* 117 (15 March 1992): 131.
Some other translated books written by Bohumil Hrabal: *I Served the King of England*; *Dancing Lessons for the Advanced in Age*; *The Little Town Where Time Stood Still*; *The Death of Mr. Baltisberger*; *Closely Watched Trains*; *Total Fears: Letters to Dubenka*

Ivan Klíma. ***The Ultimate Intimacy.***
Translated by A. G. Brain. New York: Grove Press, 1997. 387 pages.

Genre/literary style/story type: mainstream fiction

Daniel Vedra is all that one could ask for in a pastor, but he is emotionally distant from his second wife, Hana, because of the love that he still bears for his first wife, Jitka, who died of cancer. Thus, it is almost inevitable that he begins an affair with a congregant who reminds him of his first wife. The author uses journal entries and letters to narrate this story of personal and spiritual searching.

Subject keyword: family histories

Original language: Czech

Sources consulted for annotation:

Amazon.com (reviews from *Kirkus Reviews* and other editorial reviews).

Kloszewski, Marc A. *Library Journal* 122 (1 November 1997): 116.

O'Laughlin, Jim. *Booklist* 94 (1 January/15 January 1998): 777.

Some other translated books written by Ivan Klíma: *Judge on Trial*; *Waiting for the Dark, Waiting for the Light*; *Lovers for a Day*; *Love and Garbage*; *My Merry Mornings: Stories from Prague*; *No Saints or Angels*; *My First Loves*; *A Summer Affair*; *My Golden Trades*

Alexandr Kliment. *Living Parallel.*

Translated by Robert Wechsler. North Haven, CT: Catbird Press, 2001. 238 pages.

Genre/literary style/story type: mainstream fiction

Mikulaš Svoboda, a middle-aged architect, has spent his entire career building shoddy and bland apartment buildings in Prague. His personal and professional dreams are unfulfilled, so he retreats to a self-created world of beauty that provides a modicum of comfort in his humdrum life. But in 1967, just before the short-lived Prague Spring of 1968, his ordered life receives a jolt when a former lover and painter, now a widow, plans to move to Paris and suggests that he join her.

Subject keywords: identity; social roles

Original language: Czech

Sources consulted for annotation:

Amazon.com (book description).

Engberg, Gillian. *Booklist* 98 (15 February 2002): 992.

Kempf, Andrea Caron. *Library Journal* 126 (15 November 2001): 97.

Schubert, Peter Z. *World Literature Today* 77 (October/December 2003): 136.

Zaleski, Jeff. *Publishers Weekly* 249 (4 February 2002): 54.

Pavel Kohout. *I Am Snowing: The Confessions of a Woman of Prague.*

Translated by Neil Bermel. New York: Farrar, Straus and Giroux, 1994. 308 pages.

Genres/literary styles/story types: thrillers; political thrillers

In 1991, Petra Marova is ecstatic when she learns that Victor Kral, a former lover, is back in Prague and working for the government after the overthrow of communist rule. But Victor is soon accused of having been a communist collaborator. Victor's wife begs Petra to help clear her husband's name, so Petra must begin a convoluted journey into the past to uncover the truth about Victor.

Subject keyword: politics

Original language: Czech

Sources consulted for annotation:

Iggers, Wilma A. *World Literature Today* 68 (Autumn 1994): 849.

Otten, Anna. *The Antioch Review* 53 (Spring 1995): 241.

Ross, Ruth M. *Library Journal* 119 (January 1994): 162.

Taylor, Gilbert. *Booklist* 90 (1 February 1994): 994.

Some other translated books written by Pavel Kohout: *From the Diary of a Counterrevolutionary*; *The Widow Killer*; *White Book*; *The Hangwoman*

Milan Kundera. ***Ignorance.***
Translated by Linda Asher. New York: HarperCollins, 2002. 195 pages.
Genre/literary style/story type: mainstream fiction
In 1989, at the Paris airport, Irena accidently meets Josef. Both are on their way back to the Czech Republic after an absence of some 20 years; they arrange to have a more formal meeting in Prague once they return. They hope that with the fall of communism, everything will have changed for the better, but they soon discover that things are not so black and white. They also discover that some things have not changed at all. About 20 years ago, Josef and Irena almost had an affair—a touchstone for Irena but an incident that Josef has no recollection of, although he claims that he does.
Related title by the same author:
Readers may also enjoy *Slowness*, which, as Michiko Kakutani writes, is not only about "the failure of our speed-obsessed age to appreciate the delights of slowness (in lovemaking, in travel, in the rituals of daily life)" but also about "the means by which the facts of real life are turned into fiction, the means by which people sell one version of themselves to the world, to friends, to lovers and to political rivals."
Subject keyword: social roles
Original language: Czech
Sources consulted for annotation:
Amazon.com (all editorial reviews).
Engberg, Gillian. *Booklist* 99 (1 September 2002): 57.
Kakutani, Michiko. *The New York Times*, 14 May 1996 (online).
Tinney, Christopher. *Library Journal* 127 (15 October 2002): 94.
Zaleski, Jeff. *Publishers Weekly* 249 (26 August 2002): 38.
Some other translated books written by Milan Kundera: *Immortality*; *The Art of the Novel*; *Slowness*; *Identity*; *The Joke*; *The Unbearable Lightness of Being*; *Farewell Waltz*; *Laughable Loves*; *The Farewell Party*; *Life Is Elsewhere*

Vladimír Páral. ***Lovers & Murderers.***
Translated by Craig Cravens. North Haven, CT: Catbird Press, 2001. 409 pages.
Genre/literary style/story type: mainstream fiction
If you want to know about the absurdities and bleakness of life in communist Czechoslovakia in the 1960s, this satire is for you. In the dilapidated housing complex of a chemical factory, employees are thrust into a Darwinian world of bitter competition, endless struggle, and raw displays of power; the winners get the apartments that actually have hot water. It is a mean-spirited and soul-sapping world, where every action and sentence has an ulterior motive and where untold amounts of intellectual and physical energy are devoted to petty schemings to best one's rivals.
Subject keywords: power; social roles
Original language: Czech
Sources consulted for annotation:
Amazon.com (book description).
Kempf, Andrea Caron. *Library Journal* 127 (1 February 2002): 132.
Zaleski, Jeff. *Publishers Weekly* 249 (28 January 2002): 272.
Some other translated books written by Vladimír Páral: *Catapult*; *The Four Sonyas*

Josef Skvorecký. ***The Bride of Texas.***
Translated by Káca Poláckova Henley. New York: Alfred A. Knopf, 1996. 436 pages.
Genre/literary style/story type: historical fiction
During the U.S. Civil War, a small group of Czech soldiers fought for the Union. Skvorecký imaginatively retells this little-known episode by bringing together an assortment of diverse characters,

including Jan Kapsa, who murdered an army officer during the short-lived 1848 Czech revolution, fled Prague, and served under General William Tecumseh Sherman, a controversial figure well-known for his scorched-earth march through the southern states; Lida Toupelik, a Moravian woman who immigrates to Texas and marries the debauched son of a plantation owner; and her brother Cyril, who has an affair with a slave.

Subject keywords: family histories; war

Original language: Czech

Sources consulted for annotation:

Amazon.com (book description; review from *Midwest Book Review*).

Czerwinski, Edward J. *World Literature Today* 70 (Autumn 1996): 988.

Falbo, Sister M. Anna. *Library Journal* 121 (1 February 1996): 100.

Publishers Weekly 243 (22 April 1996): 56.

Seaman, Donna. *Booklist* 92 (15 December 1995): 668.

Some other translated books written by Josef Skvorecký: *The Miracle Game*; *Dvorak in Love: A Light-Hearted Dream*; *The Republic of Whores: A Fragment from the Time of the Cults*; *When Eve Was Naked: Stories of a Life's Journey*; *Two Murders in My Double Life*; *The Engineer of Human Souls*; *The Bass Saxophone: Two Novellas*; *The Mournful Demeanour of Lieutenant Boruvka*

Jáchym Topol. *City, Sister, Silver.*

Translated by Alex Zucker. North Haven, CT: Catbird Press, 2000. 508 pages.

Genre/literary style/story type: mainstream fiction

After the so-called Velvet Revolution of 1989, profound changes occurred in the Czech Republic. It was a tumultuous era, filled with euphoric turmoil and uncertainty. Potok, ostensibly an actor, survives on the margins of the law—a small-time criminal involved in real estate chicanery and other swindles. When his girlfriend, She-Dog, disappears, he is accused of her murder. At the same time, he meets She-Dog's doppelganger, takes up residence at a garbage dump, and tries to avoid a crazed killer. According to *Publishers Weekly*, the author's Dantesque vision attains "a level of horrific lyricism reminiscent of the ravings of a minor, denunciatory Old Testament prophet."

Subject keyword: social problems

Original language: Czech

Sources consulted for annotation:

Bermel, Neil. *The New York Times Book Review*, 4 March 2001, p. 24.Crossley, James. *Review of Contemporary Fiction* 20 (Fall 2000): 142.

Schubert, Peter Z. *World Literature Today* 74 (Summer 2000): 670.

Steinberg, Sybil S. *Publishers Weekly* 247 (28 February 2000): 59.

Another translated book written by Jáchym Topol: *A Trip to the Train Station*

Hungary

Ferenc Barnás. *The Ninth.*

Translated by Paul Olchváry. Evanston, IL: Northwestern University Press, 2009. 159 pages.

Genres/literary styles/story types: mainstream fiction; coming-of-age

In a poverty-stricken town deep in the northern hinterlands of Hungary in the 1960s, the ninth child of a deeply religious Catholic family observes and comments on the life around him. He is both guileless and naïve; he knows nothing of larger social and political currents; he simply watches, makes no judgements about what he sees, and reports his impressions and thoughts. As his parents struggle to make ends meets and put food on the table; as his brothers and sisters endure harsh labor in various factories; as his father peddles religious memorabilia; as he develops a unique view of death, he is the shrewdest and most honest of commentators—an enigmatic witness to monochromatic survival.

Subject keywords: family histories; rural life
Original language: Hungarian
Source consulted for annotation:
Waxman, Jeff. Three Percent website (book review), http://www.rochester.edu/College/translation/threepercent.

Attila Bartis. *Tranquility.*
Translated by Imre Goldstein. Brooklyn, NY: Archipelago Books, 2008. 325 pages.
Genre/literary style/story type: mainstream fiction
The writer Andor Weér lives with his mother, a former actress who has an exaggerated sense of her own importance. She is not exactly anyone's idea of a good mother, betraying her daughter for political favors. As Andor recounts the wretechedness of his life, he begins to discover what really happened to his father and sister as well as why his girlfriend keeps having nervous breakdowns. As Jeff Waxman observes, this is a novel in which "nothing is sacrosanct: not religion, not government, not life, love, or motherhood."
Subject keywords: family histories; identity
Original language: Hungarian
Sources consulted for annotation:
McCulloch, Alison. *The New York Times Book Review*, 16 November 2008 (online).
Waxman, Jeff. Three Percent website (book review), http://www.rochester.edu/College/translation/threepercent.

György Dalos. *The Circumcision.*
Translated by Judith Sollosy. London: Marion Boyars, 2006. 140 pages.
Genres/literary styles/story types: mainstream fiction; coming-of-age
Robi Singer's life is far from perfect. His family is one step away from sliding out of the middle class; his mother has a variety of psychological ailments; and his father is long dead. His grandmother is the financial mainstay of the family. Robi is one of only two boys in his class who is as yet uncircumcised. Naturally, he begins to reflect on the possibility of a botched circumcision, which will detrimentally affect not only his physique but also his chances of marriage.
Subject keyword: family histories
Original language: Hungarian
Sources consulted for annotation:
Amazon.com (about the author; book description).
Danny Yee's Book Reviews (book review), http://dannyreviews.com.
Another translated book written by György Dalos: *1985: What Happens After Big Brother Dies*

György Dragoman. *The White King.*
Translated by Paul Olchváry. Boston: Houghton Mifflin, 2008. 263 pages.
Genres/literary styles/story types: mainstream fiction; coming-of-age
In a country that resembles Romania, 11-year-old Djata has been dealt a bad hand. His father's political activism has meant the ruin of the family: Everyone is either imprisoned or out of work. Djata's career prospects are next to nonexistent—the usual educational avenues closed as a result of his father's principled stands. Thus, Djata must learn—in the words of Danielle Trussoni—to "fend for himself, like a cold war Huck Finn tramping through concrete apartment blocks and facing down bullies."
Subject keywords: family histories; urban life
Original language: Hungarian

Sources consulted for annotation:
Global Books in Print (online) (reviews from *Booklist*, *Library Journal*, and *Publishers Weekly*).
Trussoni, Danielle. *The New York Times Book Review*, 29 June 2008 (online).

Péter Esterházy. *Celestial Harmonies*.
Translated by Judith Sollosy. New York: Ecco, 2004. 846 pages.
Genres/literary styles/story types: historical fiction; literary historical
This epic novel, which spans some seven centuries, is about Esterházy's own family members, who were influential pillars of the Hungarian aristocracy. In their glory years, among numerous other accomplishments, they were Haydn's main financial patrons, but they faced countless struggles after the imposition of communism in 1945.
Related titles by the same author:
Readers may also enjoy *The Book of Hrabal*. Anna is a Hungarian mother of three who finds herself pregnant again. As she considers abortion, she reflects on her family and Hungarian history. *Not Art* is perhaps Esterházy's most accessible novel: a eloquent meditation on how soccer was the saving grace for the narrator's mother through the darkest years of twentieth-century Hungarian history.
Subject keyword: family histories
Original language: Hungarian
Sources consulted for annotation:
Amazon.com (book description).
Bermel, Neil. *The New York Times Book Review*, 30 May 2004, p. 13.
Bernstein, Michael Andre. *The New Republic*, 12 April/19 April 2004, p. 42.
Drabelle, Dennis. *The Washington Post*, 11 April 2004, p. T7.
Global Books in Print (online) (review from *Library Journal* for *The Book of Hrabal*).
McCullough, Alison. *The New York Times Book Review*, 16 May 2010 (online).
The New Yorker 80 (10 May 2004): 103.
Zaleski, Jeff. *Publishers Weekly* 251 (2 February 2004): 58.
Some other translated books written by Péter Esterházy: *She Loves Me*; *Helping Verbs of the Heart*; *The Book of Hrabal*; *A Little Hungarian Pornography*; *The Glance of Countess Hahn-Hahn: Down the Danube*; *Not Art*

Ferenc Karinthy. *Metropole*.
Translated by George Szirtes. London: Telegram Books, 2008. 179 pages.
Genre/literary style/story type: mainstream fiction
On his way to a linguistic conference in Finland, Budai finds himself totally flummoxed. He has mysteriously landed in a city where the inhabitants speak the strangest of languages. Simply put, he cannot understand a single word. Isolated and adrift in a world he literally cannot understand, Budai begins to feel like a prisoner. The book has been compared with Franz Kafka's *The Trial* and *Amerika*.
Subject keywords: identity; social roles
Original language: Hungarian
Sources consulted for annotation:
Global Books in Print (online) (reviews from *Booklist*, *Library Journal*, and *Publishers Weekly*).
Derbyshire, Jonathan. *New Humanist* (May/June 2008) (online).
Telegram Books (book description), http://www.telegrambooks.com.

Imre Kertész. *Liquidation*.
Translated by Tim Wilkinson. New York: Alfred A. Knopf, 2004. 129 pages.
Genre/literary style/story type: mainstream fiction

A man referred to only as B. committed suicide 10 years ago, leaving a manuscript of a play whose events and dialogue uncannily anticipate what actually happened in the years after his self-induced drug overdose. In the chaotic postcommunist era, his friend—an editor for a Hungarian publisher—must decide what to do with this strange manuscript, which shows the lingering effects of the Holocaust on the psyche long after the end of World War II.
Related titles by the same author:
Readers may also wish to explore *Fatelessness*, which centers on the perceptions of a child deported to the horrors of Auschwitz and Buchenwald. In *Detective Story*, an imprisoned member of the secret police in a South American country recalls his role in the murders of two wealthy individuals. Also noteworthy is *The Pathseeker*, where a government commissioner is sent to inspect a factory site but finds that it is an empty plot of land returning to nature.
Subject keywords: anti-Semitism; writers
Original language: Hungarian
Sources consulted for annotation:
Amazon.com (book description).
Bukiet, Melvin Jules. *The Washington Post* (14 November 2004): p. T7.
Eder, Richard. *Los Angeles Times*, 24 October 2004, p. R4.
Franklin, Ruth. *The New York Times Book Review*, 19 December 2004, p. 24.
Global Books in Print (online) (review from *Publishers Weekly* for *The Pathseeker*).
"Imre Kertész." *Contemporary Authors Online*. Thomson Gale, 2007.
Olson, Ray. *Booklist* 101 (15 October 2004): 389.
Rich, Nathaniel. *The New York Times Book Review*, 17 February 2008 (online).
Some other translated books written by Imre Kertész: *Fatelessness*; *Kaddish for a Child Not Born*; *Detective Story*; *Pathseeker*

György Konrád. *Stonedial.*
Translated by Ivan Sanders. New York: Harcourt, 2000. 290 pages.
Genre/literary style/story type: mainstream fiction
In the fictitious Hungarian city of Kandor after the fall of communism, the famous writer Janos Dragomán returns home to visit friends: the university rector; the mayor; and a media commentator. As he makes the rounds of his old haunts, he is beset by memories, including his role in the 1956 Hungarian revolution where his actions led to the inadvertent deaths of six individuals.
Subject keywords: identity; writers
Original language: Hungarian
Sources consulted for annotation:
Amazon.com (book description; review from *Kirkus Reviews*).
Bernstein, Richard. *The New York Times*, 7 June 2000, p. E8.
Lourie, Richard. *The New York Times Book Review*, 2 July 2000, p. 19.
Steinberg, Sybil S. *Publishers Weekly* 247 (20 March 2000): 70.
Some other translated books written by György Konrád: *The Case Worker*; *The Loser*; *The City Builder*; *A Feast in the Garden*

László Krasznahorkai. *The Melancholy of Resistance.*
Translated by George Szirtes. New York: New Directions, 2000. 314 pages.
Genre/literary style/story type: mainstream fiction
Written in the style of Nikolai Gogol's *Dead Souls*, this surreal book recounts the events in a small Hungarian town when a mysterious circus arrives. And while everyone marvels at the behemoth-sized

stuffed whale on display, the true oddity in the circus is a malevolent being called Prince, whose existence terrorizes even the circus director. Mayhem quickly ensues, and just as quickly, people gravitate to anyone or anything promising a modicum of order and stability.
Subject keywords: politics; social problems
Original language: Hungarian
Sources consulted for annotation:
Amazon.com (book description).
Pinker, Michael. *Review of Contemporary Fiction* 21 (Spring 2001): 188.
Wilkinson, John W. *World Literature Today* 76 (Winter 2002): 168.
Another translated book written by László Krasznahorkai: *War and War*

Péter Lengyel. *Cobblestone: A Detective Novel.*
Translated by John Bátki. Columbia, LA: Readers International, 1993. 526 pages.
Genres/literary styles/story types: crime fiction; historical mysteries
This book is ostensibly about the immaculately planned and executed theft of a diamond destined for royalty. But it is really a detailed examination of criminal behavior, as seen through the eyes of the gang responsible for the theft and the man tasked with catching them. The novel also offers insight into the late eighteenth- and early nineteeth-century history of Transylvania, specifically Romanian oppression of the Hungarian minority.
Subject keyword: politics
Original language: Hungarian
Source consulted for annotation:
Green, Maria. *World Literature Today* 68 (Winter 1994): 175.

Sándor Márai. *Casanova in Bolzano* (or ***Conversations in Bolzano*).**
Translated by George Szirtes. New York: Alfred A. Knopf, 2004. 294 pages.
Genre/literary style/story type: mainstream fiction
In late 1756, Casanova breaks out of a Venetian jail and seeks refuge at a Bolzano inn. Living close by is the Duke of Parma, who triumphed over Casanova in a duel and therefore won the hand of Fransesca. But Fransesca still pines for Casanova. The duke offers not to turn Casanova over to the authorities if he seduces and then leaves Francesca, thus forever curing her of her love for Casanova. Critics have compared Márai to Gabriel García Márquez.
Related titles by the same author:
Readers may also enjoy *The Rebels*, which follows the tragic adventures of four young men from the Austro-Hungarian empire during World War I. Also of interest may be *Embers*, in which two old military friends who have not seen each other for some 40 years finally meet and reflect on the events that drove them apart. Also noteworthy may be *Esther's Inheritance*, which focuses on Esther, whose love for Lajos—the husband of her late sister—becomes a nightmare when he convinces her to give him the deed to her house.
Subject keywords: identity; power
Original language: Hungarian
Sources consulted for annotation:
Amazon.com (book description).
Craig Nova. *The Washington Post*, 7 November 2004, p. T7.
Davies, Stevie. *The Independent on Sunday*, 14 November 2004, p. 32.
Driscoll, Brendan. *Booklist* 101 (1 November 2004): 464.
Eder, Richard. *The New York Times*, 21 December 2004, p. E10.
Fischer, Tibor. *The New York Times Book Review*, 29 April 2007 (online).

Global Books in Print (online) (reviews from *Booklist*, *Library Journal*, and *Publishers Weekly* for *Embers* and *Esther's Inheritance*).
The Washington Post, 12 September 2004, p. T8.
Some other translated books written by Sándor Márai: *Casanova in Bolzano*; *Embers*; *The Rebels*; *Esther's Inheritance*

Péter Nádas. *A Book of Memories*.
Translated by Ivan Sanders with Imre Goldstein (Imri Goldshtain). New York: Farrar, Straus and Giroux, 1997. 705 pages.
Genres/literary styles/story types: mainstream fiction; postmodernism
A writer considers all aspects of the act of writing in this multilayered work of autobiographical fiction. Interweaving social and political history and personal reminiscences, Nádas creates a series of narrators who think and care deeply about the survival of the novelistic form. The *Seattle Times* reviewer said that this novel "will endure as a great moral expression of the European crucible of public and private souls, genuinely worthy of Proust, Henry James, Musil, and Mann as an authoritative testimony to the intellectual and emotional lives of an epoch." Susan Sontag referred to it as "[t]he greatest novel written in our time, and one of the great books of the century."
Subject keywords: philosophy; writers
Original language: Hungarian
Sources consulted for annotation:
Amazon.com (reviews from *Kirkus Reviews* and *Seattle Times*).
Falbo, Sister M. Anna. *Library Journal* 122 (15 April 1997): 118.
Gyorgyey, Clara. *World Literature Today* 71 (Autumn 1997): 838.
Macmillan website (book description and reviews), http://www.macmillan.com.
Steinberg, Sybil S. *Publishers Weekly* 244 (21 April 1997): 59.
Some other translated books written by Péter Nádas: *Love*; *The End of a Family Story*; *A Lovely Tale of Photography: A Film Novella*

Miklós Vámos. *The Book of Fathers*.
Translated by Peter Sherwood. New York: Other Press, 2009. 474 pages.
Genres/literary styles/story types: historical fiction; magical realism
This novel is a rich and multihued tapestry about the past 300 years of Hungarian social and political history, as told through the eyes of 12 generations of the Csillag family. Some of the male members of the clan have the power to view the past and the future, with the result that the book has been compared to Márquez's *One Hundred Years of Solitude*. Jane Smiley praised Vámos for his "virtuoso portraits of his idiosyncratic characters" and the "evocative portrayal of the world they live in and the history they live through."
Subject keyword: family histories
Original language: Hungarian
Sources consulted for annotation:
Books Briefly Noted. *The New Yorker* (7 December 2009) (online).
Smiley, Jane. *The New York Times Book Review*, 25 October 2009 (online).

Péter Zilahy. *The Last Window-Giraffe*.
Translated by Tim Wilkinson. Derry, NH: Anthem Press, 2008. 130 pages.
Genres/literary styles/story types: mainstream fiction; postmodernism
According to the publisher's website, this novel, which includes photographs and was "inspired by a Hungarian children's dictionary entitled *Window–Giraffe*, which explained the whole world in

simple terms," is "a playful and personal journey through the political unrest" of the 1970s and 1980s in Eastern Europe.
Subject keywords: politics; power
Original language: Hungarian
Sources consulted for annotation:
Anthem Press (book description), http://www.anthempress.com.

Macedonia

Meto Jovanovski. ***Faceless Men and Other Macedonian Stories.***
Translated by Jeffrey Folks, Milne Holton, and Charles Simic. London: Forest Books, 1992. 77 pages.
Genres/literary styles/story types: mainstream fiction; short stories
These 10 stories describes the impact of social and cultural change on the everyday life of common people in Braychino, a small village in Macedonia. In one of the stories, a man casts off his aversion to killing when so requested by new political rulers. Another story examines the nature of authority when an asylum escapee in a blue suit restores order in a bus queue. In a third story, an elderly woman traveling by plane for the first time is taken aback by such modern conveniences as indoor toilets.
Subject keyword: rural life
Original language: Macedonian
Sources consulted for annotation:
Kaganoff, Penny. *Publishers Weekly* 240 (22 February 1993): 87.
Mitrevski, George. *Slavic and East European Journal* 38 (Winter 1994): 715–716.
Another translated book written by Meto Jovanovski: *Cousin*

Goce Smilevski. ***Conversation with Spinoza: A Cobweb Novel.***
Translated by Filip Korenski. Evanston, IL: Northwestern University Press, 2006. 136 pages.
Genre/literary style/story type: mainstream fiction
This novel explores the life of the seventeenth-century philosopher Baruch Spinoza through such important events as the death of his mother; his relationships with his teachers and disciples; his participation in the Jewish community of Amsterdam; his excommunication from that community; and his controversial philosophical and ethical ideas. Critics have seen resemblances to the work of Günter Grass and José Saramago in Smilevski's fiction.
Subject keywords: philosophy; religion
Original language: Macedonian
Sources consulted for annotation:
Northwestern University Press (book description), http://nupress.northwestern.edu.
Publishers Weekly 253 (27 March 2006): 58.

Montenegro

Danilo Kiš. ***Hourglass.***
Translated by Ralph Manheim. New York: Farrar, Straus and Giroux, 1990. 274 pages.
Genre/literary style/story type: mainstream fiction
This novel, which is the final volume in a trilogy that also consists of *Early Sorrows* and *Garden Ashes*, is an imaginatively autobiographical rendering of Kiš's father's life and death at Auschwitz. In *Hourglass*, E. S. is a former railway clerk still overwhelmed by daily concerns: property ownership, squabbles over pensions, disputes with his siblings. As he frets and despairs about such matters, the dark shadow of anti-Semitism and the Holocaust hangs over everything.

Related title by the same author:
Readers may also wish to explore *The Encyclopedia of the Dead*, a collection of stories and philosophical asides that are supposedly contained in an encyclopedia being prepared by a religious sect in anticipation of the apocalypse.
Subject keyword: anti-Semitism
Original language: Serbo-Croatian
Sources consulted for annotation:
Balitas, Vincent D. *Library Journal* 115 (July 1990): 131.
Global Books in Print (online) (review from *Publishers Weekly* for *The Encyclopedia of the Dead*).
Halpern, Daniel Noah. *National Post*, 7 November 1998, P 10.
Newman, Charles. *The New York Times Book Review*, 7 October 1990 (online).
Pearl, Nancy. *Library Journal* 128 (1 March 2003): 144.
Steinberg, Sybil S. *Publishers Weekly* 237 (8 June 1990): 47.
Some other translated books written by Danilo Kiš: *The Encyclopedia of the Dead*; *A Tomb for Boris Davidovich*; *Early Sorrows*; *Garden Ashes*; *Mansarda*

Borislav Pekić. *How to Quiet a Vampire.*
Translated by Stephen M. Dickey and Bogdan Rakić. Evanston, IL: Northwestern University Press, 2005. 410 pages.
Genre/literary style/story type: mainstream fiction
According to David Binder, this book "somberly explores and dissects the minds of the midlevel practitioners of a totalitarian system." In this case, it is Konrad Rutkowski, a former Gestapo officer who is now a professor of medieval history at a German university. He has just returned from a vacation to a small Dalmatian town, where he was stationed during the war. It is trip that dredged up the most horrific of memories and causes him to write 26 confessions about his abysmal wartime actions; it also psychologically unhinges him, deluding him into thinking that vampire-like beings are constantly pursuing him.
Subject keywords: anti-Semitism; identity
Original language: Serbian
Sources consulted for annotation:
Amazon.com (book description).
Binder, David. *The New York Times*, 21 January 2004, p. 3.
Pinker, Michael. *Review of Contemporary Fiction* 24 (Fall 2004): 135.
Some other translated books written by Borislav Pekić: *The Houses of Belgrade*; *The Time of Miracles: A Legend*

Poland

Janusz Anderman. *The Edge of the World.*
Translated by Nina Taylor. Columbia, LA: Readers International, 1988. 100 pages.
Genre/literary style/story type: mainstream fiction
On a foggy day in contemporary Warsaw in an area that was known as the Jewish Ghetto during the German-occupation of Poland, a group of citizens waits for a bus. As they strike up a series of conversations about such topics as immigration and politics, a scathing and often hilarious portrait of modern Polish life emerges.
Subject keywords: politics; social problems
Original language: Polish
Source consulted for annotation:
Kaganoff, Penny. *Publishers Weekly* 234 (9 September 1988): 125.
Another translated book written by Janusz Anderman: *Poland Under Black Light*

Marek Bienczyk. *Tworki.*
Translated by Benjamin Paloff. Evanston, IL: Northwestern University Press, 2008. 179 pages.
Genre/literary style/story type: mainstream fiction
On the outskirts of Warsaw, in the psychiatric hospital in Tworki, staff members go about their business in the midst of World War II, enjoying picnics and dancing in the institution's gardens during their off hours. But as the harsh realities of the war creep ever closer to the walls of their refuge, their lives and routines are forever changed.
Subject keyword: war
Original language: Polish
Sources consulted for annotation:
Amazon.com (book description).
Northwestern University Press (book description), http://nupress.northwestern.edu.

Kazimierz Brandys. *Rondo.*
Translated by Jaroslaw Anders. New York: Farrar, Straus and Giroux, 1989. 265 pages.
Genre/literary style/story type: mainstream fiction
In the late 1930s and early 1940s, Tom is madly in love with Tola, whose acting career has been short-circuited by World War II. He creates a fictive resistance group called Rondo so Tola can feel passionately involved in something. But Tom's creation takes on a life of its own, and when he is forced to tell Tola the truth, she is psychologically shattered.
Subject keywords: politics; power
Original language: Polish
Sources consulted for annotation:
Baranczak, Stanislaw. *The New Republic* 201 (9 October 1989): 37.
Steinberg, Sybil S. *Publishers Weekly* 236 (18 August 1989): 49.
Urbanska, Wanda. *Los Angeles Times*, 8 October 1989, p. BR2.
Waldhorn, Arthur. *Library Journal* 114 (15 September 1989): 134.
Some other translated books written by Kazimierz Brandys: *A Question of Reality*; *Sons and Comrades*; *A Novel of Modern Poland*; *Letters to Mrs. Z*

Stefan Chwin. *Death in Danzig.*
Translated by Philip Boehm. Orlando, FL: Harcourt, 2004. 260 pages.
Genres/literary styles/story types: historical fiction; literary historical
The time is 1945 during World War II. The place is the German city of Danzig, which would later become the Polish city of Gdansk. As Russian forces advance into the city, much of the German citizenry departs while Polish citizens enter in search of refuge. The transformation of Danzig into Gdansk is told through the experiences of a German professor who chooses to remain and a Polish family who finds shelter in an empty apartment in the professor's building.
Subject keywords: family histories; war
Original language: Polish
Sources consulted for annotation:
Amazon.com (book description).
Boehm, Philip. *The Independent*, 11 March 2005, p. 23.
Mundow, Anna. *The Boston Globe*, 5 December 2004, p. D6.
Rungren, Lawrence. *Library Journal* 129 (August 2004): 64.
Spinella, Michael. *Booklist* 101 (15 September 2004): 206.
Zaleski, Jeff. *Publishers Weekly* 251 (25 October 2004): 28.

Ida Fink. *The Journey.*
Translated by Joanna Weschler and Francine Prose. New York: Farrar, Straus and Giroux, 1992. 249 pages.
Genres/literary styles/story types: mainstream fiction; women's lives
This book is a chilling drama of the Holocaust. Two Jewish sisters posing as Christians try to flee to safety across Germany and Poland. After escaping from a prison camp, they continue their journey, searching for any type of work that will allow them to survive, relying on their disguises as peasants, and hoping against hope that their shoddy documents will ultimately prove convincing. As Molly Abramowitz wrote, the book provides "extraordinary insights into the lives of people in hiding: how they distinguish friends from enemies, maintain their identities, and survive in a world gone mad."
Subject keywords: anti-Semitism; war
Original language: Polish
Sources consulted for annotation:
Abramowitz, Molly. *Library Journal* 117 (July 1992): 121.
Amazon.com (review from *Kirkus Reviews*).
Angier, Carole. *New Statesman & Society* 6 (15 January 1993): 40.
Merkin, Daphne. *Los Angeles Times*, 27 September 1992, p. 2.
Steinberg, Sybil S. *Publishers Weekly* 239 (1 June 1992): 50.
Some other translated books written by Ida Fink: *A Scrap of Time and Other Stories*; *Traces*

Pawel Huelle. *Who Was David Weiser?*
Translated by Michael Kandel. New York: Harcourt Brace Jovanovich, 1992. 304 pages.
Genres/literary styles/story types: mainstream fiction; coming-of-age
In the 1950s, three boys named Piotr, Szymek, and Heller are interrogated by school authorities. They wish to find out about the sudden disappearance of two of the boys' friends, especially David Weiser, who is Jewish. The novel recounts the summer activities of the five companions, when David mesmerized everyone with what appeared to be powers of hypnotism and levitation. He also led them to a secret cache of weaponry. But eventually, David and his companion Elka disappear, leaving Heller perplexed about their fate.
Related titles by the same author:
Readers may also enjoy *Castorp*, a titular reference to Hans Castorp, who is the central figure of Thomas Mann's *The Magic Mountain*. Huelle imaginatively recounts Castorp's student days in Gdansk, conjuring up a plausible scenario about the place of Polish culture in Castorp's life. Also of interest may be *The Last Supper*, where an artist convenes 12 men to participate in a contemporary reenactment of Christ's last meal with his disciples. *Mercedes-Benz* follows the narrator's multiple adventures in taking driving lessons at the wheel of a very pedestrian Fiat—a story made all the more resonant because the glue that held his family together was its love of classic cars, such as the Mercedes-Benz.
Subject keywords: anti-Semitism; power
Original language: Polish
Sources consulted for annotation:
Frick, Thomas. *Los Angeles Times*, 26 April 1992, p. 9.
Mehegan, David. *Boston Globe*, 23 February 1992, p. B43.
Opello, Olivia. *Library Journal* 117 (January 1992): 174.
Publishers Weekly 241 (19 September 1994): 66.
Serpent's Tail website (book description), http://www.serpentstail.com.
Some other translated books written by Pawel Huelle: *Moving House*; *Mercedes-Benz: From Letters to Hrabal*; *Castorp*; *The Last Supper*

Tadeusz Konwicki. *Bohin Manor.*
Translated by Richard Lourie. New York: Farrar, Straus and Giroux, 1990. 240 pages.
Genres/literary styles/story types: mainstream fiction; women's lives
Helena must choose between her fiancé, a pompous local aristocrat, and a dynamic Jewish activist. In late nineteenth-century Lithuania, ethnic and racial prejudices run strong, so Helena must fight against her upbringing as she makes her fateful choice. Looming over her personal and family dilemmas is the impending violence and totalitarianism of the twentieth century, foreshadowed by authoritarian police chiefs and ravenous monsters.
Subject keywords: anti-Semitism; politics
Original language: Polish
Sources consulted for annotation:
Beres, Stanislaw. *Review of Contemporary Fiction* 14 (Fall 1994): 189.
Coates, Joseph. *Chicago Tribune*, 29 July 1990, p. 7.
The Economist 324 (18 July 1992): 92.
Hutchison, Paul E. *Library Journal* 115 (15 June 1990): 134.
Steinberg, Sybil S. *Publishers Weekly* 237 (18 May 1990): 69.
Urbanska, Wanda. *Los Angeles Times*, 12 August 1990, p. 3.
Some other translated books written by Tadeusz Konwicki: *A Minor Apocalypse*; *The Polish Complex*; *Moonrise, Moonset*; *A Dreambook for Our Time*; *New World Avenue and Vicinity*

Stanisław Lem. *Memoirs Found in a Bathtub.*
Translated by Michael Kandel and Christine Rose. San Diego, CA: Harcourt Brace Jovanovich, 1986. 204 pages.
Genre/literary style/story type: speculative fiction
Some critics have observed that Lem's futuristic novels are really about the contemporary world. This is certainly the case with *Memoirs Found in a Bathtub*, which is an allegorical treatment of the Cold War. In 3149, there is a new disease to worry about: papralysis, which destroys paper-based writing. But volcanic rock has preserved one man's memoirs, giving insight into a strange and sordid world where spies spied on each other, where secrets were preserved from enemies, and where no one knew exactly why they were doing what they were doing.
Related title by the same author:
Readers may also be interested in *Peace on Earth*, a satire in which the world's entire supply of military weapons is stored on the moon. But there is a great deal of worry that these machines will take it upon themselves to invade Earth, so decision makers send the bumbling Ijon Tichy to investigate.
Subject keywords: politics; power
Original language: Polish
Sources consulted for annotation:
Back cover of the book.
Global Books in Print (online) (reviews from *Booklist* and *Publishers Weekly* for *Peace on Earth*).
"Stanislaw Lem." *Contemporary Authors Online*. Thomson Gale, 2006.
"Stanislaw Lem." *Contemporary Literary Criticism*. Thomson Gale, 2006.
Some other translated books written by Stanisław Lem: *Return from the Stars*; *Solaris*; *Eden*; *The Star Diaries*; *Tales of Pirx the Pilot*; *More Tales of Pirx the Pilot*; *Peace on Earth*; *Memoirs of a Space Traveler: Further Reminiscences of Ijon Tichy*; *The Futurological Congress (From the Memoirs of Ijon Tichy)*; *The Cyberiad*; *Fables for the Cybernetic Age*; *Hospital of the Transfiguration*; *The Chain of Chance*; *One Human Minute*; *A Perfect Vacuum*; *His Master's Voice*; *Imaginary Magnitude*

Dorota Maslowska. *Snow White and Russian Red* (or *White and Red*).
Translated by Benjamin Paloff. New York: Black Cat., 2005. 291 pages.

Genre/literary style/story type: mainstream fiction
What is it like to be young and angry in contemporary Eastern Europe? This despair-soaked novel, which has been compared stylistically to Irvine Welsh's *Trainspotting*, provides all the answers you need. Andrzej Robakoski, nicknamed Nails, begins a series of drug-filled one-night stands when his girlfriend finally has had enough and breaks off their relationship.
Subject keyword: social problems
Original language: Polish
Sources consulted for annotation:
Fishman, Boris. *The New York Times Book Review*, 1 May 2005, p. 18.
Maslowska, Dorota. *The Globe and Mail* (Toronto), 30 April 2005, p. 15.

Jerzy Pilch. *His Current Woman*.
Translated by Bill Johnston. Evanston, IL: Northwestern University Press, 2002. 131 pages.
Genre/literary style/story type: mainstream fiction
Justyna, Pawel Kohoutek's current mistress, is determined to take up residence in Pawel's home. But he is just as determined to keep her arrival secret from his loved ones. It is easier than it seems because he is also providing shelter to numerous lodgers and relatives. Thus, he hides Justyna in the attic, triggering an elaborate farce in the best traditions of late seventeenth-century English Restoration comedy. Equally hilarious is *The Mighty Angel*, which centers on a novelist who undergoes rehab for his alcohol addiction no fewer than 18 times.
Subject keyword: family histories
Original language: Polish
Sources consulted for annotation:
Amazon.com (book description).
Budzynski, Brian. *Review of Contemporary Fiction* 22 (Fall 2002): 158.
Johnston, Bonnie. *Booklist* 98 (15 April 2002): 1383.
Post, Chad W. Three Percent website, http://www.rochester.edu/College/translation/threepercent.
Rohrbaugh, Lisa. *Library Journal* 127 (15 May 2002): 127.
Schurer, Norbert. *World Literature Today* 77 (April/June 2003): 149.
Zaleski, Jack. *Publishers Weekly* 249 (18 March 2002): 77.
Another translated book written by Jerzy Pilch: *The Mighty Angel*

Andrzej Stasiuk. *Nine*.
Translated by Bill Johnston. Orlando, FL: Harcourt, 2007. 229 pages.
Genre/literary style/story type: mainstream fiction
Things are looking bad for Pawel. Pursued by increasingly violent loan sharks, he has little recourse but to turn to the staunchest of his remaining friends: a drug dealer and an addict. As this unlikely trio makes its way through the crumbling ruins and detrituts of old and new Warsaw, the book—in the eyes of Irvine Welsh—paints an unforgettable "portrait of an uprooted and restless generation of Eastern Europeans and of a city resigned to the fact that post-Communism is not quite as advertised." Seeing echoes of Jean-Paul Sartre, Jean Genet, and Franz Kafka in Stasiuk's writing, Welsh calls *Nine* a stunning revelation that "reminds us how much bland fiction we publish in the English-speaking world," where "our imagination is increasingly filtered through the marketing lens of escapist genre fiction, and our so-called literary novels often feel like rehashed classics brazenly trumpeted as original work."
Subject keywords: social problems; urban life
Original language: Polish
Sources consulted for annotation:
Boykewich, Stephen. *Chicago Review* 51 (Spring 2005): 298.

Krzyzanowski, Jerzy R. *World Literature Today* 78 (May/August 2004): 90.
Pinker, Michael. *Review of Contemporary Fiction* 23 (Fall 2003): 123.
Welsh, Irvine. *The New York Times Book Review*, 10 June 2007 (online).
Some other translated books written by Andrzej Stasiuk: *White Raven*; *Tales of Galicia*; *Fado*

Andrzej Szczypiorski. *The Shadow Catcher.*
Translated by Bill Johnston. New York: Grove Press, 1997. 161 pages.
Genres/literary styles/story types: mainstream fiction; coming-of-age
In 1939, history is about to take a dramatic turn. Krzys is 15, and he is spending the summer in the countryside at the home of a friend of his father. When he falls in love, he begins to mull over the larger questions connected with national, religious, and ethnic identity.
Subject keyword: family histories
Original language: Polish
Sources consulted for annotation:
Amazon.com (all editorial reviews).
Grandfield, Kevin. *Booklist* 93 (15 March 1997): 1227.
Michalowski, Piotr. *The New York Times Book Review*, 28 September 1997, p. 20.
Taylor, Robert. *The Boston Globe*, 2 April 1997, p. D5.
Veale, Scott. *The New York Times Book Review*, 14 June 1998, p. 32.
Yardley, Jonathan. *The Washington Post*, 16 April 1997, p. D2.
Some other translated books written by Andrzej Szczypiorski: *The Beautiful Mrs. Seidenman*; *Self-Portrait with Woman*; *A Mass for Arras (A Mass for the Town of Arras)*

Tomek Tryzna. *Miss Nobody* (or ***Girl Nobody***).
Translated by Joanna Trzeciak. New York: Doubleday, 1999. 296 pages.
Genres/literary styles/story types: mainstream fiction; coming-of-age
In a small Polish town during the last gasp of communist rule, Marysia Kawczak is 15 years old and the object of desire of two rival female schoolmates: one is an ethereal, intellectually oriented yet angst-filled musician; the other is a seductive and lusty beauty who always gets what she wants.
Subject keyword: identity
Original language: Polish
Sources consulted for annotation:
Czerwinski, E. J. *World Literature Today* 73 (Summer 1999): 559.
Hall, Brian. *The New York Times Book Review*, 27 December 1998, p. 9.
Havel, Amy. *Review of Contemporary Fiction* 19 (1 October 1991): 180.
Steinberg, Sybil S. *Publishers Weekly* 245 (7 December 1998): 52.

Magdalena Tulli. *Dreams and Stones*.
Translated by Bill Johnston. New York: Archipelago Books, 2004. 110 pages.
Genres/literary styles/story types: mainstream fiction; experimental fiction
If only stones could tell their stories. In this novel, they actually do. The development of an urban metropolis is told through the individual histories of the stones that form its basic building blocks as well as through the dreams of some of its residents.
Related title by the same author:
Readers may also enjoy *Flaw*, another tale about changes in the urban landscape. What would you do if a motley group of people suddenly descended from a streetcar and promptly began to build a camp in your neighborhood?
Subject keywords: philosophy; urban life
Original language: Polish

Sources consulted for annotation:
Amazon.com (about the author; book description).
Global Books in Print (online) (reviews from *Booklist*, *Library Journal*, and *Publishers Weekly*).
Salm, Arthur. *The San Diego Union-Tribune*, 20 June 2004, p. 1.
Some other translated books written by Magdalena Tulli: *Moving Parts*; *Flaw*

Andrzej Zaniewski. *The Rat*.
Translated by Ewa Hryniewicz-Yarbrough. New York: Arcade, 1994. 157 pages.
Genre/literary style/story type: mainstream fiction
There are fables—and then there are fables. This book falls decidedly into the latter category. It is the life of a rat as told from a rat's perspective. And what a life it is: almost humanlike in its intensity—a life that is marked by all-pervasive fear and emotional complexity. You will never be able to look at a rat in the same way again.
Subject keyword: philosophy
Original language: Polish
Sources consulted for annotation:
Amazon.com (review from *Kirkus Reviews*).
Diamond, Ann. *The Gazette*, 24 September 1994, p. I3.
Geary, Brian. *Library Journal* 119 (1 September 1994): 217.
Roraback, Dick. *Los Angeles Times*, 18 December 1994, p. 6.
Steinberg, Sybil S. *Publishers Weekly* 241 (18 July 1994): 235.

Romania

Augustin Buzura. *Refuges*.
Translated by Ancuta Vultur and Fred Nadaban. Boulder, CO: East European Monographs, 1994. 461 pages.
Genres/literary styles/story types: mainstream fiction; women's lives
A woman works as a translator for a mining company in Romania. Her life is an unhappy one: a failed marriage and two failed affairs. One of her lovers has tried to kill her, and she now finds herself in a psychiatric ward. As she tries to make sense of these turbulent personal events, she also paints a devastating picture of the systematically oppressive social and political environment in which she was raised. Critics have referred to this book as one of the classics of contemporary Romanian literature.
Subject keywords: family histories; social problems
Original language: Romanian
Sources consulted for annotation:
Amazon.com (book description).
Dorian, Marguerite. *World Literature Today* 70 (January 1996): 178.
Another translated book written by Augustin Buzura: *Requiem for Fools and Beasts*

Vladimir Colin. *Legends from Vamland*.
Translated from Romanian. Abridged by Luiza Carol. Iali, Romania: Center for Romanian Studies, 2001. 104 pages.
Genre/literary style/story type: speculative fiction
An allegory about fear, this novel brings a new twist to the age-old myth of a struggle between the gods and humankind. At the beginning of time, on a Black Sea island, Ormag—the supreme God—engages in a test of wills with the heroic Vam, who emerges victorious.
Subject keyword: power

Original language: Romanian
Sources consulted for annotation:
Arama, Horia. *Utopian Studies. High-Beam Encyclopedia.* Society for Utopian Studies, 2002, http://www.highbeam.com/doc/1G1-97724936.html.
Global Books in Print (online) (synopsis/book jacket).

Paul Goma. ***My Childhood at the Gate of Unrest.***
Translated by Angela Clark. Columbia, LA: Readers International, 1990. 266 pages.
Genres/literary styles/story types: mainstream fiction; coming-of-age
This autobiographical coming-of-age novel set during World War II describes the multifaceted and tragic history of the Bessarabian region—caught between Romania and the Soviet Union and now incarnated as Moldova. When the author's father, a well-respected teacher, is deported to Siberia for his outspokenness, his mother faces a life of constant struggle.
Subject keywords: family histories; war
Original language: Romanian
Sources consulted for annotation:
Kaganoff, Penny. *Publishers Weekly* 237 (22 June 1990): 49.
Schwartz, Stephen. *The San Francisco Chronicle*, 26 August 1990, p. REV-6.

Norman Manea. ***The Black Envelope.***
Translated by Patrick Camiller. New York: Farrar, Straus and Giroux, 1995. 329 pages.
Genre/literary style/story type: mainstream fiction
In 1980s Bucharest, the totalitarian regime of Ceausescu is an overwhelming presence that affects every aspect of everyday life: shortages of basic necessities; a penumbral atmosphere of debilitating fear; and ubiquitous spies. Against this malefic background, Tolea is haunted by the death of his father 40 years ago and sets out to discover the truth.
Subject keywords: family histories; social problems
Original language: Romanian
Sources consulted for annotation:
Eder, Richard. *Los Angeles Times*, 25 May 1995, E11.
Green, Maria. *World Literature Today* 70 (22 September 1996): 943.
Lewis, Tess. *Partisan Review* 64 (Fall 1997): 666.
McQuade, Molly. *Booklist* (May 1, 1995): 1552.
Steinberg, Sybil S. *Publishers Weekly* (22 May 1995): 49.
Wolff, Larry. *The New York Times Book Review*, 25 June 1995, p. 7.
Some other translated books written by Norman Manea: *October*; *Eight O'Clock*; *Compulsory Happiness*

Dumitru Tsepeneag. ***Pigeon Post.***
Translated by Jane Kuntz. Champaign, IL: Dalkey Archive Press, 2008. 190 pages.
Genre/literary style/story type: mainstream fiction
Ed is at loose ends in Paris. Alone, trying to write, and caught up in his memories, he spends his time watching everything and nothing. As noted by the reviewer in *Publishers Weekly*, he eventually "resolves to write a novel by introducing anecdotes helter-skelter and enlisting the ideas of his three childhood friends named, suspiciously, Edmund, Edgar and Edward." The end result is "a kind of journal of spontaneous writing centered on his upbringing in Agen and a present flirtation with an older man who plays chess in a café for a living."
Subject keywords: family histories; writers
Original language: French

Source consulted for annotation:
Global Books in Print (online) (review from *Publishers Weekly*).
Another translated book written by Dumitru Tsepeneag: *Vain Art of the Fugue*

Serbia

David Albahari. *Bait*.
Translated by Peter Agnone. Evanston, IL: Northwestern University Press, 2001. 117 pages.
Genres/literary styles/story types: mainstream fiction; literary historical
Now in exile in Canada, the unnamed narrator considers his former life in Yugoslavia, chiefly by focusing on a series of audiotapes left to him by his dead mother in which she recounts her experiences. He wants to fashion a coherent narrative from the tapes but is unable to do so, overwhelmed by the array of details and emotions contained therein.
Related title by the same author:
Readers may also be interested in *Götz and Meyer*, which revolves around two low-level German soldiers whose job it is to gas concentration camp inmates after driving them into a forest near Belgrade.
Subject keywords: family histories; war
Original language: Serbian
Sources consulted for annotation:
Amazon.com (book description; back cover of the book).
Global Books in Print (online) (reviews from *Booklist*, *Library Journal*, and *Publishers Weekly* for *Götz and Meyer*).
Gorup, Radmila J. *World Literature Today* 76 (Spring 2002): 228.
Green, Jon. *Booklist* 97 (1 June/15 June 2001): 1834.
Publishers Weekly 248 (9 July 2001): 49.
Tepper, Anderson. *The Village Voice* 46 (14 August 2001): 55.
Some other translated books written by David Albahari: *Götz and Meyer*; *Words Are Something Else*; *Tsing*; *Snow Man*

Svetislav Basara. *Chinese Letter*.
Translated by Ana Lucic. Normal, IL: Dalkey Archive Press, 2004. 132 pages.
Genres/literary styles/story types: mainstream fiction; postmodernism
In communist Yugoslavia, paranoia is literally everywhere, structuring every human interaction. Two bureaucrats pay a visit to Fritz and order him to write a 100-page essay. No reasons for their request are provided. Thus, Fritz starts to write, fearing the consequences if he does not. His essay becomes Basara's novel. Critics have seen connections with the work of Samuel Beckett, Franz Kafka, and Nikolai Gogol.
Subject keyword: power
Original language: Serbian
Sources consulted for annotation:
Adams, Sarah. *The Guardian*, 11 December 2004, p. 30.
Nosowsky, Ethan. *Artforum* 11 (December 2004/January 2005): 45.
Power, Chris. *The Times*, 15 January 2005, p. 14.
Another translated book written by Svetislav Basara: *Civil War Within*

Milorad Pavić. *Last Love in Constantinople: A Tarot Novel for Divination*.
Translated by Christina Pribichevich-Zoric. Chester Springs, PA: Dufour Editions, 1998. 184 pages.
Genre/literary style/story type: historical fiction

This novel has the usual array of combustible elements: love, death, and family rivalries. Then, add the setting of Eastern Europe and the timeframe of the Napoleonic wars. But what really makes this book unique is the fact that it is modeled after the Major Arcana of a set of Tarot cards. Containing 21 chapters (the same number of cards in the Major Arcana) and a pack of cards, it can be read sequentially or the pack of cards can be used to determine the order in which the chapters are read. Critics have observed that one can trace this episodic approach back to such classic works as *Don Quixote* and *The Decameron*, not to mention the postmodern experimentations of Jorge Luis Borges and Gabriel García Márquez.

Related titles by the same author:

Readers may also enjoy *Dictionary of the Khazars*: *A Lexicon Novel in 100,000 Words*. As with *Last Love in Constantinople*, half the fun is reading this novel out of order and selectively skipping sections. The book consists of a series of dictionary entries about the long-disappeared Khazars, a people with a rich history living in the northern Caucasus region about 1,000 years ago and who have been identified as being related to the Turkic people. In the best postmodern traditions, readers can generate their own multiple and unique histories of the Khazars; no two readings of this book will ever be the same. *Landscape Painted with Sea* is also a unique book that can be read in multiple ways. Taking the form of a crossword, this novel about the life of an architect can be read either across or down.

Subject keyword: family histories

Original language: Serbian

Sources consulted for annotation:

Amazon.com (review from *Kirkus Reviews*).

Editors. *The New York Times Book Review*, 4 December 1988 (online).

Falbo, Sister M. Anna. *Library Journal* 123 (15 May 1998): 116.

Fox, Margalit. The New York Times, 16 December 2009 (online).

Paddock, Christopher. *Review of Contemporary Fiction* 18 (Fall 1998): 238.

Steinberg, Sybil S. *Publishers Weekly* 245 (18 May 1998): 70.

Some other translated books written by Milorad Pavić: *Dictionary of the Khazars: A Lexicon Novel in 100,000 Words*; *Landscape Painted with Tea*; *The Inner Side of the Wind, or The Novel of Hero and Leander*

Slobodan Selenić. *Premeditated Murder.*

Translated by Jelena Petrovic. London: Harvill, 1996. 186 pages.

Genre/literary style/story type: mainstream fiction

This novel recounts the parallel lives of two women named Jelena, one of whom is the granddaughter of the other. The story of Jelena the elder takes place in 1944, when a communist government under Tito assumed control in Yugoslavia. The story of Jelena the younger is set in 1994, in the midst of the Serbian-Croatian war. When Jelena the younger finds a trove of her grandmother's letters and personal effects, she becomes preoccupied with uncovering the real story about her life and death.

Subject keywords: family histories; war

Original language: Serbo-Croatian

Sources consulted for annotation:

Amazon.com (from the publisher).

Dyer, Richard. *Boston Globe*, 23 February 1997, p. N15.

Falbo, Sister M. Anna. *Library Journal* 122 (15 April 1997): 120.

Norris, David. *The Guardian*, 12 August 1993, p. 28.

Another translated book written by Slobodan Selenić: *Fathers and Forefathers*

Aleksandar Tišma. *The Book of Blam*.
Translated by Michael Henry Heim. New York: Harcourt Brace, 1998. 126 pages.
Genre/literary style/story type: mainstream fiction
Thanks to help from his mother's lover and because his wife is non-Jewish, Miroslav Blam, a Jewish resident of Novi Sad (Serbia), manages to stay alive during the war years. But he is traumatized and haunted by survivor's guilt, and he is unable to act on his feelings of vengeance. He succumbs to a form of psychological and emotional paralysis, deeply regretting his very existence.
Related title by the same author:
Readers may also be interested in *The Use of Man*, which again explores life in Novi Sad, focusing on the many divisions and rivalries between and among the various Slavic ethnic groups living there as well as their relationship with German forces. One of the main themes of this critically acclaimed novel is that fear leaves an indelible mark on the human spirit, trampling its optimism forever.
Subject keywords: identity; social roles
Original language: Serbo-Croatian
Sources consulted for annotation:
Amazon.com (book description; all editorial reviews).
Falbo, Sister M. Anna. *Library Journal* 123 (1 September 1998): 217.
Marx, Bill. *Boston Globe*, 24 November 1998, p. D5.
Pearl, Nancy. *Library Journal* 128 (1 March 2003): 144.
Perlez, Jane. *The New York Times*, 13 August 1997, p. C9.
Steinberg, Sybil S. *Publishers Weekly* 245 (31 August 1998): 45.
Taylor, Gilbert. *Booklist* 95 (1 October 1998): 309.
Wolff, Larry. *The New York Times Book Review*, 28 March 1999, p. 20.
Zimmerman, Zora Devrnja. *World Literature Today* 73 (Autumn 1999): 780.
Some other translated books written by Aleksandar Tišma: *Kapo*; *The Use of Man*

Zoran Zivković. *The Fourth Circle*.
Translated by Mary Popović. Tallahassee, FL: Ministry of Whimsy Press, 2004. 240 pages.
Genre/literary style/story type: speculative fiction
This novel brings together such individuals as Archimedes, Stephen Hawking, Nikola Tesla, Ludolph Van Ceulen, Sherlock Holmes, Dr. Watson, and Sir Arthur Conan Doyle—all of whom form part of an organization called the Circle, whose purpose is to sketch out the premises of a new world. As the review in *Publishers Weekly* stated, the author excels at "communicating the befuddlement, confusion and awe of individual characters as they wrestle with mysteries that exceed the understanding that their time, place and intellectual capacity permits."
Related title by the same author:
Readers may also be interested in *Hidden Camera*, where a man who is invited to a private showing of a movie at which there is only one other attendee becomes convinced that it is all an elaborate gag. Critics have seen echoes of Franz Kafka in Zivković's work.
Subject keyword: philosophy
Original language: Serbian
Sources consulted for annotation:
Cassada, Jackie. *Library Journal* 129 (15 May 2004): 119.
Dalkey Archive Press (book description), http://www. dalkeyarchive.com.
Jonas, Gerald. *The New York Times Book Review*, 18 April 2004, p. 25.
Publishers Weekly 251 (9 February 2004): 63.
Schroeder, Regina. *Booklist* 100 (15 April 2004): 1435.
Wilson, Scott Bryan. *Review of Contemporary Fiction* 24 (Summer 2004): 129.

Some other translated books written by Zoran Zivković: *Hidden Camera*; *Time Gifts*; *Impossible Stories*; *The Book*; *The Library*; *The Writer*; *Seven Touches of Music*; *Twelve Collections, and, The Teashop*; *The Devil in Brisbane*; *Impossible Encounters*

Slovakia

Martin M. Simecka. *The Year of the Frog.*
Translated by Peter Petro. Baton Rouge, LA: Louisiana State University Press, 1993. 247 pages.
Genres/literary styles/story types: mainstream fiction; coming-of-age
Milan's father is a political activist, which prevents Milan from entering university, which in turn prevents him from getting a professional position. Thus, he is forced to take a series of menial jobs: hospital orderly and clerk. The only bright spots are Tania, the love of his life, and marathons. But even these joys are transient: He has an affair, and his child is born prematurely and ends up being incinerated in a hospital furnace. As the last days of the communist regime tick by, is the system ultimately responsible for Milan's difficulties or is it Milan?
Subject keywords: family histories; power
Original language: Slovak
Sources consulted for annotation:
Amazon.com (book description; review from *Kirkus Reviews*).
Czerwinski, E. J. *World Literature Today* 68 (Summer 1994): 604.
Opello, Olivia. *Library Journal* 118 (1 September 1993): 223.
Shreffler, John. *Booklist* 90 (1 October 1993): 255.
Steinberg, Sybil S. *Publishers Weekly* 240 (6 September 1993): 84.

Pavel Vilikovský. *Ever Green Is . . . : Selected Prose.*
Translated by Charles Sabatos. Evanston, IL: Northwestern University Press, 2002. 193 pages.
Genres/literary styles/story types: mainstream fiction; short stories
Praised for its originality and compared with some of the work of Virginia Woolf and James Joyce, this collection is superbly inventive. In one story, the narrator meets Albert Camus while on his way to be a judge in a beauty contest. In another story, a man who struggles with the question of whether he really loved his mother, whose life he has just terminated because of severe cerebral dysfunction. In a third story, the object of a seduction attempt by an important bureaucrat begins to philosophize.
Subject keywords: politics; social roles
Original language: Slovak
Sources consulted for annotation:
Amazon.com (book description; back cover of the book).
Davis, Robert Murray. *World Literature Today* 76 (Spring 2002): 232.

Slovenia

Andrej Blatnik. *Skinswaps.*
Translated by Tamara Soban. Evanston, IL: Northwestern University Press, 1998. 109 pages.
Genres/literary styles/story types: mainstream fiction; short stories
This book consists of a series of short vignettes and what *Publishers Weekly* calls "comic pieces ranging from aphorisms to spare dialogues and explorations of cultural differences" in which recurrent themes are "philosophy, eroticism and everyday grit, as well as music, death, betrayal and the fragility of the individual's hold on reality."
Subject keyword: identity
Original language: Slovenian

Sources consulted for annotation:
Lincoln, Allen. *The New York Times Book Review*, 28 February 1999, p. 17.
Steinberg, Sybil S. *Publishers Weekly* 245 (12 October 1998): 59.

Drago Jančar. *Mocking Desire*.
Translated by Michael Biggins. Evanston, IL: Northwestern University Press, 1998. 267 pages.
Genre/literary style/story type: mainstream fiction
This novel explores the life of Gregor Gradnik, a Slovenian writer and a visiting professor at a university in New Orleans. Despite his attempts to remain a neutral observer of the American urban landscape, he is inevitably drawn into the midst of its gawdy cacophony, especially the raucousness of Mardi Gras and the bars of the French Quarter. He discovers that he has more in common with the gritty and seamy denizens of these bars than with Professor Fred Blaumann, his mentor at the university, whose life work is a never-finished book about melancholy. Some critics have compared the author to Milan Kundera.
Subject keyword: urban life
Original language: Slovenian
Sources consulted for annotation:
Amazon.com (review from *Library Journal*).
Glusic, Helga. *Slavic and East European Journal* 44 (Fall 2000): 488.
Northwestern University Press (book description), http://nupress.northwestern.edu.
Steinberg, Sybil S. *Publishers Weekly* 245 (22 June 1998): 84.
Some other translated books written by Drago Jančar: *Northern Lights*; *Joyce's Pupil*

Miha Mazzini. *The Cartier Project*.
Translated by Maja Visenjak-Limon. Seattle, WA: Scala House Press, 2004. 216 pages.
Genre/literary style/story type: mainstream fiction
Hugely popular in Slovenia, this novel is set in a squalid industrial town in the dying days of Tito's Yugoslavia. Egon works at the local foundry, where the food is abominable and workers must contend with less than hygienic working conditions. He considers himself a secret writer of romances, but, alas, the secret is out. Things get worse when his much-prized stock of Cartier perfume runs low. Egon is therefore forced into a series of tragic-comic situations to ensure a continued supply of his one vice.
Subject keywords: social problems; writers
Original language: Slovenian
Sources consulted for annotation:
Amazon.com (book description).
Scott, Whitney. *Booklist* 101 (1 October 2004): 311.
Another translated book written by Miha Mazzini: *Guarding Hanna*

Brina Svit. *Con Brio*.
Translated by Peter Constantine. London: Harvill, 2002. 167 pages.
Genre/literary style/story type: mainstream fiction
In Paris, a well-known writer impulsively proposes to a stranger who is his daughter's age. Against all likelihood she accepts, and they begin their new life together in his apartment. The marriage is based on only one condition: no questions about anything in the past and no thinking about the future. But curiosity eventually gets the better of the writer.
Subject keywords: identity; social roles
Original language: Slovenian

Sources consulted for annotation:
The Bookseller, 14 December 2001 (from Factiva databases).
STA, 2 May 2003 (from Factiva databases).
Thompson-Noel, Michael. *Financial Times*, 23 March 2002, p. 5.
Another translated book written by Brina Svit: *Death of a Prima Donna*

ANNOTATIONS FOR TRANSLATED BOOKS FROM RUSSIA AND UKRAINE

Russia

Vasilii Aksenov (Vassily Aksyonov). *Generations of Winter.*
Translated by John Glad and Christopher Morris. New York: Random House, 1994. 592 pages.
Genres/literary styles/story types: historical fiction; literary historical
Nothing is the same for the family of Boris Gradov, a surgeon, after Stalin's purges in the 1930s. His sons—a high-ranking Red Army officer named Nikita and the staunchly communist Kirill—are imprisoned in the Gulag; daughter Nina, a poet, escapes to Georgia. But as the Germans advance on Moscow, Nikita is seen as a redoubtable military strategist and rehabilitated. This novel has drawn comparisons with Boris Pasternak's *Doctor Zhivago*, Anatolii Rybakov's *Fear*, Aleksandr Solzhenitsyn's *The Gulag Archipelago*, the works of John Dos Passos, and Tolstoy's epics. Its sequel is *The Winter's Hero*.
Subject keywords: family histories; war
Original language: Russian
Sources consulted for annotation:
Allen, Brooke. *Wall Street Journal*, 10 Aug 1994, p. A6.
Hoffert, Barbara. *Library Journal* 119 (15 May 1994): 96.
Steinberg, Sybil S. *Publishers Weekly* 241 (18 April 1994): 43.
Taylor, Gilbert. *Booklist* 90 (1 June 1994): 1768.
Some other translated books written by Vasilii Aksenov: *The Burn: A Novel in Three Books*; *In Search of Melancholy Baby*; *The Island of Crimea*; *Say Cheese!*; *The New Sweet Style*; *Surplussed Barrelware*; *Our Golden Ironburg: A Novel with Formulas*; *The Destruction of Pompeii & Other Stories*

Boris Akunin (pseudonym for Grigorii Chkhartishvili). *Murder on the Leviathan.*
Translated by Andrew Bromfield. New York: Random House, 2004. 223 pages.
Genres/literary styles/story types: crime fiction; police detectives
Lord Littleby, a famous British antiquities collector, is murdered in Paris; a priceless statue of a Hindu god is stolen, as is a shawl; the culprit(s) is aboard the maiden voyage of the luxury liner *Leviathan* as it sails to India in 1878. Inspector Gustave Gauche, a bumbling French detective, is not making much progress, although the suspects—each of whom comes from a different nation—all have something to hide. The methodical and intellectual Erast Fandorin comes to the rescue each time Gauche thinks (wrongly) that he has solved the crime. In its hermetic setting and structural development, the book evokes the cerebral and classic tradition of Agatha Christie, especially *Death on the Nile* and *Murder on the Orient Express*. The exotic and multifaceted tale of the stolen goods pays homage to the work of Wilkie Collins. With his wry, sophisticated, and intellectual observations, Fandorin has been called a combination of Arthur Conan Doyle's Sherlock Holmes and such Russian literary characters as Lermontov's Pechorin (*A Hero of Our Time*) and Fyodor Dostoyevsky's Prince Myshkin (*The Idiot*). This period mystery contains much historical detail about the nineteenth century—sometimes with an overlay of nostalgia and melancholy that has reminded some commentators of Nikolai Gogol and Anton Chekhov. A different character narrates each chapter; viewpoints shift from the first person to the third.

Subject keyword: social roles
Original language: Russian
Sources consulted for annotation:
Cannon, Peter. *Publishers Weekly* 251 (22 March 2004): 66.
Levy, Anne Boles. *Los Angeles Times*, 30 June 2004, p. E6.
Pearl, Nancy. *Library Journal* 130 (1 April 2005): 135.
Vignovich, Ray. *Library Journal* 130 (1 June 2005): 186.
Some other translated books written by Boris Akunin: *The Death of Achilles*; *Pelagia & the White Bulldog*; *The Turkish Gambit*; *The Winter Queen*; *Special Assignments*; *Sister Pelagia and the Black Monk*; *Sister Pelagia and the Red Cockerel*

Iuz Aleshkovskii (Yuz Aleshkovsky). *Kangaroo.*
Translated by Tamara Glenny. New York: Farrar, Straus and Giroux, 1986. 278 pages.
Genre/literary style/story type: mainstream fiction
A pickpocket named Fan Fanych, or Citizen Etcetera, is accused by the KGB of raping and murdering a kangaroo. The murder cannot quite be pinned down to an exact date; just to be on the safe side, the authorties calculate that it took place somewhere between the Fall of the Bastille in 1789 and the beginning of the Russian Revolution in 1905. Absurdity follows absurdity in this devastating account of Soviet history.
Subject keyword: politics
Original language: Russian
Sources consulted for annotation:
Amazon.com (book description).
Florence, Ronald. *Los Angeles Times*, 6 July 1986, p. 6.
Steinberg, Sybil S. *Publishers Weekly* 229 (7 March 1986): 82.
Some other translated books written by Iuz Aleshkovskii: *A Ring in a Case*; *The Hand, or, The Confession of an Executioner*

Nina Berberova. *The Book of Happiness.*
Translated by Marian Schwartz. New York: New Directions, 1999. 205 pages.
Genre/literary style/story type: mainstream fiction; women's lives
This is an autobiographical novel about the infinite possibilities of love. The ever-balanced and rational Vera has had three significant romances in her life: her youthful affair with Sam, a musical genius who later commits suicide; her marriage to Alexander, an invalid and tyrant who takes her to Paris; and her love for Karelov, with its happy conclusion.
Subject keyword: identity
Original language: Russian
Sources consulted for annotation:
Amazon.com (book description).
Phillips, Adam. *The New York Times Book Review*, 25 July 1999, p. 26.
Steinberg, Sybil S. *Publishers Weekly* 246 (22 February 1999): 64.
Some other translated books written by Nina Berberova: *The Accompanist*; *The Ladies from St. Petersburg: Three Novellas*; *The Tattered Cloak and Other Novels*; *Cape of Storms*; *Billancourt Tales*; *The Revolt*

Andrei Bitov. *Pushkin House.*
Translated by Susan Brownsberger. New York: Farrar, Straus and Giroux, 1987. 371 pages.
Genre/literary style/story type: mainstream fiction

This is a semiautobiographical novel about the life of Lyova Odoevtsev, a philologist. As he goes about his work at Pushkin House and as intellectual life slowly crumbles around him under Soviet rule, he recalls his childhood during the siege of Leningrad; his education during the last years of Stalin's regime; and his passionate love for Faina. Some critics have invoked Proust when speaking about Bitov.
Subject keywords: family histories; war
Original language: Russian
Sources consulted for annotation:
Amazon.com (book description and review from *Library Journal*).
Brent, Frances Padorr. *Chicago Tribune*, 10 January 1988, p. 4.
Remnick, David. *The Washington Post*, 29 November 1987, p. X5.
Some other translated books written by Andrei Bitov: *Life in Windy Weather: Short Stories*; *The Monkey Link*; *A Land the Size of Binoculars*

Leonid Borodin. *Partings*.
Translated by David Floyd. San Diego, CA: Harcourt Brace Jovanovich, 1987. 221 pages.
Genre/literary style/story type: mainstream fiction
While in Siberia, Gennadi falls in love with and proposes to the enigmatic Tosya, whose father is a priest. He returns to his native Moscow to end his relationship with Irina, a psychologically unstable producer of television shows who is pregnant. As Gennadi undergoes a welter of emotions and as he assumes responsibility for his actions, his spiritual growth stands in stark contrast to the vapid and stultifying hothouse atmosphere of what passes for Moscow intellectual life.
Subject keywords: politics; social roles
Original language: Russian
Sources consulted for annotation:
Hagstrom, Suzy. *Orlando Sentinel*, 26 January 1989, p. E6.
Steinberg, Sybil S. *Publishers Weekly* 232 (11 September 1987): 80.
Some other translated books written by Leonid Borodin: *The Year of Miracle and Grief*; *The Third Truth*; *The Story of a Strange Time*

Iurii Buida (Yuri Buida). *The Zero Train*.
Translated by Oliver Ready. Monroe, OR: Dedalus, 2001. 135 pages.
Genre/literary style/story type: mainstream fiction
Ivan Ardabyev, nicknamed Don Domino, was orphaned at a young age when his parents were killed for ideological reasons. He inhabits a desolate village, which was erected for the sole purpose of ensuring that the mysterious Zero Train passes through its station at exactly midnight. No one knows what or whom this train carries, where it comes from, or where it is going. No one dares to ask questions because the curious are executed or crushed under the train wheels. Ironically, the train gives purpose to the villagers' existence, but it is a purpose bereft of meaning, driving many to drunkenness and madness. When the train stops running, people slowly abandon the village in search of better lives. Critics have compared this novel to works by Chingiz Aitmatov, George Orwell, Franz Kafka, and Viktor Pelevin.
Subject keywords: power; social problems
Original language: Russian
Sources consulted for annotation:
Massie, Allan. *The Scotsman*, 21 July 2001, p. 15.
Mozur, Joseph. *World Literature Today* 77 (Spring 2003): 150.
Another translated book written by Iurii Buida: *The Prussian Bride*

Kirill Bulychev (Kir Bulychev). ***Those Who Survive.***
Translated by John H. Costello. Peabody, MA: Fossicker Press, 2000. 384 pages.
Genre/literary style/story type: speculative fiction
The doomed space expedition Polar Star crashes on a planet populated by man-eating plants and ferocious animals. The book, whose setting is reminiscent of Harry Harrison's *Deathworld*, portrays a group of survivors battling against difficult circumstances and forging indestructible bonds in a quest to ensure their future.
Subject keyword: power
Original language: Russian
Sources consulted for annotation:
Amazon.com (book description).
Cassada, Jackie. *Library Journal* 125 (15 November 2000): 100.
D'Ammassa, Don. *Science Fiction Chronicle* 26 (September 2004): 34.
D'Ammassa, Don. *Science Fiction Chronicle* 22 (October–November 2000): 61.
Some other translated books written by Kirill Bulychev: *Alice: Some Incidents in the Life of a Little Girl of the Twenty-First Century, Recorded by Her Father on the Eve of Her First Day in School*; *Half a Life, and Other Stories*; *Gusliar Wonders*; *Earth and Elsewhere*

Irina Denezhkina. ***Give Me: Songs for Lovers.***
Translated by Andrew Bromfield. New York: Simon & Schuster, 2005. 214 pages.
Genres/literary styles/story types: mainstream fiction; coming-of-age
These stories were first published on the Internet when the author was 19 years old. The characters are wannabe hipsters who do not know anything about life under the Soviets and really do not care. Their interests and concerns are the interests and concerns of adolescents everywhere: sex, music, and drugs. But as they do their utmost to be cool and what Liesl Schillinger calls "hardboiled," they show a touching vulnerability, finally realizing that "holding hands is more compromising than sex, because tenderness isn't a pose." Some critics have compared this collection to Christopher Isherwood's *Berlin Stories*.
Subject keyword: social problems
Original language: Russian
Sources consulted for annotation:
Caso, Frank. *Booklist* 101 (1 January/15 January 2005): 813.
Publishers Weekly 252 (10 January 2005): 38.
Schillinger, Liesl. *The New York Times Book Review*, 3 April 2005, p. 21.

Nikolai Dezhnev. ***In Concert Performance.***
Translated by Mary Ann Szporluk. New York: Nan A. Talese/Doubleday, 1999. 269 pages.
Genres/literary styles/story types: mainstream fiction; magical realism
With echoes of Mikhail Bulgakov, Gabriel García Márquez, and Wim Wenders, the book tells the story of Lukary, a fallen angel who infuriated the Department of Light Powers because of his high-handedness and presumptuousness. But Lukary is given a chance to rehabilitate himself by serving as a presiding spirit in the house of a widow. When she dies, Lukary then falls in love with Anna, her niece and a television news producer who is married to a physicist. Lukary promptly wreaks havoc in their lives—time-traveling and ultimately developing a plan to murder Stalin.
Subject keyword: identity
Original language: Russian
Sources consulted for annotation:
Caso, Frank. *Booklist* 96 (1 October 1999): 343.
Fisher, Ann H. *Library Journal* 124 (15 October 1999): 104.
Steinberg, Sybil S. *Publishers Weekly* 246 (27 September 1999): 72.

Iurii Dombrovskii (Yury Dombrovsky). *The Faculty of Useless Knowledge.*
Translated by Alan Myers. London: Harvill, 1996. 533 pages.
Genre/literary style/story type: mainstream fiction
In 1937, in Kazakhstan, Georgi Zybin is a museum curator, archeologist, and a student at the Faculty of Law and Humanities, otherwise known as the Faculty of Useless Knowledge. When a golden diadem that was uncovered during excavations supervised by Zybin is stolen, he is accused of theft and other anti-Soviet activities. Jailed, he is forced to endure humiliation upon humiliation as all his associates betray him, but he clings tightly to his humanistic beliefs. Critics have seen parallels to Mikhail Bulgakov's *Master and Margarita.*
Subject keywords: politics; power
Original language: Russian
Sources consulted for annotation:
Amazon.com (book description; review from *Kirkus Reviews*).
Falbo, Sister M. Anna. *Library Journal* 121 (15 September 1996): 95.
Steinberg, Sybil S. *Publishers Weekly* 243 (2 September 1996): 112.
Another translated book written by Iurii Dombrovskii: *The Keeper of Antiquities*

Sergei Dovlatov. *The Suitcase.*
Translated by Antonina W. Bouis. New York: Grove Weidenfeld, 1990. 128 pages.
Genres/literary styles/story types: mainstream fiction; short stories
Each of the eight stories in this poignantly funny autobiographical novel is based on an item found in a dust-covered suitcase in a closet of the author's immigrant home in Queens, New York. It was the only luggage that he was allowed to take when leaving the Soviet Union, and it is still unpacked four years after immigration. The objects become talismans—evocative touchstones of a former life in 1960s Leningrad.
Subject keywords: family histories; identity
Original language: Russian
Sources consulted for annotation:
Adams, Phoebe-Lou. *The Atlantic* 265 (June 1990): 120.
Morace, Robert A. *Magill Book Review* (retrieved from the *NoveList* database).
Steinberg, Sybil S. *Publishers Weekly* 237 (13 April 1990): 54.
Sweedler, Ulla. *Library Journal* 115 (15 May 1990): 93.
Some other translated books written by Sergei Dovlatov: *A Foreign Woman*; *The Compromise*; *The Zone: A Prison Camp Guard's Story*; *The Invisible Book: (Epilogue)*

Iurii Druzhnikov (Yuri Druzhnikov). *Angels on the Head of a Pin.*
Translated by Thomas Moore. London: Peter Owen, 2002. 566 pages.
Genre/literary style/story type: mainstream fiction
One's entire life can turn on the most picayune of decisions. And so it is in this satiric look at a Soviet newspaper that is struggling to stay on the right side of the KGB. Makartsev, the editor, has the misfortune of discovering a mysterious manuscript in his office. Because it contains a potentially incendiary passage from the French author known as the Marquise de Custine, who visited Russia in the 1830s, the manuscript attracts the attention of the KGB. Soon, Makartsev suffers a heart attack, and Stephan Yagubov, the deputy editor, assumes control and tries to minimize any possible damage from the incident.
Subject keywords: politics; power
Original language: Russian
Sources consulted for annotation:
Pinker, Michael. *Review of Contemporary Fiction* 24 (Spring 2004): 139.
Publishers Weekly 250 (3 November 2003): 56.

Wright, Heather. *Library Journal* 128 (August 2003): 129.
Some other translated books written by Iurii Druzhnikov: *Passport to Yesterday: A Novel in Eleven Stories*; *Madonna from Russia*

Venedikt Erofeev. *Moscow to the End of the Line.*
Translated by H. William Tjalsma. Evanston, IL: Northwestern University Press, 1994. 164 pages.
Genre/literary style/story type: mainstream fiction
An underground classic that was circulated from hand-to-hand in the Soviet Union of the early 1970s, this book was not officially published there until the late 1980s. After losing his job, Venya gets royally drunk and decides to visit his girlfriend and child in a nearby city. He takes a commuter train, and before long he is waxing eloquent about seemingly every topic under the sun. The book is an acute dissection of Soviet social and problems, leavened with gruff and bawdy humor and circumstances.
Subject keywords: philosophy; urban life
Original language: Russian
Sources consulted for annotation:
Northwestern University Press (book description), http://www.nupress.northwestern.edu/
Wikipedia (entry for *Moscow-Petushki*), http://en.wikipedia.org.

Viktor Erofeev (Victor Erofeyev). *Russian Beauty.*
Translated by Andrew Reynolds. New York: Viking, 1993. 343 pages.
Genres/literary styles/story types: mainstream fiction
In this irreverent gem of a book, Irina Tarakanova, to whom the title of this novel refers, takes Moscow by storm, using untold charms and wiles to become an influential and feared member of various cultural and political circles. But things never quite work out as planned: one of her lovers dies during sex; she becomes pregnant and religious; has sex with a ghost and a figure described as Mother Earth. *Kirkus Reviews* hailed this raucous novel as worthy of the French satirist Rabelais because readers will be "laughing one minute and horrified the next."
Related Title by the Same Author:
Readers may also enjoy *Life with an Idiot*. In the title story of this collection, the unnamed narrator's punishment consists of being forced to look after an idiot for the rest of his life. In this peculiarly Soviet hell, there is nothing but despair and misery, where everyone and everything is conspiring against the possibility of happiness. The author has been referred to as a contemporary Chekhov.
Subject keywords: identity; urban life
Original language: Russian
Sources consulted for annotation:
Amazon.com (book descriptions for both books; reviews from *Kirkus Reviews* and *Publishers Weekly* for *Russian Beauty*).
Groskop, Viv. *The Daily Express*, 4 February 2005, p. 55.
Lynskey, Anna. *The Observer*, 9 January 2005, p. 17.
McElvoy, Anne. *The Times*, 29 March 1995, p. 1.
Another translated book written by Viktor Erofeev: *Life with an Idiot*

Anatolii Gladilin (Anatoly Gladilin). *Moscow Racetrack: A Novel of Espionage at the Track.*
Translated by R. P. Schoenberg and Janet G. Tucker. Ann Arbor, MI: Ardis, 1990. 216 pages.
Genres/literary styles/story types: crime fiction; suspense
Igor Kholmogorov is a fervent anticommunist who has written surreptious and subversive essays about Soviet history. He also has a penchant for gambling. One day, he hits a huge jackpot at a Moscow racetrack. But it is not quite his lucky day. Short of money, government authorities expropriate

his winnings and pack him off to Paris, where he is expected to win even more money to fill state coffers.
Subject keywords: politics; social problems
Original language: Russian
Sources consulted for annotation:
Amazon.com (book description).
Callendar, Newgate. *The New York Times*, 17 February 1991, p. A19.
Steinberg, Sybil S. *Publishers Weekly* 238 (11 January 1991): 89.

Irina Grekova. *The Ship of Widows.*
Translated by Cathy Porter. Evanston, IL: Northwestern University Press, 1994. 179 pages.
Genres/literary styles/story types: mainstream fiction; women's lives
This novel explores the multidimensional relationships among five women in a Moscow communal apartment during World War II. They come from various walks of life, and these socioeconomic and sociocultural differences gives rise to many tension-filled moments, especially given the lack of privacy in their home and their constant battles with bureaucratic entities. But when one of the women becomes a new mother, everything changes.
Subject keyword: social problems
Original language: Russian
Sources consulted for annotation:
McCombie, Brian. *Booklist* 90 (1 May 1994): 1582.
Simson, Maria. *Publishers Weekly* 241 (4 April 1994): 71.
Another translated book written by Irina Grekova: *Russian Women: Two Stories*

Fazil Iskander. *Sandro of Chegem.*
Translated by Susan Brownsberger. New York: Vintage Books, 1983. 368 pages.
Genres/literary styles/story types: adventure; quest
Sandro of Chegem is a true descendant of Huckleberry Finn, making his way through the ever-shifting political and social landscape of his native Abkhazia, a mountainous region on the edge of the Caucasus mountains. His many adventures, which span a period between the late nineteenth century and the 1950s, are humourously subversive and serve as the basis for penetrating commentary about such topics as sex; Stalinism; the tangled ethnic conflicts among Georgians, Abkhazians, and Russians; agricultural reforms; and the wisdom of animals. Susan Jacoby, who sees Iskander as a worthy successor to Mark Twain, has described this book is a "comic epic that, like Milan Kundera's novel *The Joke*, both depends upon and transcends the political context from which it arises."
Subject keyword: power
Original language: Russian
Source consulted for annotation:
Jacoby, Susan. *The New York Times*, 15 May 1983, p. A9.
Some other translated books written by Fazil Iskander: *The Gospel According to Chegem: Being the Further Adventures of Sandro of Chegem*; *Rabbits & Boa Constrictors*; *The Goatibex Constellation*; *Chik and His Friends*; *The Thirteenth Labour of Hercules*; *The Old House Under the Cypress Tree*

Sergei Iur'enen (Sergey Yuryenen). *The Marksman.*
Translated by Roger and Angela Keys. London: Quartet Books, 1985. 246 pages.
Genres/literary styles/story types: thrillers; spy thrillers
The Soviet spy Kirill Karayev is tasked with finding compromising material about Ivan Inoseltsev, a writer who is a potential defector with a strong yearning to go to France. The goal is simple: Gather

enough material to blackmail Inoseltsev with a view to turning him into a spy who would provide information about French activities and other Russian exiles in Paris. But Karayev's humanity prevails over his professional duty. The two men become friends, and as they engage in bouts of drinking and womanizing in the Baltics, they are given ample opportunity to ponder the true nature of authority and freedom. In its mood and style the novel has been described by *Publishers Weekly* as "Dostoyevsky-ridden and Hemingway-haunted."
Subject keyword: philosophy
Original language: Russian
Source consulted for annotation:
Steinberg, Sybil S. *Publishers Weekly* 229 (16 May 1986): 69.

Aleksandr Kabakov (Alexander Kabakov). *No Return.*
Translated by Thomas Whitney. New York: William Morrow, 1994. 94 pages.
Genre/literary style/story type: speculative fiction
When the KGB wants to find out what life will be like after Gorbachev's perestroika reforms, it turns to Yuri Illich, a well-known scientist who travels through time. What he discovers is not pleasant: Almost everything has gone to hell in a handbasket. It is the Great Depression redux: rampant poverty; economic meltdown; political chaos; street battles between rival gangs; and drug-crazed youth. Mayhem and anarchy are everywhere, and Illich has little choice but to become a gun-toting outlaw if he wants to survive.
Subject keyword: social problems
Original language: Russian
Sources consulted for annotation:
Hutchison, Paul E. *Library Journal* 115 (1 October 1990): 117.
Steinberg, Sybil S. *Publishers Weekly* 237 (3 August 1990): 63.

Evgenii Kharitonov (Yevgeny Kharitonov). *Under House Arrest.*
Translated by Arch Tait. London: Serpent's Tail, 1998. 208 pages.
Genres/literary styles/story types: mainstream fiction; short stories
It was not easy to be gay in the former Soviet Union, and this collection of fiction and poetry is ample testimony of that. The book was never officially published in the Soviet Union; many of the stories were carefully preserved by poet Mikhail Aizenberg and made available as samizdat. Some critics have found echoes of William S. Burroughs in Kharitonov's accounts of relationships marked by obsession, alienation, torment, loneliness, fear, and nihilism.
Subject keyword: identity
Original language: Russian
Sources consulted for annotation:
McMillin, Arnold. *World Literature Today* 73 (Spring 1999): 355.
Neskow, Vesna. *The New York Times Book Review*, 28 March 1999, p. 18.
Steinberg, Sybil S. *Publishers Weekly* 246 (18 January 1999): 328.

Mark Kharitonov. *Lines of Fate.*
Translated by Helena Goscilo. New York: New Press, 1996. 332 pages.
Genres/literary styles/story types: mainstream fiction; postmodernism
The scholar Anton Lizavin has made a stupendous discovery: the long-lost novel of the imaginary Simeon Milashevich, which has been jotted entirely on candy wrappers. As Lizavin works to bring a sense of coherency to the wrappers, which describe the mundane and seemingly random events that occur in a small Russian town, he begins to identify with the dead author. Many critics invoke Umberto Eco's *The Name of the Rose* when discussing this classic of postmodernism.

Subject keyword: writers
Original language: Russian
Sources consulted for annotation:
Cavanagh, Clare. *The New York Times Book Review*, 11 August 1996, p. 18.
McMillin, Arnold. *World Literature Today* 70 (Fall 1996): 984.

Sigizmund Krzhizhanovsky. *Memories of the Future*.
Translated by Joanne Turnbull with Nikolai Formozov. New York: New York Review Books, 2009. 228 pages.
Genres/literary styles/story types: speculative fiction; horror/paranormal
These seven stories were never published in the author's lifetime. Nightmarish, surreal, phantasmagoric, and hallucinatory are just four adjectives that have been used to describe Krzhizhanovsky's work. As Liesl Schillinger notes, Krzhizhanovsky writes "dream diaries" in which "the line between sleep and waking, real and unreal, life and death" is fluid. Readers who enjoy the tales of Edgar Allan Poe might wish to explore *Memories of the Future*. There are also affinities with the work of Nikolai Gogol and Andrei Bely.
Subject keyword: identity
Original language: Russian
Sources consulted for annotation:
Blair, Elaine. *The Nation* (30 November 2009) (online).
Schillinger, Liesl. *The New York Times Book Review*, 22 November 2009 (online).

Andrei Kurkov (Andrey Kurkov). *Death and the Penguin*.
Translated by George Bird. London: Harvill, 2001. 227 pages.
Genre/literary style/story type: mainstream fiction
In Ukraine after the fall of the Soviet Union, times are hard. Viktor Zolotaryov struggles to stay afloat in a dysfunctional world—to contain what seems to be an all-encompassing melancholy. He leads a mundane existence, except for the fact that he has a pet penguin named Misha, whom he adopted when the Kiev Zoo ran out of money to care for its animals. Suddenly, he is hired to write obituaries for the local newspaper in advance of the deaths of their subjects—a common practice in the newspaper industry. But when these subjects begin dying in mysterious circumstances, Viktor slowly realizes that he is an unwitting participant in a diabolical criminal conspiracy. Critics have invoked the name of Donald Barthelme when describing Kurkov's prose. This novel's sequel is called *Penguin Lost*.
Subject keyword: social problems
Original language: Russian
Sources consulted for annotation:
Kalfus, Ken. *The New York Times Book Review*, 11 November 2001, p. 8.
Nazarenko, Tatiana. *World Literature Today* 76 (Summer 2002): 146.
Some other translated books written by Andrei Kurkov: *A Matter of Death and Life*; *The Case of the General's Thumb*

Eduard Limonov (Edward Limonov). *Memoir of a Russian Punk*.
Translated by Judson Rosengrant. New York: Grove Weidenfeld, 1990. 312 pages.
Genres/literary styles/story types: mainstream fiction; coming-of-age
In the late 1950s in the Ukrainian city of Kharkov, Eddie is a 15-year-old gang member who nevertheless writes wonderful poetry. His neighborhood is poverty-stricken and the epitome of bleak. Everyone is bored, so it is little wonder that gangs are rife and that criminal activity is woven into the fabric of everyday existence. But Eddie quickly realizes that he is different from his friends;

his ticket out of the futureless miasma of the industrial wasteland that is his ostensible home is his abiding intellectual curiosity. This novel is part of the author's imaginative retelling of his life. Other volumes include *His Butler's Story* and *It's Me, Eddie*, which recount his experiences after he emigrates to New York.
Subject keyword: social problems
Original language: Russian
Sources consulted for annotation:
Adams, Phoebe-Lou. *The Atlantic* 267 (January 1991): 111.
Dirlam, Sharon. *Los Angeles Times*, 30 December 1990, p. 6.
Hutchison, Paul E. *Library Journal* 115 (1 November 1990): 126.
Steinberg, Sybil S. *Publishers Weekly* 237 (12 October 1990): 46.
Some other translated books written by Eduard Limonov: *His Butler's Story*; *It's Me, Eddie: A Fictional Memoir*; *Diary of a Loser*

Sergei Luk'ianenko (Sergei Lukyanenko). *The Nightwatch.*
Translated by Andrew Bromfield. New York: Miramax Books/Hyperion, 2006. 455 pages.
Genre/literary style/story type: speculative fiction
Anton Gorodetsky is an idealistic member of a group of other-worldly entities called Others residing in a supernatural dimension that allows them to be at once of the earth and not of it. Others are born human, but as they come of age, they choose to join either the Light Ones or the Dark Ones, who are in a constant battle that nonetheless preserves the balance between good and evil. But when Anton falls in love with Svetlana, a beautiful doctor, he starts questioning the dizzying labyrinth of compromises that underpin the status quo. As he attempts to shatter the existing order, he brings human civilization to the brink of collapse. This volume, which has been compared to Philip Pullman's *His Dark Materials*, is the first of a quartet.
Subject keyword: power
Original language: Russian
Sources consulted for annotation:
Amazon.com (book description).
Charles, Ron. *The Washington Post Book World*, 13 August 2006, p. T15.
Publishers Weekly 253 (5 June 2006): 42.
Santella, Andrew. *The New York Times Book Review*, 20 August 2006, p. 14.
Some other translated books written by Sergei Luk'ianenko: *Day Watch*; *Twilight Watch*; *Last Watch*

Vladimir Makanin. *Escape Hatch & The Long Road Ahead: Two Novellas.*
Translated by Mary Ann Szporluk. Dana Point, CA: Ardis, 1996. 193 pages.
Genre/literary style/story type: mainstream fiction
In the first novella, Klyucharyov, a middle-aged man whose main joy is reading, discovers a secret passage to an underground world that is an intellectual's paradise: no privations of any kind, all the capitalist luxuries that one could hope for, not to mention stimulating conversations on important philosophical questions. But moving between quotidian reality and his underground paradise becomes an increasingly fraught proposition, especially because his family and friends face dangers and risks. In the second novella, an engineer is horrified to discover what underpins the supposedly utopian society in which he lives. What exactly is the composition of the meat that humans now consume? Clare Cavanagh adroitly summarized this book by saying that it gives the impression that Chekhov's "Uncle Vanya had wandered into a painting by de Chirico."
Related title by the same author:
Readers may also be interested in *Baize-Covered Table with Decanter*, which follows the psychological torments and self-doubts of a man undergoing an endless interrogation.

Subject keywords: philosophy; urban life
Original language: Russian
Sources consulted for annotation:
Amazon.com (book description).
Cavanagh, Clare. *The New York Times Book Review*, 8 September 1996, p. 25.
Global Books in Print (online) (review from *Kirkus Reviews* for *Baize-Covered Table with Decanter*).
Steinberg, Sybil S. *Publishers Weekly* (1 April 1996): 57.
Some other translated books written by Vladimir Makanin: *The Loss: A Novella and Two Stories*; *Baize-Covered Table with Decanter*

Valeriia Narbikova (Valeria Narbikova). *In the Here and There.*
Translated by Masha Gessen. Dana Point, CA: Ardis, 1999. 145 pages.
Genre/literary style/story type: mainstream fiction
Petia is madly in love with Boris, an older sculptor, who is also head over heels in love with her. So, it would take an event of monumental proportions to separate them. Not so. One day Petia oversleeps, and Boris ends up in bed with her older sister Yezdandukta, a middle-aged virgin whose world revolves around domestic chores.
Subject keyword: identity
Original language: Russian
Sources consulted for annotation:
Marshall, Bonnie. *World Literature Today* 74 (Spring 2000): 435.
Steinberg, Sybil S. *Publishers Weekly* 246 (13 September 1999): 60.
Another translated book written by Valeriia Narbikova: *Day Equals Night, or, The Equilibrium of Diurnal and Nocturnal Starlight*

Viktor Pelevin (Victor Pelevin). *The Life of Insects.*
Translated by Andrew Bromfield. New York: Farrar, Straus and Giroux, 1998. 179 pages.
Genre/literary style/story type: mainstream fiction
This novel describes a world where humans are insects—and insects are humans. Arnold and Arthur are two Russian businessmen in the post-Soviet era interested in starting a company; they meet with Sam Sacker, a globetrotting American entrepreneur. As they discuss business prospects in the Crimea; as the conversation turns to grapes, glucose, and hemoglobin, Sam becomes a mosquito. Indeed, all the characters are insect-humans, including a woman wearing stiletto heels who becomes an ant. Michael Upchurch has labeled this novel as a combined "political allegory, antic fantasy, [and] willful enigma." As other critics have pointed out, it is an updated version of both Ovid's *Metamorphoses*, with a sly nod at Franz Kafka.
Related titles by the same author:
Also of interest may be *Omen Ra*, a satire about the space program in the Soviet Union, and *Homo Zapiens*, in which a translator of poetry becomes an advertising guru and darling of the nouveau-riche. Readers may also enjoy *The Sacred Book of the Werewolf*, which features, in the words of Liesl Schillinger, "a shape-shifting nymphet named A Hu-Li, a red-haired Asiatic call girl who is some 2,000 years old but looks 14" whose main claim to fame is the fact the she "ensorcells her clients by whipping out her luxuriant fox tail before each tryst and setting it a-whir like a pinwheeling ray gun, beaming hypnotic carnal fantasies into her customers' minds."
Subject keywords: power; social problems
Original language: Russian
Sources consulted for annotation:
Amazon.com (book description; review from *Kirkus Review*).

Caso, Frank. *Booklist* 94 (15 February 1998): 983.
Falbo, Sister M. Anna. *Library Journal* 123 (1 February 1998): 112.
Schillinger, Liesl. *The New York Times Book Review*, 28 September 2008, p. 14.
Steinberg, Sybil S. *Publishers Weekly* 244 (22 December 1997): 37.
Some other translated books written by Viktor Pelevin: *Buddha's Little Finger*; *A Werewolf Problem in Central Russia and Other Stories*; *Homo Zapiens*; *Omon Ra*; *The Yellow Arrow*; *The Blue Lantern and Other Stories*; *The Helmet of Horror: The Myth of Theseus and the Minotaur*; *The Clay Machine-Gun*; *Babylon*; *The Sacred Book of the Werewolf*

Liudmila Petrushevskaia (Ludmilla Petrushevskaya). *There Once Lived a Woman Who Tried to Kill Her Neighbor's Baby: Scary Fairy Tales.*
Translated by Keith Gessen and Anna Summers. New York: Penguin Books, 2009. 206 pages.
Genres/literary styles/story types: speculative fiction; horror/paranormal
Widespread critical praise has been accorded this collection of 19 scary fairy tales. As Liesl Schillinger observes, all "inhabit a borderline between this world and the next, a place where vengeance and grace may be achieved only in dreams." Reality metamorophoses into unreality and horror and then back again, creating a literary cauldron of the fantastic and supernatural. Readers for whom H. P. Lovecraft is a touchstone may wish to explore this work.
Subject keyword: identity
Original language: Russian
Sources consulted for annotation:
Amazon.com (book description).
Novikov, Tatyana. *World Literature Today* 71 (Spring 1997): 411.
Opello, Olivia. *Library Journal* 121 (1 April 1996): 121.
Schillinger, Liesl. *The New York Times Book Review*, 22 November 2009 (online).
Some other translated books written by Liudmila Petrushevskaia: *The Time: Night*; *Clarissa and Other Stories*; *Immortal Love*

Evgenii Popov (Evgeny Popov). *The Soul of a Patriot, or, Various Epistles to Ferfichkin.*
Translated by Robert Porter. Evanston, IL: Northwestern University Press, 1994. 194 pages.
Genre/literary style/story type: mainstream fiction
Evgeny, the narrator and author's namesake, is traveling on business by train and writing letters to Ferfichkin, an imaginary friend. The letters describe his memories of the fateful period surrounding the death of Leonid Brezhnev in late 1982.
Subject keyword: politics
Original language: Russian
Sources consulted for annotation:
Battersby, Eileen. *Irish Times*, 29 June 1996 (supplement).
Prednewa, Ludmila. *World Literature Today* 69 (Autumn 1995): 822.
Another translated book written by Evgenii Popov: *Merry-Making in Old Russia and Other Stories*

Valentin Rasputin. *Live and Remember.*
Translated by Antonina W. Bouis. Evanston, IL: Northwestern University Press, 1992. 216 pages.
Genre/literary style/story type: mainstream fiction
This is a profoundly moving story about a couple from the Siberian village of Atamanovka. During the last years of World War II, the wounded Andrei Guskov deserts and returns home to his wife Nastyona. They try to keep his presence a secret, but Nastyona's unexpected pregnancy complicates matters. Thus, she must resolve a series of excruciating dilemmas—all turning on the question of

whether individual or collective rights should take precedence. Should she support her husband, whom she married because she at the time was an orphan and was therefore expected to marry him; who often abused her; with whom she could not for the longest time conceive a child; whom she may not even love; yet to whom she is blindly loyal because he offered her protection and security? Or should she dutifully report him to the authorities because the entire village is turning against her and because wartime has its own peculiar laws? Ultimately, the novel explores the tragic fate of Russian women who must make untold sacrifices, including that of their unborn children. At once stoic and fragile; resilient and resigned; devoted and desperate, Nastyona becomes an everywoman caught in a maelstrom of conflicting philosophies and brutal oppression.
Subject keywords: rural life; social problems
Original language: Russian
Some other translated books written by Valentin Rasputin: *Siberia on Fire: Stories and Essays*; *Farewell to Matyora*; *You Live and Love and Other Stories*; *Money for Maria and Borrowed Time: Two Village Tales*

Irina Ratushinskaia (Irina Ratushinskaya). *Fictions and Lies*.
Translated by Alyona Kojevnikova. London: John Murray, 1999. 277 pages.
Genre/literary style/story type: mainstream fiction
Pavel Pulin has written a virulent anti-Soviet essay, but a sudden heart attack kills him. KGB agents are sent to recover the document and to hunt down whoever is hiding it. When suspicion falls on a children's book author, one of Pulin's friends, a hilariously vertiginous series of events reveals the corruption, petty ambitions, and hidden humanity of the literary circles in which Pulin moved and the world of spies during the Brezhnev era.
Subject keywords: politics; writers
Original language: Russian
Sources consulted for annotation:
Johnston, Bonnie. *Booklist* 96 (15 March 2000): 1331.
Lourie, Richard. *The New York Times*, 26 March 2000 (online)
Steinberg, Sybil S. *Publishers Weekly* 247 (14 February 2000): 175.
Ziolkowski, Margaret. *World Literature Today* 73 (Fall 1999): 770.
Another translated book written by Irina Ratushinskaia: *The Odessans*

Anatolii Rybakov (Anatoli Rybakov). *The Arbat Trilogy* (vol. 1: *Children of the Arbat*; vol. 2: *Fear*; vol. 3: *Dust and Ashes*).
Translated by Harold Shukman (vol. 1) and Antonina W. Bouis (vols. 2–3). Boston: Little, Brown, 1988 (vol. 1, 685 pages), 1992 (vol. 2, 686 pages), 1996 (vol. 3, 473 pages).
Genre/literary style/story type: historical fiction
This trilogy depicts the life of Sasha Pankratov, a youthfully naïve, romantic, and courageous law student from Moscow who is exiled to the Siberian Gulag for writing satirical poetry in a student newspaper. His ordeal is presented against the background of Stalin's purges and state-installed terror in the pre–World War II era in the Soviet Union. Taken together, the three books offer a riveting psychological portrait of Stalin, political assassinations, and intrigues. Critics have drawn comparisons to the writing of Upton Sinclair and Frank Norris.
Subject keywords: family histories; power
Original language: Russian
Sources consulted for annotation:
Amazon.com (review from *Kirkus Reviews*).
Hazard, John N. *Slavic Review* 48 (Fall 1989): 484.
Hoffert, Barbara. *Library Journal* 121 (15 March 1996): 97.

Ross, Ruth M. (1992, September 1). *Library Journal* 117 (1 September 1992): 216.
Steinberg, Sybil S. (1992, August 3). *Publishers Weekly* 239 (3 August 1992): 62.
Steinberg, Sybil S. (1996, January 29). *Publishers Weekly* 243 (29 January 1996): 84.
Some other translated books written by Anatolii Rybakov: *The Bronze Bird*; *The Dirk*; *Heavy Sand*

Yuri Rytkheu. *A Dream in Polar Fog.*
Translated by Ilona Yazhbin Chavasse. Brooklyn, NY: Archipelago Books, 2005. 337 pages.
Genres/literary styles/story types: adventure; survival and disaster stories
In 1910, in the Bering Strait, John MacLennan's ship, the *Belinda*, is ice-bound. His unsuccessful attempts to extricate it with dynamite lead only to disaster; his maimed and gangrened hands must be amputated by a medicine woman belonging to the Chukchi indigenous people. Eventually, gale-force winds free the ship, but MacLennan is left behind. According to the publisher's website, the novel's central theme is MacLennan's "integration into the Chukchi world: adapting to his handicap, adopting Chukchi ways and finding friendship—and love—among his hosts."
Subject keyword: identity
Original language: Russian
Sources consulted for annotation:
Archipelago Books (book description), http://www.archipelagobooks.org.
Global Books in Print (online) (review from *Publishers Weekly*).

Iulian Semenov (Julian Semyonov). *TASS Is Authorized to Announce . . .*
Translated by Charles Buxton. New York: Riverrun Press, 1987. 352 pages.
Genres/literary styles/story types: thrillers; political thrillers
Cold War politics was a deadly game that was played on all continents. The Soviet Union has friendly relations with Nagonia, an African nation led by a pro-Moscow government. Naturally, the CIA wants to bring about a right-wing coup and install its own puppet regime, but the KGB has a nefarious plan to prevent such an overthrow. The author is primarily known for his series about Stirlitz (Colonel Maksim Maksimovich Isaev), a Soviet spy operating as a Nazi officer in fascist Germany during World War II.
Subject keywords: politics; power
Original language: Russian
Sources consulted for annotation:
Alley, Brian. *Library Journal* 112 (15 September 1987): 96.
Steinberg, Sybil S. *Publishers Weekly* 232 (14 August 1987): 92.
Some other translated books written by Iulian Semenov: *Petrovka, 38*; *Seventeen Moments of Spring*; *The Himmler Ploy*; *In the Performance of Duty*; *Intercontinental Knot*

Olga Slavnikova. *2017.*
Translated by Marian Schwartz. New York: Overlook Press, 2010. 448 pages.
Genre/literary style/story type: mainstream fiction
Invoking the 100-year anniversary of the Russian Revolution, this novel revolves around a sordid environmental disaster and an equally sordid love triangle in an isolated northern region of Russia that the novelist calls the Riphean Mountains. There is a mysterious cyanide leak, and no one quite knows who or what is responsible for it, but the region's funeral director, Tamara, is benefitting from the resulting deaths. In fact, everyone is out to rake in as much money as possible, including Professor Anfilogov, even though they really do not know what to do with it once they have it. With the environmental scandal looming larger and larger, personal relationships become increasingly tangled. Tamara's ex-husband is Krylov, a gem-cutter who is having an affair with Tanya, the wife

of Anfilogov, Krylov's former teacher. But Tamara would not mind a reconciliation with Krylov, which may or may not explain the spy who tracks Krylov's every move. K. E. Semmel writes that this novel "uses farcical elements and outlandish, oversized characters to beguile you into reading further."
Subject keywords: politics; power
Original language: Russian
Source consulted for annotation:
Semmel, K. E. Three Percent website (book review), http://www.rochester.edu/College/translation/threepercent.

Sasha Sokolov. ***Astrophobia.***
Translated by Michael Henry Heim. New York: Grove Weidenfeld, 1989. 385 pages.
Genres/literary styles/story types: mainstream fiction; postmodernism
In this hilariously absurd recounting of Soviet history, it is the year 2044, and Palisander Dahlberg is looking back at his life and career. And what a life it has been. Abandoned as a child, he was raised in the lap of luxury in the Kremlin's orphange. As he grew older, he not only observed the political machinations of Stalin, Khrushchev, Brezhnev, and Andropov, but he also participated in various intrigues and political plots. After his thwarted attempt to assassinate Brezhnev (on Andropov's order), Palisander is imprisoned and then exiled to an imaginary country called Belvedere. Institutionalized in an asylum, he is discovered to be a hermaphrodite. But in 1999, he triumphantly returns to Russia and becomes the country's new ruler.
Subject keywords: politics; power
Original language: Russian
Sources consulted for annotation:
Steinberg, Sybil S. *Publishers Weekly* 236 (22 September 1989): 39.
Sweedler, Ulla. *Library Journal* 114 (15 September 1989): 137.
Zholkovsky, Alexander. *Los Angeles Times*, 11 February 1990, p. 2
Another translated book written by Sasha Sokolov: *A School for Fools*

Vladimir Sorokin. ***Ice.***
Translated by Jamey Gambrell. New York: New York Review Books, 2007. 321 pages.
Genre/literary style/story type: speculative fiction
In a violence-soaked and drug-wracked contemporary Moscow, blond and blue-eyed citizens are being targeted by a shadowy group. Victims are captured, and their chests are opened with ice hammers made from a Siberian meteorite. Most are left to die. But some experience rebirth and begin to speak the language of their attackers: heart-language, which has only 23 words. As they integrate into the murderous group, they learn that they only have two tasks: kill others until they find the 23,000 scattered heart-language speakers. They form a new race of beings, and their ultimate goal is to bring about the apocalypse. This novel has received the highest praise from numerous critics. It has been compared to the works of Phillip K. Dick and Michel Houellebecq. *Publishers Weekly* referred to it as "a *Master and Margarita* for the age of *Buffy the Vampire Slayer*."
Subject keywords: identity; social roles
Original language: Russian
Sources consulted for annotation:
Amazon.com (book description).
Gannon, Michael. *Booklist* 103 (1 December 2006): 23.
Kalfus, Ken. *The New York Times Book Review*, 15 April 2007 (online).
Publishers Weekly 253 (2 October 2006): 38.
Another translated book written by Vladimir Sorokin: *The Queue*

Tat'iana Tolstaia (Tatyana Tolstaya). ***The Slynx.***
Translated by Jamey Gambrell. Boston: Houghton Mifflin, 2003. 278 pages.
Genre/literary style/story type: speculative fiction
Some 200 years into the future, Russia is a wasteland after a devasting nuclear explosion. It never stops snowing; people have tails and extra appendages and organs; their diet consists of mice; and each new ruler renames Moscow in his own honor. Pre-explosion literature is forbidden, and the only books that can be read are those by Fyodor Kuzmich, who employs scribes to copy classic literary works that are issued under his name. But the Oldeners, a small colony of blast survivors, have preserved a clandestine library, and they introduce one of the scribes, Benedikt, to literature and reading. Inspired by his discoveries, Benedikt yearns to be the catalyst for a new Russian Revolution, eventually metamorphosing into a mysterious, opportunistic, and powerful slynx. Critics have compared this novel to Anthony Burgess's *A Clockwork Orange*.
Subject keywords: identity; power
Original language: Russian
Sources consulted for annotation:
Amazon.com (book description; reviews from *Kirkus Reviews* and *The New Yorker*).
Hoffert, Barbara. *Library Journal* 128 (January 2003): 160.
Spinella, Michael. *Booklist* 99 (15 December 2002): 736.
Zaleski, Jeff. *Publishers Weekly* 249 (25 November 2002): 41.
Some other translated books written by Tat'iana Tolstaia: *On the Golden Porch*; *Sleepwalker in a Fog*

Edward Topol. ***The Jewish Lover.***
Translated by Christopher J. Barnes. New York: St. Martin's Press, 1998. 403 pages.
Genres/literary styles/story types: thrillers; political thrillers
Iosef Rubinchik is a Jewish journalist who is also an inveterate seducer of young innocent girls, including the daughter of a KGB agent, Oleg Barsky. Thus, the agent starts an elaborate anti-Jewish campaign, an important component of which is to discredit Rubinchik. But his plan backfires when one of his colleagues, who has had an affair with Rubinchik, resents his prosecutory zeal and begins to dig up incriminating evidence about Barsky's past.
Subject keyword: power
Original language: Russian
Sources consulted for annotation:
Amazon.com (book description).
Kloszewski, Marc A. *Library Journal* 123 (15 November 1998): 92.
Quinn, Mary Ellen. *Booklist* 95 (15 November 1998): 569.
Some other translated books written by Edward Topol: *Red Snow*; *Submarine U-137*; *Red Gas*; *The Russian Seven* (with Emiliya Topol); *Deadly Games* (with Fridrikh Neznanskii); *Red Square* (with Fridrikh Neznanskii)

Leonid Tsypkin. ***Summer in Baden-Baden.***
Translated by Roger Keys and Angela Keys. New York: New Directions, 2001. 146 pages.
Genre/literary style/story type: mainstream fiction
This novel recounts the author's obsession with Fyodor Dostoyevsky. He undertakes both a literal and figurative pilgrimage through the key places and moments of his hero's life: Dostoyevsky's incarceration under the tsars; his disputes with Turgenev and Goncharov; his demise in St. Petersburg. But the focus is on the summer Dostoyevsky spent in 1867 in Baden-Baden with Anna Grigoryevna, his second wife, a poverty-stricken period caused in no small part by his gambling addiction. The novel also explores the unlikely kinship that Tsypkin, who is Jewish, feels toward Dostoyevsky, who was anti-Semitic.
Subject keywords: anti-Semitism; writers

Original language: Russian
Sources consulted for annotation:
Angier, Carole. *The Independent*, 25 March 2005, p. 23.
Bergman, David. *Review of Contemporary Fiction* 22 (Summer 2002): 225.
Rosen, Jonathan. *The New York Times Book Review*, 3 March 2002 (online).

Liudmila Ulitskaia (Ludmila Ulitskaya). *The Funeral Party.*
Translated by Cathy Porter; translation edited by Arch Tait. New York: Schocken Books, 2001. 154 pages.
Genre/literary style/story type: mainstream fiction
Alik, an artist, is dying in his scaldingly hot apartment in New York, which has always been a hub for the émigré Russian community. As his muscles degenerate day by day, the apartment fills with people—with their own memories of Alik's key role in their lives and wondering how best to pay their respects. Because the story takes places in the summer of 1991, it coincides with the last gasps of the Soviet Union. Thus, his friends and loved ones are to be bereft not only of Alik's beneficent guidance and wisdom but also of a political system that left indelible marks on their emotions and psyches.
Subject keywords: culture conflict; identity
Original language: Russian
Sources consulted for annotation:
Caso, Frank. *Booklist* 97 (15 January 2001): 919.
Pinker, Michael. *Review of Contemporary Fiction* 21 (Fall 2001): 213.
Rohrbaugh, Lisa. *Library Journal* 126 (January 2001): 158.
Steinberg, Sybil S. *Publishers Weekly* 247 (18 December 2000): 57.
Some other translated books written by Liudmila Ulitskaia: *Medea and Her Children*; *Sonechka: A Novella and Stories*

Vladimir Voinovich. *Monumental Propaganda.*
Translated by Andrew Bromfield. New York: Alfred A. Knopf, 2004. 365 pages.
Genre/literary style/story type: mainstream fiction
Aglaya Stepanovna Revkina, who lives in the isolated town of Dolgov, is a fanatical supporter of Stalin. In contrast with myriad feckless chameleons who shift their political loyalties to conform to new political situations, Aglaya refuses to change. She stoically preserves her allegiance to Stalin during Khrushchev's Thaw, the Brezhnev era, and the first years of capitalism—even going so far as to install in her living room the town's statue of Stalin, rescued before it could be turned into scrap metal. This novel operates within the best traditions of Jonathan Swift or George Orwell—an outrageously dark comedy that raises uncomfortable questions about history and loyalty.
Subject keywords: politics; power
Original language: Russian
Sources consulted for annotation:
Amazon.com (review from *The Washington Post Book World*).
Caso, Frank. *Booklist* 100 (August 2004): 1902.
Wright, Heather. *Library Journal* 129 (15 April 2004): 127.
Zaleski, Jeff. *Publishers Weekly* 251 (24 May 2004): 41.
Some other translated books written by Vladimir Voinovich: *The Life and Extraordinary Adventures of Private Ivan Chonkin*; *Pretender to the Throne: The Further Adventures of Private Ivan Chonkin*; *Moscow 2042*; *In Plain Russian*; *The Fur Hat*

Iuliia Voznesenskaia (Julia Voznesenskaya). *The Women's Decameron.*
Translated by W. B. Linton. Boston: Atlantic Monthly Press, 1986. 302 pages.

Genres/literary styles/story types: mainstream fiction; women's lives

Quarantined in a Leningrad maternity hospital for 10 days, 10 women—who are are meant to be representative of Soviet society—spend the evenings talking about everything and anything. No topic is taboo, including sex. As they discuss their various trials and tribulations and their joys and minor triumphs, it becomes clear that the humiliations and tragedies they faced were in no small way a function of the Soviet system.

Subject keywords: power; social problems

Original language: Russian

Sources consulted for annotation:

See, Carolyn. *Los Angeles Times*, 22 September 1986, p. 6.

Steinberg, Sybil S. *Publishers Weekly* 230 (22 August 1986): 78.

Zirin, Mary F. *Library Journal* 111 (1 October 1986): 111.

Another translated book written by Iuliia Voznesenskaia: *The Star Chernobyl*

Yevgeny Yevtushenko. *Don't Die before You're Dead.*

Translated by Antonina W. Bouis. New York: Random House, 1995. 415 pages.

Genre/literary style/story type: historical fiction

August 1991 was a momentous time in Russian history: Gorbachev, Yeltsin, coups, and countercoups. To get a good sense of this exciting period, this novel is almost a must. Numerous plotlines bring together fictional and historical characters, including high-ranking police officers; an ex-soccer player and his girlfriend; Korzinkina, an émigré poet; Gorbachev; Eduard Shevardnadze, then Minister of Foreign Affairs; Mstislav Rostropovich, the legendary cellist; and the author.

Subject keywords: politics; social problems

Original language: Russian

Sources consulted for annotation:

Goldenberg, Judy. *Richmond Times-Dispatch*, 17 March 1996, p. F4.

Opello, Olivia. *Library Journal* 120 (15 November 1995): 101.

Park, Catherine. *The Plain Dealer* (Cleveland), 3 March 1996, p. I13

Steinberg, Sybil S. *Publishers Weekly* 242 (2 October 1995): 54.

Some other translated books written by Yevgeny Yevtushenko: *Wild Berries*; *Ardabiola*; *A Dove in Santiago: A Novella in Verse*

Zinovii Zinik (Zinovy Zinik). *The Mushroom-Picker.*

Translated by Michael Glenny. New York: St. Martin's Press, 1987. 282 pages.

Genre/literary style/story type: mainstream fiction

Konstantin is a Russian foodie and intellectual—in no particular order. When Clea, a drab Englishwoman and vegetarian on a visit to Moscow, succumbs to his charms, they marry and move to England, where Konstantin hopes to indulge his gourmand tendencies. But matters go seriously awry at a party when Konstantin eats food intended for a cat—an incident that haunts him to no end. In due course, he indulges in a spate of deranged activities, culminating in a trip to a British nuclear installation, where he intends to gather rare mushrooms.

Subject keywords: culture conflict

Original language: Russian

Sources consulted for annotation:

Amazon.co.uk (synopsis).

Donald, Anabel. *The New York Times Book Review*, 19 February 1989, p. A10.

Some other translated books written by Zinovii Zinik: *Mind the Doors: Long Short Stories*; *One-Way Ticket*; *The Lord and the Gamekeeper*

Aleksandr Zinoviev (Alexander Zinoviev). ***Homo Sovieticus.***
Translated by Charles Janson. Boston: Atlantic Monthly Press, 1985. 206 pages.
Genres/literary styles/story types: mainstream fiction; postmodernism
As part of a diabolical plan called Operation Emigration to get rid of dissidents and at the same time to infilitrate key Westen counties, the KGB recruits a bored Moscow intellectual and dispatches him to Munich. He proclaims himself to be a spy, takes up residence in a boardinghouse, and creates a taxonomy of disaffected Russina émigrés. The novel consists of 215 diary fragments that amount to a scathing critique of the Soviet Union and the type of individuals created by it. The author's style has echoes of Rabelais, Swift, and Voltaire.
Subject keyword: politics
Original language: Russian
Sources consulted for annotation:
Wasserman, Steve. *Los Angeles Times*, 25 May 1986, p. 2.
Schmieder, Rob. *Library Journal* 111 (1 June 1986): 144.
Steinberg, Sybil S. *Publishers Weekly* 229 (18 April 1986): 48.
Some other translated books written by Aleksandr Zinoviev: *The Yawning Heights*; *Perestroika in Partygrad*; *The Radiant Future*; *The Madhouse*

Ukraine

Iurii Andrukhovych (Yuri Andrukhovych). ***Recreations.***
Translated by Marko Pavlyshyn. Edmonton, AB: Canadian Institute of Ukrainian Studies Press, 1998. 132 pages.
Genre/literary style/story type: mainstream fiction
In the fictional city of Chortopil, the Festival of the Resurrecting Spirit is an occasion for gaudy national celebration and sexual debauchery. The narrative is presented from the perspective of four poets, an aging prostitute, and the wife of one of the poets. Their alcohol-influenced stories and conversations give probing insight into the cultural and political contradictions of contemporary Ukraine.
Related title by the same author:
Readers may also be interested in *Perverzion*, which focuses on the mystery surrounding the death of Stanislav Perfetsky, a key figure in avant-garde Ukrainian cultural circles. Was it suicide or was he forced into it? Is there some connection with a Munich religious ceremony or his job as a stripper? Stylistically, the novel combines documentary reports, interviews, and fragmentary jottings.
Subject keywords: politics; social problems
Original language: Ukrainian
Sources consulted for annotation:
Amazon.com (book description).
Chernetsky, Vitaly. *The Slavic and East European Journal* 43 (Fall 9999): 543.
Nazarenko, Tatiana. *World Literature Today* 73 (Spring 1999): 365.
Northwestern University Press (book description), http://nupress.northwestern.edu.
Another translated book written by Iurii Andrukhovych: *Perverzion*

Volodymyr Dibrova. ***Peltse and Pentameron.***
Translated by Halyna Hryn. Evanston, IL: Northwestern University Press, 1996. 198 pages.
Genre/literary style/story type: mainstream fiction
This book contains two short novels. *Peltse* explores the rise and fall of a bureaucrat, describing his petty triumphs, setbacks, rivalries, office infighting, and eventual marginaliation and decline. *Pentameron* recounts 24 hours in the life of a group of scientific translators whose lives have been so

traumatic that they are wracked by perpetual doubts, angst, and self-censorship. Dibrova's work has been hailed as a breakthrough for Ukrainian literature and has been compared with that of Samuel Beckett and Eugène Ionesco.
Subject keywords: politics; power
Original language: Ukrainian
Sources consulted for annotation:
Owchar, Nick. *Los Angeles Times*, 28 February 1997, p. 4
Steinberg, Sybil S. *Publishers Weekly* 243 (4 November 1996): 67.

Oles' Honchar. *The Cathedral.*
Translated by Yuri Tkach and Leonid Rudnytzky. Philadelphia, PA: St. Sophia Religious Association of Ukrainian Catholics, 1989. 308 pages.
Genre/literary style/story type: mainstream fiction
In the quiet and sleepy fictional town of Zachiplianka on the Dnipro River, nothing much happens beyond the usual environmental pollution, haphazard violence, and bureaucratic silliness. The only thing that makes Zachiplianka noteworthy is its ancient cathedral, which is now being used as a museum. But Mykola Bahlay, a student, recognizes the cathedral as what Leonid Rudnytzky calls "a valued symbol of man's free-soaring spirit, a precious link with the past, and the embodiment of man's ability to create beauty." When officials decide to raze the building, townspeople rise to its defense.
Subject keyword: social problems
Original language: Ukrainian
Source consulted for annotation:
Rudnytzky, Leonid. Introduction to the book.
Some other translated books written by Oles' Honchar: *The Shore of Love*; *The Cyclone*; *Man and Arms*; *The Cathedral*; *Standard-Bearers*; *Golden Prague*; *Tronka: A Novel in Novellas*

Igor *Klekh. A Land the Size of Binoculars.*
Translated by Michael M. Naydan and Slava I. Yastremski. Evanston, IL: Northwestern University Press, 2004. 216 pages.
Genres/literary styles/story types: mainstream fiction; magical realism
This book collects the author's famous novella *Kallimakh's Wake* as well as seven other short fictional works. Taking as his setting the city of Lviv, he paints a rich portrait of Ukrainian cultural history, which has Polish, Russian, German, and Galician influences. *Kallimakh's Wake* imaginatively recounts the psychological and spiritual life of Filippo Buonaccorsi, an influential fifteenth-century historian and humanist who was instrumental in founding the Roman Academy. After being accused of plotting against Pope Paul II, he fled to Ukraine and Poland. Other stories describe a pilgrimage to the town where Nikolai Gogol set some of his stories; a trip to a region of the Carpathians where Hutsul culture lives on; and the author's experiences as a high school teacher. Klekh's work has drawn favorable comparisons with that of Gabriel García Márquez because of its magical realistic componets and that of Umberto Eco because of what the translators call his "medieval mentality and his encyclopedic knowledge of a bygone era."
Subject keywords: culture conflict; social problems
Original language: Russian
Sources consulted for annotation:
Naydan, Michael M., and Yastremski, Slava I. Translator's introduction.
Northwestern University Press, http://nupress.northwestern.edu.
Paddock, Chris. *Review of Contemporary Fiction* 25 (Summer 2005): 141.

CHAPTER 7

The Iberian Peninsula and Latin America

Language groups:	Chile	Nicaragua
Basque	Colombia	Panama
Catalan	Costa Rica	Paraguay
Galician	Cuba	Peru
Portuguese	Dominican Republic	Portugal
Spanish	Ecuador	Puerto Rico
Countries represented:	El Salvador	Spain
Argentina	Guatemala	Uruguay
Bolivia	Honduras	Venezuela
Brazil	Mexico	

INTRODUCTION

This chapter contains annotations of books translated from the languages spoken in the countries of the Iberian Peninsula (i.e., Spain and Portugal) and many of the countries in Central and South America (as well as the Caribbean) that are often referred to collectively as Latin America (e.g., Argentina, Bolivia, Brazil, Chile, Colombia, Costa Rica, Cuba, Dominican Republic, Guatemala, Honduras, Mexico, Panama, Paraguay, Peru, Puerto Rico, Uruguay, and Venezuela). The books in this chapter were originally written in Spanish, Catalan, Galician, or Portuguese.

Among the translated novels in Spanish from Central American and Caribbean countries are Tatiana Lobo's *Assault on Paradise* (Costa Rica); Jesús Díaz's *The Initials of the Earth* (Cuba); Marisela Rizik's *Of Forgotten Times* (Dominican Republic); Arturo Arias's *Rattlesnake* (Guatemala); Horacio Castellanos Moya's *Senselessness* (Honduras); Guillermo Arriaga Jordán's *The Night Buffalo* (Mexico); and Mayra Montero's *Deep Purple* (Puerto Rico).

Among the translated novels in Spanish from South American countries are Eduardo Sguiglia's *Fordlandia* (Argentina); Edmundo Paz Soldán's *The Matter of Desire* (Bolivia); Roberto Bolaño's *The Savage Detectives* and *2666* (Chile); Laura Restrepo's *The Dark Bride* (Colombia); Laura

Riesco's *Ximena at the Crossroads* (Peru); Antonio Larreta's *The Last Portrait of the Duchess of Alba* (Uruguay); and Ana Teresa Torres's *Doña Inés vs. Oblivion* (Venezuela).

Translated novels from Spain (written in Spanish, Catalan, or Galician) include Bernardo Atxaga's *The Accordionist's Son*; Alicia Giménez-Bartlett's *Dog Day*; Ray Loriga's *Tokyo Doesn't Love Us Anymore*; Eduardo Mendoza's *The Year of the Flood*; Jesús Moncada's *The Towpath*; Quim Monzo's *The Enormity of the Tragedy*; Arturo Pérez-Reverte's *The Club Dumas*; Manuel Rivas's *Vermeer's Milkmaid and Other Stories*; Mercè Rodoreda's *The Time of the Doves* and Carlos Ruiz Zafón's *The Shadow of the Wind* and *The Angel's Game*.

Translated novels from Portugal include António Lobo Antunes's *The Inquisitor's Manual*; Lídia Jorge's *The Painter of Birds*; and José Saramago's *Death with Interruptions* and *Blindness*. Among the novels in Portuguese from Brazil are Patrícia Melo's *Black Waltz*; Luís Fernando Veríssimo's *Borges and the Eternal Orangutans*; and Moacyr Scliar's *Max and the Cats*, which controversially came into the public eye as an alleged source for Yann Martel's award-winning *Life of Pi*.

Earlier Translated Literature

Any reader interested in exploring classic Spanish novels must necessarily start with Miguel de Cervantes's *Don Quixote*, first published in the early seventeenth century and almost immediately translated into English. Of the many English versions of this picaresque masterpiece, critics suggest that those by Charles Jarvis; the eighteenth-century English novelist Tobias Smollett; and Burton Raffel in the late twentieth century are the best. Other notable picaresque novels from the same general period are *The Life of Lazarillo de Tormes* and *The Life of a Swindler* [*El Buscón*]—both conveniently published in a Penguin edition in 1969. Important nineteenth-century and early twentieth-century Spanish novelists include Pedro de Alarcón (*The Three-Cornered Hat*) and Vicente Blasco Ibáñez (*The Four Horsemen of the Apocalypse* and *The Holding*). In the mid- and late twentieth century, two of the most noteworthy Spanish authors are the Nobel Prize laureate Camilo José Cela (*San Camilo*; *The Hive*; and *The Family of Pascual Duarte*) and Juan Goytisolo (*Quarantine* and *The Marx Family Saga*).

When discussing the rich heritage of Latin American Spanish-language fiction in English translation, the inevitable starting point is the Argentinean Jorge Luís Borges, whose multilayered stories first entranced and intrigued readers in the 1960s. His work has never stopped being read and discussed since then; two convenient places to begin exploring Borges are his *Complete Fictions* and *Labyrinths: Selected Stories*. Equally important is the little-known Macedonio Fernández, who critics say was a strong influence on Borges. An accessible and representative work by Fernández is *The Museum of Eterna's Novel (The First Good Novel)*.

In some respects, Borges could be said to have inspired or paved the way for the tidal wave of magic realist novels emanating from Central and South America. Many of these writers are well-known, especially Gabriel García Márquez (*One Hundred Years of Solitude* and *Love in the Time of Cholera*); Carlos Fuentes (*The Death of Artemio Cruz* and *Christopher Unborn*, along with the more recent *The Eagle's Throne*); and Mario Vargas Llosa (*The Green House* and *Conversation in the Cathedral*). Other significant Spanish-language writers associated with magic realism from Latin America include Isabel Allende; Alejo Carpentier (*Explosion in a Cathedral*); Julio Cortázar (*Hopscotch*); and Manuel Puig (all writing in Spanish) as well as Jorge Amado, a Brazilian writing in Portuguese (*Dona Flor and Her Two Husbands*).

With regard to Portuguese fiction, the renowned stature of nineteenth-century author Eça de Queiróz has ensured numerous English-language translations of his work, including *The City and the Mountains*, *The Relic*, *The Maias*, *The Crime of Father Amaro*, *Cousin Bazilio*, *The Tragedy of the Street of Flowers*, and *Yellow Sofa*. Also of interest may be the epic poem *The Lusíads* by Luís Vaz de Camões, which was first published in 1572 and is a magnificent account of the Portuguese explorer Vasco da Gama's voyage to India in the late 1490s.

SOURCES CONSULTED

France, Peter. (Ed.). (2000). "Hispanic Languages." In *The Oxford Guide to Literature in English Translation*, pp. 405–446. Oxford: Oxford University Press.

Williams, Raymond Leslie. (2007). *The Columbia Guide to the Latin American Novel Since 1945*. New York: Columbia University Press.

BIBLIOGRAPHIC ESSAY

Spain

One would be very hard-pressed indeed to find a better introduction to Spanish literature than *The Cambridge History of Spanish Literature*, edited by David T. Gies. Certainly, there are brilliant essays and sections about such classic authors as Cervantes, Federico García Lorca, and Carmen Martín Gaite, so the reader is treated to the entire majestic panorama of Spanish literature from the medieval period to the present day. But the book also contains articles that deal with such less well-known topics as eighteenth-century prose writing; the naturalist novel; nineteenth-century women writers; modernism and the avant-garde in Catalonia; prose in Franco Spain; and Spanish literature and the language of the new media. As one loses oneself in these essays, such unknown novelists as Benito Pérez Galdós, Emilia Pardo Bazán, Javier Tomeo, and Cristina Fernández capture the imagination. As a worthy substitute for Gies's edited volume, we suggest the revised edition of *A New History of Spanish Literature* by Richard E. Chandler and Kessel Schwartz, which takes a more genre-based approach, chronologically tracing the evolution of Spanish epic poetry, lyric poetry, fictional prose, nonfictional prose, and drama in separate chapters. And because so much of Spanish literature is best understood through a historical and social lens, we believe that *The Cambridge Companion to Modern Spanish Culture*, edited by David T. Gies, will be of immeasurable benefit to readers. This volume features three essays about the multifaceted relationship among history, politics, and literature in various periods from 1875–1996; more than 15 essays about narrative prose, poetry, theater, painting, sculpture, cinema, architecture, dance, media, and music; and essays about the importance of the Catalan and Basque cultures within Spain.

These historical and cultural overviews will no doubt spur readers to want to discover more about Spanish novels. The obvious place to turn is *The Cambridge Companion to the Spanish Novel from 1600 to the Present*, edited by Harriet Turner and Adelaida López de Martínez. There are articles about the continuing significance of picaresque novels, such as *Don Quixote*; the regional novel; the realist novel; the relationship of history and fiction; the testimonial novel and the novel of memory; women and fiction in post-Franco Spain; the intersection of film and literature between 1982 and 1995; and postmodern novels. Readers will find the names of so many intriguing novelists that they will immediately want more information about them. One likely source of that information is *The Oxford Companion to Spanish Literature*, edited by Philip Ward, which gives pithy overviews of novelists, poets, and dramatists and their works but also includes historians, religious writers, and philosophers. It covers the period from Roman Spain (which began around 206 B.C.E. and continued for some seven centuries thereafter) to 1977. A book that has more substantial biographical and critical information about Spanish novelists is a volume in the Dictionary of Literary Biography (DLB) series entitled *Twentieth-Century Spanish Fiction Writers*, edited by Marta E. Altisent and Cristina Martínez-Carazo (2006; vol. 322). Medieval Spanish literature—with its confluence of Muslim, Jewish, and Christian traditions—is sensitively and respectfully written about in two other DLB volumes: *Castilian Writers, 1200–1400* (2008; vol. 337) and *Castilian Writers, 1400–1500* (2004; vol. 286). Both these volumes expand the typical DLB focus on authors to include articles on significant works, genres, and themes. As they range even further afield, adventurous readers will be pleased to learn about the Spanish detective tradition in *The Detective Novel in Post-Franco Spain: Democracy, Disillusionment, and Beyond* by Renée W. Craig-Odders.

These texts should be supplemented by *Spanish Women Writers: A Bio-Bibliographical Source Book*, edited by Linda Gould Levine, Ellen Engelson Marson, and Gloria Feiman Waldman, which contains an excellent introduction to six centuries of Spanish women writers as well as articles about such authors as Rosa Chacel, Ana Diosdado, Gloria Fuertes, Carmen Laforet (whose striking 1945 novel *Nada* was reissued in an English translation in 2007 by The Modern Library), Julia Maura, Carme Riera, Concha Romero, Ana Rossetti, and Esther Tusquets. Where applicable, lists of English translations of their works are included. Just as valuable—if not more so—is *The Feminist Encyclopedia of Spanish Literature*, a two-volume set edited by Janet Pérez and Maureen Ihrie. Here, readers will find detailed entries on literary periods, genres, authors (e.g., Carmen Conde, Carmen de Icaza, Clara Janés, Mercedes Salisachs), important literary works, characters, and such general topics as: lesbianism in early modern Spanish literature (1500–1700); Catalan women writers; women's education in Spain (1860–1993); detective fiction by Spanish women writers; Galician women writers; Basque women writers; eroticism in contemporary Spanish women writers' narratives; Hispano-Arabic poetry by women; and fairy tales in novels by Spanish women. An appendix lists entries by specific time periods, and each author entry contains a list of works by and about the author in question. The intention is "to present the cultural background against which Spanish women writers have produced their works, the climate in which they were formed, and in many cases, against which they react in their writings" (p. viii).

Portugal

Spain of course shares the Iberian Peninsula with Portugal, which has a rich literary heritage of its own, as demonstrated most recently by the international acclaim given to Nobel Prize winner José Saramago for his novels that have variously been described as metaphysical and surreal allegories—the most famous of which (*Blindness*) was made into a film in 2008. Although originally published in 1922, Aubrey F. G. Bell's *Portuguese Literature* is still considered a classic of the field, and it is highly recommended for its erudite analysis of literary movements and writers from the period 1185–1910. For a contemporary perspective on many of the topics discussed by Bell, *A Revisionary History of Portuguese Literature*, edited by Miguel Tamen and Helena C. Buescu, is a good choice.

Recent Portuguese history may be said to have been fundamentally altered with a coup staged on April 25, 1974, so it is natural that much cultural criticism and analysis also uses 1974 as a reference point to discuss key transformations in the literary landscape. An example of this is *After the Revolution: Twenty Years of Portuguese Literature, 1974–1994*, edited by Helena Kaufman and Anna Klobucka. The book begins with two important background articles about Portuguese politics and society; these are followed by rewarding essays about numerous contemporary Portuguese writers, such as António Lobo Antunes. Many of his novels (e.g., *South of Nowhere*; *Fado Alexandrino*; and *The Inquisitor's Manual*) have been translated into English; they recount the tragic history of Portugal under the dictatorship of António de Oliveira Salazar as well as the bleak history of Portuguese colonialism in Angola and Mozambique. Such female novelists as Joana Ruas, Wanda Ramos, and Lídia Jorge are also given extensive consideration in the volume's final two chapters.

Anyone wishing to know more about these three writers (and others) is urged to consult *Women, Literature and Culture in the Portuguese-Speaking World*, edited by Cláudia Pazos Alonso, which contains articles about women's writing in Portugal, Brazil, and Portuguese (Luosophone) Africa. Likewise, the volume entitled *Portuguese Writers* (2004; vol. 287 in the Dictionary of Literary Biography series) is invaluable, providing detailed biographical information and critical analyses of such authors as Helena Marques, Jorge de Sena, Salette Tavares, and Miguel Torga. Some of the novels mentioned in the preceding books are annotated in *The Babel Guide to the Fiction of Portugal, Brazil & Africa in English Translation* by Ray Keenoy, David Treece, and Paul Hyland. Finally, readers of Saramago may enjoy exploring the *The Dedalus Book of Portuguese Fantasy*, edited by Eugénio

Lisboa and Helder Macedo. This book not only introduces readers to such famous Portuguese novelists as Eça de Queiroz and Mário de Sá-Carneiro but also gives insight into some of the possible literary antecedents of magical realism, which characterizes much of Latin American literature.

Because Portugal and Spain share the Iberian Peninsula, it is appropriate that their literatures should sometimes be seen in tandem, as in *Spanish and Portuguese Literatures and Their Times (The Iberian Peninsula)*, edited by Joyce Moss. This valuable reference source contains in-depth social, historical, and political information necessary for the contextual understanding of such novels as Saramago's *Baltasar and Blimunda* (e.g., Portuguese exploration, the convent of Mafra); Lídia Jorge's *The Murmuring Coast* (e.g., the Portuguese colonial war in Mozambique, Timor, and Angola); and Pío Baroja's *The Quest* (e.g., Spain after 1898; working-class life in Madrid; anarchism). Another reference works that considers Spanish and Portuguese literatures together is the *Dictionary of the Literature of the Iberian Peninsula*, edited by Germán Bleiberg, Maureen Ihrie, and Janet Pérez. Here, Spanish, Portuguese, Catalan, and Galician authors, works, and literary movements are extensively described, with a special emphasis on "traditionally neglected or forgotten female authors" (p. xvi).

Latin America

One could literally drown among the many top-notch reference sources and monographs devoted to Latin American literature. To retain one's sanity, the ideal place to start is *The Columbia Guide to the Latin American Novel Since 1945* by Raymond Leslie Williams. We cannot say enough wonderful things about this elegantly written and thoughtfully conceived book. It contains an introductory survey that explains the colonial legacy of Latin American literature, the so-called dictator novel and its critique of the colonial legacy, and the novels of exile and resistance. Williams then provides a detailed chronological survey of the Latin American novel, which is followed by regional surveys about the cultural context for the development of novels in Mexico; Central America; the Caribbean; the Andes (Columbia, Venezuela, Ecuador, Peru, Bolivia); the Southern Cone (Argentina, Chile, Uruguay, and Paraguay); and Brazil. Last but not least, there are alphabetically arranged entries about major and minor authors; key works; and significant topics of pertinence for Latin American literature. If you can only read one book on this topic, this is it. A good alternate choice is *A Companion to Latin American Literature* by Stephen M. Hart, which has detailed chapters about the Amerindian legacy, colonial literature, and century-by-century accounts up to the end of the twentieth century.

We then direct your attention to the three volumes of *The Cambridge History of Latin American Literature*, edited by Roberto González Echevarría and Enrique Pupo-Walker. Each of the essays in these volumes is a gem; taken as a whole, the three volumes are probably the last word about Latin American literature for a very long time. The first volume considers such topics as historians of the conquest and colonial period between 1550 and 1700; the nineteenth-century Latin American novel; and the essays of nineteenth-century Mexico and Central America. The second volume deals with twentieth-century Latin American literature; Afro-Hispanic American literature; the novels of the Mexican Revolution; the Spanish American novel from 1950 to 1990; and Chicano literature, among many others. The third volume is devoted to the Brazilian literary heritage, with separate chapters on the Brazilian novel, Brazilian poetry, and Brazilian drama in various time periods. It also contains an exhaustive bibliography of about 450 pages, carefully subdivided according to the primary and secondary sources referred to in each of the essays of the three volumes.

The excellence on display on each page of the foregoing text is replicated in the three volumes of *A History of Literature in the Caribbean*, edited by A. James Arnold. While the first volume is concerned with the Spanish- and French-speaking cultural regions of the Caribbean, the second is devoted to the English- and Dutch-speaking regions; the third volume intelligently discusses what one of the essays calls the "cross-cultural unity of Caribbean literature." For readers who would prefer shorter overviews, three essays in *The Cambridge History of African and Caribbean Literature*, edited by

F. Abiola Irele and Simon Gikandi, are of particular importance: Caribbean literature in Spanish; Caribbean literature in French; and postcolonial African and Caribbean literature. For Mexican literature, no better sources exist than *Mexican Literature: A History*, edited by David William Foster, and *History of Mexican Literature* by Carlos González Peña. In fact, one of the best ways to appreciate different approaches to the same subject is to read these two books one after the other. The essays collected in Foster's volume represent, for the most part, Mexican literary scholarship from the perspective of the United States, while Peña's book—first published in 1928 and republished in its ninth edition in 1966—interprets Mexican literary history from the Mexican vantage point.

To be sure, historical panoramas of literary traditions are necessary, but some readers will want to focus exclusively on Latin American novelists. One of the best one-volume guides is *The Modern Latin American Novel* by Raymond Leslie Williams, which has excellent introductory chapters about such major novelists as Alejo Carpentier, Carlos Fuentes, Julio Cortázar, and Gabriel García Márquez. But Philip Swanson's *The New Novel in Latin America: Politics and Popular Culture After the Boom* and the same author's edited *Landmarks in Modern Latin American Fiction* are equally valuable because they insightfully discuss the novels of Jorge Luis Borges, José Donoso, Manuel Puig, Clarice Lispector, and Isabel Allende. For individuals primarily interested in Brazilian fiction, there is *Brazilian Writers*, edited by Monica Rector and Fred M. Clark (2005; vol. 307 of the Dictionary of Literary Biography series), and *The Babel Guide to Brazilian Fiction in English Translation* by David Treece and Ray Keenoy. Equally germane is *Latin American Writers on Gay and Lesbian Themes: A Bio-Critical Sourcebook*, edited by David William Foster, which contains detailed entries about such writers as Marta Traba, Herbert Daniel, and Reinaldo Arenas. And for the ever-increasing number of people whose passion is mystery and crime writing, *Latin American Mystery Writers: An A-to-Z Guide*, edited by Darrell B. Lockhart, will be an eye-opener. It includes a well-wrought introductory essay about the tradition of hard-boiled detective fiction in Latin America as well as bio-bibliographic essays about 50 little-known writers, such as Sergio Sinay, Hiber Conteris, Marco Denevi, Miriam Laurini, Gabriel Trujillo Muñoz, and Enrique Serna. Lockhart's valuable contribution can be profitably supplemented with Persephone Braham's *Crimes Against the State, Crimes Against Persons: Detective Fiction in Cuba and Mexico* as well as *Hispanic and Luso-Brazilian Detective Fiction: Essays on the Género Negro Tradition* by Renée W. Craig-Odders. Once individuals have selected two or three novels for their reading pleasure, they may wish to know everything there is to know about those novels so as to immerse themselves as fully as possible into new worlds. For this purpose, *Latin American Literature and Its Times*, edited by Joyce Moss, has indispensable articles about such famous novels as Clarice Lispector's *The Hour of the Star*; Manuel Puig's *The Kiss of the Spider Woman*; Laura Esquivel's *Like Water for Chocolate*; and Oscar Hijuelos's *The Mambo Kings Play Songs of Love*.

Just as there are untold numbers of books surveying various aspects of Latin American literature and the novel, so there are numerous reference resources. The three-volume *Literary Cultures of Latin America*, edited by Mario J. Valdés and Djelal Kadir, is the kind of item that comes along once in a lifetime. It is divided into three parts: configurations of literary culture; institutional modes and cultural modalities; and Latin American literary culture. The first part "establishes the geographic, demographic, linguistic, and social dimensions of Latin American literatures as social discourse"; the second part examines the social forces that have contributed to the diversity of various cultural centers; and the third part looks at the "profoundly split vision of Latin American writing, forever caught between celebration and lament" (p. xxii). There is an amazing wealth of articles on such topics as oral literature in Brazil; contemporary Mayan theater; linguistic diversity in Colombia; the social history of the Latin American writer; various cultural centers in Latin America (from Caracas to Havana to Montevideo to Santiago); Puerto Rican literature in the United States; indigenous literatures in the Andes; and the Latin American "boom" novel. Just as extensive and authoritative is the three-volume set (with supplements) entitled *Latin American Writers*, edited by Carlos A. Solé and Maria Isabel Abreu, which contains detailed essays (with bibliographies and indicated translations) of such authors as Isabel Allende, Alberto Girri, Elena Garro, Ida Vitale, Pedro Prado, Alfonso Reyes, Octavio Paz, Pabló Neruda, Mario Vargas Llosa, Gabriela Mistral, and Miguel Ángel Asturias.

For quick information on just about everything, the *Encyclopedia of Latin American Literature*, edited by Verity Smith, is an obvious choice. All countries in Latin and Central America have articles devoted to them. There are also essays about such topics as African-Brazilian literature; Jewish writing; detective fiction; science fiction; prison writing; protest literature; and pornography—not to mention a wide range of entries about significant works as well as such authors as Carlos Fuentes, Jorge Amado, and Jorge Luis Borges. The *Encyclopedia of Latin American and Caribbean Literature, 1900–2003*, edited by Daniel Balderston and Mike Gonzalez, serves a similar purpose, with articles about fantastic literature; music and literature; Spanish- and French-speaking Caribbean literary traditions; and author bio-bibliographic entries—each with further readings listed. These two omnibus encyclopedias can be readily supplemented by more targeted reference works, such as the two-volume *Encyclopedia of Caribbean Literature*, edited by D. H. Figueredo. It contains entries about hundreds of authors as well as important literary works; genres and types of literatures (e.g., slave narratives; negrista literature; magical realism; and children's literature in the Hispanic-Caribbean literature); cultural or national identity; journals; literary generations; literary movements; and numerous national literatures (e.g., history of Guyanese literature; Francophone-Caribbean literature; Haitian literature; and literature from Martinique). More specific still are the *Dictionary of Mexican Literature*, edited by Eladio Cortés; the *Dictionary of Twentieth-Century Cuban Literature*, edited by Julio A. Martínez; and the *Dictionary of Brazilian Literature*, edited by Irwin Stern. Each of these has roughly 300–500 entries about authors (with full bio-bibliographic information); literary movements in various time periods; genres; and significant cultural occurrences with an impact on literature in the country in question.

As readers work their way through these encyclopedias and dictionaries, they will notice a large number of entries for women novelists, poets, and dramatists. To locate more detailed information about them, we are fortunate to have *Latin American Women Writers: An Encyclopedia*, edited by María Claudia André and Eva Paulino Bueno. Entries are arranged alphabetically, but there is also a handy list of entries subdivided according to country and theme, which makes it easy to locate information about such authors as Argentinian Rosa Guerra; Chilean Gabriela Mistral; Cuban Lydia Cabrera; Mexican Sara Sefchovich; Uruguayan Amanda Berenguer; and Venezuelan Antonia Palacios. There are also thematic entries on eroticism, humor in contemporary fiction, testimonial literature, and lesbian literature in Latin America. This phenomenal book should be read side by side with *Latin American Women Writers: A Resource Guide to Titles in English* by Kathy S. Leonard, which alphabetically lists authors (with the titles of their works) translated into English; titles of translated works (with their authors); and also provides a convenient subdivision of authors by their country of origin.

SELECTED REFERENCES

Alonso, Cláudia Pazos. (Ed.). (1996). *Women, Literature and Culture in the Portuguese-Speaking World*. Lewiston, NY: Edwin Mellen Press.

André, María Claudia, and Bueno, Eva Paulino. (Eds.). (2008). *Latin American Women Writers: An Encyclopedia*. New York: Routledge.

Arnold, A. James. (Ed.). (1994–2001). *A History of Literature in the Caribbean*. (3 vols.). Amsterdam, The Netherlands: John Benjamins Publishing.

Balderston, Daniel, and Gonzalez, Mike. (Eds.). (2004). *Encyclopedia of Latin American and Caribbean Literature, 1900–2003*. London: Routledge.

Bell, Aubrey F. G. (1922/1970). *Portuguese Literature*. Oxford: Clarendon Press.

Bleiberg, Germán; Ihrie, Maureen; and Pérez, Janet. (Eds.). (1993). *Dictionary of the Literature of the Iberian Peninsula*. (2 vols.). Westport, CT: Greenwood Press.

Braham, Persephone. (2004). *Crimes Against the State, Crimes Against Persons: Detective Fiction in Cuba and Mexico*. Minneapolis, MN: University of Minnesota Press.

Chandler, Richard E., and Schwartz, Kessel. (1991). *A New History of Spanish Literature*. (rev. ed.). Baton Rouge, LA: Louisiana State University Press.

Cortés, Eladio. (Ed.). (1992). *Dictionary of Mexican Literature*. Westport, CT: Greenwood Press.

Craig-Odders, Renée W. (1999). *The Detective Novel in Post-Franco Spain: Democracy, Disillusionment, and Beyond*. New Orleans, LA: University Press of the South.

Craig-Odders, Renée W. (2006). *Hispanic and Luso-Brazilian Detective Fiction: Essays on the Género Negro Tradition*. Jefferson, NC: McFarland.

Echevarría, Roberto González, and Pupo-Walker, Enrique. (Eds.). (1996). *The Cambridge History of Latin American Literature*. (3 vols.). New York: Cambridge University Press.

Figueredo, D. H. (Ed.). (2006). *Encyclopedia of Caribbean Literature*. (2 vols.). Westport, CT: Greenwood Press.

Foster, David William. (Ed.). (1994). *Latin American Writers on Gay and Lesbian Themes: A Bio-Critical Sourcebook*. Westport, CT: Greenwood Press.

Foster, David William. (Ed.). (1994). *Mexican Literature: A History*. Austin, TX: University of Texas Press.

Gies, David T. (Ed.). (1999). *The Cambridge Companion to Modern Spanish Culture*. New York: Cambridge University Press.

Gies, David T. (Ed.). (2004). *The Cambridge History of Spanish Literature*. New York: Cambridge University Press.

Hart, Stephen M. (2007). *A Companion to Latin American Literature*. (rev. ed.). Rochester, NY: Tamesis.

Irele, F. Abiola, and Gikandi, Simon. (Eds.). (2004). *The Cambridge History of African and Caribbean Literature*. (2 vols.). New York: Cambridge University Press.

Kaufman, Helena, and Klobucka, Anna. (Eds.). (1997). *After the Revolution: Twenty Years of Portuguese Literature*. Cranbury, NJ: Associated University Presses.

Kennoy, Ray; Treece, David; and Hyland, Paul. (1995). *The Babel Guide to the Fiction of Portugal, Brazil & Africa in English Translation*. London: Boulevard.

Leonard, Kathy S. (2007). *Latin American Women Writers: A Resource Guide to Titles in English*. Lanham, MD: Scarecrow Press.

Levine, Linda Gould; Marson, Ellen Engelson; and Waldman, Gloria Feiman. (Eds.). (1993). *Spanish Women Writers: A Bio-Bibliographical Source Book*. Westport, CT: Greenwood Press.

Lisboa, Eugénio, and Macedo, Helder. (Eds.). (1995). *The Dedalus Book of Portuguese Fantasy*. (Trans. by Margaret Jull Costa). New York: Hippocrene.

Lockhart, Darrell B. (Ed.). (2004). *Latin American Mystery Writers: An A-to-Z Guide*. Westport, CT: Greenwood Press.

Martínez, Julio A. (Ed.). (1990). *Dictionary of Twentieth-Century Cuban Literature*. New York: Greenwood Press.

Moss, Joyce. (Ed.). (1999). *Latin American Literature and Its Times*. Detroit, MI: Gale.

Moss, Joyce. (Ed.). (2002). *Spanish and Portuguese Literatures and Their Times (The Iberian Peninsula)*. Detroit, MI: Gale.

Peña, Carlos González. (1968). *History of Mexican Literature*. (Trans. by Gusta Barfield Nance and Florene Johnson Dunstan). Dallas, TX: Southern Methodist University Press.

Pérez, Janet, and Ihrie, Maureen. (Eds.). (2002). *The Feminist Encyclopedia of Spanish Literature*. (2 vols.). Westport, CT: Greenwood Press.

Smith, Verity. (Ed.). (1997). *Encyclopedia of Latin American Literature*. London: Fitzroy Dearborn.

Solé, Carlos A., and Abreu, Maria Isabel. (Eds.). (1989–ongoing). *Latin American Writers*. (3 vols. with supplements). New York: Charles Scribner's Sons.

Stern, Irwin. (Ed.). (1988). *Dictionary of Brazilian Literature*. Westport, CT: Greenwood Press.

Swanson, Philip. (Ed.). (1990). *Landmarks in Modern Latin American Fiction*. London: Routledge.

Swanson, Philip. (1995). *The New Novel in Latin America: Politics and Popular Culture After the Boom*. Manchester, UK: Manchester University Press.

Tamen, Miguel, and Buescu, Helena C. (Eds.). (1999). *A Revisionary History of Portuguese Literature*. New York: Garland.

Treece, David, and Keenoy, Ray. (2001). *The Babel Guide to Brazilian Fiction in English Translation*. London: Boulevard.

Turner, Harriet, and de Martínez, Adelaida López. (Eds.). (2003). *The Cambridge Companion to the Spanish Novel from 1600 to the Present*. New York: Cambridge University Press.

Valdés, Mario J., and Kadir, Djelal. (Eds.). (2004). *Literary Cultures of Latin America*. (3 vols.). New York: Oxford University Press.
Ward, Philip. (Ed.). (1978). *The Oxford Companion to Spanish Literature*. Oxford: Clarendon Press.
Williams, Raymond Leslie. (2007). *The Columbia Guide to the Latin American Novel Since 1945*. New York: Columbia University Press.
Williams, Raymond Leslie. (1998). *The Modern Latin American Novel*. New York: Twayne.

ANNOTATIONS FOR TRANSLATED BOOKS FROM CENTRAL AMERICA

Costa Rica

Tatiana Lobo. *Assault on Paradise*.
Translated by Asa Zatz. Willimantic, CT: Curbstone Press, 1998. 297 pages.
Genre/literary style/story type: historical fiction
After a night of drunken debauchery in Seville, Pedro Abaran barely escapes the long arm of the Spanish Inquisition, embarking on a journey that eventually takes him to Cartago, Costa Rica. At first, he finds refuge in a Catholic monastery and then becomes a government clerk, befriends a local shoemaker, and falls in love with a mute native Indian woman, with whom he has a child. The novel provides a rich and raucous portrait of colonial life in Central America as well as insight into the troubled relationship between Mayan culture and oppressive Spanish authorities. This novel will appeal to fans of Gabriel García Márquez and Eduardo Galeano.
Subject keywords: colonization and colonialism; indigenous culture
Original language: Spanish
Sources consulted for annotation:
Benson, Margaret. *Library Journal* 123 (1 November 1998): 126.
Global Books in Print (online) (review from *Kirkus Reviews*).
Lindstrom, Naomi. *World Literature Today* 73 (Spring 1999): 312.
Parini, Jay. *The New York Times Book Review*, 3 January 1999, p. 10.
Steinberg, Sybil S. *Publishers Weekly* 245 (28 September 1998): 73.

Óscar Núñez Olivas. *Cadence of the Moon*.
Translated by Joanna Griffin. Laverstock, Wiltshire, UK: Aflame Books, 2007. 274 pages.
Genres/literary styles/story types: crime fiction; suspense
According to the publisher's website, this book combines elements of romance and mystery to tell the story of Costa Rica's "first known case of a serial killer." As the police and media try to solve the horrid crimes, political and financial considerations get in the way of the search for truth.
Subject keyword: power
Original language: Spanish
Sources consulted for annotation:
Aflame Books (book description), http://www.aflamebooks.com.
Bol.it (book description), http://www.bol.it/books.
Global Books in Print (online) (synopsis/book jacket).

Cuba

Eliseo Alberto. *Caracol Beach*.
Translated by Edith Grossman. New York: Alfred A. Knopf, 2000. 286 pages.
Genre/literary style/story type: mainstream fiction
Beto Milanés lives in Caracol Beach, Florida. He is a Cuban veteran of the 1976 Angolan war who suffers from posttraumatic stress disorder and who has failed in two previous suicide attempts. The

tormented world of Beto soon intersects with a raucous high school party, the inquisitive neighbor disturbed by the goings-on at the party, the denizens of a seedy bar, and a conscientious police officer.

Subject keyword: social problems
Original language: Spanish
Sources consulted for annotation:
Bronfman, Alejandra. *Washington Times*, 21 May 2000, p. B8.
Polk, James. *The New York Times Book Review*, 13 August 2000, p. 21.
Shreve, Jack. *Library Journal* 125 (15 June 2000): 111.
Steinberg, Sybil S. *Publishers Weekly* 247 (17 April 2000): 51.

Reinaldo Arenas. *The Color of Summer, or The New Garden of Earthly Delights.*
Translated by Andrew Hurley. New York: Viking, 2000. 417 pages.
Genres/literary styles/story types: mainstream fiction; magical realism
Fifo, an oppressive Cuban dictator, brings his enemies back to life to celebrate his enduring rule and his 50th anniversary. But even the dead try to escape Fifo's so-called utopia. Against this political background, the author presents the tragic semiautobiographical story of a gay man with a triple name: Skunk in a Funk, Gabriel, and Reinaldo. Because the oppressive regime considers homosexuality to be antirevolutionary, the protagonist's life is filled with terror and hardship. Allegory mixes with the grotesque, and both combine with political satire to make this book a devastatingly frank history of modern Cuba. This novel is the fourth in the five-part Pentagonia series.
Subject keywords: politics; power
Original language: Spanish
Sources consulted for annotation:
Amazon.com (review from *Kirkus Reviews*).
Hooper, Brad. *Booklist* 96 (June 1/June 15 2000): 1807.
Kempf, Andrea. *Library Journal* 127 (1 April 2002): 168.
Menton, Seymour. *Hispanic Review* 66 (Autumn 1998): 501.
"Reinaldo Arenas." *Dictionary of Literary Biography Online*. Thomson Gale databases.
Shreve, Jack. *Library Journal* 125 (July 2000): 136.
Siegel, Lee. *The New York Times Book Review*, 15 October 2000, p. 28.
Steinberg, Sybil S. *Publishers Weekly* 247 (22 May 2000): 72.
Some other translated books written by Reinaldo Arenas: *Singing from the Well*; *The Palace of the White Skunks*; *Farewell to the Sea: A Novel of Cuba*; *The Assault*; *Old Rosa: A Novel in Two Stories*; *The Doorman*

Antonio Benítez-Rojo. *Sea of Lentils.*
Translated by James Maraniss. Amherst, MA: University of Massachusetts Press, 1990. 201 pages.
Genre/literary style/story type: historical fiction
This novel, which begins in 1598, portrays the discovery of America and analyzes how the experience of colonization irrevocably colored Europeans' views of themselves and others. Dying King Philip II of Spain ponders difficult questions about the defeat of the Spanish Armada by England; the slave trade; the conquest of Florida; and the atrocities against native peoples committed by the soldiers who accompanied Columbus. This book is part of a trilogy exploring Caribbean history. The other two volumes are *The Repeating Island* and *A View from the Mangrove*.
Subject keywords: colonization and colonialism; indigenous culture
Original language: Spanish
Sources consulted for annotation:
Beck, Mary Ellen. *Library Journal* 115 (August 1990): 138.

Fisher, Barbara. *The New York Times Book Review*, 25 October 1998, p. 36.
Steinberg, Sybil S. *Publishers Weekly* 237 (31 August 1990): 50.
Another translated book written by Antonio Benítez-Rojo: *The Magic Dog and Other Stories*

Daina Chaviano. *The Island of Eternal Love*.
Translated by Andrea Labinger. New York: Penguin, 2008. 336 pages.
Genres/literary styles/story types: mainstream fiction; magical realism
Cecilia is a Miami journalist of Cuban-American descent who is working on an unbelievable story: a phantom house that suddenly appears and then disappears—only to appear somewhere else. As she tries to get to the bottom of this perplexing phenomenon, she meets the elderly Amalia at a Little Havana bar. Listening to Amalia's stories about her heritage that includes Spanish, African, and Chinese roots, Cecilia begins to understand that the phantom house may be a manifestation of supernatural forces.
Subject keyword: family histories
Original language: Spanish
Source consulted for annotation:
Global Books in Print (online) (reviews from *Library Journal* and *Publishers Weekly*).

Arnaldo Correa. *Cold Havana Ground*.
Translated by Marjorie Moore. New York: Akashic Books, 2003. 317 pages.
Genres/literary styles/story types: crime fiction; police detectives
The body of the last surviving member of a secret Chinese society is stolen from the Havana cemetery, and retired detective Alvaro Antonio Molinet is called back to duty to take on the case. His pursuit of the thieves leads him into a strange world of secret societies and international hijinks. The novel contains multiple references to Afro-Cuban and Chinese religious practices. Some reviewers drew comparison with the work of Janwillem Van de Wetering and Eliot Pattison.
Subject keyword: urban life
Original language: Spanish
Sources consulted for annotation:
Artalejo, Lucrecia. *World Literature Today* 79 (January/April 2005): 107
Cannon, Peter. *Publishers Weekly* 250 (27 October 2003): 47.
Graff, Keir. *Booklist* 100 (15 November 2003): 583.
Lunn, Bob. *Library Journal* 128 (1 November 2003): 122.
Stasio, Marilyn. *The New York Times Book Review*, 23 November 2003, p. 29.
Another translated book written by Arnaldo Correa: *Spy's Fate*

Jesús Díaz. *The Initials of the Earth*.
Translated by Kathleen Ross. Durham, NC: Duke University Press, 2006. 430 pages.
Genre/literary style/story type: historical fiction
If you ever wanted to know what the Cuban Revolution was really like, this book provides the definitive answer. It traces the life of Carlos Pérez Cifredo, who is preparing to submit himself to the judgment of a committee of peers as to whether he has been a good communist. Thus, he reviews his history and accomplishments: his coddled childhood; early success as a leader of university students; the Bay of Pigs invasion and the Cuban missile crisis; and his superhuman efforts in 1970 as the manager of a sugar mill to meet the extraordinarily large production quota assigned by Fidel Castro. As Terrence Rafferty observed, the novel can be understood as "one long dark night of a Cuban revolutionary soul awaiting eternal salvation or eternal damnation."
Subject keywords: politics; power
Original language: Spanish

Sources consulted for annotation:
Global Books in Print (online) (synopsis/book jacket; review from *Choice*).
Rafferty, Terrence. *The New York Times Book Review*, 7 January 2007 (online).

Abilio Estévez. *Distant Palaces*.
Translated by David L. Frye. New York: Arcade, 2004. 268 pages.
Genre/literary style/story type: mainstream fiction
Victorio, a 46-year-old gay man, becomes homeless after his building is demolished. Lonely, broke, and disheartened, he wanders the streets of contemporary Havana, filled with crumbling and demolished buildings. Finally, he befriends Selma, a young prostitute, and Don Fuco, an old acrobatic clown. The three companions rely on one another to cope with a hostile outside world.
Subject keyword: urban life
Original language: Spanish
Sources consulted for annotation:
Chadwell, Faye A. *Library Journal* 129 (15 February 2004): 160.
Leber, Michele. *Booklist* 100 (15 November 2003): 580.
Publishers Weekly 250 (24 November 2003): 41.
Another translated book written by Abilio Estévez: *Thine Is the Kingdom*

Norberto Fuentes. *The Autobiography of Fidel Castro*.
Translated by Anna Kushner. New York: W. W. Norton, 2009. 572 pages.
Genre/literary style/story type: historical fiction
It is hard to find any critic who has had a negative word to say about this novel that takes the form of an imagined autobiography. Fuentes, who finally left Cuba in 1994 after Gabriel García Márquez intervened on his behalf, has expertly captured the nuances, megalomania, and ultimate tragedy of Fidel Castro in a breathtaking fictional account that allows readers not only to relive the central events of the Cuban revolution but to also gain insight into the tangled social and cultural consequences of Castro's self-aggrandizing and bombastic worldview. The Castro that emerges is at once a fascinating and frightening figure. As Michiko Kakutani points out, Fuentes's book can be placed in the Latin American Strongman Novel category—to be read alongside such classics as Mario Vargas Llosa's *Feast of the Goat* and Márquez's *Autumn of the Patriarch*.
Subject keywords: politics; power
Original language: Spanish
Source consulted for annotation:
Kakutani, Michiko. *The New York Times*, 15 December 2009 (online).

Pedro Juan Gutiérrez. *Dirty Havana Trilogy*.
Translated by Natasha Wimmer. New York: Farrar, Straus and Giroux, 2001. 392 pages.
Genre/literary style/story type: mainstream fiction
Set in 1990s Havana, this novel is a scathing critique of Cuban society under Castro. It focuses on Pedro Juan, an ex-journalist who has been abandoned by his wife. After losing his job because of his intolerance for sundry political machinations, Pedro Juan survives as best he can: garbage collector, black market operative, drug dealer, hustler, and gigolo. Readers may also wish to explore *Tropical Animal*, which follows Pedro Juan into his late forties. Some critics have observed that Gutiérrez can be linked with Jean Genêt and Charles Bukowski because of the brutal honesty with which all three writers eviscerate social and cultural hypocrisies.
Subject keywords: social problems; urban life
Original language: Spanish

Sources consulted for annotation:
Amazon.com (book description).
Bernstein, Richard. *The New York Times*, 5 February 2001, p. E7.
Garret, Daniel. *Review of Contemporary Fiction* 21 (Fall 2001): 215–216.
Publishers Weekly 252 (7 November 2005): 49.
Steinberg, Sybil S. *Publishers Weekly* 247 (16 October 2000): 46.
Tepper, Anderson. *The New York Times Book Review*, 27 March 2005.
Some other translated books written by Pedro Juan Gutiérrez: *The Insatiable Spider Man*; *Tropical Animal*

Leonardo Padura (Leonardo Padura Fuentes). *Adiós Hemingway*.
Translated by John King. Edinburgh, UK: Canongate, 2005. 229 pages.
Genres/literary styles/story types: crime fiction; police detectives
When the remains of an FBI agent shot 40 years ago in Hemingway's Cuban home are discovered, Mario Conde—a retired police officer who is now a writer and a bookseller—becomes involved in the murder investigation. All his life, Conde has been befuddled by his love-hate relationship with Hemingway; now he has a chance to get an unmediated look at the famous author's past. This book, which alternates between 1958 and the present, will appeal to those who are interested in Hemingway's life as well as those who like Paul Auster's work and the Inspector Espinosa series by L. A. García-Roza. Readers may also enjoy Padura's Havana Quartet, a series of four books that further chronicle Conde's experiences in the crime-ridden, poverty-stricken, yet exotic Cuban capital.
Subject keyword: urban life
Original language: Spanish
Sources consulted for annotation:
Gargan, William. *Library Journal* 130 (15 May 2005): 110.
Ott, Bill. *Booklist* 101 (1 May 2005): 1522.
Parker, James. *The New York Times Book Review*, 17 April 2005, p. 22
Salter Reynolds, Susan. *Los Angeles Times*, 1 May 2005, p. R11.
Some other translated books written by Leonardo Padura: *Havana Red*; *Havana Black*; *Havana Gold*; *Havana Blue*

José Manuel Prieto. *Rex*.
Translated by Esther Allen. New York: Grove Press, 2009. 288 pages.
Genre/literary style/story type: mainstream fiction
This is a witty and sly novel about the adventures of a tutor in a nouveau-riche Russian family in the Costa del Sol region of Spain. His ostensible task is to educate Petya, the 11-year-old son of Vasily and Nelly, but he teaches him nothing but lessons from Proust's *Remembrance of Things Past*. Soon, he becomes involved in the byazantine world of Russian crime, discovering that Vasily and Nelly owe their wealth to fake diamonds.
Related title by the same author:
Readers may also enjoy *Nocturnal Butterflies of the Russian Empire*, a book that invokes Nabokov's fascination with collecting butterflies. Here, the narrator-smuggler is commissioned to catch a rare butterfly that makes its home near the Black Sea. But while in Istanbul, he meets a young woman working as a prostitute who wants to return home to Russia.
Subject keywords: politics; power
Original language: Spanish
Sources consulted for annotation:
Global Books in Print (online) (reviews for both novels from *Library Journal* and *Publishers Weekly*).

Wimmer, Natasha. *The Nation* (20 May 2009) (online).
Another translated book written by José Manuel Prieto: *Nocturnal Butterflies of the Russian Empire*

Sonia Rivera-Valdés. *The Forbidden Stories of Marta Veneranda.*
Translated by Dick Cluster, Marina Harss, Mark Schafer, and Alan West-Duran. New York: Seven Stories Press, 2000. 158 pages.
Genres/literary styles/story types: mainstream fiction; short stories
Marta Veneranda, a student in New York, gathers 10 stories about sex from immigrant Cubans. Her aim to is explore how individuals deal with what is typically an embarrassing topic and how they adjust their frames of reference to accommodate the erotic.
Subject keyword: social roles
Original language: Spanish
Sources consulted for annotation:
Hoffert, Barbara. *Library Journal* 125 (15 October 2000): 55.
Hove, Thomas. *Review of Contemporary Fiction* 22 (Spring 2002): 141.
"Sonia Rivera-Valdes." *Contemporary Authors Online*. Gale databases, 2002.
Steinberg, Sybil S. *Publishers Weekly* 248 (1 January 2001): 70.

Severo Sarduy. *Cobra and Maitreya: Two Novels.*
Translated by Suzanne Jill Levine. Normal, IL: Dalkey Archive Press, 1995. 273 pages.
Genres/literary styles/story types: mainstream fiction; postmodernism
Both novels feature unpredictable metamorphoses and unexpected transpositions through space and time. Together with a group of friends, a transvestite changes into a Tibetan lama interested in Tantric Buddhism. A Cuban-Chinese cook becomes Buddha. The action moves from Tibet to Pakistan, Ceylon, and Cuba; then to Miami, Washington, and New York; and later to Iran and Afghanistan. Critics have pointed out that the author draws on the philosophies of such postmodern writers as Roland Barthes, Jacques Derrida, and Gilles Deleuze.
Subject keyword: identity
Original language: Spanish
Sources consulted for annotation:
Dalkey Archive Press website, http://www.dalkeyarchive.com.
Perez, Rolando. *Review of Contemporary Fiction* 24 (1 April 2004): 94.
Rogers, Michael. *Library Journal* 120 (1 May 1995): 138.
West, Alan. *The Washington Post*, 31 July 1995, p. D2.
Another translated book written by Severo Sarduy: *From Cuba with a Song*

Zoé Valdés. *Dear First Love.*
Translated by Andrew Hurley. New York: HarperCollins, 2002. 291 pages.
Genres/literary styles/story types: mainstream fiction; magical realism
Middle-aged Danae is unhappily married and depressed. Smothered by family obligations, she escapes from Havana to a rural area where she and others performed backbreaking agricultural work in the 1970s at the behest of Fidel Castro. Here, Danae fell in love with a girl named Tierra Fortuna Munda, to whom she now returns. The novel contrasts life in the economically and morally decaying Cuban capital with the vibrancy and spiritedness of rural life. The author introduces elements of fantasy into her narrative, drawing on symbols from Catholic and Yoruba religions.
Subject keywords: rural life; urban life
Original language: Spanish

Sources consulted for annotation:
Amazon.com (book description).
Anders, Gigi. *Hispanic* 15 (October 2002): 56.
Burkhardt, Joanna. *Library Journal* 127 (15 September 2002): 94.
Ortiz, Ricardo L. *Lambda Book Report* 11 (November/December 2002): 23.
Schuessler, Jennifer. *The New York Times Book Review*, 1 September 2002, p. 4.
Some other translated books written by Zoé Valdés: *I Gave You All I Had*; *Yocandra in the Paradise of Nada*

Dominican Republic

Marisela Rizik. *Of Forgotten Times.*
Translated by Isabel Zakrzewski Brown. Willimantic, CT: Curbstone Press, 2004. 215 pages.
Genres/literary styles/story types: mainstream fiction; magical realism
This novel by the Santa Domingo–born writer and filmmaker relates a tragic and multifaceted story about four generations of characters, including Herminia and Lorenza Parduz, who have supernatural powers and practice voodoo. Set on a fictional island in the Caribbean, it is a story of romance, domestic lives, oppressive men, abused women, and complicated relationships between mothers and daughters. The island is governed by a dictator resembling the Dominican ruler Rafael Trujillo. Fusing magical and conventional realism, the novel is reminiscent of works by Gabriel García Márquez, Jamaica Kincaid, and Derek Walcott.
Subject keywords: family histories; politics
Original language: Spanish
Sources consulted for annotation:
Amazon.com (book description).
Maristed, Kai. *Los Angeles Times*, 9 June 2004, p. E5.
St. John, Janet. *Booklist* 100 (15 March 2004): 1267.

Viriato Sención. *They Forged the Signature of God.*
Translated by Asa Zatz. Willimantic, CT: Curbstone Press, 1995. 250 pages.
Genres/literary styles/story types: historical fiction; magical realism
Denounced by the Dominican authorities, this book became a bestseller in the author's native country—no doubt partly because of said denunciation. It is a scathing depiction of the dictatorial regimes of Rafael Trujillo, civilian and then military ruler of the Dominican Republic from 1930 until his assassination in 1961, and Joaquín Balaguer, successor to Trujillo and three-term president from the early 1960s to 1996—with intermittent gaps. It focuses on three seminarians who must not only come to terms with the Catholic church's patriarchal oppressiveness and quiescence in the face of the tyrannical rule of Trujillo-Balaguer but also survive in an atmosphere of ruthless politics and bloody power struggles.
Subject keywords: power; religion
Original language: Spanish
Sources consulted for annotation:
Amazon.com (book description).
Schroeder, Steve. *Booklist* 92 (15 February 1996): 992.
Simson, Maria. *Publishers Weekly* 243 (8 January 1996): 63.
Unger, David. (Back cover of the book).

El Salvador

Manlio Argueta. *Little Red Riding Hood in the Red Light District.*
Translated by Edward Waters Hood. Willimantic, CT: Curbstone Press, 1998. 237 pages.

Genre/literary style/story type: mainstream fiction
In the late 1970s, Alfonso writes poetry and studies at the university but soon enters the fight against El Salvador's dictatorship. At first, he prints and distributes illegal literature, but then he joins the guerilla movement, to which he is blindly devoted. But political commitment has a significant cost: He abandons his pregnant girlfriend, who idolizes Alfonso with the simplicity of true and abiding love.
Related title by the same author:
Readers may also be interested in *One Day of Life*, which, as the title indicates, describes 24 harrowing hours of a peasant family's ordeal in a violence-ridden region of northern El Salvador.
Subject keywords: politics; power
Original language: Spanish
Sources consulted for annotation:
Diaz, Katharine A. *Hispanic* 12 (October 1999): 96.
Markee, Patrick. *The New York Times Book Review*, 17 January 1999, p. 13.
Steinberg, Sybil S. *Publishers Weekly* 245 (19 October 1998): 56.
Some other translated books written by Manlio Argueta: *One Day of Life*; *Magic Dogs of the Volcanoes*; *A Place Called Milagro del la Paz*; *Cuzcatlán: Where the Southern Sea Beats*

Mario Bencastro. *Odyssey to the North*.
Translated by Susan Giersbach Rascon. Houston, TX: Arte Público Press, 1998. 192 pages.
Genre/literary style/story type: mainstream fiction
Set in the 1980s and early 1990s in Washington, D.C., this novel recounts the story of Calixto, a Salvadoran immigrant who must adjust to a new life in an unfamiliar culture. Like many Central American refugees who fled persecution, civil war, and famine, he lives in a hovel, sharing his roof with 19 other people. He passes his days under the constant threat of deportation and survives on low-paid temporary jobs. Although his native village was destroyed, Calixto stays emotionally bound to his family in Salvador.
Subject keyword: culture conflict
Original language: Spanish
Sources consulted for annotation:
Amazon.com (book description).
Mujica, Barbara. *Americas* 51 (May/June 1999): 62.
Steinberg, Sybil S. *Publishers Weekly* 245 (26 October 1998): 44.
Some other translated books written by Mario Bencastro: *A Shot in the Cathedral*; *The Tree of Life: Stories of Civil War*; *A Promise to Keep*

Horacio Castellanos Moya. *Senselessness*.
Translated by Katherine Silver. New York: New Directions, 2008. 142 pages.
Genre/literary style/story type: mainstream fiction
This novel recounts the experiences of a writer who has taken a job at the palace of an archbishop of the Roman Catholic church copyediting a voluminous report about a series of human rights violations committed by army personnel against indigenous peoples in a Central American country. As he works on the report, he is not only affected by the grisly and haunting details of the various atrocities and massacres, but he becomes increasingly paranoid. He also becomes obsessed with seducing his coworker Fátima, who eventually reveals that her boyfriend is an Uruguyan army officer, which only increases the writer's paranoia.
Related title by the same author:
Dance with Snakes revolves around Eduardo Sosa's fascination with a dilapidated yellow Chevrolet that is a constant presence in his neighborhood. Sosa soon discovers that the car is inhabited by

Jacinto Bustillo, whom he feels compelled to kill, after which he moves into the car—only to find that it is home to four snakes. As Sosa, a failed sociologist, retraces Bustillo's once-prosperous life, the snakes escape, causing a reign of terror.
Subject keywords: politics; power
Original language: Spanish
Sources consulted for annotation:
Global Books in Print (online) (reviews from *Library Journal* and *Publishers Weekly*).
Wimmer, Natasha. *The Nation* (14 December 2009) (online).
Some other translated books written by Horacio Castellanos Moya: *Dance with Snakes*; *The She-Devil in the Mirror*

Guatemala

Arturo Arias. *Rattlesnake*.
Translated by Seán Higgins and Jill Robbins. Willimantic, CT: Curbstone Press, 2003. 245 pages.
Genres/literary styles/story types: thrillers; political thrillers
A rekindled romantic flame gets in the way of a dangerous mission undertaken by Tom Wright, a CIA agent, who must locate an underground political group known as EGP that has kidnapped an Australian banker. But Sandra Herrera, Wright's first love, places the protagonist in danger and undermines the success of his task. She has married into one of the richest Guatemalan families and has become involved with international drug dealers and the EGP.
Subject keyword: social problems
Original language: Spanish
Sources consulted for annotation:
Amazon.com (book description).
Martinez, Ani. *Hispanic* 16 (December 2003): 68.
Pitt, Davic. *Booklist* 100 (1 December 2003): 648.
Another translated book written by Arturo Arias: *After the Bombs*

Ronald Flores. *Final Silence*.
Translated by Gavin O'Toole. Laverstock, Wiltshire, UK: Aflame Books, 2008. 108 pages.
Genre/literary style/story type: mainstream fiction
Ernesto Sandoval is a successful psychologist in Minnesota with a unique speciality: coming to the aid of victims of torture. When he decides to return to Guatemala, he envisions using his skills to treat and counsel the numerous victims of Guatamela's bloody internecine struggles, autocratic military rule, and violent counterinsurgencies. But his first patient is General Jorge Camacho, a man who regularly gave orders to inflict torture on others.
Subject keywords: politics; power
Original language: Spanish
Sources consulted for annotation:
Global Books in Print (online) (review from *School Library Journal*).
New Internationalist (May 2008) (Issue 411) (online).

Rodrigo Rey Rosa. *The Good Cripple*.
Translated by Esther Allen. New York: New Directions, 2004. 116 pages.
Genre/literary style/story type: crime fiction; suspense
Juan Luis Luna, a resident of Guatemala City, has been kidnapped. His new home away from home could not be more rancid: a decaying fuel holding tank under an old gas station. When his wealthy father does not respond to ransom demands, the kidnappers begin to mutilate their captive. The

book explores the psychology of survival against the background of degrading physical and emotional hardships.
Subject keyword: social problems
Original language: Spanish
Source consulted for annotation:
Amazon.com (book description; all editorial reviews).
Some other translated books written by Rodrigo Rey Rosa: *The Beggar's Knife*; *Dust on Her Tongue*; *The Pelcari Project*; *The Path Doubles Back*

Oswaldo Salazar. *From the Darkness*.
Translated by Gavin O'Toole. Laverstock, Wiltshire: Aflame Books, 2007. 191 pages.
Genres/literary styles/story types: crime fiction; historical mysteries
In 1939, Mauricia Hernández—an ordinary woman in a small rural village—fatally poisoned her abusive husband. The case was a cause célèbre in Guatamala, raising important social and philosophical issues. Should the asbtract norms of legal justice prevail—norms that were instituted and administered by an unyielding patriarchal and authoritarian society? Or should the special circumstances of each case enter into the picture?
Subject keywords: family histories; rural life
Original language: Spanish
Sources consulted for annotation:
Aflame Books (book description), http://www.aflamebooks.com.
Carey, Eugene. *Latin American Review of Books* (online).

Honduras

Roberto Quesada. *The Big Banana*.
Translated by Walter Krochmal. Houston, TX: Arte Público Press, 1999. 248 pages.
Genre/literary style/story type: mainstream fiction
Eduardo Lin is an aspiring actor from Honduras nicknamed the Big Banana. A construction worker by day and an inveterate party regular by night, Eduardo has a big ego and even bigger dreams. Leaving his fiancée behind in Honduras, he came to New York in the late 1980s and now lives in the Bronx. Although he fantasizes about being famous and impressing directors such as Woody Allen, his life consists of seducing women, heavy drinking, and debating Latin American politics with other immigrants. But he finally gets an audition with Steven Spielberg.
Subject keyword: culture conflict
Original language: Spanish
Sources consulted for annotation:
Olszewski, Lawrence. *Library Journal* 124 (15 February 1999): 185.
Steinberg, Sybil S. *Publishers Weekly* 246 (1 February 1999): 77.
Tsing Loh, Sandra. *The New York Times Book Review*, 12 September 1999, p. 43.
Some other translated books written by Roberto Quesada: *Never Through Miami*; *The Ships*

Mexico

Homero Aridjis. *The Lord of the Last Days: Visions of the Year 1000*.
Translated by Betty Ferber. New York: Morrow, 1995. 259 pages.
Genre/literary style/story type: historical fiction
Medieval Spain was a rough and tumble place, with political and religious rivalries galore. Alfonso de Leon is a monk. His brother is Abd Allah, part of a group of Muslims intent on attacking

Alfonso's monastery. As Alfonso struggles with his sexual desires and false prophets and as he watches for signs of the apocalypse, he is caught up in the age-old tale of Cain and Abel.
Subject keyword: religion
Original language: Spanish
Sources consulted for annotation:
Flanagan, Margaret. *Booklist* 92 (1 September 1995): 37.
Olzhewski, Lawrence. *Library Journal* 120 (August 1995): 113.
Steinberg, Sybil S. *Publishers Weekly* 242 (17 July 1995): 217.
Some other translated books written by Homero Aridjis: *1492: The Life and Times of Juan Cabezón of Castile*; *Persephone*

Guillermo Arriaga Jordán. *The Night Buffalo*.
Translated by Alan Page. New York: Atria Books, 2006. 228 pages.
Genres/literary styles/story types: crime fiction; urban fiction
Themes of passion, insanity, loyalty, and guilt are the focus of this novel by one of Mexico's most popular screenwriters. Manuel and Gregorio are bound by a blood oath that is sealed by a buffalo tattoo on their left arms, but Tania, Gregorio's girlfriend, has been cheating on him with Manuel for a few years. Even after Gregorio slips into madness and commits suicide, he keeps haunting his friend from his grave. Menacing, vengeance-filled notes left behind by Gregorio drive Manuel insane. Gradually, Manuel deteriorates into delusions and lunacy—a state of affairs exacerbated by Tania's disappearance.
Subject keyword: identity
Original language: Spanish
Sources consulted for annotation:
Olszewski, Lawrence. *Library Journal* 131 (1 April 2006): 80.
Publishers Weekly 253 (27 February 2006): 33.
Segedin, Benjamin. *Booklist* 102 (June1/June 15 2006): 33.
Another translated book written by Guillermo Arriaga Jordán: *A Sweet Scent of Death*

Carmen Boullosa. *Leaving Tabasco*.
Translated by Geoff Hargreaves. New York: Grove Press, 2001. 244 pages.
Genres/literary styles/story types: mainstream fiction; magical realism; coming-of-age
This novel, which has evoked comparisons with the work of Toni Morrison, Laura Esquivel, Gabriel García Márquez, and Isabel Allende, focuses on Delmira Ulloa, a Mexican woman whose political activity forced her into exile in Germany. Here, her life is nothing compared with her wondrous childhood in a small town in Tabasco, where Delmira's days were filled with her grandmother's stories about extraordinary events: albino crocodiles; nonflying birds; and wondrous saints.
Subject keyword: rural life
Original language: Spanish
Sources consulted for annotation:
Augenbraum, Harold. *Library Journal* 126 (January 2001): 151.
Global Books in Print (online) (reviews from *Booklist* and *Kirkus Reviews*).
Tsing Loh, Sandra. *The New York Times Book Review*, 13 May 2001, p. 16.
Williams, Monica L. *Boston Globe*, 14 May 2001, p. B8.
Some other translated books written by Carmen Boullosa: *Cleopatra Dismounts*; *They're Cows, We're Pigs*; *The Miracle Worker*

Sara Levi Calderón. *The Two Mujeres*.
Translated by Gina Kaufer. San Francisco, CA: Aunt Lute Books, 1991. 211 pages.

Genre/literary style/story type: mainstream fiction' women's lives

This novel focuses on Valeria, a sophisticated middle-aged woman completing her Ph.D. in sociology. She comes from a Jewish family of Russian-Lithuanian descent who settled in Mexico to escape the Holocaust. Valeria narrates the story of her bicultural childhood as a Jewish Mexican, her failed marriage to an exacting and abusive man, and her lifelong love for a woman named Genovesa. Because she is from a relatively wealthy and privileged background, her struggles have little in common with the experiences of urban and rural middle-class lesbian characters. But even Valeria is not immune to homophobia, discrimination, and sexism, not to mention anti-Semitism.

Subject keyword: identity

Original language: Spanish

Sources consulted for annotation:

Havens, Shirley E. *Library Journal* 117 (15 June 1992): 128.

de la Pena, Terri. *Lambda Book Report* 3 (January 1992): 22.

Julieta Campos. *The Fear of Losing Eurydice*.

Translated by Leland H. Chambers. Normal, IL: Dalkey Archive Press, 1993. 121 pages.

Genres/literary styles/story types: mainstream fiction; experimental fiction

Monsieur N. is a French teacher, and as he sits in his favorite seaside café reading Jules Verne's *The Mysterious Island*, he is inspired to keep his own diary. He starts to collect interesting quotations about islands, supplementing these with reflective commentary about his efforts. The book echoes Italo Calvino's *Invisible Cities* in its narrative style.

Subject keyword: writers

Original language: Spanish

Sources consulted for annotation:

Ingraham, Janet. *Library Journal* 118 (January 1993): 163.

Steinberg, Sybil S. *Publishers Weekly* 239 (28 December 1992): 58.

Some other translated books written by Julieta Campos: *Celina or The Cats*; *She Has Reddish Hair and Her Name Is Sabina*

Martha Cerda. *Señora Rodríguez and Other Worlds*.

Translated by Sylvia Jiménez-Andersen. Durham, NC: Duke University Press, 1997. 133 pages.

Genres/literary styles/story types: mainstream fiction; postmodernism

Resembling the works of Jorge Luis Borges and Italo Calvino, this collection consists of some 30 vignettes about Señora Rodríguez and her surreal purse, which contains her entire world and defines her identity. There are the usual things: her marriage certificate, old bills, prophylactics, but also a picture autographed by Dorian Gray. When she reads a fiction book about herself, which is the same book as the reader is reading about her, she suddenly realizes that she may be no more than just a figment of someone's imagination.

Subject keyword: identity

Original language: Spanish

Sources consulted for annotation:

Guy, David. *The New York Times Book Review*, 26 October 1997, p. 40.

Pearl, Nancy. *Library Journal* 130 (15 June 2005): 119.

Steinberg, Sybil S. *Publishers Weekly* 244 (10 March 1997): 51.

Brianda Domecq. *The Astonishing Story of the Saint of Cabora*.

Translated by Kay S. García. Tempe, AZ: Bilingual Review Press, 1998. 362 pages.

Genre/literary style/story type: historical fiction

Teresa Urrea was a legendary figure in late nineteenth-century Mexican history. An illegitimate child of a wealthy landowner and an indigenous servant, Teresa educates herself and rises beyond her preordained social level. She even gains the recognition and acceptance of her unsympathetic father. In her late teenage years, she acquires miraculous healing powers and spends her life helping the sick and impoverished, earning the title of the Saint of Cabora. But her natural empathy makes her vulnerable to the manipulations of rebels fighting against the dictator Porfirio Diaz. Jailed and exiled to the United States along with her father, she continues to cure people. Never finding personal happiness, she dies at a young age.
Subject keywords: politics; power
Original language: Spanish
Sources consulted for annotation:
Cole, Melanie. *Hispanic* 11 (July/August 1998): 94.
Flanagan, Margaret. *Booklist* 94 (15 May 1998): 1594.
Gonzalez, Carolyn Ellis. *Library Journal* 123 (15 June 1998): 105.
Steinberg, Sybil S. *Publishers Weekly* 245 (27 April 1998): 46.
Some other translated books written by Brianda Domecq: *Eleven Days*; *When I Was a Horse*

Laura Esquivel. *Like Water for Chocolate.*
Translated by Carol and Thomas Christensen. New York: Doubleday, 1992. 245 pages.
Genres/literary styles/story types: mainstream fiction; magical realism; women's lives
This lyrical and sensuous book, which is subtitled "A Novel in Monthly Installments, with Recipes, Romances, and Home Remedies," revolves around the kitchen—the heart of a traditional Mexican household. Set at the turn of the twentieth century at the de la Garza ranch on the border with Texas, it tells the story of Tita, the youngest daughter of an affluent family. Her destiny is not to marry but to care for her aging Mama Elena. But Tita, a talented cook who has the magical power to communicate her feelings and passions through food, is not ready to give in to fate. She keeps fighting for her true love, Pedro, married to her older sister against his will; she also keeps fighting for the personal happiness of other women in her family. The book mixes folktales and magical realism with historical events, such as the Mexican Revolution. Critics have referred to this novel as an exotic blend of Whitney Otto's *How to Make an American Quilt* and the novels of Gabriel García Márquez.
Related title by the same author:
Readers may also enjoy *Malinche*, a book of historical fiction about La Malinche, a mysterious Mexican princess who—as the mistress of the Spanish conquistador Hernán Cortés—is traditionally looked upon as complicit in the subjugation and destruction of the Aztecs.
Subject keyword: family histories
Original language: Spanish
Sources consulted for annotation:
Amazon.com (review from *Kirkus Reviews*).
Mujica, Barbara. *Americas* 45 (July 1993): 60.
Parini, Jay. *The New York Times Book Review*, 18 June 2006 (online).
Partello, Peggie. *Library Journal* 117 (1 September 1992): 213.
Steinberg, Sybil S. *Publishers Weekly* 239 (24 August 1992): 61.
Some other translated books written by Laura Esquivel: *The Law of Love*; *Swift as Desire*; *Malinche*

Carlos Fuentes. *The Eagle's Throne.*
Translated by Kristina Cordero. New York: Random House, 2006. 336 pages.
Genre/literary style/story type: mainstream fiction

In 2020, when Mexican president Lorenzo Terán antagonizes the United States by calling for the withdrawal of American troops from Colombia and suggesting that Mexico should halt all northward oil exports, U.S. president Condoleezza Rice severs Mexico's access to a telecommunications satellite, thus ensuring that there is no possibility of phone or e-mail service. As epistolary communication makes a comeback, Fuentes's book becomes a delicious political satire and thriller as well as a contemporary piece of erotica along the lines of Choderlos de Laclos's *Les Liaisons Dangereuses* and Samuel Richardson's *Pamela* and *Clarissa*.

Related titles by the same author:

Readers may also enjoy *Christopher Unborn*, which is narrated by an unborn child endowed with stupendous intellectual skills. To say the least, it is a chaotic world into which very few people would want to be born. When Mexico finds itself financially bankrupt, it splits apart: The Mexican north joins the American south, forming a violence-infested region known as Mexamerica, while multinational oil companies take over Mexico's south. Also of interest may be Fuentes's memoir, *This I Believe: An A to Z of a Life*.

Subject keywords: politics; power

Original language: Spanish

Sources consulted for annotation:

Prose, Francine. *New York Times Book Review*, 28 September 2008 (online).

Rafferty, Terrence. *The New York Times Book Review*, 21 May 2006 (online).

Ruta, Suzanne. *The New York Times Book Review*, 20 August 1989 (online).

Some other translated books written by Carlos Fuentes: *Happy Families*; *The Old Gringo*; *Christopher Unborn*; *The Death of Artemio Cruz*; *The Years with Laura Diaz*; *This I Believe: An A to Z of a Life*

Juan García Ponce. *The House on the Beach*.

Translated by Margarita Vargas and Juan Bruce-Novoa. Austin, TX: University of Texas Press, 1994. 201 pages.

Genre/literary style/story type: mainstream fiction

As in much of life, this novel is devoid of significant events; there are neither adventures, nor steamy erotic scenes, nor intrigues, nor magical metamorphoses. But there is a house on the beach, situated in a rural community near Merida in Yucatan. And there are four protagonists gathered in the house one summer in the 1960s: Elena, a young lawyer from Mexico City; her childhood friend, Marta; Marta's alcoholic husband Eduardo; and Rafael, Eduardo's best friend and Marta's former lover. Unable to make sense of their desires and preferences, the characters are caught in constant soul searching and personal conflicts. They think about how their lifestyles transformed them; they deal with feelings of guilt, betrayal, friendship, and duty; and they desperately try to find a way to fill their vacuous lives.

Subject keywords: identity; social roles

Original language: Spanish

Sources consulted for annotation:

Amazon.com (book description).

Mujica, Barbara. *Americas* 47 (May 1995): 60.

Simson, Maria. *Publishers Weekly* 241 (4 July 1994): 57.

Another translated book written by Juan García Ponce: *Encounters*

Javier González-Rubio. *Loving You Was My Undoing*.

Translated by Yareli Arizmendi and Stephen A. Lytle. New York: Henry Holt, 1998. 155 pages.

Genre/literary style/story type: mainstream fiction

Set during the Mexican Revolution, this novel interweaves discussions of sociopolitical struggles with an exhilarating story about the love affair between Valentin Cobelo, the leader of a group of

revolutionaries and a military general of privileged ancestry, and Rosario Alomar, a recently widowed woman raised in a traditional Catholic family. Struggling with the carapace of authoritarian patriarchy, they find that passion is an ultimately liberating force.
Subject keyword: politics
Original language: Spanish
Sources consulted for annotation:
Joyce, Alice. *Booklist* 95 (January 1/January 15 1999): 831.
Olszewski, Lawrence. *Library Journal* 123 (December 1998): 158.
Steinberg, Sybil S. *Publishers Weekly* 246 (4 January 1999): 70.

Jorge Ibargüengoitia. *Two Crimes.*
Translated by Asa Zatz. New York: Avon Books, 1984. 197 pages.
Genres/literary styles/story types: crime fiction; suspense
Marcos arrives in the small town of Muerdago, Mexico, to seek his wealthy disabled uncle's money and estate, but he is only one of many relatives hovering over the aging Ramon. Marcos is also worried about the Mexican police, who once arrested him on trumped-up terrorist charges. He further complicates his situation by seducing his female cousins and getting in the middle of dormant family disputes. This book is written in the best traditions of the suspense stories of Friedrich Durrenmatt and Jorge Luis Borges.
Related title by the same author:
The author is perhaps most famous for *The Lightning of August*, where a group of amateurish and ultimately backstabbing generals—imbued with their own importance and the unquestioned righteousness of their cause—seek political power by any means possible, even if it means wholescale executions of the innocent.
Subject keywords: family histories; politics
Original language: Spanish
Sources consulted for annotation:
Dorfman, Ariel. *The New York Times Book Review*, 23 February 1986 (online).
The New York Times Book Review, 19 May 1985, p. 38.
Slung, Michele. *The Washington Post*, 16 September 1984 (from Factiva databases).
Some other translated books written by Jorge Ibargüengoitia: *The Lightning of August*; *The Dead Girls*

José López Portillo. *They Are Coming: The Conquest of Mexico.*
Translated by Beatrice Berler. Denton, TX: University of North Texas Press, 1992. 372 pages.
Genre/literary style/story type: historical fiction
Written by a former president of Mexico, this book recounts the love story between a Spanish Conquistador and a native Indian woman, but its real focus is the Spanish Conquest of 1522, the arrival of Hernán Cortés in the New World, the ensuing collision of cultures and religions, and the triumph of European Christian invaders. The author makes extensive use of primary documents and includes 103 drawings. It can be profitably read alongside historical works by William Prescott (*History of the Conquest of Mexico & History of the Conquest of Peru*) and Ronald Wright (*Stolen Continents: 500 Years of Conquest and Resistance in the Americas*).
Subject keywords: colonization and colonialism; indigenous culture
Original language: Spanish
Sources consulted for annotation:
Leonard, Louise. *Library Journal* 117 (15 March 1992): 126.
Stuttaford, Genevieve. *Publishers Weekly* 239 (2 March 1992): 56.
Some other translated books written by José López Portillo: *Quetzalcoatl*; *Don Q*

Angeles Mastretta. *Women with Big Eyes*.
Translated by Amy Schildhouse Greenberg. New York: Riverhead Books, 2003. 372 pages.
Genres/literary styles/story types: mainstream fiction; women's lives
This book consists of 39 stories, each of which features a female protagonist affectionately called tía (aunt). They are ordinary women from different walks of life at the beginning of the twentieth century: wives, mothers, and sisters from the author's native Puebla de los Angeles. Together, they symbolize strong Mexican women who must cope with grave illnesses, marital infidelity, and harmful rumors. Critcis noted that the book will appeal to those who like the fiction of Isabel Allende and Laura Esquivel.
Related title by the same author:
Readers may also be interested in *Lovesick*. Set during the Mexican Revolution at the beginning of the twentieth century, it focuses on the difficult choices Emilia Sauri must make. As someone whose father is a herbalist of Mayan ancestry and who has aspirations to be a medical doctor herself, should she give her heart to a physician or to a childhood friend who fervently partakes in the revolutionary cause?
Subject keyword: family histories
Original language: Spanish
Sources consulted for annotation:
Benson, Mary Margaret. *Library Journal* 128 (December 2003): 170.
Donovan, Deborah. *Booklist* 100 (1 November 2003): 479.
Global Books in Print (online) (reviews from *Kirkus Reviews* and *Publishers Weekly* for *Lovesick*).
Martín, Jorge Hernández. *Americas* 46 (May 1994): 60.
Mujica, Barbara. *Americas* 56 (July/August 2004): 59.
Publishers Weekly 250 (15 September 2003): 40.
Some other translated books written by Angeles Mastretta: *Lovesick*; *Mexican Bolero*; *Tear This Heart Out*

Miguel Méndez M. *The Dream of Santa María de las Piedras*.
Translated by David William Foster. Tempe, AZ: Bilingual Review Press, 1989. 194 pages.
Genres/literary styles/story types: mainstream fiction; magical realism
In the small town of Santa María de las Piedras in the Sonoran desert, there is not much to do, except talk and remember. Thus, a group of old men—good-natured bickerers and grumblers all—reconstruct their own lives and the life of their town, poignantly blending fact and fiction, drawing on an accumulated store of dreams and memories.
Subject keyword: rural life
Original language: Spanish
Sources consulted for annotation:
"Miguel Méndez M." *Contemporary Authors Online*. Thomson Gale, 2005.
"Miguel Méndez M." *Dictionary of Literary Biography Online*. Thomson Gale databases.
Some other translated books written by Miguel Méndez M.: *Pilgrims in Aztlán*; *From Labor to Letters: A Novel Autobiography*

Silvia Molina. *The Love You Promised Me*.
Translated by David Unger. Willimantic, CT: Curbstone Press, 1999. 152 pages.
Genre/literary style/story type: mainstream fiction
Marcela, an advertising writer from Mexico City married to a lawyer, has been an exemplary wife and mother for many years. But she recently had a passionate and short-lived extramarital affair with an older man. Abandoned, confused, and guilt-ridden, Marcela searches for her roots in the

small deserted village of San Lázaro. As she uncovers disconcerting secrets about her ancestors, she begins a slow and painful journey to self-acceptance and self-reconciliation.

Related title by the same author:

Readers may also be interested in the parly autobiographical novel *Gray Skies Tomorrow*, which focuses on the author's affair in 1969 in London, England, with Jose Carlos Becerra, a famous Mexican poet residing there on a Guggenheim grant.

Subject keyword: identity

Original language: Spanish

Sources consulted for annotation:

Fill, Grace. *Booklist* 96 (1 November 1999): 509.

Global Books in Print (online) (reviews for *Gray Skies Tomorrow* from *Kirkus Reviews* and *Library Journal*).

Hoffert, Barbara. *Library Journal* 124 (1 November 1999): 124.

Steinberg, Sybil S. *Publishers Weekly* 246 (11 October 1999): 57.

Tompkins, Cynthia. *World Literature Today* 74 (Autumn 2000): 899.

Another translated book written by Silvia Molina: *Gray Skies Tomorrow*

Alejandro Morales. *Barrio on the Edge*.

Translated by Francisco A. Lomelí. Tempe, AZ: Bilingual Review Press, 1998. 216 pages.

Genres/literary styles/story types: mainstream fiction; coming-of-age

Morales, an American writer of Mexican descent, provides insight into the life of the Mexican community in the United States through the eyes of two teenagers: Mateo and Jullán. Although both experience prejudice and cultural shock, Mateo adjusts better than Jullán by making a more concerted effort to assimilate. Jullán's experience is particularly dramatic because his problems of ethnic identity are exacerbated by ongoing conflict with his father.

Subject keyword: culture conflict

Original language: Spanish

Sources consulted for annotation:

"Alejandro Morales."*Dictionary of Literary Biography Online*. Thomson Gale databases.

Amazon.com (book description; back cover of the book).

Hispanic 11 (Jun 1998): 70.

Other books in English written by Alejandro Morales: *The Rag Doll Plagues*; *The Brick People*; *Death of an Anglo*; *Old Faces and New Wine*; *Waiting to Happen*

Ignacio Padilla. *Shadow Without a Name*.

Translated by Peter Bush and Anne McLean. New York: Farrar, Straus and Giroux, 2003. 192 pages.

Genres/literary styles/story types: thrillers; political thrillers

Chess is a game of rules and order, but in this novel, chess is more fluid and polyvalent. The metaphorical chessboard of the book covers Europe and the Middle East; chronologically, it continues through two world wars into the second half of the twentieth century. On an Austro-Hungarian train going to the front lines in 1916, two men play chess, with the winner getting to avoid the carnage of war by taking on the identity and job of a civilian railway worker. But the players become lost in a maze of secrets and intrigue. The story is related by four different narrators who give the reader clues about the developing mystery.

Subject keywords: identity; war

Original language: Spanish

Sources consulted for annotation:

Acle-Menendez, Ana. *Hispanic* 16 (May 2003): 66.

Polk, James. *The New York Times Book Review*, 30 May 2004 (online).
Post, Chad W. *Review of Contemporary Fiction* 23 (Summer 2003): 147.
Renner, Coop. *School Library Journal* 51 (July 2005): 46.
Unsworth, Barry. *The New York Times Book Review*, 27 April 2003, p. 7.
Another translated book written by Ignacio Padilla: *Antipodes*

Fernando del Paso. *Palinuro of Mexico.*
Translated by Elizabeth Plaister. Normal, IL: Dalkey Archive Press, 1996. 557 pages.
Genre/literary style/story type: mainstream fiction
Palinuro (a namesake of Virgil's Palinurus) is a medical student in Mexico City in the 1950s; he is having an affair with his first cousin, Estefania, a nurse. But this commonplace plot conceals a multilayered novel that encompasses picaresque adventures, medical discoveries, and a strange family genealogy stretching from Hungary to Latin America. It contains explorations into the hidden potential of the human body, spirit, and imagination; fantastic investigations into the lives of inanimate objects; and meditations on important philosophical questions. Critics have detected allusions to Rabelais, Cervantes, Jonathan Swift, Laurence Sterne, Dante, Antoine de Saint-Exupéry, and James Joyce in this novel.

Related title by the same author:
Readers may also enjoy *News from the Empire*, which focuses on the intricacies of Mexican history in the 1850s and 1860s. When Benito Juárez was elected president in 1858, some disgruntled Mexicans asked the Austrian archduke Maximilian and Marie Carlota of Belgium to be their emperor and empress. They are eventually enthroned in 1863, and a prolonged war ensues between Juárez and European forces. Some critics invoked Tolstoy's *War and Peace* in describing this novel.
Subject keywords: family histories; philosophy
Original language: Spanish
Sources consulted for annotation:
Amazon.com (book description; review from *Kirkus Reviews*).
Fox, Lorna Scott. *The Nation* (May 20, 2009) (online).
Global Books in Print (review from *Publishers Weekly* for *News from the Empire*).
Hoffert, Barbara. *Library Journal* 121 (July 1996): 156.
Kenney, Brian. *Booklist* 92 (1 June/15 June 1996): 1673.
Simson, Maria. *Publishers Weekly* 243 (3 June 1996): 77.
Another translated book written by Fernando del Paso: *News from the Empire*

Francisco Rebolledo. *Rasero.*
Translated by Helen R. Lane. Baton Rouge, LA: Louisiana State University Press, 1995. 552 pages.
Genres/literary styles/story types: historical fiction
Fausto Hermenegildo de Rasero y Oquendo is a Spanish aristocrat who lives in eighteenth-century Paris and frequents the same intellectual circles as such luminaries as Voltaire and Diderot. He is a philosopher and scientist who engages in discussions about politics, ideals, and the future. He is both blessed and cursed with the gift of clairvoyance, which brings him horrifying glimpses into the twentieth and twenty-first centuries. Worse still, these visions occur during sex: He sees Hiroshima and Auschwitz, wars, and the unintended consequences of technological progress. Rasero connects his visions back to what is referred to as the Age of Reason, the catalyst of lofty human progress and abysmal failure. Eventually, his relationship with a Mexican actress provides a salutary balm for his tortured imagination.
Subject keywords: philosophy; power
Original language: Spanish
Sources consulted for annotation:
Larson, Deanna. *Booklist* 92 (15 October 1995): 386.

Olszewski, Lawrence. *Library Journal* 120 (1 September 1995): 209.
Stavans, Ilan. *World Literature Today* 70 (Spring 1996): 373.
Steinberg, Sybil S. *Publishers Weekly* 242 (4 September 1995): 49.

Tomás Rivera. *This Migrant Earth.*
Translated by Rolando Hinojosa. Houston, TX: Arte Público Press, 1987. 128 pages.
Genre/literary style/story type: mainstream fiction
The setting is the American Midwest of the 1950s and 1960s, and the events are presented through the eyes of a young Chicano boy whose migrant family must live and work in a hostile foreign environment without any legal protections. Rivera was an American writer of Mexican descent.
Subject keyword: culture conflict
Original language: Spanish
Sources consulted for annotation:
Lee, James W. *The Dallas Morning News*, 7 June 1987, p. 10C.
Ramírez, Arturo. *Hispania* 72 (March 1989): 166-167.
Santana, Eduardo. *EFE News Services*, 14 January 2004.
"Tomás Rivera." *Dictionary of Literary Biography Online*. Thomson Gale databases.
Another translated book written by Tomás Rivera: *The Harvest: Short Stories*

Ignacio Solares. *Lost in the City: Two Novels* (*Tree of Desire* and *Serafín*).
Translated by Carolyn and John Brushwood. Austin, TX: University of Texas Press, 1998. 144 pages.
Genre/literary style/story type: mainstream fiction
In *Tree of Desire*, 10-year-old Cristina runs away from her middle-class home to escape her father's abusiveness. In the second novel, Serafín, a preteen boy, comes to Mexico City searching for his father. Although the two stories are independent narratives, both protagonists encounter Angustias and Jesús, a slum-dwelling couple. Their lifestyle, which is full of drunken orgies, animalistic sex, and violence, bears an eerie resemblance to that of Cristina's parents and Serafín's estranged father.
Subject keywords: social problems; urban life
Original language: Spanish
Sources consulted for annotation:
Mojica, Rafael H. *World Literature Today* 73 (Autumn 1999): 709.
Mujica, Barbara. *Americas* 50 (September/October 1998): 63.
Some other translated books written by Ignacio Solares: *Madero's Judgment*; *The Great Mexican Electoral Game*

Martín Solares. *The Black Minutes.*
Translated by Aura Estrada and John Pluecker. New York: Grove/Atlantic, 2010. 436 pages.
Genres/literary styles/story types: crime fiction; police detectives
Endemic corruption in the police department; drug trafficking; and numerous deaths. These are the main components of this noir mystery set in the fictional Mexican city of Paracuán, which some commentators see as a stand-in for the port of Tampico. Here, police investigators Vicente Rangel and Ramón Cabrera struggle to solve the murder of a journalist—a case that soon intersects with a decades-old investigation of a series of murders of young girls. Everyone in any position of authority—whether political, religious, or financial—seems to be implicated somehow, and the two detectives must orient themselves in a bleak and penumbral landscape in which everything is for sale. The book has been compared to the work of Paco Ignacio Taibo II and Robert Bolaño's *2666*.
Subject keyword: social problems

Original language: Spanish
Sources consulted for annotation:
Global Books in Print (online) (reviews from *Booklist* and *Publishers Weekly*).
Rohter, Larry. *The New York Times*, 31 May 2010 (online).

Paco Ignacio Taibo II. *An Easy Thing*.
Translated by William I. Neuman. New York: Viking, 1990. 230 pages.
Genres/literary styles/story types: crime fiction; private investigators
This is the first in a series of novels featuring Hector Belascoarán Shayne, a private detective who has fled his previous job of analyzing businesses in an attempt to increase their efficiency. He is an idealistic fighter for social justice in a corrupt and chaotic country. In addition to investigating the kidnapping of the daughter of a former porn star and a murder during a bloody labor dispute at a factory, he also looks into the whereabouts of Emiliano Zapata, the legendary hero of the Mexican Revolution long thought to have been killed in 1919. These three seemingly unrelated cases gradually become pieces of the same puzzle. Other books in the series include *No Happy Ending*; *Return to the Same City*; *Some Clouds*; and *Frontera Dreams*.
Subject keyword: social problems
Original language: Spanish
Sources consulted for annotation:
Amazon.com (book description).
Kaufmann, James. *St. Petersburg Times*, 28 January 1990, p. 7D.
Lambert, Pam. *Wall Street Journal*, 30 January 1990, p. A16.
"Paco Ignacio Taibo, II." *Contemporary Authors Online*. Thomson Gale databases, 2004.
Stasio, Marilyn. *The New York Times Book Review*, 21 January 1990, p. 35.
Steinberg, Sybil S. *Publishers Weekly* 236 (10 November 1989): 51.
Some other translated books written by Paco Ignacio Taibo: *Calling All Heroes: A Manual for Taking Power*; *Life Itself*; *Leonardo's Bicycle*; *Four Hands*; *Just Passing Through*; *The Shadow of the Shadow*; *Returning as Shadows*

David Toscana. *Tula Station*.
Translated by Patricia J. Duncan. New York: St. Martin's Press, 2000. 277 pages.
Genre/literary style/story type: mainstream fiction
The author, who appears as a character in this novel, is asked to edit the manuscript left behind by his friend, Froylán Gómez, who disappeared in a hurricane. But Patricia, Froylán's wife, suspects that her husband is still alive. The manuscript, which is the biography of Juan Capistrán, Froylán's supposed grandfather, tells the story of Juan's adventures during the Mexican Revolution and his passionate love for a rich woman named Carmen. But because Juan's and Froylán's fates are intertwined, it is clear that Froylán himself ran away with a woman named Carmen.
Subject keyword: family histories
Original language: Spanish
Sources consulted for annotation:
Benson, Mary Margaret. *Library Journal* 124 (December 1999): 189.
Markee, Patrick. *The New York Times Book Review*, 6 February 2000, p. 17.
Medina, David D. *Hispanic* 13 (September 2000): 100.
Steinberg, Sybil S. *Publishers Weekly* 246 (13 December 1999): 66.
Another translated book written by David Toscana: *Our Lady of the Circus*

Jorge Volpi. *In Search of Klingsor*.
Translated by Kristina Cordero. New York: Scribner, 2002. 414 pages.

Genres/literary styles/story types: historical fiction; literary historical
Francis Bacon, an American physicist, is forced out of Princeton's Institute for Advanced Study following a problematic romantic relationship. Now he is in post–World War II Germany pursuing a mysterious person with the code name of Klingsor, the namesake of a magician in Wagner's opera *Parsifal*. Klingsor served as the chief advisor to the Nazis for nuclear weapon development. As Bacon searches for Klingsor, he takes on a partner, Gustav Links, a brilliant mathematician. Links is himself troubled by distressing love affairs. As the narrative shifts back and forth between the mid-1940s and 1989, the mystery of Klingsor deepens: Just who is Links, and what is his relationship to Klingsor?
Related title by the same author:
Season of Ash is a wide-ranging and linguistically inventive historical novel covering the fall of communism and the rise of consumer culture in the former Soviet Union; the paradoxes of the economic plans developed by International Monetary Fund; environmental activism; and the power of multinational companies. Volpi, a member of the anti–magic realism literary movement Crack, has earned high praise from Carlos Fuentes.
Subject keywords: identity; war
Original language: Spanish
Sources consulted for annotation:
Augenbraum, Harold. *Library Journal* 127 (July 2002): 124.
Bissell, Tom. *The New York Times Book Review*, 13 December 2009 (online).
Dowling, Brendan. *Booklist* 98 (1 June/15 June 2002): 1689.
Morton, Oliver. *The Guardian*, 10 May 2003, p. 28.
Open Letter website (book description), http://www.catalog.openletterbooks.org.
Post, Chad W. *Review of Contemporary Fiction* 23 (Spring 2003): 141.
Another translated book written by Jorge Volpi: *Season of Ash*

Nicaragua

Rosario Aguilar. *The Lost Chronicles of Terra Firma.*
Translated by Edward Waters Hood. Fredonia, NY: White Pine Press, 1997. 186 pages.
Genres/literary styles/story types: historical fiction; feminist fiction
This novel presents a feminist view of the Spanish conquest of the New World. Traveling in the company of her Spanish colleague and lover, a young Nicaraguan journalist researches her country's past and collects six narratives from a diverse array of women, including indigenous and mestiza representatives. Her trip takes place just before the elections that will reject the Sandinista government and elect Violeta Chamorro. The collected narratives become more than just unearthed fragments of a little-known history; they point the way to reconciliation between past and present; America and Europe; and traditional and contemporary life.
Subject keywords: colonization and colonialism; indigenous culture
Original language: Spanish
Sources consulted for annotation:
Amazon.com (book description; review from *Kirkus Reviews*).
Burns, Erik. *The New York Times Book Review*, 2 March 1997, p. 18.

Gioconda Belli. *The Inhabited Woman.*
Translated by Kathleen March. Willamantic, CT: Curbstone Press, 1994. 412 pages.
Genres/literary styles/story types: historical fiction; literary historical
Lavinia Alarcon is a 23-year-old Italian-trained architect who lives in the fictitious city of Faguas, situated in an imaginary Central American country struggling for liberation from the brutal regime

of the Great General. Lavinia is oblivious to politics and social causes until she is inhabited by the spirit of Itza, a sixteenth-century native woman warrior who died fighting the conquistadors alongside Yarince, her lover. Lavinia is romantically involved with Felipe, her boss and the leader of the National Liberation Movement. Before Felipe dies, he convinces Lavinia to carry on as a member of the assault team.

Subject keywords: politics; power

Original language: Spanish

Sources consulted for annotation:

Amazon.com (review from *Kirkus Reviews*).

Augenbraum, Harold. *Library Journal* 119 (15 July 1994): 92.

Hooper, Brad. *Booklist* 90 (July 1994): 1921.

Jones-Davis, Georgia. *Los Angeles Times*, 23 August 1994, p. 4.

Steinberg, Sybil S. *Publishers Weekly* 241 (30 May 1994): 36.

Another translated book written by Gioconda Belli: *The Butterfly Workshop*

Panama

Enrique Jaramillo Levi. *Duplications and Other Stories.*

Translated by Leland H. Chambers. Pittsburgh, PA: Latin American Literary Review Press, 1994. 188 pages.

Genres/literary styles/story types: mainstream fiction; short stories

These short stories take place primarily in urban settings and examine thorny issues in everyday human relationships through the prism of the absurd and fantastic. As the author transforms people into lampposts, lawn tables, or the sunset, readers are given glimpses into these characters' tormented spiritual lives and their disparate ways of coping with cruelty, betrayal, and rejection. The book has evoked comparisons with Julio Cortázar's *End of the Game* and Jorge Luis Borges.

Subject keyword: identity

Original language: Spanish

Sources consulted for annotation:

Amazon.com (review from *Kirkus Reviews*).

Olszewski, Lawrence. *Library Journal* 119 (1 September 1994): 218

Simson, Maria. *Publishers Weekly* 241 (15 August 1994): 91.

Some other translated books written by Enrique Jaramillo Levi: *Contemporary Short Stories from Central America*; *The Shadow: Thirteen Stories in Opposition*

Puerto Rico

Rosario Ferré. *The Youngest Doll.*

Translated by the author. Lincoln, NE: University of Nebraska Press, 1991. 169 pages.

Genres/literary styles/story types: mainstream fiction; women's lives

In this collection of short stories by an author who has been compared with Isabel Allende, Luisa Valenzuela, and Clarice Lispector, women are objectified, oppressed, infantilized, and disregarded. The recurrent image of dolls is used to blur the line between real women and inanimate objects. This book is part of a feminist trilogy that also includes *Eros Besieged*, a collection of essays, and *Fables of a Bleeding Crane*, a volume of poetry.

Subject keywords: identity; social roles

Original language: Spanish

Sources consulted for annotation:

Hart, Patricia. *The Nation* 252 (6 May 1991): 597.

"Rosario Ferré." *Dictionary of Literary Biography Online*. Thomson Gale databases.

Other books in English written by Rosario Ferré: *Sweet Diamond Dust*; *Eccentric Neighborhoods*; *House on the Lagoon*

Mayra Montero. *Deep Purple.*
Translated by Edith Grossman. New York: HarperCollins, 2003. 182 pages.
Genres/literary styles/story types: mainstream fiction; magical realism
Agustín Cabán is a prominent music critic for a San Juan newspaper. Now retired, he is writing a memoir about his sexual affairs with both male and female musicians. To be sure, the novel depicts numerous sexual encounters, threesomes, passionate infatuations, dull marital relationships, and infidelities. But through an adroit use of magic realism, it also explores links between eroticism and music as well as the relationship between freedom and sexual creativity. It has evoked comparisons with *The Decameron*, *The Canterbury Tales*, and Mario Vargas Llosa's *Notebooks of Don Rigoberto*.
Related title by the same author:
Readers may also enjoy *Dancing to "Almendra."* Set in the late 1950s as the regime of Fulgencio Batista gave way to the Cuban Revolution of Fidel Castro, this novel focuses on a young Havana reporter who is working on a story about an escaped hippopotamus and its eventual death. He discovers that the animal's death is related to the murder of Umberto Anastasia in a New York City barbershop.
Subject keyword: identity
Original language: Spanish
Sources consulted for annotation:
Briggs, Carolyn S. *The Washington Post*, 15 June 2003, p. 8.
Lewis, Jim. *The New York Times Book Review*, 18 February 2007.
Olszewski, Lawrence. *Library Journal* 128 (1 May 2003): 156.
Zaleski, Jeff. *Publishers Weekly* 250 (2 June 2003): 35.
Zeidner, Lisa. *The New York Times Book Review*, 1 June 2003, p. 6.
Some other translated books written by Mayra Montero: *In The Palm of Darkness*; *The Messenger*; *Captain of the Sleepers*; *The Last Night I Spent with You*; *The Red of His Shadow*; *You, Darkness*; *The Moon Line*; *Dancing to "Almendra"*

Edgardo Rodríguez Juliá. *The Renunciation.*
Translated by Andrew Hurley. New York: Four Walls Eight Windows, 1997. 135 pages.
Genre/literary style/story type: historical fiction
In the Puerto Rico of the eighteenth century, a scheming bishop convinces Baltasar Montañez, a black man whose father Ramon spearheaded an African-American revolt on the island in 1734, to marry Josefina Prats, the white daughter of the secretary of state. In the bishop's opinion, the arranged marriage will avert racial conflict. But the newlyweds are unhappy, and Baltasar is persecuted by the authorities, excommunicated, and jailed. Structured as three academic lectures, the novel makes use of letters, governmental records, poetry, and diaries.
Subject keywords: politics; power
Original language: Spanish
Sources consulted for annotation:
Olszewski, Lawrence. *Library Journal* 122 (August 1997): 135.
Steinberg, Sybil S. *Publishers Weekly* 244 (25 August 1997): 43.
Some other translated books written by Edgardo Rodríguez Juliá: *Cortijo's Wake; San Juan: Memoir of a City*

Mayra Santos-Febres. *Sirena Selena.*
Translated by Stephen A. Lytle. New York: Picador, 2000. 214 pages.

Genre/literary style/story type: mainstream fiction
Martha Divine is transsexual and owns the Blue Danube, a louche nightclub in a sophisticated sort of way. She rescues Leocadio, a 15-year-old gay hustler addicted to cocaine, from a life on the streets. Leocadio has a golden voice, and Martha turns him into a successful singer known as Sirena Selena. After conquering the entertainment market in Puerto Rico, Sirena Selena travels to the Dominican Republic, where she wins over the wealthy businessman Hugo Graubel.
Subject keywords: identity; urban life
Original language: Spanish
Sources consulted for annotation:
Giles, Jana. *The New York Times Book Review*, 20 August 2000, p. 17.
Lopez, Adriana. *School Library Journal* 1 (1 July 2001): 31.
Steinberg, Sybil S. *Publishers Weekly* 247 (3 July 2000): 46.
Some other translated books written by Mayra Santos-Febres: *Urban Oracles*; *Any Wednesday I'm Yours*

ANNOTATIONS FOR TRANSLATED BOOKS FROM SOUTH AMERICA

Argentina

César Aira. *How I Became a Nun.*
Translated by Chris Andrews. New York: New Directions, 2007. 117 pages.
Genre/literary style/story type: mainstream fiction
Tragedy looms when a small child eats poisoned ice cream. The child is a young girl, but when she wakes up in the hospital, she is addressed by medical staff as a boy. Thus, the book becomes the story of a girl who struggles to escape from her imposed fate as a boy.
Related titles by the same author:
Readers may also wish to explore *An Episode in the Life of a Landscape Painter*, which recounts a German painter's disastrous journey to South America in 1837. Everything goes wrong: lightning strikes, disfigurement, morphine addiction. And yet, his devotion to his art only grows. Also of interest may be *Ghosts*, in which the soon-to-be residents of an unfinished apartment building come to look at their future home, currently populated only by a security guard, his family, and a diverse assortment of ghosts. Finally, *The Literary Conference* is a delicious send-up of science fiction conventions in which the author hatches a plot to achieve world domination by creating innumerable clones of the Mexican novelist Carlos Fuentes.
Subject keyword: identity
Original language: Spanish
Sources consulted for annotation:
The Complete Review (book review), http://www.complete-review.com.
Esposito, Scott. *The National* (Australia), 13 May 2010 (online).
Global Books in Print (online) (reviews from *Publishers Weekly* for both novels).
Hoffman, Jascha. *The New York Times Book Review*, 13 May 2007 (online).
Some other translated books written by César Aira: *The Hare*; *An Episode in the Life of a Landscape Painter*; *Ghosts*; *The Literary Conference*

Federico Andahazi. *The Anatomist.*
Translated by Alberto Manguel. New York: Doubleday, 1998. 215 pages.
Genre/literary style/story type: historical fiction
While examining a female patient, sixteenth-century Italian physician Mateo Colombo accidentally discovers the clitoris. But his scientific discovery scandalizes everyone, and he is perceived to be the

very incarnation of the devil. Denounced as a heretic, a blasphemer, and a practioner of the occult, he is jailed in a location far away from Mona Sofia, the woman whom he pines for and who just happens to be a prostitute. The book presents a vivid portrait of Renaissance society, where illustrious advances mingle with pseudo-scholarship against the background of the Inquisition. It will appeal to fans of Umberto Eco and Patrick Süskind.
Subject keywords: culture conflict; religion
Original language: Spanish
Sources consulted for annotation:
Blackburn, Jimmy. *Melody Maker* 76 (16 October 1999): 9.
Coulehan, Jack. *Literature, Arts, and Medicine Database* (LAMD), http://litmed.med.nyu.edu.
Seaman, Donna. *Booklist* 94 (July 1998): 1827.
Shreve, Jack. *Library Journal* 123 (August 1998): 128.
Steinberg, Sybil S. *Publishers Weekly* 245 (6 July 1998): 50.
Another translated book written by Federico Andahazi: *The Merciful Women*

Alicia Borinsky. *All Night Movie*.
Translated by Cola Franzen with the author. Evanston, IL: Northwestern University Press, 2002. 204 pages.
Genre/literary style/story type: mainstream fiction; women's lives
Recently released from jail, the scornful, unpredictable, and roguish Felipa (who also calls herself Matilde, Lucía, or Juana depending on the situation) engages in a sex transaction in a phone booth. Felipa/Juana loves Pascual; runs away from him; shoots him; keeps a vigil for him; and eventually kills him. She accuses her mother of killing her father; testifies at the trial; and is charged with Pascual's murder. Felipa can be understood as a contemporary picara on a quest to stretch the boundaries of the acceptable in Argentina.
Subject keywords: identity; urban life
Original language: Spanish
Sources consulted for annotation:
Amazon.com (book description).
Dewey, Joseph. *Review of Contemporary Fiction* 23 (Summer 2003): 128.
Gies, Martha. *The Women's Review of Books* 20 (July 2003): 34.
Kirkus Reviews 70 (1 November 2002): 1547.
Some other translated books written by Alicia Borinsky: *Mean Woman*; *Dreams of the Abandoned Seducer*

Humberto Costantini. *The Long Night of Francisco Sanctis*.
Translated by Norman Thomas di Giovanni. New York: Harper & Row, 1985. 184 pages.
Genre/literary style/story type: mainstream fiction
A radical activist during his university days, Francisco Sanctis is now middle-aged and content with choosing neutrality amidst the wave of kidnappings, murders, and tortures besetting Argentina during its military dictatorship. He has traded his literary and political aspirations for a stable career in accountancy, a happy family with two children, a comfortable home, and a passion for classical music. But a long-ago classmate suddenly informs him of an imminent kidnapping and asks him to warn the potential victims. Should he get involved in tangled political machinations or should he preserve his much cherished neutrality? In a totalitarian society, are murders ultimately the responsibility of those whose claims of neutrality mask an indifference to the plight of others?
Subject keywords: politics; power
Original language: Spanish

Sources consulted for annotation:
Carey, Barbara. *The Whig-Standard*, 7 September 1985, p. 1.
French, William. *The Globe and Mail* (Toronto), 31 August 1985, p. E13.
Gibson, Sharan. *Houston Chronicle*, 20 October 1985, p. 23.
Shvoong.com, http://www.shvoong.com.
Another translated book written by Humberto Costantini: *The Gods, the Little Guys, and the Police*

Juan Filloy. *Op Oloop*.
Translated by Lisa Dillman. Champaign, IL: Dalkey Archive Press, 2009. 251 pages.
Genre/literary style/story type: mainstream fiction
Op Oloop is a stereotypical statistician and mathematician: obsessed with quantifying everything and intent upon and satisfied with a regimented and predictable life. By the way, he is getting ready to sleep with his 1,000th prostitute. And he is more than a bit strange—well on his way to madness—as his speeches and pontifications make crystal clear. He is also a Finn working in Argentina's capital of Buenos Aires who has become engaged to the niece of a local Finnish diplomat. Originally published in 1934 and long neglected, this novel was praised by Sigmund Freud and Julio Cortazar, author of the Latin American classic *Hopscotch*.
Subject keywords: identity; social roles
Original language: Spanish
Sources consulted for annotation:
The Complete Review (book review), http://www.complete-review.com.
Post, Chad W. Three Percent website, http://www.rochester.edu/College/translation/threepercent.

Mempo Giardinelli. *The Tenth Circle*.
Translated by Andrea G. Labinger. Pittsburgh, PA: Latin American Literary Review Press, 2001. 93 pages.
Genres/literary styles/story types: crime fiction; suspense
Alfredo Romero, a successful twice-divorced businessman in his late 40s, is having an affair with Griselda Antonutti, the wife of Antonio, his business partner. When Alfredo kills Antonio in a particularly gruesome manner, the murder excites them, prompting them to similar excesses. Eventually, there is nothing left but to kill one another. Although the novel was described by *Publishers Weekly* as "a kind of *Natural Born Killers* crossed with *Peyton Place*," some critics have said that one of its important themes is business writ large. Only a very blurry boundary separates business in general from the murderous business of the novel's characters.
Subject keyword: social problems
Original language: Spanish
Sources consulted for annotation:
Foster, David William. *World Literature Today* 75 (Summer 2001): 226.
Steinberg, Sybil S. *Publishers Weekly* 247 (30 October 2000): 46.
Tinkler, Alan. *Review of Contemporary Fiction* 22 (Spring 2002): 136.
Another translated book written by Mempo Giardinelli: *Sultry Moon*

Angélica Gorodischer. *Kalpa Imperial: The Greatest Empire That Never Was*.
Translated by Ursula K. Le Guin. Northampton, MA: Small Beer Press, 2003. 246 pages.
Genre/literary style/story type: speculative fiction
Critics have said that this collection of short stories—translated to great acclaim by the noted science fiction writer Ursula K. Le Guin—is reminiscent of the works of Jorge Luis Borges and Stanislaw Lem. The setting is Kalpa Imperial, an imaginary empire in which rulers—some more

successfully than others—attempt to come to grips with intractable social problems and thorny political issues. The actors in these tales are people from all walks of life: royalty, peasantry, and military; the poor and the rich; and scientific geniuses.
Subject keywords: power
Original language: Spanish
Sources consulted for annotation:
Fail, John W. *Review of Contemporary Fiction* 24 (Spring 2004): 147.
Jonas, Gerald. *The New York Times Book Review*, 4 January 2004, p. 14.

Sylvia Iparraguirre. *Tierra del Fuego.*
Translated by Hardie St. Martin. Willimantic, CT: Curbstone Press, 2000. 199 pages.
Genres/literary styles/story types: adventure; survival and disaster stories
In 1830, Jemmy Button, a Yámana Indian from Tierra del Fuego, was taken by Captain Robert FitzRoy, commander of the first voyage of the *HMS Beagle*, to Europe against his will to serve as an interepreter, to be educated, and to be made a Christian. One year later, during the *Beagle*'s famous second voyage on which Charles Darwin participated, Button was returned to his home. He quickly divested himself of the trappings of European civilization, integrating fully with his native tribe. In 1859, he was alleged to have murdered English missonaries but denied complicity at an official inquiry. This historically based story is narrated by a fictitious seaman named John William Guevara, who accompanied Button on his voyage.
Subject keyword: culture conflict
Original language: Spanish
Sources consulted for annotation:
Olszewski, Lawrence. *Library Journal* 125 (December 2000): 189.
Quinn, Mary Ellen. *Booklist* 97 (1 January/15 January 2001): 915.

Vlady Kociancich. *The Last Days of William Shakespeare.*
Translated by Margaret Jull Costa. New York: William Morrow, 1991. 297 pages.
Genre/literary style/story type: mainstream fiction
What is one to make of a theatrical company in a major South American city that has performed *Hamlet*—to the exclusion of all else—over 855,000 times since 1920? When a U.S. publication reveals this mind-boggling information—not to mention the fact that the theater employs more than 400 people—there is much hand-wringing and jaw-dropping disbelief. The country's politicians and military leaders get involved, instituting what they call a Campaign for Cultural Reconstruction (CCR), whose aim is to privilege national manifestations of cultural accomplishment instead of English literary relics. But violence quickly ensues, and the country is engulfed in a civil war when pro-Shakespeare factions form in opposition to the CCR.
Subject keywords: politics; power
Original language: Spanish
Sources consulted for annotation:
Dorfman, Ariel. *The New York Times Book Review*, 28 July 1991 (online).
Global Books in Print (online) (reviews from *Library Journal* and *Publishers Weekly*).

Alicia Kozameh. *Steps Under Water.*
Translated by David E. Davis. Berkeley, CA: University of California Press, 1996. 149 pages.
Genre/literary style/story type: mainstream fiction
Sara is in her mid-20s and in love with Hugo. But love depends not only on the human heart but also on politics. Hugo disappears in a country that has been turned into a giant prison, where everybody is a suspect and no friend is trustworthy. Sara is arrested shortly thereafter and sent to prison, where

she forges tight bonds with fellow inmates. Partly autobiographical, this novel features letters, diary entries, and official documents; it has evoked critical comparisons to Elie Wiesel's *Night* and Jerzy Kosinski's *The Painted Bird*. The author was arrested a few months before the overthrow of Isabel Perón and remained incarcerated for more than three years; her partner disappeared during the Dirty War in Argentina.
Subject keywords: politics; power
Original language: Spanish
Sources consulted for annotation:
Olszewski, Lawrence. *Library Journal* 121 (15 October 1996): 90.
Simson, Maria. *Publishers Weekly* 243 (7 October 1996): 67.
Stavans, Ilan. *World Literature Today* 71 (Spring 1997): 361.

Guillermo Martínez. *The Oxford Murders*.
Translated by Sonia Soto. San Francisco, CA: MacAdam/Cage, 2005. 197 pages.
Genres/literary styles/story types: crime fiction; amateur detectives
A young graduate student in mathematics returns to England from Argentina and finds his landlady dead in her wheelchair. At about the same time, Arthur Seldom—a famous mathematician, logician, and author of a book about serial killers—receives a series of coded notes. In fact, Seldom keeps getting unfathomable cryptograms as more and more murders are committed. It soon becomes clear that the notes are warnings that point to the next victim. There are numerous allusions to the theorems of Gödel and Fermat as well as to Wittgenstein's paradox and Heisenberg's principle of uncertainty. Critics have noted similarities to Agatha Christie's *Ten Little Indians*.
Subject keyword: philosophy
Original language: Spanish
Sources consulted for annotation:
Fletcher, Connie. *Booklist* 102 (1 September 2005): 70.
Publishers Weekly 252 (1 August 2005): 41.
Stasio, Marilyn. *The New York Times Book Review*, 23 October 2005, p. 19.
Another translated book written by Guillermo Martínez: *Regarding Roderer*

Tomás Eloy Martínez. *Santa Evita*.
Translated by Helen R. Lane. New York: Alfred A. Knopf, 1996. 371 pages.
Genres/literary styles/story types: historical fiction; literary historical
Eva Perón was a woman who left a deep imprint on Argentina's sociopolitical landscape—posthumously turning into a cultural touchstone, national icon, and symbolic saint. *Santa Evita* is a glittering account of the often bizarre legacy of Eva Perón. The daughter of a low-ranking rural politician, she arrived in Buenos Aires to become an actress. Conquering the heart of Juan Perón, she gradually became the real political force of Argentina. After her death, her body was confiscated by her husband's opponents, who feared that it would be used to stoke political fervor against them. Numerous ersatz copies of her body were produced to conceal the real one, which was spirited away to a series of hiding places. Readers may find that *The Perón Novel* is the perfect complement to *Santa Evita* because it focuses on Juan Perón's return to Argentina in 1973 after almost 20 years of exile. Interweaving past and present to create an indelible portrait of a self-aggrandizing, power-hungry, and delusional politician, the book was described by Jay Cantor as "a brilliant image of a national psychosis."
Subject keywords: politics; power
Original language: Spanish
Sources consulted for annotation:
Brzezinski, Steve. *The Antioch Review* 55 (Spring 1997): 241.

Cantor, Jay. *The New York Times Book Review*, 22 May 1988, p. 16.
Fornes, Jose M. *Library Journal* 122 (July 1997): 68.
Foster, David William. *World Literature Today* 70 (Spring 1996): 368.
Fox, Margalit. *The New York Times*, 6 February 2010 (online).
Kakutani, Michiko. *The New York Times*, 20 September 1996, p. C31.
Some other translated books written by Tomás Eloy Martínez: *The Perón Novel*; *The Tango Singer*

Elsa Osorio. *My Name Is Light.*
Translated by Catherine Jagoe. New York: Bloomsbury, 2003. 356 pages.
Genres/literary styles/story types: mainstream fiction; coming-of-age
Luz's mother was a political prisoner who was killed as she tried to escape during Argentina's Dirty War in the 1970s and early 1980s; her father was driven out of the country by the junta. Orphaned, Luz is adopted by an upper-class and politically connected family who keep her past from her. As Luz grows up, her psychological estrangement from her adoptive home becomes stronger, as does her desire to uncover her true heritage. Now 20, married, and a mother herself, Luz is in Madrid, ostensibly on a family vacation. But she is really searching for her biological father.
Subject keywords: family histories; politics
Original language: Spanish
Sources consulted for annotation:
Amazon.com (book description).
Seymenliyska, Elena, and Thompson, Sam. *The Guardian*, 18 September 2004, p. 30.

Ricardo Piglia. *The Absent City.*
Translated by Sergio Gabriel Waisman. Durham, NC: Duke University Press, 2000. 147 pages.
Genres/literary styles/story types: crime fiction; suspense
Junior is a descendant of English immigrants and a reporter for a Buenos Aires newspaper. Along with a Korean gangster and Julia, he embarks on a quest to track down a computer-like device invented by an Argentinian writer. The machine's claim to fame is that it has been imbued with the thoughts of a woman named Elena. But the police are also trying to find Elena because cyber-Elena is broadcasting what they consider to be subversive stories about the atrocities committed by the government during the Dirty War (1976–1983). Critics have compared this novel to some of the works by James Joyce, Italo Calvino, Jorge Luis Borges, Don DeLillo, and Thomas Pynchon.
Subject keyword: politics
Original language: Spanish
Sources consulted for annotation:
Caso, Frank. *Booklist* 97 (1 November 2000): 519.
Hove, Thomas. *Review of Contemporary Fiction* 21 (Summer 2001): 152.
McQueen, Lee. *Library Journal* 125 (December 2000): 192.
Steinberg, Sybil S. *Publishers Weekly* 247 (27 November 2000): 55.
Some other translated books written by Ricardo Piglia: *Money to Burn*; *Artificial Respiration*; *Assumed Name*

Abel Posse. *Daimon.*
Translated by Sarah Arvio. New York: Atheneum, 1992. 275 pages.
Genres/literary styles/story types: historical fiction; literary historical
This book is the sequel to *The Dogs of Paradise*, which provided an account of the devastating effects of the European conquest of Peru. *Daimon* continues the theme of the evils of colonialism, suggesting that Lope de Aguirre—nicknamed the Madman and who was one of Francisco Pizarro's

men—did not perish in battle in 1561. Instead, along with his comrades, he kept haunting the continent for another 400 years—a whirlwind of destruction and mayhem. Megalomania and brutality took Aguirre to the legendary city of Eldorado, but the sight of bountiful gold killed his adventurous spirit and murderous resolve. Abandoning his warlike ways, he chose a quiet life with a woman in Machu Picchu.
Subject keyword: colonization and colonialism
Original language: Spanish
Sources consulted for annotation:
Beck, Mary Ellen. *Library Journal* 117 (1 November 1992): 118.
Christensen, Thomas. *The San Francisco Chronicle*, 10 January 1993, p. 7.
Steinberg, Sybil S. *Publishers Weekly* 239 (28 September 1992): 65.
Another translated book written by Abel Posse: *The Dogs of Paradise*

Manuel Puig. *Tropical Night Falling*.
Translated by Suzanne Jill Levine. New York: Simon & Schuster, 1992. 189 pages.
Genre/literary style/story type: mainstream fiction
Luci and Nidia are sisters in their 80s; the former lives in Rio de Janeiro and the latter is a visitor to Luci's home. Despite numerous life-altering events and losses, they are fiercely independent and intellectually dynamic, working in their garden, learning a foreign language, and taking a keen interest in the lives of their neighbors. Eventually, Luci's son convinces her to move to Switzerland to be cared for, but it is a plan that does not have a happy ending. Now alone, Nidia befriends a night watchman who swindles her, but her inner strength allows her to persevere. Although the nightfall of the title is a clear metaphor for old age, this book paints an eloquent and vibrant picture of the transcendent joys of a well-lived life.
Related title by the same author:
Readers may also enjoy *Pubis Angelical*, which focuses on an Argentinian woman hospitalized in Mexico in the 1970s. As she is visited by friends with whom she has little in common and as she recalls her former charmed life, she becomes what Steve Erickson calls "a supporting character in her own memories, the wasted shadow of two fantasy women: a Viennese actress bearing a face and life rather like Hedy Lamarr's, who marries a weapons maker in the years before World War II and then winds up in Hollywood; and W218, a sexual conscript in an alternative present where no one has a name and the state regulates matters of love and liaison."
Subject keywords: aging; family histories
Original language: Spanish
Sources consulted for annotation:
Erickson, Steve. *The New York Times Book Review*, 28 December 1986 (online).
Mujica, Barbara. *Americas* 44 (March/April 1992): 60.
Shreve, Jack. *Library Journal* 116 (15 October 1991): 122.
Steinberg, Sybil S. *Publishers Weekly* 238 (23 August 1991): 47.
Some other translated books written by Manuel Puig: *Pubis Angelical*; *Eternal Curse on the Reader of These Pages*; *Betrayed by Rita Hayworth*; *Mystery of the Rose Bouquet*; *The Buenos Aires Affair*; *Blood of Requited Love*; *Heartbreak Tango*

Juan José Saer. *The Sixty-Five Years of Washington*.
Translated by Steve Dolph. Rochester, NY: Open Letter, 2010. 203 pages.
Genre/literary style/story type: mainstream fiction
In 1961, during a walk along the streets of Santa Fe, Argentina, the past, present, and future intersect in the thoughts of two young men. As Jascha Hoffman comments about this minimalist masterpiece, the friends spend only an hour walking 21 blocks in which they recount "their fleeting

sensations, memories, epiphanies and distractions in exquisite detail," but it is more than enough time for Saer to give "omniscient glimpses of not just his characters' pasts but also their dark futures under a series of volatile Argentine regimes."

Related title by the same author:

Some readers may also be interested in *The Witness*, which gives insight into the life of a Spanish adolescent after he is captured by a group of indigenous people during Spain's colonization expeditions in the sixteenth century. *Publishers Weekly* described the book as "a swashbuckling philosophical treatise that combines anthropology, semiotics and a dose of cannibal gore."

Subject keyword: identity

Original language: Spanish

Sources consulted for annotation:

Amazon.com (review from *Publishers Weekly*).

Hoffman, Jascha. *The New York Times Book Review*, 19 December 2010 (online).

Some other translated books written by Juan José Saer: *The Witness; Nobody Nothing Never; The Event; The Investigation*

Patricia Sagastizábal. *A Secret for Julia*.

Translated by Asa Zatz. New York: W. W. Norton, 2001. 249 pages.

Genre/literary style/story type: mainstream fiction

Mercedes Beecham and her adolescent daughter Julia live in 1990s London, where Mercedes has settled after escaping from an Argentine prison. Although Mercedes has started a new life by going to graduate school, forming friendships, and raising Julia, she is never free from her terrifying memories. Her husband and sister were murdered during Argentina's Dirty War, and she was a victim of torture and rape during her imprisonment. Mercedes is also determined never to tell Julia about her real father, but her secrecy leads to deterioration in their relationship. When Mercedes's former jailer shows up in London, she is compelled to tell Julia about her painful past.

Subject keywords: family histories; power

Original language: Spanish

Sources consulted for annotation:

Gaztambide, Elsa. *Booklist* 97 (July 2001): 1983.

Olszewski, Lawrence. *Library Journal* 126 (August 2001): 166.

Rubin, Merle. *Los Angeles Times*, 2 September 2001, p. E3.

Zaleski, Jeff. *Publishers Weekly* 248 (6 August 2001): 32.

Pablo De Santis. *The Paris Enigma*.

Translated by Mara Lethem. New York: HarperCollins, 2008. 256 pages.

Genres/literary styles/story types: crime fiction; private investigators

The World's Fair was held in Paris in 1889. Among the many organizations on hand was an association comprising the top 12 detectives in the world. They have gathered to take stock of their profession, relive old cases, and develop new techniques. But Renaldo Craig, an Argentinian detective, refuses to attend, instead sending Sigmundo Salvatrio, one of his aides. When one of the illustrious 12 meets an inglorious death in a fall from the Eiffel Tower, Salvatrio joins forces with a Polish exile to prevent further tragedy.

Subject keyword: urban life

Original language: Spanish

Sources consulted for annotation:

Global Books in Print (online) (reviews from *Booklist* and *Publishers Weekly*).

Stasio, Marilyn. *The New York Times Book Review*, 16 November 2008 (online).

Eduardo Sguiglia. *Fordlandia.*
Translated by Patricia J. Duncan. New York: Thomas Dunne Books/St. Martin's Press, 2000. 245 pages.
Genres/literary styles/story types: historical fiction; literary historical
In the late 1920s and 1930s, Henry Ford hatched an ambitious yet far-fetched plan to ensure that his North American automobile factories would always have a steady supply of rubber. And what better place to extract that rubber from than the Amazon? Horacio is given the job of recruiting workers for the rubber plantations. As he travels around the Amazon, he has to deal with a host of problems, including raging epidemics, political corruption, and antipathy on the part of indigenous populations. But he is nothing if not persistent—a would-be Prometheus bringing the civilizing light of modern capitalism to the beknighted who turns into a Sisyphean figure as he confronts a haunting and primordial universe with its own implacable and eternal laws. This allegoric fable—a clear denunciation of the excesses of social and cultural imperialism—has been compared to the novels of Joseph Conrad and the tragedies of William Shakespeare. Readers may wish to supplement this fictional account with Greg Grandin's nonfiction book *Fordlandia: The Rise and Fall of Henry Ford's Forgotten Jungle City.*
Subject keyword: colonization and colonialism
Original language: Spanish
Sources consulted for annotation:
Augenbraum, Harold. *Library Journal* 125 (15 September 2000): 114.
Seaman, Donna. *Booklist* 97 (15 September 2000): 219.
Steinberg, Sybil S. *Publishers Weekly* 247 (21 August 2000): 46.
Ulin, David L. *The New York Times Book Review*, 1 October 2000, p. 19.
Yardley, Jonathan. *The Washington Post*, 1 October 2000, p. X2.

Ana María Shua. *The Book of Memories.*
Translated by Dick Gerdes. Albuquerque, NM: University of New Mexico Press, 1998. 178 pages.
Genre/literary style/story type: mainstream fiction
This lighthearted novel chronicles the lives of three generations of a Polish Jewish family who immigrated to Argentina during World War I. Grandfather Gedalia is the curmudgeonly patriarch, and his is the typical story of an East European immigrant to the Americas at the beginning of the twentieth century. He tries to survive in a foreign land and secure his children's future by working as an intinerant salesman who dabbles in loans.
Subject keyword: family histories
Original language: Spanish
Sources consulted for annotation:
Amazon.com (book description).
Friedman, Paula. *The New York Times Book Review*, 24 January 1999, p. 19.
Another translated book written by Ana María Shua: *Patient*

Alicia Steimberg. *Call Me Magdalena.*
Translated by Andrea G. Labinger. Lincoln, NE: University of Nebraska Press, 2001. 137 pages.
Genre/literary style/story type: mainstream fiction
Set in Buenos Aires at the beginning of the twenty-first century, this novel is narrated by a middle-aged woman who uses several names, one of which is Magdalena. She tirelessly searches for self-identity and faith in a fast-moving urban milieu, attempting to reconcile being Jewish in a predominantly Catholic society whose culture and lifestyle she nevertheless embraces as her own. Magdalena's grandparents, who emigrated from Russia to Argentina at the dawn of the twentieth century, remained traditional Jews, but her parents assimilated into local society.

Subject keyword: culture conflict
Original language: Spanish
Sources consulted for annotation:
"Alicia Steimberg." *Contemporary Authors Online*. Gale, 2003.
McQueen, Lee. *Library Journal* 126 (1 September 2001): 236.
Zaleski, Jeff. *Publishers Weekly* 248 (13 August 2001): 282.
Some other translated books written by Alicia Steimberg: *Musicians and Watchmakers*; *The Rainforest*

Pablo Urbanyi. *Silver.*
Translated by Hugh Hazelton. Oakville, ON: Mosaic Press, 2005. 224 pages.
Genre/literary style/story type: mainstream fiction
Silver is a white gorilla who has been forcefully removed from Gabon and brought to the United States for a series of inane scientific experiments. But in the course of the experiments, Silver becomes increasingly humanized. Not only does he acquire sophisticated manners and impeccable hygiene habits, but he also becomes an inveterate consumer of the Western lifestyle, especially fast food, alcohol, and women. Simply put, he cannot get enough. When he becomes too human, he is shipped back to Africa, where he can never adjust to the jungle lifestyle again. Insightful and witty, this book is a satire of pseudo-intellectuals in academia; a critique of stereotypical thinking that attempts to fit others into preconstructed frames; and an allegory about immigrants who have been forced to leave their homelands and struggle to adapt to a foreign culture.
Subject keyword: identity
Original language: Spanish
Sources consulted for annotation:
Amazon.com (review from *Publishers Weekly*).
Gessell, Paul. *The Ottawa Citizen*, 2 January 2006, p. C1.
Some other translated books written by Pablo Urbanyi: *The Nowhere Idea*; *Sunset*

Luisa Valenzuela. *Clara.*
Translated by Andrea G. Labinger. Pittsburgh, PA: Latin American Literary Review Press, 1999. 159 pages.
Genres/literary styles/story types: mainstream fiction; women's lives
Clara Hernandez is a young prostitute in Buenos Aires. Disowned by her parents at age 17, she leaves Tres Lomas in rural Argentina and comes to the capital in hopes of a better life. The sea—a talisman that recurs in Clara's dreams as a symbol of a brighter future—is near the hotel where she works, but it is out of reach. Eventually, she meets Alejandro, a magician, and soon appears in his performances. No matter the agony-ridden circumstances of her bleak life, she remains ever optimistic.
Subject keyword: urban life
Original language: Spanish
Sources consulted for annotation:
Benson, Mary Margaret. *Library Journal* 125 (January 2000): 163.
Quinn, Mary Ellen. *Booklist* 96 (1 January/15 January 2000): 881.
See, Carolyn. *The Washington Post*, 28 January 2000, p. C8.
Steinberg, Sybil S. *Publishers Weekly* 246 (20 December 1999): 55.
Some other translated books written by Luisa Valenzuela: *He Who Searches*; *The Censors*; *Other Weapons*; *Bedside Manners*; *Black Novel with Argentines*; *Open Door*

Bolivia

Edmundo Paz Soldán. *The Matter of Desire*.
Translated by Lisa Carter. Boston: Houghton Mifflin, 2003. 214 pages.
Genre/literary style/story type: mainstream fiction
Pedro Zabalaga, a Bolivian-born professor of Latin American studies in upstate New York, returns to his home in Río Fugitivo, a fictitious city, in order to escape his personal woes, including a tortuous love affair with Ashley, a married graduate student, and untangle his past. Once in his homeland, he devotes himself to reconstructing the multifaceted story of the betrayal and death of his father, a novelist and political activist.
Related title by the same author:
Readers may also enjoy *Turing's Delirium*, which revolves around Ramírez-Graham, who works for the National Security Agency. He is summoned to Bolivia to hacker-proof the government's computer systems against increasingly malicious attacks. He quickly comes into contact with a group of cyberterrorists as well as the notorious head of Bolivia's intelligence agency. Along with Alberto Fuguet, author of *The Movies of My Life*, Soldán belongs to the so-called McOndo literary school, which opposes magic realism and embraces urban realism.
Subject keywords: family histories; politics
Original language: Spanish
Sources consulted for annotation:
Block, Allison. *Booklist* 100 (1 April 2004): 1349.
Global Books in Print (online) (review from *Publishers Weekly* for *Turing's Delirium*).
Iyer, Pico. *The New York Times Book Review*, 16 July 2006 (online).
Polk, James. *The Washington Post*, 2 May 2004, p. T13.
Santiago, Fabiola. *Hispanic* 17 (April 2004): 68.
Shreve, Jack. *Library Journal* 129 (1 April 2004): 124.
Zaleski, Jeff. *Publishers Weekly* 251 (10 May 2004): 38.
Another translated book written by Edmundo Paz Soldán: *Turing's Delirium*

Giancarla de Quiroga. *Aurora*.
Translated by Kathy S. Leonard. Seattle, WA: Women in Translation, 1999. 178 pages.
Genre/literary style/story type: mainstream fiction
Aurora and her longtime companion Alberto, whom she ran off with while in her teens, are in many ways polar opposites. Alberto, who prides himself on his European sophistication and is prejudiced against Indians, rejects every form of conventional thinking, inveighing against religion and marriage. Aurora is naïve, impractical, and yearns for a traditional family; she teaches Indian laborers and adopts an Indian baby girl. Spanning three decades from the 1930s to the 1950s, the novel limns some of the reasons for the Bolivian Revolution and ensuing social unrest.
Subject keywords: identity; social roles
Original language: Spanish
Sources consulted for annotation:
Llumina Press (book description), http://www.llumina.com.
Mujica, Barbara. *Americas* 52 (March/April 2000): 62.

Jesús Urzagasti. *In the Land of Silence*.
Translated by Kay Pritchett. Fayetteville, AR: University of Arkansas Press, 1994. 366 pages.
Genres/literary styles/story types: mainstream fiction; experimental fiction
This novel, which begins in 1980, is organized into five notebooks written by three alter egos of the same person: Jursafu, who lives in a big city, works for a newspaper, and writes poetry. He has

internalized European social and cultural mores, but he is caught in a veritable no-man's-land between warring elements of his psyche: his urbanity and sophistication; his link to his native heritage and the spiritual realm; and his notions of death. This book, which contains numerous autobiographical elements, has been compared to *The Passion According to G.H.* by Clarice Lispector and *The Book of Disquiet* by Fernando Pessoa.
Subject keyword: identity
Original language: Spanish
Sources consulted for annotation:
Amazon.com (review from *Kirkus Reviews*).
Evenson, Brian. *Review of Contemporary Fiction* 15 (Summer 1995): 216.

Chile

Isabel Allende. *Portrait in Sepia*.
Translated by Margaret Sayers Peden. New York: HarperCollins, 2001. 304 pages.
Genre/literary style/story type: mainstream fiction; women's lives
The closing volume in the trilogy that began with *Daughter of Fortune* and *House of the Spirits*, this book examines the relentless search for self-identity of three generations of characters over the course of 50 years, starting in the early 1860s. Aurora del Valle Aurora, now 30, reflects on her birth and early childhood in San Francisco's Chinatown as well as her family history, which includes a Chilean grandmother and a Chinese grandfather. She also recalls her upbringing in the home of a wealthy family in Chile and her less-than-happy marriage.
Related titles by the same author:
Readers may also wish to explore *Inés of My Soul*, which imaginatively retells the story of Inés Suárez, a dynamic and enterprising woman of the sixteenth century who is considered to be a Spanish Conquistadora. Braving hardships and perils, she embarked on a voyage to South America, became the lover of the expedition's leader, Pedro de Valdivia, and cofounded Santiago de la Nueva Extremadura in 1541. Also of interest may be *Island Beneath the Sea*, which gives insight into Haitian history from the late eighteenth century onward through the figure of a Zarité, a mixed-blood slave whose mistress eventually becomes insane and who is forced to sleep with the owner of the plantation where she works. The book is particularly good at detailing the various competing political and social interests in Haiti as well as voodoo-inspired supernatural elements.
Subject keyword: family histories
Original language: Spanish
Sources consulted for annotation:
Bahdur, Gaiutra. *The New York Times Book Review*, 1 May 2010 (online).
Erwin, Andrew. *The New York Times Book Review*, 4 November 2001 (online).
Galehouse, Maggie. *The New York Times Book Review*, 14 January 2007 (online).
Heredia, Sylvia. *School Library Journal* 1 (Spring 2001): 20.
Hoffert, Barbara. *Library Journal* 126 (15 October 2001): 105.
Hooper, Brad. *Booklist* 98 (1 September 2001): 3.
"Isabel Allende." *Contemporary Authors Online*. Thomson Gale databases, 2006.
Zaleski, Jeff. *Publishers Weekly* 248 (16 July 2001): 164.
Some other translated books written by Isabel Allende: *Daughter of Fortune*; *The House of the Spirits*; *Of Love and Shadows*; *Eva Luna*; *The Infinite Plan*; *Paula*; *City of the Beasts*; *Inés of My Soul*; *Zorro*; *Island Beneath the Sea*

Roberto Bolaño. *The Savage Detectives*.
Translated by Natasha Wimmer. New York: Farrar, Straus and Giroux, 2007. 577 pages.

Genres/literary styles/story types: mainstream fiction; postmodernism

Partly autobiographical, this book focuses on a motley and marginalized group of Mexican writers, led by Ulises Lima and Arturo Belano, who are known as visceral realists. Lima and Belano develop an obsession for a 1920s poet by the name of Cesárea Tinajero, whom they consider to be a much neglected literary forebearer. They embark on a quixotic quest to locate their vanished muse, dramatically setting out from Mexico City for the eerie expanses of the Sonoran desert, where she is reputed to have vanished many decades before. It is almost—but not quite—beside the point that they eventually discover, in an obscure magazine that was issued only once, Tinajero's single published work: a poem that has no words but consists of three cryptic squiggles—lines that could mean everything or nothing. In a broader sense, the poem captures both the richness and futility of Lima's and Belano's lives as they become world-weary wanderers and drifters, chasing evanescent mysteries only to discover an utter bleakness at the core of longed-for certainties. Ultimately, the overarching mood of the novel is one of inexplicable sadness and regret—both for what never was because it never, ever could have been and for the possibility that, given different circumstances, something indeed could have been. As told by more than 50 narrators in a symphonic tour de force that results in a multidimensional appreciation for the agonies and ecstasies experienced by the peripatetic Lima and Belano, there are indelible portraits of the cultural underground of Mexico City in the mid-1970s, told through the perspective of Juan García Madero, a young man in his late teens whose uncle wants him to be a lawyer but who is drawn into the circle of the visceral realists; Mexican literary politics through the prism of the adventures of a delegation of writers visiting Nicaragua; a heart-wrenching meeting between Octavio Paz, an icon of Mexican literature, and Lima, drained of aspiration, rebellion, and even the wispiest of illusions; war-ravaged Africa; and poverty-stricken Barcelona. As Thomas McGonigle observed, the novel "becomes nothing less than a broad portrait of the Hispanic diaspora, spreading from Central and South America to Israel, Europe, Africa and every place in between, from the late 1960s through the 1990s."

Related titles by the same author:

Readers may also enjoy *By Night in Chile*. On his return to Chile after a tour of Italy and other European countries to write about the state of their churches, the Jesuit Sebastián Urrutia Lacroix finds nothing but political turmoil and economic chaos. On orders from Opus Dei, he begins to tutor General Augusto Pinochet and his key supporters in the subtleties of Marxism. For a time, he enjoys the tangible benefits of his new-found role as a member of the inner circle of Pinochet's regime. His remorse and confession come only when he slips into delirium; in his hallucinatory state, he encounters such imaginary and real-life characters as Pablo Neruda and Ernst Jünger. This novel raises disquieting questions not only about political apathy and conformity but also about the role of the church and intellectuals in speaking up against oppression. Also of interest may be *2666*. As Janet Maslin notes, this novel, also translated by Natasha Wimmer, is grounded in a "chronicle of [the] unsolved sex crimes in Ciudad Juárez, Mexico, with hundreds of women dead and the identities of their killers still unclear." But that description only scratches the surface of this almost 900-page book that explores the fascination of four Europeans for a little-known German writer by the name of Benno von Archimboldi, whom they believe vanished into the deserts of northern Mexico; the enigmatic and forlorn existence of Amalfitano, a middle-aged university teacher single-handedly raising his 17-year-old daughter Rosa in Santa Teresa (a stand-in for Ciudad Juárez), who helps the Europeans in their search for von Archimboldi at the same time as he tries to prevent his daughter from falling victim to the city's swirling violence; the trials and tribulations of an African-American reporter, Oscar Fate, who is dispatched to cover a boxing match in Santa Teresa and becomes involved with Rosa; and the rocambolesque life of Hans Reiter, a German who fought in World War II and whose battlefield experiences later led him to become a novelist writing under the pseudonym of Benno von Archimboldi. Klaus Haas, another mysterious German who runs a computer shop in Santa Teresa and turns out to be the son of von Archimboldi's sister, is eventually arrested and charged with carrying out the serial mutilations and killings that have terrified the region. But the murders continue unabated, despite the intervention of a leading Mexican politician who takes a keen interest in the sordid circumstances. Even at some 900 pages, *2666* deserves repeated readings—simply because there is so much there on so many levels. Intricate and subtle connections abound; layers upon layers of meaning are hidden at every turn of the page. And the writing, imbued with a polyphonic and mesmerizing grace, is nothing less than breathtakingly elegant. Numerous critics have invoked such names as Gabriel García Márquez, David Lynch, Marcel Duchamp, Bob Dylan, and David Foster Wallace to describe the intellectual brilliance of Bolaño's work.

Subject keywords: identity; writers

Original language: Spanish

Sources consulted for annotation:

Hagendoorn, Ivar. Review of *The Savage Detectives*, http://www.ivarhagendoorn.com.
Lethem, Jonathan. *The New York Times Book Review*, 9 November 2008 (online).
Levin, Kate. *The Nation* 278 (29 March 2004): 33.
Maslin, Janet. *The New York Times*, 13 November 2008 (online).
McGonigle, Thomas. *The Los Angeles Times*, 8 April 2007 (online).
Mujica, Barbara. *Americas* 56 (January/February 2004): 62.
Post, Chad W. *Review of Contemporary Fiction* 24 (Spring 2004): 158.
Wood, James. *The New York Times Book Review*, 15 April 2007 (online).

Some other translated books written by Roberto Bolaño: *By Night in Chile*; *Distant Star*; *The Romantic Dogs*; *Last Evenings on Earth*; *Amulet*; *2666*; *Nazi Literature in the Americas*; *The Skating Rink*; *Monsieur Pain*; *The Return*; *Antwerp*; *The Insufferable Gaucho*

Carlos Cerda. *To Die in Berlin*.

Translated by Andrea G. Labinger. Pittsburgh, PA: Latin American Literary Review Press, 1999. 176 pages.

Genre/literary style/story type: mainstream fiction

Mario, a doctoral student and writer; Lorena, his wife; and Don Carlos, an elderly and ailing politician, have fled the 1973 Pinochet coup and live in communist-controlled East Berlin. Displaced and adrift, they must make the best of it in their new homeland. For some, new possibilities beckon. Mario wants to leave his wife after falling in love with a young German woman; Don Carlos is smitten with an adolescent girl who aspires to be a ballerina. On the other hand, Lorena pines to return to Chile with her family.

Subject keyword: culture conflict

Original language: Spanish

Sources consulted for annotation:

Olszewski, Lawrence. *Library Journal* 124 (July 1999): 128.
Robbins, Eric. *Booklist* 95 (July 1999): 1921.
Steinberg, Sybil S. *Publishers Weekly* 246 (14 June 1999): 52.

Another translated book written by Carlos Cerda: *An Empty House*

Ariel Dorfman. *The Last Song of Manuel Sendero*.

Translated by George R. Shivers with the author. New York: Viking, 1987. 450 pages.

Genres/literary styles/story types: mainstream fiction; postmodernism

This novel has a distinctly original premise: Fetuses are on strike, refusing to be born until there is a significant amelioration of political freedom and human rights. One of them is the future son of Manuel Sendero, a broken-spirited singer who is modeled after the famous Chilean singer Victor Jara. While in the womb, Sendero's son falls in love with Pamela; when Pamela chooses to be born

along with the rest of the fetuses, Sendero's son has no choice but to follow. This plot is interwoven with the story of David and Felipe, two émigré cartoonists in Mexico who aspire to publish a magazine for South American exiles fleeing authoritarian regimes.
Subject keywords: identity; politics
Original language: Spanish
Sources consulted for annotation:
Cryer, Dan. *Newsday*, 8 February 1987, p. 16.
Freeman, Judith. *Los Angeles Times*, 5 April 1987, p. 1.
Shorris, Earl. *The New York Times Book Review*, 15 Feb 1987, p. 9.
Other books in English written by Ariel Dorfman: *Widows*; *The Rabbits' Rebellion*; *Hard Rain*; *Blake's Therapy*; *Burning City*; *My House Is on Fire*; *Konfidenz*; *Mascara*

Diamela Eltit. *The Fourth World.*
Translated by Dick Gerdes. Lincoln, NE: University of Nebraska Press, 1995. 113 pages.
Genre/literary style/story type: mainstream fiction
The fourth world of the title is a symbolic place for those excluded from the mainstream of Chilean society under General Augusto Pinochet. Maria Chipia and his twin sister try to survive in their fourth world; they pass the days in isolation and cope as best they can. They were violently conceived by a violent father who raped their ailing mother. Their uterine intimacy eventually develops into an incestuous relationship, which results in the sister's pregnancy with a potentially malformed baby girl.
Subject keyword: family histories
Original language: Spanish
Sources consulted for annotation:
Olszewski, Lawrence. *Library Journal* 120 (1 October 1995): 119.
Simson, Maria. *Publishers Weekly* 242 (25 September 1995): 54.
University of Nebraska Press (publisher's description), http://www.nebraskapress.unl.edu.
Some other translated books written Diamela Eltit: *E. Luminata*; *Sacred Cow*; *Custody of the Eyes*

Alberto Fuguet. *The Movies of My Life.*
Translated by Ezra E. Fitz. New York: Rayo, 2003. 287 pages.
Genres/literary styles/story types: mainstream fiction; coming-of-age
Beltrán Soler was born in Chile but grew up in Encino, California, as a happy and assimilated child. When he is 10, his family moves back to Santiago after the coup bringing General Pinochet to power. The repatriation triggers a chain of disasters: Beltrán's family dissolves, and he must wend his way through episodes of school bullying and awkward infatuation. He must also adjust to the language and culture of what is for him a foreign country. When first introduced, Beltrán is a brooding and alienated seismologist; eventually, he writes his memoirs in a hotel room in Los Angeles. Popular culture enters the novel through famous movies, the titles of which serve both as chapter headings and as key markers of Beltrán's evolving identity.
Subject keyword: culture conflict
Original language: Spanish
Sources consulted for annotation:
Garrett, Daniel. *World Literature Today* 79 (January/April 2005): 108.
Graff, Keir. *Booklist* 100 (1 September 2003): 54.
Olszewski, Lawrence. *Library Journal* 128 (August 2003): 129.
Publishers Weekly 250 (14 July 2003): 52.
Some other translated books written by Alberto Fuguet: *Bad Vibes*; *Shorts*

Luis Sepúlveda. *The Name of a Bullfighter.*
Translated by Suzanne Ruta. New York: Harcourt Brace, 1996. 211 pages.
Genres/literary styles/story types: thrillers; historical thrillers
This novel centers on Juan Belmonte, a Chilean named after a world-famous matador who was featured in Hemingway's *Death in the Afternoon* and *The Sun Also Rises*. At one time, he was a radical leftist but is now a bouncer in Hamburg who becomes entwined in a murky adventure revolving around medieval gold coins. Safely hidden in rural Chile for many years, the coins are being traced by Galinsky, a former East German spy. When a German insurance company hires Belmonte to thwart Galinsky, he travels back to his homeland, where his painful memories catch up to him.
Subject keywords: identity; politics
Original language: Spanish
Sources consulted for annotation:
Benson, Mary Margaret. *Library Journal* 121 (July 1996): 163.
Eder, Richard. *Los Angeles Times*, 23 October 1996, p. 5.
Steinberg, Sybil S. *Publishers Weekly* 243 (12 August 1996): 64.
Another translated book written by Luis Sepúlveda: *The Old Man Who Read Love Stories*

Antonio Skármeta. *Love-Fifteen.*
Translated by Jonathan Tittler. Pittsburgh, PA: Latin American Literary Review Press, 1996. 126 pages.
Genre/literary style/story type: mainstream fiction
Raymond Papst is an affluent 52-year-old sports doctor living in Berlin. He abandons his settled life, prosperous career, and beautiful wife to pursue Sophie Moss, a 15-year-old tennis star who becomes his Lolita. But his pursuit turns out to be essentially futile: Sex occurs only once, as Sophie manipulates and exploits her middle-aged lover.
Related title by the same author:
Readers may also enjoy *The Dancer and the Thief*, which explores the lives of a small-time thief, Ángel Santiago, and Nico, a famous criminal kingpin, after they are released from prison through an amnesty program. Ángel has developed a plan to steal the illicitly gotten gains of a top-level supporter of General Augusto Pinochet, but he needs help. Thus, he turns to Nico and a more recent acquaintance, Victoria Ponce, a woman in her late teens who never knew her father.
Subject keyword: family histories
Original language: Spanish
Sources consulted for annotation:
Amazon.com (review from *Midwest Book Review*).
"Antonio Skármeta." *Dictionary of Literary Biography Online*. Thomson Gale databases.
Proctor, Minna. *The New York Times Book Review*, 9 March 2008 (online).
Simson, Maria. *Publishers Weekly* 243 (23 September 1996): 71.
Some other translated books written by Antonio Skármeta: *The Composition*; *Watch Where the Wolf Is Going*; *Burning Patience*; *The Postman*; *The Insurrection*; *The Dancer and the Thief*

Elizabeth Subercaseaux. *A Week in October.*
Translated by Marina Harss. New York: Other Press, 2008. 224 pages.
Genre/literary style/story type: mainstream fiction
Afflicated with cancer and psychologically troubled, Clara Griffin is a woman in her mid-40s and the wife of a wealthy architect, Clemente Balmaceda. She decides to keep a journal that she knows her husband will find and read. She confides her deepest secrets and fears to this journal as well as her knowledge of Clemente's infidelity with Eliana, his mistress. As the book shifts viewpoints from wife to husband, the betrayals and agonies of married life are revealed in all their pettiness and treachery.

Subject keyword: social roles
Original language: Spanish
Source consulted for annotation:
Global Books in Print (online) (reviews from *Booklist*, *Library Journal*, and *Publishers Weekly*).
Another translated book written by Elizabeth Subercaseaux: *Song of the Distant Root*

Alejandro Zambra. *Bonsai*.
Translated by Carolina de Robertis. Brooklyn, NY: Melville House, 2008. 83 pages.
Genres/literary styles/story types: mainstream fiction; postmodernism
Julio and Emilia were lovers, but Emilia dies, and Julio is left to reminisce about their life together. Above all, he remembers their mutual love of books. Indeed, reading was, as *The Complete Review* website notes, "an act of foreplay for them, everything from Marcel Schwob and Mishima Yukio to Georges Perec, Ted Hughes, even Cioran," not to mention Flaubert's *Madame Bovary* and the book that they both claim to have read: Proust's *In Search of Lost Time*.
Subject keyword: philosophy
Original language: Spanish
Sources consulted for annotation:
The Complete Review (book review), http://www.complete-review.com.
Melville House website, http://www.mhpbooks.com.

Colombia

Fanny Buitrago. *Señora Honeycomb*.
Translated by Margaret Sayers Peden. New York: HarperCollins, 1996. 232 pages.
Genre/literary style/story type: mainstream fiction; women's lives
Despite her sensuous body, irresistible charm, and loving heart, Teodora Vencejos is anything but happy. Orphaned and stripped of her large inheritance by dishonest relatives, she marries Galaor Ucrós, a selfish and idle philanderer. In a desperate attempt to pay his debts, she moves to Madrid, where she works for Dr. Amiel, who makes his living as a supplier of aphrodisiac foods. Although Amiel falls in love with Teodora, she misses her husband. But her homecoming is not at all what she expected. Some critics observed that this novel will be appreciated by fans of Jorge Amado and Laura Esquivel's *Like Water for Chocolate*.
Subject keyword: family histories
Original language: Spanish
Sources consulted for annotation:
Arrington, Teresa R. *World Literature Today* 71 (Autumn 1997): 759.
Hanly, Elizabeth. *The Washington Post*, 28 April 1996, p. X9.
Mujica, Barbara. *Americas* 49 (January/February 1997): 60.

Jorge Franco Ramos. *Rosario Tijeras*.
Translated by Gregory Rabassa. New York: Seven Stories Press, 2004. 171 pages.
Genres/literary styles/story types: thrillers; political thrillers
Rosario Tijeras is not someone to be messed with; she once castrated a man with scissors. Now she lies on the verge of death in a hospital in violence- and drug-ridden 1980s Medellín after being shot while being kissed. Antonio, her friend and admirer, watches and waits, recounting her daring and dangerous life as an assassin. *Publishers Weekly* labeled this book "an energetic but awkward combination of *As I Lay Dying* and a Quentin Tarantino splatter-fest."
Subject keyword: urban life
Original language: Spanish

Sources consulted for annotation:
Bird, Rosa Julia. *World Literature Today* 75 (Summer 2001): 219.
Zaleski, Jeff. *Publishers Weekly* 251 (19 January 2004): 54.

Eduardo García Aguilar. *Boulevard of Heroes*.
Translated by Jay Anthony Miskowiec. Pittsburgh, PA: Latin American Literary Review Press, 1993. 192 pages.
Genres/literary styles/story types: mainstream fiction; magical realism
Petronio Rincon, a devoted guerrilla fighter betrayed by his own comrades, is living in exile in Europe, where he becomes a disillusioned dreamer who gets by working odd jobs. Through his involvement with Adela, he becomes a murderer, eventually slipping into lunacy and nightmares. A forgotten military hero, he is adrift in a treacherous world where reality and magic blur and injustice reigns. Critics have detected echoes of Julio Cortázar's *Hopscotch*, among others, in *Boulevard of Heroes*.
Subject keywords: culture conflict; urban life
Original language: Spanish
Sources consulted for annotation:
Augenbraum, Harold. *Library Journal* 118 (December 1993): 174.
Kaganoff, Penny. *Publishers Weekly* 240 (15 November 1993): 75.
Stavans, Ilan. *World Literature Today* 68 (Spring 1994): 353.
Another translated book written by Eduardo García Aguilar: *Luminous Cities*

Gabriel García Márquez. *The General in His Labyrinth*.
Translated by Edith Grossman. New York: Alfred A. Knopf, 1990. 285 pages.
Genre/literary style/story type: historical fiction
This novel describes the last days of Simón Bolivar, a charismatic revolutionary leader who was instrumental in securing South American independence from Spanish colonial rule. President from 1819 to 1830 of what was then called Gran Colombia—a union of such modern-day countries as Venezuela, Ecuador, and Colombia—he was hailed as a visionary liberator and spoken of in the same terms as Otto von Bismarck, Abraham Lincoln, and even Alexander the Great. Suffering from tuberculosis, he died in 1830 at age 47. Gabriel García Márquez is one of the giants of South American literature—well-known for his magical realist approach to writing as most forcefully expressed in two famous novels: *The Autumn of the Patriarch* and *One Hundred Years of Solitude*. The former is about a Latin American tyrant whose rule is seemingly perpetual; the latter is a captivating story about Macondo, a magical, shimmering, and imaginary town that is founded by José Arcadio Buendía and where multiple generations of the Buendía clan experience extraordinary events, tragedies, and grace.
Related titles by the same author:
Readers may also wish to take note of *Memories of My Melancholy Whores*. Soon-to-be 90-year-old Professor Gloomy Hills decides that his birthday present to himself will be a night with a 14-year-old virgin. Also of interest may be *Love in the Time of Cholera*, in which 70-year-old Florentino Ariza assiduously courts the same woman who rejected him some 50 years ago. Finally, readers may wish to consult *Living to Tell the Tale*, the author's memoir.
Subject keywords: politics; power
Original language: Spanish
Sources consulted for annotation:
"Gabriel García Márquez." *Contemporary Authors Online*, Gale, 2003.
Kakutani, Michiko. *The New York Times*, 22 November 2005 (online).
Rafferty, Terrence. *The New York Times Book Review*, 6 November 2005 (online).

Steinberg, Sybil S. *Publishers Weekly* 237 (6 July 1990): 58.
Thompson, Ian. *The Spectator*, 12 January 1991, p. 26.
Some other translated books written by Gabriel García Márquez: *Love in the Time of Cholera*; *One Hundred Years of Solitude*; *Of Love and Other Demons*; *Chronicle of a Death Foretold*; *The Autumn of the Patriarch*; *Memories of My Melancholy Whores*; *No One Writes to the Colonel*; *Living to Tell the Tale*

Alvaro Mutis. *The Adventures and Misadventures of Maqroll.*
Translated by Edith Grossman. New York: New York Review of Books, 2002. 700 pages.
Genres/literary styles/story types: adventure; survival and disaster stories
This book describes the extraordinary and multidimensional adventures of Maqroll, a good-hearted sailor who is constantly on the wrong side of the law. The story begins when the author discovers Maqroll's diary, which has been written on old financial forms. His life is full of perpetual challenges and dangerous tribulations: affairs with insane women; life-threatening illnesses; weapons trafficking; and burning ships. Maqroll's travels take him from the fictitional Xurando River to Peru, Panama, Helsinki, Madrid, Costa Rica, and Jamaica. Motifs and images from novels by Joseph Conrad, Charles Dickens, Proust, Cortázar, Borges, Herman Melville, and García Márquez are sprinkled throughout.
Subject keyword: identity
Original language: Spanish
Sources consulted for annotation:
"Alvaro Mutis." *Contemporary Authors Online*, Gale, 2003.
"Alvaro Mutis." *Dictionary of Literary Biography Online*. Thomson Gale databases.
Hooper, Brad. *Booklist* 91 (15 February 1995): 1061.
Publishers Weekly 242 (16 January 1995): 438.
Shreve, Jack. *Library Journal* 120 (1 March 1995): 103.
Updike, John. *The New Yorker* 78 (13 January 2003): 81.
Another translated book written by Alvaro Mutis: *The Mansion*

Laura Restrepo. *The Dark Bride.*
Translated by Stephen A. Lytle. New York: HarperCollins, 2001. 358 pages.
Genre/literary style/story type: mainstream fiction
Sayonara, who was conceived from the union of a Guahibo Indian and a white man, is by all accounts a sublimely beautiful woman, not to mention the most popular prostitute in the ramshackle part of town that serves as a brothel for all those who work for the Tropical Oil Company. Breaking one of the cardinal rules of her trade, Sayonara falls in love with a client, a married worker named Payanes. She herself is loved by Sacramento, who dreams of rescuing her from prostitution. Caught in a fatal love triangle, Sayonara ultimately brings about her own demise.
Related title by the same author:
Readers may also enjoy *Delirium*, which focuses on Aguilar, an unemployed intellectual whose wife Agustina is psychologically ill. As Aguilar tries to come to terms with his wife's condition, he meets an old friend of hers: a man who works for Pablo Escobar and who is privy to the tangled history of Agustina's state.
Subject keywords: culture conflict; social problems
Original language: Spanish
Sources consulted for annotation:
Ferrer, Sabrina. *Library Journal* 127 (August 2002): 145.
Pearl, Nancy. *Library Journal* 130 (15 June 2005): 119.
Rafferty, Terrence. *The New York Times Book Review*, 15 April 2007 (online).

Santiago, Fabiola. *Hispanic* 15 (November 2002): 59.
Zaleski, Jeff. *Publishers Weekly* 249 (5 August 2002): 54.
Some other translated books written by Laura Restrepo: *Isle of Passion*; *The Angel of Galilea*; *A Tale of the Dispossessed*; *Leopard in the Sun*; *Delirium*

Juan Gabriel Vásquez. *The Informers.*
Translated by Anne McLean. New York: Riverhead Books, 2009. 351 pages.
Genre/literary style/story type: mainstream fiction
During the World War II era, the United States instituted the Enemy Alien Control Program (EACP), an initiative whereby its intelligence agencies compiled a list of individuals in Latin America suspected of being Nazi and Facist sympathizers and asked various governments in Latin America to detain those individuals favorable to the Axis powers. Of course, the plan worked imperfectly, with numerous innocent people imprisoned along with true sympathizers. As the novel begins, Gabriel Santoro has just completed a book about the EACP in Colombia. Proud of his achievement, he is stunned when his father, a law professor, writes a scathing review of the book. When Gabriel sets out to find out the reason for his father's anger, he discovers a tangled web of political deceit and betrayal. Larry Rohter compared *The Informers* to Joseph Conrad's *Under Western Eyes*, eagerly anticipating Vásquez's second novel, *The Secret History of Costaguana*, which is a contemporary update of Conrad's *Nostromo*.
Subject keywords: power; war
Original language: Spanish
Source consulted for annotation:
Rohter, Larry. *The New York Times Book Review*, 3 August 2009 (online).
Another translated book written by Juan Gabriel Vásquez: *The Secret History of Costaguana*

Ecuador

Alicia Yánez Cossío. *Bruna and Her Sisters in the Sleeping City.*
Translated by Kenneth J. A. Wishnia. Evanston, IL: Northwestern University Press, 1999. 228 pages.
Genres/literary styles/story types: mainstream fiction; magical realism; women's lives
Bruna lives in the Sleeping City, modeled on Ecuador's capital city of Quito, which afflicts its residents with the desire to sleep. Rebelling against an authoritarian and sclerotic regime, she undertakes a valiant quest to uncover the true story of her ancestors, attempting to cut through the fog of secretiveness in which her outlandish relatives wrapped the family history. Instead of being descended from European aristocracy, Bruna's great-great-grandmother was an indigenous person; her grandmother forced a nephew to don girls' clothes; and another relative was obsessed with creating what would have been the world's longest red carpet for a papal visit.
Subject keywords: culture conflict; identity
Original language: Spanish
Sources consulted for annotation:
Flanagan, Margaret. *Booklist* 96 (15 December 1999): 755.
Olszewski, Lawrence. *Library Journal* 124 (15 October 1999): 104.
Steinberg, Sybil S. *Publishers Weekly* 246 (11 October 1999): 52.
Another translated book written by Alicia Yánez Cossío: *The Potbellied Virgin*

Paraguay

Rosario Castellanos. *The Book of Lamentations.*
Translated by Esther Allen. New York: Penguin Books, 1998. 381 pages.

Genre/literary style/story type: historical fiction
In Chiapas, a poverty-stricken Mexican state bordering on Guatemala, not much has changed over the course of the decades and centuries. Tensions have always existed between landowning *ladinos* (non-Indians) and the indigenous population. In 1867, there was a revolt by Chamula Indians against their oppressors. This novel, in which the author has transferred the 1860s incident into the 1930s, centers on the conflict between Leonardo Cifuentes, an aristocratic landowner with political hopes who sees the Tzotizil Indians as a moral blight on the land, and Catalina, a prophet who leads a native revolt against the *ladinos*. The author was Mexico's ambassador to Israel, where she died in 1974 in a domestic accident.
Subject keywords: culture conflict; power
Original language: Spanish
Sources consulted for annotation:
Global Books in Print (online) (book description; review from *Publishers Weekly*).
Williams, Raymond Leslie. *The Columbia Guide to the Latin American Novel Since 1945.*
Another translated book written by Rosario Castellanos: *Nine Guardians*

Augusto Roa Bastos. *I the Supreme.*
Translated by Helen R. Lane. Normal, IL: Dalkey Archive Press, 1986. 381 pages.
Genres/literary styles/story types: literary historical; magical realism
This novel centers on the dictatorial rule of José Gaspar Rodriguez Francia, Paraguay's iron-fisted leader from the mid-1810s to 1840. It paints a horrific picture of tyranny in a South America divesting itself of colonial Spanish rule. One morning, an anonymous pamphlet appears that gives precise instructions on what is to be done when El Supremo dies. Of course, El Supremo is peeved and orders that the author of this scurrilous attack be located and brought to justice. In the meantime, he rants and raves, and his thoughts are transcribed by his secretary. These musings are supplemented by a notebook that El Supremo writes himself as well as a variety of historical documents, including children's responses to an assigned essay question about their view of El Supremo's government. This book is in the tradition of Gabriel García Márquez's *The Autumn of the Patriarch* and Mario Vargas Llosa's *The Feast of the Goat*.
Subject keywords: politics; power
Original language: Spanish
Sources consulted for annotation:
Fuentes, Carlos. *The New York Times Book Review*, 6 April 1998 (online).
Williams, Raymond Leslie. *The Columbia Guide to the Latin American Novel Since 1945.*

Peru

Alfredo Bryce Echenique. *Tarzan's Tonsillitis.*
Translated by Alfred MacAdam. New York: Pantheon Books, 2001. 262 pages.
Genres/literary styles/story types: mainstream fiction; epistolary fiction
Fernanda, a Swiss-educated Salvadoran woman from a privileged family, and Juan Manuel Carpio, a Peruvian musician and a descendant of the Quechua indigenous peoples, meet in Paris in 1967. Their brief relationship ends in recrimination and separation. But their passion never ends, stretching over three decades through vast correspondence and furtive meetings.
Subject keywords: culture conflict; identity
Original language: Spanish
Sources consulted for annotation:
Howard, Gregory. *Review of Contemporary Fiction* 22 (Spring 2002): 120.

Owchar, Nick. *Los Angeles Times*, 27 December 2001, p. E10.
Ruta, Suzanne. *The New York Times Book Review*, 17 February 2002, p. 14.
Another translated book written by Alfredo Bryce Echenique: *A World for Julius*

Isaac Goldemberg. *The Fragmented Life of Don Jacobo Lerner.*
Translated by Robert S. Picciotto. Albuquerque, NM: University of New Mexico Press, 1999. 213 pages.
Genre/literary style/story type: mainstream fiction
Set in 1930s Peru, this novel focuses on Don Jacobo Lerner, a Ukrainian Jew who is on his death bed. His fragmented life slowly emerges through stories told by his friends and family; the recollections of his illegitimate son Efrain; and the clippings of the local Jewish newspaper and other documents. The book, which received critical acclaim but was also accused of being anti-Semitic, deals with such unsettling topics as xenophobia; the reluctance to adapt; apathy toward contemporary developments; and religion.
Subject keyword: culture conflict
Original language: Spanish
Sources consulted for annotation:
Amazon.com (book description).
Stavans, Ilan. *Judaism* 52 (Summer 2003): 246.
Szichman, Mario. *Associated Press Newswires*, 30 August 1999 (from Factiva databases).
Another translated book written by Isaac Goldemberg: *Play by Play*

Laura Riesco. *Ximena at the Crossroads.*
Translated by Mary G. Berg. Fredonia, NY: White Pine Press, 1998. 269 pages.
Genres/literary styles/story types: mainstream fiction; coming-of-age
Ximena, the only daughter of an affluent Peruvian family, lives in a small town near Lima in the 1940s. Her personality unfolds through interactions with eccentric relatives and strangers, the many books that she reads, and her exposure to classical myths and legends. As she discovers the economic cruelties and social injustices of the world, she becomes aware of the immense power of the written word.
Subject keyword: family histories
Original language: Spanish
Sources consulted for annotation:
Augenbraum, Harold. *Library Journal* 123 (15 March 1998): 95.
Grandfield, Kevin. *Booklist* 94 (15 April 1998): 1429.
Steinberg, Sybil S. *Publishers Weekly* 245 (6 April 1998): 61.

Mario Vargas Llosa. *The Way to Paradise.*
Translated by Natasha Wimmer. New York: Farrar, Straus and Giroux, 2003. 373 pages.
Genres/literary styles/story types: historical fiction; women's lives.
The well-known painter Paul Gaugin's grandmother was Flora Tristan, a proto-feminist, socialist, and labor activist in Peru in the first half of the nineteenth century. Although the latter is a more obscure figure than the former, both were highly significant in their respective fields. This book traces the many parallels between these two utopian visionaries and globetrotters. Moving back and forth between France, Peru, and England, Tristan attempts to mobilize supporters in her social and political struggles. Gaugin crisscrosses Europe, eventually leaving for Tahiti, where he seeks unification with nature, primordial purity, and inspiration. While Tristan is contemptuous toward the workers for whom she is advocating, Gaugin is indifferent toward his offspring and the young Tahitian women whom he knowingly infects with syphilis. Neither reaches their respective

paradise—their actions losing some of their altruistic sheen as they become increasingly preoccupied with their quest for self-determination and absolute freedom.

Related title by the same author:

Readers may also enjoy *The Feast of the Goat*, a magisterial account of the absolutist rule of Rafael Trujillo in the Dominican Republic. Urania Cabral, a young New York lawyer for the World Bank, returns to Santo Domingo to visit her dying father, a former minister in the Domincan government who lost his position due to the whims of Trujillo. Focusing on the final days of Trujillo's life, the novel gives detailed insight into the sources of his power, his overzealous acolytes, his compulsive womanizing, and the motives of the numerous enemies who plotted to assassinate him.

Subject keywords: family histories; identity

Original language: Spanish

Sources consulted for annotation:

Amazon.com (review from *Booklist*).

Eder, Richard. *The New York Times Book Review*, 23 November 2003 (online).

Kakutani, Michiko. *The New York Times*, 16 November 2001 (online).

Kirn, Walter. *The New York Times Book Review*, 25 November 2001 (online).

"Mario Vargas Llosa." *Contemporary Authors Online*. Thomson Gale, 2006.

Mujica, Barbara. *Americas* 56 (March/April 2004): 45.

Pearl, Nancy. *Library Journal* 130 (15 June 2005): 119.

Shreve, Jack. *Library Journal* 128 (15 October 2003): 100.

Some other translated books written by Mario Vargas Llosa: *Aunt Julia and the Scriptwriter*; *The Green House*; *Conversation in the Cathedral*; *The War of the End of the World*; *The Time of the Hero*; *The Notebooks of Don Rigoberto*; *The Bad Girl*

Uruguay

Napoleón Baccino Ponce de León. *Five Black Ships: A Novel of the Discoverers*.

Translated by Nick Caistor. New York: Harcourt Brace, 1994. 347 pages.

Genres/literary styles/story types: adventure; survival and disaster stories

This novel is about Ferdinand Magellan's tragic voyage of 1519. Narrated by Juanillo Ponce, a crew member, the book focuses on the human element that is the often unspoken center of expeditionary sagas. The illegitimate son of a Jewish prostitute, Juanillo enlisted for financial reasons; he was Magellan's jester, but his name does not appear on any official records or lists. Hoping to be reinstated on the crew list and therefore receive a pension from the king of Spain, he recounts the doomed naval adventure in eloquent and hallucinatory prose. Magellan is revealed as smug, obstinate, and imbued with megalomania; he disregards the mounting agonies and fears of his crew. But he is also capable of kindnesses despite being wracked by guilt about the pregnant wife he left back home, personal insecurities, and a growing sense of helplessness.

Subject keyword: social roles

Original language: Spanish

Sources consulted for annotation:

Amazon.com (reviews from *Publishers Weekly* and *Library Journal*).

Mujica, Barbara. Americas 47 (January 1995): 61.

Platt, Edward. *The Sunday Times*, 2 November 1997.

Veale, Scott. *The New York Times Book Review*, 14 August 1994, p. 718.

Eduardo Galeano. *The Book of Embraces*.

Translated by Cedric Belfrage with Mark Schafer. New York: W. W. Norton, 1991. 281 pages.

Genres/literary styles/story types: mainstream fiction; short stories

In a work of about 280 pages, Galeano gives readers 191 short passages that, taken together, are characterized by Jay Parini as "an ingenious blend of image and text that moves from autobiographical vignettes to philosophical musings, from reporting to storytelling." Galeano's traumatic experiences—illnesses, his wife's miscarriage, his friend's death—are mixed with incisive political commentaries about the oppressive dictatorial regimes that plagued many Latin American countries.

Related titles by the same author:

The Book of Embraces may be productively read in conjunction with the author's *Memory of Fire*, a trilogy that is meant to be what Ronald Christ calls a "a sort of Bible, a recorded collation of the mythological and historical soul of the peoples of North, Central and South America." Also of interest may be *Mirrors: Stories of Almost Everyone*, which recreates the entire history of the world in about 600 dictionary-like entries. Readers who enjoy *Mirrors* may also be drawn to *Dictionary of the Khazars: A Lexicon Novel* by Milorad Pavić.

Subject keywords: philosophy; politics

Original language: Spanish

Sources consulted for annotation:

Christ, Ronald. *The New York Times Book Review*, 27 October 1985 (online).
Gordon, Neil. *The New York Times Book Review*, 20 August 2009 (online).
Harris, Michael. *Los Angeles Times*, 12 May 1991, p. 6.
Olszewski, Lawrence. *Library Journal* 116 (1 April 1991): 121.
Parini, Jay. *The New York Times Book Review*, 21 April 1991 (online).
Stuttaford, Genevieve. *Publishers Weekly* 238 (8 March 1991): 59.
West, Alan. *The Village Voice*, 2 July 1991, p. 71.

Some other translated books written by Eduardo H. Galeano: *Memory of Fire*; *Walking Words*; *Mirrors: Stories of Almost Everyone*

Antonio Larreta. *The Last Portrait of the Duchess of Alba*.

Translated by Pamela Carmell. Bethesda, MD: Adler & Adler, 1988. 214 pages.

Genres/literary styles/story types: biographical fiction; historical fiction

The 13th Duchess of Alba died suddenly at age 40 in 1802. Untold rumors surrounded her death: She could have been poisoned by any one of her many enemies at the royal court or she could have committed suicide because of her drug addiction and what she perceived as the decline of her beauty. But the mystery of her death remains, especially since she had a close relationship with Goya, who painted many portraits of her. This novel begins from the premise that a memoir written by an important government official has come to light. Revealing much about the politics and culture of the age, the memoir also reveals information that may solve the puzzle of the Duchess's death.

Subject keywords: identity; social roles

Original language: Spanish

Sources consulted for annotation:

Koger, Grove. *Library Journal* 113 (15 May 1988): 93.
Steinberg, Sylvia. *Publishers Weekly* 233 (6 May 1988): 95.

Cristina Peri Rossi. *The Museum of Useless Efforts*.

Translated by Tobias Hecht. Lincoln, NE: University of Nebraska Press, 2001. 156 pages.

Genres/literary styles/story types: mainstream fiction; short stories.

This collection of 30 short stories about the ultimately meaningless nature of life has echoes of Jorge Luis Borges. In the first story, a museum undertakes an inventory to end all inventories, focusing on the futile endeavours that individuals take to change themselves or their surroundings. In other stories, children dig sand holes and watch them being washed away; a man attempts to teach his dog to speak; a man is so paralyzed by fear and a variety of phobias that he can hardly bear to leave his bed; and an insomniac who counts sheep in order to fall asleep starts hitting one of the stubborn animals.

Subject keyword: philosophy
Original language: Spanish
Sources consulted for annotation:
Alibris.com (book description).
Gerlach, T. J. *Review of Contemporary Fiction* 21 (Fall 2001): 208.
Zaleski, Jeff. *Publishers Weekly* 248 (26 March 2001): 64.
Some other translated books written by Cristina Peri Rossi: *The Ship of Fools*; *Solitaire of Love*; *Dostoevsky's Last Night*; *A Forbidden Passion*; *Panic Signs*

Carmen Posadas. *Little Indiscretions*.
Translated by Christopher Andrews. New York: Random House, 2003. 305 pages.
Genres/literary styles/story types: crime fiction; suspense
It goes without saying that Nestor Chaffino, a notoriously arrogant chef who had a penchant for snooping, gathering secrets, and recording incriminating information, had numerous enemies. It is therefore not a great surprise when he is found dead after catering an event for a rich art collector. Culinary fiction meets the crime genre.
Related titles by the same author:
Readers may also enjoy *The Last Resort*, in which Rafael Molinet Rojas's plans to commit suicide are temporarily put on hold as he attempts to save the beautiful Mercedes Algorta from being charged with her husband's murder. In *Child's Play*, a writer develops a plot for a novel revolving around the murder of a child, but this imaginary scenario soon has real-world consequences.
Subject keyword: social roles
Original language: Spanish
Sources consulted for annotation:
Cohen, Patricia. *The New York Times Book Review*, 19 August 2009 (online).
DeCandido, Grace Anne A. *Booklist* 99 (July 2003): 1871.
Mosley, Shelly. *Library Journal* 128 (July 2003): 131.
Waldman, Debby. *People* 60 (8 September 2003): 50.
Some other translated books written by Carmen Posadas: *The Last Resort*; *Mister North Wind*; *Child's Play*

Venezuela

Alicia Freilich de Segal. *Cláper*.
Translated by Joan E. Friedman. Albuquerque, NM: University of New Mexico Press, 1998. 182 pages.
Genres/literary styles/story types: mainstream fiction; coming-of-age
This story of a Jewish family who immigrated to Venezuela from Poland spans a period of some 30 years from the 1950s to the 1970s. The family struggles to adjust and survive; the father works as a peddlar and tries to secure the future of his children. Later, his daughter is faced with a different kind of struggle: a quest for self-identity and autonomy in a swiftly changing sociopolitical climate.
Subject keyword: family histories
Original language: Spanish

Sources consulted for annotation:
Amazon.com (book description).
Lindstrom, Naomi. *World Literature Today* 72 (Summer 1998): 591.

Ana Teresa Torres. *Doña Inés vs. Oblivion.*
Translated by Gregory Rabassa. Baton Rouge, LA: Louisiana State University Press, 1999. 243 pages.
Genres/literary styles/story types: historical fiction; magical realism
Told through the story of the obsessive quest of Doña Inés Villegas y Solorzano, the widow of a former plantation owner in Caracas, to recover the family's lost estate, this novel traces more than 300 years of Venezuelan history, starting from the early eighteenth century. First as an old woman and then as a ghost, Doña Inés does everything in her power to get the necessary deeds to support her claims against what she considers to be illegitimate heirs. But as the centuries move forward, Caracas becomes an ever-expanding urban center that surrounds and infringes on the plantation. The past is irretrievable, and the present is relentless. Finally, the plantation becomes a golf course and tourist center—the result of an agreement between Doña Inés's descendants and the black descendants of her husband's relationship with a plantation slave. Some critics have invoked Isabel Allende's *House of Spirits* and Gabriel García Márquez's *One Hundred Years of Solitude* when discussing this book.
Subject keywords: culure conflict; family histories
Original language: Spanish
Sources consulted for annotation:
Mujica, Barbara. *Americas* 45 (July 1993): 61.
Quinn, Mary Ellen. *Booklist* 96 (15 September 1999): 235.
Shreve, Jack. *Library Journal* 124 (1 October 1999): 136.
Vernon, John. *The New York Times Book Review*, 7 November 1999 (online).

ANNOTATIONS FOR TRANSLATED BOOKS FROM SPAIN (INCLUDING BASQUE, CATALAN, AND GALICIAN)

Núria Amat. *Queen Cocaine.*
Translated by Peter Bush. San Francisco, CA: City Lights Books, 2005. 222 pages.
Genre/literary style/story type: mainstream fiction
Wilson Cervantes is a melancholy former journalist who intends to write a novel, and Mona is a young Catalan woman and Wilson's lover. They have come to the jungle village of Bahía Negra on the Colombian Pacific coast, where the impoverished residents rely on growing coca for drug production and where a bloody three-sided conflict among left-wing revolutionaries, right-wing defense forces, and drug lords rages uncontrollably. Critics have referred to Joseph Conrad's *Heart of Darkness* to describe this violence-soaked account of contemporary Colombia.
Subject keywords: politics; power
Original language: Spanish
Sources consulted for annotation:
Amazon.com (book description).
Driscoll, Brendan. *Booklist* 101 (1 March 2005): 1140.
Publishers Weekly 252 (14 February 1005): 53.
Tepper, Anderson. *The New York Times Book Review*, 5 June 2005, p. 28.

J. J. Armas Marcelo. *Ships Afire.*
Translated by Sarah Arvio. New York: Avon Books, 1988. 310 pages.

Genres/literary styles/story types: adventure; survival and disaster stories
In the early sixteenth century, Juan Rejon, a Spanish pirate, built the city of Royal on the fictitious island of Salbago. Years later, Juan's son Alvaro leaves Salbago to make conquests of his own. Eventually, he becomes a drug-addicated slave owner in the Dominican Republic. He is obsessed to the point of madness with finding the elusive and chimerical Eldorado. Returning to Salbago, he witnesses the Dutch invasion, which destroys the world that his father built. The novel can be viewed as a cautionary parable about the disastrous effects of human greed.
Subject keyword: colonization and colonialism
Original language: Spanish
Sources consulted for annotation:
Johnson, George. *The New York Times*, 17 April 1988, p. 40.
Kaganoff, Penny. *Publishers Weekly* 233 (13 May 1988): 269.
Polk, James. *The New York Times*, 14 August 1988, p. A16.

Bernardo Atxaga. *The Accordionist's Son.*
Translated by Margaret Jull Costa. Saint Paul, MN: Graywolf Press, 2009. 370 pages.
Genre/literary style/story type: historical fiction
Critics agree that this is a sensitive and superlative novel about Basque culture and history, with particular emphasis on the period 1936–1999. Now living in exile on a California ranch, David Imaz recalls key events of his life: the discovery that his father may have been a sympathizer of General Franco during the Spanish Civil War; his father's involvement in the executions of some of Franco's opponents; his own gradual political awakening; and his participation in Basque separatist activities, some of which turned violent. The book was first translated from Basque into Spanish.
Related titles by the same author:
Readers may also enjoy *The Lone Man* and *The Lone Woman*. Both of these books center on former Basque terrorists who attempt to begin new lives but cannot escape their respective pasts.
Subject keywords: politics; power
Original language: Basque/Spanish
Sources consulted for annotation:
Amazon.com (book description; review from *Kirkus Reviews*).
Fisher, Barbara. *Boston Globe*, 6 June 1999, p. 4.
Kaske, Michelle. *Booklist* 95 (1/15 June 1999): 1788.
Steinberg, Sybil S. *Publishers Weekly* 246 (28 June 1999): 54.
Some other translated books written by Bernardo Atxaga: *Obabakoak*; *The Lone Man*; *The Lone Woman*; *Two Brothers*

Félix de Azúa. *Diary of a Humiliated Man.*
Translated by Julie Jones. Cambridge, MA: Lumen Editions, 1996. 294 pages.
Genre/literary style/story type: mainstream fiction
This novel describes a Barcelona native who meticulously records and cynically reflects on his everyday experiences in a diary for eight months. An orphan and a man of independent means by virtue of a modest inheritance, he does not do much of anything except read and walk, frequently indulging in sex, drink, and occasional louche encounters. In short, he drifts placidly and aimlessly through a penumbral Barcelona, a superfluous soul who some critics have seen as being a close literary relative of Jean-Baptiste Clamence in Albert Camus's *The Fall*.
Subject keyword: urban life
Original language: Spanish
Sources consulted for annotation:
Amazon.com (book description; review from *Kirkus Reviews*).

Howard, Eric. *Library Journal* 121 (1 October 1996): 126.
Simson, Maria. *Publishers Weekly* 243 (26 August 1996): 90.
Steinberg, Sybil S. *Publishers Weekly* 243 (4 November 1996): 37.

Lluís-Anton Baulenas. *For a Sack of Bones.*
Translated by Cheryl Leah Morgan. San Diego, CA: Harcourt, 2008. 368 pages.
Genres/literary styles/story types: mainstream fiction; coming-of-age
Niso was entrusted with a sacred mission by his father on his deathbed. Killed by Franco's troops for his political activism, the father enjoined his son to provide a formal burial to a man who played a crucial role in saving him from imprisonment. Leaving behind the orphanage where he spent his younger days, Niso is compelled to serve in Franco's military, where he distinguishes himself as part of the Spanish Foreign Legion. When he returns to Spain, he sets out to perform his dying father's wish.
Subject keywords: family histories; power
Original language: Catalan
Source consulted for annotation:
Global Books in Print (online) (reviews from *Booklist*, *Library Journal*, and *Publishers Weekly*).

Juan Luis Cebrián. *Red Doll.*
Translated by Philip W. Silver. New York: Weidenfeld & Nicolson, 1987. 162 pages.
Genres/literary styles/story types: thrillers; political thrillers
Juan Altamirano is middle-aged, married, and an advisor to the Spanish president. While working in Paris, he falls in love with Begona Aizpuri, a politically active student who may be a KGB agent. Later, when Altamirano participates in negotiations with Basque separatists and his Basque counterpart is killed, Juan realizes that byzantine political games have been set in motion.
Subject keyword: power
Original language: Spanish
Sources consulted for annotation:
Los Angeles Times, 13 December 1987, p. 14.
Shreve, Jack. *Library Journal* 112 (1 October 1987): 106.
Steinberg, Sybil S. *Publishers Weekly* 232 (9 October 1987): 78.

Javier Cercas. *Soldiers of Salamis.*
Translated by Anne McLean. New York: Bloomsbury, 2004. 210 pages.
Genre/literary style/story type: historical fiction
Javier Cercas, a Spanish journalist and the author's namesake, is tracing the story of Rafael Sánchez Mazas, one of the founders of the Spanish Falange, a small fascist party. During the Spanish Civil War in the late 1930s, the party was banned, and he was jailed. Subsequently condemned to death, he nevertheless escaped. Later in France, Cercas discovers a Spanish Civil War veteran by the name of Miralles, a soldier who likely spared Sánchez Mazas's life after his hiding place was found.
Related title by the same author:
Readers may also enjoy *The Speed of Light*, which, like *Soldiers of Salamis*, examines the dark legacies of war. This time Cercas is a Spanish teacher in Illinois, where he meets Rodney Falk, a Vietnam veteran with a haunted past. Rodney vanishes, and Rodney's father wants Cercas to find him.
Subject keywords: politics; war
Original language: Spanish
Sources consulted for annotation:
Fraiser, Tom. *The Independent on Sunday*, 20 August 2004, p. 33.
Pawel, Rebecca. *Los Angeles Times*, 29 February 2004, p. R10.

Wimmer, Natasha. *The New York Times Book Review*, 3 June 2007 (online).
Zaleski, Jeff. *Publishers Weekly* 251 (19 January 2004): 54.
Some other translated books written by Javier Cersas: *The Tenant and the Motive*; *The Speed of Light*

Rafael Chirbes. *Mimoun*.
Translated by Gerald Martin. London: Serpent's Tail, 1992. 117 pages.
Genre/literary style/story type: mainstream fiction
Manuel, a writer, has come to Morocco to get away from the hectic life of Madrid and to complete his novel. Taking up residence near the Atlas Mountains, he teaches Spanish at a nearby university, but he quickly becomes disillusioned with his new surroundings. Scared, lonely, and aliented, he escapes reality through drinking and sex. Readers interested in another view of expatriate life in Morocco might like *The Sheltering Sky* by American writer Paul Bowles.
Subject keyword: culture conflict
Original language: Spanish
Sources consulted for annotation:
Dawood, Nessim J. *The Times*, 27 June 1992.
Kaganoff, Penny. *Publishers Weekly* 240 (28 June 1993): 68.
Salter Reynolds, Susan. *Los Angeles Times*, 8 August 1993, p. 8.

Unai Elorriaga. *Plants Don't Drink Coffee*.
Translated by Amaia Gabantxo. Brooklyn, NY: Archipelago Press, 2009. 208 pages.
Genres/literary styles/story types: mainstream fiction; coming-of-age
This book contains an interlinked set of stories about the oddities and epiphanies of life in a small rural village. One of the most endearing characters is Tomas, who, along with his cousin, searches for the elusive blue dragonfly. There is also an uncle who schemes to play rugby on the nearby golf course as well as an aunt who runs a dress shop that attracts women who tell stories of lost love.
Subject keyword: rural life
Original language: Basque
Source consulted for annotation:
Kyzer, Larissa. Three percent website, http://www.rochester.edu/College/translation/threepercent.

Javier García Sánchez. *Lady of the South Wind*.
Translated by Michael Bradburn Ruster and Myrna R. Villa. San Francisco, CA: North Point Press, 1990. 221 pages.
Genre/literary style/story type: mainstream fiction
Hans Kruger is passionately in love with the mysterious Olga Dittersdorf, a fellow employee at an explosives factory. But when she rejects him, Hans's anguish knows no bounds. He becomes a psychological wreck, is institutionalized, engages in rambling conversations with himself about his obsession, and is finally released. He returns to the explosives factory but ultimately blows himself up in despair.
Subject keyword: identity
Original language: Spanish
Sources consulted for annotation:
Kettmann, Steve. *The San Francisco Chronicle*, 8 August 1990, p. REV8.
Shreve, Jack. *Library Journal* 115 (15 February 1990): 212.
Steinberg, Sybil S. *Publishers Weekly* 237 (5 January 1990): 61.
Another translated book written by Javier García Sánchez: *The Others*

Eduardo Garrigues. *West of Babylon.*
Translated by Nasario García. Albuquerque, NM: University of New Mexico Press, 2002. 308 pages.
Genres/literary styles/story types: adventure; survival and disaster stories
As Dick Davis writes, this novel is "a retelling of the epic of *Gilgamesh* in a 19th-century New Mexican setting." Featuring the Navajo Gil Gómez and his companion Decoy, it describes "the lawlessness of the New Mexico frontier between immigrants of European heritage and American Indians in the mid-19th century" as well as Navajo and Apache lore connected with hunting and warfare.
Subject keyword: culture conflict
Original language: Spanish
Sources consulted for annotation:
Amazon.com (book description).
Benson, Mary Margaret. *Library Journal* 127 (1 September 2002): 212.
Davis, Dick. *The New York Times Book Review*, 29 September 2002, p. 18.
Smith Nash, Susan. *World Literature Today* 77 (July/September 2003): 149.
Another translated book written by Eduardo Garrigues: *The Grass Rain: A Tail of Modern Africa*

Alicia Giménez-Bartlett. *Dog Day.*
Translated by Nick Caistor. New York: Europa Editions, 2006. 208 pages.
Genres/literary styles/story types: crime fiction; police detectives
This novel features Barcelona detectives Petra Delicado and Fermin Garzon. After a vagrant named Lucena is found beaten, the two police officers discover a large sum of money in his squalid apartment. Soon, they are thrust into the sordid world of animal abuse, where dogs are sold to universities and pharmaceutical companies for scientific experiments and where dogfighting is a lucrative business.
Subject keyword: social problems
Original language: Spanish
Source consulted for annotation:
Global Books in Print (online) (reviews from *Booklist*, *Library Journal*, and *Publishers Weekly*).
Some other translated books written by Alicia Giménez-Bartlett: *Prime Time Suspect*; *Death Rites*

Irene González Frei (pseudonym). *Your Name Written on Water.*
Translated by Kristina Cordero. New York: Grove Press, 1999. 196 pages.
Genres/literary styles/story types: mainstream fiction; feminist fiction
Twenty-eight-year-old Sofia works at an art gallery. She marries Santiago, an architect, but their marriage disintegrates when Santiago's jealously and violence become overwhelming. Sofia then falls in love with Marina, her doppelganger. They run away to Italy, where they invent an imaginary person named Clara, a symbolic represenatation of their unity. Six months later, a vindictive Santiago tracks his wife down. Critics compared this erotically charged psychological novel to Pauline Réage's *The Story of O* and books by Anaïs Nin.
Subject keyword: identity
Original language: Spanish
Sources consulted for annotation:
Amazon.com (book description; review from *Kirkus Reviews*).
Steinberg, Sybil S. *Publisher Weekly* 246 (16 August 1999): 58.

Juan Goytisolo. *State of Siege.*
Translated by Helen R. Lane. San Francisco, CA: City Lights Books, 2002. 155 pages.
Genres/literary styles/story types: historical fiction; magical realism
During the blockade of Sarajevo in the mid-1990s, a Goytisolo-like visitor is killed. As Sarajevo authorities try to discover the murdered man's identity and as they wonder about the sexually charged poems he left behind, readers are introduced to a series of narrators who comment on the larger tragedy of the destruction of Sarajevo's cultural heritage, including its library. The novel has been compared to works by Jorge Luis Borges, Eduardo Galeano, and Cervantes.
Related title by the same author:
Readers may also wish to explore *Landscapes After the Battle*, in which the walls of a French neighborhood are suddenly covered by undecipherable texts and where street and shop signage now appear in Arabic. This novel is a profound reflection on the meaning of colonization in a postmodern world.
Subject keywords: war; writers
Original language: Spanish
Sources consulted for annotation:
Amazon.com (book description).
Eberstadt, Fernanda, *The New York Times Magazine* (16 April 2006): 32.
Feehily, Gierry. *The Independent*, 24 October 2003, p. 20–21.
Kiley, Robert. *The New York Times Book Review*, 14 June 1987 (online).
McDowell, Megan A. *Review of Contemporary Fiction* 23 (Spring 2003): 148.
Sennett, Franc. *Booklist* 99 (1 October 2002): 301.
Wilson, Charles. *The New York Times Book Review*, 29 December 2002, p. 17.
Some other translated books written by Juan Goytisolo: *Quarantine*; *The Virtues of the Solitary Bird*; *Landscapes After the Battle*; *The Garden of Secrets*; *The Marx Family Saga*

Almuseda Grandes. *The Ages of Lulu.*
Translated by Sonia Soto. New York: Grove Press, 1994. 216 pages.
Genres/literary styles/story types: mainstream fiction; women's lives
At age 15, Lulu is seduced by Pablo, the best friend of her older brother. Eventually, they marry and have a daughter. But Lulu's world revolves around the increasingly violent Pablo, who introduces her to a variety of sexual practices. She is an eager student, participating in threesomes, sodomy, and much more. When she is raped by her brother, she begins to realize the abnegation to which she has exposed herself, fitfully struggling to establish an existence independent of Pablo. The novel has been compared to the works of Marquis de Sade and Pauline Réage's *The Story of O.*
Subject keyword: identity
Original language: Spanish
Sources consulted for annotation:
Amazon.com (book description; review from *Kirkus Reviews*).
Berona, David A. *Library Journal* 119 (1 June 1994): 158.
Shreffler, John. *Booklist* 90 (1 June 1994): 1770.
Steinberg, Sybil S. *Publishers Weekly* 241 (2 May 1994): 280.
Another translated book written Almudena Grandes: *The Wind from the East*

Julio Llamazares. *The Yellow Rain*.
Translated by Margaret Jull Costa. Orlando, FL: Harcourt, 2003. 130 pages.
Genre/literary style/story type: mainstream fiction
There is only person left in an isolated village in the Spanish Pyrenees; the mill closed some time ago, so there was very little reason for people to stay. Andres and his wife remained, but after

Sabine committed suicide, it is only Andres now and his dog. Andres recalls the key events of his life, including the death of his daughter Sara at age four; the death of his son Camilo in the Spanish Civil War; and the departure of another son who left to find happiness elsewhere. Critics used such adjectives as somber and elegiac in describing this taut novel about inexorable solitude.
Subject keywords: aging; rural life
Original language: Spanish
Sources consulted for annotation:
Amazon.com (book description).
Gies, David T. *Virginia Quarterly Review* 80 (Summer 2004): 263.
Publishers Weekly 250 (24 November 2003): 41.
St. John, Janet. *Booklist* 100 (15 November 2003): 581.

Manuel de Lope. *The Wrong Blood*.
Translated by John Cullen. New York: Other Press, 2010. 288 pages.
Genre/literary style/story type: mainstream fiction
It is the eve of the Spanish Civil War, and Isabel Cruces is about to be married. On their way to her wedding, three of her guests stop off at an inn, where one of them suddenly dies. An unlikely event, to be sure, but one that forges the closest of bonds between Isabel and the innkeeper's teenage daughter, María Antonia, especially when Isabel's husband dies soon after in the war and when María Antonia is raped by a soldier. As both women draw closer together because of their isolation and pregnancies, María Antonia becomes Isabel's maid, and they make a startling pact that will be revealed decades later when Isabel's grandson visits the estate that his grandmother has bequeathed to María Antonia. The novel can be viewed as a phantasmagoric examination of the consequences of war on noncombatants.
Subject keyword: family histories
Original language: Spanish
Sources consulted for annotation:
Howard, Erika. Three Percent website (book review), http://www.rochester.edu/College/translation/threepercent.
Other Press website (book description), http://www.otherpress.com.
Thompson, Andrea. *The New York Times Book Review*, 29 October 2010 (online).

Ray Loriga. *Tokyo Doesn't Love Us Anymore*.
Translated by John King. New York: Grove Press, 2003. 260 pages.
Genre/literary style/story type: speculative fiction
Bewitched by the concepts of change and progress, we think the future will unfold in a wonderful way. Perhaps; perhaps not. What would happen if a corporation invented an omnipotent product that erases unwelcome memories? Of course, the firm is interested in getting as much market share as possible, so it sends an agent on an international selling trip, where he peddles the newly developed elixir to anyone with a need to forget the previous night's debauchery or unpleasant memories. But as the sales representative crisscrosses the globe, he also indulges in actions that will have to be pharmaceutically erased. On its face, the perpetual possibility of a clean slate is a seductive one, but it raises profound questions about the nature of responsibility, sin, and forgiveness—to mention only three important topics. This book has been compared with J. G. Ballard's *Crash*, William S. Burroughs's *Naked Lunch*, and fiction by William Gibson and Philip K. Dick.
Subject keyword: identity
Original language: Spanish
Sources consulted for annotation:
Amazon.com (book description; review from *Bookmarks Magazine*).

Hays, Carl. *Booklist* 100 (July 2004): 1828.
Lipsyte, Sam. *The New York Times Book Review*, 17 October 2004, p. 12.
Zaleski, Jeff. *Publishers Weekly* 251 (26 April 2004): 37.
Another translated book written by Ray Loriga: *My Brother's Gun*

Javier Marías. *The Man of Feeling.*
Translated by Margaret Jull Costa. New York: New Directions, 2003. 182 pages.
Genres/literary styles/story types: mainstream novels; postmodernism
Léon de Nápoles is an opera singer on his way to Madrid to perform the role of Cassio in Verdi's *Otello*. On the train, he meets a Belgian banker, Hieronimo Manur, and his wife Natalia. Four years later, Léon narrates the story of his affair with Natalia and his subsequent confrontation with Manur, who reveals that their marriage was undertaken only for financial reasons having to do with Natalia's father. This book has been compared with Henry James's *The Turn of the Screw*.
Related titles by the same author:
Readers may also enjoy *Voyage Along the Horizon*, in which a motley assortment of supposedly sophisticated European savants are portrayed as guileless fools during a feckless scheme to sail to Antarctica. It has been compared with Katherine Anne Porter's allegorical *Ship of Fools*. Also of interest may be the three volumes of *Your Face Tomorrow*, which revolve around a mysterious spy whose task is never clearly defined but who spends his days in a state of perpetual fear and guilt, reliving the violence that he has seen, ceaselessly thinking about and analyzing each aspect and relationship of his life, but never coming to any clear conclusion. Searching how best to describe *Your Face Tomorow*, one critic situated it at the intersection of the work of Roberto Bolaño, José Saramago, Ian Fleming, Laurence Sterne, Henry James, and the long-ago television show *The Prisoners*.
Subject keyword: family histories
Original language: Spanish
Sources consulted for annotation:
Amazon.com (book description).
Global Books in Print (online) (review from *Library Journal* for *Voyage Along the Horizon*; review from *Publishers Weekly* for *Your Face Tomorrow* (vol. 2: *Dance and Dream*)).
Green, Zoe. *The Observer*, 15 February 2004, p. 17.
"Javier Marías." *Dictionary of Literary Biography Online*. Thomson Gale databases.
Kellman, Steven G. *Review of Contemporary Fiction* 23 (Summer 2003): 132.
Mason, Wyatt. *The New York Times Book Review*, 27 August 2006 (online).
Venuti, Lawrence. *The New York Times Book Review*, 29 June 2003, p. 13.
Some other translated books written by Javier Marías: *A Heart So White*; *All Souls*; *Tomorrow in the Battle Think on Me*; *When I Was Mortal*; *Dark Back of Time*; *Your Face Tomorrow* (which consists of three volumes: *Fever and Spear*; *Dance and Dream*; and *Poison, Shadow and Farewell*); *Voyage Along the Horizon; While the Women Are Sleeping*

Estaban Martin. *The Gaudi Key.*
Translated by Andreu Carranza. New York: William Morrow, 2008. 384 pages.
Genres/literary styles/story types: thrillers; religious thrillers
In Barcelona, Antoni Gaudi, a famous architect who died in 1926, devoted an inordinate amount of his life and energy to building the Roman Catholic church known as La Sagrada Família. Begun in the early 1880s, it remains unfinished. Controversies and secrets surround Gaudi's work and life, not the least of which is the disjunction between his arch-conservatism and his architectural modernism. This novel takes as its premise that Gaudi did not die in a streetcar accident but was murdered by a cabal interested in destroying a secret religious organization in possession of a sacred

relic some 3,000 years old. This book will be appreciated by fans of Dan Brown's *The Da Vinci Code*.
Subject keyword: urban life
Original language: Spanish
Source consulted for annotation:
Global Books in Print (online) (reviews from *Booklist*, *Library Journal*, and *Publishers Weekly*).

Eduardo Mendoza. *The Year of the Flood.*
Translated by Nick Caistor. London: Harvill, 1995. 118 pages.
Genre/literary style/story type: mainstream fiction
In the 1950s, Sister Consuelo, the young Mother Superior of a Catalonian convent, wants to establish a residence for senior citizens in their building, formerly used as hospital. During the course of her visits to one of the wealthiest men in the village, Don Augusto Aixelà, to solicit funds for this project, she falls in love with him, eventually learning that he sided with Franco during the Spanish Civil War. When apocalyptic rains beset the region and when a mountain bandit is wounded and kidnaps the Mother Superior, she discovers numerous secrets about Don Augusto.
Related title by the same author:
Readers may also be interested in *The Truth About the Savolta Case*, which recounts the effervescent social and political history of post–World War II Barcelona, especially as it relates to labor unrest and the movement for Catalonian independence.
Subject keywords: politics; power
Original language: Spanish
Sources consulted for annotation:
Amazon.com (book descriptions for both mentioned novels).
Annan, Gabriele. *The Spectator* 275 (7 October 1995): 49.
Steinberg, Sybil S. *Publishers Weekly* 243 (11 March 1996): 44.
Some other translated books written by Eduardo Mendoza: *The City of Marvels*; *A Light Comedy*

Ana María Moix. *Julia.*
Translated by Sandra Kingery. Lincoln, NE: University of Nebraska Press, 2004. 164 pages.
Genres/literary styles/story types: mainstream fiction; coming-of-age
Subject to frequent panic attacks, Julia has spent her entire life being terror-stricken and angst-ridden, with one sleepless night following another. Now, at age 20, she reflects on her life and past relationships with her mother, grandmother, and boyfriends, trying to trace the causes of her fears and despair. As her thoughts drift to her grandfather, Don Julio, she takes comfort from his political idealism and his staunch opposition to Franco.
Subject keyword: family histories
Original language: Spanish
Sources consulted for annotation:
Amazon.com (book description).
Scott, Whitney. *Booklist* 101 (1 September 2004): 63.
Another translated book written by Ana María Moix: *Dangerous Virtue*

Jesús Moncada. *The Towpath.*
Translated by Judith Willis. New York: HarperCollins, 1995. 256 pages.
Genre/literary style/story type: historical fiction
This novel focuses on the life of a small Catalan town, portraying both its vitality and gradual economic and social decline after World War I. At the center of the town's life was its coal mine and its

strategic location on a river. In the first decades of the twentieth century, the town was prosperous, but the Spanish Civil War and the rush to modernity conspired to rob it of vibrancy and of its very existence. A hydroelectric dam project means that the entire town has to be relocated; the subsequent destruction of houses is an apt and haunting symbol for the melancholic fate of Catalan cultural life.
Subject keyword: rural life
Original language: Catalan
Source consulted for annotation:
Think Spain website (book review), http://www.thinkspain.com.

Rosa Montero. ***Absent Love: A Chronicle.***
Translated by Cristina de la Torre and Diana Glad. Lincoln, NE: University of Nebraska Press, 1991. 187 pages.
Genre/literary style/story type: mainstream fiction
The death of Franco unleashed a torrent of changes in Spain. Cultural life began to flourish, and changing social and religious mores meant that previously unmentionable taboos could be legitimately explored and discussed. Thus, as in this novel written in the form of a quasi-diary, middle-aged women at the height of their personal and professional powers began to question what had always been taken for granted in their marriages: deference, patriarchal authority, and monogamy. Other issues also came to the forefront: unsatisfying and poorly remunerated work, terminal illnesses, divorce, same-sex relationships, and gnawing social isolation in an alienating urban environment.
Subject keyword: identity
Original language: Spanish
Sources consulted for annotation:
Amazon.com (review from *Kirkus Reviews*).
Beck, Mary Ellen. *Library Journal* 116 (December 1991): 198.
Another translated book written by Rosa Montero: *The Delta Function*

Quim Monzo. ***The Enormity of the Tragedy.***
Translated by Peter Bush. New York: Peter Owen, 2007. 222 pages.
Genre/literary style/story type: mainstream fiction
Ramon-Maria is a failed publisher; his house is filled with a stupendous number of unsold and unsellable books. As if that were not enough, he is also bald, a widower, and must find some way to deal with an angry stepdaughter who wants to kill him. Soon, he develops priapism, and he is told that he has mere months to live. The often hilarious and poignant book explores the nature of loneliness and alienation in the contemporary world.
Subject keywords: identity; urban life
Original language: Catalan
Sources consulted for annotation:
Global Books in Print (online) (jacket description).
Post, Chad W. Three Percent website (book review), http://www.rochester.edu/College/translation/threepercent.
Another translated book written by Quim Monzo: *Gasoline*

Antonio Muñoz Molina. ***Sepharad.***
Translated by Margaret Sayers Peden. Orlando, FL: Harcourt, 2003. 385 pages.
Genre/literary style/story type: historical fiction
Amalgamating historical facts and fiction, this novel focuses on the experience of exile and the unremitting psychological shock experienced by, among others, Sephardic Jewish families as they were

forced to cross borders. Themes include suffering and nostalgia; love and separation; and despair and hope. Throughout 17 chapters with diverse historical, geographical, and sociopolitical settings—where a common denominator is the image of a train that takes many to horrible deaths—the author suggests that the past can only be understood by looking deeply into the often chaotic recesses of an individual's mind.

Subject keyword: culture conflict

Original language: Spanish

Sources consulted for annotation:

Amazon.com (book description).

Eder, Richard. *The New York Times*, 1 January 2004 (online)

Pye, Michael. *The New York Times Book Review*, 21 December 2003, p. 9.

Seaman, Donna. *Booklist* 100 (15 December 2003): 728.

Zaleski, Jeff. *Publishers Weekly* 250 (1 December 2003): 42.

Some other translated books written by Antonio Muñoz Molina: *Prince of Shadows*; *Winter in Lisbon*

Arturo Pérez-Reverte. *The Club Dumas*.

Translated by Sonia Soto. New York: Harcourt Brace, 1996. 362 pages.

Genres/literary styles/story types: crime fiction; suspense

In the rarefied world of antiquarian bookdealers, Lucas Corso is something of a legend—a bloodhound of a man whose specialty is locating rare books for well-paying clients. As he works on authenticating a manuscript that is presumably a chapter from *The Three Musketeers* by Alexander Dumas, he must also solve the mystery of why there are three copies of a necromancer's book called *The Book of the Nine Doors of the Kingdom of Shadows*, when all but one were destroyed during the Spanish Inquisition. As Corso travels from Madrid to Toledo, to Portugal, and then to Paris, he is unexpectedly thrust into the middle of an elaborate criminal enterprise woven by devil worshippers, occultists, and murderers. Critics have compared this book to works by Umberto Eco and Anne Rice.

Related titles by the same author:

Readers may also enjoy *Captain Alatriste* and *Purity of Blood*, two nihilism-tinged adventure novels set against the backdrop of the defeat of the Spanish Armada and the Inquisition. Terrence Rafferty said that *Purity of Blood* reminded him of "an end-of-the-trail Peckinpah western or one of those noble, tragic Japanese pictures about the masterless samurai known as *ronin*." Also of interest may be *The Painter of Battles*, where a famous war photographer who has decided to paint a mural of human suffering is visited by one of the subjects of his photographs.

Subject keyword: identity

Original language: Spanish

Sources consulted for annotation:

Adams, Lorraine. *The New York Times Book Review*, 30 December 2007 (online).

Amazon.com (book description; review from *Kirkus Reviews*).

"Arturo Pérez-Reverte." *Dictionary of Literary Biography Online*. Thomson Gale databases.

Dibdin, Michael. *The New York Times*, 1 August 2004 (online).

Hoffert, Barbara. *Library Journal* 121 (1 September 1996): 211.

Kenney, Brian. *Booklist* 93 (1 October 1996): 292.

Livesey, Margot. *The New York Times Book Review*, 23 March 1997, p. 10.

Maslin, Janet. *The New York Times*, 28 April 2005 (online).

Rafferty, Terrence. *The New York Times Book Review*, 26 February 2006 (online).

Steinberg, Sybil S. *Publishers Weekly* 243 (18 November 1996): 61.

Some other translated books written by Arturo Pérez-Reverte: *The Flanders Panel*; *The Seville Communion*; *The Fencing Master*; *The Nautical Chart*; *Captain Alatriste*; *Purity of Blood*

Juan Manuel de Prada. *The Tempest.*
Translated by Paul Antill. Woodstock, NY: Overlook Press, 2003. 341 pages.
Genres/literary styles/story types: crime fiction; suspense
Alejandro Ballesteros, a Spanish art historian visiting Venice to study Giorgione's painting *The Tempest*, witnesses the murder of Fabio Valenzin, an art dealer. Alejandro takes an active part in the investigation; has an affair with the murdered man's adopted daughter, who works in the field of art restorationa and conservation; and eventually uncovers a forgery plot.
Subject keyword: urban life
Original language: Spanish
Sources consulted for annotation:
Amazon.com (book description).
Briggs, Carolyn S. *The Washington Post*, 10 August 2003, p. T14.
Ott, Bill. *Booklist* 99 (15 May 2003): 1649.
Zaleski, Jeff. *Publishers Weekly* 250 (12 March 2003): 45.

Benjamín Prado. *Never Shake Hands with a Left-Handed Gunman.*
Translated by Kristina Cordero. New York: St. Martin's Press, 1999. 150 pages.
Genres/literary styles/story types: crime fiction; urban fiction
Israel Lacasa knows everything about being a nonconformist—just as he knows almost everything about books, movies, and music, including the most obscure facts. When he disappears, three of his friends try to trace his whereabouts, delving into his ambiguous past and discovering his painful and abysmal childhood. The book has numerous literary, cinematic, and musical allusions to such figures as Franz Kafka, Chester Himes, and the Sex Pistols.
Subject keyword: identity
Original language: Spanish
Sources consulted for annotation:
Amazon.com (book description; review from *Kirkus Reviews*).
Lunn, Bob. *Library Journal* 124 (June 1999): 158.
Zaleski, Jeff. *Publishers Weekly* 245 (21 December 1998): 57.
Some other translated books written by Benjamín Prado: *Not Only Fire*; *Snow Is Silent*

Soledad Puértolas. *Bordeaux.*
Translated by Francisca González-Arias. Lincoln, NE: University of Nebraska Press, 1998. 143 pages.
Genre/literary style/story type: mainstream fiction
Pauline Duvivier, Lilly Skalnick, and Réne Dufour live in the French city of Bordeaux, where their desire for happiness collides with the reality of a seemingly purposeless existence. Overwhelmed by loneliness, they struggle as best they can—adrift, disengaged, and emotionally paralyzed. One critic has invoked the work of Alice Munro to describe this novel.
Subject keyword: social roles
Original language: Spanish
Sources consulted for annotation:
Atamian, Christopher. *The New York Times Book Review*, 21 June 1998, p. 24.
Ireland, Susan. *Review of Contemporary Fiction* 19 (Spring 1999): 190.
Shreve, Jack. *Library Journal* 123 (1 June 1998): 156.

Rafael Reig. *Blood on the Saddle.*
Translated by Paul Hammond. London: Serpent's Tail, 2007. 192 pages.
Genres/literary styles/story types: crime fiction; postmodernism

This book is a surreal, metaphysical, and amusing account of the work of Dickens & Clot Investigations, a detective agency that specializes in helping authors find characters who have escaped from their fictional homes. This novel, which also features the diabolical head of a genetic-engineering company, takes place in a world dominated by a political federation between the United States and the Iberian Peninsula.
Subject keywords: urban life; writers
Original language: Spanish
Source consulted for annotation:
Serpent's Tail website (book description), http://www.serpentstail.com.
Another translated book written by Rafael Reig: *A Pretty Face*

Julián Ríos. *Loves That Bind.*
Translated by Edith Grossman. New York: Alfred A. Knopf, 1998. 243 pages.
Genres/literary styles/story types: mainstream fiction; epistolary fiction
This novel is composed of 26 letters that Emil writes to the women who abandoned him. While each of the letters purports to describe his own failed relationships, they really describe such fictional women as Marcel Proust's Albertine, F. Scott Fitzgerald's Daisy, and Vladimir Nabokov's Lolita.
Subject keyword: identity
Original language: Spanish
Sources consulted for annotation:
Amazon.com (book description; review from *Kirkus Reviews*).
"Julián Ríos." *Dictionary of Literary Biography Online*. Thomson Gale databases.
Kakutani, Michiko. *The New York Times*, 9 June 1998, p. E7.
Kenney, Brian. *Booklist* 94 (15 May 1990): 1597.
Malin, Irving. *Review of Contemporary Fiction* 18 (Fall 1998): 234.
Some other translated books written by Julián Ríos: *Larva: Midsummer Night's Babel*; *Poundemonium*; *Monstruary*

Manuel Rivas. *Vermeer's Milkmaid and Other Stories.*
Translated by Jonathan Dunne. New York: Overlook Press, 2008. 120 pages.
Genres/literary styles/story types: mainstream fiction; coming-of-age
Containing 16 short stories that resurrect images and events from the Galician author's childhood, this book is the embodiment of lyrical gracefulness. Two of the most memorable tales are about the narrator's memory of his mother and the fate of one of his school teachers during the Spanish Civil War.
Subject keyword: rural life
Original language: Galician
Sources consulted for annotation:
Global Books in Print (online) (reviews from *Library Journal* and *Publishers Weekly*).
Hunter, Margaret. *The Southland Times*, 15 May 2004, p. 7.
Nash, Elizabeth. *The Independent*, 1 February 2003, p. 20.
Urquhart, James. *The Independent*, 29 January 2002, p. 5.
Some other translated books by Manuel Rivas: *In the Wilderness*; *The Carpenter's Pencil*; *Butterfly's Tongue*

Mercè Rodoreda. *The Time of the Doves.*
Translated by David H. Rosenthal. St. Paul, MN: Graywolf Press, 1986. 201 pages.
Genre/literary style/story type: mainstream fiction
This novel focuses on the hardships experienced by Natalia after she marries Quimet. Against the backdrop of the Spanish Civil War and a poverty-stricken existence, she experiences childbirth,

her husband's death, and remarriage. This stream-of-consciousness novel received the highest praise from Gabriel García Márquez and Sandra Cisneros.

Related titles by the same author:

Readers may also enjoy *A Broken Mirror*, which, according to the website of the University of Nebraska Press, is a rich historcal saga about "a matriarchal dynasty" that was founded in the 1870s in Barcelona when Teresa Goday, the daughter of a fishmonger, marries an older and wealthier man. The story extends for three generations through the Spanish Civil War and Franco's assumption of power. Rodoreda's *Death in Spring* is also a powerful novel that has invoked comparisons to Shirley Jackson's story "The Lottery." In this book, a teenage boy lives in a rural village where life is oppressive, dangerous, and violent. The village's very existence is threatened by its precarious location, residents engage in brutal activities, and the boy senses that he has no real place in this world. As he wanders the streets and as he swims in the river, he fends off attacking bees and tries to deal with a gnawing sense of impending doom.

Subject keyword: family histories

Original language: Catalan

Sources consulted for annotation:

Global Books in Print (online) (review from *Publishers Weekly Annex Reviews*).

Munning, Kate. *Bookslut* (book review), http://www.bookslut.com.

Post, Chad W. Three Percent website (book review), http://www.rochester.edu/College/translation/threepercent.

University of Nebraska Press website (book description), http://www.nebraskapress.unl.edu.

Some other translated books written by Mercè Rodoreda: *A Broken Mirror*; *Death in Spring*

Luis Manuel Ruiz. *Only One Thing Missing.*

Translated by Alfred J. Mac Adam. New York: Grove Press, 2003. 308 pages.

Genres/literary styles/story types: crime fiction; suspense

In Seville, Alicia has just experienced a tragedy to end all tragedies: the death of her husband and child. Soon, she is not only overcome by nightmares, but she also begins to see evidence of those nightmares in the people and objects that make up her waking hours. When no one believes her and when psychiatrists consider her paranoid, she turns to her brother-in-law Estaban. Together, they unearth an occult conspiracy that has its roots in medieval Lisbon.

Subject keyword: family histories

Original language: Spanish

Sources consulted for annotation:

Amazon.com (book description).

Canfield, Kevin. *Booklist* 99 (15 December 2002): 734.

Shreve, Jack. *Library Journal* 127 (December 2002): 181.

Zaleski, Jeff. *Publishers Weekly* 249 (28 October 2002): 46.

Carlos Ruiz Zafón. *The Shadow of the Wind.*

Translated by Lucia Graves. New York: Penguin, 2004. 486 pages.

Genres/literary styles/story types: crime fiction; historical mysteries

In post–World War II Barcelona, 10-year-old Daniel Sempere's father takes him to what is described as The Cemetery of Forgotten Books. Here, Daniel reads a novel called *The Shadow of the Wind* and becomes fascinated with its author, Julián Carax, an obscure Spanish author who has taken up residence in Paris between the two World Wars. He wants more of Carax's works but soon learns that they are extremely rare. For the past 10 years, someone has been purchasing all available copies and stealing those in libraries and personal collections. Thus begins Daniel's lifelong quest to find out as much as he can about Carax.

Related title by the same author:
Also of interest may be *The Angel's Game*. Daniel Martin pseudonymously writes gothic-oriented pulp fiction about the seamy underside of Barcelona; his one attempt at literary fiction was not well-received. Suddenly, he is asked by Andreas Corelli, a mystery-enshrouded French editor who may not be what he seems, to write a book that is supposed to fundamentally change the course of humanity. Critics have detected echoes of Jorge Luis Borges, Gabriel García Márquez, Umberto Eco, Arturo Pérez-Reverte, Paul Auster, Victor Hugo, A. S. Byatt, and Ross King in Zafón's work.
Subject keywords: philosophy; writers
Original language: Spanish
Sources consulted for annotation:
Amazon.com (book description).
Dirda, Michael. *The Washington Post*, 25 April 2004, p. T15.
Eder, Richard. *The New York Times Book Review*, 25 April 2004, p. 6.
Graff, Keir. *Booklist* 100 (1 March 2005): 1102.
Zaleski, Jeff. *Publishers Weekly* 251 (16 February 2004): 148.
Another translated book written by Carlos Ruiz Zafón: *The Angel's Game*

Albert Sánchez Piñol. *Cold Skin.*
Translated by Cheryl Leah Morgan (from Catalan). New York: Farrar, Straus and Giroux, 2005. 182 pages.
Genres/literary styles/story types: speculative fiction; horror/paranormal
On a desolate island near Antarctica, a weather researcher cannot find his predecessor; there is only Gruner, a mysterious Austrian living in a lighthouse. Dangers lurk everywhere, and strange human-like amphibians populate the surrounding sea and attack the island each night. The weather researcher joins forces with Gruner in a desperate struggle to ward off the attackers. This gothic novel has been compared to *The Tempest*, *Lord of the Flies*, and *Robinson Crusoe*.
Related title by the same author:
Readers may also enjoy *Pandora in the Congo*, which is a postmodern mystery about an author, Tommy Thomson, hired by a lawyer to write about what really happened when two British brothers are killed during a trip to the Belgian Congo in search of diamonds. Critics have pointed out that the book has echoes of Joseph Conrad and Jules Verne.
Subject keyword: culture conflict
Original language: Catalan
Sources consulted for annotation:
Lewis, Debi. *Booklist* 102 (1 Sep 2005): 66.
Publishers Weekly 252 (15 Aug 2005): 27.
Salvatore, Joseph. *The New York Times Book Review*, 29 May 2009 (online).
Shreve, Jack. *Library Journal* 130 (15 Sep 2005): 57.
Theroux, Marcel. *The New York Times Book Review*, 11 Dec 2005, p. 13.
Some other translated books written by Albert Sánchez Piñol: *A Blow to the Heart*; *Pandora in the Congo*

Javier Sierra. ***The Secret Supper.***
Translated by Alberto Manguel. New York: Atria Books, 2006. 329 pages.
Genres/literary styles/story types: thrillers; religious thrillers
At the end of the fifteenth-century, Father Agostino Leyre, a papal emissary, is dispatched from Rome to Milan to investigate a claim that Leonardo da Vinci, who is in the process of completing his masterpiece *The Last Supper* at the Santa Maria delle Grazie monastery, is encrypting heretical messages in the painting. In an era of fervent religiosity—where heresies were intensely ideological

and where the church was deeply involved in politics and intrigue—Father Agostino struggles to understand the hidden meanings of da Vinci's work. This book will appeal to those who like Dan Brown's *The Da Vinci Code* and Umberto Eco's *The Name of the Rose*.
Subject keywords: power; religion
Original language: Spanish
Sources consulted for annotation:
O'Hara, Lisa. *The Library Journal* 131 (1 February 2006): 74.
Publishers Weekly 253 (2 January 2006): 33.
Segura, Jonathan. *Publishers Weekly* 253 (9 January 2006): 30.
Another translated book written by Javier Sierra: *The Lady in Blue*

José Carlos Somoza. *The Athenian Murders*.
Translated by Sonia Soto. New York: Farrar, Straus and Giroux, 2002. 262 pages.
Genres/literary styles/story types: crime fiction; historical mysteries
Murder can happen anywhere and anytime; Athens in the late fifth century B.C.E. is no exception, as a modern-day translator working on an ancient Greek text discovers. At Plato's school of philosophy, when someone begins to kill young male students, two teachers begin to unravel a series of clues that eventually lead them into the inner sanctums of Athenian wealth and power. But in a macabre metafictional twist, the ancient text is no longer a static entity; references to the translator start to appear, and soon enough, he is also at risk of being killed.
Subject keyword: identity
Original language: Spanish
Sources consulted for annotation:
Amazon.com (about the author; book description).
Gerling, David Ross. *World Literature Today* 77 (October/December 2003): 148.
Ponce, Pedro. *Review of Contemporary Fiction* 23 (Spring 2003): 150.
Zaleski, Jeff. *Publishers Weekly* 249 (6 May 2002): 33.
Another translated book written by José Carlos Somoza: *The Art of Murder*

Nora Strejilevich. *A Single, Numberless Death*.
Translated by Cristina de La Torre in collaboration with the author. Charlottesville, VA: University of Virginia Press, 2002. 176 pages.
Genre/literary style/story type: mainstream fiction
According to the publisher's website, this is a "gripping story of survival" in Argentina under the military junta, which ruled the country from 1976 to 1983. Combining "autobiography, documentary journalism, fiction, and poetry," the book paints a grim and uncompromising picture of violence, imprisonment, abuse, state anti-Semitism, and political murders. Many of the author's family fell victim to the abusive regime, and she herself was kidnapped and tortured.
Subject keyword: power
Original language: Spanish
Source consulted for annotation:
University of Virginia Press website (book description), http://www.upress.virginia.edu.

Esther Tusquets. *Stranded*.
Translated by Susan E. Clark. Elmwood Park, IL: Dalkey Archive Press, 1991. 230 pages.
Genres/literary styles/story types: mainstream fiction; stream of consciousness; women's lives
Elia, a writer whose husband Jorge has just left her, joins her friends Eva and Pablo on their summer vacation in Costa Brava. The marriage of Eva and Pablo is also on the verge of collapse, and the

presence of young Clara, who is madly in love with Eva, only aggravates the situation. Critics have compared the author's style to that of Dorothy Richardson and Virginia Woolf.
Subject keyword: social roles
Original language: Spanish
Sources consulted for annotation:
Amazon.com (review from *Kirkus Reviews*).
Beck, Mary Ellen. *Literary Journal* 116 (August 1991): 148.
Center for Book Culture. Dalkey Archive Press (book review), http://www.aboutus.org/CenterForBookCulture.org.
Steinberg, Sybil S. *Publishers Weekly* 238 (12 July 1991): 53.
Some other translated books written by Esther Tusquets: *Love Is a Solitary Game*; *The Same Sea as Every Summer*; *Never to Return*

Angela Vallvey. *Hunting the Last Wild Man*.
Translated by Margaret Jull Costa. New York: Seven Stories Press, 2002. 190 pages.
Genre/literary style/story type: mainstream fiction
Candela March—a lover of solitude of who nonetheless lives with her five sisters, mother, grandmother, and aunt—has a job that is decidedly out of the ordinary. She is an embalmer. When she works on the corpse of a man who was the head of an extended family of Romani (typically yet erroneously referred to as Gypsies), she not only becomes the lover of his nephew but also makes a discovery that could mean untold riches. Critics have seen resemblances to the films of Pedro Almodóvar in the author's ironic yet touching literary style.
Related title by the same author:
Readers may also want to explore *Happy Creatures*, in which Penelope leaves her adulterous husband Ulysses and her son. Two years later, having transformed herself into a sexy and successful blonde, she returns. As with *Hunting the Last Wild Man*, this novel, which evokes Homer's *The Odyssey*, takes place in what Amaia Gabantxo calls "a postmodern Spain where all the values of the 20th century have collapsed: the family is finished, feminism is dead, the sexual revolution a fiasco, middle-class-ness and even comfortable wealth are not the hot tickets to happiness, and people no longer believe in the ideology of self-fulfillment."
Subject keyword: social roles
Original language: Spanish
Sources consulted for annotation:
Amazon.com (book description).
Gabantxo, Amaia. *The Independent*, 2 July 2004, p. 25.
Zaleski, Jeff. *Publishers Weekly* 249 (11 February 2002): 161.
Another translated book written by Angela Vallvey: *Happy Creatures*

Manuel Vázquez Montalbán. *The Buenos Aires Quintet*.
Translated by Nick Caistor. London: Serpent's Tail, 2003. 377 pages.
Genres/literary styles/story types: crime fiction; private investigators
This is one of a series of novels featuring Pepe Carvalho, a private detective who loves food and the good life. Here, he reluctantly travels to Buenos Aires to search for his missing cousin Raul, a former prisoner of the Argentine military junta who inexplicably returned to the country. In the course of his investigation, Carvalho meets with individuals on both sides of the political spectrum who knew his cousin. Readers may also be drawn to *The Man of My Life*, where Carvalho delves into the world of religious cults when a wealthy man's son is killed.
Subject keyword: power
Original language: Spanish

Sources consulted for annotation:
Amazon.com (book descriptions for both mentioned novels; about the author; review extracts).
Cleary, James. *The Belfast News Letter*, 20 December 2003, p. 21.
Danny Yee's Book Reviews (book review), http://dannyreviews.com.
Yager, Susanna. *The Sunday Telegraph*, 21 December 2003, p. 13.
Some other translated books written by Manuel Vázquez Montalbán: *The Pianist*; *Southern Seas*; *Galíndez*; *The Angst-Ridden Executive*; *An Olympic Death*; *Murder in the Central Committee*; *Off Side*; *The Man of My Life*

Horacio Vázquez Rial. *Triste's History.*
Translated by Jo Labanyi. Columbia, LA: Readers International, 1990. 216 pages.
Genre/literary style/story type: mainstream fiction
This novel chronicles the life of Cristobal Artola, nicknamed Triste. Born in an impoverished neighborhood in Buenos Aires, he is an assassin for hire who begins to work for a priest who is in cahoots with the Argentinian junta. Triste does his new job well, firing into crowds of demonstrators, killing indiscriminately, and kidnapping enemies of the regime. But he finally realizes his complicity in the suffering of the victims after he sees the torture that they undergo.
Subject keyword: power
Original language: Spanish
Sources consulted for annotation:
Kaganoff, Penny. *Publishers Weekly* 237 (21 December 1990): 49.
Polk, James. *Los Angeles Times*, 13 June 1991, p. 5.

Enrique Vila-Matas. *Bartleby & Co.*
Translated by Jonathan Dunne. New York: New Directions, 2004. 178 pages.
Genres/literary styles/story types: mainstream fiction; experimental fiction
Melville's Bartleby the Scrivener famously said "I would prefer not to" when asked to do certain tasks at his office. And so it is in this novel, where another clerk in another time and place considers Bartleby to be a hero. He keeps a notebook of footnotes with jottings about books that were never written or never finished—a mysterious universe or anti-universe of silence that features famous authors such as Arthur Rimbaud, Marcel Duchamp, and J. D. Salinger as well as such lesser-known figures as Juan Rulfo and Clément Cadou.
Subject keywords: philosophy; writers
Original language: Spanish
Sources consulted for annotation:
Amazon.com (book description).
McGonigle, Thomas. *Los Angeles Times*, 19 December 2004, p. R2.
Post, Chad W. *Review of Contemporary Fiction* 25 (Spring 2005): 144.
Tepper, Anderson. *The New York Times Book Review*, 5 June 2005, p. 28.

ANNOTATIONS FOR TRANSLATED BOOKS FROM PORTUGAL AND BRAZIL

Portugal

António Lobo Antunes. *The Inquisitor's Manual.*
Translated by Richard Zenith. New York: Grove Press, 2003. 435 pages.
Genre/literary style/story type: historical fiction
This novel describes the authoritarian regime of Portugal's Antonio de Oliveira Salazar, who almost single-handly controlled Portugal from 1932 to the 1968; his right-wing party's grip on power

effectively ended in the military coup called the Carnation Revolution of 1974. One of the major figures in the novel is Senhor Francisco, a former minister in Salazar's government who is now residing in a nursing home. But numerous other characters speak, and together, their testimonies provide withering evidence of Salazar's tyranny and debauchery. As William Deresiewicz notes, the book is "not so much an allegory of fascism as an anatomy of the way it penetrates societies—families, psyches, bodies—and of the scars it leaves." He also observes that the book has the same tone and style as many of William Faulkner's novels; both writers are masters of creating "a rank atmosphere of illusion and cowardice, futility and neglect."

Related title by the same author:

Readers may also enjoy *What Can I Do When Everything's on Fire?* Set in the nightclubs of Lisbon, this novel focuses on the troubled Paolo as he tries to come to terms with his transvestite father's horrific death as well as the suicide of his father's lover.

Subject keywords: politics; power

Original language: Portuguese

Sources consulted for annotation:

Amazon.com (book description; review from *The New Yorker*).

Blythe, Will. *The New York Times Book Review*, 23 November 2008 (online).

Deresiewicz, William. *The New York Times Book Review*, 2 March 2003, p. 12.

Eder, Richard. *The New York Times*, 15 January 2003 (online).

Post, Chad W. *Review of Contemporary Fiction* 23 (Summer 2003): 134

Spinella, Michael. *Booklist* 99 (15 December 2002): 731.

Three Percent website (link to publisher), http://www.rochester.edu/College/translation/threepercent.

Zenith, Richard. *Publishers Weekly* 249 (2 December 2002): 32.

Some other translated books by António Lobo Antunes: *South of Nowhere*; *The Return of the Caravels*; *Fado Alexandrino*; *An Explanation of the Birds*; *Act of the Damned*; *The Natural Order of Things*; *The Fat Man and Infinity*; *What Can I Do When Everything's on Fire?*

Mário de Carvalho. *A God Strolling in the Cool of the Evening.*

Translated by Gregory Rabassa. Baton Rouge, LA: Louisiana State University Press, 1997. 265 pages.

Genre/literary style/story type: historical fiction

At the end of the second century, Lucius Valerius Quintius rules Tarcisis on the Iberian Peninsula. Constantly battling invading Moors from North Africa, he must also make important decisions about what to do about Christianity, which is rapidly expanding. The latter task is made particularly difficult when he falls in love with a young Christian woman.

Subject keywords: power; religion

Original language: Portuguese

Sources consulted for annotation:

Amazon.com (book description).

Burns, Erik. *The New York Times Book Review*, 23 November 1997, p. 28.

Flanagan, Margaret. *Booklist* 94 (15 November 1997): 541.

Rohrbaugh, Lisa. *Library Journal* 122 (1 October 1997): 120.

Steinberg, Sybil S. *Publishers Weekly* 244 (15 September 1997): 52.

The Virginia Quarterly Review 74 (Spring 1998): 59.

Lídia Jorge. *The Painter of Birds.*

Translated by Margaret Jull Costa. New York: Harcourt, 2001. 233 pages.

Genre/literary style/story type: mainstream fiction

Walter Dias has left his wife, wanders the world, sketches and paints birds, and finds comfort in the company of women. He has a daughter, and he sends her letters filled with pictures of birds. From time to time, he visits her, but she is always told that he is her uncle because her mother has married Walter's brother. But she has the bird drawings, and she is content. One night, he comes into her room, and nothing is ever the same.
Subject keyword: family histories
Original language: Portuguese
Sources consulted for annotation:
Amazon.com (about the author; book description).
Bolton-Fasman, Judith. *The New York Times Book Review*, 29 April 2001 (online).
Guyer, Leland. *World Literature Today* 76 (Winter 2002): 233.
Kaske, Michelle. *Booklist* 97 (1 February 2001): 1040.
Nesbitt, Robin. *Library Journal* 126 (1 January 2001): 154.
Another translated book by Lídia Jorge: *The Murmuring Coast*

João De Melo. ***My World Is Not of This Kingdom.***
Translated by Gregory Rabassa. Minneapolis, MN: Aliform Publishing, 2003. 248 pages.
Genres/literary styles/story types: mainstream fiction; magical realism
In the town of Rozario in the Portuguese Azores, life moves at a glacial pace until an airplane crashes into the nearby mountains. In addition, the mayor becomes politically ambitious and the priest sinks into ecclesiastic rigidity. Blending realistic episodes and magical events, the author vividly describes the live of João-Maria, a poor farmer; the resurrection of João-Lazaro, a beggar; an unceasing 99-day-long rain; and animals that cry.
Subject keyword: rural life
Original language: Portuguese
Sources consulted for annotation:
Amazon.com (book description).
Crossley, James. *Review of Contemporary Fiction* 24 (Spring 2004): 153.
Owchar, Nick. *Los Angeles Times*, 9 July 2004, p. E19.

José Luís Peixoto. ***The Implacable Order of Things.***
Translated by Richard Zenith. New York: Nan A. Talese/Doubleday, 2008. 224 pages.
Genres/literary styles/story types: mainstream fiction; magical realism
In a poverty-stricken and timeless Portuguese village, a series of extraordinary and symbolism-laden events occur: The devil tells a shepherd that his wife is being untrue to him; one Siamese twin falls in love with a cook; and a crippled man marries a blind prostitute. Critics have lauded the book's haunting lyricism and deep philosophical insights about love and death.
Subject keyword: rural life
Original language: Portuguese
Sources consulted for annotation:
Global Books in Print (online) (reviews from *Library Journal* and *Publishers Weekly*).
Nan. A. Talese (book description), http://nan-a-talese.knopfdoubleday.com.

Fernando Pessoa. ***The Book of Disquiet.***
Translated by Margaret Jull Costa. London: Serpent's Tail, 2002. 272 pages.
Genre/literary style/story type: mainstream fiction
This novel is the purported diary of an assistant bookkeeper in Lisbon, Bernardo Soares, whose self-obsession soars to philosophical and existential heights. Fernanda Eberstadt referred to this book as

a "compendium of dull days and transfiguring epiphanies" that "is so distilled it should be dipped into in small doses over a lifetime." It has been critically acclaimed as a masterpiece.
Subject keyword: identity
Original language: Portuguese
Sources consulted for annotation:
Eberstadt, Fernanda. *The New York Times Book Review*, 1 September 1991 (online).
Serpent's Tail website (book description), http://www.serpentstail.com.

José Cardoso Pires. *Ballad of Dogs' Beach: Dossier of a Crime.*
Translated by Mary Fitton. New York: Beaufort Books, 1987. 181 pages.
Genres/literary styles/story types: crime fiction; police detectives
In 1960s Lisbon, a body is found on a beach. Inspector Elias Santana, nicknamed Graveyard, starts to investigate the murder of Major Castro, a political opponent of Salazar's regime who led a failed coup. The trail quickly leads to Mena, Castro's seductive mistress, and two former members of the armed forces—all of whom Santana subjects to harsh interrogations despite the fact that he fantasizes about Mena.
Subject keyword: power
Original language: Portuguese
Sources consulted for annotation:
Manguel, Alberto. *The Whig-Standard*, 10 January 1987, p. 1.
Steinberg, Sybil S. *Publishers Weekly* 231 (13 Match 1987): 71.
Another translated book by José Cardoso Pires: *O Delfim: Romance*

José Saramago. *Death with Interruptions.*
Translated by Margaret Jull Costa. San Diego, CA: Harcourt, 2008. 256 pages.
Genre/literary style/story type: mainstream fiction
Saramago's typical procedure is to create an implausible eventuality and then work out how people might react and what the societal consequences might be. *Death with Interruptions* examines the unimaginable chaos that occurs when no one dies for a period of some seven months. Death, a rickety old skelton living in a mysterious underground location, has decided to take a holiday. At first, everyone is ecstatic at what they consider to be the coming of utopia, but it quickly dawns on people that the government will not be able to financially support everyone. And families begin to realize what a huge burden it will be to perpetually tend to the infirm and the aged. Hoping to avoid bankruptcy, the government contracts with a secretive organization to transport the frail and ailing to neighboring countries, where death is still operating in full force. There is also ecclesiastical chaos because, as the Catholic church recognizes, deathless life has severe repercussions for the existence of the soul. Soon, Death decides to return from holiday, but he has a new plan: A few weeks before he is to swoop down on those whose time has come, he will send them notifications in violet letters.
Related titles by the same author:
Readers may also be interested in *Blindness*, a novel that explores the very thin line between civilization and violence when everyone, except one person, becomes blind. Also noteworthy is *Seeing*, where more than 80 percent of voters on a rainy election day refuse to mark their ballots. Although the government sees this as an act of insurrection, the author views it as the ultimate act of freedom. *The Elephant's Journey* also deserves mention: Based on a mid-sixteenth-century incident, it focuses on the epic travels of Solomon, an elephant, and his retinue from Lisbon to Vienna after the Portuguese monarch decides to give Solomon as a gift to the archduke of Austria. Ursula K. Le Guin observed that this book, with its "reminder of the importance of the nonhuman," solidifies Saramago's reputation as being "perhaps closer in spirit and in humour to our first great novelist, Cervantes, than any novelist since." Perhaps the author's most powerful work is *The Cave*, which

examines the tragic and nightmarish ramifications of a gigantic shopping center on the life of a simple potter, Cipriano Alger, whose clay pots are deemed no longer good enough to be sold at such an upscale mecca. For a similar view of the perfidy of consumerism run amok as symbolized by shopping centers, readers may find that J. G. Ballard's *Kingdom Come* is enlightening.
Subject keywords: philosophy; religion
Original language: Portuguese
Sources consulted for annotation:
Banville, John. *The New York Times Book Review*, 10 October 2004, p. 17.
Eder, Richard. *The New York Times*, 28 November 2002 (online).
Eder, Richard. *The New York Times*, 27 October 2004, p. E10.
Hooper, Brad. *Booklist* 101 (1 September 2004): 7.
Le Guin, Ursula K. *The Guardian*, 24 July 2010 (online).
Millet, Lydia. *The Globe and Mail* (Toronto), 11 October 2008, p. D14.
Rafferty, Terrence. *The New York Times Book Review*, 9 April 2006 (online).
Woods, James. *The New Yorker*, 27 October 2008 (online).
Zaleski, Jeff. *Publishers Weekly* 251 (16 August 2004): 40.
Some other translated books by José Saramago: *Baltasar and Blimunda*; *The Year of the Death of Ricardo Reis*; *The Stone Raft*; *The History of the Siege of Lisbon*; *All the Names*; *The Tale of the Unknown Island*; *The Double*; *The Elephant's Journey*

Brazil

Caio Fernando Abreu. *Whatever Happened to Dulce Veiga?*
Translated by Adria Frizzi. Austin, TX: University of Texas Press, 2000. 200 pages.
Genres/literary styles/story types: crime fiction; amateur detectives
A down-and-out journalist undertakes a week-long search for Dulce Veiga, a singer who was last seen some 20 years ago. As Jana Giles writes, the journalist "navigates the social jungle that is Sao Paulo in the 1990s, with its beggars, junkies, transvestites, shattered revolutionaries, fortune-tellers and social climbers," eventually finding happiness and strength in memories of his former life and first lover.
Subject keyword: urban life
Original language: Portuguese
Sources consulted for annotation:
Giles, Jana. *New York Times Book Review*, 18 February 2001, p. 21.
Scott, Whitney. *Booklist* 97 (1 February 2001): 1041.
Treece, Dave, and Ray Keenoy. *The Babel Guide to Brazilian Fiction in English Translation*. Oxford: Boulevard Books, 2001, pp. 15–17.
Another translated book written by Caio Fernando Abreu: *Dragons*

Ignácio de Loyola Brandão. *Zero*.
Translated by Ellen Watson. Normal, IL: Dalkey Archive Press, 2004. 305 pages.
Genre/literary style/story type: mainstream fiction
José, who has a foot deformity and passes out from time to time, works in a dilapidated movie theater catching mice. Rosa has a checkered sexual past, lies, struggles with her weight, and yearns for a house of her own. After the two meet through a marriage agency, José does everything to make her dream come true. He turns to robbery, does not sneer at gunplay, and ends up as a political outlaw sought by the authorities. As indicated on the publisher's website, this novel set in 1960s Brazil "depict[s] the absurdity of a repressive political regime with exceptional daring and humor."

Related title by the same author:
Readers may also wish to explore *Anonymous Celebrity*, in which the only thing that matters to the book's central character is being famous. He yearns to be an integral part of celebrity culture so badly that he is willing to do anything. He wants to brand every aspect of his life, including his sexual activities; he keeps a stable of consultants for every imaginable eventuality; he cannot get enough of listening to the applause at the end of recorded concert performances. The novel is an utterly uproarious examination of the emptiness of contemporary life and the struggle for success no matter the cost.
Subject keywords: social problems; urban life
Original language: Portuguese
Sources consulted for annotation:
The Complete Review (book review), http://www.complete-review.com.
Dalkey Archive Press (book description), http://www.dalkeyarchive.com.
Rogers, Michael. *Library Journal* 129 (August 2004): 131.
Some other translated books written by Ignácio de Loyola Brandão: *And Still the Earth: An Archival Narration*; *Teeth Under the Sun*; *Anonymous Celebrity*

Chico Buarque. *Budapest*.
Translated by Alison Entrekin. New York: Grove Press, 2004. 183 pages.
Genres/literary styles/story types: mainstream fiction; postmodernism
José Costa ghostwrites books. On his way back to Brazil from an Istanbul convention, his plane is forced to land in Budapest, where he is smitten with the Hungarian language. Back in Brazil, he begins to talk in Hungarian during his sleep; soon, he flies back to Hungary, where a local woman succumbs to his sexual charms and begins to teach him the numerous intricacies of her native language until he is deported.
Subject keyword: identity
Original language: Portuguese
Sources consulted for annotation:
Hooper, Brad. *Booklist* 101 (15 September 2004): 206.
Reynolds, Susan Salter. *Los Angeles Times*, 3 October 2004, p. R11.
Shreve, Jack. *Library Journal* 129 (15 October 2004): 52.
Zaleski, Jeff. *Publishers Weekly* 251 (30 August 20040: 29.
Some other translated books written by Chico Buarque: *Turbulence*; *Benjamin*

Paulo Coelho. *Eleven Minutes*.
Translated by Margaret Jull Costa. New York: HarperCollins, 2004. 273 pages.
Genre/literary style/story type: mainstream fiction
Originally from Brazil, Maria now earns her living in Switzerland as a high-class prostitute. She is mystified by the fact that an act of sex that takes, on average, 11 minutes is so central to so many people. Thus, she begins to study what makes sexuality so powerful—physically, emotionally, and psychologically. With her newfound knowledge, she returns to Brazil, where she falls in love with an artist.
Related titles by the same author:
Readers may also enjoy *Brida*, which focuses on Brida O'Fern, whose serpentine path through life leads her to discover humility and the extraordinary power of sex. Together with a budding scientist, she embarks on an emotional journey characterized by spiritual grace and passion. Also of interest may be *The Winner Stands Alone*, which chronicles the gaudy excesses of the Cannes Film Festival through the life and loves of a megalomaniac nouveau-riche Russian.
Subject keyword: identity

Original language: Portuguese
Sources consulted for annotation:
Di Filippo, Paul. *The Washington Post* (from Amazon.com).
Global Books in Print (online) (reviews from *Booklist*, *Library Journal*, and *Publishers Weekly* for *Brida*).
Harris, Michael. *Los Angeles Times*, 23 May 2004, p. R11.
Mujica, Barbara. *Americas* 56 (November/December 2004): 61.
Pearl, Nancy. *Library Journal* 130 (15 June 2005): 119.
Publishers Weekly 251 (15 March 2004): 54.
Some other translated books written by Paulo Coelho: *The Alchemist*; *The Zahir: A Novel of Obsession*; *The Fifth Mountain*; *Veronika Decides To Die*; *By the River Piedra I Sat Down and Wept*; *The Devil and Miss Prym*; *The Fifth Mountain*; *The Valkyries: An Encounter with Angels*; *The Witch of Portobello*; *Brida*; *The Winner Stand Alones*

Rubem Fonseca. *Vast Emotions and Imperfect Thoughts*.
Translated by Clifford E. Landers. Hopewell, NJ: Ecco Press, 1998. 312 pages.
Genre/literary style/story type: mainstream fiction
A Brazilian movie director moonlighting as a director of television commercials finds himself in the middle of an incredibly fantastic set of circumstances. Entrusted with a box of valuable jewels by a mysterious woman who is later found dead, he discovers that his every move is being watched. When he is presented with the chance to turn Isaac Babel's story collection *Red Cavalry* into a film, he is only too happy to seize the chance, in turn entrusting the gems to a Russian Jewish intellectual. Travelling to Berlin, he learns about a lost novel written by Babel, purchases it, and smuggles it back to Brazil. But before he can have it translated by his Jewish friend, he is kidnapped by jewel smugglers keen on having their gems returned. Critics have compared Fonseca's works with that of the Spanish film director Pedro Almodóvar because of their insouciant spirit and poignant undertexts.
Related title by the same author:
Readers may also enjoy *The Taker and Other Stories*, which consists of a series of fragmentary episodes exploring the often nihilistic violence, mayhem, and anarchy of Rio de Janeiro. Noting that Fonseca "has been famously championed by [Thomas] Pynchon, among others," Anderson Tepper called him "a depraved poet-prophet of Rio's street terror."
Subject keyword: writers
Original language: Portuguese
Sources consulted for annotation:
Bukiet, Melvin Jules. *Los Angeles Times*, 7 July 1998, p. 11.
Global Books in Print (online) (review from *Kirkus Reviews*).
Ott, Bill. *Booklist* 94 (15 April 1998): 1382.
Smith, Margaret A. *Library Journal* 123 (1 May 1998): 137.
Steinberg, Sybil S. *Publishers Weekly* 245 (20 April 1998): 46.
Tepper, Anderson. *Time Out New York*, 13-19 November 2008 (online).
Some other translated books written by Rubem Fonseca: *High Art*; *Bufo & Spallanzani*; *The Taker and Other Stories*

L. A. (Luiz Alfredo) García-Roza. *A Window in Copacabana*.
Translated by Benjamin Moser. New York: Henry Holt, 2005. 243 pages.
Genres/literary styles/story types: crime fiction; police detectives
This is the fourth book in the series about Inspector Espinosa, a wry police detective who loves books. As the head of a Rio de Janeiro precinct, he must solve the murder of three policemen, but

matters get particularly complicated when the mistresses of the murdered policemen also start getting killed.
Subject keyword: urban life
Original language: Portuguese
Source consulted for annotation:
Amazon.com (reviews from *Booklist* and *Publishers Weekly*).
Some other translated books in the Inspector Espinosa series: *The Silence of the Rain*; *December Heat*; *Southwesterly Wind*; *Pursuit*; *Blackout*

Milton Hatoum. *The Brothers.*
Translated by John Gledson. New York: Farrar, Straus and Giroux, 2002. 226 pages.
Genre/literary style/story type: mainstream fiction
Although they are twins, Omar and Yaqub have little in common except their dysfunctional family. After fighting with his brother, Yaqub strikes out on his own, eventually becoming an engineer in São Paulo. But Omar remains a dissolute drunk in his hometown of Manaus, forced to contend with a jealous mother who interferes with every aspect of his life. Family secrets abound, especially because the reputed son of the family servant, who is the book's narrator, is firmly convinced that his real father is one of the twins.
Related title by the same author:
Readers may also enjoy *The Tree of the Seventh Heaven*, which describes the extraordinary journey of a Lebanese family who decides to emigrate to the Amazon port city of Manaus, Brazil. Flabbergasted by the news, the ultra-pious Emilie flees Beirut to become a nun and then is eventually persuaded by her brother to come to Brazil to join the rest of the family. Here, Emilie marries a Muslim man but remains fervently attached to Christian icons, worshipping saints and talking to birds and animals.
Subject keyword: family histories
Original language: Portuguese
Sources consulted for annotation:
Global Books in Print (online) (reviews from *Library Journal* and *Publishers Weekly* for *The Tree of Seventh Heaven*).
Hallsworth, Caroline. *Library Journal* 127 (August 2002): 142.
Montgomery, Isobel, and David Jays. *The Guardian*, 15 March 2003, p. 30.
Zaleski, Jeff. *Publishers Weekly* 249 (29 April 2002): 40.
Some other translated books written by Milton Hatoum: *The Tree of the Seventh Heaven*; *Tale of a Certain Orient*

Patrícia Melo. *Black Waltz.*
Translated by Clifford E. Landers. London: Bloomsbury, 2004. 209 pages.
Genre/literary style/story type: mainstream fiction
After an unsuccessful first marriage, an orchestra conductor in São Paulo weds Marie, a talented Jewish violinist who is some 30 years younger than him. Wracked by persistent jealousy, he soon begins to hate everything and everyone, suspecting the housemaid, Marie's parents, and fellow musicians of malicious conspiracies. Bewildered and isolated, Marie withdraws into her own world of obsessions, where the Israeli intifada and drugs take center stage. But her longing for Israel only broadens the gap between them, fueling her husband's perfervidly paranoid imagination even more.
Subject keywords: culture conflict; identity
Original language: Portuguese
Sources consulted for annotation:
Hopkinson, Amanda. *The Observer*, 19 December 2004, p. 16.

International Impac Dublin Literary Award, http://www.impacdublinaward.ie.
Lewis, Trevor. *The Sunday Times*, 20 November 2005, p. 54.
Montgomery, Isobel, and David Jays. *The Guardian*, 11 September 2004, p. 30.
Some other translated books written by Patrícia Melo: *The Killer*; *In Praise of Lies*; *Inferno*

Ana Maria Miranda. *Bay of All Saints and Every Conceivable Sin.*
Translated by Giovanni Pontiero. New York: Viking, 1991. 305 pages.
Genre/literary style/story type: historical fiction
This novel is about the late seventeenth-century political assassination of the infamous captain-general of the Brazilian state of Bahia, who was killed by the insurgents struggling against the rule of autocratic Antonio De Souza De Menezes. Also featured prominently are the Baroque poet Gregório de Mattos, best known for his trenchant satires, and an enlightened Jesuit, Father António Vieira.
Subject keyword: power
Original language: Portuguese
Sources consulted for annotation:
Cosin, Elizabeth M. *The Washington Times*, 22 March 1992, p. B8.
Miller, Lucasta. *New Statesman & Society* 5 (27 March 1992): 41.
Partello, Peggie. *Library Journal* 117 (1 February 1992): 127.
Ryan, Alan. *The Washington Post*, 7 August 1992, p. C5.
Steinberg, Sybil S. *Publishers Weekly* 238 (20 December 1991): 66.
Sutherland, John. *The Seattle Times*, 21 June 1992, p. K6.

Alberto Mussa. *Riddle of Qaf.*
Translated by Lennie Larkin. Laverstock, Wiltshire, UK: Aflame Books, 2008. 208 pages.
Genres/literary styles/story types: mainstream fiction; magical realism
The Muallaqat, typically referred to as a famous pre-Islamic Arab literary masterpiece, consists of seven long poems. But a Lebanese-Brazilian, convinced that there is a lost eighth poem, undertakes an arduous journey to the Middle East to find it. According to the *New Internationalist* reviewer, the book, which is "elaborately structured with 28 narrative chapters corresponding to the 28 letters of the Arabic alphabet," makes use of "myths and legends such as *Aladdin*, *Scheherazade* and *Ali Baba and the 40 Thieves*."
Subject keyword: philosophy
Original language: Portuguese
Sources consulted for annotation:
Aflame Books (book description), http://www.aflamebooks.com.
Global Books in Print (online) (synopsis/book jacket).
New Internationalist (October 2008) (Issue 416) (online).

Nélida Piñon. *Caetana's Sweet Song.*
Translated by Helen R. Lane. New York: Alfred A. Knopf, 1992. 401 pages.
Genre/literary style/story type: mainstream fiction
Caetana Toledo's acting career has not made her famous; for the most part, she has made a living touring backwater towns. She returns to Trindade, a small town where 20 years ago, she and wealthy local landowner, Polidoro Alves, were lovers. Trapped in a marriage in name only, Alves has spent the past two decades in a fog of despair and illusion. But Caetana does not want to revive their former passion; instead, she wants to put on a production of Verdi's *La Traviata*. As the whole town gets caught up in the enthusiasm of the moment, Caetana briefly succeeds in stirring up the town's dormant dreams, but reality soon intrudes in the form of legal restrictions. The

book may be read as a tribute to female perseverance, independence, and sense of self-worth in the face of fading beauty and professional failure.
Subject keywords: identity; rural life
Original language: Portuguese
Sources consulted for annotation:
Amazon.com (reviews from *Publishers Weekly* and *Library Journal*).
Krueger, Lesley. *The Globe and Mail* (Toronto), 13 June 1992, p. C14.
Mujica, Barbara. *Americas* 44 (July/August 1992): 61.
Ruta, Suzanne. *The New York Times*, 24 May 1992 (online).
Another translated book written by Nélida Piñon: *The Republic of Dreams*

João Ubaldo Ribeiro. *The Lizard's Smile*.
Translated by Clifford E. Landers. New York: Atheneum, 1994. 355 pages.
Genres/literary styles/story types: thrillers; conspiracy thrillers
Ângelo Marcos Barreto is a hypocritical politician who indulges in homophobic, sexist, and racist diatribes. When he goes to Itaparica, an island in the Brazilian state of Bahia, for chemotherapy treatment, his wife starts an affair with João Pedroso, a local fishseller who once was a biologist. When João discovers that Lúcio, chief of the island hospital, is participating in dubious genetic research that uses African-American women as subjects, numerous ethical questions come to the forefront. Readers may wish to explore John le Carré's *The Constant Gardener* for a similar view of the stakes involved when scientific research intersects with financial profit.
Subject keyword: social problems
Original language: Portuguese
Sources consulted for annotation:
Amazon.com (review from *Publishers Weekly*).
Evenson, Brian. *Review of Contemporary Fiction* 15 (Spring 1995): 175.
Mujica, Barbara. *Americas* 48 (July/August 1996): 61.
Ott, Bill, and Cooper, Ilene. *Booklist* 96 (1 January 2000): 985.
Some other translated books written by João Ubaldo Ribeiro: *Sergeant Getúlio*; *An Invincible Memory*

Moacyr Scliar. *Max and the Cats*.
Translated by Eloah F. Giacomelli. New York: Plume, 2003. 115 pages.
Genre/literary style/story type: mainstream fiction
This novel is best known as the inspiration for Yann Martel's award-winning *Life of Pi*. Max Schmidt, born in Berlin in the early 1910s, has a fear of cats, not the least because his father is a furrier with a keen interest in taxidermy. While at university, he resumes an affair with Frida, who is now married to a supporter of the Nazis. Max flees to Brazil onboard a ship carrying animals. But the ship sinks, and Max must share a lifeboat with a jaguar. Rescued and brought to Brazil, Max builds a new life but realizes that one of his neighbors may be a Nazi. With nowhere else to run, he must finally confront his phobias.
Subject keyword: anti-Semitism
Original language: Portuguese
Sources consulted for annotation:
Amazon.com (review from *Library Journal*).
Morra, Linda. *Canadian Literature* 183 (Winter 2004): 166.
Patterson, Troy. *Entertainment Weekly* 740 (5 December 2003): 107.
Publishers Weekly 250 (3 November 2003): 52.

Some other translated books written by Moacyr Scliar: *The Strange Nation of Rafael Mendes*; *The Centaur in the Garden*; *The Volunteers*; *The Enigmatic Eye*; *The Carnival of the Animals*; *The One-Man Army*; *Tieta*; *The Gods of Raquel*; *The Ballad of the False Messiah*

Jô Soares. *Twelve Fingers: Biography of an Anarchist.*
Translated by Clifford E. Landers. New York: Pantheon Books, 2001. 303 pages.
Genres/literary styles/story types: historical fiction; literary historical
Born in Bosnia in 1897, Dimitri Borja Korozec is the walking definition of a bungling killer. He also happens to have 12 fingers but is missing his right testicle as a sign of membership in a left-wing cult-like organization. In pursuit of assassination targets, he attempts to murder Archduke Ferdinand in Sarajevo; Jean Jaurés in Paris; and President Franklin D. Roosevelt in the United States. Of course, he fails. When he reaches Brazil in 1954, he stalks Getúlio Vargas, a murderous dictator and his own uncle.
Subject keyword: politics
Original language: Portuguese
Sources consulted for annotation:
Mujica, Barbara. *Americas* 54 (March/April 20020: 61.
Olson, Ray. *Booklist* 97 (1 June/15 June): 1849.
Shreve, Jack. *Library Journal* 126 (15 June 2001): 105.
Zaleski, Jeff. *Publishers Weekly* 248 (4 June 2001): 56.
Another translated book written by Jô Soares: *A Samba for Sherlock*

Edla van Steen. *Scent of Love.*
Translated by David Sanderson George. Pittsburgh, PA: Latin American Literary Review Press, 2001. 110 pages.
Genres/literary styles/story types: mainstream fiction; short stories
In the title novella, a reporter writing an obituary about a famous woman becomes overly involved in her life. In the two stories that complete the collection, the theme of the dead or the near-dead having an outsize influence on the living is once again present: An ordinary conversation between two friends turns into anything but ordinary when one woman drops a deep dark secret about the other woman's husband and a 90-year-old man who has had nothing to do with his daughters throughout his life decides to visit them.
Subject keyword: family histories
Original language: Portuguese
Sources consulted for annotation:
Scott, Whitney. *Booklist* 97 (1 December 2000): 694.
Steinberg, Sybil S. *Publishers Weekly* 247 (27 November 2000): 55.
Some other translated books written by Edla van Steen: *Early Mourning*; *Village of the Ghost Bells: A Novel*; *A Bag of Stories*

Luís Fernando Veríssimo. *Borges and the Eternal Orangutans.*
Translated by Margaret Jull Costa. New York: New Directions, 2005. 135 pages.
Genres/literary styles/story types: crime fiction; postmodernism
Volgenstein is a translator attending a meeting of a scholarly society that studies the work of Edgar Allan Poe. Here, he hopes to meet Jorge Luis Borges. He certainly does meet Borges but not under the circumstances that he had envisioned. When Rotkopf, another conference participant is stabbed, Volgenstein and Borges team up to solve the crime. They soon discover that Rotkopf had numerous enemies, including Oliver Johnson, who was roundly embarrassed by Rotkopf in the best traditions of vigorous academic cut-and-thrust. But because Rotkopf's body was found in front of a mirror

arranged in the form of an X, the mystery takes Volgenstein and Borges into the shadowy world of cryptograms, the Necronomicon, the Kaballah, and the sixteenth-century hermetic philosophy of John Dee.
Subject keyword: writers
Original language: Portuguese
Sources consulted for annotation:
Amazon.com (book description).
Bukiet, Melvin Jules. *The Washington Post*, 5 June 2005, p. T7.
Kirkus Reviews, 15 March 2005 (from Factiva databases).
Publishers Weekly 252 (11 April 2005): 32.
Another translated book written by Luís Fernando Veríssimo: *The Club of Angels*

CHAPTER 8

Northern Europe: Low Countries, Scandinavia, and Baltic Countries

Language groups:		
Danish	Lithuanian	Finland
Dutch	Norwegian	Iceland
Estonian	Swedish	Latvia
Finnish	**Countries represented:**	Lithuania
Icelandic	Belgium	Netherlands
Latvian	Denmark	Norway
	Estonia	Sweden

INTRODUCTION

This chapter contains annotations of books from various regions of Northern Europe: the Low Countries (i.e., the Netherlands and Belgium); Scandinavia (i.e., Denmark, Iceland, Norway, Sweden, and Finland); and the Baltic states (Estonia, Latvia, and Lithuania). Please note that titles from French-speaking Belgium are covered in Chapter 9. The most common languages represented in this chapter are Dutch, Danish, Icelandic, Norwegian, Swedish, and Finnish, with a handful of books in each of Estonian, Latvian, and Lithuanian.

Some of the Dutch authors included in this chapter are Arnon Grunberg (*Blue Mondays*); Harry Mulisch (*The Discovery of Heaven*); and Cees Nooteboom (*All Souls' Day*), who is often mentioned as a possible Nobel Prize laureate. Perhaps the most well-known Belgian novelist is Hugo Claus (*The Sorrow of Belgium* and *Wonder*), who died in 2008.

A number of contemporary Scandinavian novelists are much better known than Dutch and Belgian writers, but many other important novelists fly under the radar. Some readers may be familiar with Danish authors Peter Høeg (*Smilla's Sense of Snow*) and Henrik Stangerup (*Snake in the Heart*) but may not recognize Peter H. Fogtdal (*The Tsar's Dwarf*); Christian Jungersen (*The Exception*); or Morten Ramsland (*Doghead*). With regard to Icelandic novels, the mystery writer Arnaldur

Indriđason (*Silence of the Grave*) has established quite a reputation. But Bragi Ólafsson (*The Pets*) and Sjón (*The Blue Fox*) may be less familiar names, despite Sjón's fame as the lyricist for some of Björk's songs.

Norwegian authors with name recognition that have been translated into English include Karin Fossum (*Don't Look Back*); Jan Kjærstad (*The Seducer, The Conqueror*, and *The Discoverer*); Jo Nesbø (*The Redbreast* and *The Devil's Star*); and Per Petterson, whose book *Out Stealing Horses* was unanimously hailed as a masterpiece. Some of the best-known contemporary Swedish novelists in English translation are Karin Alvtegen (*Missing*); Åke Edwardson (*Never End*); Kerstin Ekman (*Blackwater*); Per Olov Enquist (*The Royal Physician's Visit*); Stieg Larsson (*The Girl with the Dragon Tattoo, The Girl Who Played with Fire*, and *The Girl Who Kicked the Hornet's Nest*); and Henning Mankell, whose Kurt Wallander mystery series—two of which are *The Dogs of Riga* and *Before the Frost*—have brought him international attention.

Compared with readers' knowledge of translated Swedish and Norwegian novels, knowledge of translated Finnish novels is almost nonexistent. But with authors such as Elina Hirvonen (*When I Forgot*); Arto Paasilinna (*The Year of the Hare*); and Marja-Liisa Vartio (*The Parson's Widow*), this may soon change. With regard to Baltic novels, readers may want to pay particular attention to Mati Unt's *Things in the Night* and *Diary of a Blood Donor* (Estonia) and Ričardas Gavelis's *Vilnius Poker* (Lithuania).

Earlier Translated Literature

The nonnovelistic prose tradition of Northern Europe is impressive. Any discussion of this heritage must start with the Old Norse/Icelandic sagas, which are available to the English reader in the five-volume *The Complete Sagas of Icelanders Including 49 Tales*. Some of the most famous sagas, such as *Njal's Saga, Hrafnkel's Saga*, and *Laxdoela Saga*, are also available separately in various Penguin editions. The Finnish epic *Kalevala* may also be of great interest. Sometimes translated as epic poetry and sometimes as prose, the *Kalevala* is the national touchstone of Finland. It has inspired countless writers, including Henry Wadsworth Longfellow, who based *The Song of Hiawatha* on it. Readers may also not want to overlook the fairy tales and stories of the Danish author Hans Christian Andersen; the children's stories of Swedish writer Astrid Lindgren (*Pippi Longstocking*); and Anne Frank's *Diary of a Young Girl*, originally in Dutch.

With regard specifically to novels, a bountiful feast awaits. From Denmark, there is the nineteenth-century author Herman Bang (*Tina*); from Finland, the nineteenth-century author Aleksis Kivi (*Seven Brothers*) and 1939 Nobel Prize winner F. E. Sillanpää (*Fallen Asleep While Young* and *People in the Summer Night*); from Iceland, 1955 Nobel Prize laureate Halldór Laxness (*Independent People* and *Paradise Regained*); from Norway, 1920 Nobel Prize winner Knut Hamsun (*Hunger*) and 1928 Nobel Prize winner Sigrid Undset (*Kristin Lavransdatter*); and from Sweden, 1909 Nobel Prize laureate Selma Lagerlöf (*The Löwensköld Ring*).

SOURCES CONSULTED

France, Peter. (Ed.). (2000). "Northern European Languages." In *The Oxford Guide to Literature in English Translation*, pp. 551–581. Oxford: Oxford University Press.

BIBLIOGRAPHIC ESSAY

Scandinavian Countries

Scandinavian literature is not just Henrik Ibsen (Norway), August Strindberg (Sweden), and Halldór Laxness (Iceland). An excellent overview that will allow readers to situate themselves within the diverse and relatively little-known Scandinavian literary landscape is Sven H. Rossel's *A History of Scandinavian Literature, 1870–1980*. Rossel admirably surveys Norwegian, Swedish, Finnish, Danish, Icelandic, and Faroese literatures, enabling readers to discover such obscure (yet significant) topics as Fenno-Swedish modernism and nature worship and national literature in Norway as well as the writings of Vilhelm Moberg, Karin Boye, Aksel Sandemose, Toivo Pekkanen, Leif Panduro, Gunnar Gunnarsson, and Per Gunnar Evander, among numerous others. This general history should be used in conjunction with the *Dictionary of Scandinavian Literature*, edited by Virpi Zuck, which contains entries about notable Scandinavian authors (always indicating their translated works) as well as important literary topics. The extensive bibliography lists a wide variety of English-language anthologies of authors and their works from each of the countries in question.

Readers who are smitten with one or more of the individual Scandinavian literatures after reading Rossel's overview can then consult one of the five country-specific literary histories published by the University of Nebraska Press in conjunction with The American Scandinavian Foundation. One could spend years (and never be bored) paging through these magnificently detailed, nuanced, and sensitively written volumes. We begin with *The History of Swedish Literature*, edited by Lars G. Warme. It has chapters about Swedish writing during the Middle Ages; the Reformation; Sweden's centuries as a great power (1523–1718); the breakthrough into realism from 1830–1890; literature after 1950; women writers; and literature for children and young people. Subsections deal with such issues as democratic theater; the documentary novel; the melodramatic tale and the novel of intrigue; historical fiction; and working-class writers of the 1930s. Readers will be delighted to learn about such neglected yet significant authors as John Landquist, Martin Koch, Eyvind Johnson, Artur Lundkvist, Harry Martinson, Stig Dagerman, Lars Ahlin, Lars Gyllensten, Birgitta Trotzig, Sara Lidman, Per Olof Sundman, Per Olov Enquist, Kerstin Ekman, Lars Ardelius, Hans Granlid, and Bosse Gustafson. Bibliographies indicate writers translated into English.

Everything that one ever wanted to know about Icelandic literature is contained in *A History of Icelandic Literature*, edited by Daisy Neijmann. There are substantial chapters about Old Icelandic poetry and prose that discuss the historical and social circumstances that gave rise to the eddic and saga traditions. Subsequent chapters deal with romanticism, realism, and neo-romanticism in the nineteenth century; the politicization of literature in the 1930s; prose literature from 1940–2000 (with an emphasis on such thematic subtopics as urban epics and the hinterlands, minimalism and fantasy, sexuality and family, and the Reykjavík cityscape novel); Icelandic poetry and theater; the female tradition in Icelandic literature; Icelandic children's literature; and Icelandic-Canadian literature. Authors well worth discovering include Einar H. Kvaran, Mikael Torfason, Rúnar Helgi Vignisson, Olaf Olafson, Ólafur Gunnarsson, Birgitta H. Halldórsdóttir, and Hallgrimu Helgason, who wrote the much commented-upon novel *101 Reykjavík*. Again, there are bibliographies that indicate literary works available in English translation.

A History of Danish Literature, edited by Sven H. Rossel, is equally compelling. Topics discussed here include the medieval ballad; the Lutheran reformation; the philosophy of nature; absolute monarchy and the sciences; poets of the baroque period; the secular challenge to theology; Biedermeier culture; the roles of Hans Christian Andersen, Frederik Paludan-Müller, and Søren Kierkegaard; the rural rebellion; the chaos and disillusionment of the years between World War I and World War II; the inclination toward fantasy; satirical realism; existential humanism; and politicization and social experimentation in poetry and prose. Likewise, there are lengthy chapters about literature from the Faroe Islands (typically described as a "self-governing overseas administrative division of Denmark"); Danish women writers; and the historical development of Danish children's literature. Danish authors that may pique the interest of readers include Martin A. Hansen, Peter Seeberg, Sven Holm, Kirsten Thorup, and Karen Blixen, author of *Babette's Feast*.

Edited by Harald S. Naess, *A History of Norwegian Literature* begins with the runic and the Old Germanic tradition, surveys the age of the Vikings, and discusses the oral tradition of the fourteenth and fifteenth centuries before moving on to such famous authors of the nineteenth century as Johan Sebastian Welhaven, Henrik Arnold Wergeland, Knut Hamsun, and Hans Knick. The book is particularly masterful in its consideration of such early and late twentieth-century writers as Sigrid Undset, Olav Duun, Kristofer Uppdal, Johan Falkberget, Tarjei Vesaas, Cora Sandel, Johan Borgen, Sigurd Evensmo, Terje Stigen, and Alfred Hauge.

George C. Schoolfield's edited volume entitled *A History of Finland's Literature* completes the journey around Scandinavia. It starts with Finnish oral poetry, of which the epic *Kalevala* is perhaps the most famous example. It then tackles the thorny question of Swedish and Latin hegemony in the world of Finnish literature. However, by 1860, Finnish-language literature had been established; there are thoughtful sections on the importance of Aleksis Kivi, Teuvo Pakkala, and Juhani Aho. And in the later twentieth century, Antti Tuuri, Heikki Turunen, Matti Pulkkinen, Arto Paasilinna, Annika Idström, and Daniel Katz are writers worth knowing about. Schoolfield's volume concludes with a detailed consideration of the phenomenon of Finland-Swedish literature.

It is inevitable that readers will find in these books at least four or five writers about whom they wish to know much more. Thus, they should waste little time in consulting the following six volumes of the Dictionary of Literary Biography series: *Icelandic Writers*, edited by Patrick J. Stevens (2004; vol. 293); *Danish Writers from the Reformation to Decadence, 1550–1900*, edited by Marianne Stecher-Hansen (2004; vol. 300); *Twentieth-Century Danish Writers*, again edited by Marianne Stecher-Hansen (1999; vol. 214); *Twentieth-Century Norwegian Writers*, edited by Tanya Thresher (2004; vol. 297); *Twentieth-Century Swedish Writers Before World War II*, edited by Ann-Charlotte Gavel Adams (2002; vol. 259); and *Twentieth-Century Swedish Writers After World War II*, also edited by Ann-Charlotte Gavel Adams (2002; vol. 257). Among the many fine essays contained in the Icelandic volume is the one about Laxness, with a complete list of his works available in English. We cannot emphasize the relevancy and importance of Laxness in the modern age. Also worth mentioning are the essays about the Swedish authors Pär Lagerkvist and Selma Lagerlöf, who in 1909 was the first woman to receive the Nobel Prize for Literature. Essays about the Danish writer Herman Bang, who is curiously forgotten in the English-speaking world despite two early translations in the 1920s, and Peter Høeg, author of many works translated into English in the 1990s and 2000s (e.g., *The Quiet Girl*, *Smilla's Sense of Snow*, *Borderliners*), are also rewarding.

If you cannot resist learning still more about Scandinavian literature, we suggest Janet Garton's *Norwegian Women's Writing, 1850–1990* and Helena Forsås-Scott's *Swedish Women's Writing, 1850–1995*. Lovers of Norwegian literature will be only too happy to make the acquaintance of such writers as Amalie Skram, Cora Sandel, Camilla Collett, Bjørg Vik, Cecilie Løveid, Herbjørg Wassmo, Gerd Brantenberg, and Mari Osmundsen. Swedish literary aficionados will likewise be pleased to be introduced or reintroduced to Frederika Bremer, Moa Martinson, Kerstin Ekman, Agneta Pleijel, and Mare Kandre. Finally, there is the *Babel Guide to Scandinavian and Baltic Fiction* by Paul Binding, which provides an annotated list of many famous books translated into English from Norway, Sweden, Finland, Denmark, and Iceland as well as a handful of translated books from Estonia, Latvia, and Lithuania.

Baltic Countries

There is some information about the literature of the Baltic countries in English but not too much. It is probably best to start with two volumes in the Dictionary of Literary Biography series called *Twentieth-Century Eastern European Writers Second Series* (2000; vol. 220) and *Twentieth-Century Eastern European Writers Third Series* (2001; vol. 232), both edited by Steven Serafin. Here, readers will meet such Estonian writers as Betti Alver, Jaan Kross, Gustav Suits, Marie Under, Mati Unt, and Eduard Wilde; such Latvian writers as Aspazija, Rudolfs Blaumanis, Jánis Rainis, Alberts Bels, Regína Ezera, and Imants Ziedonis; and such Lithuanian writers as Jonas Aistis, Jonas Maironis, and Sigitas Geda.

With this background, one can profitably consult *Lithuanian Literature*, a series of interlinked essays tracing the historical development of Lithuanian literature by Vytautas Kubilius and colleagues. Topics covered include: ancient written literature and belles lettres; literature of the national movement; Soviet literature; and literature of the resistance. Attention is also paid to émigré literature as well as developments up to 1995. The book concludes with an invaluable bibliography of translations of Lithuanian literature into non-Lithuanian languages from 1927–1995. For brief histories of Latvian and Estonian literature, Aleksis Rubulis's 1970 book *Baltic Literature: A Survey of Finnish, Estonian, Latvian, and Lithuanian Literatures* will prove to be useful to many individuals as an introductory text. These books can then be supplemented by three anthologies: *Bear's Ears: An Anthology of Latvian Literature*, compiled by Ieva Zauberga, Andrejs Veisbergs, and Andrew Chesterman; *The Earth Remains: An Anthology of Contemporary Lithuanian Prose*, translated and edited by Laima Sruoginis; and *From Baltic Shores*, edited by Christopher Moseley. Finally, *Baltic Postcolonialism*, a collection of essays edited by Violeta Kelertas, is also an important source of information. Here, readers will find fruitful and challenging essays about twentieth-century Estonian, Latvian, and Lithuanian literature as seen through the perspectives of such political and cultural theorists as Franz Fanon and Homi Bhabha.

Low Countries

The Low Countries are typically considered to be the Netherlands, Belgium, and Luxembourg. Belgium has a complex linguistic situation, with both French and Dutch spoken; in Luxembourg, the French, German, and Luxembourgish languages are prevalent. We will briefly mention French-language literature emanating from Belgium in Chapter 9. Here, we are concerned with Dutch literature in the Netherlands and the Flemish part of Belgium as well as Luxembourgish literature. Four historical works stand out. The first is Reinder P. Meijer's *Literature of the Low Countries: A Short History of Dutch Literature in the Netherlands and Belgium*, which begins with the twelfth century and continues to the twentieth century. Paying due attention to social and historical developments, Meijer expertly introduces readers to such forgotten figures as Willem van Haren; Willem Bilderdijk; Anthonie C. W. Starling; Nicolaas Beets; Louis Couperus; Herman Teirlinck; Paul Van Ostaijen; Simon Vestdijk; and Gerrit Krol. Just as eye-opening is Vernon Mallinson's *Modern Belgian Literature, 1830–1960*, which has a particularly compelling chapter about the work and influence of Nobel Prize winner Maurice Maeterlinck (in 1911) as well as pithy overviews about such novelists as Félix Timmermans and Ernest Claes.

For those who are able to read French, there is no better introduction to Dutch literature than *Histoire de la Littérature Néerlandaise*, edited by Hanna Stouten, Jaap Goedegebuure, and Frits van Oostrom. There are chapters about all the major periods in Dutch literature, with special emphasis on the Middle Ages, the Renaissance, and the eighteenth and nineteenth centuries. The book is particularly good in relating the evolution of Dutch literature to external cultural and historical forces. Among the key authors discussed are Herman Gorter, Willem Kloos, Cyriel Buysse, Stijn Streuvels, W. F. Hermans, and Gerard Reve. One hopes that this definitive 915-page book will eventually be translated into English. Also in French is a history of literature in Luxembourg by Jul Christophory entitled *Précis d'histoire de la Littérature en Langue Luxembourgeoise*, which is an updated and expanded version of the same author's 1994 *A Short History of Literature in Luxembourgish*. If there ever was an unknown literary tradition, it is safe to say that this is it. Christophory surveys poetry and theater in Luxembourg but concentrates on the rise of the novel starting around the middle 1980s, highlighting the work of Guy Rewenig, Josy Braun, Nico Helminger, Georges Kieffer, and Georges Hausemer.

These literary histories should be supplemented by *Women Writing in Dutch*, edited by Kristiaan Aercke, and *Making the Personal Political: Dutch Women Writers, 1919–1970* by Jane Fenoulhet.

Aercke's book has extensive biographical introductions about and translations of such authors as Anna Bijns, Maria Petijt, Elizabeth Wolff, Hella S. Haasse, Marga Minco, Anne Frank, Eva Gerlach, and Maria Stahlie. Fenoulhet's book discusses the work of Carry van Bruggen, Ina Boudier-Bakker, Jo van Ammers-Küller, Etty Hillesum, Anna Blaman, and others. Finally, readers should consult *New Trends in Dutch Literature*, edited by Gillis J. Dorleijn, where such essays as "Patterns of Change in Recent Dutch Literature" and "Women Authors and Women's Writing in the Declining Years of Modernism" may be of special interest. Individuals choosing to read one or more of these books about literature from the Low Countries are sure to be astounded by the rich cultural heritage and diversity of these nations.

SELECTED REFERENCES

Aercke, Kristiaan. (Ed.). (1994). *Women Writing in Dutch*. New York: Garland.

Binding, Paul. (1999). *The Babel Guide to Scandinavian and Baltic Fiction*. London: Boulevard Books.

Christophory, Jul. (2005). *Précis d'histoire de la Littérature en Langue Luxembourgeoise*. Luxembourg: Paul Bauler.

Dorleijn, Gillis J. (Ed.). (2006). *New Trends in Modern Dutch Literature*. Leuven, Belgium: Peeters.

Fenoulhet, Jane. (2007). *Making the Personal Political: Dutch Women Writers, 1919–1970*. London: Modern Humanities Research Association and Maney Publishing.

Forsås-Scott, Helena. (1997). *Swedish Women's Writing, 1850–1995*. London: Athlone.

Gratton, Janet. (1993). *Norwegian Women's Writing, 1850–1990*. London: Athlone.

Kelertas, Violeta. (Ed.). (2006). *Baltic Postcolonialism*. Amsterdam, The Netherlands: Rodopi.

Kubilius, Vytautas; Samulionis, Algis; Zalatorius, Albertas; and Vanagas, Vytautas. (1997). *Lithuanian Literature*. Vilnius, Lithuania: Vaga.

Mallinson, Vernon. (1966). *Modern Belgian Literature, 1830–1960*. London: Heinemann.

Meijer, Reinder P. (1978). *Literature of the Low Countries: A Short History of Dutch Literature in the Netherlands and Belgium*. Cheltenham, UK: Stanley Thornes.

Naess, Harald S. (Ed.). (1993). *A History of Norwegian Literature*. Lincoln, NE: University of Nebraska Press.

Neijmann, Daisy. (Ed.). (2006). *A History of Icelandic Literature*. Lincoln, NE: University of Nebraska Press.

Rossel, Sven H. (Ed.). (1992). *A History of Danish Literature*. Lincoln, NE: University of Nebraska Press.

Rossel, Sven H. (Ed.). (1982). *A History of Scandinavian Literature, 1870–1980*. (Trans. by Anne C. Ulmer). Minneapolis, MN: University of Minnesota Press.

Rubulis, Aleksis. (1970). *Baltic Literature: A Survey of Finnish, Estonian, Latvian, and Lithuanian Literatures*. Notre Dame, IN: University of Notre Dame Press.

Schoolfield, George C. (Ed.). (1998). *A History of Finland's Literature*. Lincoln, NE: University of Nebraska Press.

Stouten, Hanna; Goedegebuure, Jaap; and van Oostrom, Frits. (Eds.). (1999). *Histoire de la Littérature Néerlandaise*. Paris: Fayard.

Warme, Lars G. (Ed.). (1996). *A History of Swedish Literature*. Lincoln, NE: University of Nebraska Press.

Zuck, Virpi. (Ed.). (1990). *Dictionary of Scandinavian Literature*. New York: Greenwood.

ANNOTATIONS FOR TRANSLATED BOOKS FROM THE LOW COUNTRIES, SCANDINAVIA, AND THE BALTIC COUNTRIES

Belgium

Hugo Claus. *The Sorrow of Belgium.*

Translated by Arnold J. Pomerans. New York: Pantheon Books, 1990. 608 pages.

Genres/literary styles/story types: mainstream fiction; coming-of-age

Reminiscent of Günter Grass's *The Tin Drum*, this book—which ironically juxtaposes the mundane life of a middle-class family with the horrors of the Nazi regime—focuses on Belgian school boy Louis Seynaeve during the war years. His mother works in a German arms factory, his father revels about his connections in the Gestapo, and almost every relative imaginable has positive things to say about the German love of precision and order. As Suzanne Ruta observes, the novel contains "lively dialogue about food, sex and the minutiae of right-wing Flemish politics between the wars" and is structured as "a long succession of short, vivid genre scenes set in cafes, bars, schoolyards, theaters, churches, kitchens and parlors."

Related title by the same author:

Readers may also be interested in *Wonder*, in which a Flemish teacher, drifting through life, allows a series of events to happen to himself that ultimately cause him to be institutionalized. After briefly meeting a mysterious woman at a party, he later conducts a search for her, in the company of a young male student. They end up at a meeting of former Nazi sympathizers, where the teacher pretends to have knowledge of their leader and engages in other dubious activities. Originally published in the early 1960s, this novel addresses the little-known Flemish role in World War II.

Subject keywords: family histories; war

Original language: Dutch

Sources consulted for annotation:

Amazon.com (book description).

The Complete Review (book review), http://www.complete-review.com.

Danny Yee's Book Reviews (book review), http://dannyreviews.com.

Global Books in Print (online) (review from *Kirkus Reviews* for *The Swordfish*).

"Hugo Claus." *Contemporary Authors Online*. Thomson Gale, 2008.

Hutchison, Paul E. *Library Journal* 115 (1 June 1990): 176.

Roter, Danielle. *Los Angeles Times*, 22 July 1990, p. 3.

Ruta, Suzanne. *The New York Times Book Review*, 1 July 1990 (online).

Some other translated books written by Hugo Claus: *The Swordfish*; *Desire*; *The Duck Hunt*; *Sister of Earth*; *Wonder*

Dirk Draulans. *The Red Queen: A Novel of the War Between the Sexes*.

Translated by Sam Garrett. New York: St. Martin's Press, 1998. 212 pages.

Genre/literary style/story type: speculative fiction

Diana hates men; she really and truly despises them. Thinking of herself as a messiah, she unleashes a plague designed to wipe out men. Her plan works to perfection, and her dream of an exclusively female society is about to be realized. But power has a way of corrupting all regimes, so it is not surprising when legal representatives of the new order begins to trample on individual rights even as they track down and kill the last few remaining men. As cloning and other similar techniques do not turn out to be the hoped-for panacea to repopulate Earth and as birth defects multiply, some of the women think that their only chance for survival lies in tracking down the last man on Earth.

Subject keyword: power

Original language: Dutch

Sources consulted for annotation:

Amazon.com (review from *Kirkus Reviews*).

D'Ammassa, Don. *The Science Fiction Chronicle* 19 (July/August 1998): 45.

Erwin Mortier. *My Fellow Skin*.

Translated by Ina Rilke. London: Harvill, 2003. 200 pages.

Genres/literary styles/story types: mainstream fiction; coming-of-age

Anton is a small boy who subconsciously prefers the world of men. Two traumatic events occur early on in his life: His uncle dies while playing with him; shortly thereafter, he is attacked by his cousin Roland. When he begins to attend school, he meets Willem, who will become his friend and lover—the person who liberates him from the religious and social strictures of his

circumscribed life. But just when they are about to take up their university studies, tragedy strikes again. A. S. Byatt compared the author to Proust for his "resurrection of lost significant moments."
Subject keywords: family histories; identity
Original language: Dutch
Sources consulted for annotation:
Byatt, A. S. *The Guardian*, 22 November 2003, p. 26.
Tonkin, Boyd. *The Independent*, 12 December 2003, p. 27.
Some other translated books written by Erwin Mortier: *Marcel*; *Shutterspeed*

Anne Provoost. *In the Shadow of the Ark.*
Translated by John Nieuwenhuizen. New York: A. A. Levine, 2004. 368 pages.
Genre/literary style/story type: historical fiction
When the waters rise, Re Jana and her family leave the marshlands where they have eked out a living by fishing and seek work in the desert. Here, they discover Noah, who is constructing a large ship to escape an impending flood. Re Jana's father begins to help with the ark's construction, while Re Jana and Ham, Noah's son, fall in love. Eventually, her father decides to build a boat of his own in this poignant retelling of the well-known biblical story.
Related title by the same author:
Readers may also enjoy *Looking into the Sun*, which features a perceptive eight-year-old girl living with her mother, who is slowly going blind, on an Australian ranch.
Subject keyword: religion
Original language: Dutch
Sources consulted for annotation:
Amazon.com (all editorial reviews).
Krug, Nora. *The New York Times Book Review*, 19 September 2004, p. 17.
McCay, Mary. *Booklist* 101 (15 February 2005): 1088.
Richards, Kelly Berner. *School Library Journal* 50 (October 2004): 193.
Roback, Diane, Brown, Jennifer M., and Joy Bean. *Publishers Weekly* 251 (25 October 2004): 49.
Some other translated books written by Anne Provoost: *My Aunt is a Pilot Whale*; *Falling*; *The Rose and the Swine*; *Looking into the Sun*

Peter Verhelst. *Tonguecat.*
Translated by Sherry Marx. New York: Farrar, Straus and Giroux, 2003. 331 pages.
Genre/literary style/story type: speculative fiction
Prometheus, who is known in Greek mythology for bringing fire to humankind, leaves the mythical world and descends to Earth, taking up residence in a constantly metamorphosing and transmogrifying city. He befriends the orphan Ulrike, who leads him into the city's impoverished bowels—a Hades-like place filled with social outcasts.
Subject keyword: urban life
Original language: Dutch
Sources consulted for annotation:
Amazon.com (book description).
Maristed, Kai. *Los Angeles Times*, 27 August 2003, p. E11.
Publishers Weekly 250 (14 July 2003): 53.

Léon de Winter. *God's Gym.*
Translated by Jeanette K. Ringold. New Milford, CT: Toby Press, 2009. 350 pages.
Genres/literary styles/story types: thrillers; political thrillers

Suspense and unrelenting action characterize this novel, which spans a single day in Los Angeles in 2000. Joop Koopman, a Dutch screenwriter, becomes involved in international espionage at the behest of a longtime friend, who works for an Israeli intelligence agency. He must also decide to remove his daughter Muriel from life support after a horrific motorcycle accident caused by a brawny gym owner whom he nevertheless befriends. At about the same time, he is drawn into the schemes and machinations of a Tibetan monk who turns up in the company of a distant relative with whom he was sexually obsessed as a teenager. It could only happen in Los Angeles, and de Winter makes it all seem highly plausible.
Subject keyword: urban life
Original language: Dutch
Sources consulted for annotation:
Global Books in Print (review from *Publishers Weekly*) (online).
Toby Press website (book description), http://www.tobypress.com.
Another translated book written by Léon de Winter: *Hoffman's Hunger*

The Netherlands

Gerbrand Bakker. *The Twin.*
Translated by David Colmer. Brooklyn, NY: Archipelago Press, 2009. 343 pages.
Genre/literary style/story type: mainstream fiction
Helmer is 19 years old and studying in Amsterdam when his life irrevocably changes. His twin brother Henk dies in a car accident, and Helmer is summoned home to take over the family farm. He does so reluctantly but has dutifully stayed for more than 30 years, peacefully doing what needs to be done, forging tight bonds with the animals, brooding about what could have been. His father has remained on the farm, a sullen presence whom Helmer, now in his mid-50s, moves to an upstairs room. He has the whole ground floor to himself—a milestone of independence. And then Henk's former girlfriend, now a widow, expresses a desire to visit Helmer's farm and leave her almost fully grown son with him.
Subject keywords: family histories; rural life
Original language: Dutch
Sources consulted for annotation:
Archipelago Books (book description), http://www.archipelagobooks.org.
The Complete Review (book review), http://www.complete-review.com.
Post, Chad W. Three Percent website, http://www.rochester.edu/College/translation/threepercent.

Abdelkader Benali. *Wedding by the Sea.*
Translated by Susan Massotty. New York: Arcade, 1999. 211 pages.
Genres/literary styles/story types: mainstream fiction; magical realism
In this humor-filled novel about the return of immigrants to their land of origin, Lamart Minar and his family travel back to their North African village for his sister Rebekka's wedding to their uncle, Mosa. But when Mosa gets cold feet and disappears on the day of the marriage, Lamart must convince him to come to his senses. The author is Dutch-Moroccan.
Subject keywords: family histories; rural life
Original language: Dutch
Sources consulted for annotation:
Amazon.com (review from *Kirkus Reviews*).
Mian, Emran. *The Herald*, 14 June 1999, p. 12.
Rohrbaugh, Lisa. *Library Journal* 125 (July 2000): 136.
Steinberg, Sybil S. *Publishers Weekly* 247 (29 May 2000): 52.

J. Bernlef (a pseudonym for Hendrik J. Marsman). *Eclipse*.
Translated by Paul Vincent. London: Faber and Faber, 1996. 149 pages.
Genre/literary style/story type: mainstream fiction
After a car accident in which he is plunged into a body of water, Kees Zomer is partially paralyzed. He has a full range of cognitive and intellectual powers, but his speech patterns are—to say the least—confused, and he has no physical feeling on his left side. As he struggles to express himself and to make himself understood, he is overwhelmed by frustration, isolation, and the eerie feeling that there has been a profound break in his perception of the world.
Subject keyword: identity
Original language: Dutch
Sources consulted for annotation:
Foundation for the Production and Translation of Dutch Literature (book description), http://www.nlpvf.nl.
Hermans, Theo, and Price, Barry. *The Babel Guide to Dutch & Flemish Fiction in English Translation*. Oxford, UK: Boulevard, 2001, p. 30.
Some other translated books written by J. Bernlef: *Out of Mind*; *Public Secret*

Arno Bohlmeijer. *To an Angel Who Is New*.
Translator unknown. Grand Rapids, MI: W. B. Eerdmans, 2004. 164 pages.
Genre/literary style/story type: mainstream fiction
Arno, Marian, and their two young daughters suffer serious injuries in a car accident. While Arno and the daughters are being treated at the hospital, Marian becomes comatose. Unable to communicate with her in person, Arno starts writing his wife letters from his hospital bed about the trials and tribulations of their psychological and emotional states. After Marian dies, her presence is an ongoing constant in the lives of the bereaved family. The novel is based on real events in the author's life.
Subject keyword: family histories
Original language: Dutch
Sources consulted for annotation:
Back cover of the book.
Ryan, Antonia. *National Catholic Reporter* 41 (12 November 2004): 21.
Another translated book written by Arno Bohlmeijer: *Something Very Sorry*

H. M. van den Brink. *On the Water*.
Translated by Paul Vincent. New York: Grove Press, 2001. 134 pages.
Genres/literary styles/story types: mainstream fiction; coming-of-age
Under the tutelage of an inscrutable and enigmatic German, Anton—a naïve teenager who lives with his morose and poverty-stricken family in government-assisted housing—learns to row competitively with David, whose wealth gives him the confidence and brashness that Anton lacks. As they become an almost unbeatable tandem in the coxless pair and as visions of participation in the Olympics dance before them, Anton briefly allows himself to dream of an existence far removed from the humdrum and cowardly life of his beaten-down father. But it is the summer of 1939, and even though the water shimmers and glows on the rivers of Amsterdam, the impeding tragedy of World War II is just around the corner.
Subject keyword: identity
Original language: Dutch
Sources consulted for annotation:
Amazon.com (book description).
Solomon, Chris. *The New York Times Book Review*, 22 July 2001, p. 16.

Topolski, Daniel. *The Guardian*, 17 February 2001, p. 10.
Zaleski, Jeff. *Publishers Weekly* 248 (2 April 2001): 40.

Renate Dorrestein. *A Heart of Stone*.
Translated by Hester Velmans. New York: Viking, 2001. 243 pages.
Genre/literary style/story type: mainstream fiction; women's lives
After the birth of Ida, Ellen van Bemmel's mother Margje degenerated into madness, conversing with a supernatural being who incites her to harm her loved ones. Previously, the family had lived a storybook life, operating a news-clipping service from their home. Now in her 30s and about to become a mother herself, Ellen recalls her mother's raging insanity, her sister's spate of injuries, her father's obliviousness, and the inexorable denouement, experiencing survivor's guilt and a harrowing sense of loss. This novel has been compared with Shirley Jackson's *We Have Always Lived in the Castle*.
Subject keyword: family histories
Original language: Dutch
Sources consulted for annotation:
Amazon.com (book description).
Huntley, Kristine. *Booklist* 97 (15 November 2000): 614.
Steinberg, Sybil S. *Publishers Weekly* 247 (13 November 2000): 84.
Some other translated books written by Renate Dorrestein: *Without Mercy*; *Unnatural Mothers*; *A Crying Shame*

Anna Enquist. *The Secret*.
Translated by Jeannette K. Ringold. London: Toby Press, 2000. 262 pages.
Genre/literary style/story type: mainstream fiction; women's lives
This novel focuses on the life of concert pianist Wanda Wiericke, including her relationship with her husband, whom she abandons when she has to choose between him and music. She has always used music as a refuge—a safe place to escape the intruding chaos of the world. But her peace is shattered when her dying mother reveals a secret that forces Wanda into isolation, resolved never to play again until she can digest what she has learned.
Related title by the same author:
Readers may also enjoy *The Homecoming*, which imaginatively retells the story of Elizabeth Batts, wife of the eighteenth-century explorer James Cook. As one after another of their six children dies during Cook's long absences and as she edits the reports of his travels, he is revealed to be less than the conquering historical hero.
Subject keyword: family histories
Original language: Dutch
Sources consulted for annotation:
Foundation for the Production and Translation of Dutch Literature, http://www.nlpvf.nl.
Hermans, Theo and Price, Barry. *The Babel Guide to Dutch & Flemish Fiction in English Translation*. Oxford, UK: Boulevard, 2001, p. 70.
The Toby Press (book review), http://www.tobypress.com.
Some other translated books written by Anna Enquist: *The Ice Carriers*; *The Masterpiece*; *The Injury*; *The Homecoming*

Carl Friedman. *Nightfather*.
Translated by Arnold and Erica Pomerans. New York: Persea Books, 1994. 129 pages.
Genre/literary style/story type: mainstream fiction; coming-of-age

This novel explores the profound impact of the Holocaust on its survivors and their children. An eight-year-old girl and her two older brothers must cope with a father, Ephraim, who never stops talking about his horrific death camp experiences. Eventually, he tells them about a murder that he committed and his liberation, which allowed him to reunite with his wife.
Subject keywords: anti-Semitism; family histories
Original language: Dutch
Sources consulted for annotation:
Graeber, Laurel. *The New York Times*, 17 September 1995 (online).
Klein, Richard. *School Library Journal* 41 (January 1995): 145.
Opello, Olivia. *Library Journal* 119 (1 September 1994): 215.
Publishers Weekly 241 (1 August 1994): 71.
Some other translated books written by Carl Friedman: *The Shovel and the Loom*; *The Gray Lover*

Arnon Grunberg. *Blue Mondays*.
Translated by Arnold and Erica Pomerans. New York: Farrar, Straus and Giroux, 1997. 278 pages.
Genres/literary styles/story types: mainstream fiction; coming-of-age
Arnon Grunberg has a world of adolescent problems: acne; a troubled home life; and authoritarian teachers. After deciding to drop out of high school, he cycles his way through numerous low-paying and futureless clerical jobs and consoles himself in the arms of prostitutes. When he runs out of money, he becomes a male escort. The novel has been compared with Philip Roth's *Goodbye, Columbus* in its depiction of a disaffected youth trying to find himself.
Related titles by the same author:
Under the heteronym of Marek van der Jagt, the author wrote *The Story of My Baldness*, which focuses on Marek, a teenager whose worries about the size of his penis lead to a series of tawdry conquests of women with self-esteem lower than his own. Readers may also enjoy *Jewish Messiah*, a biting satire about a young man from Switzerland whose fascination with Judaism knows no bounds. Setting out to atone for the tragic fate of the Jewish people during World War II; his grandfather's Nazi affiliation; and his mother's praise of Hitler's actions, he undergoes an unsuccessful circumcision, begins a love affair with a Jewish boy, translates *Mein Kampf* into Yiddish, is elected prime minister of Israel, and eventually leads the world toward Armageddon when he begins to sell nuclear arms. *Jewish Messiah* may profitably be read in conjunction with Joshua Cohen's *Witz*, which numerous critics have described as a comic masterpiece about the world's last remaining Jew. Benjamin Israelien, the sole survivor of a deadly plague and other nefarious machinations, suddenly becomes a celebrity to end all celebrities, with Jewishness as the newest cultural phenomenon.
Subject keyword: identity
Original language: Dutch
Sources consulted for annotation:
Amazon.com (reviews from *Kirkus Reviews* and other editorial reviews).
Biersdorfer, J. D. *The New York Times Book Review*, 2 February 1997, p. 11.
Cohen, Joshua. *Library Journal* 122 (January 1997): 146.
Dalkey Archive Press website (book descriptions), http://www.dalkeyarchive.com.
Global Books in Print (online) (reviews from *Booklist*, *Kirkus Reviews*, *Library Journal*, and *Publishers Weekly* for all novels).
Hooper, Brad. *Booklist* 93 (1 January/15 January 1997): 818.
Munson, Sam. *The New York Observer*, 13 December 2004, p. 1.
Steinberg, Sybil S. *Publishers Weekly* 243 (9 December 1996): 61.
Zaleski, Jeff. *Publishers Weekly* 251 (11 October 2004): 56.

Zeitchik, Steven. *Wall Street Journal*, 17 December 2004, p. W8.
Some other translated books written by Arnon Grunberg: *Silent Extras*; *Phantom Pain*; *Jewish Messiah*

Arthur Japin. *The Two Hearts of Kwasi Boachi.*
Translated by Ina Rilke. New York: Alfred A. Knopf, 2000. 384 pages.
Genres/literary styles/story types: mainstream fiction; coming-of-age
Based on historical events, this book describes the story of two Ashanti princes whom the Ashanti king sends to the Netherlands in the 1830s as part of a political exchange that will allow the Dutch to continue the practice of slavery under a more euphemistic term. They are to be educated in the ways of colonial aristocracy in their new surroundings among European royalty. They do their best to fit in, but their presence is met with a wary ambivalence that soon degenerates into barely concealed racism. Eventually, the princes lose their tight bond of friendship: One ends up in the Dutch East Indies, a repository of the memories of their arduous journey and experiences; the other returns to an Africa he no longer knows.
Subject keyword: colonization and colonialism
Original language: Dutch
Sources consulted for annotation:
Amazon.com (book description).
Huntley, Kristine. *Booklist* 97 (15 November 2000): 621.
Maslin, Janet. *The New York Times*, 21 December 2000, p. E12.
Pye, Michael. *The New York Times Book Review*, 10 December 2000, p. 9.
Steinberg, Sybil S. *Publishers Weekly* 247 (23 October 2000): 59.
Another translated book written by Arthur Japin: *In Lucia's Eyes*

Tim Krabbé. *The Vanishing.*
Translated by Claire Nicolas White. New York: Random House, 1993. 108 pages.
Genres/literary styles/story types: crime fiction; suspense
On their way to southern France from Holland for a well-deserved vacation, Rex Hofman and Saskia Ehlvest make an ordinary decision that will have momentous consequences. Who does not stop at a gas station on a long trip? And so they do; Saskia goes to the restroom in a course of events that is the epitome of banality. But she does not come back; she simply vanishes. Of course, Rex is wracked with guilt, even eight years later. When he is contacted by Saskia's alleged kidnapper, Rex puts himself at the mercy of this mysterious man in the hopes that he can discover what happened to her.
Subject keyword: social roles
Original language: Dutch
Sources consulted for annotation:
Keymer, David. *Library Journal* 118 (1 May 1993): 116.
Steinberg, Sybil S. *Publishers Weekly* 240 (12 April 1993): 47.
Some other translated books written by Tim Krabbé: *The Cave*; *The Rider*; *Delay*

Tessa de Loo. *The Twins.*
Translated by Ruth Levitt. New York: Soho, 2000. 352 pages.
Genre/literary style/story type: mainstream fiction
At age five, Anna and Lotte, twin German sisters, lost their parents. Raised separately, they do not meet again until 1990 at a Belgian hotel. Their different upbringings have given them very different views about society and politics, so their conversations about their respective pasts are sometimes fraught with tension. Anna lived with her impoverished grandmother in rural Germany and fell in

love with an Austrian SS officer, while Lotte grew up in the Netherlands, eventually marrying a Jewish man and working with war refugees. As the sisters discuss their divergent paths and as Anna's eagerness to re-establish their sisterly bonds meets with Lotte's recalcitrance, the ambiguities of family loyalty come to the forefront.

Subject keyword: family histories

Original language: Dutch

Sources consulted for annotation:

Ferguson, William. *The New York Times Book Review*, 27 August 2000, p. 18.

Henderson, David W. *Library Journal* 125 (July 2000): 138.

Hoover, Danise. *Booklist* 96 (July 2000): 2006.

Zaleski, Jeff. *Publishers Weekly* 250 (10 February 2003): 162.

Another translated book written by Tessa de Loo: *A Bed in Heaven*

Marga Minco. ***An Empty House.***

Translated by Margaret Clegg. London: Peter Owen, 1990. 151 pages.

Genre/literary style/story type: mainstream fiction

After Holland is freed from Nazi occupation, Yona and Sepha, two Jewish women—the only surviving members of their family—emerge from their hiding places. They find their houses to be forlorn and hollow carcasses, vacant of all warmth, joy, and future possibilities—a perfect representation of their own anomie.

Subject keyword: family histories

Original language: Dutch

Sources consulted for annotation:

Devereaux, Elizabeth. *The Village Voice*, 20 August 1991, p. 69.

Steinberg, Sybil S. *Publishers Weekly* 238 (4 January 1991): 57.

Some other translated books written by Marga Minco: *The Fall*; *The Glass Bridge*; *The Other Side*

Margriet de Moor. ***The Storm.***

Translated by Carol Brown Janeway. New York: Alfred A. Knopf, 2010. 257 pages.

Genre/literary style/story type: mainstream fiction

This is a numinous account of the multidimensional consequences of an innocent joke that tragically backfires. Lidy and Armanda are two sisters who bear an uncanny resemblance to each other; as a result, they decide to switch identities for a day in late January 1953. Lidy, who has a family, sets out to a party in Zeeland—a southern Dutch province bordering on Belgium that is largely made up of islands and river deltas—while Armanda stays in Amsterdam. Lidy dies almost immediately, swept up and drowned in the fierce hurricane that devastated Zeeland, killing almost 2,000 people and submerging large parts of the area. Armanda lives on into the first years of the twenty-first century, caught in a perpetual vortex of guilt and sorrow.

Related titles by the same author:

Readers may also be interested in *The Kreutzer Sonata*, which centers on Marius van Vlooten, a music critic who shoots himself in the head due to a failed love affair. Now blind, he is introduced to a violinist, whom he hastily marries after hearing her stunning interpretation of Beethoven's Kreutzer Sonata. But Marius becomes jealous of Suzanna's supposed relationship with another musician and tries to kill her. Also worthwhile may be *The Virtuoso*, in which a woman falls in love with a castrato singer. Readers may also enjoy *Duke of Egypt*, which explores the little-known world of the European Romani (typically though erroneously referred to as Gypsies). The Dutch owner of a horse farm marries a member of the Romani, who leaves each spring but returns in the fall.

Subject keyword: identity
Original language: Dutch
Sources consulted for annotation:
Global Books in Print (online) (reviews from *Kirkus Reviews* and *Publishers Weekly* for *Duke of Egypt*).
Haggas, Carol. *Booklist* 101 (1 January/15 January 2005): 813.
Harrison, Kathryn. *The New York Times Book Review*, 13 February 2005, p. 14.
Kline, Nancy. *The New York Times Book Review*, 4 April 2010 (online).
Publishers Weekly 252 (10 January 2005): 38.
Pye, Michael. *The New York Times Book Review*, 6 January 2002 (online).
Some other translated books written by Margriet de Moor: *Duke of Egypt*; *First Gray, Then White, Then Blue*; *The Virtuoso*; *The Kreutzer Sonata*

Marcel Möring. *The Dream Room*.
Translated by Stacey Knecht. New York: HarperCollins, 2003. 128 pages.
Genres/literary styles/story types: mainstream fiction; coming-of-age
The Speijir family leads what appears to be a placid existence in 1960s Holland, although storm clouds are brewing. They live above a toy shop. David is twelve and loves to cook, and one day he comes up with the idea that he and his unemployed father—a war pilot later injured while crop dusting—could build model planes for the shop owner. David's mother reluctantly goes along with the plan, hoping that it might spark her angst-ridden husband. But then they receive a visit from a wartime friend of his father. Now a food writer, Humbert Coe is pleased by David's interest in cooking, but he also becomes the key to unlocking the tensions that lie at the heart of the Speijirs's troubled existence.
Subject keywords: family histories; war
Original language: Dutch
Sources consulted for annotation:
Global Books in Print (online) (review from *Kirkus Reviews*).
Huntley, Kristine. *Booklist* (1 February 2002): 923.
Zaleski, Jeff. *Publishers Weekly* 249 (28 January 2002): 269.
Some other translated books written by Marcel Möring: *The Great Longing*; *In Babylon*

Harry Mulisch. *The Discovery of Heaven*.
Translated by Paul Vincent. New York: Viking, 1996. 730 pages.
Genre/literary style/story type: mainstream fiction
God is none too pleased with mankind; after all, they are collectively on the verge of discovering the fundamental secrets of creation through their work in the field of genetics. In fact, He wants to rescind the original biblical covenant, setting humanity adrift to fend for itself. But first He has to get the Ten Commandments back; to do this, He puts his faith in two angels who will then work out a plan to create an agent who will then return the tablets to their rightful heavenly home. The novel is full of the kind of metaphysical and linguistic arcana favored by Umberto Eco as well as profound philosophical and religious speculations that are reminiscent of the work of Thomas Mann and Dostoyevsky.
Related title by the same author:
Readers may also enjoy *Siegfried*, in which a Dutch novelist promoting his book meets Ullrich and Julia Falk, who were servants at Berchtesgaden, where Hitler often vacationed. Here, they were privy to a dark secret: Hitler and Eva Braun had a child, Siegfried. The Falks are ordered to pretend that the boy is theirs and then Ullrich is commanded to kill him because it is feared that he, because of his mother, is partly Jewish.

Subject keywords: religion; philosophy
Original language: Dutch
Sources consulted for annotation:
Amazon.com (book description; review from *Kirkus Reviews*).
Louire, Richard. *The New York Times Book Review*, 16 November 2003 (online).
Miles, Jack. *The New York Times Book Review*, 5 January 1997 (online).
Ross, Patricia. *Library Journal* 121 (15 October 1996): 91.
Steinberg, Sybil S. *Publishers Weekly* 243 (23 September 1996): 55.
Some other translated books written by Harry Mulisch: *The Assault*; *The Procedure*; *Last Call*; *Siegfried*; *Two Women*; *The Stone Bridal Bed*; *The Pupil*

Cees Nooteboom. *All Souls' Day*.
Translated by Susan Massotty. New York: Harcourt, 2001. 338 pages.
Genre/literary style/story type: mainstream fiction
Middle-aged Arthur Daane lives in Berlin and makes documentary films; he has cerebral friends with whom he converses about history and philosophy. His world is shattered when his wife and son die in a plane crash. In the throes of recovery from this ghastly incident, he meets Elik, a mysterious university student with her own traumatic past, as evidenced by her scarred face. As they become lovers and as they relocate to Spain, their lives are continually haunted by death, evil, and the past. The *Booklist* reviewer noted that the novel shows "the quiet heroics of individual lives lived in a world perpetually poised on the brink of chaos."
Related title by the same author:
Readers may also enjoy *Lost Paradise*, which centers on two Brazilian women who travel to Australia to escape a violent past, find employment at a literary festival where they dress as angels, and meet a venomous Dutch literary critic.
Subject keywords: family histories; identity
Original language: Dutch
Sources consulted for annotation:
Barbash, Tom. *The New York Times Book Review*, 9 December 2007 (online).
Global Books in Print (online) (reviews from *Booklist* and *Kirkus Reviews*).
Hall, Emily. *The New York Times Book Review*, 23 December 2001, p. 17.
Sullivan, Patrick. *Library Journal* 126 (August 2001): 163.
Zaleski, Jeff. *Publishers Weekly* 248 (8 October 2001): 41.
Some other translated books written by Cees Nooteboom: *Rituals*; *The Following Story*; *In the Dutch Mountains*; *A Song of Truth and Semblance*; *The Knight Has Died*; *Philip and the Others*; *Mokusei!: A Love Story*, *Lost Paradise*

Connie Palmen. *The Friendship*.
Translated by Ina Rilke. London: Harvill, 2000. 261 pages.
Genres/literary styles/story types: mainstream fiction; coming-of-age
Kit, a 10-year-old schoolgirl, befriends 13-year-old Ara, a new student who has a learning disability. As they become emotionally and psychologically inseparable, their friendship is frowned upon by just about everyone: other students, their mothers, and their teachers. As adults, they drift apart—Kit working at a university and studying psychology and philosophy; Ara finding employment as a dog trainer.
Subject keyword: identity
Original language: Dutch
Sources consulted for annotation:
Nussbaum, Lisa. *Library Journal* 125 (November 2000): 97.

Steinberg, Sybil S. *Publishers Weekly* 247 (25 September 2000): 86.
Another translated book written by Connie Palmen: *The Laws*

Ilja Leonard Pfeijffer. *Rupert: A Confession.*
Translated by Michele Hutchison. Rochester, NY: Open Letter, 2009. 172 pages.
Genres/literary styles/story types: crime fiction; suspense
Rupert, who used to work at a peep show emporium, has been accused of a crime against a female victim, but he vehemently proclaims his innocence. For three days, he tries to convince a jury that he is incapable of acting in any capacity whatsoever. He is merely a spectator, not a perpetrator of evil. But is he really innocent or is his claim of passivity the very proof of his guilt?
Subject keyword: social roles
Original language: Dutch
Sources consulted for annotation:
The Complete Review (book review), http://www.complete-review.com.
Open Letter Press (book description), http://catalog.openletterbooks.org.

Maya Rasker. *Unknown Destination.*
Translated by Barbara Fasting. New York: Ballantine Books, 2000. 215 pages.
Genre/literary style/story type: mainstream fiction
On the day that would have been the sixth birthday of Lizzy—their deceased daughter—Gideon Salomon's wife Raya goes to a bar and then abruptly vanishes. Poring over letters and photographs, Gideon desperately tries to unravel the mystery of his wife's disappearance, finally realizing that his wife's struggle to reconcile motherhood and art was unsuccessful. He also makes a shattering discovery about her role in the death of their daughter.
Subject keyword: family histories
Original language: Dutch
Sources consulted for annotation:
Amazon.com (book description).
Johnston, Bonnie. *Booklist* 98 (1 January/15 January 2002): 813.
Rohrbaugh, Lisa. *Library Journal* 127 (January 2002): 154.

Helga Ruebsamen. *The Song and the Truth.*
Translated by Paul Vincent. New York: Alfred A. Knopf, 2000. 355 pages.
Genres/literary styles/story types: mainstream fiction; coming-of-age
In the Dutch East Indies before World War II, five-year-old Lulu and her parents, Cees and Helene Benda, live a relatively comfortable existence far from the center of things. But with the arrival of ominous news about the political and military situation in Europe, Lulu's father, a physician, is called back in 1939 to the Netherlands, now occupied by the Germans. Lulu accompanies him, but her mother and younger brother opt for the perceived safety of London. Eventually, she and her father must hide from Nazi forces—an arduous and transformative experience that will leave indelible scars.
Subject keywords: family histories; war
Original language: Dutch
Sources consulted for annotation:
Amazon.com (book description).
Chadwell, Faye A. *Library Journal* 125 (August 2000): 161.
McFall, Gardner. *The New York Times Book Review*, 5 November 2000, p. 23.
Rochman, Hazel. *Booklist* 97 (1 September 2000): 67.
Steinberg, Sybil S. *Publishers Weekly* 247 (24 July 2000): 66.

Philibert Schogt. *Daalder's Chocolates.*
Translated by Sherry Marx. New York: Thunder's Mouth Press, 2000. 322 pages.
Genre/literary style/story type: mainstream fiction
Joop Daalder used to study art history, but he has now become a chocolatier. He moves to Toronto with his wife Emma, where he earns renown for the delicacy and sophistication of his creations. But when his small shop is threatened by the arrival of a multinational food store, he must make a difficult choice, especially because the new superstore has three chocolatiers on staff.
Related title by the same author:
Readers may also enjoy *The Wild Numbers*, in which a mid-level mathematics professor, Isaac Swift, believes that he has solved what is referred to as Beauregard's Wild Number Problem. With visions of fame dancing in his head, Swift is quickly brought down to Earth by a rival who scoffs at Swift's solution. Soon, plagiarism charges follow, and violence is not far behind.
Subject keyword: urban life
Original language: Dutch
Sources consulted for annotation:
Amazon.com (book description for *The Wild Numbers*).
Back cover of the book (*Daalder's Chocolates*).
Global Books in Print (online) (reviews from *Library Journal* and *Publishers Weekly* for *Daalder's Chocolates*).
Steinberg, Sybil S. *Publishers Weekly* 247 (6 March 2000): 83.
Sullivan, Patrick. *Library Journal* 125 (1 April 2000): 132.

Janwillem van de Wetering. *Just a Corpse at Twilight.*
Translator unknown. New York: Soho, 1994. 265 pages.
Genres/literary styles/story types: crime fiction; private investigators
This book is part of the author's popular Grijpstra and de Gier detective series featuring Henk Grijpstra and Rinus de Gier, retirees from the Amsterdam police force. Grijpstra, now a private detective, receives a disturbing late-night call from his former partner, who is afraid that he has caused the death of his girlfriend while he was in an alcoholic stupor. Likewise, he is now being blackmailed by two friends who claim to have disposed of the girlfriend's body. Grijpstra makes the long journey to Maine, where de Gier lives on an island, to help solve this tangled mystery. Other books in the *Amsterdam Cop* series are: *Outsider in Amsterdam*; *Tumbleweed*; *The Corpse on the Dike*; *Death of a Hawker*; *The Japanese Corpse*; *The Blond Baboon*; *The Maine Massacre*; *The Mind Murders*; *The Streetbird*; *The Rattle-Rat*; *Hard Rain*; *The Hollow-Eyed Angel*; *The Perfidious Parrot*; and *The Amsterdam Cops: Collected Stories*.
Subject keyword: rural life
Original language: Dutch
Sources consulted for annotation:
Amazon.com (review from *Kirkus Reviews*).
Brainard, Dulcy. *Publishers Weekly* 241 (5 September 1994): 94.
San Francisco Chronicle, 12 November 1994, p. D8.
Some other translated books written by Janwillem van de Wetering: *The Butterfly Hunter*; *Seesaw Millions*

Lulu Wang. *The Lily Theater: A Novel of Modern China.*
Translated by Hester Velmans. New York: Nan A. Talese/Doubleday, 2000. 434 pages.
Genres/literary styles/story types: mainstream fiction; coming-of-age
In the early 1970s during the Chinese Cultural Revolution, 12-year-old Lian's parents have been sent to rural re-education camps. Allowed home visits on the weekend, Lian's mother, a history

professor, persuades a communist official to allow her to take Lian back with her to the camp. Here, Lian is given a first-rate education by an array of banished intellectuals who become her friends and guardians. Soon, she is giving history lessons of her own to the wildlife in a nearby pond, which she calls the Lily Theater. When Lian returns to the city, her friendship with Kim, whose parents are peasants, is irretrievably changed because of class differences.
Subject keywords: politics; power
Original language: Dutch
Sources consulted for annotation:
Amazon.com (book description).
Huntley, Kristine. *Booklist* 97 (1 September 2000): 64.
Schwartz, John Burnham. *The New York Times Book Review*, 10 September 2000, p. 9.
Steinberg, Sybil S. *Publishers Weekly* 247 (24 July 2000): 67.

Denmark

Solvej Balle. *According to the Law: Four Accounts of Mankind.*
Translated by Barbara Haveland. New York: HarperCollins, 1996. 89 pages.
Genres/literary styles/story types: mainstream fiction; short stories
Four people—a biochemist, a law student, a mathematician, and a sculptor—struggle with the most basic of questions: their sense of their emotional and physical selves. The mathematician and the sculptor want to dissolve into the surrounding atmosphere and approach nothingness; the law student has the extraordinary capacity to inflict physical pain on others just by looking at them; and the biochemist ponders official guidelines for death.
Subject keywords: identity; philosophy
Original language: Danish
Source consulted for annotation:
Global Books in Print (online) (reviews from *Publishers Weekly*).

Leif Davidsen. *The Russian Singer.*
Translated by Jørgen Schiøtt. New York: Random House, 1991. 277 pages.
Genres/literary styles/story types: thrillers; political thrillers
Jack Andersen, a Danish diplomat posted to Moscow, has a big problem. His secretary apparently has committed suicide, slitting her wrists while in a bathtub. But there is also the problem of a dead prostitute in the next room. And while the Soviet police are content to label the crime as a murder-suicide involving lesbians, Andersen is not convinced, especially when it turns out that the two women were involved in pornography.
Subject keyword: power
Original language: Danish
Sources consulted for annotation:
Callendar, Newgate. *The New York Times*, 6 October 1991, p. A33.
Publishers Weekly 238 (7 June 1991): 55.
The Virginia Quarterly Review 68 (Winter 1992): 23.
Some other translated books written by Leif Davidsen: *Lime's Photograph*; *The Sardine Deception*; *The Serbian Dane*; *The Unholy Alliances*

Peter H. Fogtdal. *The Tsar's Dwarf.*
Translated by Tiina Nunnally. Portland, OR: Hawthorne Books & Literary Arts, 2008. 286 pages.
Genre/literary style/story type: historical fiction

In the early 1800s, when Peter the Great visits Denmark, the Russian tsar is presented with an unusual gift: a disfigured female dwarf named Sørine. The tsar takes her to St. Petersburg to serve as a court jester and then sends her to a cloister to be violently purged of any vestiges of postlapsarian evil. Eventually, she is displayed in the tsar's famous cabinet of curiosities—a room-sized collection of a motley assortment of odd and rare items that testified to the aristocratic owner's interest in all aspects of natural history: fossils, stuffed animals, relics, rocks, and even fetuses. At first, Sørine rebels against her harsh fate, lashing out at her captors in numerous and aggressive shows of independence, and then she slowly begins to accept her situation.
Subject keywords: identity; power
Original language: Danish
Sources consulted for annotation:
Global Books in Print (online) (synopsis/book jacket).
Kyzer, Larissa. Three Percent website (book review), http://www.rochester.edu/College/translation/threepercent.

Jens Christian Grøndahl. ***An Altered Light.***
Translated by Anne Born. Orlando, FL: Harcourt, 2004. 271 pages.
Genres/literary styles/story types: mainstream fiction; women's lives
Irene Beckmen is in her mid-50s, a well-respected lawyer, and an ultra-sophisticated beauty. But when her husband Martin informs her that he is in love with a woman decidedly younger than her, Irene is hurt but soon enough takes matters into her own hands. She resurrects a love affair from the past, eventually discovering that her real father is a cellist with whom her mother had an affair.
Related titles by the same author:
Readers may also enjoy *Lucca*, which focuses on an actress whose husband has just informed her that he wants a divorce. In the throes of anger, she has a tragic car accident. At the hospital, a surgeon named Robert saves her life but not her eyesight. As Lucca recuperates and as the doctor takes the time to watch and wait by her bedside during his off hours, a bond slowly develops, and each opens up to the other about their failed personal lives. Also of interest may be *Silence in October*, a melancholy rumination about the effects of divorce after 18 years of marriage.
Subject keyword: family histories
Original language: Danish
Sources consulted for annotation:
Amazon.com (book description).
Evans, Janet. *Library Journal* 130 (15 March 2005): 70.
Global Books in Print (online) (reviews from *Publishers Weekly* and *Library Journal* for *Lucca*; review from *Booklist* for *Silence in October*).
Publishers Weekly 252 (31 January 2005): 46.
Wilkinson, Joanne. *Booklist* 101 (1 March 2005): 1137.
Some other translated books written by Jens Christian Grøndahl: *Lucca*; *Silence in October*; *Virginia*

Peter Høeg. ***Smilla's Sense of Snow.***
Translated by Tiina Nunnally. New York: Farrar, Straus and Giroux, 1993. 453 pages.
Genres/literary styles/story types: thrillers; conspiracy thrillers
Smilla Jaspersen, a Greenlander of Inuit ancestry now living in Copenhagen, knows everything that there is to know about snow and ice, having published a handful of academic papers on how to classify various types of these substances. When a small Inuit boy who lives in her apartment building allegedly falls off the roof, Smilla does not believe the official explanations, partly because she has examined the boy's tracks in the snow and concluded that he was fleeing from

something at the time of his fatal plunge. Of course, no one takes her seriously, but Smilla persists in her investigation, eventually discovering that the boy's father, who worked for a Danish mining corporation, was mysteriously killed just a few years ago and his heirs were handsomely compensated with an extravagant pension. As she learns more and more about the corporation, she is drawn ever deeper into a scientific conspiracy of unimaginable proportions that extends back to World War II.

Related titles by the same author:

Readers may find *The Woman and the Ape* to be the perfect follow-up to *Smilla's Sense of Snow*. Adam is a dissolute British zoologist whose sister discovers an ape named Erasmus—a representative of a new species. If true, Adam would be famous. Thus, Erasmus is hidden away in a building behind Adam's home. But Adam's Danish wife Madelene suspects that something is not quite right: Too many people are visiting the building, and too many inexplicable events are occurring. Soon, she befriends Erasmus, discovers that he can talk, and helps him escape. In time, they become lovers, and she teaches him English and Danish. Then, she must choose between the ape and Adam. Some critics have invoked Marian Engel's *The Bear* and William Boyd's *Brazzaville Beach* when discussing this novel. Also of interest may be Høeg's *Tales of the Night*, in which each of the Kafkaesque-like stories comes to a close on March 19, 1929, and *Borderliners*, a scathing indictment of the Danish educational system.

Subject keyword: politics

Original language: Danish

Sources consulted for annotation:

Dunn, Katherine. *The Washington Post*, 26 April 1998, p. X4.

Global Books in Print (online) (reviews from *Kirkus Reviews* and *Publishers Weekly*).

Ott, Bill. *Booklist* 94 (1 January/15 January 1998): 776.

Parini, Jay. *The New York Times Book Review*, 1 March 1998, p. 34.

Queenan, Joe. *The New York Times Book Review*, 22 December 1996 (online).

Schillinger, Liesl. *The New York Times Book Review*, 11 November 2007 (online).

Steinberg, Sybil S. *Publishers Weekly* 245 (5 January 1998): 60.

Some other translated books written by Peter Høeg: *Tales of the Night*; *Borderliners*; *The Woman and the Ape*; *The History of Danish Dreams*; *The Quiet Girl*

Christian Jungersen. *The Exception*.

Translated by Anna Paterson. New York: Nan A. Talese/Doubleday, 2006. 502 pages.

Genres/literary styles/story types: thrillers; political thrillers

This novel focuses on five staff members who work at the Danish Center for Information on Genocide. When threatening e-mails are sent to two of them, they immediately suspect a war criminal from Serbia whom they have investigated. But suspicion quickly devolves onto one of their office mates, resulting in a series of concerted physiological attacks on the alleged perpetrator that mirrors the type of behavior that they regularly denounce on the world stage. As Marcel Theroux writes, the book expertly captures "the texture of office life, the appalling inconsistencies and lacunas in our perceptions of our own characters, the way intelligent people use the insights of psychology not to deepen their self-awareness but to calumniate one another with more sophisticated accusations."

Subject keywords: politics; power

Original language: Danish

Sources consulted for annotation:

Global Books in Print (online) (reviews from *Booklist*, *Library Journal*, and *Publishers Weekly*).

Theroux, Marcel. *The New York Times Book Review*, 22 July 2007 (online).

Michael Larsen. *Uncertainty.*

Translated by Lone Thygesen Blecher and George Blecher. New York: Harcourt Brace, 1996. 260 pages.

Genres/literary styles/story types: crime fiction; amateur detectives

As a newspaper reporter in Denmark's capital, Martin Molberg is accustomed to the odd and the strange. But when his girlfriend, a flight attendant, is murdered, things really get strange. Martin becomes the prime suspect despite vociferously proclaiming his innocence. As every clue leads to a dead end and as the truth recedes further and further, Martin has only one chance left to find out what really happened: tracing the man with whom his girlfriend had sex in a Los Angeles luxury hotel.

Subject keyword: urban life

Original language: Danish

Sources consulted for annotation:

Amazon.com (book description; review from *Kirkus Reviews*).

Armstrong, Robert. *Star Tribune*, 5 April 1998, p. 16F.

Gaughan, Thomas. *Booklist* 92 (August 1996): 1886.

Steinberg, Sybil S. *Publishers Weekly* 243 (15 July 1996): 55.

Another translated book written by Michael Larsen: *The Snake in Sydney*

Morten Ramsland. *Doghead.*

Translated by Tiina Nunnally. New York: Thomas Dunne Books/St. Martin's Press, 2009. 383 pages.

Genre/literary style/story type: historical fiction

This book is a ribald, rambunctious, and ultimately generous saga about three generations of a Norwegian family, the Erikssons, who have endured more than their share of difficulties and absurdities. As the matriarch of the family lies on her deathbed, she debunks the stories and legends that have grown up around the family, lifting the veil from people who have been war profiteers, alcoholics, voyeurs, and adulterers. The author has referred to his novel as an example of grotesque realism. European literary critics have been unanimous in praising this novel, variously comparing it to Günter Grass's *The Tin Drum*, Frank McCourt's *Angela's Ashes*, Isabel Allende's *The House of Spirits* as well as making comparisons with the work of John Irving, T. C. Boyle, Jonathan Franzen, Peter Høeg, and Gabriel García Márquez.

Subject keyword: family histories

Original language: Danish

Sources consulted for annotation:

Clark, Clare. *The New York Times Book Review*, 1 March 2009 (online).

Thomas Dunne Macmillan website (book description), http://us.macmillan.com.

Henrik Stangerup. *Snake in the Heart.*

Translated by Anne Born. London: Marion Boyars, 1996. 315 pages.

Genre/literary style/story type: mainstream fiction

The Danish journalist Max Mollerup is in a bad way. His best days lie behind him—the heady promise of a limitless career long dissipated. All he has left is the crumbling present, which he is spending in 1960s Paris. Or, rather, wasting away in 1960s Paris because his main activities include visiting prostitutes, stalking ex-lovers, making paper airplanes, and plagiarizing the work of others. As he grows increasingly misanthropic, his gloom and alienation deepen.

Subject keyword: identity

Original language: Danish

Sources consulted for annotation:
Amazon.com (review from *Midwest Book Review*).
Harris, Michael. *Los Angeles Times*, 8 July 1996, p. 6.
Steinberg, Sybil S. *Publishers Weekly* 243 (12 February 1996): 60.
Some other translated books written by Henrik Stangerup: *The Man Who Wanted To Be Guilty*; *The Road to Lagoa Santa*; *Brother Jacob*; *The Seducer: It Is Hard To Die In Dieppe*

Hanne Marie Svendsen. *The Gold Ball.*
Translated by Jørgen Schiøtt. New York: Alfred A. Knopf, 1989. 245 pages.
Genres/literary styles/story types: mainstream fiction; magical realism
Some critics have invoked Gabriel García Márquez's *One Hundred Years of Solitude* in describing *The Gold Ball*, which recounts the intertwining story of numerous generations of a family who live on a fictional island near the Danish coast. Thus, in the course of some 400 years, extraordinary legends, folktales, and accumulated oral wisdom have combined to render the island a mythical place that encapsulates a wider social and cultural history.
Subject keyword: family histories
Original language: Danish
Sources consulted for annotation:
Hughes, Mary Gray. *Chicago Tribune*, 10 December 1989, p. 146.
Koger, Grove. *Library Journal* 114 (July 1989): 111.
Schott, Webster. *The Washington Post*, 21 December 1989, p. D9.
Steinberg, Sybil S. *Publishers Weekly* 235 (9 June 1989): 52.
Another translated book written by Hanne Marie Svendsen: *Under the Sun*

Dorrit Willumsen. *Marie: A Novel About the Life of Madame Tussaud.*
Translated by Patricia Crampton. London: Bodley Head, 1986. 213 pages.
Genres/literary styles/story types: historical fiction; women's lives
If you have ever been to a wax museum, you have probably heard the name of Madame Tussaud. There's a real person behind all that wax, and this novel explores the origins and evolution of that real person—from her days as an apprentice to a Swiss physician; her early wax models of such luminaries as Jean-Jacques Rousseau; her work as an art teacher at the court of Louis XVI; her fraught life during the French Revolution; her emigration to London; and the founding of a permanent home for her growing collection.
Subject keyword: family histories
Original language: Danish
Sources consulted for annotation:
Review of Contemporary Fiction 15 (Spring 1995): 137.
Schack, May. *Danish Literary Magazine* (2006), http://www.danishliterature.info.
Another translated book written by Dorrit Willumsen: *If It Really Were a Film*

Estonia

Jaan Kross. *The Czar's Madman.*
Translated by Anselm Hollo. New York: Pantheon Books, 1993. 362 pages.
Genre/literary style/story type: historical fiction
Timotheus von Bock, a nineteenth-century Estonian aristocrat, was very much his own man and someone decades ahead of his time. As narrated through a diary kept by Jakob Mattik, his lowly brother-in-law, von Bock scorned the privileges associated with his birth and station. He married a chambermaid; freed serfs working his lands; was imprisoned for almost 10 years when he sent

the Russian tsar a letter critically analyzing the many shortcomings of Russia as a nation and the tsar as a person; and underwent house arrest as a madman.
Subject keywords: politics; power
Original language: Estonian
Sources consulted for annotation:
Brennan, Geraldine. *The Guardian*, 10 April 1994 (from Proquest databases).
Kempe, Frederick. *Wall Street Journal*, 23 May 1994, p. A13.
Montgomery, Isobel. *The Guardian*, 24 March 1994, (from Proquest databases).
Opello, Olivia. *Library Journal* 117 (15 November 1992): 101.
Steinberg, Sybil S. *Publishers Weekly* 239 (26 October 1992): 54.
Some other translated books written by Jaan Kross: *The Conspiracy & Other Stories*; *Professor Martens' Departure*; *Treading Air*; *The Rock from the Sky*

Viivi Luik. *The Beauty of History.*
Translated by Hildi Hawkins. Norwich, UK: Norvik Press, 2007. 152 pages.
Genre/literary style/story type: mainstream fiction
A young Estonian woman who resembles the author visits Riga (Latvia) to meet Lion, her Jewish Latvian lover. It is 1968, and there is possibility in the air, especially in Czechoslovakia. But the Baltics are a different story. Here, everything is a struggle: cramped living quarters; finding a common language; deciphering the meaning of the clothes that one wears; the legacy of the Baltic underground resistance movement; and interminable train journeys. When Lion goes to Moscow to discuss possible military exemption; when his Estonian friend stays behind in his apartment surrounded by an unbelievable accumulation of odds and ends; when she finally travels back to Estonia, history has moved on and yet it has not. According to Eric Dickens, this lyrical and poetic novel limns "what it was like to live in an vassal state of the Soviet Union."
Subject keywords: politics; power
Original language: Estonian
Sources consulted for annotation:
Dickens, Eric. Three Percent website (book review), http://www.rochester.edu/College/translation/threepercent.
Global Books in Print (online) (synopsis/book jacket).

Emil Tode (a.k.a. Tõnu Õnnepalu and Anton Nigov). *Border State.*
Translated by Madli Puhvel. Evanston, IL: Northwestern University Press, 2000. 100 pages.
Genre/literary style/story type: mainstream fiction
This novel focuses on a lonely gay man who wanders the streets of Paris and entertains notions of drowning himself in the Seine. Drifting back and forth between hallucinations and reality and between the fleeting comfort that evanescent hope brings and monochromatic despair, he has no real sense of himself, of belonging anywhere, of being fully human.
Subject keyword: identity
Original language: Estonian
Sources consulted for annotation:
Mikiver, Ilmar. *World Literature Today* 74 (Autumn 2000): 835.
Miller, Gregory. *The San Diego Union-Tribune*, 16 July 1000, p. Books 8.

Mati Unt. *Things in the Night.*
Translated by Eric Dickens. Normal, IL: Dalkey Archive Press, 2006. 316 pages.
Genres/literary styles/story types: mainstream fiction; postmodernism

Tallinn, Estonia's capital, may soon be without electricity when the protagonist devises a plan to sabotage the local power plant. Originally published in 1990 when Estonia was part of the Soviet Union, the book describes an ice-bound postapocalyptic city shivering in the dark and waiting for a possible savior. Brendan Driscoll praises Unt for the "mastery of postmodern literary form, fracturing and recombining werewolf tales and other traditional Estonian tropes into an ironic, multivocal sprawl through subjectivity itself."
Related titles by the same author:
Readers may also enjoy *Diary of a Blood Donor*, where Joonatan Hark travels to Leningrad to meet a mysterious stranger on board the *Aurora*, a ship associated with the Russian Revolution. Here, he is initiated into a supernatural world populated by vampires. Critics have referred to this book as an update of Bram Stoker's *Dracula*. Also of interest may be *Brecht at Night*, a historically based book that imaginatively reconstructs the dramatist Bertolt Brecht's sojourn in Finland at a particularly fraught moment. It is 1940, and Brecht wants to take his family to the safety and comforts of the United States. In addition to examining the tense relations between Finland and the Soviet Union, the book also depicts the historical background of the Soviet annexation of the Baltic states, especially Estonia.
Subject keywords: power; urban life
Original language: Estonian
Sources consulted for annotation:
Back cover of the book.
The Complete Review (book reviews), http://www.complete-review.com.
Dickens, Eric. Afterword in the book.
Driscoll, Brendan. *Booklist* 102 (15 February 2006): 46.
Global Books in Print (online) (review from *Publishers Weekly* for *Diary of a Blood Donor*).
Saunders, Kate. *The Times*, 25 March 2006, p. 15.
Some other translated books written by Mati Unt: *The Autumn Ball: Scenes of City Life*; *Brecht at Night*; *Diary of a Blood Donor*

Finland

Elina Hirvonen. *When I Forgot*.
Translated by Douglas Robinson. Portland, OR: Tin House Books, 2009. 184 pages.
Genre/literary style/story type: mainstream fiction
This is an elegant and searing novel about the effects of 9/11 on people in Finland, especially Anna Louhinitty and her older brother Joona, who is battling psychological demons. The book is set some 18 months after the tragic events in New York, when Anna sits alone at a Helsinki coffeehouse trying to read Michael Cunningham's *The Hours*. However, it is a lost cause because her thoughts inexorably circle back to her numerous preoccupations. She worries about her job as a reporter, her boyfriend, and her mother. But above all, she worries about Joona. As the twin towers collapsed, all of Anna's hopes that her brother would get better also collapsed. She finally realizes the stark reality of who he is and who she is. As Liesl Schillinger points out, Hirvonen's unforgettable novel invokes and mirrors Virginia Woolf's *Mrs. Dalloway*, revealing the way in which "a lifetime may be contained and revealed in small, seemingly inconsequential details."
Subject keywords: family histories; identity
Original language: Finnish
Source consulted for annotation:
Schillinger, Liesl. *The New York Times Book Review*, 10 May 2009 (online).

Matti Yrjänä Joensuu. *The Priest of Evil*.
Translated by David Hackston. London: Arcadia, 2006. 204 pages.

Genres/literary styles/story types: crime fiction; police detectives
Detective Sergeant Timo Harjunpaa is a specialist in arson and explosives for the Helsinki police department. His skills have never been more needed than now. At the behest of a religious cult leader, teenagers are carrying bombs, concealed in their backpacks, aboard the city's subway system. The novel has been compared to Graham Greene's *The Third Man*; critics have also seen affinities between the tormented Harjunpaa and Henning Mankell's Kurt Wallander.
Subject keyword: urban life
Original language: Finnish
Sources consulted for annotation:
The Independent, 23 June 2006, p. 22.
Millar, Peter. *The Times*, 10 June 2006, p. 14.
Some other translated books written by Matti Yrjänä Joensuu: *The Stone Murders*; *To Steal Her Love*

Leena Krohn. *Tainaron: Mail from Another City.*
Translated by Hildi Hawkins. Holicong, PA: Prime Books, 2004. 124 pages.
Genres/literary styles/story types: mainstream fiction; epistolary fiction
A woman has mysteriously arrived in Tainaron, a mythological city of insects at the gates of Hades. She writes her lover a series of letters—30 in all—but she gets no replies. Thus, she begins to explore her new home, accompanied by an enigmatic guide. The author is well-known as a fabulist; she has also published *Pereat Mundus*, a novel about a shape-shifting being who assumes the oddest appearances, including a vendor of ice cream.
Subject keyword: aging
Original language: Finnish
Sources consulted for annotation:
Global Books in Print (online) (book description for *Pereat Mundus*).
Nestingen, Andrew. *Scandinavian Studies* 76 (1 July 2004): 233.
Publishers Weekly 251 (15 November 2004): 45.
Some other translated books written by Leena Krohn: *Doña Quixote and Other Citizens*; *Gold of Ophir*; *Pereat Mundus*

Sofi Oksanen. *Purge.*
Translated by Lola Rogers. New York: Grove/Atlantic, 2010. 416 pages.
Genres/literary styles/story types: mainstream fiction; women's lives
The Soviet occupation of the Baltic states, including Estonia, was politically and socially charged—a sordid and messy affair with contemporary repercussions. Aliide Truu is a survivor; she lives alone in a rural part of Estonia—far from the excesses of modernity. But modernity has a way of catching up with people, and one morning in the early 1990s, Aliide discovers Zara, a young woman very much the worse for wear, in her front garden. Zara is an escapee from a sex-trafficking organization, but her appearance in Aliide's yard is almost foreordained because they share a dark history that goes to the heart and soul of Estonia's past, especially the long years spent under Soviet occupation in the twentieth century.
Subject keywords: power; war
Original language: Finnish
Source consulted for annotation:
Grove/Atlantic website (book description), http://www.groveatlantic.com.

Arto Paasilinna. *The Year of the Hare.*
Translated by Herbert Lomas. London: Peter Owen, 1995. 135 pages.

Genres/literary styles/story types: adventure; quest
When a journalist and a photographer accidently hit a rabbit on a rural road, the journalist's life is fundamentally altered. Disconsolate, he gets out of their vehicle and sets off in search of the hare. As man and animal becomes inseparable friends, they embark on a poignant series of adventures that reveal to them the extent to which humans are vile, backstabbing, and hypocritical, not to mention drones with no sense of the myriad possibilities of a life well-lived. These adventures transform the journalist's perspective on just about everything: his job; his marriage; his finances; and his possessions.
Related title by the same author:
Readers may also enjoy *The Howling Miller*, which focuses on a socially uncouth man who restores a mill in the far northern reaches of Finland.
Subject keywords: identity; philosophy
Original language: Finnish
Sources consulted for annotation:
Amazon.com (review from *Publishers Weekly*).
St. John, Janet. *Booklist* 92 (1 September 1995): 42.
Van Lanen, E. J. Three Percent website (book review), http://www.rochester.edu/College/translation/threepercent.
Another translated book written by Arto Paasilinna: *The Howling Miller*

Kalle Päätalo. *After the Storm*.
Translated by Richard A. Impola. New Paltz, NY: FATA, 2002. 422 pages.
Genre/literary style/story type: historical fiction
This is the fourth book of a five-part Finnish historical saga that focuses on three interconnected families. This novel is set after World War II, when not much was left of Finland in the wake of retreating armies. Almost everything had to be rebuilt from the ground up. As families struggle with impoverished conditions, the vague premises of national recovery glimmer on the horizon. The first book in the series is *Our Daily Bread*, which describes how Finns survived during the 1930s, a time of worldwide economic depression. In the last book of the series, *The Winter of the Black Snow*, the author examines some of the consequences of modernization, including television and the desire of young people to move to Sweden.
Subject keyword: family histories
Original language: Finnish
Source consulted for annotation:
Kellam Book Shop, http://www.kellamknives.com.
Some other translated books written by Kalle Päätalo: *Our Daily Bread*; *Before the Storm*; *Storm Over the Land: A Novel About War*; *Before the Storm*; *The Winter of the Black Snow*

Antti Tuuri. *The Winter War*.
Translated by Richard A. Impola. Beaverton, ON: Aspasia Books, 2003. 208 pages.
Genre/literary style/story type: historical fiction
This novel is an authentic and detailed examination of the lives of the Finnish soldiers who fought against the Russians during Russia's invasion of Finland in 1939. During the 100 or so days that the Winter War lasted, there were innumerable acts of heroism by men committed to upholding Finnish national pride and repelling the invading forces. Writing about the movie that was made from this book, Kevin Thomas observed that it provides "a collective portrait of sturdy, resilient men, most of whom are taciturn farmers sustained by a strong sense of community, a deep reverence for God and an earthy sense of humor."
Subject keywords: power; war

Original language: Finnish
Sources consulted for annotation:
Chapters.Indigo.ca (book description).
Northwindbooks.com (book review), http://northwindbooks.com.
Thomas, Kevin. *Los Angeles Times*, 8 December 1989, p. 4.
Another translated book written by Antti Tuuri: *A Day in Ostrobothnia*

Marja-Liisa Vartio. *The Parson's Widow.*
Translated by Aili Flint. Champaign, IL: Dalkey Archive Press. 2008. 256 pages.
Genre/literary style/story type: mainstream fiction
How many versions of the truth are there, and why do we keep telling stories over and over again in search of a definitive version? In the cloistered world of a Finnish village in the first decades of the twentieth century, a parson's widow and her maid undertake—in the words of the *Booklist* reviewer—"an exquisitely choreographed memory dance about mental instability, addiction, threats, disputed inheritance, assault, and a devastating parsonage fire." As they recall the same events from numerous perspectives; as they bicker about stuffed birds; as they tell lies that may contain some element of truth; as they relate the truth through lies, they move ever closer to an inexorable conclusion.
Subject keywords: rural life; social roles
Original language: Finnish
Source consulted for annotation:
Global Books in Print (online) (reviews from *Booklist* and *Publishers Weekly*).

Iceland

Böðvar Guðmundsson. *Where the Winds Dwell.*
Translated by Keneva Kunz. Winnipeg, MB: Turnstone Press, 2000. 363 pages.
Genre/literary style/story type: mainstream fiction
Born in Iceland, a famous opera singer now resides in London, England, with his family. When he travels to Vancouver for a performance, he meets a Canadian-Icelandic opera singer to whom he is related by way of a common great-grandfather. This meeting inspires him to write a letter to his daughter to share their family history, including the story of how the children of his poverty-stricken great-grandfather were placed in foster homes. This book is no less than a poignant account of Icelandic history and emigration writ large, starting in the early nineteenth century with a decision by an Icelandic leader to free prisoners.
Subject keyword: family histories
Original language: Icelandic
Source consulted for annotation:
Winnipeg Free Press, 17 December 2000: p. D4.

Einar Már Guðmundsson. *Angels of the Universe.*
Translated by Bernard Scudder. New York: St. Martin's Press, 1997. 164 pages.
Genre/literary style/story type: mainstream fiction
When Paul Olafsson begins to experience paranoia and schizophrenia, he reluctantly enters the clutches of the medical system: heavy-handed physicians; the haze of medication; psychiatric hospitals; and halfway houses. When he is finally cleared to go home, he must deal with his parents, who have very little idea about the psychological and emotional needs of their son. The book is a thoughtful account of the often minuscule differences between social conventions, eccentricities, and madness.

Related title by the same author:
Readers may also be interested in *Epilogue of the Raindrops*, which traces the aftermath of a storm in one Icelandic region. You will never take weather for granted again.
Subject keywords: identity; family histories
Original language: Icelandic
Sources consulted for annotation:
Amazon.com (review from *School Library Journal*).
Amazon.co.uk (reader comments for *Epilogue of the Raindrops*).
Augenbraum, Harold. *Library Journal* 123 (1 March 1998): 152.
Steinberg, Sybil S. *Publishers Weekly* 244 (20 January 1997): 392.
Another translated book written by Einar Már Guðmundsson: *Epilogue of the Raindrops*

Ólafur Gunnarsson. *Troll's Cathedral.*
Translated by David McDuff and Jill Burrows. London: Mare's Nest, 1996. 294 pages.
Genre/literary style/story type: mainstream fiction
Sigurbjörn Helgason is an ambitious architect who dreams of building the Icelandic version of Antoni Gaudi's Sagrada Família in 1950s Reykjavík but has to make do with a less glamorous project: a department store reputed to be the first of its kind in Iceland. But this setback is nothing compared with a more profound tragedy. Sigurbjörn's son, just on the cusp of his teenage years, is sexually molested by a neighbor. As the architect's personal and professional world collapses, he loses his faith and trust in others, seeing betrayal and perfidy everywhere.
Subject keyword: family histories
Original language: Icelandic
Sources consulted for annotation:
Hutchison, Paul. *Library Journal* 122 (August 1997): 128.
Scandinavian Review 85 (Autumn 1997): 97.
Wolf, Kirsten. *World Literature Today* 72 (Winter 1998): 151.
Some other translated books written by Ólafur Gunnarsson: *Potter's Field*; *Gaga*

Hallgrímur Helgason. *101 Reykjavík.*
Translated by Brian FitzGibbon. New York: Scribner, 2002. 339 pages.
Genre/literary style/story type: mainstream fiction
Hlynur Bjorn is an unemployed man in his mid-30s who lives in his mother's basement. Here, he leads a less-than-stressful life, existing on a steady diet of pornography and endless Internet use. At night, he partakes of the heady club scene in Reykjavík, indulging in alcohol and drugs. When he learns that not only his on-again, off-again girlfriend is pregnant but also his sister and his mother's partner, his placid routine is shattered. And although he turns out not to be the father, he decides it is time that he took a break from the rigors of Icelandic slackerdom and saw the world. But self-loathing and self-destructive impulses know no geographic boundaries: While in Europe, he makes a deliberate attempt to become HIV positive through encounters with prostitutes.
Subject keyword: urban life
Original language: Icelandic
Sources consulted for annotation:
Cohen, Joshua. *Library Journal* 127 (1 November 2002): 129.
Fitzgibbon, Brian. *The New York Times Book Review*, 27 April 2003, p. 16.
Spinella, Michael. *Booklist* 99 (1 November 2002): 474.
Wolf, Kirsten. *World Literature Today* 71 (Autumn 1997): 810.
Zaleski, Jeff. *Publishers Weekly* 249 (14 October 2002): 62.

Arnaldur Indriðason. *Silence of the Grave*.
Translated by Bernard Scudder. London: Vintage Books, 2006. 290 pages.
Genres/literary styles/story types: crime fiction; police detectives
Even in Iceland, there is no stopping suburban development. As the city of Reykjavík extends its tentacles, the bones of a man and a small child are found during excavations for the upscale residences of the Millennium Quarter. Previously, this had been a sparsely inhabited rural area that became the site of a large American military base during World War II. Detective Erlendur—a forlorn and guilt-ridden man whose drug-addicted daughter, Eva Lind, clings to life in a hospital—notices red currant bushes close to the discovered bones—a sign that someone had once tried to homestead there. Making use of local archives and the memories of a former American soldier who remained in Iceland after the war, he undertakes a detailed reconstruction of the social milieu of 1940s Reykjavík. Sensational tales about an orgy in the city's gasworks on the eve of Halley's Comet intersect with heartrending stories about domestic abuse perpetrated by Grímur upon his terrified wife Margrét and their three children: Mikkelína, Símon, and Tómas. When Grímur is incarcerated for stealing and reselling supplies from the military depot, Margrét has a romantic idyll with David Welch, one of the soldiers, by whom she becomes pregnant. But when Grímur is released from jail, matters worsen. Welch is shipped to Europe; Margrét's attempts at poisoning Grímur fail; and Símon kills his father with a pair of scissors and buries him, along with Welch's stillborn baby, in what will become the Millennium Quarter. After seeing an elderly woman, who turns out to be Mikkelína, tending to the ravaged yet resilient red currant bushes, Erlendur gradually discovers the truth about the bones. He is taken by Mikkelína to meet Símon, who suffers from hebephrenia and is thus enveloped in a childlike peaceful world. This stark novel eloquently captures numerous aspects of twentieth-century Icelandic history, weaving a multifaceted tapestry whose recurring motif is that the brooding alienation experienced in early twenty-first-century Reykjavík is not so very different from that prevalent on the isolated farms of Iceland's past.
Related titles by the same author:
Another excursion into the Icelandic past by the same author is *The Draining Lake*, which examines life in Iceland during the Cold War when the Soviet Union and the United States exerted pressure on Icelandic citizens to become their respective ideological supporters. In *Arctic Chill*, the focus is on the racism experienced by Asian immigrants to Iceland. A small Thai boy is stabbed to death outside the bleak apartment building where he, his half-brother, and mother eke out a meager existence. The boy's death as well as his half-brother's catatonia awaken painful memories for Erlunder, who was unable to protect his own brother from death in a raging snowstorm many decades ago.
Subject keyword: family histories
Original language: Icelandic
Sources consulted for annotation:
Batten, Jack. *The Toronto Star* (19 November 2006), p. D8.
Stasio, Marilyn. *The New York Times Book Review*, 22 October 2006 (online).
Stasio, Marilyn. *The New York Times Book Review*, 28 September 2008 (online).
Stasio, Marilyn. *The New York Times Book Review*, 17 September 2009 (online).
Some other translated books written by Arnaldur Indriðason: *Arctic Chill*; *The Draining Lake*; *Tainted Blood* (or *Jar City*); *Voices*; *Hypothermia*

Bragi Ólafsson. *The Pets*.
Translated by Janice Balfour. Rochester, NY: Open Letter, 2008. 157 pages.
Genre/literary style/story type: mainstream fiction
Emil Halldorsson has just returned from an English vacation; the best part of his trip may have been meeting Greta on the plane back to Icelandic. As Emil waits for Greta to call him, he gets an

unexpected visit from Havard Knutsson, his former roommate who, at last report, was institutionalized in a Swedish asylum. To say the least, Emil has no desire to see Havard nor anyone else, especially since his thoughts are preoccupied with Greta. Thus, his decision to hide under his bed is perhaps understandable. But as with every spur-of-the-moment decision, it goes massively awry when Havard, sensing the opportunity of an empty house, stays true to his violence-prone and loutish character. Not satisfied with breaking into someone's home and drinking the owner's stock of alcohol, he also hosts an unusual party that progressively becomes downright weird.
Subject keyword: urban life
Original language: Icelandic
Sources consulted for annotation:
Global Books in Print (online) (book synopsis).
Open Letter Press (book description), http://catalog.openletterbooks.org.

Ólafur Jóhann Ólafsson (Olaf Olafsson). *Absolution.*
Translated by Bernard Scudder. New York: Pantheon, 1991. 259 pages.
Genre/literary style/story type: mainstream fiction
Although he made a fortune as a businessman in New York, Peter Peterson probably would not win any popularity contests. A mean-spirited and acerbic man, he did not much like his two wives nor his children. Now old and retired and in between bouts of trying to seduce his Cambodian maid, he broods about the past. And what a past it was. Some 50 years ago, after a privileged adolescence in Iceland, he lived in Denmark during the German occupation. There, he fell in love with an Icelandic woman, who rejected him. Peterson did not take rejection lightly, falsely accusing the woman's boyfriend of complicity with the Nazis.
Subject keyword: family histories
Original language: Icelandic
Source consulted for annotation:
Global Books in Print (online) (reviews from *Library Journal* and *Publishers Weekly*).
Some other translated books written by Ólafur Jóhann Ólafsson: *Walking into the Night*; *The Journey Home*

Yrsa Sigurdardottir. *My Soul to Take.*
Translated by Bernard Scudder and Anna Yates. New York: William Morrow, 2009. 346 pages.
Genres/literary styles/story types: crime fiction; amateur detectives
This is the second of the author's novels to feature Thora Gudmundsdottir, a lawyer who has a penchant for taking on thorny cases. In the first book of the series, *Last Rituals*, she looks into the murder of a German university student who was fascinated by the little-known story of Icelandic witch hunts, whose primary victims were men. In *My Soul To Take*, Jonas Juliusson, the owner of a health spa who believes his property is haunted, asks Gudmundsdottir to get to the bottom of the matter, but when an architect is murdered nearby, he himself has much to answer for.
Subject keyword: social roles
Original language: Icelandic
Sources consulted for annotation:
Fantastic Fiction (book review), http://www.fantasticfiction.co.uk.
Global Books in Print (online) (reviews from *Booklist* and *Publishers Weekly*).
Some other translated books written by Yrsa Sigurdardottir: *Last Rituals*; *Ashes to Dust*

Sjón. *The Blue Fox.*
Translated by Victoria Cribb. London: Telegram Books, 2008. 112 pages.
Genres/literary styles/story types: adventure; survival and disaster stories

Critics have referred to this novel as either a fable or parable. It focuses on two individuals—each of whose lives mirror and refract elements of the other. In 1883, a pastor successfully kills the blue fox that he has been tracking across the desolate snows, but almost at once, he falls victim to an avalanche. A naturalist makes preparations for the funeral of a Down syndrome woman who was instrumental in saving his life when his ship ran aground off the coast of Iceland in 1868. As A. S. Byatt comments, "The world of 19th-century Iceland is brilliantly and economically present—the bareness of the dwellings, the roughness of the churches and congregations, the meagre food." The author is perhaps best known for his musical association with Björk, especially his work on *Dancer in the Dark*.
Subject keyword: rural life
Original language: Icelandic
Sources consulted for annotation:
Byatt, A. S. *The Times* (September 25, 2008) (online).
Global Books in Print (online) (synopsis/book jacket).
Telegram Books (book description), http://www.telegrambooks.com.

Thor Vilhjálmsson. *Justice Undone.*
Translated by Bernard Scudder. London: Mare's Nest, 1995. 222 pages.
Genre/literary style/story type: mainstream fiction
According to Schulte Annotations, this historically based book focuses on "the trial of half-siblings accused of incest and infanticide." The publisher's synopsis noted the author's "narrative fervor of Late-Romanticism" and "astonishing psychological depth."
Subject keyword: identity
Original language: Icelandic
Sources consulted for annotation:
Barnesandnoble.com (all editorial reviews).
Schulte Annotations, http://www.utdallas.edu/~schulte/annotations.
Some other translated books written by Thor Vilhjálmsson: *Quick Quick Said the Bird*; *Faces Reflected in a Drop*

Latvia

Alberts Bels. *The Voice of the Herald and The Investigator.*
Translated by David Foreman. Moscow: Progress Publishers, 1980. 367 pages.
Genre/literary style/story type: mainstream fiction
This collection of two novels and 10 short stories is focused on what Anatoly Bocharov calls "moral quests, doubts and convictions." *The Voice of the Herald* explores the life of a Latvian revolutionary: Luthers Karlsons. In *The Investigator*, Juris Rigers and his conscience have an extremely detailed discussion about the philosophical and existential aspects of life. As he embarks on his quest to find the "good in man," the author examines such universal themes as self-determination, mortality, spirituality, time, and "the revolutionary spirit of transformation."
Subject keyword: philosophy
Original language: Latvian
Source consulted for annotation:
Bocharov, Anatoly. "The Prose of Alberts Bels" (contained in the book).
Another translated book written by Alberts Bels: *The Cage*

Marģeris Zariņš. *Mock Faustus, or The Corrected Complemented Cooking-Book.*
Translated by Raissa Bobrova. Moscow: Raduga, 1987. 301 pages.

Genre/literary style/story type: mainstream fiction
An update of Christopher Marlowe's *Dr. Faustus*, this book explores Latvian social and political history in the 1930s and during World War II. It features Trampedahs, described as an apothecary; a minstrel and budding author who goes by the name of Christopher Marlowe; and Margareta, a poet. While Trampedahs throws in his lot with the Nazis, eventually becoming a brutal killer, Marlowe emerges as a tormented figure who—despite and indeed perhaps because of his trials and tribulations—resolves to fight against looming horror.
Subject keywords: politics; power
Original language: Latvian
Source consulted for annotation:
Rudenko-Desnyak, Alexander. "About the Novel" in the book.

Lithuania

Ričardas Gavelis. *Vilnius Poker.*
Translated by Elizabeth Novickas. Rochester, NY: Open Letter, 2009. 485 pages.
Genre/literary style/story type: mainstream fiction
After what he has experienced, Vytautas Vargalys has every right to be paranoid. In the 1970s and 1980s, Vilnius, Lithuania's capital, is a grimly monochromatic city wracked by the overwhelming weight of its painful history. Vargalys, who has been in Soviet labor camps, now works at the forbidding National Library, developing an electronic catalog for inaccessible collections. No one much comes to the library, so he can devote his time to identifying and ferreting out ubiquitous and omnipresent conspirators who are responsible for the world's accumulated evil. They have killed his wife and his best friend; they lurk in books; and they might have even take control of Lolita, his young coworker who may turn out to be his saving grace. Some critics have invoked Albert Camus, James Joyce, and Franz Kafka to describe this penumbral and melancholic novel, which is considered to be a Lithuanian landmark.
Subject keywords: identity; power
Original language: Lithuanian
Sources consulted for annotation:
Global Books in Print (online) (book reviews from *Booklist*, *Library Journal*, and *Publishers Weekly*).
Open Letter Press (book description), http://catalog.openletterbooks.org.

Norway

Gerd Brantenberg. *The Four Winds.*
Translated by Margaret O'Leary. Seattle, WA: Women in Translation, 1994. 353 pages.
Genres/literary styles/story types: mainstream fiction; coming-of-age
Inger Holm grows up in a small Norwegian town in the 1960s. It is a household marred by tragedy: Her sister dies of polio; her parents drink; and her father abuses her mother while doting on her. Thus, it is with a certain sense of relief that she goes to Scotland to work as a nanny, where she falls in love with her employers' daughter. Later, in Oslo during her university years, she continues her exploration of sexuality, finding necessary psychological and emotional comfort in relationships with other women.
Subject keywords: family histories; identity
Original language: Norwegian
Sources consulted for annotation:
Alther, Lisa. *The Women's Review of Books* 13 (July 1996): 35.

Amazon.com (review from *Midwest Book Review*).
Upchurch, Michael. *The Seattle Times*, 25 February 1996, p. M3.
Some other translated books written by Gerd Brantenberg: *Egalia's Daughters: A Satire of the Sexes (The Daughters of Egalia)*; *What Comes Naturally*

Finn Carling. *Diary for a Dead Husband.*
Translated by Louis A. Muinzer. London: Peter Owen, 1998. 136 pages.
Genre/literary style/story type: mainstream fiction; women's lives
This lyrical novel describes one year of Felicia's life—the first year after her husband of 20 years dies. Felicia's sadness is limitless, but she is also wracked with guilt as she recalls the domineering man who prevented her from realizing her potential as an artist. As she writes to her dead husband to tell him news of the world that he is missing and as she tells him of her increasing hatred for her children and friends, her act of writing evolves from an act of duty and consolation into a nascent realization that she is now free to pursue her dreams.
Subject keyword: identity
Original language: Norwegian
Source consulted for annotation:
Johnston, Bonnie. *Booklist* 95 (1 April 1999): 1384.
Some other translated books written by Finn Carling: *Commission*; *Under the Evening Sky*

Lars Saabye Christensen. *The Half Brother.*
Translated by Kenneth Steven. New York: Arcade, 2004. 682 pages.
Genre/literary style/story type: mainstream fiction
This novel is a sensitively wrought saga of some 50 years in the life of a Norwegian family in Oslo. As in all families, there are tragic secrets and eccentricities, and the Nilsens are no exception. The father is a ne'er-do-well and small-time grifter. The mother, Vera, is raped in the mid-1940s, and after giving birth to Fred, she retreats into silence. The narrator is Barnum, a failed screenwriter and Fred's half-brother. As the boys grow up in a household made rich by the presence of their grandmother and great-grandmother, Fred is a moody and angry young man whom Barnum tries to protect as best he can. But Fred runs off to sea, and Barnum must make the best of things, finding solace with Vivian, his future wife, who eventually has a child despite Barnum's infertility. Critics specifically invoked Péter Nádas's *Book of Memories* and Péter Esterházy's *Celestial Harmonies* when discussing this novel as well as, more generally, such writers as Halldór Laxness and August Strindberg.
Subject keyword: family histories
Original language: Norwegian
Sources consulted for annotation:
Global Books in Print (online) (review from Library Journal and Publishers Weekly).
Scandinavian Review 92 (Autumn 2004): 90.
Some other translated books written by Lars Saabye Christensen: *Herman*; *The Joker*; *The Model*; *Beatles*

K. O. Dahl. *The Fourth Man.*
Translated by Don Bartlett. New York: St. Martin's Press, 2008. 276 pages.
Genres/literary styles/story types: crime fiction; police detectives
Detective Inspector Frank Frølich works in Oslo and has just saved the life of Elizabeth Faremo, who was caught in the crossfire of a police raid. When Elizabeth later seduces him, Frank discovers that he has been used. Elizabeth's brother, Jonny, has been charged with murder, and Elizabeth's affair with Frølich is part of a well-conceived alibi to help him. Things only get worse for Frølich

when both Faremos as well as a friend of Elizabeth's are killed, and his colleagues begin to suspect him of the crimes.
Subject keyword: urban life
Original language: Norwegian
Sources consulted for annotation:
Global Books in Print (online) (reviews from *Booklist*, *Library Journal*, and *Publishers Weekly*).
Macmillan (book description), http://us.macmillan.com.
Some other translated books written by K. O. Dahl: *The Man in the Window*; *The Last Fix*

Karin Fossum. *Don't Look Back.*
Translated by Felicity David. London: Vintage Books, 2003. 421 pages.
Genres/literary styles/story types: crime fiction; police detectives
In the hamlet of Lundeby, where the houses are close together and everyone knows everyone else's business, 15-year-old Annie Sofie Holland is found dead beside a mountain pool called Serpent Tarn. Naked except for a jacket carefully placed around her shoulders, she appears not to have been sexually attacked. Inspector Konrad Sejer, a widower who lives alone with his dog, and Jacob Skarre, a young officer who was formerly a taxi driver in Oslo, are stumped. Annie, a dynamic young woman who excelled at handball and ran 20 miles per week, was liked by everyone, especially the households for which she babysat. The tiny village has an assortment of individuals who initially arouse suspicion: Fritzner, a man who has a boat in his living room in which he sits and drinks; Halvor Muntz, Annie's boyfriend, who apparently shot his father in self-defense and now works at a nearby ice cream factory and takes care of his grandmother; Raymond Låke, a man in his 30s with Down syndrome who raises rabbits; and an athletics coach convicted of rape more than a decade ago. But one by one, they prove to be innocent. Sejer and Skarre eventually learn that Annie's personality had recently changed; she was no longer as optimistic and confident as before. They also discover that Annie was severely affected by the seemingly accidental death of a young hyperactive child, Eskil Johnas, whom she alone could deal with. But Eskil's death was no accident; his father—a dealer in rare carpets and unable to endure the child's hyperactivity—choked him to death by stuffing too much food in his mouth. Annie's inadvertent knowledge of this domestic tragedy ultimately seals her own fate.
Subject keyword: rural life
Original language: Norwegian
Sources consulted for annotation:
Cannon, Peter. *Publishers Weekly* 251 (5 January 2004): 43.
Klett, Rex. *Library Journal* 129 (1 February 2004): 128.
Ott, Bill. *Booklist* 100 (15 March 2004): 1270.
Some other translated books written by Karin Fossum: *Black Seconds*; *Calling Out for You*; *Don't Look Back*; *He Who Fears the Wolf*; *When the Devil Holds the Candle*; *The Water's Edge*

Jostein Gaarder. *Sophie's World.*
Translated by Paulette Møller. New York: Farrar, Straus and Giroux, 1994. 403 pages.
Genres/literary styles/story types: mainstream fiction; postmodernism
Sophie Amundsen is a 14-year-old Norwegian teenager who lives with her mother in the suburbs. It is an ordinary life until, one day, her mailbox starts to fill up with correspondence from an ultra-mysterious man named Alberto Knox. His letters are an introduction into the vertiginous subject of Western philosophy. As Sophie works her way through the tangle of pre-Socratics, Plato, and Aristotle as well as modern luminaries, such as Sartre, she also begins to receive postcards intended for a girl whom she has never met. Eventually, she and Albert Knox discover that they are characters in a novel.

Subject keyword: philosophy
Original language: Norwegian
Sources consulted for annotation:
Global Books in Print (online) (review from *Kirkus Reviews*).
Irvine, Ann. *Library Journal* 119 (1 September 1994): 215.
Steinberg, Sybil S. *Publishers Weekly* 241 (15 August 1994): 87.
Some other translated books written by Jostein Gaarder: *The Solitaire Mystery*; *The Orange Girl*; *Maya*; *The Ringmaster's Daughter*; *The Christmas Mystery*; *Through a Glass, Darkly*; *The Castle in the Pyrenees*

Erik Fosnes Hansen. *Tales of Protection.*
Translated by Nadia Christensen. New York: Farrar, Straus and Giroux, 1998. 500 pages.
Genre/literary style/story type: mainstream fiction
We either like to think that there is nothing new in the world—that everything is a mere repetition of the past—or we sneer at such a notion. But Wilhelm Bolt, a former engineer turned amateur scientist, is firmly convinced that there is great truth in what he calls the theory of serialisation. For him, nothing is random; everything relates somehow to what has gone before. He derived this theory from Paul Kammerer, and he devoted a large part of his life to collecting examples of coincidence. When Bolt dies, his grand-niece Lea inherits her great-uncle's notebooks, filled with jottings and stories about the interrelationship of diverse events and phenomena, including bees, nineteenth-century lighthouses, and fifteenth-century artists.
Subject keyword: philosophy
Original language: Norwegian
Sources consulted for annotation:
Dowling, Brendan. *Booklist* 98 (July 2002): 1821.
The Independent, 16 August 2002 (online).
Zaleski, Jeff. *Publishers Weekly* 249 (3 June 2002): 59.
Another translated book written by Erik Fosnes Hansen: *Psalm at Journey's End*

Edvard Hoem. *Ave Eva: A Norwegian Tragedy.*
Translated by Frankie Belle Shackelford. Riverside, CA: Xenos Books, 2000. 295 pages.
Genre/literary style/story type: mainstream fiction
His father was considered to a be a traitor, and he is something of a vagabond. But Edmund Saknevik has finally come home to Norway. He intends to resume farming on his family's lands but finds that there have been sweeping changes, especially the growth of the oil industry and the baleful influence of homogenizing westernization. But the past still lingers, manifested in ancient customs, religious practices, and a gnawing social divide about Norway's role during World War II. Caught between the past and the present, he attempts to reclaim his heritage and find meaning in a contemporary world he barely recognizes. His work, written in what is called Nynorsk (New Norwegian), has been compared with that of Knut Hamsun.
Subject keyword: family histories
Original language: Norwegian
Sources consulted for annotation:
Publishers Weekly 248 (26 February 2001): 61.
Xenos Books website (book description), http://www.xenosbooks.com.
Another translated book written by Edvard Hoem: *The Ferry Crossing*

Jan Kjærstad. *The Seducer.*
Translated by Barbara J. Haveland. New York: Overlook Press, 2007. 606 pages.

Genres/literary styles/story types: thrillers; conspiracy thrillers
Jonas Wergeland is a television producer at the peak of his career. He also has a well-deserved reputation as a stupendous lover, not to mention a perhaps too-healthy self-regard about his role in prominent world events. But his life is irrevocably transformed when he returns from yet another international trip to discover that his wife has been killed. His investigations into her death are both wildly funny and unbearably sad.
Related titles by the same author:
The Conqueror and *The Discoverer* complete the Wergeland trilogy. When Jonas is accused of murdering his wife, he becomes even more famous than before. Thus, it is almost inevitable that every facet of his life will be poked and probed for clues about his true character and his rise to the pinnacle of broadcast media. After serving time in prison, he joins a scientific expedition. Critics have compared the series to James Joyce's *A Portrait of the Artist as a Young Man*.
Subject keyword: urban life
Original language: Norwegian
Sources consulted for annotation:
Amazon.com (all editorial reviews).
Global Books in Print (online) (synopsis/book jacket).
Powell's Books (book review), http://www.powells.com.
Santella, Andrew. *The New York Times Book Review*, 20 August 2006, p. 14.
Shone, Tom. *The New York Times Book Review*, 25 October 2009, p. 8.
Some other translated books written by Jan Kjærstad: *The Conqueror*; *The Discoverer*

Gunnar Kopperud. *The Time of Light*.
Translated by Tiina Nunnally. New York: Bloomsbury, 2000. 247 pages.
Genre/literary style/story type: mainstream fiction
Markus Wagner was captured and imprisoned by the Soviets during the Battle of Stalingrad in the fall and winter of 1942–1943. After the war, he never returned to Germany, settling in Armenia to build his life anew and to serve as a Russian spy. Tormented by a past filled with episodes of arson, rape, and murder, he unburdens himself to an Armenian priest against the background of the late 1980s to early 1990s war over the disputed territory of Nagorno-Karabakh, claimed by both Armenia and Azerbaijan. The novel has been compared to Erich Maria Remarque's *All Quiet on the Western Front*.
Subject keywords: identity; war
Original language: Norwegian
Sources consulted for annotation:
Kloszewski, Marc. *Library Journal* 125 (15 June 2000): 116.
Steinberg, Sybil S. *Publishers Weekly* 247 (3 July 2000): 50.
Some other translated books written by Gunnar Kopperud: *Longing*; *The Backpacker's Father*

Øystein Lønn. *The Necessary Rituals of Maren Gripe*.
Translated by Barbara Haveland. London: Flamingo, 2001. 151 pages.
Genre/literary style/story type: mainstream fiction
By all accounts, Maren Gripe has a good life in an isolated fishing village on the North Sea. Her marriage is a happy and faithful one, and she can still turn the heads of every man who comes in contact with her. Her days assume meaning and resonance from a series of rituals that are somewhat out of the ordinary. But when a Dutch sailor proves to be resistant to her charms, everything changes for the worse: The village is engulfed in chaos and Maren becomes insane.
Subject keyword: rural life
Original language: Norwegian

Sources consulted for annotation:
Book Depository (book description), http://www.bookdepository.com.
Montgomery, Isobel. *The Guardian*, 23 November 2002, p. 30.
Tillman, Jo. *M2 Best Books*, 31 May 2002 (from Factiva databases).
Another translated book written by Øystein Lønn: *Tom Reber's Last Retreat*

Jo Nesbø. *The Redbreast*.
Translated by Don Bartlett. New York: Random House, 2007. 521 pages.
Genres/literary styles/story types: crime fiction; police detectives
Harry Hole is a renegade Oslo police inspector who is at once brilliant, moody, quixotic, and a borderline alcoholic; in the opinion of some critics, he is much like Michael Connelly's detective Harry Bosch. During a visit by the president of the United States to Norway, Hole wounds a suspicious unidentified man, who turns out to be a Secret Service agent. In order to keep the incident under wraps, Hole is officially commended, promoted, and transferred to a national security bureau posting, where he is assigned to keep tabs on the Norwegian neo-Nazi underground—a supposedly low-level task meant to keep him away from inquiring reporters. But when he finds out that one of the rarest—and deadliest—guns in the world has been clandestinely shipped into Norway and when his former police partner, Ellen Gjelten, is killed by a neo-Nazi, Hole launches an investigation that leads him into the byzantine tangle of Norway's collaborationist history during World War II—the serpentine aftereffects of which still ramify in contemporary political life.
Related titles by the same author:
In *The Devil's Star*, Hole returns to the unsolved murder of Gjelten, discovering additional sordid facts about the extent of fascist ideology in Norway. In the first book of the series, translated in French as *L'homme Chauve-Souris*, Hole is sent to Australia to investigate the murder of a Norwegian woman—a journey that also exposes him to aboriginal culture. In the second book, *Les Cafards*, he is dispatched to Thailand, where his job is to provide a whitewashed explanation for the death of the Norwegian ambassador, who has been stabbed with a rare ceremonial knife in a hotel known as a venue for sexual rendezvous. As Hole investigates the circumstances of the assassination with the help of Bangkok policewoman Liz Crumley, he discovers a corrupt Norwegian expatriate milieu involved in pedophilia, brutal gang violence, and extensive financial machinations that, taken together, bespeak a kind of twenty-first-century colonialism every bit as insidious as its nineteenth-century forerunner.
Subject keywords: politics; power
Original language: Norwegian
Source consulted for annotation:
Batten, Jack. *The Toronto Star*, 11 February 2007, p. D6.
Some other translated books written by Jo Nesbø: *The Devil's Star*; *The House of Pain*; *Nemesis*; *The Snowman*; *Redeemer*

Per Petterson. *Out Stealing Horses*.
Translated by Anne Born. St. Paul, MN: Graywolf Press, 2007. 258 pages.
Genre/literary style/story type: mainstream fiction
Three years after a horrible automobile accident on a rain-slicked Norwegian highway in which his wife dies, Trond Sander, the novel's narrator, has had enough of life and loss. It is 1999, a few scant months before the dawn of a new century. He decides to move to a remote village in northern Norway, where—at age 66—he buys a tumbledown house on the outskirts of a village. Here, he intends to live out his remaining years, with only a dog for company, cut off from any vestiges of his past, including his daughters. In part, it may be because his blood-stained and agony-ridden face at the accident site was captured by a freelance photographer and splashed across the front pages of

newspapers, a modern-day Edvard Munch–like *The Scream* that eventually wins a prize. All he wants is solitude, a slow accretion of days in which to refurbish his crumbling house, and a chance to forget. But the past intrudes in the form of a neighbor whom he remembers from the late 1940s, when Trond and his father would spend their summers in a cabin deep in the forest in the vicinity of an isolated Norwegian hamlet near the Swedish border, traversed by a river that meandered through both countries. The neighbor is Lars Haug, who as a boy accidentally shot his twin brother with a gun that his older brother Jon had forgotten to take the bullets out of. It was a mystery to Trond why his father would take him to this cabin, leaving the rest of the family behind in Oslo, but in the fateful summer of 1948, at age 15, he begins to discern the contours of the enigma. His father, part of the Norwegian underground resisting the Nazi occupation of Norway during World War II, used this same cabin as a base from which to smuggle documents and people to Sweden, which had declared itself neutral. Many of the hamlet's residents, including Lars's mother, were also part of the resistance, so Trond's father was by no means a stranger in the area. In 1948, Trond's father hatches a plan to cut down a large swath of trees on his property and float the trunks on the river to a Swedish paper mill. As neighbors pitch in to help with the difficult work and as Lars's father is severely injured in a senseless competition to stack logs higher and higher, Trond discovers that his father and Lars's mother are having an affair. At the end of the summer, Trond goes back to Oslo; his father stays behind, promising to return in a few weeks. But he never reappears; it is clear that he has begun a new life with Lars's mother and that, as a result, Lars has been raised by Trond's father. A few months later, a letter comes from his father, explaining to Trond and his mother that money from the sale of the lumber is being held for them in a bank in the Swedish city of Karlstad. In a devastatingly poignant scene, Trond and his mother set out for Karlstad to retrieve the money that is supposed to be their future nest egg. But it turns out to be a paltry amount, sufficient only to buy Trond a suit that, in the end, is the entire legacy of his father. Thus, in 1999, as Trond and Lars prepare for the coming winter by clearing fallen trees, their long separate lives intertwine yet again in a resonant echo of a distant summer. With nary a false note, the novel explores the hidden effect of the war on a teenage boy whose father chooses to vanish and start a new life—a boy now a widower who moves back to the same cabin in an attempt to fathom the signs, codes, and significations of his father's disappearance after their last summer together.

Related title by the same author:

Readers may also find Petterson's *To Siberia* the perfect companion piece to *Out Stealing Horses* because it examines from a female perspective the emotional and psychological consequences of escape afforded by World War II. On a rural farm in Denmark before the war, Jesper and his sister grow up in a pious, strict, yet ultimately hypocritical household. Against the backdrop of the German occupation of Denmark, brother and sister dream of escape—he to the deserts of Morocco; she to the vast silent expanses of Siberia. And while the circumstances of Jesper's life do lead him to Morocco, his sister must content herself with humdrum jobs and evanescent affairs in the loneliness of Copenhagen, Stockholm, and Oslo—until, pregnant, she returns home to an affective tundra more bitterly cold than any Siberia she could have imagined. Readers of *Out Stealing Horses* who may be interested in how other novelists portray the fate of children who accidentally shoot one of their siblings may wish to delve into the world depicted in Larry Brown's *Father and Son*, a tragedy worthy of William Shakespeare set in the hill country of northern Mississippi in the 1960s.

Subject keyword: family histories

Original language: Norwegian

Sources consulted for annotation:

Frank, Jeffrey. *The New Yorker*, 20 October 2008 (online).

Global Books in Print (online) (reviews from *Booklist*, *Library Journal*, and *Publishers Weekly*).

McGuane, Thomas. *The New York Times Book Review*, 24 June 2007 (online).

Miles, Jonathan. *The New York Times Book Review*, 12 October 2008 (online).
Rohrbaugh, Lisa. *Library Journal* 124 (1 May 1999): 112.
Steinberg, Sybil S. *Publishers Weekly* 246 (15 March 1999): 48.
Some other translated books written by Per Petterson: *In the Wake*; *To Siberia; I Curse the River of Time*

Pernille Rygg. *The Butterfly Effect.*
Translated by Joan Tate. London: Harvill, 1997. 220 pages.
Genres/literary styles/story types: crime fiction; amateur detectives
When her father, an Oslo private detective, is killed in an alleged hit-and-run accident, Igi Heitmann, a psychologist researching chaos theory who is married to a transvestite, launches her own investigation. As she goes through her father's office, she locates pieces of evidence that her father collected just before his death about the murder of a young woman abandoned in a snowdrift. When she discovers the body of another woman in a church, Igi is caught in the middle of a mystery that touches on the occult and child abuse. Critics have invoked Ross Macdonald, Raymond Chandler, and Peter Høeg in discussing this novel.
Subject keyword: urban life
Original language: Norwegian
Sources consulted for annotation:
Brainard, Dulcy. *Publishers Weekly* 245 (9 February 1998):78.
Ott, Bill. *Booklist* 94 (15 April 1998): 1393.
Another translated book written by Pernille Rygg: *The Golden Section*

Stig Saeterbakken. *Siamese.*
Translated by Stokes Schwartz. Champaign, IL: Dalkey Archive Press, 2009. 164 pages.
Genre/literary style/story type: mainstream fiction
This is the first of the author's "S" trilogy to be published in English. It focuses on the power struggles and bleakness that accompany the aging process. Edwin is a typical curmudgeon who has come to the end of his life. With a diverse array of health problems, he makes life miserable for his wife Sweetie and the superintendent of the building where they reside. Jim Krusoe invoked the "desperation" of Knut Hamsun and the "haunted compulsions" of Thomas Bernhard in discussing this book, which—according to Larissa Kyzer—eloquently invokes such themes as "the fear of death or inadequacy, the frailty of the body, the need to feel in control, the desire for power."
Subject keyword: aging
Original language: Norwegian
Sources consulted for annotation:
Krusoe, Jim. *The New York Times Book Review*, 7 January 2010 (online).
Kyzer, Larissa. Three Percent website (book review), http://www.rochester.edu/College/translation/threepercent.

Gunnar Staalesen. *The Writing on the Wall.*
Translated by Hal Sutcliffe. London: Arcadia, 2004. 264 pages.
Genres/literary styles/story types: crime fiction; private investigators
Varg Veum is a former children's social worker who has become a private detective. While investigating the case of a disappeared 16-year-old girl, he discovers not only a prostitution ring consisting of wealthy young women who have been lured into the Bergen (Norway) underworld but also a dead judge wearing women's undergarments.
Subject keyword: urban life
Original language: Norwegian

Sources consulted for annotation:
Back cover of the book.
Batten, Jack. *Toronto Star*, 26 June 2005, p. D8.
Some other translated books written by Gunnar Staalesen: *At Night All Wolves Are Grey*; *Yours Until Death*

Linn Ullmann. *Stella Descending*.
Translated by Barbara Haveland. New York: Alfred A. Knopf, 2003. 243 pages.
Genre/literary style/story type: mainstream fiction
This novel, which is set in Oslo in 2000, begins when Stella, the wife of Martin and the mother of Amanda and Bee, falls nine floors to her death from a rooftop. Amanda suspects Martin, her stepfather. But there are many obvious questions: Was there a struggle; did Stella lose her footing; or was Martin just a passive observer, not trying to save Stella as she teetered on the edge of the precipice? These questions in turn lead to less obvious ones, focusing on the state of Amanda and Martin's marriage.
Related title by the same author:
Readers may also enjoy *A Blessed Child*, which chronicles the journeys of three half-sisters attempting to reach their father, a retired gynecologist living reclusively on an island, before he puts into practice his vow to commit suicide after the death of his wife. The book can be read semiautobiographically: Ullmann is one of the nine children of Ingmar Bergman, who lived on the remote Swedish island of Faro until his death.
Subject keyword: family histories
Original language: Norwegian
Sources consulted for annotation:
Andersen, Beth E. *Library Journal* 128 (15 June 2003): 103.
D'Erasmo, Stacey. *The New York Times Book Review*, 15 August 2008 (online).
Johnson, Roberta. *Booklist* 99 (August 2003): 1959.
Publishers Weekly 250 (21 July 2003): 174.
Some other translated books written by Linn Ullmann: *Before You Sleep*; *Grace*; *A Blessed Child*

Sweden

Karin Alvtegen. *Missing*.
Translated by Anna Paterson. Toronto, ON: Penguin Canada, 2007. 347 pages.
Genres/literary styles/story types: crime fiction; suspense
Sibylla Forsenström was once the cosseted daughter of a wealthy family in a small Swedish industrial town, where her father owned the metal foundry and was its most influential citizen. Raised to be a proper young woman in the traditional provincial style, she rebels against her staid upbringing, befriending a group of young men whose main interest is cars. Her rebelliousness is diagnosed as a psychiatric condition, and she is institutionalized. When she becomes pregnant and is forced to give her child up for adoption, she breaks all bonds with her family, escaping from the hospital and becoming a street person in Stockholm. Now 32, she has lived incognito for the last 14 years, embracing the freedom of homelessness and drifting from hostel to hostel. Occasionally, she runs scams on lonely businessmen in posh hotels, convincing them to buy her dinner and book her a room so she can bathe and get a good night's sleep. But her hard-won independence is shattered when one of these businessmen is found mutilated and murdered in his hotel room. Although innocent of the ghastly crime, Sibylla is the obvious suspect, and when other similar ritualistic murders occur, a nationwide hunt commences for her. With nowhere to turn and few resources to call upon,

Sibylla takes it upon herself—in the company of Patrik, a teenage boy whom she meets when she hides in the attic of a school—to solve the murders. As the unlikely pair slowly piece together the clues, they realize that all the victims were the recipients of donated organs from a single dead individual.

Subject keyword: family histories

Original language: Swedish

Sources consulted for annotation:

Dawson, Jonathan. *Hobart Mercury*, 13 January 2007, p. B9.

Dawson, Jonathan. *Hobart Mercury*, 24 June 2006, p. B13.

Keenan, Catherine. *The Sun Herald*, 15 January 2006, p. 58.

Some other translated books written by Karin Alvtegen: *Guilt*; *Betrayal*; *Shame*; *Shadow*

Ingmar Bergman. *The Best Intentions*.

Translated by Joan Tate. New York: Arcade, 1993. 298 pages.

Genre/literary style/story type: mainstream fiction

The author, who was an internationally renowned film director, explores the relationship of his parents, especially the tumultuous early years. His parents brought two different perspectives and worldviews to their new life—a cause of protracted friction. His father was a divinity student; as befitted his position, he was the epitome of seriousness. His mother was studying nursing, and her aristocratic family was opposed to her choice of a future member of the clergy as a husband.

Subject keyword: family histories

Original language: Swedish

Sources consulted for annotation:

Global Books in Print (online) (review from *Booklist*).

Holston, Kim. *Library Journal* 118 (15 April 1993): 124.

Nolan, Margaret. *School Library Journal* 40 (January 1994): 144.

Steinberg, Sybil S. *Publishers Weekly* 240 (22 March 1993): 69.

Some other translated books written by Ingmar Bergman: *Sunday's Children*; *Private Confessions*

Kjell-Olof Bornemark. *The Messenger Must Die* . . .

Translated by Laurie Thompson. New York: Dembner Books, 1986. 236 pages.

Genres/literary styles/story types: thrillers; political thrillers

When he is not earning his living as a freelance journalist, Greger Tragg spends his time spying for the East Germans. Infact, he has been doing it for some 30 years, using a reliable informant in the Swedish government. But the East Germans have now decided that they do not need Tragg to serve as a middleman; they will deal directly with his source. Things get even more problematic when Tragg arouses the suspicions of Swedish security forces. The *Publishers Weekly* reviewer referred to this book as being in "John le Carré territory, but colder and bleaker and with no real traitors."

Subject keywords: politics; power

Original language: Swedish

Source consulted for annotation:

Steinberg, Sybil S. *Publishers Weekly* 230 (5 September 1986): 88.

Some other translated books written by Kjell-Olof Bornemark: *The Henchman*; *The Dividing Line*

Carina Burman. *The Streets of Babylon: A London Mystery*.

Translated by Sarah Death. London: Marion Boyars, 2008. 288 pages.

Genre/literary style/story type: historical fiction

This novel, which is the first volume of a trilogy, introduces Euthanasia Bondeson, a famous Swedish author. In 1851, she and a female companion have gone to London for both business and pleasure. First, there is the matter of getting Euthanasia's latest book translated and published; second, they are eager to see the Crystal Palace Exhibition in Hyde Park. But all plans are put on hold when the companion suddenly disappears. Euthanasia is therefore compelled to explore the teeming, poverty-stricken, debauched, and violent underworld of London in search of her friend.
Subject keywords: identity; urban life
Original language: Swedish
Sources consulted for annotation:
Global Books in Print (online) (review from *Library Journal*).
Marion Boyars website (book description), http://www.marionboyars.co.uk.

Åke Edwardson. *Never End.*
Translated by Laurie Thompson. New York: Viking, 2006. 308 pages.
Genres/literary styles/story types: crime fiction; police detectives
This is the second novel in the author's Erik Winter series. Middle-aged Erik Winter is a police inspector in Göteborg; he has been brooding over a five-year-old unresolved case of rape and murder. During an unusually sweltering summer, a series of brutal murders strikingly similar to the one five years ago occurs. Winter traces and tracks connections, wracked with guilt over not spending time with his new family. Some critics have said that the novel resembles the work of Henning Mankell and Ian Rankin.
Subject keyword: social problems
Original language: Swedish
Sources consulted for annotation:
Moritz, Susan O. *Library Journal* 131 (1 June 2006): 94.
Ott, Bill. *Booklist* 102 (August 2006): 49.
Some other translated books written by Åke Edwardson: *Sun and Shadow*; *Frozen Tracks*; *Death Angels*; *The Shadow Woman*

Kerstin Ekman. *Blackwater.*
Translated by Joan Tate. New York: Doubleday, 1996. 434 pages.
Genres/literary styles/story types: crime fiction; suspense
Life in the north of Sweden is hard and bleak. The town of Blackwater is no exception; forests are being sacrificed to the maw of giant corporations, and drinking oneself into a blissful haze is as good an answer as any to surviving the penumbral winters. It is a place of no return—somewhere to go when there are no other options. There is a commune nearby, and when Annie Raft and her young daughter come to participate in the back-to-the-land movement in 1974, they stumble upon the bodies of two dead campers and spot someone running off in the distance. Eighteen years later, Annie suddenly recalls that horrific scene when she sees Mia, her daughter, in the company of a young man. Some critics have said that this narrative combines the ruthlessness of Truman Capote's *In Cold Blood*, the grimness of Joseph Conrad's *Heart of Darkness*, and the fatalistic outlook of Thomas Hardy. Others have said that this book will appeal to fans of *Smilla's Sense of Snow* by Peter Høeg.
Subject keyword: rural life
Original language: Swedish
Sources consulted for annotation:
Bernstein, Richard. *The New York Times*, 17 April 1996, p. C15.
Global Books in Print (online) (reviews from *Library Journal*, *Kirkus Reviews*, and *Publishers Weekly*).

Lowry, Beverly. *The New York Times Book Review*, 17 March 1996, p. 24.
Merritt, Stefanie. *The Observer*, 24 October 1999, p. 15.
Scott, Bede. *Sunday Star-Times*, 15 September 1996, p. E4.
Some other translated books written by Kerstin Ekman: *Under the Snow*; *Witches' Rings*; *The Spring*; *The Forest of Hours*; *The Angel House*; *City of Light*; *God's Mercy*; *The Dog*

Per Olov Enquist. *The Royal Physician's Visit* (or ***The Visit of the Royal Physician***).
Translated by Tiina Nunnally. Woodstock, NY: Overlook Press, 2001. 312 pages.
Genre/literary style/story type: historical fiction
During the early 1770s in Denmark, the real ruler was not King Christian VII but rather the monarch's physician, a man named Johann Friedrich Struensee who issued more than 600 orders and rulings on behalf of the king, most of which were intended to relieve the socioeconomic plight of the Danish lower classes and make the government less authoritarian. When Christian VII ascended to the throne at age 16, he was already on the verge of insanity. Two years later, upon his marriage to King George III's sister, Caroline Mathilde, matters became worse. Afraid of sex, Christian turned to Struensee, who from that moment on exerted wide-ranging political influence. He also began an affair with the young queen but lost his influence and power when the queen's teacher discovered the relationship. Struensee was executed in 1772; the queen was sent into exile; and the teacher became prime minister.
Related title by the same author:
Readers may also enjoy *The Book About Blanche and Marie*, a lyrical and philosophical novel about a woman who spent 16 years as a patient at the Salpêtrière asylum. After her release, Blanche worked for Marie Curie. Excessively exposed to radiation while performing her assigned tasks, she had multiple amputations such that she could no longer walk. But she kept a notebook in which she made nuanced observations about love.
Subject keywords: politics; power
Original language: Swedish
Sources consulted for annotation:
Bawer, Bruce. *The New York Times Book Review*, 18 November 2001, p. 74.
Olson, Ray. *Booklist* 98 (1 November 2001): 459.
Prose, Francine. *The New York Times Book Review*, 2 April 2006 (online).
Scandinavian Review 90 (Spring 2003): 70.
Tonkin, Boyd. *The Independent*, 12 April 2003, p. 39.
Zaleski, Jeff. *Publishers Weekly* 248 (22 October 2001): 48.
Some other translated books written by Per Olov Enquist: *The Book About Blanche and Marie*; *Lewi's Journey*; *The Legionnaires*; *Downfall*; *The March of the Musicians*; *Captain Nemo's Library*; *The Magnetist's Fifth Winter*

Kjell Eriksson. *The Princess of Burundi*.
Translated by Ebba Segerberg. New York: Thomas Dunne Books/St. Martin's Minotaur, 2006. 300 pages.
Genres/literary styles/story types: crime fiction; police detectives
A welder by trade, John Harald Jonsson has a singularly unique passion: the cichlid fish in his aquarium. Not only did he lovingly care for these African fish, but he seemed to know everything about them. When he is murdered in his small Swedish town, police detectives Ola Haver and Ann Lindell are stumped. Could his death be related to his expensive hobby? What about his rumored big win at poker? And what—if anything—does an old school acquaintance who was perpetually tormented by others, including Jonsson, have to do with it? Numerous critics have pointed out that this book evokes Ed McBain's 87th Precinct series.

Related titles by the same author:
Readers may also enjoy *The Cruel Stars of The Night* and *The Demon of Dakar*. Critics have seen elements of Ruth Rendell in these two later books: an amalgam of psychological thriller and police procedural. *The Demon of Dakar* is especially well wrought, focusing on an upscale restaurant in Uppsala that becomes the theater for murder after one of the partners is killed.
Subject keyword: social problems
Original language: Swedish
Sources consulted for annotation:
Kim, Ann. *Library Journal* 130 (1 October 2005): 63.
Leber, Michele. *Library Journal* 130 (December 2005): 103.
Publishers Weekly 252 (28 November 2005): 26.
Some other translated books written by Kjell Eriksson: *The Cruel Stars of The Night*; *The Demon of Dakar*

Aris Fioretos. *The Truth About Sascha Knisch.*
Translated by the author. New York: Overlook Press, 2008. 320 pages.
Genres/literary styles/story types: crime fiction; amateur detectives
In late 1920s Berlin, Sascha Knisch is a movie projectionist who likes to cross-dress. When his enigmatic friend Dora Wilms, who helped him accept his sexuality, is the victim of an apparent murder, Sascha becomes the primary suspect. Naturally, he tries to clear his name by trying to find out everything he can about Dora. As he peels back the layers of her baffling past, he discovers a mysterious organization called the Foundation for Sexual Research.
Subject keywords: identity; urban life
Original language: Swedish
Source consulted for annotation:
Global Books in Print (online) (reviews from *Library Journal* and *Publishers Weekly*).

Marianne Fredriksson. *Two Women* (or *Inge & Mira.*)
Translated by Anna Paterson. New York: Ballantine Books, 2001. 195 pages.
Genres/literary styles/story types: mainstream fiction; women's lives
Inge and Mira, two middle-aged divorcées, meet while shopping for gardening supplies, eventually becoming the best of friends. The Swedish Inge has had a difficult life; her husband was a drunkard who abused her. But her story pales beside that of Mira, a Chilean refugee who, along with remaining family members, fled her native country after the disappearance of her son and daughter during the regime of General Augusto Pinochet.
Subject keyword: family histories
Original language: Swedish
Sources consulted for annotation:
Kubisz, Carolyn. *Booklist* 97 (15 February 2001): 1115.
Leber, Michele. *Library Journal* 126 (1 March 2001): 130.
Zaleski, Jeff. *Publishers Weekly* 248 (5 March 2001): 63.
Some other translated books written by Marianne Fredriksson: *Hanna's Daughters*; *Simon's Family (Simon & the Oaks)*; *According to Mary Magdalene*; *Elisabeth's Daughter*

Lars Gustafsson. *The Tale of a Dog: From the Diaries and Letters of a Texan Bankruptcy Judge.*
Translated by Tom Geddes. New York: New Directions, 1999. 182 pages.
Genres/literary styles/story types: mainstream fiction; postmodernism
When Erwin Caldwell, a Texas bankruptcy judge, finds out that one of the people whom he respected the most misrepresented himself, he cannot quite get over it. Jan van de Rouwers was

his friend, his mentor, and supposedly an inveterate enemy of the Nazis in Holland during World War II. Caldwell now discovers him to have been a staunch German supporter instead. And what is one to make of the fact that van de Rouwers, wearing only pajamas, drowns in a Texas river, especially when Caldwell starts to tell everyone he meets about killing a stray dog?

Related titles by the same author:

Readers may also enjoy *Funeral Music for Freemasons*, which explores the life of Jan Bohman, now a tourist guide in Western Africa but once a poet in Sweden. Also of interest may be *Bernard Foy's Third Castling*, a postmodern thriller about a genre novel—featuring a rabbi and a skull—written by an octogenarian poet.

Subject keyword: war

Original language: Swedish

Sources consulted for annotation:

Amazon.com (book description).

Gerzina, Gretchen Holbrook. *The New York Times Book Review*, 4 April 1999, p. 17.

Global Books in Print (online) (review from *Publishers Weekly* for *Funeral Music for Freemasons*).

Scammell, William. *New Statesman* 11 (19 June 1998): 49.

Steinberg, Sybil S. *Publishers Weekly* 245 (14 December 1998): 57.

Some other translated books written by Lars Gustafsson: *The Death of a Beekeeper*; *The Tennis Players*; *Stories of Happy People*; *Bernard Foy's Third Castling*; *Sigismund: From the Memories of a Baroque Polish Prince*; *Funeral Music for Freemasons*; *A Tiler's Afternoon*

Ninni Holmqvist. *The Unit.*

Translated by Marlaine Delargy. New York: Other Press, 2009. 268 pages.

Genre/literary style/story type: speculative fiction

A dystopia to end all dystopias—or just a natural extrapolation of the utilitarianism of contemporary society, where everyone and everything must have measurable worth? In Sweden, childless men over 60 years of age and childless women over 50 are obligated by law to be housed in special medical units where they are compelled either to participate in scientific experiments or donate body parts—all for the good of society at large. To say the least, life in these units is luxurious and completely state-supported—a stark contrast to the increasingly bleak circumstances present in the external world.

Subject keyword: power

Original language: Swedish

Source consulted for annotation:

Valdes, Marcela. *The Washington Post*, 30 June 2009 (online).

P. C. Jersild. *Children's Island.*

Translated by Joan Tate. Lincoln, NE: University of Nebraska Press, 1986. 288 pages.

Genres/literary styles/story types: mainstream fiction; coming-of-age

Reine Larsson is not your average 10-year-old boy. He wants to know everything, and he wants to know it now—or at least before the onset of puberty, which he fears like the plague, having read in an encyclopedia all about how puberty causes everyone to become sex-obsessed. So, all of life's really important questions must be resolved as soon as possible. Tricking his mother into believing he is at a summer camp, he roams the streets of Stockholm on the lookout for answers as well as his unknown father. He takes a job writing messages on funeral wreaths, falls in with a crowd of auto enthusiasts, and then meets Nora, a 22-year-old woman with whom he briefly resides.

Subject keyword: urban life

Original language: Swedish

Sources consulted for annotation:
Sensibar, Judith L. *The New York Times Book Review*, 21 December 1986 (online).
Steinberg, Sybil S. *Publishers Weekly* 230 (24 October 1986): 57.
Sweedler, Ulla. *Library Journal* 111 (December 1986): 136.
Some other translated books written by P. C. Jersild: *After the Flood*; *House of Babel*; *The Animal Doctor*; *A Living Soul*

Reidar Jönsson. *My Life as a Dog*.
Translated by Eivor Martinus. New York: Farrar, Straus and Giroux, 1989. 219 pages.
Genres/literary styles/story types: mainstream fiction; coming-of-age
It is the late 1950s, when Swedish pride was centered on the boxer Ingemar Johansson, who improbably defeated Floyd Patterson, then world champion, in 1959. The Ingemar of this novel has just started his teenage years, and his mother has already died of tuberculosis; his father is absent; and his siblings live with relatives elsewhere. He is therefore sent to stay with his uncle's family in the isolated Swedish province of Småland. It is a whole new world for him, and he gets more than his fair share of bumps and bruises as he tries to accustom himself to the peculiarities of the village and its eccentric residents. As he experiences life in a glass factory; as he makes a flying saucer; and as he learns about outhouses, all his adventures are presented with a luminous nostalgia for a bygone age when life was less hectic.
Subject keyword: rural life
Original language: Swedish
Sources consulted for annotation:
Belden, Elizabeth A., and Judith M. Beckman. *English Journal* 80 (February 1991): 85.
Cart, Michael. *School Library Journal* 37 (January 1991): 110.
Steinberg, Sybil S. *Publishers Weekly* 237 (27 April 1990): 54.
Another translated book written by Reidar Jönsson: *My Father, His Son*

Mari Jungstedt. *The Inner Circle*.
Translated by Tiina Nunnally. New York: St. Martin's Press, 2008. 288 pages.
Genres/literary styles/story types: crime fiction; police detectives
There is much to discover in the historic town of Visby, on the no-less-historic island of Gotland, off the Swedish coast. So, it is not surprising that the island attracts archeologists seeking Viking remains and other medieval artefacts. But there are strange things afoot: A pony has had its head severed, and one of the young archeology students has been gruesomely murdered in what appears to be a ritualistic killing. Then, two more victims meet a similar fate. Police inspector Anders Knutas knows that he must confront a psychopathic and brutal killer well-versed in ancient mythology. The Inspector Knutas mystery series starts with *Unseen*, where another serial killer terrorizes Gotland, causing a media storm that the tourist-dependent authorities of Gotland could do without.
Subject keyword: rural life
Original language: Swedish
Source consulted for annotation:
Global Books in Print (online) (reviews from *Booklist*, *Library Journal*, and *Publishers Weekly*).
Some other translated books written by Mari Jungstedt: *Unseen*; *Unspoken*; *The Killer's Art*

Christer Kihlman. *The Downfall of Gerdt Bladh*.
Translated by Joan Tate. London: Peter Owen, 1989. 221 pages.
Genre/literary style/story type: mainstream fiction
Gerdt Bladh runs a family department store in Finland; he has built his life and his business on the strictest of moral and ethical principles. But his world begins to shatter when he learns about his

wife's affair. Distraught and isolated, he has no friends to fall back on for support. Even his three adult children sympathize with their mother. As he begins to rethink the premises of his professional success and as he examines the crumbling foundations of his personal life, he realizes he knows very little about anyone else nor about himself. Soon, Gerdt's troubles deepen when the store becomes the object of a hostile takeover and when a sensationalistic newspaper publishes sexually based pictures of him.
Subject keyword: family histories
Original language: Swedish
Sources consulted for annotation:
Hornik, Peter David. *Jerusalem Post*, 9 February 1990, p. 44.
Steinberg, Sybil S. *Publishers Weekly* 236 (10 November 1989): 50.
Some other translated books written by Christer Kihlman: *The Blue Mother*; *All My Sons*; *Sweet Prince*

Camilla Läckberg. *The Ice Princess*.
Translated by Steven T. Murray. New York: Pegasus, 2010. 393 pages.
Genres/literary styles/story types: crime fiction; amateur detectives
Erica Falck, a writer, returns to her rural birthplace to attend to the funeral arrangements for her parents. But she is drawn into the mystery surrounding the horrid death of a longtime friend. Alex, a woman who preferred solitude despite her popularity, has apparently committed suicide in her bathtub. When the water in the tub freezes, she is entombed, literally becoming an ice princess. Of course, Erica is intrigued, delves further into the life of Alex with the idea of writing a book about her, and eventually joins the police investigation led by Patrik Hedstrom. In the second book of the series, *The Preacher*, Erica and Patrik are now lovers, with Erica expecting a child. Their idyll is shattered when two decomposed corpses from a long-ago double murder are found nearby—together with the body of a young girl recently killed. Suspicion quickly falls on an eccentric and violence-prone family with rabid religious convictions. Some critics have compared Läckberg to Agatha Christie.
Subject keyword: rural life
Original language: Swedish
Source consulted for annotation:
Fantastic Fiction (book review), http://www.fantasticfiction.co.uk.
Some other translated books written by Camilla Läckberg: *The Preacher*; *The Stone Cutter*; *The Gallow's Bird*

Åsa Larsson. *Sun Storm*.
Translated by Marlaine Delargy. New York: Pegasus, 2006. 310 pages.
Genres/literary styles/story types: crime fiction; amateur detectives
The amateur detective in this series is Rebecca Martinsson, a tax lawyer in Stockholm, who returns to her native village in the north of Sweden after a frenzied appeal by an old friend, Sanna, whose brother—the founder of a fundamentalist church—has been murdered. When Sanna becomes the primary suspect, Rebecca is thrust back into the middle of a past she thought she left behind. The series also features Inspector Anna-Maria Mella, a local detective with whom Rebecca joins forces.
Subject keyword: rural life
Original language: Swedish
Sources consulted for annotation:
Fantastic Fiction (book review), http://www.fantasticfiction.co.uk.
Global Books in Print (online) (reviews from *Booklist*, *Library Journal*, and *Publishers Weekly*).
Some other translated books written by Åsa Larsson: *The Blood Spilt*; *The Black Path*

Björn Larsson. *The Celtic Ring.*
Translated by George Simpson. Rendlesham, Woodbridge, Suffolk, UK: Seafarer Books, 1997. 387 pages.
Genres/literary styles/story types: adventure; survival and disaster stories
Two Swedish friends, Ulf and Torben, are given a mysterious logbook by a mysterious sailor whom they meet in a Danish harbor in the 1990s. The logbook speaks of a secret organization called the Celtic Ring, whose goal is Celtic independence. As the two friends make a treacherous winter crossing of the North Sea, they are thrust into the world of druids, bloody rituals, cults, and contemporary politics, especially the IRA. Some critics have compared this book to Erskine Childers's *The Riddle of the Sands*.
Subject keyword: power
Original language: Swedish
Sources consulted for annotation:
Amazon.com (book description).
Green, Roland. *Booklist* 93 (15 March 1997): 1226.
Publishers Weekly 247 (20 November 2000): 48.
Sheridan House website (book description and reviews), http://sheridanhouse.com.
Another translated book written by Björn Larsson: *Long John Silver: The True and Eventful History of My Life of Liberty and Adventure as a Gentleman of Fortune & Enemy to Mankind*

Stieg Larsson. *The Girl with the Dragon Tattoo.*
Translated by Reg Keeland. New York: Alfred A. Knopf, 2008. 465 pages.
Genres/literary styles/story types: thrillers; conspiracy thrillers
Things are not going well for Carl Mikael Blomkvist, a reporter. He and his newspaper have been successfully sued for libel by Hans-Erik Wennerström, a Swedish tycoon. When Henrik Vanger, another prominent Swedish businessman, wants to hire Blomkvist to get to the bottom of his niece's disappearance in 1960, Blomkvist is more than happy to take on the case, especially since Vanger promises him a large fee and inside information about Wennerström. Blomkvist teams up with Lisbeth Salander, an unconventional dynamo described by Michiko Kakutani as "Angelina Jolie's Lara Croft endowed with Mr. Spock's intense braininess and Scarlett O'Hara's spunky instinct for survival." Blomkvist and Salander's investigation reveals the dark paradoxes of Stockholm—at once an aristocratic and corrupt metropolis on the cusp of gentrification and globalization.
Related titles by the same author:
Readers may also enjoy *The Girl Who Played with Fire*, a sequel where Blomkvist undertakes a desperate search for Salander, who has gone into hiding after the police become convinced she is involved in three murders. In the final volume of this trilogy, *The Girl Who Kicked the Hornet's Nest*, Salander and Blomkvist's struggles become intertwined with international intrigue and conspiracy theories involving government agencies. As Salander lies on the edge of death in a hospital and as Blomkvist fulminates in jail, the backstory underpinning the trilogy becomes clear. It involves Salander's father, a rough-hewn Soviet spy whose defection to Sweden was such a coup for the Swedish intelligence apparatus that they mandated a special detail to constantly keep watch over him. Salander had an extremely tense relationship with her father—to the extent that the Swedish government committed her to an asylum. But the days of the Soviet Union are over, as are the days when Cold War spying mattered. But revealing any of these extraordinary events would threaten Swedish prestige, so various agencies work together to forestall incriminating revelations.
Subject keywords: politics; power
Original language: Swedish
Sources consulted for annotation:
Kakutani, Michiko. *The New York Times*, 30 September 2008 (online).

Kakutani, Michiko. *The New York Times*, 17 July 2009 (online).
Kakutani, Michiko. *The New York Times*, 21 May 2010 (online).
Some other translated books written by Stieg Larsson: *The Girl Who Played with Fire*; *The Girl Who Kicked the Hornet's Nest*

Torgny Lindgren. *Hash.*
Translated by Tom Geddes. Woodstock, NY: Overlook Press, 2004. 236 pages.
Genre/literary style/story type: mainstream fiction
In 1947, a journalist who is in the middle of writing an article about two new arrivals in a small Swedish village is abruptly fired after being accused of making things up. Now 107 years old and living in a retirement community, the same journalist seems to have drunk copiously at the fountain of youth; his hair is no longer white, and his eyesight is much improved. He decides to pick up the threads of his never-completed story about the two strangers, one of whom he believes was the notorious Martin Bormann, an influential Nazi and longtime associate of Hitler.
Subject keyword: identity
Original language: Swedish
Sources consulted for annotation:
Amazon.com (review from *Booklist*).
Mattsson, Margareta. *World Literature Today* 78 (September/December 2004): 128.
Zaleski, Jeff. *Publishers Weekly* 251 (1 March 2004): 50.
Some other translated books written by Torgny Lindgren: *Bathsheba*; *Sweetness*; *Merab's Beauty and Other Stories*; *Light*; *In Praise of Truth: The Personal Account of Theodore Marklund, Picture-Framer*; *The Way of a Serpent*

John Ajvide Lindqvist. *Let the Right One In.*
Translated by Ebba Segerberg. New York: St Martin's Press, 2008. 480 pages.
Genres/literary styles/story types: speculative fiction; horror/paranormal
A bullied 12-year-old boy by the name of Oskar; a new neighborhood girl who has an uncanny ability to solve puzzles, such as the Rubik's Cube; and the strange murder of one of Oskar's tormentors. It all adds up to a gothic coming-of-age tale set in Sweden.
Related title by the same author:
Readers may also enjoy *Handling the Undead*, in which the dead really do come back to life and cause untold problems for the people who have already mourned their loss. And what will the country as a whole do? Are the undead to be considered citizens or zombies, and what are their rights and responsibilities? This book could be profitably be read together with José Saramago's *Death with Interruptions*. Both function as social satires while focusing on personal issues that arise from an apocalyptic-like scenario.
Subject keyword: identity
Original language: Swedish
Source consulted for annotation:
Global Books in Print (online) (synopsis).
Another translated book written by John Ajvide Lindqvist: *Handling the Undead*

Henning Mankell. *The Dogs of Riga: A Kurt Wallander Mystery.*
Translated by Laurie Thompson. New York: New Press, 2001. 326 pages.
Genres/literary styles/story types: crime fiction; police detectives
In the early 1990s, the bodies of two dead men—both victims of gangland execution—wash ashore in the small southern Swedish town of Ystad, where the introspective, gloomy, and divorced Kurt Wallander works. It is eventually determined that the men are from Latvia, a former republic of

the disintegrating Soviet Union. Unable to come to terms with the collapse of traditional social values and ever-increasing amounts of violence, Wallander is hospitalized for psychological reasons. Beset by personal problems—the death of his police partner, fraught relationships with his father and daughter, his infatuation with the local district attorney—Wallander struggles to remain on an even keel. Karlis Liepa, a Latvian detective, arrives to help Wallander in his investigation, but after Liepa returns to Latvia, he is murdered. Wallander travels to Latvia—a place where criminal activity is inextricably linked with political machinations—to unravel the already vexed situation but becomes entangled even more as he falls in love with Liepa's young widow and discovers the extent of corruption in a Baltic state caught in the throes of postcommunism and the difficult transformation to a working democracy. Part international spy thriller and part police procedural, the book focuses on the moody and unconventional Wallander, who has been compared with Georges Simenon's Inspector Maigret and John Le Carré's George Smiley.

Related titles by the same author:

Readers may also enjoy *Before the Frost*, which introduces Linda Wallander, Kurt's daughter, who is about to follow in her father's footsteps and become a police officer in Ystad. Here, the theme centers on the violence of religious cults. In *The Return of the Dancing Master*, the theme is neo-Nazism. In *The Man from Beijing*, no less than 19 grisly murders stun a quiet Swedish village.

Subject keywords: politics; power

Original language: Swedish

Sources consulted for annotation:

Cannon, Peter. *Publishers Weekly* 250 (31 March 2003): 46.

Ellmann, Lucy. *The New York Times Book Review*, 15 April 2007 (online).

Lipez, Richard. *The Washington Post*, 27 April 2003, p. T13.

Stasio, Marilyn. *The New York Times Book Review*, 21 October 2007 (online).

Stasio, Marilyn. *The New York Times Book Review*, 23 January 2005 (online).

Stasio, Marilyn. *The New York Times Book Review*, 28 March 2004 (online).

Some other translated books written by Henning Mankell: *Faceless Killers*; *The Return of the Dancing Master*; *The White Lioness*; *Chronicler of the Winds*; *Depths*; *Kennedy's Brain*; *Sidetracked*, *The Fifth Woman*, *One Step Behind*, *Firewall*; *Before the Frost*; *The Pyramid*; *Italian Shoes*; *The Man from Beijing*

Håkan Nesser. *Borkmann's Point.*

Translated by Laurie Thompson. New York: Pantheon Books, 2006. 321 pages.

Genres/literary styles/story types: crime fiction; police detectives

Chief Inspector Van Veeteren, a reflective chess player who likes good food, subscribes to the theory that too much information in police investigations may often be detrimental to solving the crimes in question; careful reasoning is all that is really needed. This theory is put to the test when he is forced to terminate his vacation to solve a series of brutal murders that have occurred in the small town of Kaalbringen. What do the deaths of a real estate developer, a female detective, and two others have in common? Critics have noted the similarities between Nesser's detective and the protagonists of novels by Fred Vargas and Henning Mankell.

Related titles by the same author:

Readers may also enjoy *The Return*, where Van Veeteren must get to the bottom of the grisly dismemberment of a man who has served 24 years in prison for two murders that he claims he did not commit. Also of interest may be *The Mind's Eye*, in which Van Veeteren investigates the murder of a man in a mental hospital who had been institutionalized after allegedly drowning his newlywed wife. In *Woman with Birthmark*, two cases of murder—in which the victims are shot multiple times in the groin and chest—pique the interest of Van Veeteren.

Subject keyword: social problems

Original language: Swedish
Sources consulted for annotation:
Publishers Weekly 253 (2 January 2006): 38.
Ott, Bill. *Booklist* 102 (1 April 2006): 25.
Stasio, Marilyn. *The New York Times Book Review*, 24 April 2009 (online).
Some other translated books written by Håkan Nesser: *The Return*; *Mind's Eye*; *Woman with Birthmark*; *The Inspector and Silence*

Leif G. W. Persson. *Between Summer's Longing and Winter's End: The Story of a Crime.*
Translated by Paul Norlen. New York: Pantheon, 2010. 608 pages.
Genres/literary styles/story types: crime fiction; suspense
If you thought that Stieg Larsson's trilogy featuring Lisbeth Salander was full of conspiracies, you have not seen anything yet. Everything is connected, and everyone and everything is being manipulated by powerful systemic forces—of which we have very little inkling. After an American falls to his death from a Stockholm building, a suspicious Swedish policeman travels to the United States in an attempt to discover clues about what may or may not be a suicide. His investigation quickly becomes international in scope, with connections to the defining moment in recent Swedish history: the murder of former prime minister Olaf Palme in 1986. This is the first volume of a trilogy whose final two volumes are projected to be translated into English in the near future.
Subject keywords: politics; power
Original language: Swedish
Sources consulted for annotation:
Amazon.com (reviews and product description).
Global Books in Print (online) (synopsis).

Helene Tursten. *Detective Inspector Huss.*
Translated by Steven T. Murray. New York: Soho Press, 2003. 371 pages.
Genres/literary styles/story types: crime fiction; police detectives
Irene Huss is a middle-aged policewoman assigned to violent crime in the coastal city of Göteborg, Sweden's second largest. As she tries to find a balance in her personal and professional life, she is faced with an apparent suicide to end all suicides. One of Göteborg's wealthiest men lies at the bottom of his swank apartment building. And even though Huss and her colleagues are warned that he had numerous social and political connections to the top echelons of Swedish society, her investigation soon involves a motley assortment of small-time criminals and neo-Nazis. Critics have compared the author to P. D. James.
Related title by the same author:
Readers may also enjoy *The Glass Devil*, in which Huss is perplexed by a series of occult symbols found on the computer screens of a murdered teacher and his parents.
Subject keyword: urban life
Original language: Swedish
Sources consulted for annotation:
Cannon, Peter. *Publishers Weekly* 249 (18 November 2002): 44.
Global Books in Print (online) (reviews from *Booklist* and *Publishers Weekly* for *The Glass Devil*).
Helene Tursten fansite (book description), http://heleneturst en.com.
Pearl, Nancy. *Library Journal* 128 (1 April 2003): 156.
Some other translated books written by Helene Tursten: *The Torso*; *The Glass Devil*

CHAPTER 9

Western Europe: Austria, Germany, France, Switzerland, French-Speaking Belgium, and French-Speaking Caribbean

Language groups:	**Countries represented:**	
French	Austria	Guadeloupe
German	Belgium	Haiti
	France	Martinique
	Germany	Switzerland

INTRODUCTION

This chapter contains annotations of books from France; Belgium; Caribbean countries, such as Haiti, Guadeloupe, and Martinique; Germany; Austria; and Switzerland. Please note that titles from Dutch-speaking Belgium are covered in Chapter 8 and that titles from French-speaking Africa are covered in Chapter 1. All books represented in this chapter were translated either from French or German.

Translated titles from France include Jacques-Pierre Amette's *Brecht's Mistress*; Stéphane Audeguy's *The Only Son*; Muriel Barbery's *The Elegance of the Hedgehog*; Tonino Benacquista's *Holy Smoke*; Didier van Cauwelaert's *One-Way*; Phillipe Claudel's *By a Slow River*; Michel Houellebecq's *The Elementary Particles* and *Platform*; 2008 Nobel Prize winner J.-M. G. Le Clézio's *Wandering Star* and *Desert*; Jonathan Littell's highly controversial *The Kindly Ones*; Irène Némirovsky's *Suite Française*; Jean-Christophe Rufin's *Brazil Red*; Shan Sa's *Alexander and Alestria*; and Fred Vargas's *Have Mercy on Us All*. One of the most popular Belgian authors writing in French is Amélie Nothomb (*Fear and Trembling* and *The Stranger Next Door*).

Some of the translated books from French-speaking Caribbean countries are Patrick Chamoiseau's *Texaco* (Martinique); Maryse Condé's *The Story of the Cannibal Woman* and *Windward Heights* (Guadeloupe); and Lyonel Trouillot's *Children of Heroes* (Haiti).

Among the novels from Germany mentioned in this chapter are Nobel Prize winner Günter Grass's *Crabwalk* and *Too Far Afield*; Katharina Hacker's *The Lifeguard*; Christoph Hein's *Willenbrock*; Michael Kumpfmüller's *The Adventures of a Bed Salesman*; Bernhard Schlink's *The Reader*; Ingo Schulze's *New Lives*; Patrick Süskind's *Perfume* and *The Pigeon*; and Uwe Timm's *The Invention of Curried Sausage*.

Some of the more well-known Austrian writers include Thomas Bernhard (*Frost*); Peter Handke (*Don Juan: His Own Version*); and 2004 Nobel Prize winner Elfriede Jelinek—an extremely contested selection that caused major rifts in the selection committee. Readers may want to peruse Jelinek's *The Piano Teacher* to gain some insight into the politics of contemporary literary awards. Of the Swiss novelists mentioned in this chapter—Otto F. Walter (*Time of the Pheasant*)—may be the most recognized name.

Earlier Translated Literature

The history of French literature reads like a who's who of influential and famous writers. In the sixteenth century, there are two comic masterpieces by François Rabelais: *Pantagruel* and *Gargantua*; the seventeenth century is marked by the *Fables* of Jean de la Fontaine. The list of important and popular nineteenth- and early and mid-twentieth-century French novelists is nearly endless. In the nineteenth century, some of these authors are Henri Beyle, better known as Stendhal (*The Red and the Black* and *The Charterhouse of Parma*); Victor Hugo (*Les Misérables* and *The Hunchback of Notre-Dame*); Alexandre Dumas (*The Count of Monte Cristo* and *The Three Musketeers*); George Sand (*Indiana*); Guy de Maupassant (*Selected Short Stories*); Jules Verne (*Twenty Thousand Leagues Under the Sea*; *Around the World in Eighty Days*; and *Journey to the Center of the Earth*); Gustave Flaubert (*Madame Bovary* and *A Sentimental Education*); and Émile Zola (*Germinal*; *Nana*; and *L'Assommoir*). Of particular note is Honoré de Balzac's *La Comédie Humaine*, a series of 89 novels that provide an incisive examination of every facet of French society; some of the more popular individual titles of the series are *Cousin Bette*; *Père Goriot*; *The Wild Ass's Skin*; and *Eugénie Grandet*. In the twentieth century, at least five novelists stand out: Marcel Proust, universally known for his *A La Recherche Du Temps Perdu* (*Remembrance of Things Past*); Nobel Prize laureate Albert Camus, whose *The Stranger* [or *The Outsider*], *The Plague*, and *The Fall* are classics of existentialism; Nobel Prize laureate Claude Simon (*The Wind*; *The Flanders Road*; and *Grass*); Alain Robbe-Grillet (*The Erasers* and *In the Labyrinth*); and Marguerite Duras (*The Lover*).

Probably the most famous figure in German literature is Johann Wolfgang von Goethe, best known for his play *Faust*. But Goethe—whose output spans the late eighteenth and early nineteenth century—also wrote two important novels, collectively referred to as the *Wilhelm Meister* novels, which were translated by the British essayist and philosopher Thomas Carlyle. The list of canonical German fiction writers of the later nineteenth century and twentieth century includes Theodor Fontane (*Effi Briest*); Franz Kakfa (*The Metamorphosis*; *The Castle*; and *The Trial*); Thomas Mann (*The Magic Mountain*; *Joseph and His Brothers*; and *Death in Venice*); Robert Musil (*The Man Without Qualities*); Herman Hesse (*Siddhartha*; *Steppenwolf*; and *The Glass Bead Game*); Erich Maria Remarque (*All Quiet on the Western Front*); and Heinrich Böll (*Billiards at Half Past Nine* and *The Lost Honor of Katharina Blum*).

Robert Walser is perhaps the most respected Swiss writer. Producing the majority of his work in the first quarter of the twentieth century, he is relatively obscure—partly because he spent more than 25 years of his life in an asylum. But his fiction has been praised by such major international writers as Franz Kafka and W. G. Sebald. Two of his most accessible novels are *The Assistant* and *The Tanners*. In the former, a clerk has ambiguous feelings about his employer—a man on the verge of bankruptcy who spends his time inventing far-fetched gizmos. In the latter, which critics have said is partly autobiographical, Simon Tanner is content to be an absolute nobody. But this stance is the ultimate act of liberation because it frees him to not only be as unconventional and strange as he wants but to also say the things that no one else dares to.

SOURCES CONSULTED

Bartram, Graham. (Ed.). (2004). *The Cambridge Companion to the Modern German Novel*. New York: Cambridge University Press.

France, Peter. (Ed.). (2000). "French" and "German." In *The Oxford Guide to Literature in English Translation*, pp. 251–347. Oxford: Oxford University Press.

McCullough, Alison. (2007). "Fiction Chronicle." *The New York Times Book Review*, 19 August 2007 (online).

Toal, Drew. (2009). "Book Review." *TimeOut New York*, 20–26 August 2009 (online).

BIBLIOGRAPHIC ESSAY

France

We recommend that readers start with Sarah Kay, Terrence Cave, and Malcolm Bowie's *A Short History of French Literature*, which presents historical and cultural overviews and literary closeups of three periods: the Middle Ages up to 1470; the early modern period from 1470 to 1789; and the modern period 1789–2000. It reads almost like a novel, with subsections with titles such as: "Inventing Love Poetry"; "Humanism, Didacticism, Licence, and Death"; "The Sentimental and the Erotic"; "Prose Fiction Prepares for Victory"; and "Flaubert's War on Stupidity." It is a literary history for individuals who do not wish to be overwhelmed by long lists of famous and not-so-famous names but who wish to understand the role and place of literature within French society writ large. The same could be said of *A New History of French Literature*, edited by Denis Hollier. As the introduction puts it, "[T]his volume presents French literature not as a simple inventory of authors or titles, but rather as a historical and cultural field viewed from a wide array of contemporary critical perspectives" (p. xix). Each of the essays "individually and cumulatively . . . question our conventional perception of the historical continuum" (p. xix). Thus, we are treated to sparkling discussions of Rabelais and textual architecture; manners and mannerisms at court; pastoral fiction; the age of the technician; the politics of epistolary art; beauty in context; civil rights and the wrongs of women; the novel and gender difference; class struggles in France; orientalism; colonialism; the scandal of realism; Americans in Paris; literature and collaboration; and many others. It is not too much of an exaggeration to say that one will never look at French literary history in the same way again.

Nevertheless, readers will want some sense of the key figures in French literature that comes with a more traditional chronological narrative. For these individuals, David Coward's *A History of French Literature: From Chanson de Geste to Cinema* is the first place to look. It has marvelously detailed chapters about French literature in the medieval era, the Renaissance, and the Classical Age. But Coward outdoes himself when he reaches the age of enlightenment, the nineteenth century, and twentieth century, with subsections on writers and their publics as well as such various intellectual currents and aesthetic doctrines as existentialism, symbolism, and surrealism. And there is comprehensive analysis of such major French literary figures as Racine; Marivaux; Sade; Voltaire; Rousseau; Baudelaire; Balzac; Hugo; Flaubert; Zola; Camus; Cocteau; Duras; and Yourcenar. But there are also chapters devoted to women's writing, Francophone writing outside France, humor writing, regional literature, detective novels, and graphic novels. If readers are unable to find Coward's book, they will not do themselves a disservice by turning to Jennifer Birkett and James Kearns's *A Guide to French Literature: From Early Modern to Postmodern* or the six-volume *French Literature and Its Background*, edited by John Cruickshank. Both offer original readings about many topics and authors.

By necessity, biographical information about authors is kept to a minimum in historical literary surveys. For in-depth information about specific authors, there are no better sources than Anthony Levi's *Guide to French Literature: Beginnings to 1789* and *Guide to French Literature: 1789 to the Present*. Taken together, these two volumes contain about 2,000 pages of incomparable (and lengthy) bio-bibliographic information about major French writers. For example, the essay on Denis Diderot is some 20 pages; the one on Jean-Paul Sartre is 12 pages; and the one on Pierre Loti is seven pages. *The New Oxford Companion to Literature in French*, edited by Peter France, and the *Dictionary of Modern French Literature: From the Age of Reason Through Realism* by Sandra W. Dolbow fill the same role as Levi's volumes, but both have much briefer entries. On the other hand, they cover more writers than Levi, and both also discuss famous works (such as Balzac's novel *Eugénie Grandet* and Rousseau's *The Social Contract*) and literary topics (such as printing in France until 1600 and classical influences) in separate entries.

It is impossible to discuss individual French authors without mentioning the numerous volumes in the Dictionary of Literary Biography series consecrated to them. Among the more than dozen that currently exist, we can without hesitation recommend *French Novelists, 1900–1930*, edited by Catharine Savage Brosman (1988; vol. 65); *French Novelists, 1930–1960*, also edited by Catharine Savage Brosman (1988; vol. 72); *Nineteenth-Century French Fiction Writers: Naturalism and Beyond, 1860–1900*, yet again edited by Catharine Savage Brosman (1992; vol. 123); *Seventeenth-Century French Writers*, edited by Françoise Jaouën (2002; vol. 268); *Writers of the French Enlightenment*, edited by Samia I. Spencer (2005; vols. 312 and 313); and *Twentieth-Century French Dramatists*, edited by Mary Anne O'Neil (2006; vol. 321). As with all volumes in the Dictionary of Literary Biography series, each included author is accorded a substantial bio-bibliographic entry, with complete information about any translated works.

A much-needed addition to the history of French literature is provided by *The Feminist Encyclopedia of French Literature*, edited by Eva Martin Sartori, and *French Women Writers: A Bio-Bibliographical Source Book*, edited by Eva Martin Sartori and Dorothy Wynne Zimmerman. *The Feminist Encyclopedia of French Literature* is especially valuable for its introductory essay entitled "A Feminist History of French Literature" as well as such entries as essentialism; letter writing; memoirs; prison writing; Saint-Simonianism; and many other topics of particular relevance to women's literary production. But perhaps the most valuable feature of these volumes is their detailed bio-bibliographic entries on such famous writers as George Sand, Nathalie Sarraute, Simone Weil, Monique Wittig, Flora Tristan, Violette Leduc as well as the emphasis in *The Feminist Encyclopedia of French Literature* on such less-known literary figures as Elisabeth Gille, Louise Labé, Marguerite de Lussan, Alina Reyes, Geneviève Serreau, and Suzanne Voilquin. After readers have thoroughly immersed themselves in these books, they may wish to read some of the works of French women writers. A good introductory text for this purpose is Elizabeth Fallaize's *French Women's Writing: Recent Fiction*, which not only contains a superb essay about the cultural context of women's writing in 1970s and 1980s France but also translated extracts from Marie Cardinal, Chantal Chawaf, Annie Ernaux, Claire Etcherelli, Jeanne Hyvrard, Annie Leclerc, and Marie Redonnet.

For more specialized information about various aspects of the French novel, readers will want to gravitate toward *The Cambridge Companion to the French Novel: From 1800 to the Present*, edited by Timothy Unwin. Here, they will find concise essays by world-renowned experts on such topics as popular fiction in the nineteenth century; existentialism and ideology; twentieth-century war and Holocaust novels; the colonial and postcolonial Francophone novel; French-Canadian novels; and experimental and postmodern French fiction. Additional critical analyses of some of the writers mentioned in Unwin's text are available in *The Contemporary Novel in France*, edited by William Thompson, which has essays on 20 contemporary writers grouped into four categories: continuing traditions and changing styles; innovations in language and form; writing, history, and myth; and new narratives and new traditions. Some of the authors discussed are Julien Green, Julien Gracq, Hélène Cixous,

Jean Echenoz, Michel Tournier, Monique Wittig, Patrick Drevet, and Jean-Philippe Toussaint. Readers can also turn to *The Babel Guide to French Fiction in English Translation* by Ray Keenoy, Laurence Laluyaux, and Gareth Stanton to find out which of the novels that they have read about in Unwin's and Thompson's books have been translated into English.

To put French literature into a wider context, *The Cambridge Companion to Modern French Culture*, edited by Nicholas Hewitt, should be considered a must-read item. There are fascinating articles on such topics as consumer culture (food, drink, fashions); language divisions and debates; the mass media; architecture and design; and the place of religion and politics in French life. There are also cogent overviews about poetry, theater, music, the visual arts, and cinema. One topic not included is children's literature. Fortunately, Penny Brown has written a groundbreaking two-volume work entitled *A Critical History of French Children's Literature*, which not only discusses such classic and oft-translated writers as Jules Verne and Antoine de Saint-Exupéry but also numerous other innovative authors and texts, starting from 1600 and continuing to about 2005. In addition, there are chapters about the way in which children read in the seventeenth century as well as what they read—for example, fables, fairy tales, and moral and didactic novels.

We cannot forget Belgian literature written in French. Inevitably, the best sources are written in French. Without a doubt, the definitive historical text about major writers in Francophone Belgium is *Histoire de le Littérature Belge Francophone, 1830–2000*, edited by Jean-Pierre Bertrand, Michel Biron, Benôit Denis, and Rainier Grutman. This should be supplemented with a series of essays about various aspects of Belgian culture life, entitled *Littératures Belges de Langue Française (1830–2000)* and edited by Christian Berg and Pierre Halen. Well worth reading is the article about the Belgian contribution to the birth of the modern graphic novel. But because both of these books are well over 600 pages, some readers will want to start with the more manageable *La Littérature Belge: Précis d'Histoire Sociale* by Benôit Denis and Jean-Marie Klinkenberg. In about 250 pages, they make the case that Belgian literature should not simply be equated with such famous names as 1911 Nobel Prize winner Maurice Maeterlinck, the crime and mystery writer Georges Simenon, or the bestselling contemporary writer Amélie Nothomb. Instead, they suggest that Belgian literature is just as complex and multidimensional as the country itself—pushed and pulled between divergent social, linguistic, and cultural forces. A small part of this complexity and multidimensionality can be glimpsed in *Anthologie de la Littérature Française de Belgique: Entre Réel et Suréel*, edited by Marc Quaghebeur. Certainly, there are representative extracts from Maeterlinck, Simenon, and Nothomb, but there are also samples from the writings of such overlooked authors as Edmond Picard, Jean Ray, Marie Gevers, Guy Vaes, Jean Muno, Suzanne Lilar, Pierre Mertens, Jacqueline Harpman, and Caroline Lamarche.

Germany

To get a sense of the vast sweep of German literary history, readers should be clamoring to get their hands on *The Cambridge History of German Literature*, edited by Helen Watanabe-O'Kelly. All the major authors and movements are expertly discussed, but the chapters in the book also pay close attention to "what Germans in a given period were actually reading and writing, what they would have seen at the local theatre and found in the local lending library" (p. xii). In addition to thorough coverage of the Middle Ages and the Enlightenment, of especial note are essays entitled "From Naturalism to National Socialism (1890–1945)"; "The Literature of the German Democratic Republic (1945–1990)"; and "German Writing in the West (1945–1990)," which also briefly covers German-language literature in Austria and Switzerland. The 75-page bibliography—divided according to time period, then genre, then author—is a work of artistic beauty. A more traditional approach to German literary history can be found in *A Concise History of German Literature to 1900*, edited by Kim Vivian. Here, readers will get succinct overviews of the Gothic and Old High German, Middle High

German, Baroque, Classic, Romantic, and Naturalistic periods, among others. Placed in their historical and social context, the works of Goethe, Herder, Schiller, and Heine are made all the more meaningful.

The two-volume *Encyclopedia of German Literature*, edited by Matthias Konzett, should be the next requisite stop. In-depth essays about such writers as Elias Canetti, Heinrich Böll, Günter Grass, and W. G. Sebald as well as such topics as the epistolary novel, minority literature, mysticism, the Weimar Republic, war novels, women and literature, and the relationship of films and literature make this an indispensable guide to understanding the German literary heritage. A reference work of the same kind but with shorter (but many more) entries is Henry and Mary Garland's *The Oxford Companion to German Literature* (3rd ed.). Despite the brevity of the entries, the amount of information contained in each one is breathtaking; particularly valuable are the summaries and analyses of famous German novels, such as Hermann Hesse's utopian *Das Glasperlenspiel.*

As with many of the literatures discussed in other chapters, the Dictionary of Literary Biography series has numerous volumes devoted to the authors of various time periods. Some of the most valuable of these include: *German Fiction Writers, 1914–1945*, edited by James Hardin (1987; vol. 56); the two-volume *German Fiction Writers, 1885–1913*, edited by James Hardin (1988; vol. 66); *Contemporary German Writers, First Series*, edited by Wolfgang D. Elfe and James Hardin (1988; vol. 69); *Contemporary German Writers, Second Series*, edited by Wolfgang D. Elfe and James Hardin (1988; vol. 75); *Nineteenth-Century German Writers, 1841–1900*, edited by James Hardin and Siegfried Mews (1993; vol. 129); and *Nineteenth-Century German Writers to 1840*, edited by James Hardin and Siegfried Mews (1993; vol. 133). Also noteworthy is *The Feminist Encyclopedia of German Literature*, edited by Friederike Eigler and Susanne Kord, which not only contains substantial entries on such authors as Louise Aston, Helke Sander, Christa Wolf, and Fanny Lewald but also covers such topics as Swiss-German literature, Austrian literature, and minority literature.

After becoming familiar with individual fiction writers, readers will be ready for *The Cambridge Companion to the Modern German Novel*, edited by Graham Bartram. Quite simply, this book is a stunning achievement. The individual articles are thematically focused, but taken as a group, they chronologically trace the serpentine path of German-language fiction from 1870 to the present. Some of the essay titles alone evoke the multifaceted nature of German literature: "Contexts of the Novel: Society, Politics, and Culture in German-Speaking Europe"; "The Novel in Wilhelmine Germany: From Realism to Satire"; "Gender Anxiety and the Shaping of the Self in Some Modernist Writers"; "Franz Kafka: The Radical Modernist"; "Modernism and the *Bildungsroman*: Thomas Mann's *Magic Mountain*"; "Apocalypse and Utopia in the Austrian Novel of the 1930s: Hermann Broch and Robert Musil"; "Women Writers in the 'Golden' Twenties"; "The First World War and Its Aftermath in the German Novel"; "The German Novel During the Third Reich"; "History, Memory, Fiction After the Second World War"; "Identity and Authenticity in Swiss and Austrian Novels of the Postwar Era: Max Frisch and Peter Handke"; "Subjectivity and Women's Writing of the 1970s and early 1980s"; and "The German Postmodern Novel." In sum, each of the essays is a mini-lesson in German history, culture, and literature that, collectively, allow readers to begin to understand some of the bleakness, ferocity, anger, tragedy, and anxiety at work in such famous contemporary German novels as Michael Kumpfmüller's *The Adventures of a Bed Salesman*, Günter Grass's *Crabwalk*, Bernhard Schlink's *The Reader*, or Christoph Hein's *Willenbrock*. For a perspective that is broader still, we suggest *The Cambridge Companion to Modern German Culture*, edited by Eva Kolinsky and Wilfried van der Will, which offers insightful overviews about German national identity, class structure, non-German minorities, and folk and mass culture as well as nuanced considerations of modern German poetry, music, art, architecture, cinema, and mass communication media.

Naturally, readers will then want to read as much German fiction as possible in English translation. In addition to investigating the bibliographic information in the above sources for the names of translated titles, they will quickly determine that Ray Keenoy, Mike Mitchell, and Maren Meinhardt's *The*

Babel Guide to German Fiction in English Translation: Austria, Germany, Switzerland is a convenient and valuable text. And if they read at least some of the titles therein listed, they will just as quickly discover that hotels are an important setting in German fiction. For readers intrigued enough to wish to seek an explanation, we heartily recommend *The Hotel as Setting in Early Twentieth-Century German and Austrian Literature* by Bettina Matthias, where the hotel is deconstructed as a "one of the most glamorous, colorful and, at the same time, opaque sites in the psychological topography of modern life" (p. 13).

Careful readers will have noticed that German literary history includes Austrian and Swiss writers. For much more substantial coverage of Austrian literature than individual chapters in edited essay collections or reference books can provide, *A History of Austrian Literature, 1918–2000*, edited by Katrin Kohl and Ritchie Robertson, is indispensable. To be especially noted are the chapters about the politics of Austrian literature between 1927 and 1956; the institutional and publishing context of post-1945 writing; Austrian responses to national socialism and the Holocaust; popular culture in Austria; prose fiction between 1945 and 2000; and Austrian literary responses to multiculturalism. Key figures include Joseph Roth, Thomas Bernhard, and Elfriede Jelinek. Still more information about Austrian writers can be gleaned from two volumes in the Dictionary of Literary Biography series: *Austrian Fiction Writers, 1875–1913* and *Austrian Fiction Writers After 1914*, both edited by James Hardin and Donald G. Daviau (1989; vols. 81 and 85). Also valuable are the following three reference sources—all edited (and with useful introductions) by Donald G. Daviau: *Major Figures of Nineteenth-Century Austrian Literature*; *Major Figures of Austrian Literature: The Interwar Years, 1918–1938*; and *Major Figures of Contemporary Austrian Literature*.

The literary tradition of Switzerland is even less well-known than that of Austria, but we can rectify that by turning to *The Four Literatures of Switzerland* by Iso Camartin and colleagues. Here, we discover that Switzerland is home to German, French, Italian, and Rhaeto-Romanic writers. Indeed, all four literary traditions can be experienced in H. M. Waidson's *Anthology of Modern Swiss Literature*, which includes prose from such German-language writers as Max Frisch, Gerhard Meier, Paul Nizon; such French authors as Alice Rivaz and Anne Cuneo; such Italian authors as Plinio Martini and Giovanni Bonalumi; and such Rhaeto-Romanic authors as Cla Biert and Gion Deplazes.

SELECTED REFERENCES

Bartram, Graham. (Ed.). (2004). *The Cambridge Companion to the Modern German Novel*. New York: Cambridge University Press.

Berg, Christian, and Halen, Pierre. (Eds.). (2000). *Littératures Belges de Langue Française (1830–2000)*. Bruxelles: Le Cri.

Bertrand, Jean-Pierre; Biron, Michel; Denis, Benôit; and Grutman, Rainier. (Eds.). (2003). *Histoire de le Littérature Belge Francophone, 1830–2000*. Paris: Fayard.

Birkett, Jennifer, and Kearns, James. (1997). *A Guide to French Literature: From Early Modern to Postmodern*. New York: St. Martin's Press.

Brown, Penny. (2008). *A Critical History of French Children's Literature: Volume One: 1600–1830*. New York: Routledge.

Brown, Penny. (2008). *A Critical History of French Children's Literature: Volume Two: 1830–Present*. New York: Routledge.

Camartin, Iso; Francillon, Roger; Jakubec-Vodoz, Doris; Käser, Rudolf; Orelli, Giovanni; and Stocker, Beatrice. (1996). *The Four Literatures of Switzerland*. Zurich: Pro Helvetia.

Coward, David. (2002). *A History of French Literature: From Chanson de Geste to Cinema*. Oxford: Blackwell.

Cruickshank, John. (Ed.). (1968). *French Literature and Its Background*. (6 vols.). London: Oxford University Press.

Daviau, Donald G. (Ed.). (1995). *Major Figures of Austrian Literature: The Interwar Years, 1918–1938*. Riverside, CA: Ariadne Press.

Daviau, Donald G. (Ed.). (1987). *Major Figures of Contemporary Austrian Literature*. New York: Peter Lang.

Daviau, Donald G. (Ed.). (1998). *Major Figures of Nineteenth-Century Austrian Literature*. Riverside, CA: Ariadne Press.

Denis, Benôit, and Klinkenberg, Jean-Marie. (2005). *La Littérature Belge: Précis d'histoire Sociale*. Bruxelles: Éditions Labor.

Dolbow, Sandra W. (1986). *Dictionary of Modern French Literature: From the Age of Reason Through Realism*. New York: Greenwood Press.

Eigler, Friederike, and Kord, Susanne. (Eds). (1997). *The Feminist Encyclopedia of German Literature*. Westport, CT: Greenwood Press.

Fallaize, Elizabeth. (1993). *French Women's Writing: Recent Fiction*. London: Macmillan.

France, Peter. (Ed.). (1995). *The New Oxford Companion to Literature in French*. Oxford: Clarendon Press.

Garland, Henry, and Garland, Mary. (Eds.). (1997). *The Oxford Companion to German Literature*. (3rd ed.). Oxford: Oxford University Press.

Hewitt, Nicholas. (Ed.). (2003). *The Cambridge Companion to Modern French Culture*. New York: Cambridge University Press.

Hollier, Denis. (Ed.). (1989). *A New History of French Literature*. Cambridge, MA: Harvard University Press.

Kay, Sarah; Cave, Terence; and Bowie, Malcolm. (2003). *A Short History of French Literature*. Oxford: Oxford University Press.

Kennoy, Ray; Laluyaux, Laurence; and Stanton, Gareth. (1996). *The Babel Guide to French Fiction in English Translation*. London: Boulevard.

Kennoy, Ray; Mitchell, Mike; and Meinhardt, Maren. (1997). *The Babel Guide to German Fiction in English Translation: Austria, Germany, Switzerland*. London: Boulevard.

Kohl, Katrin, and Robertson, Ritchie. (Eds.). (2006). *A History of Austrian Literature, 1918–2000*. Rochester, NY: Camden House.

Kolinsky, Eva, and van der Will, Wilfried. (Eds.). (1998). *The Cambridge Companion to Modern German Culture*. New York: Cambridge University Press.

Konzett, Matthias. (Ed.). (2000). *Encyclopedia of German Literature*. (2 vols.). Chicago: Fitzroy Dearborn.

Levi, Anthony. (1992). *Guide to French Literature: 1789 to the Present*. Detroit, MI: St. James Press.

Levi, Anthony. (1994). *Guide to French Literature: Beginnings to 1789*. Detroit, MI: St. James Press.

Matthias, Bettina. (2006). *The Hotel as Setting in Early Twentieth-Century German and Austrian Literature*. Rochester, NY: Camden House.

Quaghebeur, Marc. (Ed.). (2006). *Anthologie de la Littérature Française de Belgique: Entre Réel et Suréel*. Bruxelles: Éditions Racine.

Sartori, Eva Martin. (Ed.). (1999). *The Feminist Encyclopedia of French Literature*. Westport, CT: Greenwood Press.

Sartori, Eva Martin, and Zimmerman, Dorothy Wynne. (Eds.). (1991). *French Women Writers: A Bio-Bibliographical Source Book*. New York: Greenwood Press.

Thompson, William. (Ed.). (1995). *The Contemporary Novel in France*. Gainesville, FL: University Press of Florida.

Unwin, Timothy. (Ed.). (1997). *The Cambridge Companion to the French Novel: From 1800 to the Present*. New York: Cambridge University Press.

Vivian, Kim. (Ed.). (1992). *A Concise History of German Literature to 1900*. Columbia, SC: Camden House.

Waidson, H. M. (Ed.). (1984). *Anthology of Modern Swiss Literature*. London: Oswald Wolff.

Watanabe-O'Kelly, Helen. (Ed.). (1997). *The Cambridge History of German Literature*. New York: Cambridge University Press.

ANNOTATIONS FOR BOOKS TRANSLATED FROM FRENCH: FRANCE, FRENCH-SPEAKING BELGIUM, AND FRENCH-SPEAKING CARIBBEAN

Eliette Abécassis. *The Qumran Mystery.*

Translated by Emily Read. London: Phoenix, 2003. 336 pages.

Genre/literary style/story type: historical fiction

David Cohen, an archeologist, is asked to locate one of the Dead Sea Scrolls, which has likely been stolen. A central figure is Ary, Cohen's son. During their peregrinations around the Dead Sea,

Bedouins in 1947 discovered the long-lost Qumran parchments, which contain startling secrets about the Jewish and Christian faiths. When these sacred documents were brought to Jerusalem and word of their existence spread, their contents caused excitement, intrigue, consternation, and anguish. Many religious leaders and scientists who came into contact with the scrolls met a grisly death. As Ary and his father follow the tangled path of the murders and the missing manuscript, the novel weaves a compelling story about the intersection of religion and history, where numerous social and cultural assumptions shatter and realign based on new information about such fundamental issues as the death of Christ and the Second Coming.

Related titles by the same author:

Readers may also enjoy *Sacred*, which explores the childless marriage of Nathan and Rachel. On their 10th anniversary, Nathan—an adherent of ultra-orthodox Judaism—decides to repudiate his wife. Also of interest may be *Clandestin*, which recounts the unexpected and passionate love affair between an illegal immigrant and a French official.

Subject keyword: religion

Original language: French

Sources consulted for annotation:

Amazon.com (book description).

Amazon.fr (book description).

Another translated book written by Eliette Abécassis: *Sacred*

Alain Absire. *Lazarus*.

Translated by Barbara Bray. San Diego, CA: Harcourt Brace Jovanovich, 1988. 230 pages.

Genre/literary style/story type: historical fiction

This is an elegantly written and compelling psychological portrait of the resurrected Lazarus that plumbs the core of human desires and frailties, revealing a tangle of bewilderment, awe, anger, belief, and stoicism. Lazarus is given his life back, but it is a life where he is a mere shell of a man, unable to do everyday things. A tangible manifestation of Jesus's miraculous power and hence a source of concern for political leaders, he is the target of an assassination attempt. Although he survives, he becomes nothing if not corpse-like—a foul-smelling outcast. Naturally, he is disconsolate in his suffering, wishing to enjoy life to the fullest. Lazarus seeks out Jesus in the hope of convincing Him to restore him to his former dynamic self but arrives only to find Him crucified on the cross. Upon meeting the disciple John on his return to Jerusalem, Lazarus begins to understand why it is important for him to appear as if he were dead. The fact that he is alive is a constant reminder to others of Christian salvation and grace.

Related title by the same author:

Readers may also enjoy *The Miracle Hater*, another profound psychological meditation about a different biblical topic: the Exodus from Egypt. It focuses on Eshkar, a Hebrew slave and participant in the Exodus, who considers Moses's miracles to be harmful subterfuges. He stays behind in the desert, his proud independence and fierce cynicism masking a haunting alienation.

Subject keyword: religion

Original language: French

Sources consulted for annotation:

Amazon.com (all editorial reviews).

Boyd, Malcolm. *Los Angeles Times*, 21 February 1988, p. 12.

Steinberg, Sybil S. *Publishers Weekly* 233 (22 January 1988): 105.

Another translated book written by Alain Absire: *God's Equal*

Jacques-Pierre Amette. *Brecht's Mistress*.

Translated by Andrew Brown. New York: New Press, 2005. 228 pages.

Genres/literary styles/story types: thrillers; political thrillers

While this novel concentrates on Bertolt Brecht's personal circumstances after he returned to Berlin from the United States in late 1948 after a 15-year absence, it is also a multifaceted portrait of the cultural, social, and political tensions permeating East Germany after World War II. The mistress of the title, Maria Eich, is recruited to spy on Brecht by governmental authorities still unsure about his commitment to communism in the wake of his appearance before the House Un-American Activities Committee. As everyone waits, watches, and analyzes everyone else in a defeated nation, Brecht is caught between his ideals and cynical reality. Critics have evoked John Le Carré when discussing this book.

Subject keywords: power; writers

Original language: French

Sources consulted for annotation:

Amazon.com (all editorial reviews).

Battersby, Eileen. *Irish Times*, 18 June 2005, p. 11.

Gordon, Neil. *The New York Times Book Review*, 2 April 2006 (online).

Another translated book written by Jacques-Pierre Amette: *Country Landscapes*

Stéphane Audeguy. *The Only Son*.

Translated by John Cullen. San Diego, CA: Harcourt, 2008. 246 pages.

Genres/literary styles/story types: historical fiction; literary historical

Who knew that Jean-Jacques Rousseau had an older brother? There is only the briefest of mentions of François in Jean-Jacques's autobiographical writings. In Audeguy's novel, François sets out to correct this most unfortunate of oversights. In a word, François thinks that Jean-Jacques was a prig, maudlin sentimentalist, and romanticist who spouted the most conventional of wisdoms and had very little experience of life. On the other hand, François had more than his fair share of adventures. Introduced to sex by an aristocrat and a farm girl, he was incarcerated in Geneva for breaking curfew and then apprenticed to a watchmaker. Life in Geneva does not suit him, so he travels to Paris, where he quickly finds employment in a brothel as a sort of jack-of-all-trades and then becomes an expert in the rarefied art of making sex toys. Eventually, he is imprisoned in the Bastille, meets the Marquis de Sade, survives the increasingly repressive atmosphere of the first years after the French Revolution, finds another job in a Chinese-style bathhouse, becomes the bathhouse owner's lover, and fights alongside her on behalf of the rights of women. This book is a philosophical delight that adroitly skewers pretentiousness and hypocrisy in all their manifestations while painting a no-holds-barred portrait of the seamy realities of Geneva and Paris.

Related title by the same author:

Readers may also enjoy *The Theory of Clouds*, in which a famous Japanese fashion designer becomes obsessed with the study of clouds. He hires Virginie, a librarian, to help him organize his collection of weather-related books. As they unhurriedly go about their work, he informs her of such key figures as Luke Howard, who was the first to develop a taxonomy of clouds; a painter who went insane trying to capture the ever-changing cloudscape on canvas; and the whispered existence of a talismanic manuscript compiled by the Scot Richard Abercrombie, a weather researcher who set out to photograph the shapes and forms of clouds all over the world, with a view to creating a definitive reference work. As he traveled to Indonesia and other distant lands in the late nineteenth century, his fascination with clouds changed into a fascination for photographing women's vaginas. On his return to England, the legend of the Abercrombie Protocol grew all the more because it was hidden away due to its controversial contents. Eventually, it comes to the attention of Virginie through a convoluted set of circumstances. The novel is a poignantly lyrical consideration of the impossibility of scientific rationalism as manifested in the love of order and categorization.

Subject keywords: identity; philosophy

Original language: French
Sources consulted for annotation:
Global Books in Print (online) (reviews from *Booklist*, *Library Journal*, and *Publishers Weekly* for both novels).
Warner, Judith. *The New York Times Book Review*, 2 November 2008 (online).
Another translated book written by Stéphane Audeguy: *The Theory of Clouds*

Brigitte Aubert. *Death from the Woods*.
Translated by David L. Koral. New York: Welcome Rain, 2000. 279 pages.
Genres/literary styles/story types: crime fiction; amateur detectives
Victim of a terrorist attack in Northern Ireland that killed her fiancé and left her blind, mute, and a quadriplegic, Elsie Andrioli, a French cinema owner, tries to determine the identity of a murderer who is preying on young boys in her neighborhood. A young girl suddenly befriends her and reveals a litany of terrible secrets about the deaths, suggesting that she knows the identity of the killer.
Subject keyword: social problems
Original language: French
Sources consulted for annotation:
Amazon.com (all editorial reviews).
Stankowski, Rebecca House. *Library Journal* 125 (15 February 2000): 194.
Stasio, Marilyn. *The New York Times Book Review*, 2 April 2 2000, p. 28.
Another translated book written by Brigitte Aubert: *Death from the Snows*

Antoine Audouard. *Farewell, My Only One*.
Translated by Euan Cameron. Boston: Houghton Mifflin, 2004. 328 pages.
Genre/literary style/story type: historical fiction
The legendary love story of Heloise and the famous philosopher and theologian Peter Abelard is told through the eyes of William, a struggling young student who also loves Heloise. Abelard was hired by Fulbert, Heloise's uncle, to make her a shining beacon of intellectual attainment, but Abelard and his student fall in love, with tragic consequences once Fulbert learns of the affair. The book portrays Heloise's pregnancy and childbirth; her refuge in a convent; the lovers' secret meetings; Abelard's physical and intellectual castration by Fulbert; and their decision to join religious orders and their ensuing exchange of letters.
Subject keyword: philosophy
Original language: French
Sources consulted for annotation:
Amazon.com (all editorial reviews).
Huntley, Kristine. *Booklist* 100 (15 May 2004): 1607.
Simeone, Lisa. *Chicago Tribune*, 13 August 2004, p. 3.

Muriel Barbery. *The Elegance of the Hedgehog*.
Translated by Alison Anderson. New York: Europa Editions, 2008. 325 pages.
Genre/literary style/story type: mainstream fiction
This novel chronicles the psychological and emotional lives of the upper-class residents of a French apartment building and their concierge, Renée Michel, a widow who is a voracious reader. Indelibly scarred by her family background, Renée is content to remain invisible and within the parameters of what she believes to be her immutable social station. She befriends 12-year-old Paloma Josse, who hates her privileged family, considering them to be sanctimonious members of the intellectual and governmental elite. For her 13th birthday, she plans to commit arson and suicide unless she can find a reason for continuing to live. When a new tenant from Japan, Kakuro Ozu, moves into the

building, the widow and the young girl discover that they have much in common (e.g., grammtical precision and tea) beyond their mutual wish to live outwardly average lives. And as Renée and Kakuro become friends, the possibility of love imbues their conversations and meetings, a possibility that—thanks to Paloma's keen awareness—is on the verge of becoming a reality—only to be tragically cut short by Renée's untimely death.

Related title by the same author:

Readers may also wish to explore *Gourmet Rhapsody.* In this novel, another resident of the same Parisian apartment building is the celebrated food critic Pierre Arthens, who is much loved and also vehemently hated for his trenchant culinary opinions. On the verge of death, he has only one goal in mind: rediscovering the most exquisite taste that he has ever experienced.

Subject keywords: aging; family histories

Original language: French

Sources consulted for annotation:

Books Briefly Noted. *The New Yorker*, 20 October 2008 (online).

Dirda, Michael. *The Washington Post Book World*, 14 September 2008, p. BW10.

Europa Editions website (book description), http://www.europaeditions.com.

Global Books in Print (online) (reviews from *Booklist*, *Library Journal*, and *Publishers Weekly*).

James, Caryn. *The New York Times Book Review*, 7 September 2008 (online).

Another translated book written by Muriel Barbery: *Gourmet Rhapsody*

Christophe Bataille. *Annam.*

Translated by Richard Howard. New York: New Directions, 1996. 87 pages.

Genre/literary style/story type: historical fiction

This novel explores the multifaceted history of French involvement in Vietnam, which began in 1787 when the seven-year-old Vietnamese emperor Canh fails in his attempt to convince Louis XVI to intervene in the political disputes roiling his kingdom. Canh dies, and a year later, a retired French bishop dispatches a small group of soldiers and Dominican missionaries to help the exiled Prince Regent Nguyen Anh regain the Vietnamese throne and to spread Christianity. Forgotten by a France undergoing a cataclysmic revolution, the monks and nuns start a well-respected religious community, but their ranks are soon decimated by disease, and they eventually run afoul of Nguyen Anh in 1800. All the Dominicans are murdered at the hands of Anh's troops, except Brother Dominic and Sister Catherine, who escape to the isolated mountain village of Annam, where they lose their faith and fall in love. And it is their gentle love for each other as well as their unassuming life in Annam that adheres to the ancient rhythms of Vietnam that spares their lives when Anh's soldiers finally track them down.

Subject keywords: colonization and colonialism; religion

Original language: French

Source consulted for annotation:

Amazon.com (reviews from *Library Journal* and *Publishers Weekly*).

Some other translated books written by Christophe Bataille: *Hourmaster*; *Absinthe*

Frédéric Beigbeder. *Windows on the World.*

Translated by Frank Wynne. New York: Miramax Hyperion, 2005. 306 pages.

Genre/literary style/story type: mainstream fiction

The title of this novel refers to the restaurant on the top floor of the North Tower of the World Trade Center, where Texas real estate agent Carthew Yorston has taken his two young sons for breakfast on September 11, 2001. The minutiae of daily life (e.g., no-smoking regulations; discussions about sex, politics, and other assorted topics; references to Sinclair Lewis's George Babbitt) are a poignant backdrop to the doomed struggles of the restaurant patrons. Two years later, a writer dining at a

restaurant high atop the Parisian skyline reflects on the meaning of that fateful autumn morning in 2001. Rejecting knee-jerk anti-Americanism, the writer, Beigbeder's alter ego, suggests that 9/11 is really about the end of narcissism, hedonism, and consumerism. Readers may want to compare this vision of 9/11 with Don DeLillo's *Falling Man*. Readers can also hope that Beigbeder's 2009 book *Un Roman Français*—an achingly graceful, wise, and frank autobiographical novel alternating between an account of the ignominy of being ensnared in the French justice system and limpid insights about childhood and adolescence—will be translated into English.
Subject keyword: urban life
Original language: French
Sources consulted for annotation:
Amazon.com (all editorial reviews).
Metcalf, Stephen. *The New York Times Book Review*, 17 April 2005, p. 9.
Publishers Weekly 252 (January 24, 2005): 219.
Sullivan, Patrick. *Library Journal* 130 (January 2005): 93.
Some other translated books written by Frédéric Beigbeder: *99 Francs; Holiday in a Coma & Love Lasts Three Years: Two Novels*

René Belletto. *Machine*.
Translated by Lanie Goodman. New York: Grove Press, 1993. 359 pages.
Genres/literary styles/story types: thrillers; medical thrillers
While Marc Lacroix, a noted psychiatrist, is treating Michel Zyto, a sexually violent psychopath, he invents a machine that allows him to temporarily inhabit a patient's mind. But something goes horribly wrong: The machine permanently exchanges the two mens' minds. When the deranged Zyto becomes an almost perfect Lacroix, the result is one harrowing event after another. The question of identity (is an individual defined by the body or the mind?) is woven throughout the book, and the theme of scientific arrogance is also never far from the surface. Critics have pointed to Mary Shelley's *Frankenstein* as a literary forerunner.
Subject keyword: identity
Original language: French
Sources consulted for annotation:
Amazon.com (review from *Kirkus Reviews*).
Donovan, Ann. *Library Journal* 118 (October 15, 1993): 86.
Harris, Michael. *Los Angeles Times*, 27 December 1993, p. 3.
Another translated book written by René Belletto: *Eclipse*

Antoine Bello. *The Missing Piece*.
Translated by Helen Stevenson. Orlando, FL: Harcourt, 2003. 248 pages.
Genres/literary styles/story types: crime fiction; suspense
After establishing the International Speed Puzzle Circuit in Europe, where it has become wildly successful, millionaire Charles Wallerstein is ready to export his concept to the United States. But a tragedy suddenly strikes the new sport: Someone is killing the players and making an unusual jigsaw puzzle from their amputated body parts. Can these gruesome developments be linked to its more traditional rival, the Puzzology Society, which invents bizarre games such as the construction and immediate deconstruction of walls? The novel is both a murder mystery and a delicious satire about the nature of sports.
Subject keyword: social problems
Original language: French
Sources consulted for annotation:
Amazon.com (all editorial reviews).

Feeney, Tim. *Review of Contemporary Fiction* 23 (Fall 2003): 142.
Fletcher, Connie. *Booklist* 99 (15 March 15 2003): 1278.
Zaleski, Jeff. *Publishers Weekly* 250 (31 March 2003): 42.

Tonino Benacquista. *Holy Smoke.*
Translated by Adriana Hunter. London: Bitter Lemon Press, 2005. 200 pages.
Genre/literary style/story type: mainstream fiction
Critics are unanimous that this is a dark comedy to end all dark comedies. Mordant and caustic, it delivers an original picture of the corruption of both urban and rural life. Ever the dutiful son, Tonio visits his parents in a Paris suburb. He unexpectedly meets Dario, a former friend who is now making a living as a gigolo. Dario is soon executed, but he has been sensible enough to make a will in which he leaves a decaying vineyard near Naples to Tonio. A shocked Tonio travels to Italy, where he soon finds that everyone, including the Mafia and the Roman Catholic church, covets the vineyard.
Related title by the same author:
Readers may also enjoy *Framed*, which deploys Benacquista's customary panache and verve to satirize the art world.
Subject keywords: rural life; urban life
Original language: French
Sources consulted for annotation:
Corrigan, Maureen. *The Washington Post Book World*, 8 May 2005 (online).
Stasio, Marilyn. *The New York Times Book Review*, 14 August 2005 (online).
Some other translated books written by Tonino Benacquista: *Someone Else*; *Framed*

Philippe Besson. *In the Absence of Men.*
Translated by Frank Wynne. New York: Carroll & Graf, 2003. 166 pages.
Genres/literary styles/story types: mainstream fiction; coming-of-age
During one week in the summer of 1916 in the middle of World War I, 16-year-old Vincent de l'Etoile experiences two life-changing events: a sexual relationship with Arthur Vales, an off-duty soldier who visits his mother who works for the de l'Etoile family, and a series of platonic idylls with a middle-aged Marcel Proust in Parisian cafés and literary salons. After returning to the front lines, Arthur is soon killed at Verdun, and Proust is called away on family business. Told through diary entries and letters, this novel is a sophisticated, moving, and clear-eyed homage to a literary giant. One critic invoked Hemingway's *A Farewell to Arms.*
Subject keywords: identity; war
Original language: French
Sources consulted for annotation:
Amazon.com (all editorial reviews).
Olson, Ray. *Booklist* 99 (March 15, 2003): 1273.
Sullivan, Patrick. *Library Journal* 128 (March 1, 2003): 116.
Another translated book written by Philippe Besson: *His Brother*

Nella Bielski. *The Year is '42.*
Translated by John Berger and Lisa Appignanesi. New York: Pantheon Books, 2004. 207 pages.
Genre/literary style/story type: historical fiction
Wehrmacht officer Karl Bazinger is stationed in occupied Paris in 1942, where he travels in elite cultural circles, attending dinner parties with Coco Chanel and Jean Cocteau and listening to lectures about the poetry of William Butler Yeats. However, his friendship with an officer in the French Resistance, Hans Bielenberg, as well as his barely concealed scorn of the Nazi regime attract negative attention from his superiors, resulting in a transfer to Kiev on the Eastern Front. Far from the glamour

of his former bohemian life, he discovers hard truths about Nazi atrocities and the Babi Yar massacre. He also meets a Russian doctor, Katia, who helps him cope with a skin disease. As Bazinger's infection gradually disappears, he realizes the extent of his moral complicity in an unyielding war.
Subject keyword: war
Original language: French
Sources consulted for annotation:
Amazon.com (all editorial reviews).
Driscoll, Brendan. *Booklist* 101 (October 15, 2004): 388.
Tepper, Anderson. *The New York Times Book Review*, 27 March 2005, p. 23.
Zaleski, Jeff. *Publishers Weekly* 251 (October 4, 2004): 66.
Some other translated books written by Nella Bielski: *Oranges for the Son of Alexander Levy*; *After Arkadia*

Olivier Bleys. *The Ghost in the Eiffel Tower.*
Translated by J. A. Underwood. London: Marion Boyars, 2004. 420 pages.
Genre/literary style/story type: historical fiction
Anyone interested in the social and cultural life of Paris at the time of the building of the Eiffel Tower will gravitate toward this novel, which focuses on the after-work life of two draughtsman who are employed by Gustave Eiffel. Representatives of the forces of science and technological modernity, they become immersed in the spiritualist milieu of late 1880s Paris, participating in séances and card readings. In the background looms Gordon Hole, an American architect who wishes to sabotage Eiffel's work.
Subject keyword: urban life
Original language: French
Source consulted for annotation:
Marion Boyars website (book description), http://www.marionboyars.co.uk.

Janine Boissard. *A Different Woman.*
Translated by Mary Feeney. Boston: Fawcett, 1989. 208 pages.
Genres/literary styles/story types: mainstream fiction; women's lives
This novel recounts the transformation of Severine, a 40-year-old divorcée who resumes her interrupted singing career after she meets Vincent, a television talk show host. At the same time that Severine invents a stage persona for herself, she discovers a smoldering sexuality that shatters her formerly mundane view of herself, not to mention her ex-husband's description of her as frigid. The author also publishes under the name of Janine Oriano.
Subject keyword: identity
Original language: French
Sources consulted for annotation:
Amazon.com (all editorial reviews).
Mihram, Danielle. *Library Journal* 114 (1 April 1989): 109.
Steinberg, Sybil S. *Publishers Weekly* 235 (February 10, 1989): 57.
Some other translated books written by Janine Boissard: *A Time To Choose*; *Christmas Lessons*; *A Matter of Feeling*; *Cecile*; *A Question of Happiness*

Geneviève Brisac. *Losing Eugenio.*
Translated by J. A. Underwood. London: Marion Boyars, 1999. 157 pages.
Genres/literary styles/story types: mainstream fiction; feminist fiction
This novel explores the agony-filled and tormented world of Nouk, a single mother who leaves her husband and her artistic career behind in an attempt to live in a man-free world. Working at a library

filled with self-absorbed and unsympathetic employees, she struggles to raise her son, Eugenio, realizing that she is likely doing him more harm than good. Even a vacation at her friend Martha's beach home does not go as planned because Eugenio increasingly distances himself from her. Nouk is more alone than ever, contemplating the haunting duplicity of the feigned happiness captured briefly in old photographs and wondering about the ethics of suicide.
Subject keyword: identity
Original language: French
Sources consulted for annotation:
Amazon.com (all editorial reviews).
Irvine, Anne. *Library Journal* 125 (1 March 2000): 123.
Steinberg, Sybil S. *Publishers Weekly* 247 (31 January 2000): 79.

Emmanuel Carrère. *Class Trip*.
Translated by Linda Coverdale. New York: Metropolitan Books, 1997. 162 pages.
Genres/literary styles/story types: mainstream fiction; coming-of-age
A two-week class trip to a skiing school was supposed to be adventurous fun but instead turns into a nightmare of fears and anxieties for 10-year-old Nicholas, who—because of his timidity, small stature, and bedwetting—is not the most confident of children to begin with. Friendless and alone, he spends his time dreaming about a doll—offered by Shell gas stations to customers who collect a sufficient number of coupons—called the Visible Man, which has an anatomically correct interior. It does not help that his overprotective father, who drove him to the mountain village instead of allowing him to take the bus, forgets Nicholas's suitcase in the trunk of the car and ominously has not yet returned to drop it off. Nicholas is also slightly paranoid, ever fearful of being kidnapped by criminals who sell body parts—a fear made even more vivid and terrifying when a child disappears from a nearby town. Indeed, humiliation and terror are Nicholas's daily lot. As Nicholas returns home to an apartment made even emptier by the death of his father, his future does not look very bright at all.
Related title by the same author:
Readers may also want to delve into *The Moustache*, where the simple act of shaving off his moustache leads one man to the edge of insanity.
Subject keyword: social roles
Original language: French
Sources consulted for annotation:
Amazon.com (all editorial reviews).
Eder, Richard. *Los Angeles Times*, 1 January 1997, p. 3
Hawthorne, Mary. *The New York Times Book Review*, 2 February 1997, p. 12.
Lynch, Doris. *Library Journal* 122 (January 1997): 143.
Steinberg, Sybil S. *Publishers Weekly* 243 (9 December 1996): 62.
Some other translated books written by Emmanuel Carrère: *Gothic Romance*; *The Moustache*

Jean-Claude Carrière. *Please, Mr. Einstein*.
Translated by John Brownjohn. San Diego, CA: Harcourt, 2006. 186 pages.
Genre/literary style/story type: speculative fiction
Part time travel and part novel of ideas, this book begins when a contemporary Central European woman is escorted to a room where Albert Einstein is hard at work on his elusive theory of unity. Wanting to understand everything about his life and discoveries, she conducts an interview with Einstein, who obliges by discussing his theory of relativity; his philosophical differences with Newton and Bohr; his experiences in Nazi Germany; and his participation in the Manhattan Project, which developed the atomic bomb.

Subject keyword: philosophy
Original language: French
Sources consulted for annotation:
Global Books in Print (online) (reviews from *Booklist*, *Library Journal*, and *Publishers Weekly*).
Overbye, Dennis. *The New York Times Book Review*, 26 November 2006 (online).

Didier van Cauwelaert. *One-Way.*
Translated by Mark Polizzotti. New York: Other Press, 2003. 152 pages.
Genre/literary style/story type: mainstream fiction
Personal identity, not to mention ethnic, cultural, or national identity, is nothing more than what we ourselves believe and what we tell others. Official labels are meaningless—the contrived creation of those who, for their own reasons, wish to exercise power or at least the semblance of power. When his parents die in a car crash, the orphaned Aziz Kemal is raised as an Arab in Marseilles by the Roma people; he survives by stealing car radios. When he is arrested for a crime he did not commit, he is deported to Morocco, which authorities believe is his homeland. But Morocco is a place he knows nothing about. Aziz is accompanied by Jean-Pierre Schneider, a sad-sack bureaucrat whose role is to help him resettle. Playing on Schneider's gullibility and guilt, Aziz creates out of whole cloth an improbable story of a utopic and secluded place called Urghiz. As they travel toward the nonexistent Irghiz across an always mesmerizing and sometimes dangerous terrain, happiness remains just over the horizon—elusive as the categories and stories that are meant to define us.
Related title by the same author:
Readers may also enjoy *Out of My Head*, which focuses on Martin Harris, a botanist who—after being comatose for three days subsequent to a traffic accident—returns home from his hospital stay only to find that another Martin Harris, who everyone truly believes is the real Martin Harris, has taken his place.
Subject keyword: identity
Original language: French
Sources consulted for annotation:
Amazon.com (all editorial reviews).
Haggas, Carol. *Booklist* 100 (15 October 2003): 387.
Harrison, Sophie. *The New York Times Book Review*, 23 January 2005, p. 23.
Zaleski, Jeff. *Publishers Weekly* 250 (27 October 2003): 46.
Another translated book written by Didier van Cauwelaert: *Out of My Head*

Patrick Chamoiseau. *Texaco.*
Translated by Rose-Myriam Réjouis and Val Vinokurov. New York: Pantheon, 1997. 401 pages.
Genres/literary styles/story types: historical fiction; magical realism
This novel is an extraordinarily poignant and searing dissection of some 200 years of the history of Martinique as seen through the perspective of Marie-Sophie Laborieux. The only child of an aging father and a near-blind woman, she is the founder and chief spokesperson for a shantytown called Texaco, near a landscape-blighting oil facility that is just on the outskirts of Fort-de-France, Martinique's capital. As the shantytown grows, municipal authorities and thugs do everything in their power to raze it, but Texaco persists depite all odds—a teeming and vibrant hub of diverse memories and overlapping histories and a place where the economically and socially disadvantaged attempt to eke out an existence through day jobs and backbreaking labor in factories. When an ironically named urban planner, Christ, comes to take stock of the situation, he is perceived by Texaco's residents as yet another enemy to their continued existence. But he eventually comes to understand the importance of the concept of shantytowns, which were established in opposition to the homogenizing forces of orderly, antiseptic, and gentrifying cities, such as Fort-de-France.

As Marie-Sophie relates the specific circumstances of how she came to settle in Texaco, her story becomes the anguished and tormented history of Martinique itself: the demise of plantation life; emancipation of the slaves; the influx of Indian and Chinese workers and the resulting racial divisions; a devastating volcanic eruption that destroys the city of Saint Pierre; the growth of Fort-de-France; and the effects of World War I, World War II, and Aimé Césaire on Martinique's development. Critics have invoked Gabriel García Márquez and Salman Rushdie to describe the power of Chamoiseau's vision and language. For another view of Martinique's history, readers may wish to turn to the relatively unknown American author Lafcadio Hearn, who is invoked in *Texaco* and who wrote *Youma*, an 1890 novel about an insurrection of Martinique's slaves in the nineteenth century, as well as *Two Years in the French West Indies*.

Related title by the same author:

Readers may also be interested in Chamoiseau's *Chronicle of Seven Sorrows*, an excursion into contemporary Martinique history between the 1940s and 1970s, as told through the voice of a truck driver who knows everything about the back roads and traffic secrets of the island.

Subject keywords: colonization and colonialism; power

Original language: French/Creole

Sources consulted for annotation:

Bernstein, Richard. *The New York Times*, 31 March 1997 (online).

Bernstein, Richard. *The New York Times*, 23 March 1998 (online).

Hoffert, Barbara. *Library Journal* 124 (1 November 1999): 122.

Steinberg, Sybil S. *Publishers Weekly* 246 (4 October 1999): 61.

Some other translated books written by Patrick Chamoiseau: *Solibo Magnificent*; *School Days*; *Strange Words*; *Chronicle of Seven Sorrows*

François Cheng. *The River Below.*

Translated by Julia Shirek Smith. New York: Welcome Rain, 2000. 288 pages.

Genre/literary style/story type: historical fiction

This novel focuses on twentieth-century Chinese history, especially the degradations and depravations imposed on artists and intellectuals during the Cultural Revolution. The recipient of a scholarship, Tianyi studies art in Paris between 1948 and 1957 and then returns to a China caught in the grip of Mao's Cultural Revolution. His friends have either committed suicide or been forced into re-education camps, and Tianyi himself is soon sent to one such camp in the far north of the country. There, he meditates on his own impending death, clinging to a belief in the power of culture and his eroding memories.

Subject keywords: identity; power

Original language: French

Sources consulted for annotation:

Gambone, Philip. *The New York Times Book Review*, 18 February 2001, p. 21.

Hoover, Danise. *Booklist* 97 (15 November 2000): 611.

Steinberg, Sybil S. *Publishers Weekly* 247 (16 October 2000): 48.

Some other translated books written by François Cheng: *Green Mountain, White Cloud: A Novel of Love in the Ming Dynasty*

Eric Chevillard. *On the Ceiling.*

Translated by Jordan Stump. Lincoln, NE: University of Nebraska Press, 2000. 135 pages.

Genre/literary style/story type: mainstream fiction

This novel is about the hilarious and thought-provoking misadventures of a narrator who—despite his average height—always stoops when entering a room, always wears gray clothes, and is never

without an upside-down chair on his head. He also has a motley assortment of friends, including Kolski, who is in love with the smell of his own body, and Madame Stempf, who has decidedly unconventional views about obstetrics. Compelled to leave their provisional squat, the whole group moves in with the narrator's girlfriend, eventually taking up residence on her ceiling when they discover that they do not really like furniture. In a novel with unmistakable echoes of the surrealist drama of Eugène Ionesco and the existentialism of Samuel Beckett's *Malone Dies*, the author creates a wholly believable world that adheres to its own unique rules.
Subject keyword: philosophy
Original language: French
Sources consulted for annotation:
Evenson, Brian. *Review of Contemporary Fiction* 21 (Spring 2001): 186.
Steinberg, Sybil S. *Publishers Weekly* 247 (28 August 2000): 57.
Some other translated books written by Eric Chevillard: *The Crab Nebula*; *Palafox*

Hélène Cixous. *The Third Body.*
Translated by Keith Cohen. Evanston, IL: Hydra Books/Northwestern University Press, 1999. 161 pages.
Genres/literary styles/story types: mainstream fiction; feminist fiction
Some reviewers of this novel mocked it for its lack of conventional narrative, pointing out that a high point in plot development occurs when a fly is swallowed. But that is to miss the point of the author's work, which is a philosophically and psychologically rich exploration of states of being and states of mind. Here, readers are presented with what the *Library Journal* called an "intoxicating invocation of a woman and her male lover as one being." Written in a stream-of-consciousness style that incorporates many literary allusions, the primary emphasis of the book is on the multiple sensations that lovers experience as both separate and unified entities.
Subject keyword: philosophy
Original language: French
Sources consulted for annotation:
Amazon.com (review from *Kirkus Reviews*).
Irvine, Anne. *Library Journal* 124 (1 September 1999): 231.
Some other translated books written by Hélène Cixous: *The Book of Promethea*; *Manna: for the Mandelstams for the Mandelas*; *Inside*; *First Days of the Year*; *Angst*; *Neuter*; *The Day I Wasn't There*

Philippe Claudel. *By a Slow River.*
Translated by Hoyt Rogers. New York: Alfred A. Knopf, 2006. 194 pages.
Genre/literary style/story type: historical fiction
Against the backdrop of World War I, a French village is struck by a series of personal tragedies that, in the end, are interlinked: the murder of a small girl; a suicide; death after a long illness; death during childbirth. But this book is much more than a murder mystery because it examines the fraught psychological and emotional undercurrents of a rural town whose hierarchical power structure is fast eroding.
Related title by the same author:
In *Brodeck*, Claudel masterfully portrays the claustrophobic atmosphere of a village that is both geographically isolated and ethically bereft. This is probably one of the most terrifying visions of the philosophical underpinnings of xenophobia that exists in modern French literature. In its themes, the book complements Michael Haneke's film *The White Ribbon*.
Subject keywords: rural life; war
Original language: French

Sources consulted for annotation:
Eder, Richard. *The New York Times*, 29 June 2006 (online).
Global Books in Print (online) (reviews from *Booklist*, *Library Journal*, and *Publishers Weekly*).
Another translated book written by Philippe Claudel: *Brodeck*

Maryse Condé. *The Story of the Cannibal Woman.*
Translated by Richard Philcox. New York: Atria Books, 2007. 311 pages.
Genres/literary styles/story types: mainstream fiction; women's lives
After the murder of her long-term partner Stephen, a white professor of literature, Rosélie Thibaudin, a 50-year-old painter from Guadeloupe, is devastated. To say the least, her position is tenuous: She was not formally married and thus has no legal claim to anything except their shared house in Cape Town. As she tries to get out from under the veil of despondency that has settled over her and as she begins to participate in the murder investigation, Rosélie realizes that her relationship with Stephen was problematic from the very beginning.
Related titles by the same author:
Readers may also be interested in Condé's *Windward Heights*, which is a retelling of Emily Brontë's masterpiece *Wuthering Heights* set in Cuba and Guadeloupe in the late nineteenth century. Also worthwhile may be *Victoire*, which is a fictional chronicle of the author's grandmother. Condé is from the Caribbean island of Guadeloupe, one of France's départements d'outre-mer.
Subject keyword: identity
Original language: French
Sources consulted for annotation:
Amazon.com (all editorial reviews for *Windward Heights*).
Back cover of *Windward Heights*.
Schmidt, Elizabeth. *The New York Times Book Review*, 15 April 2007, p. 26.
Seaman, Donna. *Booklist* 103 (15 February 2007): 34.
Steinberg, Sybil S. *Publishers Weekly* 246 (12 July 1999): 76.
Some other translated books written by Maryse Condé: *I, Tituba, Black Witch of Salem*; *Tree of Life*; *Desirada*; *Crossing the Mangrove*; *Segu*; *Land of Many Colors*; *Nanna-ya* ; *The Last of the African Kings*; *Who Slashed Celanire's Throat?*; *Hérémakhonon*; *A Season in Rihata*; *Victoire*

Raphaël Confiant. *Mamzelle Dragonfly.*
Translated by Linda Coverdale. New York: Farrar, Straus and Giroux, 2000. 169 pages.
Genres/literary styles/story types: mainstream fiction; women's lives
At age 14, Adelise is no stranger to rape and has learned numerous survival strategies. At 16, she leaves rural Martinique and goes to live with her aunt in the island's capital of Fort-de-France. Soon, Adelise is following in her aunt's footsteps as a prostitute. But she soon learns to compartmentalize her life, retaining a salutary independence, outspokenness, and pride. The novel, which also provides a vivid portrait of race relations on Martinique, was originally written in Creole and then translated into French.
Subject keywords: social problems; urban life
Original language: French/Creole
Sources consulted for annotation:
Global Books in Print (online) (review from *Publishers Weekly*).
Olson, Yvette. *Library Journal* 125 (July 2000): 136.
Seaman, Donna. *Booklist* 96 (July 2000): 2006.
Another translated book written by Raphaël Confiant: *Eau de Café*

Paule Constant. *Trading Secrets.*
Translated by Betsy Wing. Lincoln, NE: University of Nebraska Press, 2001. 165 pages.

Genres/literary styles/story types: mainstream fiction; women's lives
After the conclusion of a feminist colloquium in a Kansas university town, Gloria, its African-American organizer, welcomes three houseguests. Each has her own burdens and difficulties: the consequences of colonialism, divorce, and alcohol. As the tangled lives of all four women are examined, the *Booklist* reviewer said that novel "illuminates the dark side of feminism, where women pay lip service to ideals but at the same time ruthlessly manipulate one another in the name of sisterhood."
Subject keyword: social roles
Original language: French
Sources consulted for annotation:
Amazon.com (all editorial reviews).
Johnston, Bonnie. *Booklist* (15 October 2001): 381.
Olszewski, Lawrence. *Library Journal* (December 2001): 170.
Some other translated books written by Paule Constant: *The Governor's Daughter*; *White Spirit*; *Ouregano*

Laurence Cossé. *A Corner of the Veil.*
Translated by Linda Asher. New York: Scribner, 1999. 271 pages.
Genre/literary style/story type: mainstream fiction
What would happen if the existence of God were irrefutably proved? A six-page document sent to Father Bertrand Beaulieu, editor of a Catholic religious journal, by Mauduit, a persistent correspondent who has submitted many previous attempts at proofs, turns out to be the real thing. Try as they might, even eminent theologians cannot refute Mauduit's argument. When word of the discovery leaks out and comes to the attention of political figures, general consternation ensues. After Prime Minister Petitgrand reads it, he becomes an exuberant gardener, announcing the beginning of a new earthly paradise. As elected officials and members of the church hierarchy begin to realize the implications for society and themselves of a world where God's existence is an incontrovertible fact, they decide to keep the proof a secret, fearing not only for their own job security but also for world stability.
Subject keywords: religion; politics
Original language: French
Sources consulted for annotation:
Amazon.com (reviews from *Kirkus Reviews* and others).
Burns, Erik. *The New York Times Book Review*, 1 August 1999, p. 14.

Céline Curiol. *Voice Over.*
Translated by Sam Richard. New York: Seven Stories Press, 2008. 288 pages.
Genre/literary style/story type: mainstream fiction; women's lives
We hear disembodied voices everywhere now: automated phone messages telling us to select any number of choices; subway and bus stop announcements; GPS directions in cars. We take them for granted, but there is often a real human behind that voice. What if you were that human; what if your only claim to meaningful professional existence lay in the tenuous nature of anonymous contact? Would you not live your life constantly inside your own mind, creating a fantastic imaginary existence just for the sake of it? So it is with the unnamed protagonist of this novel, whose job it is to inform passengers of arrivals and departures at a Parisian train station.
Subject keyword: urban life
Original language: French
Sources consulted for annotation:
Global Books in Print (online) (reviews from *Booklist* and *Publishers Weekly*).
McCulloch, Alison. *The New York Times Book Review*, 16 November 2008 (online).

Sijie Dai (Dai Sijie). ***Balzac and the Little Chinese Seamstress.***
Translated by Ina Rilke. New York: Alfred A. Knopf, 2001. 197 pages.
Genres/literary styles/story types: mainstream fiction; coming-of-age
In the early 1970s, the author spent four years in a re-education camp in an isolated northern Chinese province during Mao's Cultural Revolution. Two young men (the narrator and Luo) are sent to a mountain village to undergo re-education. The villagers read nothing but Mao's scientific essays. But the two young men, whose exposure to Western literature has been minimal, discover a hoard of Western classics, including Balzac's *Ursule Mirouet* and Flaubert's *Madame Bovary*. When a traveling tailor and his daughter come to their village, the young men share their literary treasures with them. It is only a matter of time before Luo falls in love with the person identified as the little Chinese seamstress, going to heroic lengths to visit her distant village. The seamstress becomes pregnant, has an abortion, and then secretly leaves for a new life in the city, having understood better than the narrator and Luo the true meaning of personal freedom.
Subject keywords: identity; rural life
Original language: French
Source consulted for annotation:
Allen, Brooke. *The New York Times Book Review*, 16 September 2001, p. 24.
Some other translated books written by Sijie Dai: *Mr. Muo's Travelling Couch*; *Once on a Moonless Night*

Antoine B. Daniel. ***Incas*** **(Vol. 1:** ***The Puma's Shadow*****; Vol. 2:** ***The Gold of Cuzco*****; Vol. 3:** ***The Light of Machu Picchu*****).**
Translated by Alex Gilly. New York: Simon & Schuster, 2001–2003.
Genre/literary style/story type: historical fiction
In the mid-1500s, Spanish conquistadors attack and occupy the Incan empire. The period is marked by violence, shifting loyalties, large-scale geopolitical concerns, internal political divisions, cultural conflicts, and social upheaval. Containing descriptions about the Incan way of life and Spanish military history, this trilogy vividly describes the era by focusing on the complex relationships among the Incan emperor Manco; Princess Anamaya; Spanish commander Francisco Pizarro; and the Spanish aristocrat Gabriel Montelucar y Flores, with whom the princess falls in love. As Pizarro struggles to quell an unbridled lust for gold (and violent destruction) among his troops, the Incas prepare for a final battle to defeat their enemy. Caught in the gearworks of epochal change, Anamaya must reconcile her love for Flores with her commitment to Incan heritage.
Subject keywords: colonization and colonialism; power
Original language: French
Sources consulted for annotation:
Amazon.com (all editorial reviews).
Zaleski, Jeff. *Publishers Weekly* 238 (9 December 2002): 62.

Marie Darrieussecq. ***Pig Tales: A Novel of Lust and Transformation.***
Translated by Linda Coverdale. New York: New Press, 1997. 151 pages.
Genres/literary styles/story types: mainstream fiction; feminist fiction
After being hired as a perfume and cosmetics salesperson in a department store, the narrator quickly attracts a loyal male clientele, who are more than pleased that she is becoming Rubenesquely voluptuous and sexually insatiable. Soon, she is offering kinky massages to an ever-expanding range of satisfied customers who do not seem to mind that she is slowly (and literally) metamorphosing into a pig, complete with grunts and tail. Eventually, she becomes the poster girl for a right-wing

political campaign, is taken to an orgy, and meets a young business executive who is a part-time wolf. There are echoes of George Orwell's *Animal Farm* as well as Franz Kafka in this satire about sexual and social mores.
Subject keyword: identity
Original language: French
Sources consulted for annotation:
Amazon.com (all editorial reviews).
Harshaw, Tobin. *The New York Times Book Review*, 6 July 1997 (online).
Steinberg, Sybil S. *Publishers Weekly* 244 (3 March 1997): 64.
Wilkinson, Joanne. *Booklist* 93 (1 April 1997): 1280.
Some other translated books written by Marie Darrieussecq: *My Phantom Husband*; *Undercurrents*; *A Brief Stay with the Living*; *Breathing Underwater*; *White*

Michèle Desbordes. *The House in the Forest.*
Translated by Shaun Whiteside. London: Faber and Faber, 2004. 186 pages.
Genre/literary style/story type: mainstream fiction
When a mother sends her son off to the Caribbean in the eighteenth century, she hopes that he will become wealthy. But he does not find fame and riches there, so he returns to France, scarred and haunted by his failures. He does not go back to his mother's house, choosing instead to live in a hovel in the nearby forest, accompanied only by a mysterious young boy and a dog. When he dies, the young boy brings the mother bundles of unsent letters written by her son, who was obsessed with records and logs detailing the minutiae of passing time.
Subject keyword: social roles
Original language: French
Sources consulted for annotation:
Atkins, Lucy. *Sunday Times*, 25 January 2004, p. 53.
Global Books in Print (online) (synopsis/book jacket).
Kellaway, Kate. *The Observer*, 1 February 2004, p. 16.
Another translated book written by Michèle Desbordes: *The Maid's Request*

Marc Dugain. *The Officers' Ward.*
Translated by Howard Curtis. New York: Soho, 2001. 135 pages.
Genre/literary style/story type: mainstream fiction
Just after beginning a job in Paris as a railway engineer, 24-year-old Adrien Fournier is inducted into the army. But this is not a traditional story about trench warfare during World War I. Sent to construct a bridge, Fournier is the victim of a sniper at the beginning of his tour of duty. He is immediately whisked back to Paris, where he becomes the first patient in a mirrorless ward designed for those who have the most atrocious wounds. His face almost completely blown to shreds, he spends the next four years and eight months in the ward, watching a parade of men with similarly grotesque injuries come and go. Together with a Breton aristocrat and a Jewish pilot, he attempts to comfort the new arrivals as best he can while watching the sometimes overly optimistic doctors try to persuade the patients that their lives will return to normal.
Subject keyword: war
Original language: French
Sources consulted for annotation:
Amazon.com (all editorial reviews).
Hooper, Brad. *Booklist* 98 (15 November 2001): 550.
McCullough, David Willis. *The New York Times Book Review*, 2 December 2001, p. 81.

Benoît Duteurtre. *The Little Girl and the Cigarette*.
Translated by Charlotte Mandell. Brooklyn, NY: Melville House, 2007. 188 pages.
Genre/literary style/story type: mainstream fiction
An author who has received words of praise from Samuel Beckett, Milan Kundera, and Guy Debord must have something going for him. And indeed he does, as this book testifies. Duteurtre has written a wicked satire about our over-regulated world, about how we make our children into little monarchs whose every behest must be obeyed as soon as possible, about the fundamental inanity and egregious absurdity of living in contemporary society. In a no-smoking prison, an inmate about to be executed makes a request for a final cigarette. His simple request makes him a cultural hero of sorts in a media-saturated world, especially for tobacco companies. But that is not all: When an insignificant municipal bureaucrat is observed smoking by a little girl, she accuses him of sexual perversion.
Related title by the same author:
If readers are in the mood for another rip-roaring satire featuring cigarettes, they may wish to consider Christopher Buckley's *Thank You for Smoking*. If they want another satire by Duteurtre, they should do their utmost to get their hands on *Customer Service*, which gleefully subverts our love affair with the cell phone. After a man loses his much-cherished communication device, he finds out just how difficult it is to get a replacement for it. His descent into the forlorn abysses of the netherworld that is called customer service, with its interminable phone menus and platitudinous rhetoric, is an insightful journey into the vacuity and vapidness of consumerism.
Subject keyword: power
Original language: French
Source consulted for annotation:
Melville House website, http://www.mhpbooks.com.
Another translated book written by Benoit Duteurtre: *Customer Service*

Jean Echenoz. *Chopin's Move*.
Translated by Mark Polizzotti. Normal, IL: Dalkey Archive Press, 2004. 135 pages.
Genres/literary styles/story types: mainstream fiction; postmodernism
The unlikely secret-agent hero of this novel is an entomologist named Franck Chopin who hunts his quarry using microphone-bearing flies that he has tamed. In a delicious parody of the espionage novel, the clueless Chopin operates in mysterious circumstances among equally mysterious beings in a world where reality is highly contingent if not elusive. One critics has pointed out that this book can be read as a satire of Dashiell Hammett's noir detective novels.
Related titles by the same author:
Readers may also want to savor *Cherokee* and *Big Blondes*, both of which are send-ups of the detective genre. Also of interest may be *Piano*, in which Echenoz tells the story of Max, a classical pianist who comes back from the dead and is granted eternal life, and *Ravel*, which concentrates on the often mundane daily activities of the French composer Maurice Ravel.
Subject keyword: philosophy
Original language: French
Sources consulted for annotation:
Cone, Edward. *Library Journal* 129 (15 April 2004): 129.
James, Caryn. *The New York Times Book Review*, 25 April 2004, p. 15.
McCulloch, Alison. *The New York Times Book Review*, 19 August 2007 (online).
Motte, Warren. *World Literature Today* 78 (September/December 2004): 115.
Zaleski, Jeff. *Publishers Weekly* 251 (5 April 2004): 251.
Some other translated books written by Jean Echenoz: *Big Blondes*; *Cherokee*; *Double Jeopardy*; *Piano*; *Plan of Occupancy*; *Ravel*; *Running*

Annie Ernaux. ***A Woman's Story.***
Translated by Tanya Leslie. New York: Four Walls Eight Windows, 1991. 92 pages.
Genres/literary styles/story types: mainstream fiction; feminist fiction
Partly autobiographical, this heart-wrenching novel tells the story of Ernaux's mother, born in 1906 in poverty-stricken rural Normandy. Devoting her life to hard work and thereby hoping to raise her family's social position, she became the owner of a small general store and café in the small town of Yvetot. Her sacrifices and frugality allowed her daughter to receive an education at a private Roman Catholic school. But as she succumbs to Alzheimer's disease in Paris, she recalls that no matter how hard she tried to make her daughter happy, she never achieved that goal.
Related titles by the same author:
The author's *Shame* is a more in-depth examination of the same social and psychological landscape, focusing on the holiday trip Ernaux and her parents take to Lourdes as well as her father's attack on her mother. Just as eloquent is *Cleaned Out*, which recounts the fragmented memories of a young woman undergoing an abortion, and *Simple Passion*, which dissects a love affair with a married man.
Subject keyword: family histories
Original language: French
Sources consulted for annotation:
Dickstein, Mindi. *St. Petersburg Times*, 14 July 1991, p. 4D.
Harrison, Kathryn. *The New York Times Book Review*, 28 November 1999, p. 34.
Ireland, Susan. *World Literature Today* 78 (September/December 2004): 115.
Messaud, Claire. *The New York Times Book Review*, 13 September 1998, p. 16.
Some other translated books written by Annie Ernaux: *A Frozen Woman*; *A Man's Place*; *Cleaned Out*; *I Remain in Darkness*; *Shame*; *Simple Passion*; *Possession*; *Things Seen*

Maxence Fermine. ***The Black Violin.***
Translated by Chris Mulhern. New York: Atria Books, 2003. 133 pages.
Genre/literary style/story type: mainstream fiction
Johannes Karelsky, a famous child-prodigy violinist, withdraws from society to live as a recluse and then is conscripted to serve in Napoleon's army in the late 1790s during the Italian campaigns. Wounded on the battlefield, he is mysteriously saved when he hears the sound of exquisite singing. He takes up residence in a Venetian boarding house owned by Erasmus, who pledges to create a violin that would have no equals. The result is the famous Black Violin, which hangs tantalizingly on the wall of the boarding house but which Erasmus forbids Karelsky to touch. As Erasmus tells the story of the violin, Karelsky envisions playing it and finding the evanescent woman who saved his life through her singing.
Subject keyword: identity
Original language: French
Sources consulted for annotation:
Amazon.com (all editorial reviews).
Isaac, Leann. *Library Journal* 129 (January 2004): 154.
Seaman, Donna. *Booklist* 100 (15 November 2003): 580.
Some other translated books written by Maxence Fermine: *Snow*; *The Beekeeper*

Dan Franck. ***My Russian Love.***
Translated by Jon Rothschild. New York: Nan A. Talese/Doubleday, 1997. 175 pages.
Genre/literary style/story type: mainstream fiction
Luca, a successful film director in his 40s, is returning from St. Petersburg, where he explored the site of his next film: a story by Pushkin that he first heard from Anna, a former lover. In 1970s Paris,

where Anna had been sent to study art by her Soviet parents, Anna and Luca engaged in a torrid romance and then separated when she returned home on learning of her father's exile to a Siberian work camp. Twenty years have passed since Luca last saw her, but now, on a night train to Paris, he spots a woman wrapped in a shawl who makes Anna's trademark gesture. With the help of a conductor, he embarks on a quest to determine the identity of the mysterious woman.
Subject keyword: social roles
Original language: French
Sources consulted for annotation:
Amazon.com (book description; review from *Kirkus Reviews*).
Bernstein, Richard. *The New York Times*, 21 March 1997 (online).
Steinberg, Sybil S. *Publishers Weekly* 243 (30 December 1996): 55.
Another translated book written by Dan Franck: *Separation*

Max Gallo. *Napoleon* (Vol. 1: *The Song of Departure*; Vol. 2: *The Sun of Austerlitz*; Vol. 3: *The Emperor of Kings*; Vol. 4: *The Eternal Man of Saint Helena*).
Translated by William Hobson. London: Macmillan, 2004-2006.
Genre/literary style/story type: historical fiction
These four novels offer a rich and multidimensional biography of Napoleon, starting from his education at a French military school as a young Corsican with only the most rudimentary knowledge of the French language. The author is particularly good when discussing Napoleon's psychological development: He was the victim of schoolyard bullying and had almost no contact with his family. The second and third volumes deal with Napoleon's successful coup, the growth of empire, and his hubristic march into Russia. The fourth volume carries readers through to Napoleon's final days amid a series of defeats and betrayals.
Subject keywords: politics; power
Original language: French
Sources consulted for annotation:
Amazon.com (book description).
Binyon, T. J. *The Sunday Telegraph*, 15 August 2004, p. 15.
Global Books in Print (online) (synopses of all four volumes).
Another translated book written by Max Gallo: *With the Victors*

Laurent Gaudé. *Death of an Ancient King* (or *The Death of King Tsongor*).
Translated by Adriana Hunter. London: Fourth Estate, 2004. 244 pages.
Genre/literary style/story type: historical fiction
King Tsongor is a fictional African ruler whose Massaba empire is powerful and feared. As the king draws near the end of his life, he prepares his transition, overseeing the preparations of the marriage of his daughter to the prince of the Lands of Salt. But scant hours before the nuptials, another suitor appears. The result is a horrific and long-running war. The book can be read as a retelling of the Trojan War.
Related title by the same author:
Readers may also enjoy *The House of Scorta*, which recounts the life of Carmela and her three brothers as they operate a small tobacco store in a southern Italian village.
Subject keywords: power; war
Original language: French
Sources consulted for annotation:
Amazon.com (reviews from *The New Yorker* and *Publishers Weekly*).
Evans, Janet. *Library Journal* 128 (December 2003): 165.
Mann, Jessica. *The Sunday Telegraph*, 8 August 2004, pages. 16.
Some other translated books written by Laurent Gaudé: *The House of Scorta*; *Eldorado*

Anna Gavalda. *Someone I Loved.*
Translated by Catherine Evans. New York: Riverhead Books, 2005. 325 pages.
Genre/literary style/story type: mainstream fiction
Chloé, a young wife and mother of two daughters, is abandoned by her husband for another woman. But Pierre, her father-in-law, is surprisingly sympathetic to her predicament, and he takes Chloé and her daughters to his rural home. As he tells her about his own infidelity, which he has kept secret for some 40 years, Chloé finds the consolation and strength to regroup.
Subject keyword: family histories
Original language: French
Sources consulted for annotation:
Peiffer, Prudence. *Library Journal* 130 (1 April 2005): 85.
Publishers Weekly 252 (14 March 2005): 45.
Scott, Whitney. *Booklist* 101 (1 March 2005): 1142.
Some other translated books written by Anna Gavalda: *95 Pounds of Hope*; *Hunting and Gathering*; *Paris Tales*; *I Wish Someone Were Waiting for Me Somewhere*

Sylvie Germain. *The Book of Nights.*
Translated by Christine Donougher. Boston: David R. Godine, 2003. 263 pages.
Genres/literary styles/story types: historical fiction; literary historical
In the tradition of Gabriel García Márquez's *One Hundred Years of Solitude*, this book recounts the wretched family history of the Peniels, who are peasants in rural France. The patriarch of the family fights in the Franco-Prussian War, but his only reward is insanity and deformation. Violence constantly stalks the family, especially his son Victor-Flandrin, who becomes a widower four times. He is born with a gold-flecked eye, and he passes on that trait to his 15 children. While the *Book of Nights* take the Peniels down to World War II, its sequel, *Night of Amber*, follows their travails through the Algerian conflict and the student revolts of 1968 Paris.
Subject keyword: family histories
Original language: French
Sources consulted for annotation:
Global Books in Print (online) (reviews from *Choice* and *Kirkus Reviews*).
Irvine, Ann. *Library Journal* 118 (December 1993): 174.
Porter, Michael. *The New York Times Book Review*, 25 June 2000 (online).
Seaman, Donna. *Booklist* 90 (15 November 1993): 601.
Steinberg, Sybil S. *Publishers Weekly* 240 (1 November 1993): 68.
Some other translated books written by Sylvie Germain: *The Song of False Lovers*; *Infinite Possibilities*; *Days of Anger*; *The Weeping Woman on the Streets of Prague*; *The Medusa Child*

Jean-Christophe Grangé. *The Stone Council.*
Translated by Ian Monk. London: Harvill, 2001. 373 pages.
Genres/literary styles/story types: thrillers; conspiracy thrillers
Diane Thiberge, a victim of sexual violence in her early teens, studies wild animals and is highly qualified in the martial arts. For the most part, she has very little to do with people, until she adopts Lucien, a small boy from an orphanage in Thailand. But her joy is short-lived when Lucien is involved in an almost-fatal car accident. Although an enigmatic doctor, Rolf van Kaen, saves Lucien, the doctor meets a gruesome death through a technique that is current in the north of Mongolia. As the investigation about this grisly ritualistic killing progresses, van Kaen's mysterious past comes into a focus: It seems he once worked at a Mongolian nuclear facility. This is too much of a coincidence for Diane, who suspects that the car accident was not really an accident at all. She

begins to delve into the identity of her adopted son and discovers his Mongolian heritage. Some critics have seen echoes of Joseph Conrad's *Heart of Darkness* in this novel.
Subject keywords: identity; power
Original language: French
Sources consulted for annotation:
Painter, Michael. *Irish Times*, 12 January 2002, p. 59.
Upson, Nicola. *New Statesman*, 10 December 2001, p. 53.
Zaleski, Jeff. *Publishers Weekly* 249 (14 January 2002): 41.
Some other translated books written by Jean-Christophe Grangé: *Empire of the Wolves*; *Blood-Red Rivers (The Crimson Rivers)*; *Flight of the Storks*

Denis Guedj. *The Measure of the World.*
Translated by Arthur Goldhammer. Chicago: University of Chicago Press, 2001. 298 pages.
Genre/literary style/story type: historical fiction
Have you ever wondered how a meter came to be exactly the length that it is? This novel is a historical account of the protracted struggle to establish the metric standard. Strange as it may seem, in the late eighteenth century, it had a lot to do with meridians, especially when the French Academy of Science hired two astronomers—Jean Baptiste Joseph Delambre and Pierre Méchain—to measure the Dunkirk-Barcelona meridian. Despite being interrupted by historical events, such as the French Revolution, their work was completed at the end of the eighteenth century and served as the basis of the modern meter.
Subject keyword: politics
Original language: French
Sources consulted for annotation:
Amazon.com (book description; inside flap).
Quinn, Mary Ellen. *Booklist* 98 (1 September 2001): 50.
Another translated book written by Denis Guedj: *The Parrot's Theorem*

Hervé Guibert. *Blindsight.*
Translated by James Kirkup. New York: George Braziller, 1996. 119 pages.
Genre/literary style/story type: mainstream fiction
Josette and Robert are married and blind; their lives are spent in an anonymous facility adapted to their needs. They lead a quiet existence, playing music. Other residents create sculptures and observe the stars—all the while trying to keep out of the way of the supercilious and smug director. But soon, their peace is shattered with the arrival of Taillegueur, who claims to be a masseur. It is not enough that he draws Josette into a web of steamy sexual frolic; he also plans to kill Robert. As the reviewer in *Publishers Weekly* stated, the book "evokes touch, taste, sound and smell so powerfully" that it becomes "a biting commentary on the opportunities for feeling and sensation squandered by those with all their senses working."
Subject keyword: power
Original language: French
Sources consulted for annotation:
Irvine, Ann. *Library Journal* 121 (July 1996): 159.
Steinberg, Sybil S. *Publishers Weekly* 243 (2 September 1996): 114.
Some other translated books written by Hervé Guibert: *To the Friend Who Did Not Save My Life*; *The Compassion Protocol*; *My Parents*; *The Gangsters*; *The Man in the Red Hat*; *Paradise*; *Incognito*

Marek Halter. *The Book of Abraham.*
Translated by Lowell Bair. New York: Henry Holt, 1986. 722 pages.

Genre/literary style/story type: historical fiction

This epic is nothing less than the full-fledged history of a Jewish family's serpentine path through the violence and horror of the last two millennia. When the Romans sack Jerusalem in 70 C.E., the scribe Abraham and his family flee, but their success is short-lived when Abraham's wife is raped and murdered. Abraham, his sons, and their descendents continue on, with each of their journeys, trials, and tribulations recorded in a book of scrolls. As they make their way through various European cities in the Middle Ages, during the Renaissance, and into the twentieth century, their individual tragic fates serve as a devastating indictment of human abjectness.

Subject keyword: family histories

Original language: French

Sources consulted for annotation:

Global Books in Print (online) (review from *Publishers Weekly*).

Irvine, Ann. *Library Journal* 128 (July 2003): SS24.

Potok, Chaim. *Wall Street Journal*, 24 April 1986, p. 1.

Wikipedia (entry for *The Book of Abraham*), http://en.wikipedia.org.

Some other translated books written by Marek Halter: *Sarah*; *The Children of Abraham*; *Zipporah, Wife of Moses*; *Lilah: A Forbidden Love, a People's Destiny*; *The Wind of the Khazars*

Jacqueline Harpman. *I Who Have Never Known Men*.

Translated by Ros Schwartz. New York: Seven Stories Press, 1997. 206 pages.

Genres/literary styles/story types: speculative fiction; feminist fiction

In a postapocalyptic world, one has to relearn everything. Even the simplest tasks are now difficult and danger-filled, as was made clear in Cormac McCarthy's *The Road*. In Jacqueline Harpman's novel, this truth also holds. Forty women are incarcerated underground—their every action watched over by heinous and sadistic male guards. Touching is not allowed; they have no memories left. Everything must be discovered anew or for the first time, as in the case of one of the younger women, who learns to think and then tell time. When the women escape, their euphoria does not last long because they realize that they are the only survivors of a destructive event of monumental proportions. The book has been compared with Margaret Atwood's *The Handmaid's Tale* as well as the work of Ursula K. Le Guin.

Subject keyword: power

Original language: French

Sources consulted for annotation:

Cassin, Erin. *Library Journal* 122 (1 April 1997): 125.

Eckhoff, Sally. *The New York Times Book Review*, 14 September 1997, p. 26.

Global Books in Print (online) (reviews from *Booklist* and *Kirkus Reviews*).

Steinberg, Sybil S. *Publishers Weekly* 244 (21 April 1997): 60.

Some other translated books written by Jacqueline Harpman: *Orlanda*; *The Mistress of Silence*

Michel Houellebecq. *The Elementary Particles*.

Translated by Frank Wynne. New York: Alfred A. Knopf, 2000. 263 pages.

Genre/literary style/story type: mainstream fiction

This novel follows the lives of two half-brothers who were abandoned in the 1960s by their selfish, pleasure-seeking mother. Raised by different sets of grandparents, both boys were less than happy adolescents. Bruno Clément, repeatedly bullied by his peers, becomes a sexually frustrated adult—a professional masturbator dreaming of inaccessible women. On the other hand, Michel Djerzinski becomes a molecular biologist whose research into cloning would mean the end of sex. As Jenny Turner writes, the novel features insightful analysis about the connections "between sexual liberation and spiritual emptiness, Judeo-Christianity and genetic manipulation." Readers who are interested in provocative views about contemporary social, cultural, and political issues will be challenged by Houellebecq's writing, which some commentators have denounced as sexist and racist but which other critics have seen as being worthy of the highest praise for its honesty and boldness. Houellebecq has been favorably compared with Albert Camus.

Related titles by the same author:

Readers may also wish to explore *Platform*, where Michel, an alienated bureaucrat, visits Thailand as a way of getting over his father's death. Here, he discovers that the future belongs to sex tourism. Teaming up with Valérie, a travel consultant and his new-found lover, he becomes the Donald Trump of sex resorts. Their life seems idyllic until a bomb explodes. Also of interest may be *The Possibility of an Island*, a philosophical novel where two narrators, Daniel-1 and Daniel-24, analyze how notions of sexuality changed over the course of time as the world came face-to-face with environmental armageddon. Readers will likely want to look forward to the English translation of Houellebecq's most critically acclaimed novel, *La Carte et le Territoire* (2010), which is a devastatingly nihilistic, but nevertheless ineffably poignant meditation on the ephemerality of all things. Jed Martin is an artist whose innovative works—a photographic reconsideration of rural maps; a series of portraits of the practitioners of traditional and contemporary professions; and video montages of vegetation and modern technology—serve as a backdrop to thoughtful discussions about mortality; the purpose of art; and the utter impossibility of ever knowing one's parents. Houellebecq himself is a central character in the novel: he writes a laudatory preface for the catalogue of Martin's "professions" exhibit; allows Martin to visit him and paint his portrait; and ends up the victim of a gruesome murder that lies unresolved for years. Deeply affected by Houellebecq's philosophy of life as well as his macabre death, Martin, now one of the wealthiest of contemporary French painters, withdraws into the far reaches of the French countryside, isolating himself in a fenced compound where he placidly awaits death, convinced that all attempts to keep it at bay through a swirl of social connections are narcissistically futile.

Subject keywords: family histories; identity

Original language: French

Sources consulted for annotation:

Hoffert, Barbara. *Library Journal* 125 (1 November 2000): 134.
Kakutain, Michiko. *The New York Times*, 10 November 2000 (online).
Maslin, Janet. *The New York Times*, 21 July 2003 (online).
Metcalf, Stephen. *The New York Times Book Review*, 11 June 2006 (online).
Quinn, Anthony. *The New York Times Book Review*, 19 November 2000 (online).
Steinberg, Sybil S. *Publishers Weekly* 247 (4 September 2000): 81.
Turner, Jenny. *The New York Times Book Review*, 20 July 2003 (online).

Some other translated books written by Michel Houellebecq: *Platform*; *The Possibility of an Island*; *Whatever*; *Lanzarote; H. P. Lovecraft: Against the World, Against Life*

Christian Jacq. *War of the Crowns: A Novel of Ancient Egypt*.

Translated by Sue Dyson. New York: Atria Books, 2004. 312 pages.

Genre/literary style/story type: historical fiction

Jacq is a well-known Egyptologist who has written numerous historically based novels about Ancient Egypt. This is the second book in the *Queen Liberty Trilogy*, of which *The Empire of Darkness: A Novel of Ancient Egypt* and *The Flaming Sword: A Novel of Ancient Egypt* are the first and the third novels, respectively. It focuses on Queen Ahotep, who is referred to as a warrior queen and the founder of a dynasty that repelled the Hyksos.

Subject keywords: politics; power

Original language: French

Sources consulted for annotation:
Amazon.com (book description).
Flanagan, Margaret. *Booklist* 100 (15 April 2004): 1425.
Wikipedia (entry for Christian Jacq), http://en.wikipedia.org.
Some other translated books written by Christian Jacq: *The Son of Light*; *The Eternal Temple*; *The Battle of Kadesh*; *The Lady of Abu Simbel*; *Nefer the Silent*; *Under the Western Acacia*; *Paneb the Ardent*; *The Wise Woman*; *The Place of Truth*; *The Temple of a Million Years*; *The Black Pharaoh*

Sébastien Japrisot. *A Very Long Engagement.*
Translated by Linda Coverdale. New York: Farrar, Straus and Giroux, 1993. 327 pages.
Genre/literary style/story type: mainstream fiction
Mathilde Donnay is confined to a wheelchair but leads a rich and full life. She is informed that her fiancé, Jean Etchevery, died in 1917 in World War I. But Mathilde does not believe the news of his death and sets out to determine what really happened. She discovers that the truth is multifaceted, not the least because Etchevery and four others—in an attempt to escape the brutality of the front lines—shot themselves in the hands. To deter other attempts of the same kind, French military authorities punished them by leaving them to die in an exposed area between the opposing armies. This book was made into a movie in 2004.
Subject keyword: war
Original language: French
Sources consulted for annotation:
Amazon.com (book description).
Global Books in Print (online) (review from *Kirkus Reviews*).
Hartshorn, Laurie. *Booklist* 101 (15 March 2005): 1312.
Steinberg, Sybil S. *Publishers Weekly* 240 (1 November 1993): 46.
Wikipedia (entry for *A Very Long Engagement*), http://en.wikipedia.org.
Some other translated books written by Sébastien Japrisot: *One Deadly Summer*; *The Passion of Women*; *The Lady in the Car with Glasses and a Gun*; *The 10:30 from Marseille*; *Women in Evidence*; *Goodbye, Friend*; *Trap for Cinderella*; *Awakening*; *The Sleeping Car Murders*

Alexandre Jardin. *Fanfan.*
Translated by Charles Penwarden. New York: St. Martin's Press, 1994. 170 pages.
Genre/literary style/story type: mainstream fiction
Alexandre Crusoe's parents are, to his mind, amoral libertines indulging in wanton sex with whomever they please. In the time-honored tradition that children always rebel against what their parents represent, Alexandre decides that he will be the most moral of men. When he affiances himself, it is to Laure, a prim and proper woman whose boring nature he initially finds to be an asset. But he does not count on the effect that Fanfan, a devil-may-care filmmaker with an independent streak, will have on him. Still, because of his fervent beliefs about the sanctity of sex, he vows to remain true to Laure.
Subject keyword: identity
Original language: French
Sources consulted for annotation:
Furtsch, Stephanie. *Library Journal* 119 (1 June 1994): 160.
Global Books in Print (online) (review from *Booklist*).
Steinberg, Sybil S. *Publishers Weekly* 241 (9 May 1994): 62.
Some other translated books written by Alexandre Jardin: *The Zebra*; *In the Fast Lane*

Michel Jouvet. *The Castle of Dreams.*
Translated by Laurence Garey. Cambridge, MA: MIT Press, 2008. 344 pages.
Genre/literary style/story type: mainstream fiction
In the eighteenth century, Hugues la Scève, an amateur scientist if there ever was one, took it upon himself to classify and categorize his own dreams. To discover still more about the nature of dreams, he also conducted a series of bizarre experiments on animals and other people. In 1982, a scientist who is a stand-in for the author purchases an old trunk containing la Scève's work and sets out to understand how and why la Scève did what he did. Jouvet also wrote the nonfiction work *The Paradox of Sleep*. *The Castle of Dreams* can be enjoyably paired with Stéphane Audeguy's *The Theory of Clouds*, which provides another viewpoint about attempts to classify the ineffable.
Subject keyword: identity
Original language: French
Sources consulted for annotation:
Global Books in Print (online) (reviews from *Booklist*, *Library Journal*, and *Publishers Weekly*).
McCulloch, Alison. *The New York Times Book Review*, 16 November 2008 (online).
The MIT Press (book description), http://mitpress.mit.edu.
Another translated book written by Michel Jouvet: *The Paradox of Sleep*

Hédi Kaddour. *Waltenberg.*
Translated by David Coward. London: Harvill Secker, 2008. 660 pages.
Genre/literary style/story type: mainstream fiction
This is a novel of ideas masquerading as a spy thriller, with succinct historical considerations of World War I and World War II. In a small Swiss village in the mid-1950s, the thirst for power and influence continues as the Cold War plays out against a backdrop of love, friendship, and geopolitical strategies. East German spies battle operatives from the Central Intelligence Agency, with betrayal as the ever-present leitmotif.
Subject keyword: politics
Original language: French
Source consulted for annotation:
Lewin, Matthew. *The Guardian*, 3 May 2008 (online).

Julia Kristeva. *Possessions.*
Translated by Barbara Bray. New York: Columbia University Press, 1998. 211 pages.
Genres/literary styles/story types: crime fiction; amateur detectives
Gloria Harrison seems to have it all: a good job as a translator, fulfillment as a mother, and a satisfying sexual life. But she meets a tragic fate in a resort in Eastern Europe. Not only is she murdered, but her head is severed from her body. Although a formal investigation is undertaken, it does not produce results. Thus, Stéphanie Delacour, Gloria's friend, sets out to solve the case. No stranger to detective work because of her professional position as a journalist, Stéphanie quickly focuses her inquiry on Gloria's disabled son as well as the intriguing question about whether murder and decapitation were carried out by one and the same person. Kristeva is a well-known French philosopher, among many other accomplishments.
Subject keyword: family histories
Original language: French
Sources consulted for annotation:
Irvine, Ann. *Library Journal* 123 (1 February 1998): 111.
Kingcaid, Renee. *Review of Contemporary Fiction* 18 (Fall 1998): 252.
Some other translated books written by Julia Kristeva: *The Old Man and the Wolves*; *The Samurai*; *Murder in Byzantium*

Philippe Labro. ***Le Petit Garçon.***
Translated by Linda Coverdale. New York: Farrar, Straus and Giroux, 1992. 259 pages.
Genres/literary styles/story types: mainstream fiction; coming-of-age
In a small town in southwest France during World War II, German occupation forces are dictating every aspect of life. One large family is particularly affected; all seven children, including the narrator of the novel, are inexorably drawn into a conflict-ridden universe when their father tirelessly helps numerous Jewish refugees escape the occupying forces. After the war, the family moves to Paris so that the children may benefit from attending superior schools. Here, the narrator meets one of the refugees—a meeting that confirms for him the value of ethical behavior no matter the circumstances.
Related titles by the same author:
Readers may also want to explore two other coming-of-age stories—both of which are set in the 1950s: *One Summer Out West*, set in Colorado, and *The Foreign Student*, set in Virginia.
Subject keywords: family histories; war
Original language: French
Sources consulted for annotation:
Global Books in Print (online) (reviews from *Booklist* and *Kirkus Reviews*).
Mihram, Danielle. *Library Journal* 117 (15 May 1992): 120.
Steinberg, Sybil S. *Publishers Weekly* 239 (6 April 1992): 50.
Some other translated books written by Philippe Labro: *The Foreign Student*; *One Summer Out West*; *Dark Tunnel, White Light*

J.-M. G. Le Clézio. ***Wandering Star.***
Translated by C. Dickson. Willimantic, CT: Curbstone Press, 2004. 316 pages.
Genres/literary styles/story types: mainstream fiction; coming-of-age
During World War II, Esther, a young Jewish girl, and her parents are living in the small French mountain village of Saint-Martin near the Italian border after fleeing Nice. Here, Italian forces are in charge, and Jews are forced to show their identity cards every day. When the Italians evacuate the village and German forces move in, the refugees of Saint-Martin struggle to reach the safety of Italy. Esther's father disappears, killed trying to help other refugees reach safety. Esther and her mother work for a time in a run-down Italian hotel, move to Paris, and then undertake a harrowing sea journey to Israel, where they hope to start a new life. Here, Esther briefly comes in contact with Nejma, a Palestinian refugee whose life is marked by as much devestation—if not more—than that experienced by Esther. Soon, the abject misery of the Palestinian refugee camps becomes unbearable. Nejma escapes, unable to bear the harsh physical conditions and the loss of hope.
Related titles by the same author:
Readers may also want to explore *Onitsha*, a partly autobiographical novel about Fintan, a 12-year-old boy traveling to Africa to live with his parents. Again, the viewpoints of children are privileged, especially in Fintan's observations about colonialism. Soon, the reconstituted family finds itself isolated, especially when the boy's mother does not adhere to the strict protocols of colonial convention. The author's masterpiece is considered by many to be *Desert*, which incisively describes the contact of African nomad cultures with the Western world. Lalla lives in a shantytown in a Moroccan city on the edge of the desert. Here, she befriends the young shepherd Hartani, who—despite being a mute—recounts legends of the desert to Lalla and introduces her to its secrets. Lalla discovers the power of nature and voices from the past; she also discovers love with Hartani. Her life takes a sudden turn when she emigrates to Marseilles, where she works as a chambermaid in a dilapidated hotel. Living what amounts to a slave's existence, she is discovered by a photographer and appears on the cover of a magazine. Pregnant with Hartani's child, she returns to her beloved

Morocco, where she gives birth in solitude and names her child after her mother. Sensitively examining two very different worlds, *Desert* suggests that the chasm between them is a deep and abiding one.
Subject keywords: power; war
Original language: French
Sources consulted for annotation:
Amazon.com (book description for *Wandering Star*; reviews from *Publishers Weekly* and *Library Journal* for *Onitsha*).
Back cover of the book (French edition of *Desert*).
Lyall, Sarah. *The New York Times*, 10 October 2008, p. A10.
Schwartz, Ignacio. *Ralph* [*Review of Arts, Literature, Philosophy and the Humanities*], http://www.ralphmag.org.
Seaman, Donna. *Booklist* 101 (15 September 2004): 208.
Some other translated books written by J.-M. G. Le Clézio: *The Round and Other Cold Hard Facts*; *Onitsha*; *The Prospector*; *The Giants*; *War; Terra Amata*; *The Flood*; *Fever*; *The Interrogation*; *Desert*

Justine Lévy. *Nothing Serious*.
Translated by Charlotte Mandell. Brooklyn, NY: Melville House, 2005. 176 pages.
Genre/literary style/story type: mainstream fiction; women's lives
Louise thought that she had the perfect marriage with Adrien, but everything falls apart when her husband leaves her for Paula, a beautiful model who was his father's lover. Louise must cope as best she can. With the help of handfuls of painkillers, Louise undertakes a brutally honest journey into her vanity-filled life and tortured psyche. The author is the daughter of the philosopher and cultural critic Bernard-Henri Lévy.
Subject keyword: identity
Original language: French
Sources consulted for annotation:
Global Books in Print (online) (review from Publishers Weekly).
Melville House website, http://www.mhpbooks.com.
Another translated book written by Justine Lévy: *The Rendezvous*

Jonathan Littell. *The Kindly Ones*.
Translated by Charlotte Mandell. New York: HarperCollins, 2009. 983 pages.
Genre/literary style/story type: mainstream fiction
As the twentieth century draws to a close, Maximilien Aue, a German, is the head of a factory in northern France that makes lace garments. He is the holder of a doctorate in constitutional law and a homosexual, and during World War II, he was a mid-level SS officer. One day, he decides to write about the nightmarish events of the war and his participation therein. Aue is an educated individual, so his account is a wide-ranging, objective, and balanced explanation of Nazi ideology. Aue's central tasks in the war effort consisted of liaison work and report writing, but he accepts his share of responsibility for the Holocaust even though he was nauseated by it. His clinically precise, stomach-turning, and frequently overwhelming story is not so much a justification of German actions as a chillingly lucid attempt at a philosophical inquiry into the psychological, legal, and administrative dynamics that led to the specious rationalizations that made the atrocities possible. In the end, the accumulation of unexpurgated details—together with the laconic manner in which those details are presented—functions as an unswerving indictment of every aspect of German conduct under Hitler. Aue begins by focusing on his homosexuality and the way in which Thomas Hauser, another Nazi officer, helped him to hide that fact when he was arrested for suspicion of

homosexual activities in 1937. Hauser is a careerist, but he becomes Aue's friend and confidant—a sounding board for his apprehensions, ambivalence, and despair. The novel then focuses on the brutally systematic march in 1941 of German forces through Ukrainian towns and cities, including Kiev; Aue's two-month stay at a Crimean sanatorium for nervous exhaustion; the conquest of various Caucasian republics and autonomous regions; Aue's transfer to Stalingrad, where German forces were completely surrounded by the Soviet army and where he receives a head wound; his hospitalization and convalescence in Berlin; and his new assignment as a strategist responsible for developing an overarching plan regarding the Jewish question. In this new capacity, he soon finds that he must navigate numerous competing interests within the Nazi hierarchy, which he discovers is an almost impossible task. As he gathers information about the fate of Jewish populations in areas under German control, he confronts evil that is made all the more ghastly by its pedestrian nature. It is a mark of Littell's artistic mastery that Aue makes intelligent observations about the short- and long-term consequences of the war, but these are then invariably undercut by cold-blooded ratiocination about political power and control. While Aue claims to adhere to universal moral and ethical standards, he is also enthused about the teachings of national socialism; in the end, he realizes that the implacable and impersonal logic of war makes individual survival directly dependent on obedience to immediate superiors, who are representatives of community will. Aue's family background (an absent father; a mother whom he grows to hate after her second marriage; an incestuous relationship with his twin sister Una; the forced separation of the twins after the discovery of their relationship; Una's marriage to a wheelchair-bound composer many years her senior; and the death of his mother and stepfather in mysterious circumstances) also plays a key part in this novel. Each event adds to the portrait of Aue as a psychopathic narcissist. For anyone wishing to better understand 1930s and 1940s German national socialism, this fictional memoir is an indispensable—if gruesome—book.
Subject keywords: anti-Semitism; politics
Original language: French
Source consulted for annotation:
Gates, David. *The New York Times Book Review*, 5 March 2009 (online).

Andreï Makine. *Music of a Life* (or ***A Life's Music*).**
Translated by Geoffrey Strachan. New York: Arcade, 2002. 109 pages.
Genre/literary style/story type: mainstream fiction
Alexei Berg is playing the piano in a railway station waiting room in the Soviet Union. Soon, Berg and the unnamed narrator begin to talk—a conversation that continues as the train moves through the bleak wintry Siberian landscape toward Moscow. Berg's life story is nothing if not tragic. On the cusp of a promising career as a pianist in 1940, he flees to Ukraine when his parents are arrested. Here, he assumes the identity of another man: a dead soldier from the peasant class. He distinguishes himself in the Soviet war effort, becomes the trusted associate of an important general, and has romantic illusions with regard to the general's daughter. But when he sits down to play the piano, his carefully constructed new life unravels. Sven Birkerts wrote that this short novel "grafts upon the tradition of the traveler's tale something of the sensibility of Borgesian modernism, with its beguiling play of doubles and transposed identities."
Related titles by the same author:
Readers may also enjoy the autobiographical novel *Dreams of My Russian Summers*, which describes the author's visits to his grandmother's home in Siberia and her multihued life story. She was originally French, then served in Russia as a nurse in World War I, and married a Russian who died from wounds received during World War II. Also of interest may be *The Woman Who Waited*, a keenly observed and poignant story about Vera, a middle-aged woman who waits some 30 years for the return of her fiancé from World War II. *Human Love* represents somewhat of a

departure for Makine. Set against the backdrop of the Angolan Civil War in the late 1970s, it focuses on three hostages captured by one of the rebel groups.
Subject keywords: power; war
Original language: French
Sources consulted for annotation:
Birkerts, Sven. *The Washington Post Book World*, 18 August 2002 (online).
Global Books in Print (online) (reviews from *Library Journal* and *Publishers Weekly* for all novels).
Harleman, Ann. *The New York Times Book Review*, 6 October 2002 (online).
Hoffert, Barbara. *Library Journal* 127 (July 2002): 120.
Hunt, Laird. *Review of Contemporary Fiction* 23 (Spring 2003): 138.
McCulloch, Alison. *The New York Times Book Review*, 16 November 2008 (online).
Slivka, Andrey. *The New York Times Book Review*, 19 March 2006 (online).
Some other translated books written by Andreï Makine: *Dreams of My Russian Summers*; *Requiem for a Lost Empire*; *Once upon the River Love*; *The Earth and Sky of Jacques Dorme*; *The Crime of Olga Arbyelina*; *The Woman Who Waited*; *Confessions of a Fallen Standard-Bearer*; *A Hero's Daughter*; *Human Love*

Patrick Modiano. *Missing Person.*
Translated by Daniel Weissbort. Boston: David R. Godine, 2005. 167 pages.
Genres/literary styles/story types: crime fiction; private investigators
Guy Roland, a private investigator in Paris, has very little recollection of anything since World War II. Thus, he begins to investigate himself and his lost past. Piecing together the most mundane of clues, he convinces himself that he has led more than one life—that he is more than one person.
Subject keyword: identity
Original language: French
Sources consulted for annotation:
Evans, Janet. *Library Journal* 130 (15 May 2005): 107.
Sennett, Frank. *Booklist* 101 (1 May 2005): 1532.
Some other translated books written by Patrick Modiano: *Out of The Dark*; *Catherine Certitude*; *Night Rounds*; *Honeymoon*; *The Search Warrant*; *Ring Roads*

Yves Navarre. *Cronus' Children.*
Translated by Howard Girven. New York: Riverrun Press, 1986. 319 pages.
Genre/literary style/story type: mainstream fiction
Henri Prouillan was part of the French elite in the post–World War II era. But then again, he was not. Ever striving to preserve his family's honor and his own career prospects within government circles, he dispatched Bertrand, the youngest of his sons, to be lobotomized because he dared to affirm his homosexuality. He then confined him under guard to the family's rural estate. While Bertrand is forever psychologically and emotionally scarred, his brothers and sisters also lead tortured lives of quiet despair, aghast at their father's sordid actions but unable to act. This novel has been compared with James Joyce's *Ulysses* and William Faulkner's *The Sound and the Fury*. There are important mythological resonances in the book's title.
Subject keyword: family histories
Original language: French
Sources consulted for annotation:
Buitenhuis, Peter. *The Globe and Mail* (Toronto), 27 September 1986, p. E23.
Global Books in Print (online) (reviews from *Choice* and *Publishers Weekly*).
Rose, Marilyn Gaddis. *Library Journal* 112 (January 1987): 108.

Some other translated books written by Yves Navarre: *Our Share of Time*; *Sweet Tooth*; *The Little Rogue in Our Flesh*; *A Cat's Life*

Irène Némirovsky. *Suite Française.*
Translated by Sandra Smith. New York: Alfred A. Knopf, 2006. 395 pages.
Genre/literary style/story type: historical fiction
This long-forgotten book, resurrected after spending about 60 years in a suitcase belonging to the author's daughter, was written a mere two years before Némirovsky's death at Auschwitz in August 1942. Containing two accounts of life in France during the summer months of 1940 and 1941 under German occupation, it was unanimously praised for its verisimilitude and profound insight. The names of Camus and Tolstoy were invoked to denote the book's power. The publication of *Suite Française* led to the discovery of other works by the author, a convert to Catholicism, including *Fire in the Blood*, which focuses on a bachelor's memories of his past life when he meets a young woman at a wedding, and *Dimanche and Other Stories*. In addition, Everyman's Library published a volume of Némirovsky's early fictional works: *David Golder*, *The Ball*, *Snow in Autumn*, *The Courilof Affair*. In the first-named work, Golder is a petroleum speculator whose actions lead to the suicide of another man. *The Courilof Affair*, which centers on a man who has been given the task of assassinating a high-ranking Russian official, recalls Joseph Conrad's *The Secret Agent*. The sudden interest in Némirovsky's work led to further examination of her life, which was full of numerous paradoxes—chief of which was that some of her novels contained startling stereotypes of Jewish people and that she published in magazines that some critics described as xenophobic. Readers interested in coming to terms with some of these paradoxes may want to explore *The Life of Irène Némirovsky, 1903–1942*, by Olivier Philipponnant and Patrick Lienhardt, translated by Euan Cameron. On a more general level, also valuable in this regard might be *Trials of the Diaspora: A History of Anti-Semitism in England* by Anthony Julius.
Subject keyword: anti-Semitism
Original language: French
Sources consulted for annotation:
Benfey, Christopher. *The New York Times Book Review*, 21 October 2007 (online).
Global Books in Print (online) (review from *Booklist* for *Fire in the Blood*).
Gray, Paul. *The New York Times Book Review*, 9 April 2006 (online).
Mallon, Thomas. *The New York Times Book Review*, 9 March 2008 (online).
Prose, Francine. *The New York Times Book Review*, 6 May 2010 (online).
Some other translated books written by Irène Némirovsky: *Fire in the Blood*; *David Golder, The Ball, Snow in Autumn, The Courilof Affair*; *All Our Wordly Goods*; *Dimanche and Other Stories*

Amélie Nothomb. *Fear and Trembling.*
Translated by Adriana Hunter. New York: St. Martin's Press, 2001. 132 pages.
Genre/literary style/story type: mainstream fiction
The fictional Japanese company Yumimoto is the epitome of hierarchical bureaucracy. For a young Belgian woman who wants to impress her new employer, the firm is a labyrinth of administrative levels that must be navigated in exactly the correct way. Of course, she can hardly fail to make a gigantic error: taking the inititiave to do something without being asked. Her immediate superior is Fubuki Mori, a stunning woman whom she secretely admires and even loves. Fubuki's superiors are, in ascending order, Saito, Omochi, and Haneda—all men and all more vociferous and intimidating than their underling. When the Belgian employee, a stand-in for the author, starts to deliver the internal company mail without authorization, her downfall begins; she is quickly told to confine herself to photocopying. But while photocopying, she meets a manager from another department who is not in any way her boss. He has an innovative project on the go with a Belgian agricultural

co-operative with regard to light butter. Thus, it is natural for him to ask a Belgian native to help him. When her second initiative is discovered, her future at the company hangs by a thread: She is reduced to filing and calculating travel expenses. After miserably failing at these clerical tasks and earning the withering scorn of Fubuki for her attempts at personal empathy, she is still further reduced to being a bathroom attendant on a single floor of the Yumimoto building. Throughout the day she must replenish towels, ensure a steady supply of toilet paper, and scrub the bowls when they become too encrusted with residue. It is a totally useless and superfluous task because there are cleaning women at night, but it is a task that assumes Sisyphean proportions because of cultural misunderstanding. Throughout her numerous miseries, she nevertheless retains a philosophical attitude—stoically and not without grace examining the consequences and implications of her actions. The author is Belgian.

Related titles by the same author:

Readers may also enjoy *The Character of Rain*, which is a fictional portrait of the author's early childhood in Japan as the daughter of a Belgian diplomat and his wife. Also noteworthy is *Tokyo Fiancée*, in which the author teaches French in Japan. Her only student is Rinri, who is interested in Sartre. Tutor and pupil begin a relationship that may be described as friends with benefits. Also of interest is *The Stranger Next Door*, where a recently retired couple who have been married for more than 40 years finally realize their lifelong dream of a solitary existence in a rural area far away from everyone and anything. But their peaceful existence comes to an end even before it begins when their only neighbor, a fat doctor with no patients, comes to visit them each and every day from 4 p.m. to 6 p.m. He merely sits, grunts a few words, expects to be entertained and fed, and then leaves promptly at 6 p.m. Eventually, the couple persuades him to bring his wife to visit. She turns out to be more obese than her physician husband. Of course, they cannot help wondering about their strange neighbors. As they slowly begin to unravel the mystery of the doctor, they realize that his wife is both a physical and psychological prisoner whose freedom can only be secured through her husband's death.

Subject keywords: culture conflict; identity

Original language: French

Sources consulted for annotation:

Chira, Susan. *The New York Times Book Review*, 25 March 2001 (online).
Eder, Richard. *The New York Times*, 17 April 2002 (online).
Fay, Sarah. *The New York Times Book Review*, 4 January 2009 (online).
Kaye, Janet. *The New York Times Book Review*, 15 February 1998 (online).
Kirkus Reviews 70 (15 March 2002): 368.

Some other translated books written by Amélie Nothomb: *The Character of Rain*; *The Book of Proper Names*; *The Stranger Next Door*; *Loving Sabotage*; *Antichrista*; *The Life of Hunger*; *Tokyo Fiancée; Hygiene and the Assassin*

Érik Orsenna. *Grammar Is a Gentle, Sweet Song.*

Translated by Moishe Black. New York: George Braziller, 2004. 126 pages.

Genres/literary styles/story types: adventure; quest

Critics have said that this book is reminiscent of Antoine de Saint-Exupéry's *The Little Prince*: Shipwrecked on a magical island, a preteen girl and her older brother are so traumatized that they are no longer able to speak. However, in due course, Monsieur Henri is of great help to them, explaining the many wonders of the island, where words have all the attributes of real people. Ultimately, the playfulness and inventiveness of language is the siblings' saving grace.

Related title by the same author:

Readers may also enjoy *Love and Empire*, in which the history of France's imperial and colonial ambitions is recounted by a mother, her son, and her grandson. As William Ferguson observes,

"The novel's French title, *L'Exposition Coloniale*, is cleverly ambiguous: the novel as a whole is a kind of 'colonial exhibition,' not so much in the sense of displaying exotic products and customs—though these abound—as of revealing the faulted essence of Europe's imperial vision."
Subject keyword: philosophy
Original language: French
Sources consulted for annotation:
Ferguson, William. *The New York Times Book Review*, 11 August 1991 (online).
Fisher, Ann H. *Library Journal* 129 (15 May 2004): 116.
Publishers Weekly 251 (19 April 2004): 39.
Some other translated books written by Erik Orsenna: *Love and Empire*; *History of the World in Nine Guitars*

Olivier Pauvert. *Noir.*
Translated by Adriana Hunter. Oxford, UK: Basic Books, 2008. 224 pages.
Genre/literary style/story type: speculative fiction
If you like dystopias, then this is likely the book for you. Twelve years ago, a man was falsely accused of murder. On his way to prison in a police van, he dies, the victim of a crash. Now he has returned under the guise of someone else's identity, intent on clearing his name. But 12 years is a long time: France is governed by a right-wing authoritarian regime. Indeed, there is something called the Ministry of Racial Differences. As he tries to solve the crime for which he was originally arrested and as he comes to terms with the fact that his stare is literally a lethal weapon, he travels across a France that has been transformed beyond all belief. Reviewers invoked classic works, such as Aldous Huxley's *Brave New World*, when discussing this book.
Subject keywords: politics; power
Original language: French
Sources consulted for annotation:
Global Books in Print (online) (reviews from *Booklist*, *Library Journal*, and *Publishers Weekly*).
Rourke, Lee. *Bookforum* (December 2008/January 2009) (online).

Daniel Pennac. *Passion Fruit.*
Translated by Ian Monk. London: Harvill, 2001. 181 pages.
Genres/literary styles/story types: crime fiction; urban fiction
Set in the Belleville quarter of Paris, this novel is part of the author's series that features the Malaussènes, whom Bill Ott describes as "the Marx Brothers of alternative families." No one can explain the upcoming marriage of Thérèse Malaussène and Marie-Colbert de Roberval, a straitlaced government official. Could it have something to do with the fact that Thérèse, a fortune teller, has an extremely good record of predicting the future and that Marie-Colbert has a burning desire to advance his political career? Thérèse's brother Benjamin and his friends try to derail the marriage but to no avail. Things go from bad to worse when their honeymoon is marred by Thérèse's decision to abandon her husband, a fire, and the murder of Marie-Colbert.
Subject keyword: family histories
Original language: French
Sources consulted for annotation:
Cannon, Peter. *Publishers Weekly* 248 (17 September 2001): 58.
Global Books in Print (online) (review from *Kirkus Reviews*).
Ott, Bill. *Booklist* 97 (August 2001): 2098.
Some other translated books written by Daniel Pennac: *Better than Life*; *Eye of the Wolf*; *Write to Kill*; *Dog*; *The Scapegoat*; *Monsieur Malaussène*; *Reads Like a Novel*; *The Fairy Gunmother*; *The Dictator and the Hammock*

Georges Perec. *A Void.*
Translated by Gilbert Adair. Boston: David R. Godine, 2005. 284 pages.
Genres/literary styles/story types: mainstream fiction; experimental fiction
Can a book be written without one single instance of the letter E? That previous sentence had many Es in it, so you can see that writing a book without that letter would be diabolically difficult. And yet, here it is. As many critics have pointed out, the formal name for what Perec has done is a lipogram. And perhaps it is not surprising because he was a member of Oulipo, a group of mathematicians who were beyond brilliant and who loved to try new things. Does this book have a hero? Of course, and his name is Anton Vowl. And he has disappeared. Can anyone say detective parody? As his friends gather to solve the mystery of his disappearance, they soon find themselves swept up by a whirlwind of just about every cliché you could ever find in a mystery book.
Subject keyword: philosophy
Original language: French
Sources consulted for annotation:
Irving, Malin. *Review of Contemporary Fiction* 15 (Summer 1995): 200.
Kincaid, James. *The New York Times Book Review*, 12 March 1995 (online).
O'Brien, Maureen. *Publishers Weekly* 241 (3 October 1994): 13.
Some other translated books written by Georges Perec: *Life, a User's Manual*; *W, or, The Memory of Childhood*; *Things: A Story of the Sixties*; *The Winter Journey*; *53 Days*

Gisèle Pineau. *Exile According to Julia.*
Translated by Betty Wilson. Charlottesville, VA: University of Virginia Press, 2003. 224 pages.
Genres/literary styles/story types: mainstream fiction; coming-of-age
The author's parents emigrated to France from Guadeloupe, so she lived in Paris during her adolescent years. Partly autobiographical, the novel features a young woman who is very unhappy and isolated—the victim of Parisian snobbery and racism. When her grandmother moves to Paris to escape from a violent husband, she discovers the richness of her Caribbean heritage in her grandmother's stories and comforting presence. Soon thereafter, both grandmother and granddaughter return to Guadeloupe and the culture of their ancestors.
Subject keyword: identity
Original language: French
Sources consulted for annotation:
Global Books in Print (online) (review from *Choice*).
University of Virginia Press website (book description), http://www.upress.virginia.edu.

Pascal Quignard. *The Salon in Württemberg.*
Translated by Barbara Bray. New York: Grove Weidenfeld, 1991. 274 pages.
Genre/literary style/story type: mainstream fiction
Charles Chenogne is a former music teacher and a French translator of the biographies of German musicians. He decides to return to his home in southwestern Germany and to devote his time and energy to his memoirs. His reminisces center around his friendship with Florent Seinece, whom he betrayed by having an affair with his wife, Isabelle. As Charles contemplates his many love affairs and the consequences thereof, he is overtaken by soul-destroying despair.
Subject keyword: family histories
Original language: French
Sources consulted for annotation:
Caprio, Anthony. *Library Journal* 115 (December 1990): 165.
Global Books in Print (online) (review from *Choice*).
Steinberg, Sybil S. *Publishers Weekly* 237 (30 November 1990): 56.

Some other translated books written by Pascal Quignard: *All the World's Mornings*; *Albucius*; *On Wooden Tablets: Apronenia Avitia*

Atiq Rahimi. ***The Patience Stone.***
Translated by Polly McLean. New York: Other Press, 2010. 160 pages.
Genre/literary style/story type: mainstream fiction; women's lives
This book is a withering indictment of the childishness and utter insanity of war. As her severely wounded husband lies in their hovel—unable to speak or to move—his wife castigates him for his futile heroism, his doomed participation in the never-ending hostilities besetting Afghanistan, and the oppressiveness of a patriarchal clan-based society. Struggling to keep him alive and struggling to stay alive herself as the war swirls around them, she confesses a multitude of dark secrets about their life together and her own sexual desires.
Related titles by the same author:
Rahimi has also written two others translated books—both originally in Dari: *Earth and Ashes* and *A Thousand Rooms of Dreams and Fears*. In *Earth and Ashes*, which has been made into a film, Dastaguir and his grandson Yassin are some of the only survivors when their Afghan village is destroyed by the advancing Soviets. They set out to find Yassin's father, who works in a distant coal mine; their journey turns into a terrifying portrait of a physically and psychologically devastated country. In *A Thousand Rooms of Dream and Fears*, Farhad, an Afghani student who overindulges in the pleasures of drink, must flee his native land after he is beaten by soldiers enforcing a curfew.
Subject keyword: religion
Original language: French
Source consulted for annotation:
Other Press website (book description), http://www.otherpress.com.
Some other translated books written by Atiq Rahimi: *Earth and Ashes*; *A Thousand Rooms of Dream and Fears*

Patrick Rambaud. ***The Battle.***
Translated by Will Hobson. New York: Grove Press, 2000. 313 pages.
Genre/literary style/story type: historical fiction
Napoleon is renowned as a military leader, but he had more than his share of defeats, including the Battle of Aspern-Essling in 1809. Balzac had plans to write about this major battle but was unable to do so before he died. Rambaud provides realistic portraits of the gruesome battlefield conditions, emphasizing the tragic fates of ordinary fighting men caught up in a vortex of imperial ambitions.
Subject keywords: power; war
Original language: French
Sources consulted for annotation:
Flanagan, Margaret. *Booklist* 96 (15 May 2000): 1731.
Keymer, David. *Library Journal* 125 (1 May 2000): 154.
Steinberg, Sybil S. *Publishers Weekly* 247 (13 March 2000): 59.
Waggoner, Jeff. *The New York Times Book Review*, 11 June 2000 (online).
Some other translated books written by Patrick Rambaud: *The Retreat*; *Napoleon's Exile*

Marie Redonnet. ***Nevermore.***
Translated by Jordan Stump. Lincoln, NE: University of Nebraska Press, 1996. 123 pages.
Genres/literary styles/story types: thrillers; conspiracy thrillers
Strange things are occurring in San Rosa, a seedy town that has had better days. Here, violence and corruption are endemic. There is another wealthier town nearby, Santa Flor, which has a golf course but also a mysterious area labeled a camp. Into this seething cauldron steps Willy Bost, who is a

bureaucrat with no sense of humor but a healthy sexual appetite—to say the least. He is an enigmatic presence; he has a past that is all shadows and no light. And his parents have died in a set of camps. He now must come to terms with his new home and troubling past. Critics have invoked Samuel Beckett in discussing Redonnet's work as well as such contemporary writers as Jean-Philippe Toussaint and Jean Echenoz. She has been described by John Taylor as writing "unsettling fables" that are "redolent of ancient legends and hallucinatory fantasy."

Related titles by the same author:

Readers may also be interested in *Hôtel Splendid*, *Forever Valley*, and *Rose Mellie Rose*, a trilogy that John Taylor calls the author's most accomplished work. Here, she "constructs troubling, multifaceted allegories out of desolate landscapes, decrepit buildings, watery surroundings, and border-crossings."

Subject keywords: politics; power

Original language: French

Sources consulted for annotation:

Boaz, Amy. *Library Journal* 121 (August 1996): 114.

Simson, Maria. *Publishers Weekly* 243 (8 July 1996): 79.

Taylor, John. *Paths to Contemporary French Literature*, pp. 214-217 (online).

Some other translated books written by Marie Redonnet: *Hôtel Splendid*; *Rose Mellie Rose, with the Story of The Triptych*; *Forever Valley*; *Candy Story*; *Understudies*; *Dead Man & Company*

Alina Reyes. *Behind Closed Doors*.

Translated by David Watson. New York: Grove Press, 1996. 167 pages.

Genres/literary styles/story types: mainstream fiction; experimental fiction

Readers are never more in charge of plot development than they are here. It is a long way from John Cleland's erotic classic *Fanny Hill, or the Memoirs of a Woman of Pleasure*. In Reyes's novel, you the reader choose your sex and what you want to have happen to you. After all, you're in the Kingdom of Eros. Start from the front or the back of the book and make decisions at the end of each chapter. No two readings are ever the same. This is the ultimate journey of sexual fantasy—or, rather, sexual fantasies.

Subject keyword: identity

Original language: French

Sources consulted for annotation:

Amazon.com (review from *Kirkus Reviews*).

Steinberg, Sybil S. *Publishers Weekly* 243 (1 April 1996): 55.

Some other translated books written by Alina Reyes: *The Butcher and Other Erotica*; *Satisfaction: An Erotic Novel*; *Lucie's Long Voyage*; *The Fatal Bodice*; *When You Love You Must Depart*; *The Politics of Love*

Yasmina Reza. *Desolation*.

Translated by Carol Brown Janeway. New York: Alfred A. Knopf, 2002. 135 pages.

Genre/literary style/story type: mainstream fiction

You have all seen cantankerous geezers rant and rave—their frail fists shaking, their lips frothing, their eyes blazing with disgust at the perfidy of the modern world. This novel is the ultimate rant and rave delivered by a septuagenarian who is not happy with anything—not the supposedly slacker life being led by his son, not his wife who is involved in trendy social causes, and certainly not his daughter. The protagonist is utterly scathing, funny, and often spot-on accurate in his caustic assessments. But there is a pronounced undertext of desolation permeating his words—a desolation that one of his friends urges him to channel into a more productive form.

Related title by the same author:
Also of interest may be *Adam Haberberg*, which some critics have seen as outdoing *Desolation* from the perspective of ribald humor and irony. The world of Adam Haberberg, a middle-aged writer, seemingly cannot get worse: His wife has more or less given up on him; he is losing his eyesight; and he is a professional failure. As he sits in a public garden morosely contemplating how life has done him wrong, along comes someone he once knew in high school some 30 years ago. She is a happy-go-lucky saleswoman who peddles magnets and pencils, loves kitchen appliances, and had a severe crush on Adam.
Subject keyword: aging
Original language: French
Sources consulted for annotation:
Global Books in Print (online) (reviews from *Booklist*, *Library Journal*, and *Publishers Weekly* for both novels).
James, Caryn. *The New York Times Book Review*, 4 March 2007 (online).
Kakutani, Michiko. *The New York Times*, 2 February 2007 (online).
Some other translated books written by Yasmina Reza: *Hammerklavier*; *Adam Haberberg*; *The Unexpected Man*

Michel Rio. *Dreaming Jungles*.
Translated by William R. Carlson. New York: Pantheon Books, 1987. 113 pages.
Genre/literary style/story type: mainstream fiction
The amateur meets the professional; the humanist confronts the implacable realities of genetics and science. Such could be some of the subtitles for this demanding novel. In the early decades of the twentieth century, a French aristocrat wants to learn about altruism. He decides to study chimpanzees in Africa, hoping to discover that their altruistic acts have moral underpinnings, that they are a result of a considered choice about right and wrong. But when he meets Jane Sheldon, an anthropologist, his beliefs are put to a rude test. According to William W. Stowe, the book, which is filled with "exotic description, parody, adventure, passion and philosophical speculation," presents the "rival claims of art and science to produce and represent meaning in the world."
Subject keyword: philosophy
Original language: French
Sources consulted for annotation:
Mutter, John. *Publishers Weekly* 231 (10 April 1987): 89.
Stowe, William W. *The New York Times Book Review*, 23 August 1987 (online).
Some other translated books written by Michel Rio: *Parrot's Perch*; *Archipelago*

Jean Rouaud. *The World More or Less*.
Translated by Barbara Wright. New York: Arcade, 1998. 218 pages.
Genres/literary styles/story types: mainstream fiction; coming-of-age
This is the concluding volume in the author's autobiographical/biographical trilogy. The first novel, *Fields of Glory*, focuses on the narrator's grandfather and his relatives, who suffered greatly during World War I. The second volume, *Of Illustrious Men*, recounts the life of Joseph, the narrator's father, who was captured by the Germans during World War II and whose death left him an orphan at age 12. The author draws a haunting picture of Joseph as he travels throughout northwestern France selling dishes and obsessing about ancient stone monuments. *The World More or Less* draws a poignant portrait of Rouaud's childhood and adolescence on France's Atlantic coast, his Catholic education, his forays into political activism and sex, and his love of films. *The World More or Less* has been compared with James Joyce's *Portrait of the Artist as a Young Man*.
Subject keyword: family histories

Original language: French
Sources consulted for annotation:
Bernstein, Richard. *The New York Times*, 9 January 1998 (online).
Carroll, Mary. *Booklist* 94 (15 March 1998): 1203.
Goodman, Richard. *The New York Times Book Review*, 20 November 1994 (online).
Steinberg, Sybil S. *Publishers Weekly* 245 (2 February 1998): 81.
Some other translated books written by Jean Rouaud: *Fields of Glory*; *Of Illustrious Men*

Jean-Christophe Rufin. *Brazil Red.*
Translated by Willard Wood. New York: W. W. Norton, 2004. 429 pages.
Genre/literary style/story type: historical fiction
Just and Colombe have always lived as brother and sister, even though they are not. Their father, during a military excursion in early sixteenth-century Italy, discovered a baby in a pillaged town and adopted her, naming her Colombe. For the longest of time, only Just is aware of this fact. In fact, Just and Colombe pretend to be brothers—a subterfuge that allows them to embark in 1555 on a quixotic colonization voyage to Brazil under the command of a French aristocrat and military hero named Villegagnon. They are to be interpreters or intermediaries to the indigenous tribes, under the theory that children can easily pick up languages. It is an arduous sea voyage, where numerous passengers—most of whom are ex-convicts, mercenaries, and religious refugees—starve or flee. But eventually, the fleet reaches an island in Guanabara Bay, the mainland of which will later become Rio de Janeiro. Here, the French found Fort Coligny and try to establish a foothold in a continent that is presumptively Portuguese. But as with all colonization endeavors, things do not go as planned. The Tupi people resist Christianity, and Villegagnon inexorably slides toward megalomania. When Villegagnon sends for reinforcements from France, they turn out to be strict French Calvinists, and internal religious strife breaks out between fervent supporters of Catholic practice and the newly arrived Huguenots. As Villegagnon's authority crumbles and as he returns to France to plead for still more reinforcements, he increasingly relies on Just, who is his designated successor and a stalwart supporter of French colonial rule. Just does his best to keep the colony alive but soon dispatches the Calvinists to the mainland after an attempt on his life. On the other hand, Columbe is more comfortable with indigenous beliefs and lives deep in the lush Brazilian forests, a convert to the animist worldview of the Tupis. Some five years after the arrival of the French, European politics and skullduggery intervene to make Fort Coligny the target of a massive Portuguese naval attack. Just and Colombe, now reunited as lovers, begin a new life in the company of indigenous tribes united in their opposition to Portugal's expanding empire. The book is historically based—the French did make a colonization effort in modern-day Brazil.
Related titles by the same author:
Readers may also enjoy *The Abyssinian*, which recounts the story of Jean-Baptiste Poncet, a doctor who is recruited in the early 1700s by a French diplomat in Egypt to help draw Abyssinia, which is present-day Ethopia and Eritrea, into France's colonial sphere of influence. It is a task that is fraught with difficulty. Not only must the doctor steer a path between competing political interests, but he must also be wary of the interests of religious orders, not to mention his own motives vis-à-vis his romantic aspirations to the diplomat's daughter's hand. The sequel is *The Siege of Isfahan*. Poncet is now living in Persia and practicing medicine at the shah's court. But he makes a long journey to Russia when he learns that an old friend has been been imprisoned by the tsar. The author is one of the founders of Doctors Without Borders.
Subject keywords: colonization and colonialism; indigenous culture
Original language: French
Sources consulted for annotation:
Bell, David A. *The New York Times Book Review*, 31 October 1999 (online).

Flannagan, Margaret. *Booklist* 97 (15 March 2001): 1355.
Friedman, Paula. *The New York Times Book Review*, 1 April 2001 (online).
Global Books in Print (online) (reviews from *Booklist* and *Publishers Weekly* for all three novels).
Zaleski, Jeff. *Publishers Weekly* 248 (12 February 2001): 186.
Some other translated books written by Jean-Christophe Rufin: *The Abyssinian*; *The Siege of Isfahan*

Sa Shan (Shan Sa). *Alexander and Alestria.*
Translated by Adriana Hunter. New York: HarperCollins, 2008. 256 pages.
Genres/literary styles/story types: historical fiction; alternate history
The image of Alexander the Great as an intrepid conqueror is well-known. But what would have happened if he had met Alestria, queen of a fierce tribe of warrior women inhabiting a vague region somewhere in eastern Europe or western Asia? He does meet her in this novel—under unique circumstances. In the midst of battle, he thinks her to be a man, but later, when the truth is revealed, they become lovers. Of course, their passion has large-scale political implications, which become even bigger when Alestria becomes pregnant and when yet another battle looms. The *Library Journal* reviewer stated that the author writes "as a poet, blending image, action, and character in a rhythmic stream and branching out from the possibility of an actual historical meeting into pure speculative fancy."
Related title by the same author:
Readers may also enjoy *The Girl Who Played Go*, which focuses on a teenage girl from Manchuria and a mid-20s Japanese military officer. As the title indicates, the young woman plays Go, and as she and the officer confront each other across the table, they reveal themselves through the various game strategies that they adopt.
Subject keywords: politics; power
Original language: French
Sources consulted for annotation:
Global Books in Print (online) (reviews from *Booklist*, *Library Journal*, and *Publishers Weekly*).
Nimura, Janice P. *The New York Times Book Review*, 26 October 2003 (online).
Another translated book written by Shan Sa: *The Girl Who Played Go*

Lydie Salvayre. *The Lecture.*
Translated by Linda Coverdale. Normal, IL: Dalkey Archive Press, 2005. 135 pages.
Genre/literary style/story type: mainstream fiction
Absolutely gut-wrenchingly funny but also absolutely gut-wrenchingly sad. It is a lecture-monologue given by possibly the world's most boring man. As he pontifcates about the superiority of French conversational skills, he draws a telling picture of his own misogynistic, dyspeptic, and ultimately futile existence.
Related title by the same author:
Readers may also be interested in *Everyday Life*, a monologue from a female perspective. Here, the speaker is Suzanne, an ad agency secretary who has worked at the firm for more than 30 years. One can forgive her for being just a touch paranoid when a new secretary arrives on the scene. Thus, she does everything to make the perfumed newcomer's working life a living hell.
Subject keywords: identity; philosophy
Original language: French
Sources consulted for annotation:
Dalkey Archive Press (book review), http://www.dalkeyarchive.com.
Evans, Janet. *Library Journal* 130 (15 June 2005): 60.
Scheeres, Julia. *The New York Times Book Review*, 17 December 2006 (online).

Some other translated books written by Lydie Salvayre: *The Award*; *The Company of Ghosts: Followed by Some Useful Advice for Apprentice Process-Servers*; *Everyday Life*

Leïla Sebbar. *Silence on the Shores*.
Translated by Mildred Mortimer. Lincoln, NE: University of Nebraska Press, 2000. 79 pages.
Genre/literary style/story type: mainstream fiction
The life of Algerian immigrants to France is not an easy one. Success in a new land is more often than not a chimerical notion—never realized despite one's best efforts. Instead of success, there is alienation and despair, the constant longing for an ever-receeding homeland, and memories of traditions and relatives that become hazier and fainter. And then one is on the verge of death, pondering the weight of accumulated miseries, regretting lost loves and ruing harsh realities, and, above all, wondering who will perform the age-old Muslim ritual of the washing of the deceased—if it is performed at all.
Subject keyword: identity
Original language: French
Sources consulted for annotation:
Flexman, Ellen. *Library Journal* 126 (January 2001): 157.
Global Books in Print (online) (reviews from *Booklist* and *Kirkus Reviews*).
Orland, Valerie. *Review of Contemporary Fiction* 21 (Summer 2001): 162.
Some other translated books written by Leïla Sebbar: *Sherazade: Missing, Aged 17, Dark Curly Hair, Green Eyes*

Pierre Siniac. *The Collaborators*.
Translated by Jordan Stump. Champaign, IL: Dalkey Archive Press, 2010. 486 pages.
Genre/literary style/story type: mainstream fiction
At one time or another, many novelists have dreamed of metaphorically eviscerating the critics who have written negative reviews of their work. Here, the dream becomes reality in a mysteriously brutal fashion. Jean-Rémi Dochin and Charles Gastinel have ostensibly co-authored a novel called *Dancing the Brown Java*, the first part of a projected multivolume opus about the seamy politics of France during World War II. But it is really Dochin (or is it?) who has written the book, and it turns out that he is being blackmailed by Gastinel in order to share credit. As Dochin recognizes, *Dancing the Brown Java* is nothing but gibberish, but Ferdinaud Céline—a rural innkeeper and former bookseller—believes in it. In fact, she becomes Dochin's lover and muse, spending untold weeks and months typing it (or is she really doing something else?). The novel becomes a hit—a bestselling cultural phenomenon that brings celebrity to the two co-authors and death to anyone planning to criticize it. Ultimately, *The Collaborators* revolves around the identity of Céline and her wartime political allegiances and views—an identity that has been kept concealed for many years in rustic exile. The book may also be read as a broad satire about all aspects of the publishing industry.
Subject keywords: politics; writers
Original language: French
Source consulted for annotation:
Nassau, Timothy. Three Percent website, http://www.rochester.edu/College/translation/threepercent.

Michel Tournier. *The Golden Droplet*.
Translated by Barbara Wright. New York: Doubleday, 1987. 206 pages.
Genre/literary style/story type: mainstream fiction
This novel is a tour de force consideration of the nature of objectification. After a tourist takes a photograph of a young Berber man in the Saharan desert, the Berber is adamant that he must retrieve

that consumerist-based usurpation of his very soul and being. Thus, Idris journeys to Paris, experiencing numerous trials, tribulations, and wretchedness along the way. When he reaches Paris, things do not get better, especially since he loses a valuable amulet that reminds him of his heritage. Anguished, disheartened, and forlorn, Idris begins to realize the hollowness of westernized urban life, not to mention its obsession with commodification when he becomes the model for a series of store mannequins. The appropriation of his body and spirit is almost complete until he meets a calligrapher from North Africa who teaches him another way of looking at the world.

Related title by the same author:

Readers may also enjoy *Friday and Robinson*, which turns Daniel Defoe's *Robinson Crusoe* on its head. No longer does Western culture and civilization emerge triumphant from its confrontation with a so-called primitive and natural world. Rather, rationalism-based civilization is shown to be far inferior. In Tournier's vision, Friday leads Crusoe to a realization about the superiority of a prelapsarian world where savagery gives way to innocence and where paradise is regained.

Subject keyword: culture conflict

Original language: French

Sources consulted for annotation:

Global Book in Print (online) (reviews from *Choice*).

Rose, Marilyn Gaddis. *Library Journal* 112 (1 October 1987): 110.

Sieburth, Richard. *The New York Times Book Review*, 1 November 1987 (online).

Steinberg, Sybil S. *Publishers Weekly* 232 (28 August 1987): 68.

Some other translated books written by Michel Tournier: *The Ogre*; *The Fetishist*; *The Four Wise Men*; *Gemini*; *Friday and Robinson: Life on Esperanza Island*; *The Mirror of Ideas*; *Eleazar, Exodus to the West*; *Gilles & Jeanne*; *The Erl-King*

Jean-Philippe Toussaint. *Television*.

Translated by Jordan Stump. Normal, IL: Dalkey Archive Press, 2004. 168 pages.

Genre/literary style/story type: mainstream fiction

A dithering art professor suffering from a severe case of writer's block vows to give up television, with scathingly funny and emotionally tragic results. Instead of completing his scholarly monograph about a little-known aspect of the life of the Italian painter Titian, he sinks ever further into an angst-ridden morass, justifying his descent with arcane rationalizations that redefine the meaning of work and thinking.

Related titles by the same author:

Readers may also enjoy *The Bathroom*, where a bathtub becomes the sole refuge for an existentially scarred protagonist. Also of interest may be *Camera*, a wryly absurd comic novel in which the hero—sinking ever deeper into a swamp of futility—juggles driving lessons and sexual encounters with a driving-school employee. *Running Away* evolves into a meditation on the malaise of globalization when the narrator is asked by his girlfriend to deliver a large amount of money to a mysterious person named Zhang in Shanghai.

Subject keywords: identity; philosophy

Original language: French

Sources consulted for annotation:

Byrd, Christopher. *The New York Times Book Review*, 27 December 2009 (online).

Global Books in Print (online) (review from *Booklist*).

McCarthy, Tom. *The New York Times Book Review*, 14 December 2008 (online).

Olszewski, Lawrence. *Library Journal* 129 (1 November 2004): 78.

Press, Joy. *The New York Times Book Review*, 2 January 2005 (online).

Zaleski, Jeff. *Publishers Weekly* 251 (18 October 2004): 48.

Some other translated books written by Jean-Philippe Toussaint: *Making Love*; *Monsieur*; *The Bathroom*; *Camera*; *Running Away*

Lyonel Trouillot. *Children of Heroes*.
Translated by Linda Coverdale. Lincoln, NE: University of Nebraska Press, 2008. 161 pages.
Genre/literary style/story type: mainstream fiction
Colin and his older sister Mariéla live in the slums of Port-au-Prince, Haiti. Their father is a violent and abusive man who inspires constant terror in their mother. His boxing career was a dismal failure, and he is now a mechanic, sullen and bitter. To defend their long-suffering mother, the children fatally beat their father, after which they attempt to flee their ravaged city—themselves victims of an endemic violence that permeates everything.
Related title by the same author:
Readers may also wish to explore *Street of Lost Footsteps*, which describes one night of politically inspired violence in Port-au-Prince as a rebellious faction with a charismatic and often messianic leader battles the representatives of a perpetual authoritarian regime.
Subject keywords: family histories; power
Original language: French
Sources consulted for annotation:
Global Books in Print (online) (review from *Publishers Weekly* for *Children of Heroes*; synopsis/book jacket for *Street of Lost Footsteps*).
University of Nebraska Press (book descriptions), http://www.nebraskapress.unl.edu.
Another translated book written by Lyonel Trouillot: *Street of Lost Footsteps*

Fred Vargas. *Have Mercy on Us All*.
Translated by David Bellos. New York: Simon & Schuster, 2005. 353 pages.
Genres/literary styles/story types: crime fiction; police detectives
The hero of Vargas's many crime novels is Chief Inspector Jean-Baptiste Adamsberg, whom some critics have pointed out has affinities with Georges Simenon's Jules Maigret. In *Have Mercy on Us All*, it appears that contemporary Paris is about to be ravaged by a black death–like plague. A series of cryptic clues suggest that someone is appropriating historical texts and signs to create the illusion that mass death is imminent. Of course, there is widespread panic and consternation, which Adamsberg and his deputy must work to contain as they search for a diabolical serial killer.
Related titles by the same author:
Readers may also enjoy *Seeking Whom He May Devour*, where Adamsberg must bring clarity to a murky situation in which a werewolf is leaving a long chain of victims in rural France. Also of interest may be *This Night's Foul Work*, where yet another serial killer draws inspiration from medieval practices.
Subject keyword: urban life
Original language: French
Sources consulted for annotation:
Global Books in Print (online) (reviews from *Booklist* for all mentioned novels).
Publishers Weekly 252 (3 October 2005): 49.
Stasio, Marilyn. *The New York Times Book Review*, 5 November 2006 (online).
Terpening, Ronnie H. *Library Journal* 130 (15 October 2005): 52.
Some other translated books written by Fred Vargas: *Seeking Whom He May Devour*; *The Three Evangelists*; *Inside Out*; *Wash This Blood Clean from My Hand*; *The Chalk Circle Man*; *This Night's Foul Work*

Myriam Warner-Vieyra. *Juletane*.
Translated by Betty Wilson. London: Heinemann, 1987. 83 pages.

Genres/literary styles/story types: mainstream fiction; women's lives

Helene is a social worker who rediscovers a journal that was given to her by a former client, Juletane, who thought that it would help Helene to understand her torments and alienation. As Helene begins to read it, she gains a better appreciation not only of the many challenges that Juletane had to face but also about her own life. Born in the French West Indies, Juletane lived in Paris with a strict relative after the death of her parents. When the relative dies, Juletane must fend for herself. Briefly optimistic after a marriage to a West African, she soon discovers that she is nothing more than a second wife. Critics have drawn comparisons to such books as Miriama Bâ's *So Long a Letter* and Bessie Head's *A Question of Power* when discussing *Juletane*.

Subject keyword: identity

Original language: French

Sources consulted for annotation:

Global Books in Print (online) (review from *Choice*).

Smith, Holly. *500 Great Books by Women* (Amazon.com).

Another translated book written by Myriam Warner-Vieyra: *As the Sorcerer Said*

Elie Wiesel. *The Time of the Uprooted.*

Translated by David Hapgood. New York: Alfred A. Knopf, 2005. 299 pages.

Genre/literary style/story type: mainstream fiction

During World War II, Gamaliel Friedman, a young Jewish boy, fled from Czechoslovakia to Hungary, where he was taken in by Ilonka, a singer and a Christian. When the Soviets seize Hungary, Friedman flees again—to Vienna, Paris, and, finally, New York. Here, he recalls his tormented past, consoling himself with his memories and a group of fellow exiles. The past is more alive for him than the present, especially when a physician enlists his help in order to communicate with a Hungarian woman at a nearby nursing home. As Gamaliel wonders whether the woman could possibly be Ilonka, he is overwhelmed by feelings of loss and love. As in his other famous books, such as *The Night Trilogy* and the memoir *All Rivers Run to the Sea*, Wiesel brilliantly examines the multidimensional facets of the Jewish experience in the twentieth century. Readers may also wish to explore *The Judges*, where one individual takes it upon himself to judge who will live and die among a group of five airline passengers whose plane has been forced to land by bad weather.

Subject keywords: anti-Semitism; family histories

Original language: French

Sources consulted for annotation:

Amazon. com (book description for *The Night Trilogy* and *The Judges*).

Carrigan, Henry L., Jr. *Library Journal* 130 (July 2005): 74.

Global Books in Print (online) (reviews from *Library Journal* and *Publishers Weekly*).

Hooper, Brad. *Booklist* 101 (1 May 2005): 1501.

Rosen, Jonathan. *The New York Times Book Review*, 25 October 2002 (online).

Some other translated books written by Elie Wiesel: *The Oath*; *The Testament*; *The Fifth Son*; *The Forgotten*; *A Beggar in Jerusalem. The Town Beyond the Wall*; *The Gates of the Forest*; *Twilight*; *The Six Days of Destruction: Meditations Towards Hope*; *The Golem: The Story of a Legend*; *Night, Dawn, The Accident*; *The Judges*

Monique Wittig. *Across the Acheron.*

Translated by David Le Vay in collaboration with Margaret Crosland. London: Peter Owen, 1987. 119 pages.

Genres/literary styles/story types: mainstream fiction; feminist fiction

This is a riveting autobiographical account of a feminist journey toward emancipation from every aspect of patriarchal society. As the protagonist moves through a phantasmagoric mix of eerie

settings—from Hades to urban California—she traces the history of womankind and its sufferings as well as its serpentine rise to power and liberation—manifested in the ethos of lesbianism and warrior women.
Subject keywords: politics; power
Original language: French
Sources consulted for annotation:
Britannica Online Encyclopedia, http://www.britannica.com.
Global Books in Print (online) (review from *Choice*).
Steinberg, Sybil S. *Publishers Weekly* 232 (30 October 1987): 52.
Some other translated books written by Monique Wittig: *The Opoponax*; *The Lesbian Body*

ANNOTATIONS FOR BOOKS TRANSLATED FROM GERMAN: AUSTRIA, GERMANY, AND SWITZERLAND

Austria

Thomas Bernhard. *Frost.*
Translated by Michael Hofmann. New York: Alfred A. Knopf, 2006. 342 pages.
Genre/literary style/story type: mainstream fiction
When you are a medical intern, your life is not your own. When your supervising surgeon tells you to do something, you do it. And when the surgeon wants you to find out what his unconventional brother, a painter, is doing in the dismal mountain village of Weng, you undertake the journey—perhaps posing as a vacationing law student. The surgeon's brother is named Strauch, and he lives in the most decrepit of inns run by the most piteous of landladies. He never paints; offers gloomy observations about the state of the world and Austria; and is a fan of Blaise Pascal, a scientist and mathematician. As the intern wanders the village, listens to Strauch's caustic comments, and tries to finish his Henry James novel, he becomes part of a bleak and ravaged world from where there is little spiritual escape.
Related titles by the same author:
Readers may also enjoy *Wittgenstein's Nephew*. Set in a hospital, it traces the interactions of two men who become the best of friends. Music-loving eccentrics, they are the very essence of curmudgeonliness. As they outdo each other in damn-the-consequences honesty, a revealingly sordid picture emerges about the underside of life in Vienna. Also of interest may be *The Voice Imitator*, a collection of 104 vignettes about the dichotomy between social façade and messy reality.
Subject keyword: rural life
Original language: German
Sources consulted for annotation:
Amazon.com (book description).
Benfey, Christopher. *The New York Times Book Review*, 22 October 2006 (online).
DeShell, Jeffrey. *Review of Contemporary Fiction* 18 (Summer 1998): 241.
Filkins, Peter. *The New York Times Book Review*, 14 December 1997, p. 28.
Global Books in Print (online) (review from *Publishers Weekly* and synopsis/book jacket for *Wittgenstein's Nephew*).
Irvine, Ann. *Library Journal* 122 (1 September 1997): 221.
Some other translated books written by Thomas Bernhard: *The Voice Imitator*; *Wittgenstein's Nephew*; *The Loser*; *Extinction*; *On the Mountain*; *Nonsense*; *The Lime Works*; *Gargoyles*; *Yes*; *Old Masters*; *Correction*; *Concrete*

Lilian Faschinger. *Magdalena the Sinner.*
Translated by Edna McCown. New York: HarperCollins, 1997. 306 pages.

Genres/literary styles/story types: mainstream fiction; feminist fiction
Magdalena is no ordinary woman. And she is very far from a saint in the conventional sense of the word. And yet,what can one say about a woman who kidnaps a priest and forces him to hear her confession about her extraordinary life in which she—among numerous other adventures—has had sex with another priest, murdered one of her lovers, and dressed herself in a nun's habit to detract attention from her forays into pickpocketing? Does she really want to repent in the best traditions of Mary Magdalene? Or is she up to something else? As the *Publishers Weekly* reviewer noted, she may just want to offer "a series of erotic provocations and observations designed to inflame the priest and confront him with his own hidden desires."
Subject keywords: identity; religion
Original language: German
Sources consulted for annotation:
Christophersen, Bill. *The New York Times Book Review*, 4 January 1998, p. 16.
Hoffret, Barbara. *Library Journal* 122 (1 September 1997): 216.
Steinberg, Sybil S. *Publishers Weekly* 244 (21 July 1997): 183.
Some other translated books written by Lilian Faschinger: *Woman with Three Aeroplanes*; *Vienna Passion*

Barbara Frischmuth. *The Shadow Disappears in the Sun.*
Translated by Nicholas J. Meyerhofer. Riverside, CA: Ariadne Press, 1998. 157 pages.
Genre/literary style/story type: mainstream fiction
A female Austrian university student takes up residence in Turkey to study religious rituals. She seems to be the perfect Westerner abroad—fluent in Turkish and sensitive and knowledgeable about relevant cultural issues. When Turgut, a political radical whom she has befriended, is killed, she begins to understand the difference between her tourist-based notion of the exotic and harsh reality.
Subject keyword: culture conflict
Original language: German
Sources consulted for annotation:
Ariadne Press (book description), http://www.ariadnebooks.com.
"Barbara Frischmuth." *Dictionary of Literary Biography Online*. Thomson Gale databases.
World Literature Today 69 (22 June 1995): 458.
Some other translated books written by Barbara Frischmuth: *Chasing After the Wind: Four Stories*; *The Convent School*

Marianne Gruber. *Calm.*
Translated by Margaret T. Peischl. Riverside, CA: Ariadne Press, 2001. 175 pages.
Genres/literary styles/story types: crime fiction; suspense
In the southern Austrian province of Carinthia, there has always been tension between German speakers and the Slovenian minority. As with most ethnic tensions, economic, historic, and cultural issues are at play. When a Slovenian domestic working in a Carinthian resort is murdered, Herman Pratt—a prosperous Austrian businessman with deep roots in neighboring Slovenia—attracts the attention of investigators. Eventually, authorities clear Pratt but not before he has had to come to terms with the contradictions and paradoxes of his past life as well as the lingering mistrust and prejudices animating the Carinthina psyche.
Subject keyword: rural life
Original language: German
Sources consulted for annotation:
Ariadne Press (book description), http:/www.ariadnebooks.com.
Back cover of the book.

Global Books in Print (online) (synopsis/book jacket).
Peischl, Margaret T. Afterword to the book.
Some other translated books written by Marianne Gruber: *The Sphere of Glass*; *The Death of the Plover and Trace of the Buckskin: Two Stories*

Norbert Gstrein. *The English Years*.
Translated by Anthea Bell. London: Harvill, 2002. 295 pages.
Genre/literary style/story type: mainstream fiction
Narrated by an unnamed young woman from Vienna, this novel is a philosophical reflection on Austrian involvement in World War II, the persecution of the Jewish people, exile, and the myriad ways we choose to identify ourselves. The narrator has gone to England to seek information about Gabriel Hirschfelder, a famous Jewish writer who escaped to London shortly before the war. But he was soon classified as an undesirable alien and held on a remote island. The narrator locates one of Hirschfelder's former wives, who discloses her husband's deathbed confession. He was not Hirschfelder at all but had simply appropriated the literary heritage of someone who had disappeared.
Subject keyword: identity
Original language: German
Sources consulted for annotation:
Dasgupta, Subhoranjan. *The Statesman* (India), 19 April 2004 (from Factiva databases).
Eve, James. *The Times*, 12 October 2002 (from Factiva databases).
Hickling, Alfred. *The Guardian*, 15 November 2003, p. 30.
Robinson, Oliver. *The Observer*, 26 October 2003, p. 18.
The Times, 5 January 2002 (from Factiva databases).
Another translated book written by Norbert Gstrein: *The Register*

Wolf Haas. *The Weather Fifteen Years Ago*.
Translated by Stephanie Gilardi and Thomas S. Hansen. Riverside, CA: Ariadne Press, 2009. 224 pages.
Genres/literary styles/story types: mainstream fiction; postmodernism
At age 30, Vittorio Kowalski is either some kind of prodigy or a total fool. He can recall the state of the weather in an Austrian village for every day of the last 15 years. It is a mind-boggling and mysterious feat. Why has he bothered to memorize such obscure and essentially useless facts? The prosaic answer is that his family went to that village for vacations, he fell in love with Anni, and her father died. But that is getting ahead of ourselves. For now, Kowalski's powerful memory has landed him on a quiz show, where he is accurately able to rattle off the village's weather history for whichever days he is asked about. He achieves a dubious celebrity status and his long-ago first love briefly comes back into his life, but alas, she is betrothed to someone else. All this might seem far-fetched, but this multilayered tale is told in the form of a five-day media interview that its author is undergoing with a contentious book critic who wants to know why the author chose to write a book about Kowalski in the way that he did. Ultimately, the novel functions as an ironic send-up of literary pretension as well as a philosophical inquiry about why some facts and ideas are considered to be more important than others.
Subject keyword: identity
Original language: German
Sources consulted for annotation:
Ariadne Press (book description), http://www.ariadnebooks.com.
The Complete Review (book review), http://www.complete-review.com.
Post, Chad W. Three Percent website, http://www.rochester.edu/College/translation/threepercent.

Peter Handke. ***Don Juan: His Own Version.***
Translated by Krishna Winston. New York: Farrar, Straus and Giroux, 2010. 101 pages.
Genre/literary style/story type: mainstream fiction
We all think we know who Don Juan was. And we all think we know what we mean when we say that someone is a Don Juan. But we would be very much in the wrong. As Don Juan himself—or the spirit of Don Juan—tells us or, rather, tells a solitude-loving Frenchman who—after failing as a chef and hotel owner—spends his time reading classic literature. Don Juan makes a great crashing entrance into the former chef's garden and then proceeds to tell him that he has been very much misunderstood. In fact, he does not much like power—or the perceived power that he has over women. It is all too much of an obligation, and what he really wants is the freedom that only langorous and unquantified time can given him. This book can be profitably read together with Milan Kundera's *Slowness*.
Related titles by the same author:
Readers may also enjoy *My Year in the No-Man's-Bay*, which is a lyrical account of some 20 years of the life of a successful author who nevertheless perceives himself to be a failure, and *On a Dark Night I Left My Silent House*, which features a failed pharmacist who—in the company of two others—undertakes a phantasmagoric journey through an ever-changing Europe. Also worthwhile may be *Crossing the Sierra de Gredos*, a book about a woman's inward journey through a lifetime's worth of fears, obsessions, and passions. One of the author's most famous books is *The Goalie's Anxiety at the Penalty Kick*, which follows the degeneration of a soccer player's life outside the sports world; unemployed, he commits murder and then begins to lose all his faculties. He is also well-known for *Across*, which focuses on an Austrian teacher who impetously kills a stranger whom he sees painting a swastika on a tree.
Subject keyword: social roles
Original language: German
Sources consulted for annotation:
Agee, Joel. *The New York Times Book Review*, 12 February 2010 (online).
Bernstein, Richard. *The New York Times*, 29 November 2000 (online).
Global Books in Print (online) (review from *Kirkus Reviews*).
Gordon, Neil. *The New York Times Book Review*, 19 August 2007 (online).
Graver, Lawrence. *The New York Times Book Review*, 27 July 1986 (online).
Kenney, Brian. *Booklist* 94 (August 1998): 1962.
Siegel, Lee. *The New York Times Book Review*, 25 October 1998, p. 20.
Steinberg, Sybil S. *Publishers Weekly* 245 (1 June 1998): 50.
Some other translated books written by Peter Handke: *Repetition*; *On a Dark Night I Left My Silent House*; *Across*; *Slow Homecoming*; *The Goalie's Anxiety at the Penalty Kick*; *The Left-Handed Woman*; *The Afternoon of a Writer*; *A Sorrow beyond Dreams*; *Crossing the Sierra de Gredos*; *My Year in the No-Man's-Bay*

Alois Hotschnig. ***Leonardo's Hands.***
Translated by Peter Filkins. Lincoln, NE: University of Nebraska Press, 1999. 146 pages.
Genre/literary style/story type: mainstream fiction
Kurt Weyrath has much to atone for. He is the likely cause of a car accident that decimates a family. Both parents are killed, and Anna—their mid-20s daughter—lies comatose. Kurt flees the scene. Later, overcome with remorse, he totally changes his life. He secures an ambulance job so he can locate Anna and be close to her. Gradually, he come to identify almost completely with her, doing what she would have done had she not been hospitalized. Inevitably, they fall in love, but Kurt soon finds out that Anna is not the woman he thought she was.

Subject keyword: identity
Original language: German
Sources consulted for annotation:
Amazon.com (book description).
Budzynski, Brian. *Review of Contemporary Fiction* 19 (Fall 1999): 178.
Steelman, Ben. *Morning Star*, 4 April 1999, p. 6D.
Steinberg, Sybil S. *Publishers Weekly* 246 (25 January 1999): 73.
University of Nebraska Press (book description), http://www.nebraskapress.unl.edu.

Elfriede Jelinek. *The Piano Teacher.*
Translated by Joachim Neugroschel. London: Serpent's Tail, 2001. 280 pages.
Genre/literary style/story type: mainstream fiction
As the title of this novel indicates, Erika Kohut is a piano teacher. She had aspirations to be much more—or at least her horror of a mother had the highest of aspirations for her. It is music-obsessed Austria after all, and Erika was placed at an early age on the fast track to renown and fame. She did not quite make it though, so she spends her days being a strict and feared instructor at the conservatory. Her personal life is a shambles; even though she is in her 30s, she still shares an apartment with her mother, meekly submitting to the old woman's draconian edicts and following a daily and nightly ritual that has has not deviated in years. She is the very image of the prim and proper career woman—but then again not. She has a dark side, indulging in trips to seedy neighborhoods, attending sex shows, and practicing self-mutilation. One of her students is Walter Klemmer, a promising yet naïve young man who falls in love with her. But Walter does not really know what he is getting himself into, and he is rather surprised when he is asked to participate in sadomasochism with a woman whom he always thought of as the epitome of respectability.
Related titles by the same author:
Some readers may also wish to explore *Greed*. As in *The Piano Teacher*, love is very close to hellish. When Kurt, a policeman, stops Gerti for a traffic intraction, it is not long before they are having sex. And despite the brutish nature of the sex, Gerti wants to think that she is in love, that Kurt is her gracious lover. But it is all an illusion, as she quickly discovers when Kurt assumes legal ownership of her home and has an affair with a 16-year-old girl whom he subsequently kills. Also of interest may be *Wonderful Wonderful Times*, which focuses on the violence perpetrated by four Austrian teenagers. Jelinek has stated that her novels are meant to counteract the idyllic and stereotyped image that the world has of Austria.
Subject keyword: identity
Original language: German
Sources consulted for annotation:
Agee, Joel. *The New York Times Book Review*, 15 April 2007 (online).
Amazon.com (book description).
Global Books in Print (online) (reviews from *Booklist* and *Publishers Weekly* for all novels).
Hutchinson, Paul E. *Library Journal* 113 (15 October 1988): 102.
Moore, Miranda. *The Guardian*, 4 December 1999, p. 11.
Morin, Carole. *New Statesman & Society*, 28 July 1989, p. 33.
Steinberg, Sybil S. *Publishers Weekly* 234 (12 August 1988): 440.
Some other translated books written by Elfriede Jelinek: *Women as Lovers*; *Wonderful Wonderful Times*; *Lust*; *Greed*

Gert Jonke. *Geometric Regional Novel.*
Translated by Johannes W. Vazulik. Normal, IL: Dalkey Archive Press, 1994. 131 pages.

Genres/literary styles/story types: mainstream fiction; experimental fiction
What happens when nothing ever changes? When nostalgia and ritual triumph over all other considerations? In a village where every human act and function is regulated by outlandish administrative and bureaucratic procedures, where everyone does what they have always done, where events recur like clockwork every year, where permission to take a walk involves submitting a formal request, what is life really like? Is there any chance for even the slightest of freedoms? With a bevy of official-looking laws, rules, and blueprints about the Dos and Don'ts of life in this fictional village, this book asks sobering questions about the nature of obedience and inertia. Some critics invoked Samuel Beckett and Franz Kafka when referring to this novel.
Related title by the same author:
Also of interest may be *Homage to Czerny: Studies in Virtuoso Technique*. Here, Fritz and his friends decide that the party they throw every year should in no way deviate in the slightest from last year's get-together. To what lengths will their love of immutable traditions take them, especially when they become imprisoned in a musty attic full of old pianos?
Subject keywords: rural life; social problems
Original language: German
Sources consulted for annotation:
Amazon.com (review from *Kirkus Reviews*).
Antonucci, Ron. *Library Journal* 119 (15 May 1994): 99.
Global Books in Print (online) (review from *Publishers Weekly* for *Homage to Czerny*).
Shreffler, John. *Booklist* 90 (1 May 1994): 1583.
Steinberg, Sybil S. *Publishers Weekly* 241 (2 May 1994): 286.
Another translated book written by Gert Jonke: *Homage to Czerny: Studies in Virtuoso Technique*

Gloria Kaiser. ***Dona Leopoldina: The Habsburg Empress of Brazil.***
Translated by Lowell A. Bangerter. Riverside, CA: Ariadne Press, 1998. 379 pages.
Genres/literary styles/story types: historical fiction; women's lives
Leopoldina was the privileged daughter of the emperor of Austria, Francis I. In 1817, she was married to Pedro de Alcantara, the man who would later become king of Portugal and Brazil. They lived in Brazil, and she bore her husband multiple children. Before she died at age 30, her life was full of major achievements. In her husband's absence, she exercised political authority in Brazil. She also collected data about Brazilian minerals; designed climate-suitable clothing and furniture; worked hard in ameliorating the life of slaves; and paid particular attention to establishing proper sanitation facilities. Isolated and often overwhelmed, she was nevertheless the embodiment of psychological strength and courage. The sequel is *Pedro II of Brazil: Son of the Habsburg Empress*.
Subject keyword: colonization and colonialism
Original language: German
Sources consulted for annotation:
Ariadne Press (book description), http://www.ariadnebooks.com.
Schlant, Ernestine. *World Literature Today* 69 (22 September 1995): 781.
Some other translated books written by Gloria Kaiser: *Pedro II of Brazil: Son of the Habsburg Empress*; *Saudade: Life and Death of Queen Maria Glória of Lusitania*

Anna Mitgutsch. ***Lover, Traitor: A Jerusalem Story.***
Translated by Roslyn Theobald. New York: Henry Holt/Metropolitan Books, 1997. 211 pages.
Genre/literary style/story type: mainstream fiction' women's lives
Devorah, an Austrian Catholic, has very little idea of who she really is, especially when she discovers that her grandmother was Jewish. She converts to Judaism, moves to the United States, and

makes visits to Jerusalem in a quest to gain some sense of clarity about her identity. Here, she meets and falls in love with Sivan, a man whom her friends warn her may be a Palestinian terrorist. Soon, both Sivan and Devorah are implicated in a fatal bus bombing.

Related title by the same author:

Readers may also enjoy *House of Childhood*, in which a New York architect with Austrian roots returns to his homeland in an attempt to recover his family's ancestral home, which was taken over by the Nazi government. As he digs deep into the family history, he meets some of the few remaining Jewish members of the town.

Subject keyword: identity

Original language: German

Sources consulted for annotation:

Amazon.com (review from *Kirkus Reviews*).

Global Books in Print (online) (reviews from *Booklist*, *Library Journal*, and *Publishers Weekly* for both novels).

O'Pecko, Michael T. *Library Journal* 122 (1 September 1997): 219.

Steinberg, Sybil S. *Publishers Weekly* 244 (4 August 1997): 65.

Some other translated books written by Anna Mitgutsch: *Three Daughters* (or *Punishment*); *Jacob*; *In Foreign Cities*; *House of Childhood*

Christoph Ransmayr. *The Terrors of Ice and Darkness*.

Translated by John E. Woods. New York: Grove Weidenfeld, 1991. 228 pages.

Genres/literary styles/story types: historical fiction; adventure

Obsession has very deep roots. In the early 1870s, a group of Austro-Hungarians set out for the North Pole. They did not reach their goal, and the only legacy of their journey was the discovery of what they called Franz Josef Land. For Josef Mazzini, this failed Arctic expedition has talismanic power; as a result, he attempts to retrace its route—only to disappear himself in 1981. And then we come to the narrator of this novel, who follows in the footsteps of Mazzini. Some critics have compared the author's language and style to that of Michael Ondaatje.

Related title by the same author:

Readers may also enjoy *The Last World*, which is—according to Robert Irvin—an "alternative literary history" about what might have happened to the unfinished original manuscript of Ovid's *Metamorphoses* if the poet had not burned it after learning that he had been banished to the small town of Tomis on the Black Sea. As time tumbles and rushes by in the contemporary town of Tomi, forlorn and isolated, a man by the name of Cotta comes to search for Nosa, which is how Ovid referred to himself.

Subject keyword: identity

Original language: German

Sources consulted for annotation:

Back cover of the book.

Global Books in Print (online) (review from *Booklist* for *The Last World*).

Irwin, Robert. *The New York Times Book Review*, 27 May 1990 (online).

Klein, T. E. D. *The Washington Post*, 11 August 1991, p. X7.

Moorhouse, Geoffrey. *The New York Times Book Review*, 11 August 1991 (online).

O'Pecko, Michael T. *Library Journal* 116 (1 June 1991): 196.

Steinberg, Sybil S. *Publishers Weekly* 238 (14 June 1991): 43.

Some other translated books written by Christoph Ransmayr: *The Last World*; *The Dog King*

Gerhard Roth. *The Calm Ocean*.

Translated by Helga Schreckenberger and Jacqueline Vansant. Riverside, CA: Ariadne Press, 1993. 239 pages.

Genre/literary style/story type: mainstream fiction
A disgraced big city doctor decides to start a new life in a small village in southeast Austria. He leaves behind everything, including his wife and family. He takes a new name, tries to blend in with traditional village life, and eventually starts practicing medicine again. But he quickly realizes that rural life has its own rhythms, codes, and outlooks, which he often finds difficult to accept. Confronted with an onslaught of rabies, he comes to face-to-face with what the publisher's website calls the "destructive uniformity of rural existence, its resulting fatalism, resignation, and latent aggressions."
Subject keyword: social problems
Original language: German
Sources consulted for annotation:
Ariadne Press (book descriptions for both novels), http://www.ariadnebooks.com.
Back cover of the book.
Schreckenberger, Helga. Afterword to the book.
Some other translated books written by Gerhard Roth: *Winterreise*; *The Lake*; *The Autobiography of Albert Einstein*; *The Story of Darkness*

Robert Schneider. *Brother of Sleep.*
Translated by Shaun Whiteside. Woodstock, NY: Overlook Press, 1995. 215 pages.
Genre/literary style/story type: mainstream fiction
In a small Alpine village in the early decades of the nineteenth century—where isolation gives rise to firmly entrenched traditions and periodic outbreaks of religious fervor—a musical prodigy, Johannes Elias Alder, is born. He has exquisite hearing, and he plays the organ divinely. Everyone is simply in awe of him. But soon, Johannes realizes that the circumstances of his upbringing—along with growing jealousies and his ambivalent relationship with God—will prevent him from achieving renown as a musician and gaining happiness in his personal life. He resolves to commit suicide in a unique way: by forcing himself to constantly stay awake. The *Library Journal* reviewer said the book may be understood as "an exploration of the roots that lead to the twisted humanity of Nazi Germany." Another book about a musical prodigy is Richard Powers's *The Time of Our Singing*, an epic consideration of what it means to be a young man, of Jewish and African-American heritage, blessed with a divine voice growing up in late 1940s, 1950s, and 1960s America. Jonah Strom is the prodigy in question, and while the novel focuses on him, it also paints an unforgettable picture of his parents and siblings, each struggling with their own cataclysms, demons, and histories as they rely on music, science, and radical activism to find their place in a tumultuous post World War II era characterized by racism and political ferment.
Subject keyword: rural life
Original language: German
Sources consulted for annotation:
Global Books in Print (online) (reviews from *Kirkus Reviews* and *Library Journal*).
Golub, Marcia. *The New York Times Book Review*, 15 October 1995 (online).
Steinberg, Sybil S. *Publishers Weekly* 242 (8 May 1995): 288.
Young, Kenneth. *Buffalo News*, 25 June 1995, p. G8.
Another translated book written by Robert Schneider: *Dirt*

György Sebestyén. *Thennberg, or Seeking to Go Home Again.*
Translated by Lisa Fleisher. Riverside, CA: Ariadne Press, 1995. 135 pages.
Genre/literary style/story type: mainstream fiction
This novel focuses on Richard Kranz, a 21-year-old man who has survived the Nazi concentration camps. He is a mere ghost of what he once was, but his memories still run strong. He longs to return to his village of Thennberg, where his family rented a summer home and where he lost his virginity.

Subject keywords: anti-Semitism; rural life
Original language: German
Sources consulted for annotation:
Ariadne Press (book descriptions for all novels), http://www.ariadnebooks.com.
Back cover of the book.
Mitchell, Michael. Afterword to the book.
Some other translated books written by György Sebestyén: *The Works of Solitude*; *A Man Too White*; *The Doors Are Closing*; *Moment of Triumph*

Erich Wolfgang Skwara. ***Ice on the Bridge.***
Translated by Michael Roloff. Riverside, CA: Ariadne Press, 1996. 149 pages.
Genre/literary style/story type: mainstream fiction
Sebastian Winter is an Austrian architect in his mid-40s. At one time he lived in San Diego, but the city no longer has much meaning for him because it is here that Claudia, his lover, left him. Nonetheless, he finds himself once again in San Diego, awash in memories. Fearing that he will see Claudia again, he gets drunk at a social event at the conference that he is attending. He compounds his mistake by driving, which leads to the death of a pedestrian, which leads to his arrest. In jail awaiting bail, he meets John, who makes him realize his humanity and his myriad failings.
Subject keyword: identity
Original language: German
Sources consulted for annotation:
Ariadne Press (book descriptions for all novels), http://www.ariadnebooks.com.
Back cover of the book.
Zohn, Harry. *World Literature Today* 71 (Autumn 1997): 783.
Some other translated books written by Erich Wolfgang Skwara: *The Cool Million*; *Plague in Siena*; *Black Sails*

Gerald Szyszkowitz. ***Murder at the Western Wall.***
Translated by Todd C. Hanlin. Riverside, CA: Ariadne Press, 2000. 134 pages.
Genres/literary styles/story types: crime fiction; amateur detectives
When a reporter for CNN is murdered in Jerusalem, one of his colleagues, Nadja Assad, attempts to solve the murder after the police reach an impasse. As one death eventually turns into three, she is caught in the middle of a tumultuous political and religious situation that she cannot fully grasp.
Related title by the same author:
Readers may also enjoy *On the Other Side*, an examination of the effect of the end of the Cold War on two cities on the border of Austria and the Czech Republic.
Subject keyword: politics
Original language: German
Sources consulted for annotation:
American Literary Translators Association. *Translation Review—Annotated Books Received* 7.1 (July 2001): 9, http://www.utdallas.edu/alta/publications/translation-review.
Ariadne Press (book descriptions for both novels), http://www.ariadnebooks.com.
Some other translated books written by Gerald Szyszkowitz: *Puntigam, or, The Art of Forgetting*; *On the Other Side*

Germany

Jakob Arjouni. ***Happy Birthday, Turk!***
Translated by Anselm Hollo. New York: Fromm International, 1993. 154 pages.

Genres/literary styles/story types: crime fiction; private investigators

This is the first in a series of novels about Kemal Kayankaya, a German private detective who—because of his Turkish name and appearance—is the victim of anti-Turkish discrimination and prejudice despite being raised by a family of Germans and being able to fluently speak German. When Ahmed Hamul meets a bloody death, his family thinks it may have something to do with drugs. His girlfriend is not so sure; she hires Kayankaya to get to the bottom of the matter. Plunging into Frankfurt's red-light district, where Ahmed's girlfriend worked on a professional basis, Kayankaya discovers a sordid netherworld of violence and police corruption as well as persistent discrimination against Turkish immigranrts. Other books in the Kayankaya series are *And Still Drink More* (or *More Beer*); *One Death to Die* (or *One Man, One Murder*); and *Kismet*. The author has been compared to Raymond Chandler and Dashiell Hammett.

Subject keyword: urban life

Original language: German

Sources consulted for annotation:

Amazon.com (review from *Kirkus Reviews*).

Brainard, Dulcy. *Publishers Weekly* 240 (6 September 1993): 86.

Freeman, Jay. *Booklist* 90 (1 November 1993): 504.

Partello, Peggie. *Library Journal* 118 (1 October 1993): 125.

Some other translated books by Jakob Arjouni: *Magic Hoffmann*; *Idiots: Five Fairy Tales and Other Stories*

Zsuzsa Bánk. *The Swimmer.*

Translated by Margot Bettauer Dembo. Orlando, FL: Harcourt, 2004. 278 pages.

Genres/literary styles/story types: mainstream fiction; coming-of-age

After the Soviets crushed the Hungarian Revolution in 1956, Kalman Velencei's wife abruptly flees to Germany, leaving him to care for two young children. As Kalman tries to fathom his new situation and as he tries to make a suitable home for his daughter Kata and son Isti, he finds himself sinking into a proverbial slough of despond. Nothing seems worthwhile, so he decides to adopt an itinerant existence—going from the house of one relative to another in various parts of Hungary and never staying very long. Longing for their mother and trying to make the best of a constant state of impermanency, the children seek refuge in their imaginations. As Kata puzzles out the logic and rationale of the adult world, Isti discovers the solace of swimming.

Subject keyword: family histories

Original language: German

Sources consulted for annotation:

McConigle, Thomas. *Los Angeles Times*, 13 March 2005, p. R10.

Tepper, Anderson. *The New York Times Book Review*, 27 March 2005, p. 23.

Whitney, Scott. *Booklist* 101 (1 December 2004): 634.

Zaleski, Jeff. *Publisher Weekly* 251 (18 October 2004): 45.

Jurek Becker. *The Boxer.*

Translated by Alessandra Bastagli. New York: Arcade, 2002. 277 pages.

Genre/literary style/story type: mainstream fiction

Aron Blank and his eight-year-old son are reunited after World War II. Both are survivors of the camps, with Blank finally locating his son in a hospital, where he has been given a new name by a rescue agency. Blank drifts through life, isolated and unable to form lasting human connections. As his son recuperates in and is then released from hospital, Blank works at a series of random jobs and has unsuccessful relationships with his son's nurse and rescue agency contact. Mark grows up as introverted and alone as his father; even boxing lessons are of little help. Decades later, he takes

part in the military conflict wracking the Middle East, sending his father monthly letters containing detailed stories of his new life. Critics have stated that the novel is a masterpiece of understated eloquence.
Subject keywords: anti-Semitism; power
Original language: German
Sources consulted for annotation:
Amazon.com (about the author; book description).
Beckman, Joshua. *The Washington Post*, 25 August 2002, p. T6.
Zaleski, Jeff. *Publishers Weekly* 249 (3 June 2002): 59.
Some other translated books by Jurek Becker: *Bronstein's Children*; *Jacob the Liar*; *Sleepless Days*

Ulla Berkéwicz. *Angels are Black and White.*
Translated by Leslie Willson. Columbia, SC: Camden House, 1997. 218 pages.
Genres/literary styles/story types: mainstream fiction; coming-of-age
Reinhold Fischer is a young man searching for meaning in life. And he thinks he has found it in the Nazi movement. A poet, he quickly finds himself imbued with an idealistic fervor all the more powerful because it draws upon some of his favorite writers. He enrolls in the German army; fights at the Russian front; gradually becomes disabused because of the horrors that he sees around him; deserts; and falls in love with a Jewish refugee. As he tries to survive the frigid temperatures and as he remembers what happened to Jewish families in his neighborhood, he realizes that he has been complicit in erecting the scaffolding for a tragedy of monumental proportions. The *Publishers Weekly* reviewer noted that the book powerfully "dramatizes how the language of heroic struggle, sacrifice and spiritual renewal found in Nietzsche, Rilke and Hölderlin was adopted and perverted by Nazi propagandists."
Subject keywords: power; war
Original language: German
Sources consulted for annotation:
Amazon.com (book description).
Conard, R. C. *Choice* 34 (May 1997): 1502.
Steinberg, Sybil S. *Publishers Weekly* 243 (28 October 1996): 58.
Some other translated books written by Ulla Berkéwicz: *Josef is Dying*; *Love in a Time of Terror*

Marcel Beyer. *Spies.*
Translated by Breon Mitchell. Orlando, FL: Harcourt, 2005. 273 pages.
Genre/literary style/story type: mainstream fiction
What do you do when you suddenly discover that your grandmother no longer appears in the family album? Four young German children become very intrigued about this startling gap; they set out to solve the mystery. It could have something to do with their grandfather's second marriage; his new wife is by all reports a harridan. But grandfather himself is a very enigmatic presence; he had something to do with the Spanish Civil War as a secret German operative. And then there is the neighbor whose only friends are birds, not to mention an inscrutable, tiny statue of a ballerina.
Subject keyword: family histories
Original language: German
Sources consulted for annotation:
Block, Allison. *Booklist* 101 (July 2005): 1896.
Charles, Ron. *The Washington Post*, 24 July 2005, p. T5.
Chicago Review 48 (Summer 2002): 335.

Jain, Priya. *The New York Times Book Review*, 21 August 2005, p. 21.
Publishers Weekly 252 (6 June 2005): 37.
Another translated book by Marcel Beyer: *The Karnau Tapes*

Horst Bienek. *Time Without Bells*.
Translated by Ralph R. Read. New York: Atheneum, 1988. 338 pages.
Genres/literary styles/story types: historical fiction; literary historical
This is the third volume in the Gleiwitz Suite tetralogy. The first two volumes were *The First Polka* and *September Light*; the fourth is *Earth and Fire*. The tetralogy gives imaginative life to the effect of World War II on the Polish-German borderlands through the lives of two families from different socioeconomic classes. Weddings and funerals dominate the first two volumes, giving good insight into the daily lives of individuals struggling with personal concerns against the backdrop of an increasingly tense situation. While these two books focus on the months just before or after the outbreak of hostilities, *Time Without Bells* is a chilling account of the utter fatigue and weariness that the war brought to every aspect of daily life. Nothing is spared; no one escapes. On Good Friday in 1943, with Nazi forces in a tenuous position, bells are taken from the local church to serve as raw material for the building of military equipment. The last volume describes the aftermath of Nazi defeat, focusing on the chaotic political circumstances that engendered countless human tragedies.
Subject keywords: politics; power
Original language: German
Sources consulted for annotation:
Birkerts, Sven. *The New York Times Book Review*, 17 January 1988 (online).
Global Books in Print (online) (reviews from *Booklist* and *Choice*).
"Horst Bienek." *Dictionary of Literary Biography Online*. Thomson Gale databases.
Huyssen, Andreas. *The New York Times Book Review*, 15 January 1989 (online).
Pelzer, Jurgen. *Los Angeles Times*, 22 May 1988, p. 13.
Smith, Starr E. *Library Journal* 113 (January 1988): 96.
Steinberg, Sybil S. *Publishers Weekly* 232 (20 November 1987): 60.
Some other translated books by Horst Bienek: *The First Polka*; *September Light*; *Earth and Fire*; *The Cell*

Alina Bronsky. *Broken Glass Park*.
Translated by Tim Mohr. New York: Europa Editions, 2010. 336 pages.
Genre/literary style/story type: mainstream fiction; coming-of-age
A publishing sensation in Germany, this novel—written by a young Russian woman—features 17-year-old Sacha Naimann: a wry take-no-prisoners heroine who—after the murder of her mother—is left an orphan who dreams of vengeance and better days.
Subject keyword: urban life
Original language: German
Source consulted for annotation:
Europa Editions (book description), http://www.europaeditions.com.

Dorothea Dieckmann. *Guantanamo*.
Translated by Tim Mohr. New York: Soft Skull Press, 2007. 192 pages.
Genre/literary style/story type: mainstream fiction
Rashid is a 20-year-old and lives in Hamburg; his mother is German, and his father is an Indian Muslim. While visiting India, he meets an Afghani man who convinces him to join an anti-American demonstration in Peshawar. Rashid is arrested and shipped to Guantánamo Bay in Cuba.

The book examines the psychological, emotional, and social consequences of his imprisonment. It has been compared with Aleksandr Solzhenitsyn's *One Day in the Life of Ivan Denisovich.*
Subject keyword: power
Original language: German
Sources consulted for annotation:
Global Books in Print (online) (reviews from *Booklist* and *Publishers Weekly*).
Soft Skull Press (book description), http://www.softskull.com.

Doris Dörrie. *Where Do We Go from Here?*
Translated by John Brownjohn. New York: Bloomsbury, 2001. 242 pages.
Genre/literary style/story type: mainstream fiction
Fred Kaufmann has a complicated life—to put it mildly. Although he has always wanted to make films, he and his wife own a coffee shop. His wife is obsessed with neatness, and Fred is partially obsessed with a young Spanish teacher. His daughter becomes involved with a Tibetan monk at a Buddhist spiritual center and wants to move to India. When Fred is given the task of preventing the impending marriage of his daughter, he really does not know what he is in for. Visiting the center, he finds himself surrounded by a motley array of blissful and blissed-out individuals as well as a daughter who is more serene than he has ever seen her. He also makes a startling discovery about his wife.
Subject keyword: family histories
Original language: German
Sources consulted for annotation:
Andersen, Beth E. *Library Journal* 126 (1 June 2001): 212.
Bissey, Carrie. *Booklist* 97 (1 June/15 June 2001): 1835.
Global Books in Print (online) (review from *Kirkus Reviews*).
Hickling, Alfred. *The Guardian*, 8 June 2002, p. 29.
Zaleski, Jeff. *Publishers Weekly* 248 (25 June 2001): 47.
Some other translated books by Doris Dörrie: *Lottie's Princess Dress*; *What Do You Want from Me? and Fifteen Other Stories*; *Love, Pain and the Whole Damn Thing*

Jenny Erpenbeck. *Visitation*
Translated by Susan Bernofsky. New York: New Directions, 2010. 150 pages.
Genre/literary style/story type: mainstream fiction
Everything changes, and nothing does. As the years turn into decades and the decades into centuries or parts thereof, a house has numerous occupants, each reflecting in some way the broader social and cultural currents of their era and geographic location. For all intents and purposes, a given house becomes a palimpsest where competing histories—evanescent shards of humanity's overwhelmingly arrogant desire to leave a legacy—are written. And when that country is Germany starting in the 1930s and continuing on into the 1990s, the house is the repository of various manifestations of evil, fear, and ideological certitude—some viscerally palpable, others conveyed in a whisper by a chiaroscuro-tinged dance of beckoning and receding shadows. But as the house's initial Jewish owners flee and as a succession of inhabitants representing every political allegiance move in and then out, the gardener is always there, an incandescent and incantatory presence. As he attends to the cycle of seasons, he is not only the keeper of rituals, a secular version of a Cistercian monk performing Gregorian chant, but also the preserver of immutable verities about the nature of sanctuary. Written in lapidary prose, *Visitation* is a novel to be treasured.
Subject keyword: family histories
Original language: German

Sources consulted for annotation:
Faber, Michael. *The Guardian*, 30 October 2010 (online).
Witte, Phillip. Three Percent website (book review), http://www.rochester.edu/College/translation/threepercent.
Some other translated books by Jenny Erpenbeck: *The Old Child; The Book of Words*

Andreas Eschbach. *The Carpet Makers*.
Translated by Doryl Jensen. New York: Tom Doherty Associates, 2005. 300 pages.
Genre/literary style/story type: speculative fiction
This book is about as speculative as they come, and it is set so far in the future that there are really no words to describe the timespan. Imagine an empire lasting one-quarter of a million years and imagine that the empire consists of innumerable planets on which the main industry is making carpets. Imagine further that the carpets are made of the hair of humans and that it takes a lifetime to make a single carpet. Imagine a grim, monochromatic world that harbors untold secrets about the process behind carpet production. Finally, imagine that the empire comes to an end. When news of its decline finally reaches one of the distant planets, what are the inhabitants to do now? How are they to survive and find meaning in a world that had been tightly regimented? The book has been compared with the work of Ursula K. Le Guin and Isaac Asimov.
Subject keyword: power
Original language: German
Sources consulted for annotation:
Amazon.com (about the author; book description).
Green, Ronald. *Booklist* 101 (15 April 2005): 1442.
Jonas, Gerald. *The New York Times Book Review*, 7 August 2005, p. 16.
Publishers Weekly 252 (7 March 2005): 54.

Hans Fallada. *Every Man Dies Alone*.
Translated by Michael Hoffman. Brooklyn, NY: Melville House, 2009. 543 pages.
Genre/literary style/story type: mainstream fiction
First published in 1947 in German, it took 60 years for this neglected novel—which is based on real events—to appear in English. The author's real name is Rudolf Ditzen; the pen name comes from Grimm's *Fairy Tales*. In 1941, in Berlin, someone is distributing postcards denouncing the Third Reich and Hitler's activities. So far, 44 of these postcards have been found in random locations, and Inspector Escherich is tasked with finding the perpetrator of this invidious act of rebellion. His mission is all the more tense because his superior has let it be known that should he fail in finding the person responsible for the postcards, he himself will die. The perpetrators turn out to be Otto and Anna Quangel, a meek couple who keep to themselves and whose son has died in the war. Their act of resistance becomes a symbol of enduring humanity among carnage, mayhem, and brutality.
Related titles by the same author:
The small independent publisher Melville House should be commended for also releasing Fallada's *The Drinker* and *Little Man—What Now? The Drinker* focuses on Erwin Sommer's descent into alcoholism and madness. His hate for his wife Magda inexorably turns into debased self-loathing. First published in German in 1932, *Little Man—What Now?* is the tenebrous story of a salesman named Pinneberg who is unable to find work in Berlin. His fall is all the more tragic because he quickly realizes that he no longer has the right to the good things he once took for granted.
Subject keywords: politics; power
Original language: German

Source consulted for annotation:
Schlillinger, Liesl. *The New York Times Book Review*, 1 March 2009 (online).
Some other translated books written by Hans Fallada: *The Drinker*; *Little Man—What Now?*

Jörg Fauser. *Snowman.*
Translated by Anthea Bell. London: Bitter Lemon Press, 2004. 190 pages.
Genres/literary styles/story types: crime fiction; urban fiction
It is a hard life when you cannot sell old Danish pornography magazines in Malta. Thus, Blum—a down-on-his-luck grifter—decides to become a drug smuggler, with tragicomic results.
Subject keyword: social problems
Original language: German
Source consulted for annotation:
Global Books in Print (online) (review from *Publishers Weekly*).

Günter Grass. *Crabwalk.*
Translated by Krishna Winston. Orlando, FL: Harcourt, 2002. 234 pages.
Genres/literary styles/story types: historical fiction; literary historical
Based on a historical incident, this book captures the unremitting tragedies and paradoxes of World War II like few others. In 1937, the Germans built the ship *Wilhelm Gustloff* to serve as a luxury liner for vacationing government officials. Starting in 1939, it was used as a hospital and military personnel ship. In 1945, on a raw January day with about 10,000 German refugees onboard hoping to escape the advancing Russian army, it sank in the Baltic Sea after being hit by Soviet torpedos in what has commonly been referred to as the worst maritime disaster in history. With end-of-war desperation and tensions mounting; with quarrels breaking out on almost any conceivable topic among the naval officers; and with the harsh grip of winter descending, it was almost inevitable that something terrible would happen. Grass's novel is narrated by Paul Pokriefke, a less-than-successful journalist born during the ship's sinking. Tulla, his mother—whose parents were Nazi supporters—also survived. As Pokriefke investigates the history of the disaster, he discovers that Konrad, his son—with whom he has at best a tenuous relationship—is a neo-Nazi obsessed by the disaster and devotes endless hours to a website memorializing it, viewing it through the prism of a war crime committed against German citizens.
Related titles by the same author:
Readers may also enjoy the controversial *Too Far Afield*, which centers on Theo Wuttke, whose job is to transform East German businesses into capitalist institutions after the fall of the Berlin Wall. Grass presents German reunification from the viewpoint of East Germans, who were less than thrilled with what they considered the abrupt and insensitive importation of Western values into their social and cultural life. Also of interest may be *Peeling the Onion*, the author's autobiography where he reveals that he was a member of the Waffen SS. It should be read in conjunction with *The Box: Tales from the Darkroom*, a memoir-like novel in which the eight children of a man very much resembling Grass deliver piercing assessments of their father and his work. Grass's most famous novel is *The Tin Drum*, in which Oskar Matzerath commits the supreme act of rebellion against a father who prosaically wants his son to become a grocer: He wills himself to physically remain a child.
Subject keywords: politics; war
Original language: German
Sources consulted for annotation:
Adler, Jeremy. *The New York Times Book Review*, 27 April 2003 (online).
Amazon.com (book description).
Caso, Frank. *Booklist* 99 (15 February 2003): 1047.

Eder, Richard. *The New York Times*, 24 April 2003 (online).
"Günter Grass." *Contemporary Authors Online*. Thomson Gale, 2007.
Irving, John. *The New York Times Book Review*, 8 July 2007 (online).
Mohr, Tim. *The New York Times Book Review*, 14 November 2010 (online).
Sheehan, James J. *The New York Times Book Review*, 5 November 2000 (online).
Zaleski, Jeff. *Publishers Weekly* 250 (3 March 2003): 51.
Some other translated books written by Günter Grass: *My Century*; *The Rat*; *The Call of the Toad*; *Too Far Afield*; *The Meeting at Telgte*; *The Danzig Trilogy*; *The Tin Drum*; *Local Anaesthetic*; *Dog Years; Peeling the Onion; The Box: Tales from the Darkroom*

Claudia Gross. *Scholarium.*
Translated by Helen Atkins. New Milford, CT: Toby Press, 2004. 294 pages.
Genres/literary styles/story types: thrillers; conspiracy thrillers
Frederico Casall is a medieval scholar at Cologne's new university; he believes strongly in the philosophy of Thomas Aquinas. But he is brutally murdered on a gloomy rain-soaked evening. When Konrad Steiner, a colleague of the dead man, investigates the murder, he finds a number of suspects, including an academic rival as well as Casall's young wife, who is also intellectually inclined. Some critics have have said that this novel recalls Umberto Eco's *The Name of the Rose* for its labyrinth exploration of scholastic debates and controversies.
Subject keyword: philosophy
Original language: German
Sources consulted for annotation:
Amazon.com (about the author; book description).
Baker, Jennifer. *Booklist* 100 (1 June 2004): 1707.
Kirkus Reviews 72 (1 May 2004): 411.

Martin Grzimek. *Shadowlife.*
Translated by Breon Mitchell. New York: New Directions, 1991. 207 pages.
Genres/literary styles/story types: thrillers; political thrillers
Felix Seyner works at the secretive Central Institute for Biographics (CIB). To say that it is secretive is an understatement. In a nation where most citizens are not allowed to write, Felix interviews people and records the facts of their lives. But a confluence of untoward events sends Felix hurtling toward the unknown. Someone dies during an interview, and there is a great deal of ambiguity about whether it is a suicide or murder. After Felix tries to get in touch with an old girlfriend, he is accused of surreptiously entering the computer system of the CIB. Hovering in the background is the question of what exactly is the CIB's purpose. How does it use its gathered information? Critics have invoked George Orwell's *1984* to describe the important social and philosophical issues raised by Grzimek's exploration of surveillance and control.
Subject keyword: power
Original language: German
Sources consulted for annotation:
Dwyer, Jim. *Library Journal* 116 (1 March 1991): 116.
Global Books in Print (online) (reviews from *Booklist*).
Kaganoff, Penny. *Publishers Weekly* 238 (8 February 1991): 53.
Another translated book by Martin Grzimek: *Heartstop: Three Stories*

Katharina Hacker. *The Lifeguard.*
Translated by Helen Atkins. New Milford, CT: Toby Press, 2002. 186 pages.
Genre/literary style/story type: mainstream fiction

Imagine yourself as a beknighted old man who has worked at one job for some 40 years. You would have a significant amount of psychological and emotional attachment to that job and to that place of employment. The protagonist of this novel is a lifeguard, and he has worked for what seems his entire life at a public swimming and bathing facility in East Berlin. But the baths are decrepit and dilapidated, and the government finally shuts them down. The lifeguard is bereft. Knowing that he would be lost without the routine of his job, he becomes a squatter in the condemned building, with ever-growing decay and rats his only companions. As the baths become a living presence, the lifeguard's memories slowly form into a devastating whole: The sinister facility had a significant role to play in the horrors of World War II.
Subject keywords: anti-Semitism; identity
Original language: German
Sources consulted for annotation:
Amazon.com (book description).
Global Books in Print (online) (review from *Kirkus Reviews*).

Peter Härtling. *Schubert.*
Translated by Rosemary Smith. New York: Holmes & Meier, 1995. 248 pages.
Genre/literary style/story type: historical fiction
This book is a fictionalized biography of the Austrian composer Franz Schubert, who lived at the beginning of the nineteenth century. The author uses Schubert's romantic Lieder as clues to the composer's inner life. Traumatized by the death of his mother and alienated from his father, Schubert seeks solace in the arms of prostitutes and pines for one of his young pupils. As he struggles with syphilis and as he drifts further and further into an abject loneliness, he appears as a tragic and misunderstood figure.
Related title by the same author:
Readers may also enjoy *A Woman*, which focuses on Katharina Wullner, a symbolic representation of German womanhood who suffers one setback after another: Within the space of two months, she not only loses her husband and her son in World War II, but she must also deal with her brother's suicide. Yet she stalwartly goes on because to not do so would be to give into the forces of history.
Subject keyword: family histories
Original language: German
Sources consulted for annotation:
Global Books in Print (online) (review from *Choice* for *A Woman*).
O'Pecko, Michael. *Library Journal* 120 (15 April 1995): 114.
Steinberg, Sybil S. *Publishers Weekly* 242 (27 March 1995): 75.
Some other translated books by Peter Härtling: *A Woman*; *Ben Loves Anna*; *Crutches*; *Old John*; *Oma*, *Theo Runs Away*

Gaby Hauptmann. *In Search of an Impotent Man.*
Translated by Shaun Whiteside. New York: Ecco Press, 1998. 312 pages.
Genre/literary style/story type: mainstream fiction
Carmen Legg is an insurance agent to end all insurance agents. She attracts men like bees to honey. But that encapsulates her problem. All her male friends—many of whom are not the brightest bulbs in the box—want to sleep with her. But Carmen is tired of all that. She wants a man who is an intellectual and impotent, and she specifically adverstises for that rare combination in a newspaper. After receiving numerous responses, she finally selects David, an architect who loves Rilke. But she eventually realizes that she wants David to be—shall we say—more than she advertised for.
Subject keyword: identity
Original language: German

Sources consulted for annotation:
Joll, William. *The Spectator* 282 (30 January 1999): 44.
Rohrbaugh, Lisa. *Library Journal* 124 (December 1999): 186.
Steinberg, Sybil S. *Publishers Weekly* 246 (6 December 1999): 55.
Some other translated books by Gaby Hauptmann: *A Handful of Manhood*; *Grabbing the Family Jewels*

Christoph Hein. *Willenbrock*.
Translated by Philip Boehm. New York: Metropolitan Books, 2003. 322 pages.
Genre/literary style/story type: mainstream fiction
Bernd Willenbrock, a former East German engineer, is sitting on a veritable gold mine: a Berlin used-car dealership. In the first heady months of German unification, he seemingly has everything he wants. But his car dealership is suddenly subject to a series of robberies—one more violent than the last. Naturally, he decides to protect his possessions. When a guard dog, a human guard, and an alarm system do not do the trick, he buys a gun. His descent into the maw of ruthless social Darwinism is complete, and he soon discovers that the fear, insecurity, and lack of freedom that lie at the heart of Western capitalism are no less oppresive than the shackles of his previous East German life.
Subject keyword: urban life
Original language: German
Sources consulted for annotation:
Caso, Frank. *Booklist* 100 (1 September 2003): 56.
Global Books in Print (online) (reviews from *Booklist* and *Library Journal* for both novels).
Publishers Weekly 250 (22 September 2003): 84.
Wolf, Gregory H. *World Literature Today* 75 (Winter 2001): 145.
Some other translated books written by Christoph Hein: *The Distant Lover*; *The Tango Player*; *Jamie and His Friends*; *Settlement*

Gert Hofmann. *Luck*.
Translated by Michael Hofmann. New York: New Directions, 2002. 266 pages.
Genres/literary styles/story types: mainstream fiction; coming-of-age
When a marriage comes to an end, it is never a happy moment. Recriminations fly, anger wells up, tears are shed. And that is just the adults. For children, it is all kind of incomprehensible. Especially the very last day. This novel examines that last day from the perspective of two adults and two children, especially the teenage son. It poignantly captures his bewildered attempts to make sense of the situation as he and his sister wend their way through their house for the final time.
Related titles by the same author:
Readers may also enjoy *The Film Explainer*, a comic novel about the author's grandfather whose job it was to be a film explainer; that is, the accompanying voice to silent motion pictures. But when the first talking picture makes his position obsolete, he can think of nothing better to do than join the Nazis. Also of interest may be *Before the Rainy Season*, which focuses on a former German solider now living in rural Bolivia. He has spent most of his time in Bolivia denying any complicity in wartime atrocities—so much so that he really does not want to return, even though he has been assured it is now safe to do so.
Subject keyword: family histories
Original language: German
Sources consulted for annotation:
Amazon.com (about the author; book description).
Bamforth, Iain. *The New York Times Book Review*, 1 September 1996 (online).
Global Books in Print (online) (review from *Publishers Weekly* for *The Film Explainer*).

Isenberg, Noah. *The New York Times Book Review*, 8 September 2002, p. 22.
Ruta, Suzanne. *The New York Times Book Review*, 28 April 1991 (online).
Zaleski, Jeff. *Publishers Weekly* 249 (1 April 2002): 49.
Some other translated books by Gert Hofmann: *The Film Explainer*; *Before the Rainy Season*; *Balzac's Horse and Other Stories*; *The Parable of the Blind*; *Our Conquest*; *The Spectacle at the Tower*

Peter Stephan Jungk. *The Perfect American*.
Translated by Michael Hofmann. New York: Handsel Books, 2004. 186 pages.
Genre/literary style/story type: mainstream fiction
Europeans have always had a love-hate relationship with Walt Disney. This tradition continues in Jungk's novel, where Wilhelm Dantine—an innovative German cartoonist who used to work for Disney before being fired for ideological reasons related to a proposed visit by former Soviet president Nikita Khrushchev to Disneyland in 1959—provides an imaginative retelling of the American cultural icon's paradoxical life.
Subject keyword: power
Original language: German
Sources consulted for annotation:
Charles, Ron. *The Christian Science Monitor*, 13 July 2004, p. 16.
Global Books in Print (online) (review from *Publishers Weekly*).
Hay, Carl. *Booklist* 100 (15 May 2004): 1609.
Schickel, Richard. *Los Angeles Times*, 13 June 2004, p. R2.
Another translated book written by Peter Stephan Jungk: *Tigor*

Daniel Kehlmann. *Measuring the World*.
Translated by Carol Brown Janeway. New York: Pantheon Books, 2006. 259 pages.
Genre/literary style/story type: historical fiction
In the early decades of the nineteenth century, two of the most famous scientists in Germany were Alexander von Humboldt and Carl Gauss. This novel captures the essence of their lives and scientific work, their philosophies, and their accomplishments. While the former travels the world—exploring isolated parts of South America and willingly putting himself in danger—the latter is a homebody, brooding over, lovingly imagining, and perfecting his mathematical theorems. Boyd Tonkin stated that Kehlmann's book has affinities with the depictions of scientists by Neal Stephenson and Richard Powers as well as Thomas Pynchon's *Mason & Dixon*.
Related title by the same author:
Readers may also enjoy *Me and Kaminski*, which focuses on Sebastian Zollner, everyone's worst nightmare of a cultural critic and biographer. Determined to unearth scandal and make a name for himself in the process, he abruptly enters the private world of an almost blind painter.
Subject keyword: philosophy
Original language: German
Sources consulted for annotation:
LeClair, Tom. *The New York Times Book Review*, 5 November 2006 (online).
Tonkin, Boyd. *The Independent* (London), 31 October 2008 (online).
Another translated book written by Daniel Kehlmann: *Me and Kaminski*

Hans Werner Kettenbach. *Black Ice*.
Translated by Anthea Bell. London: Bitter Lemon Press, 2005. 224 pages.
Genres/literary styles/story types: crime fiction; amateur detectives
When Erika Wallmann suddenly dies after a mysterious fall, Jupp Scholten is not at all sure that the death was an accident. Something does not ring true, especially because Erika once confided in him

about her unhappy marriage. But her rich older husband is also Scholten's boss; he must therefore tread carefully. And why is Scholten devoting himself to the matter? Is it revenge or an opportunity to redeem himself; after all, he is a thoroughly unlikable man who spends more time with prostitutes and his cat than his long-suffering wife.
Subject keyword: social roles
Original language: German
Sources consulted for annotation:
Kirkus Reviews, 15 October 2005 (from Factiva databases).
Publishers Weekly 252 (28 November 2005): 26.
Sennett, Frank. *Booklist* 102 (1 December 2005): 28.

Michael Kleeberg. *King of Corsica.*
Translated by David B. Dollenmayer. New York: Other Press, 2008. 392 pages.
Genre/literary style/story type: historical fiction
Theodor von Neuhoff was a most ordinary man with the most sublime of luck. In the early eighteenth century, he was a kind of diplomat and secret agent in Europe, working for a variety of governments: France, Sweden, Spain, and Austria. While in modern-day Italy, he meets Corsicans who want to make their island independent. To do this, they must get rid of their current rulers from Genoa. Neuhoff pledges to lead their crusade, and in early 1736, he is named king of Corsica. His regime only lasts some six months. He is forced to leave the island after skirmishes with the Genoese, and he flees to the Netherlands and England, where he is hounded for a series of debts.
Subject keywords: politics; power
Original language: German
Source consulted for annotation:
Global Books in Print (online) (reviews from *Library Journal* and *Publishers Weekly*).

Alexander Kluge. *The Devil's Blind Spot: Tales from the New Century.*
Translated by Martin Chalmers and Michael Hulse. New York: New Directions, 2004. 322 pages.
Genres/literary styles/story types: mainstream fiction; short stories
In 173 eloquent short stories arranged in five chapters, the author explores the nature of tragedy and evil in the contemporary world (e.g., September 11; the Chernobyl catastrophe; and the demise of the nuclear submarine *Kursk*); love; power; the cosmos; and knowledge.
Related title by the same author:
Readers may also enjoy *Learning Processes with a Deadly Outcome*, in which a horrific conflict called the Black War has almost completely destroyed civilization as we know it. There are some survivors, but they are hiding deep in the bowels of the earth or in outer space, struggling to form a new society that, paradoxically, will have many of the worst features of the annihilated world.
Subject keyword: philosophy
Original language: German
Sources consulted for annotation:
Amazon.com (book descriptions for both books).
Herter, Philip. *St. Petersburg Times*, 12 December 2004, p. 5P.
Malin, Irving. *Review of Contemporary Fiction* 25 (Spring 2005): 147.
Some other translated books written by Alexander Kluge: *Attendance List for a Funeral*; *The Battle*; *Case Histories*; *Learning Processes with a Deadly Outcome*

Helmut Krausser. *Eros.*
Translated by Mike Mitchell. New York: Europa Editions, 2008. 352 pages.

Genre/literary style/story type: mainstream fiction
It is more than a cliché to say that love is powerful, but in this novel, that trite expression literally holds true. On his death bed, the wealthy factory owner Alexander von Brücken recounts his biography to a novelist over the course of eight days. He has always loved Sofie Kurtz, a worker's daughter with whom he experienced the joys of puppy love at the tender age of 14. As time moved on, she forgot him, but he did not forget her, surreptiously exerting influence over her entire life and career.
Related title by the same author:
Readers may also enjoy *The Great Bagarozy*, which focuses on Cora Dulz, a psychiatrist who accepts Stanislaus Nagy as a new patient. Nagy has problems—and then some: He claims to be visited by Maria Callas, whom he believes to be the embodiment of evil. Nevertheless, Cora falls in love with Nagy, going so far as to leave her husband in an attempt to find Nagy when he disappears.
Subject keywords: family histories; power
Original language: German
Source consulted for annotation:
Global Books in Print (online) (reviews from *Library Journal* and *Publishers Weekly*; reviews from *Booklist* and *Publishers Weekly* for *The Great Bagarozy*).
Another translated book written by Helmut Krausser: *The Great Bagarozy*

Michael Kumpfmüller. *The Adventures of a Bed Salesman.*
Translated by Anthea Bell. New York: Picador, 2003. 420 pages.
Genre/literary style/story type: mainstream fiction
As the title indicates, these are the adventures of Heinrich Hampel, West German bed salesman extraordinaire. And what zany adventures they are. He cannot get enough sex, he has too many mistresses, and he is constantly in debt. As a way to solve his problems, he flees to East Germany, where he thinks he will be accorded a hero's welcome. Instead, he is imprisoned, sharing quarters with other refugees from the West whose lives have been ruined by excessive freedom. Eventually, Rosa—his long-suffering wife—joins him, and while Heinrich intends to begin a new life, he does not succeed. He just loves women too much. Constantly short of money, he becomes a petty criminal who is eventually recruited to be an East German informer. In time, he becomes a well-recognized apologist for the East German government.
Subject keywords: identity; politics
Original language: German
Sources consulted for annotation:
Crispin, Jessica. *Bookslut* (July 2003) (book review), http://www.bookslut.com.
Global Books in Print (online) (synopsis/book jacket).

Barbara König. *The Beneficiary.*
Translated by Roslyn Theobald in collaboration with the author. Evanston, IL: Northwestern University Press, 1993. 117 pages.
Genre/literary style/story type: mainstream fiction
As World War II draws to a close, Mommsen faces death for his alleged part in a plan to destroy a strategic bridge. In an act of supreme sacrifice, a chaplain substitutes himself for Mommsen and is shot to death by the firing squad. Thirty-five years later, the priest's action is the subject of a commemoration, and an inquisitive public wants to know how Mommsen—who is now a successful real estate agent—feels about having had a second chance at life.
Subject keywords: identity; social roles
Original language: German

Sources consulted for annotation:
Derr, Nancy. *Belles Lettres* 9 (Spring 1994): 60.
Steinberg, Sybil S. *Publishers Weekly* 240 (9 August 1993): 461.
Another translated book written by Barbara König: *Our House*

Gerhard Köpf. *There Is No Borges.*
Translated by Leslie Willson. New York: George Braziller, 1993. 196 pages.
Genres/literary styles/story types: mainstream fiction; postmodernism
When you are a marginal academic, you need spectacular theories to put yourself on the map. A less-than-middling German professor specializing in Lusitanics—defined as the science of loss—thinks that William Shakespeare wrote *Don Quixote*. On his way to Malaysia to expound on his views, he starts up a conversation with a fellow airline passenger who believes that the Argentine writer Jorge Luis Borges is a figment of everyone's imagination. As the two men exchange notes and indulge in literary exegesis, their personal lives also come into focus. Eventually, the professor encounters Borges outside a restroom—or someone whom he thinks is Borges—in the former Portuguese colony of Macao.
Related title by the same author:
Readers may also enjoy *Piranesi's Dream*, an imaginative retelling of the life of the world-famous engraver whose real goal was to be an architect.
Subject keyword: identity
Original language: German
Sources consulted for annotation:
Amazon.com (review from *Kirkus Reviews*).
Burgin, Richard. *The Washington Post*, 18 July 1993, p. X7.
Global Books in Print (online) (reviews from *Booklist* for both books).
Steinberg, Sybil S. *Publishers Weekly* 240 (10 May 1993): 49.
Walton, David. *The New York Times Book Review*, 10 October 1993, p. 20.
Some other translated books by Gerhard Köpf: *Papa's Suitcase*; *The Way to Eden*; *Piranesi's Dream*; *Nurmi*; *Innerfar & Bluff, Or the Southern Cross*

Michael Krüger. *The Cello Player.*
Translated by Andrew Shields. Orlando, FL: Harcourt, 2004. 200 pages.
Genre/literary style/story type: mainstream fiction
Gyargy is a German composer whose dream is to create an opera about Osip Mandelstam, a Russian poet. In the meantime, he spends his time writing television background music. His ordered and precise middle-aged life is turned topsy-turvy by the arrival of Judit. She is Hungarian, plays the cello, and—as the daughter of one of his former lovers—is a symbol of dynamic womanhood. She not only completely colonizes Gyargy's apartment, but she also takes over his psychological and emotional life, offering wry observations about his projected opera and his sellout to the forces of corrupting commercialism.
Subject keyword: identity
Original language: German
Sources consulted for annotation:
Amazon.com (book description).
Evans, Janet. *Library Journal* 129 (January 2004): p. 157.
Isenberg, Noah. *The New York Times Book Review*, 16 May 2004, p. 26.
Spinella, Michael. *Booklist* 100 (15 December 2003): 727.
Zaleski, Jeff. *Publishers Weekly* 250 (1 December 2003): 41.

Some other translated books by Michael Krüger: *The End of the Novel*; *The Man in the Tower*; *Himmelfarb*; *Scenes from the Life of a Best-Selling Author*

Benjamin Lebert. *Crazy.*
Translated by Carol Brown Janeway. New York: Alfred A. Knopf, 2000. 177 pages.
Genres/literary styles/story types: mainstream fiction; coming-of-age
Published when the author was 16, this novel is partly autobiographical. It focuses on the teenage Benni, whose life is a constant struggle. He is not very intellectually oriented, and his left side is almost completely paralyzed. He has been cycled through one boarding school after another, but at his latest stop, he discovers sex and the brief joys of drunken camardarie at a topless bar in Munich. Some critics have seen affinities with J. D. Salinger's *The Catcher in the Rye* and Susan E. Hinton's *The Outsiders*.
Subject keyword: identity
Original language: German
Sources consulted for annotation:
Amazon.com (review from *Kirkus Reviews*).
Eugenides, Jeffrey. *The New York Times Book Review*, 14 May 2000 (online).
Fowler, Sheryl. *School Library Journal* 46 (August 2000): 212.
Huntley, Kristine. *Booklist* 96 (15 February 2000): 1052.
Kicinski, Judith. *Library Journal* 125 (1 Apr 2000): 130.
Lehoczky, Etelka. *The New York Times Book Review*, 29 January 2006 (online).
Steinberg, Sybil S. *Publishers Weekly* 247 (20 March 2000): 73.
Another translated book written by Benjamin Lebert: *The Bird Is a Raven*

Monika Maron. *Animal Triste.*
Translated by Brigitte Goldstein. Lincoln, NE: University of Nebraska Press, 2000. 133 pages.
Genres/literary styles/story types: mainstream fiction; women's lives
An elderly woman—once a paleontologist at an East German museum—is haunted by memories of an obsessive and wildly erotic affair in her distant past. Married and the mother of a daughter, her world was forever changed, when—after the collapse of the Berlin Wall—she fell in love with Franz, a West German scientist who became her coworker. She left her family for him, and their passion knew no bounds. But a trifling quarrel led to Franz's accidental death under the wheels of a bus, and she became a recluse, constantly tormented by her guilt in his death and in her family's collapse.
Subject keyword: family histories
Original language: German
Sources consulted for annotation:
Isenberg, Noah. *The New York Times Book Review*, 19 March 2000, p. 20.
Johnson, Bonnie. *Booklist* 96 (15 March 2000): 1330.
Some other translated books by Monika Maron: *Flight of Ashes*; *The Defector*; *Silent Close No. 6*

Walter Moers. *Rumo & His Miraculous Adventures.*
Translated by John Brownjohn. London: Secker & Warburg, 2004. 686 pages.
Genres/literary styles/story types: adventure; quest
This book, which is the sequel to *The 13 Lives of Captain Bluebear*, has been characterized by most critics as wonderfully exuberant and innovative. The hero is Rumo, no ordinary animal. In fact, he is a Wolperting, described as a kind of half-deer and half-dog. He has a lovable horn, and he lives on a farm owned by a family of dwarfs in the imaginary land of Zamonia. In this novel, Rumo is taken

against his will to Roaming Rock by an evil giant in search of prey. But things are never as bad as they seem: Rumo is taught mythology, escapes, and eventually falls in love. The book contains more than 100 illustrations by the author.
Subject keyword: identity
Original language: German
Sources consulted for annotation:
Bergstrom, Jenne. *Library Journal* 131 (July 2006): 67.
Publishers Weekly 253 (24 July 2006): 40.
Schroeder, Regina. *Booklist* 102 (July 2006): 43.
Some other translated books written by Walter Moers: *A Wild Ride Through the Night*; *The 13 1/2 Lives of Captain Bluebear: Being the Demibiography of a Seagoing Bear*; *The City of Dreaming Brooks: A Novel from Zamonia by Optimus Yarnspinner* (translated from the Zamonian and illustrated by Walter Moers)

Herta Müller. *The Appointment.*
Translated by Michael Hulse and Philip Boehm. New York: Metropolitan Books, 2001. 214 pages.
Genre/literary style/story type: mainstream fiction; women's lives
A young woman working in a garment factory is so desparate to escape the constant fear that is the objective correlative of totalitarianism that she sews secret notes into men's suits exported to Italy. The notes give her address and contain a plea to the man buying the suit to marry her. But after she is caught, she loses her job and must face a seemingly endless round of humiliating interrogations. The book was described by Richard Eder as "a brooding, fog-shrouded allegory of life under the long oppression of the regime of Nicolae Ceausescu" in Romania.
Related title by the same author:
Readers may also be interested in *The Land of Green Plums*, which—according to Larry Wolff—"seeks to create a sort of poetry out of the spiritual and material ugliness of life in Communist Romania." It focuses on poverty-stricken Lola, a university student living in a squalid dormitory with five other young women. To say the least, her life is one misery after another, culminating in suicide and posthumous disgrace.
Subject keywords: politics; power
Original language: German
Sources consulted for annotation:
Bader, Eleanor J. *Library Journal* 126 (1 September 2001): 234.
Eder, Richard. *The New York Times*, 12 September 2001, p. E8.
Filkins, Peter. *The New York Times Book Review*, 21 October 2001 (online).
Kubisz, Carolyn. *Booklist* 98 (1 September 2001): 52.
Wolff, Larry. *The New York Times Book Review*, 1 December 1996 (online).
Zaleski, Jeff. *Publishers Weekly* 248 (6 August 2001): 61.
Some other translated books written by Herta Müller: *The Land of Green Plums*; *Nadirs*; *Traveling on One Leg*; *The Passport*; *Everything I Possess*; *The Fox Was Always a Hunter*

Sten Nadolny. *The Discovery of Slowness.*
Translated by Ralph Freedman. New York: Viking, 1987. 325 pages.
Genre/literary style/story type: historical fiction
This book is a fictional account of the life of Sir John Franklin, the nineteenth-century explorer whose attempts at finding the Northwest Passage did not meet with success. The author describes Franklin's agonizingly slow progress in learning everything there is to know about ships. But he was nothing if not encyclopedic in his knowledge of sails, rigging, and ropes. This deep understanding of all things naval served him well during the Battle of Copenhagen in the first years of the

nineteenth century and was partly responsible for the fact that he had the rank of captain by the time he was 30. He is chiefly remembered for his three Arctic expeditions and his governorship of Van Diemen's Land, now known as Tasmania. According to Sara Blackburn, the novel's ultimate purpose is to show Franklin's success "in harnessing his own slowness as a virtue in the service of compassion, pleasure and humane governance, while his century clangs around him to the maddened cries of empire and progress."
Subject keywords: identity; power
Original language: German
Sources consulted for annotation:
Blackburn, Sara. *The New York Times Book Review*, 20 December 1987 (online).
Coombs, Ronald L. *Library Journal* 112 (15 September 15 1987): 96.
Global Books in Print (online) (review from *Booklist*).
Rodriguez, Johnette. *Providence Journal*, 15 November 1987, p. H15.
Steinberg, Sybil S. *Publishers Weekly* 232 (21 August 1987): 56.
Another translated book by Sten Nadolny: *The God of Impertinence*

Emine Sevgi Özdamar. *The Bridge of the Golden Horn.*
Translated by Martin Chalmers. London: Serpent's Tail, 2007. 272 pages.
Genre/literary style/story type: mainstream fiction; coming-of-age
In the late 1960s, a 16-year-old Istanbul girl leaves Turkey to seek fame and fortune in Berlin. But the path to success is filled with many obstacles. She must pretend that she is older than she really is in order to be allowed to work at a tedious factory job assembling radios, which is nevertheless necessary to permit her to save money to attend a drama school. But it is a time of social and cultural ferment in Germany, and the narrator of this partly autobiographical novel becomes caught up in political upheaval and sexual discovery.
Subject keywords: identity; urban life
Original language: German
Sources consulted for annotation:
LeTourneur, Jessica. Three Percent website (book review), http://www.rochester.edu/College/translation/threepercent.
McCulloch, Alison. *The New York Times Book Review*, 6 August 2009 (online).
Serpent's Tail website (book description), http://www.serpentstail.com.

Gudrun Pausewang. *The Final Journey.*
Translated by Patricia Crampton. New York: Viking, 1996. 153 pages.
Genre/literary style/story type: mainstream fiction
There is nary a moment of optimism in this relentlessly dark and chilling account of the inhumanity experienced by an 11-year-old girl and her grandfather as they—along with thousands of others—are herded onto crowded railway cars meant for livestock. As Alice Dubsky endures the terrifying rail journey that will end at Auschwitz, recent memories of the numerous tragedies her family has lived through occupy her mind: arson at their temple; expropriation of the family business; constant hiding; unexplained disappearances; and now the final journey. The *Booklist* reviewer said that this novel can be viewed as "an extension of the autobiographical journeys of Primo Levi's *Survival in Auschwitz* (1959) and Isabella Leitner's *The Big Lie* (1992)."
Subject keyword: anti-Semitism
Original language: German
Sources consulted for annotation:
Balfour, Laura. *The Herald*, 6 January 2001, p. 17.
Global Books in Print (online) (review from *Kirkus Reviews*).

Rochman, Hazel. *Booklist* 93 (1 October 1996): 344.
Sutton, Roger. *The Horn Book Magazine* 73 (January/February 1997): 66.
Some other translated books written by Gudrun Pausewang: *Fall-Out*; *Bolivian Wedding*; *The Last Children of Schevenborn*; *Dark Hours*; *Traitor*

Akif Pirinçci. *Felidae.*
Translated by Ralph Noble. London: Fourth Estate, 1993. 262 pages.
Genres/literary styles/story types: crime fiction; suspense
This is not your ordinary mystery or detective novel. All the major characters are cats, although, of course, they have very human concerns and issues. When Francis moves into a new home, he knows at once something is wrong. There is a peculiar smell, not unlike chemicals. He soon discovers that the neighborhood has been plagued by the deaths of a handful of male cats—all killed in the throes of sexual passion. Eventually, Franics finds the records of a mysterious Professor Preterius, whose supposedly scientific experiments on hundreds of cats can be seen as manifestations of the Nazi desire to engage in purification through eugenics. The *Kirkus Books* reviewer observed that "[w]hat begins as homicidal *Watership Down* eventually resonates with echoes of Günter Grass, Umberto Eco, Hitchcock, and Spiegelman." Readers may also be interested in a sequel entitled *Felidae on the Road.*
Subject keyword: power
Original language: German
Sources consulted for annotation:
Global Books in Print (online) (reviews from *Booklist* and *Kirkus Reviews*).
Klett, Rex E. *Library Journal* 118 (January 1993): 169.
Lehmann-Haupt, Christopher. *The New York Times*, 15 March 1993, p. C17.
Steinberg, Sybil S. *Publishers Weekly* 239 (23 November 1992): 53.

Charlotte Roche. *Wetlands.*
Translated by Tim Mohr. New York: Grove Press, 2009. 229 pages.
Genres/literary styles/story types: mainstream fiction; coming-of-age
Critics either loved or hated this book that graphically recounts 18-year-old Helen Memel's numerous sexual experiences as well as her fascination with her own excreta. As she lies in a hospital recovering from an anal lesion, she analyzes her proclivities and reflects on her divorced parents. According to the *Library Journal* critic, the book is "simultaneously exhilarating, moving, sad, and scary," but for Sallie Tisdale, it has "all the nuance of *Mad* magazine and less wit." It has been translated into more than 25 languages and was a bestseller in many European countries, especially Germany.
Subject keyword: identity
Original language: German
Sources consulted for annotation:
Global Books in Print (online) (reviews from *Booklist*, *Library Journal*, and *Publishers Weekly*).
Tisdale, Sallie. *The New York Times Book Review*, 19 April 2009 (online).

Herbert Rosendorfer. *The Night of the Amazons.*
Translated by Ian Mitchell. London: Secker & Warburg, 1991. 247 pages.
Genre/literary style/story type: historical fiction
Christian Weber, a violence-prone man who worked in bars as a bouncer and was reputed to be involved in the sex trade, was one of Hitler's few close friends and an early adherent of the National Socialist party. As such, he rose to a place of prominence in Munich politics, where—in the late

1930s—he staged a summer festival that culminated with nude women on horseback. His life and career give rich insight into the growth of the Nazi movement.

Related title by the same author:

Readers may also be interested in *Grand Solo for Anton*, a book of science fiction in which a small boy awakens to find himself as one of the few survivors of a mysterious disaster. As he struggles to survive and feed himself, vegetation is slowly recolonizing the city. But there are clues to the existence of a handful of others, whose primary activity seems to be hunting for an enigmatic book that will shed light on their collective fate.

Subject keywords: politics; power

Original language: German

Sources consulted for annotation:

Global Books in Print (online) (review from *Booklist*).

Moore, John. *The Vancouver Sun*, 20 March 1993, p. C19.

Publishers Weekly 239 (23 November 1992): 54.

Some other translated books by Herbert Rosendorfer: *The Architect of Ruins*; *Stephanie or A Previous Existence*; *Letters Back to Ancient China*; *Grand Solo for Anton*; *German Suite*

Bernhard Schlink. *The Reader.*

Translated by Carol Brown Janeway. New York: Pantheon Books, 1997. 218 pages.

Genres/literary styles/story types: mainstream fiction; coming-of-age

Michael Berg at 15 is a callow and naïve youth. One October day in postwar Germany, he suddenly begins to vomit in the street—a prequel to a serious liver disease. A helpful female stranger whisks him away to her apartment and helps to clean him up. Six months later, when he has recovered, he goes in search of the woman—a bouquet of flowers in his hand. He locates her apartment and sits quietly while she irons lingerie and then cannot help but stare when she goes into the next room to change clothes. On being discovered, he flees ignominiously but spends the next eight days dreaming about her beauty and grace. On his return to her building, he helps her haul coal from the basement, is instructed to bathe, and then the inevitable happens. He and Hanna Schmidt, a streetcar ticket-taker become lovers. His frequent visits to her apartment come with a single proviso: He must read extracts from classic literature to her before sex. And she turns out to be an avid listener, literally drinking up the words Michael speaks. But the idyll ceases just as quickly as it commenced: Hanna vanishes. Some seven years later, he meets her again in circumstances that he could not have imagined. Now a law student, he monitors a war crimes trial, and Hanna suddenly reappears. Along with others, she is a defendant charged with being responsible for deaths in a burning church. But instead of presenting a defense, she meekly takes upon herself a guilt that is not wholly hers. As the trial progresses, Michael realizes that Hanna does not have the capacity to defend herself and that his oral reading of the classics to her was a ruse designed to conceal her darkest secret. And even though he knows that an intervention by him on her behalf may mitigate her sentence, he does not act—perhaps ashamed to admit their past liaison. He writes to her in prison, sends her cassettes of books that he has recorded, and when at the end of 18 years she is to be released, he visits her and plans to help her re-establish herself in the civilian world. But she abruptly commits suicide. Michael then discovers that while in prison, she has slowly learned to read, exhibiting a special interest in Holocaust literature by such authors as Primo Levi and Hannah Arendt, and that her final legacy is a bequest of her savings to one of the survivors of the church fire.

Related titles by the same author:

Readers may also enjoy *Homecoming*, in which a legal historian discovers an apologia for the German blockade of Leningrad written by a man he thinks may be his father. Schlink has also written books featuring private detective Gerhard Self: *Self's Punishment* and *Self's Deception*. Self is a cantankerous and curmudgeonly old man on the threshold of 70 who—despite the best efforts of his

younger girlfriend—staunchly holds on to his bachelordom. In *Self's Deception*, he becomes involved in the tangled world of German left-wing radicals.
Subject keywords: power; war
Original language: German
Sources consulted for annotation:
Bernstein, Richard. *The New York Times*, 20 August 1997, p. C16.
Global Books in Print (online) (review from *School Library Journal*).
Havens, Shirley E. *Library Journal* 123 (1 May 1998): 168.
Ruta, Suzanne. *The New York Times Book Review*, 27 July 1997, p. 8.
Schillinger, Liesl. *The New York Times Book Review*, 13 January 2008 (online).
Steinberg, Sybil S. *Publishers Weekly* 244 (3 November 1997): 45.
Taylor, Charles. *The New York Times Book Review*, 9 September 2007 (online).
Some other translated books by Bernhard Schlink: *Flights of Love*; *Homecoming; The Weekend*

Peter Schneider. *Couplings*.
Translated by Philip Boehm. New York: Farrar, Straus and Giroux, 1996. 293 pages.
Genre/literary style/story type: mainstream fiction
It is not easy for couples to stay together. Thus, anything helps—even bets. Three friends wager that they in fact will be able to maintain their respective relationships for a year. One of them—the molecular biologist Eduard Hoffmann—even decides to take the supreme plunge. Having a child, he decides, is the best way to counteract the impermanency of relationships. But when tests suggest that he is sterile, his resolve about his relationship goes by the wayside. After a series of affairs, things get even more complicated when the tests are determined to be false and he finds out that he has fathered two children. It could not get worse—or could it? Invoking the specter of Nazi history, animal activitists begin to claim that his research is unethical—to put it mildly.
Related title by the same author:
Readers may also enjoy *Eduard's Homecoming*, which may be viewed as a sequel to *Couplings*. After marrying an American and working at Stanford University, Eduard—now heir to an apartment building—takes up an academic position in East Berlin.
Subject keyword: social roles
Original language: German
Sources consulted for annotation:
Global Books in Print (online) (reviews from *Booklist* and *Library Journal*).
Gorra, Michael. *The New York Times Book Review*, 13 August 2000 (online).
Kessler, Rod. *Review of Contemporary Fiction* 17 (Summer 1997): 273.
Ruta, Suzanne. *The New York Times Book Review*, 22 September 1996, p. 17.
Steinberg, Sybil S. *Publishers Weekly* 243 (19 August 1996): 51.
Some other translated books by Peter Schneider: *The Wall Jumper*; *Eduard's Homecoming*; *The German Comedy: Scenes of Life After the Wall*; *Lenz*

Ingo Schulze. *New Lives*.
Translated by John E. Woods. New York: Alfred A. Knopf, 2008. 573 pages.
Genre/literary style/story type: mainstream fiction
Enrico Türmer has lived under two regimes in contemporary German. Before reunification, he experienced the ambiguities of communism in East Germany—a cosseted intellectual whom the regime supported and tolerated because of his very innocuousness. In 1990, working in Altenburg at a radical-minded newspaper, he becomes a cog in the great machine of Western capitalism when he succumbs to the blandishments of a consultant who encourages him to give the newspaper a thorough makeover, turning it into an advertising vehicle with minimal news content that will be

distributed for free. As Richard Eder noted, this novel examines the way in which "invading capitalism" undertook "a moral, social and economic plundering" of East Germany that was "unrestrained in the absence of any countervailing force."

Related title by the same author:

Readers may also be interested in *33 Moments of Happiness*, a collection of short stories in which the author focuses on mundane yet highly revealing moments in the life of ordinary people caught in the death march of a totalitarian system. For example, in Moment 22, Viktoria Federovna goes to work even though she is ill. But when she finally reaches her place of employment, a power failure prevents her from doing anything, so she has a dream about an eloquent speech she once heard. In a poignant story about illusion, a man's relationship with his dead parents is so tangibly real that he wants them to think that he leads a happy life in the company of a wonderful, supportive wife. Thus, he hires a prostitute for his next trip to the cemetery.

Subject keywords: politics; power

Original language: German

Sources consulted for annotation:

Eder, Richard. *The New York Times*, 29 October 2008 (online).

McManus, James. *The New York Times Book Review*, 22 February 1998 (online).

Some other translated books by Ingo Schulze: *33 Moments of Happiness: St. Petersburg Stories*; *Simple Stories*

Winfried Georg Sebald. *The Emigrants*.

Translated by Michael Hulse. New York: New Directions, 1996. 237 pages.

Genres/literary styles/story types: historical fiction; literary historical

Often considered as a classic of exile literature, this book focuses on four Jewish émigrés who were not incarcerated in concentration camps. Nevertheless, their lives were indelibly changed by historical forces that both antedate World War II and are an intrinsic part of it. Forced to endure prosecutions and forced to start anew, they are lost souls forever adrift, internalizing a Holocaust that for them has profound emotional and psychological ramifications. For example, there is Ambros Adelwarth, whose will to live is so fragile and tenuous that he willingly undergoes electroshock treatments at a mental health facility in the hopes that he will die. Another traumatized individual is Max Ferber, whose reclusiveness and claustrophobia are a direct result of having lost his parents to the Nazi regime. Supplemented with photographs, the book becomes—according to Larry Wolff—"a kind of scrapbook of the 20th century, set with haunting images of its victims and survivors."

Related title by the same author:

Readers may also wish to explore *Austerlitz*, which is described by Michiko Kakutani as "a memory scape—a twilight, fogbound world of half-remembered images and ghosts that is reminiscent at once of Ingmar Bergman's *Wild Strawberries*, Kafka's troubling fables of guilt and apprehension and, of course, Proust's *Remembrance of Things Past*." The book's protagonist, Austerlitz, delves into his complicated past, discovering that he was sent from Prague to England at a young age as part of the Kindertransport movement that saved European children from Nazi depredations.

Subject keywords: anti-Semitism; family histories

Original language: German

Sources consulted for annotation:

Global Books in Print (online) (reviews from *Choice*, *Kirkus Reviews*, and *Publishers Weekly*).

Kakutani, Michiko. *The New York Times*, 26 October 2001 (online).

Malin, Irving. *Review of Contemporary Fiction* 17 (Spring 1997): 173.

Olcott, Susan. *Library Journal* 122 (15 April 1997): 148.

Wolff, Larry. *The New York Times Book Review*, 30 March 1997, p. 19.

Some other translated books by Winfried Georg Sebald: *Rings of Saturn*; *Vertigo*; *Austerlitz*

Patrick Süskind. ***Perfume: The Story of a Murderer.***
Translated by John E. Woods. New York: Alfred A. Knopf, 1986. 255 pages.
Genre/literary style/story type: historical fiction
Jean-Baptiste Grenouille is no ordinary creature: His body gives off no smell, but he has what is probably the world's most acute sense of smell. In eighteenth century Paris, he grows up an orphan, works for a tanner, and in his wanderings stumbles across a small girl whose scent he cannot resist. To possess the scent, he murders her, but death destroys it. Now his life's course is set: He will do everything to recreate her fleeting scent. Thus, he apprentices himself to Giuseppe Baldini, whose once-famous perfume business has declined but is now miraculously resurrected thanks to Grenouille's ethereal scents. But he has much more to learn, and in a mélange of disgust for humanity and a craving for ascestism, he exiles himself to a forlorn mountainous region of France, where he lives alone for seven years. Then, in the town of Grasse—where he has gone to perfect his perfumery skills—Grenouille murders 25 young women in order to procure their exquisite odors. When he is finally caught and about to be put to death, he splashes himself with the perfume that he has made from the scents of the murdered women, and the throng of citizens assembled to watch his execution begin a raucous orgy. He is freed and eventually makes his way back to Paris, where he once again douses himself with his magical perfume—this time for the purpose of causing his own death.
Related title by the same author:
Readers may also enjoy *The Pigeon*, which features Jonathan Noel, a guard at a Paris bank who lives what many would say is a boring life filled with predictable routine. But it is a life that he has carefully and lovingly stitched together—thread by minimalist thread—the kind of quiet and uneventful life that he needs after the traumas of childhood and adolescence, when his mother suddenly vanished, taken away to Drancy; when he and his sister were spirited away to live with an uncle in the south of France; when he fought in the French army in Southeast Asia; and when his uncle urged him into a sham marriage. One morning, he is utterly flummoxed when a pigeon appears in the hallway of the apartment building where he has his carefully arranged one-room flat. Fear and anxiety infiltrate every pore of his being, and as he struggles to go through the motions of his daily routine at the bank and during his lunch hour, he conjures up the worst possible scenarios: He will never be able to return to his apartment nor use the washroom down the hall; he will not only be forced to live in the streets but also to defecate in public. Finally, he takes a room in a hotel, hoping to stay until the pigeon disappears, but it is here that he undergoes a fundamental transformation, finally gaining sufficient strength to face the anomalies of existence.
Subject keyword: identity
Original language: German
Sources consulted for annotation:
Ackroyd, Peter. *The New York Times Book Review*, 21 September 1986 (online).
Farrell, Beth. *Library Journal* 122 (15 June 1997): 114.
Lehmann-Haupt, Christopher. *The New York Times*, 16 September 1986, p. C21.
Retting, Ulrike S. *Library Journal* 111 (15 October 1986): 112.
Simon, Linda. *The New York Times Book Review*, 26 June 1998 (online).
Some other translated books by Patrick Süskind: *The Pigeon*; *Mr. Summer's Story*; *Three Stories and a Reflection*

Uwe Timm. ***The Invention of Curried Sausage.***
Translated by Leila Vennewitz. New York: New Directions, 1995. 217 pages.
Genres/literary styles/story types: mainstream fiction; women's lives
Have you ever wondered how curried sausage was invented? The narrator of this novel does, and he tracks down Mrs. Brücker, a sidewalk vendor in late 1940s Hamburg who sold the heavenly

delicacy that he has always remembered. He convinces her to reveal her secret. It is an extraordinary story that involves love affairs, a navy deserter, World War II politics, and the black market—all against the background of daily life in Germany under the Nazis. Some critics have seen affinities with Laura Esquivel's *Like Water for Chocolate*.

Related title by the same author:

Readers may also enjoy *Morenga*, which centers on the rebellion of indigenous African tribes against German colonial rule of South-West Africa—now called Namibia. Critics have pointed out that this same rebellion was touched upon in Thomas Pynchon's *Gravity's Rainbow*.

Subject keywords: politics; war

Original language: German

Sources consulted for annotation:

Foden, Giles. *The New York Times Book Review*, 20 April 2003 (online).

Global Books in Print (online) (reviews from *Kirkus Reviews* for both novels).

Hughes, Kathleen. *Booklist* 91 (1 June 1995): 1732.

Prose, Francine. *The New York Times Book Reviews*, 11 June 1995, p. 31.

Steinberg, Sybil S. *Publishers Weekly* 242 (27 May 1995): 74.

Some other translated books by Uwe Timm: *The Snake Tree*; *Headhunter*; *Midsummer Night*; *Morenga*

Hans-Ulrich Treichel. *Lost*.

Translated by Carol Brown Janeway. New York: Pantheon Books, 1999. 136 pages.

Genres/literary styles/story types: mainstream fiction; coming-of-age

This book is a comic masterpiece with dark, philosophical overtones that Christopher Lehmann-Haupt called an allegory "of the division and reunification of East and West Germany, with the snarling of red tape interfering with the recognition of human fraternity." In the chaos that marked the end of World War II, a German family flees Russian troops; the frightened mother entrusts her eldest son, Arnold, to a random stranger. Some 10 years later, living in West Germany, the family tries to locate Arnold. It is an unenviable and arduous task. Finally, a boy known as Foundling 2307 is determined to have all the characteristics of the lost Arnold, but before family reunification can take place, a vexing series of bureaucratic and pseudo-medical procedures must be followed—all in the presumed interests of the lost boy.

Subject keywords: family histories; war

Original language: German

Sources consulted for annotation:

Amazon.com (book description; review from *Kirkus Reviews*).

Cooper, Rand Richards. *The New York Times Book Review*, 26 December 1999 (online).

Lehmann-Haupt, Christopher. *The New York Times*, 21 October 1999 (online).

Roncevic, Mirela. *Library Journal* 124 (1 October 1999): 136.

Steinberg, Sybil S. *Publishers Weekly* 246 (6 September 1999): 77.

Another translated book by Hans-Ulrich Treichel: *Leaving Sardinia*

Iliya Troyanov. *The Collector of Worlds*.

Translated by William Hobson. New York: Ecco/Harper Collins, 2009. 454 pages.

Genre/literary style/story type: historical fiction

If you have ever wanted to know anything or everything about Sir Richard Burton, this is the novel for you. Burton, of course, is most famous for his attempt to find the source of the Nile, but he had numerous other experiences. He served in India with the British East India Company between 1842–1849; made a pilgrimage to Mecca and Medina in disguise; learned many foreign languages;

and translated the Kama Sutra. This book recounts Burton's adventures in a gregarious manner, turning a historical figure into an engaging fictional construct.
Subject keyword: identity
Original language: German
Sources consulted for annotation:
Foden, Giles. *The Guardian*, 28 June 2008 (online).
Macintyre, Ben. *The New York Times Book Review*, 10 May 2009 (online).

Kevin Vennemann. *Close to Jedenew.*
Translated by Ross Benjamin. Brooklyn, NY: Melville House, 2008. 200 pages.
Genre/literary style/story type: mainstream fiction
In a small village in Poland, a Jewish family has been living peacefully with their neighbors, intermarrying, and occasionally converting to Catholicism. But at the beginning of World War II, the arrival of German forces turns everything topsy-turvy. Suddenly, the villagers become violent and vindictive, and the family of the narrator—who is a 16-year-old Jewish girl—has little choice but to seek shelter in a tree house.
Subject keywords: family histories; rural life
Original language: German
Sources consulted for annotation:
Global Books in Print (online) (review from *Publishers Weekly*).
Melville House website, http://www.mhpbooks.com.

Martin Walser. *Breakers.*
Translated by Leila Vennewitz. New York: Henry Holt, 1987. 305 pages.
Genre/literary style/story type: mainstream fiction
What does an aging German high school teacher whose Nietzsche manuscript has once again been rejected want most in life? Fun in the California sun might be one answer, but that fun comes at a high price. Helmut Halm's friend, the head of the German department at a university in California, is in a tight spot. He needs someone to fill a lecturer's slot for a semester. And who better to call upon than the gloomy and depressed Helmut? Of course, California has a catalytic effect on Helmut, not the least because of Fran—the embodiment of youth and wealth as well as a stereotypical temptress. But California living has its dark side—something that a chastened Helmut quickly realizes when he must deal with the suicide of his friend, the drowning death of Fran, and the deaths of his in-laws and two other acquaintances.
Related title by the same author:
Readers may also enjoy *Runaway Horse*, an earlier look at Halm's life that is a moving portrait of how the slowly accreting emotional and physical distance between a long-married couple was bridged.
Subject keyword: urban life
Original language: German
Sources consulted for annotation:
Global Books in Print (online) (review from *Choice*).
Holt, Patricia. *San Francisco Chronicle*, 3 February 1988, p. E4.
Hutchison, Paul E. *Library Journal* 112 (August 1987): 145.
"Martin Walser." *Contemporary Literary Criticism*. Thomson Gale databases.
"Martin Walser." *Dictionary of Literary Biography Online*. Thomson Gale databases.
Ruta, Suzanne. *The New York Times Book Review*, 1 November 1987 (online).
Steinberg, Sybil S. *Publishers Weekly* 232 (7 August 1987): 435.

Some other translated books by Martin Walser: *Runaway Horse*; *No Man's Land*; *Letter to Lord Liszt*; *The Inner Man*; *The Swan Villa*

Grete Weil. *Last Trolley from Beethovenstraat*.
Translated by John Barrett. Boston, MA: David R. Godine, 1997. 176 pages.
Genre/literary style/story type: mainstream fiction
Andreas, a German, writes poetry. During World War II, he was a journalist in occupied Holland, where for a time he sheltered Daniel, a Jewish adolescent. Ultimately, he was unsuccessful: Daniel became yet one more victim of the Holocaust. To a much lesser degree, so did Andreas; even though he shares his life with Daniel's sister, he finds it difficult to come to terms with Daniel's fate—struggling to find any sense in life and struggling to find purpose in writing about that senslessness.
Related title by the same author:
Readers may also enjoy *The Bride Price*, which artfully juxtaposes the author's life and a consideration of Michal, most famously known in the Bible as the wife of David.
Subject keywords: anti-Semitism; identity
Original language: German
Source consulted for annotation:
Global Books in Print (online) (reviews from *Booklist*, *Library Journal*, and *Publishers Weekly* for both books).
Some other translated books written by Grete Weil: *Aftershocks*; *The Bride Price*

Natascha Wodin. *The Interpreter*.
Translated by J. Maxwell Brownjohn. San Diego, CA: Harcourt Brace Jovanovich, 1986. 326 pages.
Genre/literary style/story type: mainstream fiction
This novel centers on a young woman born in Germany to a family of Russian refugees. She does not a have a pleasant life: There is never enough money, her parents have time for everything else except her, and she is constantly on the receiving end of dismissive comments. Isolated and alienated, she is increasingly attracted to the Soviet Union, falling in love with a recently widowed and aging Russian poet who appears to her as a heroic savior. But when she follows him back to the Soviet Union, she discovers that she is no more at home there than in Germany.
Subject keyword: culture conflict
Original language: German
Sources consulted for annotation:
Chait, Sandra. *The Seattle Times*, 16 November 1986, p. L7.
Cryer, Dan. *Newsday*, 14 August 1986, p. 11.
Publishers Weekly 241 (16 May 1994): 61.
Another translated book written by Natascha Wodin: *Once I Lived*

Christa Wolf. *Accident/A Day's News*.
Translated by Heike Schwarzbauer and Rick Takvorian. New York: Farrar, Straus and Giroux. David R. Godine, 1989. 113 pages.
Genre/literary style/story type: mainstream fiction
A woman who loves to garden and cook waits for news of two events that will have a profound effect on her future life. Her brother is undergoing brain surgery, and her gardening and cooking are threatened by the fallout from the Chernobyl nuclear explosion. As she ponders the ironies and paradoxes of events and as she converses with her two daughters by phone about family life, she examines the very premises of existence. The brain surgery will prove to be a success, but Chernobyl will have devastating consequences. And what about the novel's narrator? She will

endure—a stoic presence—trying to come to terms with the vicissitudes of life, knowing full well that that whether joy or disaster looms, it is a blessing and a grace to be alive.

Related titles by the same author:

Readers may also enjoy *Cassandra*, which is a unique retelling of the Trojan War from the perspective of the visionary Trojan seer; *No Place on Earth*, which envisions the meeting of two writers who each committed suicide at different times and places; and *In the Flesh*, where a hospitalized woman experiences hallucinations and flashbacks about her life under an authoritarian regime.

Subject keywords: power; social roles

Original language: German

Sources consulted for annotation:

Evans, Janet. *Library Journal* 130 (January 2005): 101.

Gordon, Mary. *The New York Times Book Review*, 23 April 1989 (online).

Harrison Smith, Sarah. *The New Leader* 88 (January/February 2005): 29.

Seaman, Donna. *Booklist* 101 (January 1/January 15 2005): 824.

Some other translated books by Christa Wolf: *Medea: A Modern Retelling*; *What Remains and Other Stories*; *In the Flesh*; *Cassandra: A Novel and Four Essays*; *No Place on Earth*; *A Model Childhood*; *The Quest for Christa T.*

Stefanie Zweig. *Nowhere in Africa.*

Translated by Marlies Comjean. Madison, WI: University of Wisconsin Press/Terrace Books, 2004. 291 pages.

Genre/literary style/story type: mainstream fiction

This novel recounts the story of a group of Jewish refugees in the 1930s and 1940s who end up in rural Kenya. Here, Walter Redlich, formerly a lawyer, and his wife Jettel try to make a living as farm owners, but untold difficulties arise. They have endless disagreements, and although Jettel detests her Kenyan life, she refuses to leave when her husband contemplates a return to Germany. Conversely, their young daughter Regina comes into her own in Africa, learning an indigenous language and making numerous friends. The movie based on this novel received an Oscar for Best Foreign Film. The sequel is *Somewhere in Germany*, in which the Redliches move back to Germany because of Walter's ongoing desire to resume legal work.

Subject keyword: culture conflict

Original language: German

Sources consulted for annotation:

Cooper, Rand Richard. *The New York Times Book Review*, 2 May 2004, p. 24.

Global Books in Print (online) (review from *Publishers Weekly* for *Somewhere in Germany*).

Rochman, Hazel. *Booklist* 100 (15 February 2004): 1040.

Another translated book by Stefanie Zweig: *Somewhere in Germany*

Switzerland

Melitta Breznik. *Night Duty.*

Translated by Roslyn Theobold. South Royalton, VT: Steerforth Press, 1999. 131 pages.

Genres/literary styles/story types: mainstream fiction; women's lives

In a bleak post–World War II Austrian town, life is almost not worth living. But people try to do so despite everything. The unnamed narrator of this novel is a doctor, and her parents have gone their separate ways. Her father, now residing in a nursing home, is an alcoholic. He served in the Austrian army as a stopgap measure and then returned home after the war to lead a stultifying and dreary existence at the town's steelworks. He became increasingly depressed, paranoid, and violent. There is no hope and no future, especially when the steelworks is bought by a foreign

company and he loses his job. Her mother lives on her own, taking pleasure in small moments and small cermonies—finally free of an oppressive life with her husband. And the narrator herself—beset by the unyielding burdens of her thankless responsibilities at a provincial hospital—nevertheless finds time to tend to her dying father, sifting through her memories of him to find rare occasions of grace.
Subject keyword: family histories
Original language: German
Sources consulted for annotation:
Leber, Michele. *Booklist* 95 (15 March 1999): 1288.
Leber, Michele. *Library Journal* 125 (15 April 2000): 148.
Ruta, Suzanne. *The New York Times Book Review*, 1 August 1999 (online).
Steinberg, Sybil S. *Publishers Weekly* 246 (18 January 1999): 325.

Zoë Jenny. *The Pollen Room.*
Translated by Elizabeth Gaffney. New York: Simon & Schuster, 1999. 143 pages.
Genres/literary styles/story types: mainstream fiction; coming-of-age
This book recounts the life of Jo, whose parents separated when she was three. Lucy, her mother, leaves to be with an artist, Alois. Jo is left in the care of her father, a third-rate publisher of fifth-rate books. Her life is one of utter loneliness as her father struggles to make ends meet, slaving away at his press and then going off to his second job. Years later, when Alois dies, Lucy has a breakdown, and Jo goes to care for her mother, who has turned Alois's studio into a room filled with pollen. But when Lucy recovers, Jo inexorably slides into a long depression that is made all the worse by a failed romance and the need for an abortion.
Subject keyword: family histories
Original language: German
Sources consulted for annotation:
Global Books in Print (online) (reviews from *Booklist* and *Kirkus Reviews*).
Olson, Yvette Weller. *Library Journal* 124 (January 1999): 152.
Steinberg, Sybil S. *Publishers Weekly* 246 (11 January 1999): 52.

Felix Mettler. *The Wild Boar.*
Translated by Edna McCown. New York: Fromm International, 1992. 216 pages.
Genres/literary styles/story types: crime fiction; suspense
Gottfried Sonder is a widower on the verge of retirement from his job in a Swiss autopsy lab. He should be looking forward to more free time to pursue his hobby of big-game hunting. But instead, he has just been released from hospital after undergoing surgery for lung cancer. And he is out for revenge because he suspects that his disease was caused by Horst Götze, a doctor, coworker, and inveterate smoker. Drawing on his hunting prowess, he uses a poisoned dart to murder Götze. When Commissioner Haberli is called in to shed light on Götze's mysterious death, he discovers that the people who work at the autopsy lab are less than sympathetic.
Subject keyword: aging
Original language: German
Sources consulted for annotation:
Amazon.com (review from *Kirkus Reviews*).
Brainard, Dulcy. *Publishers Weekly* 239 (2 March 1992): 51.
Schierling, Ingrid. *Library Journal* 117 (1 April 1992): 148.

Peter Stamm. *Unformed Landscape.*
Translated by Michael Hofmann. New York: Handsel Books, 2004. 161 pages.

Genre/literary style/story type: mainstream fiction; women's lives

Kathrine, a young woman in her 20, works for the Norwegian customs authority in an isolated village in the far northern reaches of Finnmark. Here, she leads a desultory existence as the mother of a boy whose father still inhabits the village. She has remarried, but she despises her new husband—a distant, regimented, and lugubrious man. She longs for something more—a nebulous excitement and passion that goes beyond the tightly delimited boundaries of village life and short trips to spend time with neighbors. One day, she leaves everything; she simply disappears.

Related title by the same author:

Readers may also be interested in *On a Day Like This*, which may be seen as a man's version of *Unformed Landscape*. Here, Andreas—an unmarried teacher with a serious health problem—decides to start anew. He gives up his Parisian life and returns to Switzerland, hoping to rekindle an early romance.

Subject keyword: rural life

Original language: German

Sources consulted for annotation:

Evans, Janet. *Library Journal* 130 (1 April 2005): 89.

Global Books in Print (online) (reviews from *Library Journal* and *Publishers Weekly* for *On a Day Like This*).

Scott, Whitney. *Booklist* 101 (1 March 2005): 1143.

Some other translated books written by Peter Stamm: *In Strange Gardens and Other Stories*; *Agnes*; *On a Day Like This*

Martin Suter. *Small World*.

Translated by Sandra Harper. London: Harvill, 2001. 247 pages.

Genre/literary style/story type: mainstream fiction

Konrad has never had much of a life of his own. He has always grown up around and worked for the rich Koch family in one capacity or another. Now he tends to their summer home on Corfu. But his persistent drinking problem causes him to be less than an ideal caretaker, and there is a disastrous fire at the villa. But thanks to the oversight of Elvira Senn, the no-nonsense leader of the Koch clan, he briefly puts his life back in order. However, he soon falls victim to Alzheimer's disease. As his condition deteriorates, he starts to recall the horrors of a distant past. As Elvira tries to keep Konrad's memory in check, Simone—her new daughter-in-law—becomes intrigued with Konrad's recollections. Soon, she discovers hidden stories that put an entirely different light on her new family.

Related title by the same author:

Readers may also enjoy *A Deal with the Devil*. When Sonia Frey starts work as a hotel physiotherapist in the Swiss hinterlands, mysterious occurrences that have an eerie resemblance to those found in a specific folktale cause her more than a few sleepless nights.

Subject keyword: family histories

Original language: German

Sources consulted for annotation:

Amazon.com (book description; publisher's description).

Euro Crime Reviews, http:/www.eurocrime.co.uk.

Global Books in Print (online) (synopsis/book jacket).

Howat, Casron. *The Scotsman*, 29 March 2003, p. 6.

Lawson, Anthea. *The Times*, 3 April 2002 (from Factiva databases).

Mergendahl, Peter. *Rocky Mountain News*, 16 August 2002, p. 30D.

Otto F. Walter. *Time of the Pheasant*.

Translated by Leila Vennewitz. New York: Fromm International, 1991. 412 pages.

Genre/literary style/story type: mainstream fiction
Thom Winter is a historian who has been researching the veracity of Swiss claims to neutrality during World War II. But he also very much wants to get to the bottom of a mysterious entry that he found in his aunt's diary that claims that Thom's mother was the victim of murder in the early 1960s. Thom's visit to his family home triggers a host of memories from his childhood—a fearful time when Swiss business owners, including Thom's father, collaborated with the Nazis. Such activities caused a rift in the household, with Thom's pious mother heartily disapproving of her husband's decisions. As the story of how the Winter family's steelworks was an important cog in the German war effort during World War II intersects with the larger story of Switzerland's true role in the war, Thom discovers the real reasons for his mother's death.
Subject keywords: family histories; war
Original language: German
Sources consulted for annotation:
Global Books in Print (online) (reviews from *Choice* and *Kirkus Reviews*).
Steinberg, Sybil S. *Publishers Weekly* 238 (20 September 1991): 120.
Another translated book written by Otto F. Walter: *The Mute*

Author Index

This index contains the names of translated authors for whom there are annotated entries and who are prominently mentioned in the Introduction. Please consult the sections entitled "Earlier Translated Literature" and "Bibliographic Essay" at the beginning of each chapter for additional names of translated authors.

Subject and Keyword Index

Title Index

This index contains the titles of translated books that are the focus of each annotated entry; it also contains the titles of other prominently mentioned translated books in the annotated entries and Introduction. Please consult the sections entitled "Earlier Translated Literature" and "Bibliographic Essay" at the beginning of each chapter for additional titles of translated books.

Translator Index (Selected)

About the Authors

Juris Dilevko is an associate professor in the Faculty of Information, University of Toronto, Toronto, Canada. His publications include *Reading and the Reference Librarian: The Importance to Library Service of Staff Reading Habits*, *The Evolution of Library and Museum Partnerships: Historical Antecedents, Contemporary Manifestations, and Future Directions*, and *Readers' Advisory Service in North American Public Libraries, 1870-2005*, among others.

Keren Dali, Ph.D., is an Assistant Professor at the Faculty of Information, University of Toronto. Her research interests include reading and readers, readers' advisory, and multicultural collections and reference services. She is an author and co-author of peer-reviewed publications that appeared in the Journal of Academic Librarianship, Library Resources & Technical Services, College & Research Libraries, New Library World, and The Reference Librarian, among others. She teaches courses on reading and the foundations of LIS.

Glenda Garbutt received a master of information studies degree from the Faculty of Information, University of Toronto, Toronto, Canada.